THE PRINCE OF EDEN

Marilyn Harris

BALLANTINE BOOKS • NEW YORK

Library of Congress Catalog Card Number: 77-25420

ISBN: 0-345-32592-3

This edition published by arrangement with G.P. Putnam's Sons

Manufactured in the United States of America

First Ballantine Books Edition: December 1985

For Judge Again, Gratefully—

Great men, taken up in any way, are
profitable company. We cannot look,
however imperfectly, upon a great man
without gaining something by him. He is
the living light-fountain which it is
good and pleasant to be near, . . .
a natural luminary shining by the gift of
Heaven in whose radiance all souls feel
that it is well with them. . . .

THOMAS CARLYLE

London
Newgate Prison
May, 1836

The new turnkey looked down, alarmed, into the Common Cell where the prisoners were beginning to stir. "What's 'appening, sir?" he whispered.

Jawster Gray, head turnkey of Newgate, followed his gaze downward from their perch high atop the catwalk. The lad was right. The pit *was* breathing new life.

Jawster halted his patrol and looked closer. There was neither revulsion nor acceptance in his face. His sole reward for having spent forty-two of his sixty years in this dark, foul pit was a comforting objectivity. It was primordial slime beneath him, that's what it was, out of which would never crawl anything better or worse than humanity.

"Just shiftin' for the evening," he reassured the lad. "No cause for alarm."

The new turnkey, a boy of sixteen, adjusted his black coat with two solid rows of brass buttons and walked a hesitant step forward on his patrol around the catwalk.

Jawster Gray held his position. The vast room below was chill and dark save for wall torches flickering in their fixed standards on red brick walls blackened with years of soot. He leaned still closer to the railing. The slime never stirred without a reason. They stirred to eat and drink and

1

fornicate. But eating and drinking were over for the day, and the fornication wouldn't start until Jawster, with the help of the boy, extinguished the wall torches.

On the catwalk across the way, the new lad called out, a rising hysteria in his voice, "Raise the ladder, sir!"

Quickly Jawster glanced down. Gawd! The ladder was at the ready, left there from earlier in the afternoon when in the safety of daylight, Jawster had descended to break up a fight. Hurriedly he bent over and drew up the ladder, twelve slender rungs, the only connecting links between himself and the scabs below.

He was getting careless. Perhaps they'd sent him the new man just in time. "You, there!" he shouted to a bent old man who was passing quickly among the prisoners, whispering something. "You! Hold your tongue. If it's talk you want, I'll put you on the treadmill. That'll ease the talk out of you right enough."

The old man looked up and smiled a toothless grin. He drew open his buttonless trousers and displayed for Jawster's benefit a limp, diseased penis.

The gesture won for the old man a scattering of applause and hoarse shouts of approval. The entire floor of the Common Cell was now stirring, the whole miserable community on their feet; street thieves and pickpockets, footpads and shoplifters, whore bullies as well as a scattering of whores.

In the accelerating tension, Jawster looked down, dismayed that he'd spent most of his years in such company.

The new lad was at his elbow. "Look at 'em sir," he gasped. "Just look—"

At that moment a sharp female scream pierced the air. Jawster's head swiveled toward the far corner, dimly lit where the spill of torchlight did not fall. "You! Over there!" he shouted. "Step forward!"

When after several moments nothing had emerged from the shadows, Jawster called again. "I warn you. The crank and treadmill's waiting. Step forward!"

A cadaverous, hollow-eyed woman moved slowly out of the shadows. The top of her bodice was down about her waist, revealing two sagging breasts. "T'aint nuthin, Guv," she called up. "Me mate was hungry is all, if you know what I mean." She smiled and hurriedly drew the bodice up about her shoulders. "I wanted to feed him, 'fore—"

Abruptly she clamped a soiled hand over her mouth as though she knew she'd said too much.

"Before what?" Jawster shouted down at her.

But she was saying no more and quickly she moved back into the shadows. A few moments later Jawster heard giggling.

The mysterious activity below continued. Jawster cursed under his breath. Usually by this time of an evening, the prisoners were quiet, on the verge of sleep, which meant that Jawster could slip away for checkers and a pint in the Warden's Hall.

But not tonight. In fact if he hadn't looked up and seen black beyond the high barred ceiling windows, he would have sworn it was morning, the prisoners preparing themselves either for release or further punishment.

In a rush of anger, Jawster shouted, "Line the walls! Every rotten one of you. Put your asses flat and hands out straight."

The sixty or so faces merely gaped up at him.

"You heard what I said," he cried again, pacing back and forth on the catwalk. "Line the wall! If it's a fete you're planning, you can pass the night pressed against cold brick."

But the prisoners were paying no attention to him and continued to jostle each other, the excitement clearly rising, several now facing the broad barred iron doors through which new prisoners were placed in the Common Cell.

The new turnkey leaned close with an opinion. "It's like they was waitin' for someone, sir. Look! Look how they stand!"

The scabs did seem to be forming close to the doors. Still it made no sense. Customarily the last prisoner delivery was made by six o'clock.

The new lad pressed closer, clearly growing more frightened. "Sir, please let me call for reinforcement. We don't know what—"

But Jawster's reply was quick and firm. "No! We're here because the Warden expects us to know what to do. Remember that," he added in a scolding tone, "if you ever want to rise higher than where you are."

Chastised, the new turnkey stepped back. "But what do we do, sir?" he pleaded.

"Keep a sharp eye and ear, that's what," Jawster scolded

again. "And remember there's only twelve foot of air between you and them." Jawster glanced over his shoulder
at the lad. "Now, go along with you," he urged, softening
his tone. "Get on your side of the walk so we can keep all
in view."

Suddenly he called after the new turnkey. "Where's the
lady? The young one they brought in this afternoon?"

The boy hurried back as though grateful for a reprieve.
"Down there she is, sir," and he pointed toward the far
wall to their left, toward a mound of straw and a slight
figure crumpled as though dead upon it. "She ain't moved
since they placed her there this afternoon. I know, sir. I've
kept my eye on that one—"

"I'll just bet you have," Jawster concurred with a wink.
While the rest of the prisoners continued to gather about
the broad barred doors at the opposite end of the cell, Jawster stared downward at the isolated figure. Seldom did
they get nobs like her in the Common Cell. Jawster knew
her case well enough, as did everyone in London who
could read or had ears to hear. She was Charlotte Longford, the young wife of a rich linen merchant in Oxford
Street who had been charged by her husband with
adultery.

Jawster felt an odd surge of pity. She did not belong
here, yet here she was, and here apparently she would
stay. Only that afternoon, an old magistrate named Sir
Cedric Dalrymple, with heavy-handed and high Tory
arrogance, had come down hard on her sentencing. Apparently choosing to use her as an example for the upstart
middle class, the bewigged old man had resurrected an
ancient form of punishment for adultery, sentencing her to
be burned on the palm of her hand with a hot poker in
public court, but first to pass a week with the denizens of
the Common Cell, knowing full well that if she survived
the latter crucible, the former would be as nothing in
comparison.

Upon hearing her sentence, the young woman had collapsed and they had brought her in, and deposited her on
the mound of straw. Once or twice Jawster had seen her
stir, but for the most part, she had appeared lifeless.

Now in the face of the new and mysterious ferment
going on below, Jawster warned the new turnkey, "Keep
your eye on her. We owe her that much."

The young man nodded. Apparently the order was to his liking.

Wearily he turned his attention back to the crowd pressing closer to the iron doors. Again he shouted down, "I don't know what it is you're waiting for, friends, but you might start praying for new skin to make up for that which you'll lose come morning. Now turn to, I mean it, and line the walls."

In spite of the new harshness in his voice, the tattered rag-covered company scarcely looked up. One old man cried out, "'Tis new skin we're waitin' for right enow, Gov. Keep your eyes peeled and you'll see it as well."

A pickpocket looked up and saw him eavesdropping. "Close your traps, mates. Old Jawster's givin' us a listening ear."

Jawster stepped back, anger increasing. He had no weapon save his voice and an awesome stance of authority. "Move away!" he cried, feeling that authority begin to crumble before the now silent crowd. Stalemate! The slime were still now though they continued to press close to the doors. In all honesty they were doing no harm. If they chose to pass the night standing like cattle at Smithfield's, then Jawster was of the mind to let them. Fatigue would overtake their wasted bodies soon enough. There wasn't anything coming through those barred doors tonight, of that he was certain. They'd been locked and bolted at sunset, and they'd stay that way until sunrise.

"Then hold your places, scum," he called down, "till you drop for all I care."

Now suddenly from the front of the cell, he heard a hoarse cry. "He's comin'!" Jawster looked sharply up. All the scum were shouting now, their vow of silence forgotten in the excitement of the moment.

The new turnkey called over the din, "What are they talking about, sir? What's coming?"

Jawster ignored him and moved quickly back around the catwalk. A chorus of voices had now taken up the cry, an unruly, yet curiously measured shout of "He's comin', he's comin'!"

A grin broke out on his ruddy face. Gawd! It wasn't possible. Yet it was, and the proof was there in the yelling, stamping crowd beneath him, their glazed eyes turned expectantly toward the iron doors, hands outreaching as though to assist the still invisible presence through the doors and welcome him into their midst.

The grin on Jawster's face broadened as he shook his head. How had they known? That was what puzzled him. How had the senseless, illiterate creatures known who was coming? Yet they knew. *They knew!* The dreariness of their daily existence had lifted. In each upturned face he saw the light of hope. The chant grew to a din, a continuous refrain of "He's comin', he's comin'!"

The new turnkey was again at his side. "Who is it they're—"

As Jawster was on the verge of explaining, the vast cell fell ominously silent. Hands upraised, frozen in position. The entire milling pushing crowd fell without warning into a tableau, the only movement the red flicker of fire coming from the wall torches.

Beyond this silence Jawster heard the sound of bolts being thrown on the other side of the door. Still the tableau held, every trembling thief, pickpocket, whore turned expectantly toward the doors, emotions vaulting, yet somehow held at bay.

The new turnkey whispered, "My Gawd, what is it?"

"Shhh!" Jawster hushed him, then moved slowly down the catwalk, the better to get an unobstructed view.

At that moment the doors were flung open. A dozen Peelers rushed in, their brass buttons gleaming in the firelight. They formed a ready passage, a half dozen men on either side. The gaping criminals inched backward, their eyes still focused on someone just out of sight.

Suddenly a woman cried out, "It's him!"

Jawster leaned sharply forward against the railing. Below him, from his angle of vision, he saw first the toes of highly varnished black boots with lofty heels that clacked softly against the stone floor. Next he saw peg-top trousers, sash-cut, the fabric straining against leg muscles. And such an astounding waistcoat, crimson, like fresh blood, such a white flowing neck scarf, and such a plain, sober, but elegant black velvet cape, floor length. Hatless, the overlong fair hair appeared slightly mussed. There was a small wound over his right temple, the blood staunched, but still glistening on his strong forehead.

Now the man stood full portrait before the gaping, admiring criminals. There was a faint smile on his remarkable features which spoke of a passion for doing as one likes. Jawster himself looked admiringly down. It was him, as he had guessed.

Then a great roar went up from the crowd. As though at last given permission to move, they surged forward, their hands outreaching until they engulfed the newcomer. Two strong men lifted him to their shoulders while he, laughing, turned this way and that, greeting all, many by name.

Still leaning on the railing, Jawster found himself laughing with them.

The man was directly beneath Jawster now, still sitting astride shoulders. He looked up at Jawster high on the catwalk. "Good evening to you, sir," he called out quite cheerily.

Flattered, Jawster returned the greeting. He straightened up from his inclining position on the railing and touched his chimney-pot hat in salute. "Good evening to you, sir." He motioned toward the small wound over the man's right eye. "I see they tossed you about a bit. No lasting damage, I hope."

The man threw back his head and laughed openly, struggling for balance atop the shifting shoulders. "No lasting damage, I assure you," he grinned. "I left two broken batons and some missing teeth in my wake. It's becoming increasingly difficult to gain admittance to your nightly salon." His dark eyes burned with a hard gemlike flame, as though it were nothing to him to maintain this ecstasy.

Jawster laughed heartily. "Ask your friends there how they do it, sir," he called down. "They'll give you practical lessons enough."

The man bobbed his head, and as the shoulders were now carrying him away in the opposite direction, he craned his head back and lifted his voice to Jawster. "As soon as the festivities are over, sir, I want your ear for a moment."

Again Jawster nodded. He watched carefully as the scum bore him away, their upturned faces as bright as children's.

Then the new turnkey was there again with his unbroken refrain. "Who is he, sir, please? Who is he?"

Jawster's smile softened into a reflective angle. He leaned forward in a relaxed position on the railing. Quietly he spoke. "The Prince of Eden, lad."

Apparently the identification meant nothing to the young boy. He now pointed down into the Common Cell, his young face awash with indignation. "Look what he's doing, sir. Now, that's not permissible, is it? I mean—"

The boy was becoming tedious. Jawster considered sending him on to the Women's Ward. After all, his job for the first month was to gain experience in *all* parts of grand old Newgate. Jawster had suffered him long enough. But no. Perhaps this experience was as important as any to be gained in Newgate, the knowledge that, under certain conditions, there were forces larger than all the rules and handbooks, and against such an incomprehensible force, all that the turnkeys and wardens could do was shuck the rules, like foolish burdens borne for too many years.

Against the shocked expression in the boy's face, Jawster turned away. He knew what was going on below. He didn't have to look, but he looked anyway.

The inmates had deposited the Prince of Eden near the center of the Common Cell. Upon the instant of alighting, the man had flung open his great velvet cape, revealing carefully sewn pouches, a walking storeroom containing many bottles of gin, loaves of bread, white bread, unknown in Newgate, and pouches of tobacco. This bounty he was now distributing liberally about the floor to the eager, outstretched hands of the prisoners.

Apparently the new turnkey had been shocked into silence at the sight of the incorrigibles passing bottles and loaves around. Jawster tried again to make him understand. "Pay them no mind, lad," he counseled. "A little gin won't hurt them. Their sins will be intact come morning when, as belated punishment, you can mask the lot of them."

Obviously it was cold comfort. "Does this go on nightly, sir?" the lad asked with clenched jaw.

"Oh my, no," soothed Jawster. "Certainly not nightly. The Prince of Eden gives us the pleasure of his company perhaps once, twice a month. The rest of the time—"

Suddenly a great cheer arose from the Common Cell as apparently all felt the impulse to pay communal homage to their benefactor. Jawster looked down. Someone had arranged a firmly packed throne of straw and on this the Prince of Eden was now sitting, the bottles passing back and forth before him. The conversation had fallen so low that Jawster couldn't hear what was being said. Again, no

the game of the aristocracy. No Tory in his right mind could permit it." He saw something which resembled anger on Edward's tired face and moved to check it. "The middle classes will rise, Edward," he comforted. "The peers have no objection to that. In fact most good Tories are only too willing to make room for them." He leaned still farther over his desk. "*Make* room," he repeated pointedly. "The aristocracy will *make* room. They will not absorb them. The difference is subtle and very important."

The man appeared to be listening, but Sir Claudius couldn't be certain. He looked as troubled as ever, the damnable compulsion to confess still raging within him. "I beg you listen, Edward," Sir Claudius now pleaded. "Tell me, what would have been accomplished if I had permitted you to speak in open court?"

Edward again closed his eyes. "She would have been spared."

To that bit of nonsense, Sir Claudius could only laugh. "Spared?" he repeated. "Do you really believe that? The journalists would have had a field day, the scandal mongers would have turned a pretty penny's profit for Fleet Street, the magistrate would probably have banished you from court, and Charlotte Longford would have received exactly the same sentence."

Edward glared up at him. He sat up suddenly and drove his fingers through his hair as, apparently, his despair overtook him.

Before such a pitiable countenence, Sir Claudius felt another wave of pity. "Edward, listen, I beg you," he said softly. "The walls *are* breached on occasion. Your dear mother breached them and quite successfully, but make no mistake, there's a large portion of influential England that has never forgiven her. Oh, the scandal is dead, to be sure, but consider for a moment, if you will, what the public would do if your involvement in this sordid little affair were common knowledge? Do you think they would punish you?" he asked lightly, from the window. It was a rhetorical question, requiring no reply, and he received none. "Of course not." Sir Claudius smiled pleasurably. "You bear the onus of bastard, sufficient punishment in any man's eyes, particularly Tory eyes. No, they would turn their attention back to your dear mother. The Countess Dowager would again find herself confronting the fisherman's daughter, all her good works and exemplary life come to nothing."

He paused for effect. Edward's face was a network of pain. Sir Claudius went on, exploiting the silent agony. "She still is like a beautiful child, warm and affectionate, and doubly vulnerable now without the protection of Lord Eden. I counseled you silence then and now on her behalf." He paused again for effect, rather pleased with his impromptu speech. "There are worlds which separate us, Edward," he concluded quietly. "But on one point we stand as brothers, our mutual love for your dear mother and our desire that she should pass her remaining days in peace."

Yes, it had a nice ring. Even the expression on Edward's face was rewarding, the pathetic downward angle of defeat. Perhaps once and for all he might rid himself of this foolish need for confession.

He saw Edward lift his eyes slowly, hollow-circled from his sleepless night. "And what of Charlotte?" he asked quietly.

Annoyed, Sir Claudius returned to his desk. "What of her? She'll survive. To be sure, it's barbaric punishment," he muttered, disconcerted. "But in a way she should be grateful. A burned hand is nothing compared to the public flogging which would have been her sentence a scant fifty years ago. She should be grateful to be living in such progressive times."

Quite suddenly and without any warning whatsoever, Edward began to laugh. Sir Claudius stared at him, perplexed. Then equally abrupt, the laugh died. His face was completely changed, mocking, hard, clearly angry. Now Sir Claudius saw him leave the chair where he had sat slumped for most of the interview and lean sharply across the desk. "I wish to sell more land," he announced. "As soon as possible, as much as necessary. I have immediate need of five thousand pounds."

Sir Claudius could only gape. So! This was the true purpose of the early morning meeting. "I must protest," he began, but that was as far as he got.

"Your protestations mean nothing," Edward snapped. "I instruct you to sell, as much as necessary. You know my demands."

Sir Claudius's voice became rasping under the duress of the moment. "You sold property only a month ago—"

"And I intend to sell again, as often as I wish."

"Your brother—"

"My brother has nothing to do with it."

"Your mother has suggested that—"

"Nor has my mother anything to do with it. The property is mine. Legally, I have the right to do with it as I please."

His voice and manner were firm, without margin. Sir Claudius retreated before such resolution. It was his quiet prediction that before the century had reached its halfway mark, the Eden family would tear itself apart, due to the foolishness of old Thomas Eden, who had left his estates to his bastard, his titles to the second, legitimate son, then conveniently had died.

Now in the face of this latest madness, and as the Eden solicitor, Sir Claudius knew he should counsel prudence. To this end, he ventured, "You've sold a great deal within the last few years, Edward. The property *is* exhaustible."

"Then I shall exhaust it," Edward countered bluntly.

"You have responsibilities—"

Edward smiled. "The point of the sale."

"—other responsibilities to your mother and brother, the entire community now living in Eden Castle."

"And I will do nothing to alter that." The smile broadened. "It's not Eden I'm selling, Sir Claudius. Just a parcel of the twenty thousand acres deeded to me as an infant."

Considerably reduced now, Sir Claudius commented, "James informs me that—"

Again rage surfaced on the once smiling face. "My brother has nothing to do with it," Edward pronounced again, leaning over the desk. "His hounds and horses will always have a place. I'll see to it."

"It will take time," Sir Claudius muttered, lowering his head, knowing that now he would be detained in these chambers for the better part of the morning. There were letters to write. The Countess Dowager had insisted upon being informed when another portion of the Eden estates crumbled beneath her.

"Take all the time you need," smiled Edward graciously. "For now, give me a note in the required amount. Then when the sale is consummated, you may reimburse the account plus a generous interest for yourself."

Sir Claudius protested. "I am not a bank clerk or a lend-ing agent, Eden. I'm a solicitor."

"And a rich solicitor," Edward concurred, "your private account well lined with Eden coin."

Indignant, Sir Claudius rose. The man had never been this coarse before. And he was perspiring like a hunting dog. And what was that over his eye? A wound, no doubt the result of public brawling.

Sir Claudius turned away and stared gloomily out of the window.

Behind him, Edward prodded gently. "The money, Sir Claudius, if you will. Do you doubt my collateral?"

Sir Claudius tried a final time. "I beg you, remember your mother."

"She is never out of my mind or heart."

"If you do anything to bring additional pain down on her, I swear I will abandon you."

Edward gazed at him with delighted astonishment. "The abandonment would be twofold, Sir Claudius. You would have to go to work for a living in order to make up for the cream you skim off the top of the Eden fortune."

Sir Claudius had heard enough. Now he straightened his shoulders under his fatigue and hurried to the door. "John-son!" he shouted.

The man materialized from behind a filing cabinet. Quickly Sir Claudius gave him instructions to fetch five thousand pounds from the safe and make a careful note of it in the debit ledger complete with interest. Then he turned back into the chamber and with disgust saw Edward gazing down on the sleeping female as though he were meditating on something grand.

Slyly, still feeling a need to strike some sort of blow, Sir Claudius asked, "And what do you intend to do with that bit of soiled goods?"

Edward raised his head. His voice came softly from across the room. "I may wed her, Sir Claudius," he smiled, "a very public ceremony in Westminster, with you as my best man."

"You do that!" Sir Claudius snapped and hurriedly took refuge behind his desk as though to put that massive bar-rier between himself and the contamination.

He watched carefully, the revulsion showing on his face as Edward gently roused the child. "Come, Elizabeth," he heard him whisper. "You can finish your nap in another place."

The girl opened her eyes. For a moment there was terror in them as though she had not the slightest idea where she was. Looking up, she spied Edward and pressed close to him, her chin quivering, the mutilated hand clinging to his waistcoat.

"It's all right," he soothed. "No need to be afraid."

Sir Claudius watched the whole maudlin little scene, and wondered how long it would take to clear his chambers of the awful stench. Finally, with the girl clinging to him as the vine clings to the wall, Edward glanced in his direction. "I apologize, Sir Claudius," he began, "for this early-morning encounter. And I apologize for our harsh words and cross-purposes. The night was long and I'm out of sorts." He was on the verge of saying something else when Johnson appeared, a large brown packet in his hand. Timidly he glanced about the room, started toward Sir Claudius, who instructed him to give it to Edward.

"You now hold in your hand several acres of Eden land," Sir Claudius mused. "And prior to that, there were the thirty acres to the north of Exmoor, and prior to that the sixty acres west of Exeter—" He could have gone on, but something in Edward's face suggested he'd made his point. Satisfied, Sir Claudius leaned back in his chair.

It was quiet in the room. The girl still clung to Edward while he fingered the packet of money, head down. When he lifted his face again, the smile was back in place.

Quickly he pocketed the money and placed a protective arm about the girl. "When you write to my mother, Sir Claudius," he began, moving toward the door, "tell her that as soon as this business is over here, I intend to come home for a while." His manner lightened even more. "Tell her I'll bring her a London bonnet and news of her old friend, William Pitch." At the door, he stopped and looked back. His manner had changed again, his voice low. "And tell her I beg for forgiveness for any pain I have caused her."

Then they were gone, the both of them, leaving the stench of their presence, leaving Sir Claudius to ponder those last words. His brow furrowed. What was it the street garbage called Edward? He'd heard it before, something silly. Then he remembered. "The Prince of Eden," that was it.

Again he considered his earlier prophecy, that by the time the century reached its midpoint, the Eden family would have torn itself apart.

He called to Johnson. "Bring the writing pad," he shouted. "We'll work in the sitting room. This place is unbearable."

Situated down the corridor from his smelly chambers, he dictated two letters, one to the Countess Dowager, a letter bearing unhappy news, and the second to his land agent in Exeter, containing what was becoming a perennial and standing order: "Sell Eden Land to the first bidder."

Business over, he prepared to take his leave. The glorious Saturday was half over. The beautiful ladies in Hyde Park were waiting. He needed loveliness as an antidote to the ugliness of the morning. As he was leaving his chambers, he commanded Johnson to "Air it! Fumigate all weekend if necessary." As he passed through the door, he spied the chair where the filth had sat. "And destroy that chair," he ordered. "I don't want to see it here on Monday morning."

As he started down the steps and across the courtyard he reviewed the events of the last few hours. If the Edens were about to destroy themselves, it would behoove him to increase his fee. There was fruit enough for all on the tree as long as it stood. But in the event it fell to ground, a wise man would gather as much as he could.

Along the elegant linen and drapery establishments of Oxford Street now passed Edward Eden's private coach, long past its prime but well enough suited to Edward's purposes. Atop the high seat was John Murrey, an old friend whom Edward had plucked from the jaws of starvation beneath Westminster Bridge.

Inside the carriage, pressed against the worn velvet cushions, rode a very wide-eyed Elizabeth, and Edward himself, who felt more at peace than at any time during the last forty-eight hours.

The girl leaned forward, her head bobbing in one direction, then the other. "Where is it, sir, you're takin' me to?" she whispered.

"Home," Edward replied, finding pleasure in the small

pale face who seemed to wonder continuously at the world and its strange ways.

The pronouncement seemed to increase her agitation. "Home, sir?" she asked, clearly bewildered. "Ain't no place around here that looks right—"

Edward laughed. "Not yours, Elizabeth. Mine."

She seemed to digest this for a minute, her one good hand continuously stroking her damaged one. "And what am I to be doing there, sir?"

"Whatever you wish," he said, then added quickly, "after a wash-up and a hot meal, that is."

At length she went back to gaping, the fear in her face beginning to relax a bit. She giggled prettily. "I feel like a grand lady," she murmured, eyeing the interior of the carriage. "I ain't never been carried about so before."

"You are a grand lady," Edward graciously replied and saw the becoming blush on her face and looked hurriedly out the window to relieve her of further embarrassment.

It always pained him to see how Oxford Street had changed. Once an avenue of private dwellings, now it was an unbroken row of commercial shops. His house alone was the only remaining private establishment, and he knew it was only a matter of time before he'd have to sell and go somewhere else. Curiously, this was the one piece of property he had no desire to sell.

He looked up from his thoughts and now saw it just coming into view, wedged tightly between plate-glass museums of capricious fashion, looking rather stodgy and stubborn in its sixteenth-century lines and angles. He leaned forward as the carriage drew up alongside the pavement, the shadow of the impressive structure devouring all, horses, carriage, and occupants. No, he would postpone as long as possible the sale of the grand old house which had been in his family for over three hundred years. He felt peculiarly at home with the ghosts who resided within.

Then old John Murrey was there, opening the door. And he saw his friend, Daniel Spade, just coming through the arched doorway and down the steps, his face creased with concern.

"Edward," he shouted, still coming forward. "Are you well? Did John Murrey wait all night for you? I sent a cab to Newgate this morning, but they said you had already left." Then the man was upon him and love was in full possession of Edward as he clasped Daniel to him and reassured him that he was well.

"My God," Daniel muttered, seeing the small dried wound over Edward's eye. As Daniel examined the insignificant cut, Edward gave in to his small attentions and focused on the face of this dearest of friends. At times like now, in moments of fatigue and confusion, Edward had difficulty even remembering when this long relationship had started. They had played together as boys at Eden Point. Daniel's father, Jack Spade, had been Edward's father's loyal overseer, a mountainous, untutored man who had performed all the unpleasant tasks inherent in an estate the size of Eden. A mere two weeks had separated the boys' births, Daniel the older. But nothing had separated them since. They had grown up together, and they had been joined in 1810 by Edward's adored younger sister, Jennifer, who as soon as she was capable of steps had trailed mindlessly behind the two boys, dogging their every movement.

At some point—Edward could not say exactly when—Daniel had fallen in love with Jennifer. Now one of Edward's fondest hopes was for a union between the two, thus legally binding Daniel to him forever, this friend who was more of a brother to him than his real one.

While Daniel continued to examine the bruised flesh above Edward's eye, Edward found himself thinking briefly, sadly, on poor Jennifer, exiled to some school in the Midlands, a teacher of pianoforte. And he remembered as well the endless arguments that had raged between his mother and father on his choice of companions. But his father had been no match for the persuasive Marianne. And when the time had come for Edward to go up to Oxford, Daniel had gone with him, accepted on the strength of the Eden name and purse, not as servant, but as an equal. Unlike Edward, who had barely muddled through, Daniel had taken to his books like a thirsty man discovering a spring. He had come down with honors and a few radical and peculiar notions such as every human being had a right to enough to eat and a place to sleep, and dignity as a human being. He'd wanted to be a schoolteacher, but the public schools had not been interested in a man, no matter how brilliant, with such radical ideas. Edward had offered to share the house on Oxford Street, and had given Daniel permission to turn part of it into a Ragged School, a tuition-free establishment for abandoned children.

Now Edward looked gratefully at this friend who was asking him endless questions about his well-being. And Edward saw again the one quality that had attracted him to the man from the beginning. It was his habitually caring spirit, his deep and genuine concern, not for mankind in the abstract, but for the smallest child, the most insignificant wound.

At last Daniel shook his head, his long unruly red hair graying slightly at the temples. "The last I saw of you yesterday evening were the bottoms of your boots as they carried you out of the Blue Bell and Crown." He shook his head as though reliving the sight. "Is it always so difficult to gain admittance to Newgate?"

Again Edward tried to make light of the event. "A drunken row was a small price to pay."

Daniel leaned closer. "Did you see her? How is she faring?"

"I saw her, but did not speak with her."

Daniel looked across the street toward the Longford linen establishment. "I've not seen movement all morning."

Edward followed his gaze. In the process, he saw the young prostitute, Elizabeth, still in the carriage, apparently frozen in fear and indecision. Edward reached back and extended her his hand. "Come," he urged, "I want you to meet my friend."

Following without protest, the girl came, as always hiding her damaged hand behind her. Edward noticed Daniel's face. Nothing brought him greater delight than raw material. "Her name is Elizabeth," Edward said quietly.

Smiling, Daniel bobbed his head. "Elizabeth," he repeated.

Now as they started up the stairs, Edward noticed the vast entrance hall was deserted, yet the welcoming spirit of the old house was enough to satisfy him. With Daniel leading the way, talking quietly to the girl, they passed along until they reached what once had been the grand banqueting hall. Edward stopped at the door and admired the view before him; approximately forty children were sitting upright at desks, four volunteer teachers in attendance while the children recited their figures. In spite of the crowded room, everything seemed quiet with purpose.

He waited and watched while Daniel handed the girl over to one of the volunteers, saw the fleeting fear in her eyes as she turned a final time and looked in his direction. He smiled his reassurance at her. Then she was led off to the kitchen below, where the staff would bathe her, give her fresh garments and a hot meal. If she chose to return to her home at nightfall, she was free to do so. But based on past experience, Edward knew she wouldn't.

Now as Daniel and Edward retreated to the entrance hall, Daniel's concern was still very genuine. "Are you certain you're not seriously injured, Edward? Next time, please advise me of what you're up to."

Edward placed an affectionate arm about his shoulder. "If you'd been in on it, they would have arrested you as well. I need you here."

Daniel confronted him with a direct question. "And what was accomplished?"

"A plot," Edward replied, "or more accurately half a plot. With the help of the head turnkey, perhaps she'll never have to endure the sentence." He then remembered the packet of money inside his pocket. "And this," he smiled, withdrawing the packet, "this was accomplished as well." Carefully he separated the notes, retaining fifteen hundred pounds. The rest he handed over to Daniel. "I've brought you another mouth to feed. You may need this."

Daniel stared at the very generous sum being offered him. He seemed hesitant to take it. "I don't need that much," he protested.

But Edward insisted. "There are overdue bills. I know. I've seen them scattered about your desk. And give your volunteers something, and hire that man you want to teach the boys tailoring and shoemaking."

For a moment, their eyes held. Still Daniel seemed hesitant. "I've no right to take it," he began.

"Nonsense," Edward scoffed. "You've no right not to

take it. Now, here." And with that he thrust the sum at
Daniel and started up the stairs to his second-floor chambers. Over his shoulder he called back good-naturedly,
"You're a schoolteacher, Daniel, with absolutely no business sense. It takes money to fill empty heads and bellies."
At the top of the landing, he looked back on his friend, the
warm features which brought him such pleasure. His
fatigue was beginning to take a tremendous toll. When he
spoke, his voice was low. "You serve me well, Daniel.
Your good works compensate for my sins. Don't shut me
out."

From the bottom of the steps came the reply, soft,
earnest. "Never, Edward. Surely you know that."

The expression of friendship, instead of buttressing him,
seemed to have the opposite effect. A feeling of loneliness,
keener than any he had ever experienced before, suddenly
held him in its grip. To break its spell, he tried to alter
his mood. "Tell John Murrey to wait for me," he called
down. "I need to call on William Pitch later. I'll be down
shortly."

Then hurriedly he escaped into his chambers and closed
the door behind him. His fingers gripped the knob as
though to strangle the echo of his last words to Daniel, the
tone of voice he loathed, clearly that of master to servant.
If indeed that despicable division existed between them,
then he, Edward, was the servant and Daniel the master.

In despair he turned away from the door and faced the
spartan room, simply furnished with a pallet on the floor,
one chair, one table, one washstand, one wardrobe. There
was an enormous division between the two of them, one
consisting of thousands of acres of rich Devon land, and
an annual income of over one hundred thousand pounds
and an incredible weight of personal debt and guilt.
Peculiar, Edward had not felt the separation as acutely
when they both had been boys. But of late it seemed to be
growing stronger.

Wearily he shed his clothes and drew on a dressing robe.
Carefully he inserted the fifteen hundred pounds in a fresh
packet and placed it on the table. And finally he stretched
out on the pallet, his mind crowded with disjointed, fleeting memories of trifling episodes of home, North Devon,

mother, father. And yet, with all that poignancy of feeling which a man is capable of experiencing, he sensed an intense love and tenderness for the old ghosts. They were all dead, or living in the past, which was as good as dead. What mattered now? None of it.

A few moments' rest and he would go and pay his respects to William Pitch. His mother would want news. Indeed, he too hungered for an audience with the old man, realized with a start the number of times within the last twenty-four hours that William Pitch had entered his thoughts, as though he were calling to Edward, or Edward to him.

He relaxed upon the pallet as images of William Pitch settled over him, his white flowing hair, the features strong and resolute even under the assault of illness and age. The particular worth of William Pitch to Edward, indeed to the entire reading public of London who had so profited from his keen intellectual powers and compassionate wit, was the simple ability of the man to put everything into perspective. If the rest of the world chose to drown in the flood of the present, Pitch stood high up on the dry ground of wisdom.

In memory, Edward could hear the old man's voice, counseling patience, counseling compassion, counseling love for all, and most important, for oneself.

Then he was incapable of thinking any more. He closed his eyes. In the beginning of the dream, he saw himself just going through a door. What was on the other side, he could not say. But a feeling of quiet stole over him, as if everything was going to be put to rights again . . .

At noon, armed with the latest edition of *The Illustrated London News*—for he was a man who liked to keep abreast of events—Jawster Gray left his flat on Charing Cross and headed toward the White Bear at the top of Oxford Street. He looked forward to a cheese roll and a few pints, and a diversion of his loneliness which he always found in the crowded pub.

As he paused on the pavement to await a break in the never-ending stream of carriages, he again pondered his dilemma. Good Gawd! How many times he'd been back and forth over the same territory. Earlier that morning he'd hoped to lose himself in sleep. But his simple bed, which in the past had always granted him soothing respite, had refused for some reason to receive him. He'd turned fever-ishly for several hours and at last had surrendered to wake-fulness, lying on his back like a beached ship, staring out the soot-smudged window at the pale golden rifts in the clouds.

Fifteen hundred pounds would unsmudge those windows right enough, indeed would lift him totally free of the grim alley which served as his walkway, the black, un-varnished door which led in to the smelly stairs which in turn led to the mean, narrow, cold room in which he had passed the last forty-two years.

A few minutes later he took refuge in the White Bear, heading toward his table by the window which afforded him a safe but generous view of Piccadilly. Several of the young serving girls greeted him warmly, their faces glisten-ing with perspiration.

From across the congested room, one called cheerily, "Jawster, you're up and about early."

Usually he enjoyed giggling with the girls. Now rather cheerlessly he returned the greeting. "A cheese roll," he called out, "and a pint of ale."

He sank heavily into the chair and spread the newspaper before him. For a moment he rested his head in his hands as though his brain were on the verge of exploding. Sweet Gawd! There had to be respite somewhere. Hungry for distraction, he opened his eyes to an article concerning the arrival of the Coburg cousins, German princes, Ernest and a lad named Albert, here for Princess Victoria's seven-teenth birthday. Carefully he studied the accompanying il-lustrations. Such pretty children, all of them, although Jawster had no idea how the ship of state would manage to sail under the frail hand of a woman. And he knew, as did all of London, that it was only a matter of time before the old King died and left the slim girl in his place.

Again he stared at the pretty pampered faces before him. He would have liked to have had children. But how could a decent man ask a decent woman to share his lot of twelve shillings a week, and not even that in the beginning.

But now? Was it too late? Fifteen hundred pounds, a piece of Kent land, a comfortable cheery widow, not too old, perhaps still capable of childbearing, a couple of good horses, his own carriage? Why not!

A smile blazed across his face as he stared, unseeing, at the crowds beyond the window. The serving girl was at his elbow now. "Lord, Jawster," she grinned. "The look on your face! What is it you're seein'? The shores of Heaven?"

Hungrily he reached for the cheese roll while she was still lowering the plate. Unfortunately at that moment he remembered again the whole dread pleasure and pain of his last meeting with the Prince of Eden, the free bottle of port, the offer of fifteen hundred pounds.

He settled back in his chair, folded the newspaper to one side, and listened to the pleasant hum of voices rise about him. He stared, still unseeing, out the window at the crush of traffic. Then what was his decision? Use his keys and his position of authority to help the young woman to escape, pocket the small fortune, and never come near Newgate or London again?

Or— Refuse the bargain, endure the open court spectacle of burning flesh, endure too the bond of friendship with the Prince of Eden broken, no more bottles of port, but conscience intact, secure in the knowledge that he had served the law?

Thus he went like that, back and forth, for the better part of the afternoon. The serving girls kept him well supplied with an endless river of ale. And by four o'clock his besotted brain had at last slipped into a kind of welcome numbness.

Another hour and he was due to go back on the watch at Newgate. In the event the Prince of Eden appeared tonight, and Jawster knew he would, he must have his answer ready.

Feeling as battered as though he'd fought five hundred Waterloos, he stumbled to his feet, tossed enough coin on the table to cover his bill, and grasping his way from chair to chair, he arrived at the door and the blazing late afternoon sun beyond.

Someone called after him, but he didn't answer. Out on

the pavement he stood for a moment as though in a stupor, the street noises magnified in his ears, his bleary eyes seeing all in triplicate. Pedestrians jostled against him. A street urchin tried to slip a grimy hand into his pocket.

"Be off with you," he shouted, waving wildly at the child. Then he saw the sullen eyes in the youthful face and softened his attitude. "Don't rob old Jawster today," he smiled. "He's a poor man, as poor as you." He leaned closer, grinning. "But come tomorrow. Then you can rob old Jawster, for he'll be a rich man."

The stream of pedestrians separated them, carrying the child in one direction, Jawster in the other. It astonished him to discover that in that instant the decision had almost been made.

He looked angrily about. No one in all those passing faces was paying the slightest attention to him. Well, then nothing to do but step out into the middle of the pavement and announce his news again. Everyone must know. Someone *must* care. He drew himself up and wished that the pavement would hold steady. He lifted his head, closed his eyes, and taking a broad stride, stepped directly out into the flow of carriages.

Then here it came, that great shadow bearing down on him. A man's voice, very close or so it seemed, shouted, "Watch—"

Jawster tried to do as he was told. Glancing upward he saw six horses pulling a crowded omnibus heading straight for him. He thought quite lucidly that he'd never seen such monsters before. Where had they come from? The huge beasts seemed to be flinging themselves about, sending a flurry of white foam from their mouths.

The noise and confusion boiled around him, the brutes coming closer. He stepped back before the onslaught; his boots caught on something and he was falling backward, the giants rearing up over him, hooves striking the pavement all about while Jawster cried out, *"Jesus—"*

Then he lay quietly on the pavement, pain and darkness increasing. Now and then a hissing sound slipped from his mouth. Through a dim red moist curtain his eyes moved from one to another of the horrified onlookers. "A rich man," he muttered.

Blood filled his mouth, a stream of blood spouting from his nose, his splintered legs twisted beneath him. One hand moved up as though to hold his head together. A pain as sharp as a blade pierced through to the center of his brain. The grip of his teeth on his tongue relaxed.

A decision had been made.

At five o'clock that afternoon, hopelessly stalled in a traffic crush near the White Bear on Oxford Street, Edward gazed out his carriage window at the chaos beyond.

Old John Murrey shouted down at him. "It's a horse-drawn omnibus, sir. Gone sideways it has. A lame horse, I reckon—"

"No rush, John," Edward called out. "Do your best."

As a direct ray of late afternoon sun struck his face, he closed his eyes. The restless interval which had passed for sleep had not really revived him. His thoughts went continuously back to Newgate, to Charlotte imprisoned there.

Rapidly he lifted his head and stared fixedly out the opposite window. Pray God old Jawster Gray had lost his battle with his conscience.

With a start the carriage lurched forward. John Murrey called down, "It's a dead man, sir."

As the carriage inched slowly forward, Edward leaned toward the window. He saw ahead a stalled omnibus, passengers leaning out of the windows, and on the pavement he saw three Peelers bending over a crumpled form, the legs twisted in a macabre position, blood everywhere, the poor victim himself obscured by the Peelers and the press of curious onlookers. Somewhere in this vast city, there would be a pitiful pocket of grief this night. Corpses, if not men, were always loved.

The traffic was thinning, the scene outside his window a manageable flow. He remembered as a child his mother bringing him to William Pitch's house, delicious fortnights prowling the British Museum and the lovely empty fields beyond. He smiled openly now, remembering how his mother had given him stern instructions never to mention the family secret, that her half-sister, Jane, and William Pitch were not legally married. But then she'd always hastened to reassure him that the duration and intensity

of their union made them wed in the eyes of God. It
seemed a silly point then and now.

From atop the high seat he heard John Murrey calling
to him again. "Great Russell Street, was it, sir?"

"Yes, John, straight ahead, then to the left." As they
drew near his destination, he made an attempt to straighten
himself from the jogging ride. He'd taken certain pains
with his dress, knowing how important such matters were
to his Aunt Jane. He'd forced himself into black peg-top
trousers, a buff-colored waistcoat, and black coat. On the
seat beside him was a polished and brushed beaver hat
which he'd thought once to wear, but now upon studying
it, he changed his mind. He'd come to see, not be seen. Old
Jane would forgive him.

While he was still eyeing the hat, the carriage stopped.
He looked out. "No, John, it's just ahead—"

"Can't get no closer, sir. Look for yourself."

Quickly he leaned out of the window. On both sides the
street was lined with carriages, as many as a dozen, block-
ing the passage in front of William's house. What in the—

Puzzled, he alighted the carriage, gave John instructions
for waiting, then started down the pavement on foot. He
passed a knot of idle coachmen having a pipe and a chat,
their liveries clearly bespeaking the importance of their
masters.

Looking up, he saw a gentleman in a black frock coat just
emerging from the red brick house. Then Edward was running, his fears increasing with his speed. He took the walk
at breakneck speed and saw in his mind's eye for just a
flash a young boy, seven or eight, running belatedly for
dinner, his younger brother trailing behind him, both grimy
from their play in the empty fields.

"I beg your pardon, sir—" His breath caught in his
throat as he approached the departing priest. "Could you
tell me—"

Then beyond the priest, standing in the opened doorway,
he saw his Aunt Jane, her figure still slim and erect at
seventy, a handkerchief pressed to her lips. Her gown was
black, her face a contortion of pain.

"Edward?" she inquired gently as though age and tears
had dulled her vision.

It was a distance of a dozen steps from where he stood

to her outstretched arms, and with every step, Edward prayed, Don't let him be dead.

Then he was standing beside her on the threshold, trying to read the grief in her face. Gently he took her in his arms, felt her frail body press closer to him as though for protection.

"I just sent for you," she whispered. "He's been asking for you over and over—"

Edward closed his eyes. Thank God. He held her a moment longer, breathing deeply of her lavender scent, the young boy within him as insistent as ever. *Let Aunt Jane fix it. Come, Aunt Jane will hold you.*

"What happened?" he asked quietly, trying to send the boy away.

She stood back, making a valiant attempt to control her tears. "Late last night, he was working—at his desk. I heard him call for the girl, and the next thing—" A fresh wave of tears coursed down her wrinkled face.

Again he put his arms around her and drew her close, heard her murmur, "It's his heart. The doctors give us little hope." Then with a certain sternness she straightened her shoulders, dabbed a final time at her eyes. "But, come," she said, businesslike. "He's been asking for you since early morning."

Since early morning! As Edward walked with her through the entrance hall, he repeated those words in his head. Since morning. It had been then when his thoughts of William Pitch had almost overwhelmed him.

A few steps this side of the drawing room, Jane stopped. "The house is filled," she whispered, a slant of annoyance on her face. "I have no idea how word traveled so fast, but you'd think we were still running our salon." She leaned closer, still dabbing at her eyes. "My girls have been kept busy since midmorning, endless rounds of coffee and tea." As she spoke, she fingered the single strand of pearls about her neck. He noticed her hand, thin, blue-veined, and trembling like her shoulders.

"Must I stop in?" Edward begged. "Who am I to them?"

A look of shock momentarily displaced the expression of grief on her face. "Who are you?" she repeated. "Shame! You are Edward Eden, William's nephew and the son of Lord Thomas Eden." He saw a fierce light of pride on her face, her blue eyes as alert as ever, still reveling in her peripheral connection with one of the great names of England.

"Come," she urged now, "the introductions will take only a moment. Your mother would expect it of you."

With an air of fatality, he straightened the buff waistcoat, eyed sadly the staircase leading up to the second-floor bed-chambers where the man he loved more than life itself lay dying.

As they entered the drawing room, he narrowly avoided a collision with a young serving girl heavily laden with a tray bearing a tea service. As they passed her by, Jane murmured new instructions to her. "Prepare high tea, Esther. Our guests must be getting hungry."

For a moment, Edward felt a flare of anger surface within him. His aunt, for all her protestations, was carrying on as though her salon *was* opened again. Then the company was before him, the drawing room crowded, at least twenty people standing in small groups, quietly talking. As they caught sight of Jane, they fell silent. Some balanced tea-cups. A few of the gentlemen smoked. All were staring.

Edward had counted on a general introduction. Instead Jane took his arm and led him steadily forward to the first small group of guests. Again he felt an urgent need for haste. His aunt, however, was resolute in her attention to proprieties and guided him to a seated gentleman with a broad forehead and a head of wavy, unruly brown hair. As they approached, he stood, one hand stroking the great mustache that blended with a luxuriant chin beard. The grief which Jane had displayed earlier at the door entirely disappeared as she spoke softly, almost reverently, "Edward, may I present Mr. Dickens."

Edward took the hand extended to him. He'd seen the popular novelist from a distance and greatly admired him, his novels less than his Sketches by Boz. "My pleasure, sir," he smiled.

Mr. Dickens returned the sentiment. "I've heard of you, Mr. Eden," he said. "I only regret that we meet under such sorrowful circumstances. The world, I fear, for a long while will be a dim and colorless place without William Pitch."

Again Edward nodded his agreement and his gratitude. There was a gentleman standing to the right of Mr. Dick-

ens. Now he stepped forward, as though aware that it was
his turn.

This time, Dickens performed the introductions. "Mr.
Eden, I would like to present my house guest, Thomas De
Quincey. Down from Edinburgh."

The man himself stepped forward, the infamous opium
eater, reformed, or so Edward had heard. Edward was impressed with the man's face, shy, sensitive, gaunt, as
though he'd survived crucibles. De Quincey did not extend
his hand, but merely stood as though at attention, as though
with the slightest of movements, he might shatter like
glass. "I do not generally attend death, Mr. Eden," he commented softly. "I've met the fellow too often in other
spheres to be much impressed by his company. But the
world went black for me several years ago, and the only
man who offered me a lantern was William Pitch."

Apparently the man had succeeded in moving himself
for quickly he turned away. Behind him, Edward heard
Jane sniffling. Before him stood Mr. Dickens. The man
now leaned close. "May I suggest that you take your leave,
Mr. Eden," he murmured. "This company will wait. The
man upstairs may not."

Grateful, Edward started to follow the sound advice. But
Jane was at his side again, indomitably leading him around
the room, omitting no one. If the faces were meaningless,
the names were not: G. H. Lewes, Mr. and Mrs. Thomas
Carlyle, Mr. Thackeray, of course. Edward had met him
before in this very drawing room under happier circumstances. Also there was an elegant, though stony-faced
woman who introduced herself as Harriet Martineau, and
next to her, an arrogant-looking gentleman who extended
a limp wrist and identified himself as Thomas Babington
Macaulay. Pompous old Tory. Briefly Edward wondered
what he was doing here in this liberal atmosphere. But of
course. Then he remembered. William took no sides, political or otherwise. The world was of a piece, he'd said, human impulses not that far removed from each other. And
there, standing by the door, the most dignified of all, his
face glazed, Robert Southey, poet laureate of England.

At the conclusion of the introductions, Edward realized
with wonder that all the literary lions of London were now
gathered in William Pitch's front parlor, the men and
women who under other circumstances and in different

times had quite effectively torn each other and society in general to shreds, armed only with their pens.

Now reduced to unity by common grief for one man, they stood in silent circles, sipping tea and gazing blank-faced out the windows, their tribute mute and therefore highly effective.

But enough, and Edward signaled as much when approaching the door again, after having made the full circle, he begged of Jane, "Please, now take me to him."

And she did, apparently satisfied that he had met everyone.

As they took the stairs, he had to slow his pace for the enfeebled Jane. Heavily she leaned on his arm, her other hand pressed against her breast as though her heart were beating too rapidly. "Oh, for the ease of youth," she mourned. "I can remember the days when I took these stairs two at a time, generally in rage and ill-temper."

He smiled considerately. "You're doing fine, Aunt Jane."

She dismissed his lie for what it was. At the top of the landing, she came to a complete halt, gasping for breath. While she was still recovering, she said, "I've agonized all day for your mother, Edward. I wish she were here." With peculiar force, she added, "She should be here."

Edward tried to offer comfort. "If she had known, I'm sure she would have made the effort. You know as well as I how difficult it is to pry her loose from Eden."

Jane looked at him, a strangely soft expression on her face. "All my life I've tried to keep them apart. Now I'd give my last breath to be able to bring them together."

She walked ahead of him down the long corridor, leaving him to puzzle her last comment. Near a door at the end of the corridor, he saw two gentlemen in close huddle. They parted as Jane approached. The three of them were talking quietly as Edward drew near. Again there were introductions, two physicians, Doctor Someone and Doctor So-and-so, the blank, unrevealing expressions of all medical men on their faces.

"Only a few minutes, Mr. Eden, if you will," one of them suggested. "He needs his rest." Then one of the physicians had him by the arm and was guiding him into the dimly lit chamber. The drapes were drawn on the one broad window, partly obscuring the pink dusk which had begun to fall outside.

Edward closed his eyes and silently cursed the stern dictates of age. His memories of the man at his prime were painfully before him, playing horseshoes in the back garden, William teasing Edward for losing so soundly to a one-armed man.

Again the physician passed him by. "Only a few minutes, Mr. Eden," he repeated.

At that moment, the white head on the pillow stirred. From behind the closed eyes came a voice only slightly diminished by his faltering heart. "Pay no mind to the old cutthroat, Edward. Only by the grace of God have I survived his ministrations for all these years."

The eyes were open now, a smile warming the once lifeless features. "Come," he muttered to Edward, waving his good left hand in the air. "Earlier today I dreamed you were here. Come, let me touch you and see if the vision has substance."

As the nurse and physician retreated, Edward stepped toward the edge of the bed. *A game of marbledores, Uncle William?* the child within him cried.

As the door closed softly behind him, Edward drew a chair close to the bed, leaned forward, and took the hand extended to him. It felt like a piece of thin white parchment, cold, with sharp blue ridges like a relief map. "I'm here, William," he said. "You're not dreaming now."

The old man tried to shift his position on the bed. His sunken eyes peered intently into the dimness. "Why in hell are the drapes closed?" he grumbled. "Open them, Edward. A man has a right to light."

Quickly Edward went to the window and threw open the drapes. A stream of soft pink dusk flooded the room. "That's better," the old man sighed. "Now, come back," he urged, patting the edge of the bed. "We have business to discuss."

Edward returned to the chair and again enclosed the thin hand between his own. In the increased light he saw a purple tint to William's lips. The sight caused Edward's alarm to increase. The man resembled a cadaver. "I mustn't stay too long, William," he said. "There are others—"

"Damn the others," William snapped. "Vultures, most of them, come to pick the bones clean."

Again Edward smiled. "Not vultures, William. You

should see your front parlor. It's a galaxy of stars, the cream of London's literati—"

"Curdled now," the old man snapped. "Dickens is writing sentimental slop. Macaulay is arrogant as ever, and Carlyle's spouting like a great beached whale on such subjects as Chaos and Necessity, the Devil, and Universal Warfare—" He broke off. A smile softened his features. "Carlyle's the only man I know whose very voice can render a capitalization."

He chuckled softly and shook his head upon the pillow. For an instant his eyes fell on the tops of emerald trees beyond the window. "Not a Boswell on the horizon," he mourned, "to say nothing of a Johnson." He looked back at Edward, a gleam of pride in his eyes. "I knew them both, you know, in my youth." He closed his eyes. "I can't account for much in my life, but I can say I knew the gods."

Abruptly he shook his head as though to rouse himself out of his nostalgia. "But enough," he scolded. "Let the fools wait. I'll have to endure their farewell speeches soon enough, a fitting prelude to Hell—" Again he shifted upon the bed, and though experiencing mild discomfort, Edward noticed his nightshirt, sleeveless on one side, tailored in the fashion of all of William's garments, to conceal the absence of his right arm.

How many times Edward had heard the tale of how he'd lost it, and he'd never tired of hearing it, how William had been in Paris in '93, at the height of the Revolution, how he'd stepped before an assassin's bullet and spared the life of Mr. Thomas Paine, and in the process lost his arm.

Now as he waited for the old man to recover, he felt a strangely oceanic sense, as though all of London had dropped away and left the two of them stranded in this small room.

"Great God, what a face, Edward," William now was scolding. His left hand floated weakly up and lightly brushed across Edward's brow. "What a pretty brow," he smiled. "Still a pretty brow. Your mother's brow," he added, the delight on his face softening into sorrow.

Edward leaned forward. "She would be here if she could, William, if she knew—"

The old man nodded quickly. "I know. You must convey to her my affection." He continued to stare intently into Edward's face as though seeing beyond it. "My God," he murmured, smiling, "that woman has never been where I wanted her. It seems as though I've spent half my life waiting for her, calling for her. When I lost this—" He glanced down at his smooth right side, then abruptly broke off speaking.

Edward fought continuously against the conflict within him, the feeling that he should leave and the desire to stay. "Please, William," he begged, "try to be at ease. Don't—"

"Be at ease," the man scoffed on diminishing breath. "I'll be at ease soon enough. For now, let's talk of you."

Edward had not expected such a direct focus.

Apparently William saw the surprise on his face. "I've followed the trial, Edward," he said, his voice strong. "I know all about the young woman, and I know too of your constant attendance in the company of that jackass, Sir Claudius Potter—" He hesitated, not faltering this time, merely giving Edward a chance to assimilate his words. Slowly he went on. "What I don't know is your involvement in the affair."

Edward bowed his head. "My involvement is total," he confessed.

William nodded. "I thought as much." Again he fell into a close scrutiny of Edward's face. "Well," he sighed, "fifty years ago you would have met the offended husband in the meadows beyond Hampstead Heath and the affair would have been settled in a matter of minutes. Now, in this 'progressive age,' the two cocks go free and the poor hen is left to suffer the consequences."

"She will not suffer," Edward interjected quickly.

William looked surprised. "Sentence has been handed down, and knowing the old magistrate, it will stand—"

Edward agreed, and disagreed. "But she will never face it. I have friends in Newgate."

Suddenly the old man's face brightened. "A plot? Oh, how delicious. Tell me all, Edward. A farewell plot to warm an old man's bones—"

In spite of himself, Edward smiled. The very matter of which he'd agonized for four long weeks seemed suddenly as important as a theatrical at the Haymarket. "Some money will change hands," he began. "The head turnkey at Newgate will conveniently leave doors unlocked. My friends will spirit her out—" He came to a halt in his narrative, realizing that there his plot ended.

"And?" prompted William.

Edward shrugged. "And—nothing. She'll be free."

"To do what?"

"What she pleases," Edward replied, rather snappish. He left the bedside and went to the window.

Behind him he heard a soft inquiry. "Do you love her?"

Edward stared through the window at the patch of dwindling blue above. "I made love to her," he replied.

Again from behind, he heard a clucking noise. "Oh, Edward," William sighed. "What a waste."

As Edward looked over his shoulder, he saw the white head wagging back and forth. "Mind you, I'm not opposed to taking other men's wives. I took a few of my own in my day. But I always did it with passion." He closed his eyes as though the word tasted sweet upon his lips. "Passion," he repeated, smiling, "the true test of vulgarity *and* refinement."

In his own defense, Edward said, "She was lonely, as was I. I loved her in a fashion, still love her, perhaps—" In despair, he shook his head and again looked out the window. "My problem, William, seems to be the classic inability to define love—"

For a moment, the room was silent behind him. When that silence persisted, he turned in alarm, only to find the man staring at him. Still when he did not speak, Edward stepped back to the bed. In some confusion, he saw tears on the old man's face.

"Have I said something, William, that—"

But quickly the man shook his head. As though embarrassed by his own weakness, he hurriedly wiped the moisture away. "You'd think that at eighty plus, the word would have lost its hold on me. But it hasn't. I hear the word and I see one face, hear one voice—"

A tribute to Jane, Edward thought, and found it touching. But the man spoke on. "You should have known her as a girl, Edward, your beloved mother, the miraculous Marianne—"

Edward stepped closer, the ancient puzzle from his childhood beginning to fall into place. William was speaking quite steadily now, though his eyes were closed, his voice low. "I remember the first time I laid eyes on her, a

drowned rat she was after the coach ride from North
Devon, a mere girl of sixteen, with a scarred back"—his
voice hardened—"the handiwork of your father, I might
add." The hardness passed. "But what spirit, what light!
Jane had banished her to the storeroom, her first feeble attempt to make a servant of her." The dim eyes opened.
"What a foolish gesture that was." Again the voice fell.
"Oh, God, how I loved her, love her still, if you'll forgive
an old man's confession."

Edward held his position beside the bed. Words were
beyond him. There was nothing to forgive. It wasn't embarrassment he felt, rather a kind of relief, as more pieces
fell into place, as though he'd known forever what the man
was now confessing.

Then an urgency surfaced on the old face. He waved
wildly for Edward to come closer. "I have lived," he
whispered, "my entire life on the nourishment of what
might have been." His head pressed backward into the
pillow as though he were seized by a tremor. "What a
waste," he gasped.

Edward felt concern for him, the emotional remem-
brances obviously taking a tremendous toll. "Please, William," he begged, "no more talk—"

The old man looked up. "Do I shock you?" he grinned.
"These antics of the heart? The young always think their
elders too stupid for such knowledge. But if you are listening carefully, you will hear a lesson—aimed particularly
at you."

Distracted, Edward murmured, "I don't understand."

William laughed. "You were never dense before, Edward. Why now, when you need most to listen and to
understand?"

Hurriedly Edward shook his head. "I'm concerned for
you, William—"

The laugh faded rapidly. The enfeebled head tried to
lift. "Forget about me," he rasped. "It's you. You're the
one." He relaxed again into the pillow as though he knew
he was spending more energy than he had to spare. "I look
at you, Edward, and you become for me a flawless pier
glass. I see myself as I was forty years ago, full of the
rancor of an ambitious man who knows he has powers and
is savage because they aren't being used, feels that the
months, the years are being gnawed away—you are just at

the stage, Edward, when you are ready and willing for liberation. You are too robust a man, have too much strength and warmth of nature—"

Edward started to protest, but William cut him off. "No, hear me out. You have too much strength and warmth of nature to abide in passive despondency much longer." Again he smiled and shook his head. "Depression, yes. The two of us are born depressives. I struggled against it for a lifetime, as you will too. But like all true depressives, we have much capacity for enjoyment—and love, and I think, in your case, it is ready to break out—"

He was trembling. Edward could feel it in his hand. "Did you break out, William?" he asked softly.

A look of grief crossed the man's face. "No," he whispered. "Instead I committed the worst crime that a man can perpetrate on himself." He looked directly up at Edward. "I *accustomed* myself to it."

Edward listened closely. He leaned forward and with his handkerchief caressed the sweat-covered brow. The eyes which had been closed opened again.

"I apologize for painting such a black picture, Edward," he whispered. "And it isn't true that I'm not grateful. God grant everyone such a life." He smiled warmly. "But it might have been more, if I'd only had the will to—"

Suddenly he broke off in a spasm of coughing. The frail frame shook under the paroxysm. Edward started forward in alarm. Although the spasm passed, it left him with his head pushed backward, eyes closed. But the mind was still working, forming words.

"Remember one thing, Edward. Nature isn't to be changed. But character, by will and effort, might be—"

The cough was almost continuous now. Tears filled his eyes. "Please, William," Edward begged.

"Oh God," the old man moaned.

Edward tried to rise. The physicians were just outside. But in spite of the weakness now engulfing William, he would not release Edward's hand. The man's lips were moving. Edward leaned closer in order to hear.

"Thank you, Edward," he whispered, "for sharing this life with me. And thank your mother—" The sentences were coming in fragments now. "Much love—much indulgence—much bewilderment, suffering this hour of dreams

—this life. There is no error in the design, merely errors in—us—"

The bell for evening matins sounded in St. Mark's down the road. Edward leaned forward and kissed the man. Blind with tears, he murmured, "I love you, William."

He saw the head upon the pillow as though he might speak. But instead an awful gasp escaped through purple lips. Edward saw his mouth frozen in a final attempt to draw breath.

He sat a moment longer, clasping the hand. He tried to remember what the man had said, but the words were a jumble.

The bell in the church steeple began to ring again. As in a trance, Edward placed the hand upon the sunken chest. Again he leaned forward and kissed the beloved face.

Suddenly in a pain of grief, he bent over and bodily lifted William into his arms, cradled him close, and rocked him as though he were a child in need of comfort. Beneath the nightshirt, Edward felt the ancient stump, felt as mutilated as the man he held, something cut off, missing, gone forever.

Behind him he heard the door softly open. Then he heard a rush of footsteps and the two physicians were separating them, one guiding Edward away, the other hovering over William.

Looking up, he saw Jane clinging to the door, her face buried in her hands. Quickly he went to her and separated her from the door and took her into his arms. As the old woman clung to him, her sobs increased. To one side, Edward saw the physicians drawing the coverlet over William's face. Still he continued to hold the frail woman and absorb her distress. With his hand pressing her head to his breast, he said, "His last words were of you, Jane, how empty his life would have been without you—"

She looked up at him, tears streaming in a crisscross pattern over the wrinkles of her face. "I loved him," she whispered fiercely, as though someone had challenged her. "I loved him always, and will love him to my grave."

Edward nodded. He continued to hold her for several minutes. Sooner than he might have expected, her grief seemed to subside. There were important matters awaiting her, the physicians standing a discreet distance away. She dried her tears and with remarkable control asked Edward to stay close by. She would have need of him.

He assured her that he would, although as she turned toward the waiting physicians, he doubted her words. She had run William Pitch's life with extraordinary efficiency. She would preside over his death in a like manner.

The corridor outside the chamber was now filled with people, word of the death somehow having spread to the visitors waiting in the front parlor. As Jane rather primly arranged the dignitaries for final deathbed visitations, Edward retreated.

Hurriedly he pushed past the crowded corridor, heading for the stairs. Someone called after him, but he didn't stop in his downward progress. In fact his speed increased until he was running across the entrance hall and out into the cool May evening.

He saw the street still clogged with carriages, even more arriving. He wanted no fellowship, desired to exchange words with no man, and in an attempt to gain some privacy, he cut sharply to the left, skirted the house, and took refuge in the darkened garden.

He felt like something lost, trying to get home. The exhaustion was increasing. Slowly he sank down onto a stone bench and bowed his head.

Why couldn't he remember the man's last words? Something about looking into his face, seeing his own. And nature wasn't to be changed, but character, with— Or was it the other way around?

As his confusion mounted, tears commenced. He felt as though the death upstairs was beginning to spread. The thrust of his grief was that he could not imagine life without William Pitch.

Thank you for sharing this life with me, Edward.

The dam broke. Heavily he fell upon his knees in the moist grass, his head resting on the stone bench.

He was not at first aware of the footsteps approaching him, almost stealthily, in the dark. He thought he heard movement, but did not bother to look up. He was first aware that he was not alone when he heard the voice, deep, yet close: "Total eclipse without all hope of day."

He turned sharply and saw a gentleman standing a distance apart. "I trust, Mr. Eden," the man said, "that you do not weep from a sense of bereavement."

In darkness Edward could not clearly see the man's face and did not recognize the voice. "Please leave me," he muttered, resenting the intrusion. "I seek no consolation."

"But you're in sore need of it," the man persisted. He stepped closer. Edward started to rise.

"No," the gentleman commanded. "Hold your position. In the past, I've found it a comforting one, on my knees—"

All in the world that Edward desired at that moment was privacy. Was it too much to ask? Apparently it was.

The gentleman, still unidentified, drew nearer. "I repeat what I said, Mr. Eden. I trust you do not weep from a sense of bereavement. There is no prop withdrawn, no consolation torn away, no dear companion lost."

"The man is dead," Edward snapped angrily. "Now, please, I beg you, leave—"

"You weep for yourself," the man continued, undaunted. "All grief is selfish. All death a comfort. If only we could reconcile the two."

Edward looked up, still angry at the intrusion. "Who are you?"

The man inclined his head. "We met earlier inside. De Quincey. Thomas De Quincey."

"Why aren't you with the others?"

"Remains hold no fascination for me."

There was a certain harshness in his voice that Edward now found peculiarly comforting. The man's shadow continued to hover over the bench. He spoke softly. "All that one must bear in mind, Mr. Eden, is that earthly existence is not that precious. All our positions here are exquisitely painful. Death is merely the termination of that pain. In societies more primitive than ours, it is an occasion for great rejoicing—"

"I do not live in other societies."

"No, but does that mean you cannot benefit from their wisdom?"

The voice, coming so steadily across the darkness, began to have a strangely soothing effect. Edward felt the tears subsiding, the muddle and mystery of William's last words no longer a care.

He started to lift himself up and saw the man's hand outstretched, offering support. "Come, Mr. Eden," he invited. "Our business is finished here. As my host, Mr.

Dickens, has elected to remain, I find myself quite without transportation. Would it be an imposition if I—"

"My aunt has requested that I stay," said Edward quickly, brushing the bits of clinging earth from his trousers. In spite of the man's brief comfort, now Edward found his intimacy embarrassing, in poor taste.

Abruptly De Quincey laughed, a strange sound in a sea of grief. "Your aunt is having a glorious time, Mr. Eden. Would you rob her of a single moment of her pleasure?"

Edward moved away. "I should stay," he announced.

But the man merely followed after him, objecting. "A rare personality is gone, Mr. Eden. Come, let's toast his life and ignore his death. This earth holds us down. I have the means by which we can fly after him. No pain, no grief, floating in the arms of angels—"

Edward listened carefully. Oh God, how the prescription appealed! And what the man had said was true. Even Edward had doubted Jane's need of him. Then, too, it would be rude of him to ignore the man's request for transportation. "For an hour, De Quincey," he said finally. "Then I must return."

The man smiled. "If you want to return in an hour, I shall deliver you myself. Come—"

As they entered the front walk, Edward saw the increase of traffic passing in and out of the red brick house, lamps ablaze in every window. God, the thought of human intercourse was appalling. As the two men started hurriedly down the pavement toward Edward's carriage, De Quincey leaned close. "The fragile frame is of no interest to us, Mr. Eden. It is the strong spirit we're after. Are you game?"

Feeling the unbearable weight of grief slip from his shoulders, Edward could only nod. The night air seemed to revive him, the presence of the man beside him assisting with that revival.

As they drew near the carriage, Edward saw old John Murrey dozing atop the high seat. He shouted up to the man. But before Edward could convey a destination, De Quincey spoke. "May I? I know a pleasant place."

Edward nodded, heard the man call up the name of a street near the Embankment. A moment later both men crawled inside the carriage and the horses started forward. In the passing lamplight Edward studied the face opposite him, a most strange face.

He seemed now to be aware of Edward's close scrutiny. "I've not visited Heaven for several years, Mr. Eden," he began, as though aware that some explanation was necessary. "I've trod a straight course in Edinburgh. I've been productive both professionally and maritally." He smiled broadly. "I have a loving wife and a family of eight.

"The straight course," De Quincey repeated, "unerringly, for years." He leaned backward against the cushions, his eyes closed, on his face a dazzling smile. "But, oh God, how I have missed that cloudland, that gorgeous land which only opens to the sleep-closed eyes—" The ecstasy was fixed on his face. Edward felt the excitement spreading as, leaning forward, De Quincey revealed the object in his hand, a small glass vial filled with a red-brown liquid.

"Laudanum," De Quincey said softly. "The only passage a man needs to get from here to Heaven. Will you be so kind as to accompany me, Mr. Eden?"

Edward turned away and gazed out the window. The streets were dark and silent with the exception of a passing cab. What was there for him back at the house on Great Russell Street save a corpse? What was there waiting for him on Oxford Street save Daniel's purpose, Daniel's students, Daniel's conviction? What was there awaiting him at Newgate except the young woman whose future agony was his responsibility?

"Come, Edward," De Quincey whispered intimately. He took Edward's hand and placed the vial in his opened palm. "Let me tell you what it was that in reality made me an opium eater. Pain, was it? No, but misery. Casual overcasting of sunshine, was it? No, but black desolation. Gloom, was it, that might have departed? No, but settled and abiding darkness."

Edward looked at the vial. It was inviting, the thought of closing his tired eyes from that total eclipse without all hope of day. He knew what he held in his hand. Though he'd never indulged, still he knew the risks, the benefits.

"Well?" De Quincey prodded gently.

Edward nodded.

Hadley Park
Shrewsbury
Shropshire
May, 1836

German tutors, French dressmakers, Spanish eques-
trian masters, eighty-seven thousand pounds per annum,
and four hundred years of arrogant breeding had gone into
the making of Harriet Powels. On other occasions, in
aristocratic households, those same ingredients had produced entire generations of shy, vapid, noncommittal young
women who tended to hysteria. But in this instance, for
reasons unknown except to nature, these same ingredients
had produced Harriet.

Hadley Park was the ancestral home of the Powelses, had
been since the early fourteen hundreds when a land-rich
Englishman named Hadley Powels had raided the Welsh
border and brought back a ravishing red-haired Welsh
beauty. It was not a kidnapping. In fact her father was
grateful to the Englishman for taking the creature off his
hands and in a show of gratitude had sent along as dowry
one of the largest sheep herds in all of Wales, over ten
thousand head, or so it was estimated. Legend had it
that the continuous procession of sheep crossing the narrow
wooden bridge that spanned the border had lasted for
three days.

A direct descendant of this union, Harriet's father, like

all his ancestors, had known precisely what to do with the profitable combination of sheep and grazing land, and now the Powelses were one of the richest worsted manufacturing families in England, and had lately added ingeniously to their already burgeoning fortunes by using steam power in the manufacture of woolens.

Harriet was a beloved, pampered, only daughter, only child as well since the death of her older brother three years earlier in a senseless hunting accident. Now the entire future of the Powelses rested on her slim, straight shoulders. At twenty-five and well into spinsterhood, her parents had acted for her, and had entered into a tentative agreement with Lady Eden, the Countess Dowager of Eden Point, whose younger son, Lord James Eden, seemed as hesitant as Harriet herself.

She was not beautiful in the conventional, fashionable sense of the word. Men had never responded to her presence in a courtly manner. But for anyone who cared to look, there was a striking quality about her, as though her beauty were of another age. Her hair, fair with tints of her ancestor's reddish tinge, was long, and while it refused to curl in contemporary fashion, it gave itself quite admirably to chignons and French knots. The eyes were Welsh blue and deep, the nose, straight though small, giving the appearance of an afterthought on the part of her Creator. The mouth alone was well defined, though even that was a bit too dignified, scarcely opening for laughter or for words.

Her entire face had a stillness about it, an introspection which on certain occasions could chill to the marrow. The appearance she gave was one of aloofness and hauteur. But in fact she was neither. She was something worse. She was bright, extremely intelligent, quick to the point that she had realized at an early age that her one clear asset, her native intelligence, was neither necessary nor negotiable. In fact, under certain circumstances, it could be and was a downright liability.

Thus the stillness was accountable, the need to hold herself very rigid lest the mind commence working, then naturally the tongue. According to her mother, Harriet would have been married long ago if she hadn't caused all her suitors to feel like empty packing cases. James Eden, again as her mother had pointed out, was perhaps her last chance to avoid the curse of spinsterhood. On her parents'

strong advice, she'd better take the step as soon as possible
lest this last poor fish slip away as effortlessly as all the
rest.

It was a dilemma to which she had yet to address herself. And on this morning in early May, she was thinking
about neither James Eden nor the dreaded party at the end
of June. Now she had an appointment, with herself, and
with her magnificent brown-splotched stallion to whom she
had lovingly given the name of Falstaff.

Quite simply she adored him and once a week they had
a private appointment, just the two of them, a secret which
Harriet would die before she would tell anyone.

Now she took a quick final glimpse in her pier glass and
for a moment stared steadily back at the reflection, prim,
sober in her black silk riding habit with high-buttoned
jacket, long buttoned sleeves, longer flowing skirt, her hair
done tightly up and secured beneath the black hat with
dark veil. All that remained were the black gloves in her
hand, then not an inch of flesh would show save that of
her face.

There! Gloves were secured, everything hidden. It was
quiet in her private apartments. Even the furnishings
seemed to possess a slow pulse. She twisted her head in a
peculiar position as though trying to get a glimpse of herself without looking directly into the glass. Her excitement
was increasing, but she must not let it show.

Again she looked about her. She must remember everything. Once she had gone, it would be too late. On the near
table she spied the clean linen. That must go with her. That
was part of it. Hurriedly she folded the linen into a small
square and tucked it deftly inside her jacket. And the
comb, that too must accompany her, and the small vial of
lavender water. Now both items were scooped up and carefully plunged into the deep pocket of her riding skirt. What
else? Last time, it had occurred to her to take a brush. But
now she couldn't find it, and no matter. She'd managed in
the past without one.

She must hurry. She still had to make her way through
the vast corridors of the grand old estate, from her private
apartments on the second floor to the small ground-floor
exit where the old groom would be waiting with her horse.
Pray God she did not encounter anyone. Not that she owed
a soul an explanation. Not even her parents. This was her

riding day. She was dressed appropriately. No need to account to anyone, unless of course the tinge of red on her cheeks which spoke of excitement betrayed her.

She glanced back at the mirror. The red was there as well as something different about her eyes. Then she must obscure her face as well and this she did, drawing the dark veil forward from the back of her hat and allowing it to fall freely over her face.

Better! Now nothing was visible. Through the black veil she saw only a black figure, safe, unrevealing, proper, most proper.

Fourteen steps to the door. She counted them off, then she was out in the corridor, increasing her speed, one gloved hand shoved into her pocket, trying to still the slight jingle the comb made as it bounced against the bottle of lavender water.

A few minutes later as she was approaching the Morning Room, she stopped. Coming from inside she heard her parents' voices. She mustn't encounter them now. She had talked with them at breakfast about James Eden. And undoubtedly the subject would be the same at dinner. But for now she prayed silently, Let me pass unimpeded, please let me pass unnoticed.

The prayer was granted by one sympathetic deity or another, and a short time later, speed increasing, she approached the broad main corridor of the first floor, looking neither to the right nor left at the occasional servant who stood deferentially to one side and bowed low at her passage.

Then she saw him, through the arched door at the end of the passage, standing in full morning sun, his great head lifting in annoyance at the tight grip of the groom on his reins.

Trembling with anticipation, she deliberately broke her speed and paused a moment just this side of the door. She closed her eyes. *Patient, be patient.* Her heart was now a drumming sound, surely audible to all. *Be silent, please. Don't betray me—*

Slowly she opened her eyes and proceeded through the door at a deliberate pace. Then she was standing at his side, the groom stepping forward at her appearance and wordlessly arranging the small step near the animal's massive side so that she might effortlessly mount him and settle into the demure side-saddle position.

Her legs beneath the long black skirts seemed no longer subject to her will and just in time she settled into the saddle. Quickly certain adjustments were made, both by her and the groom, the stirrup shortened, foot inserted, reins drawn over the horse's head and placed in her gloved hands. Beneath her, she could feel the impatience of the animal. He knew. Old Falstaff knew as well as she where they were going. Neither she nor he had need of rein at all. Still, the charade must be played out.

The toothless old groom stepped back now, smiling. "Have a pleasant ride, milady. Him there is rarin' to go, so you'd best keep a tight rein—"

Patiently Harriet nodded. The lecture was always the same. "I will, Rudy," she smiled. "Thank you."

Then they were moving down the gravel drive, the great horse bobbing his head up and down, a curious sound escaping from his nostrils as though he were trying to conceal a laugh.

She leaned forward and patted his broad neck and whispered cool words. "Walk prettily, Falstaff, like a gentleman. At least to the end of the parkway—"

As they cleared the shadow of the estate, she glanced back over her shoulder. Old Rudy was still watching her. Now her eyes swept the front of the estate. Behind one of those many windows she felt certain that other eyes were watching as well, parental eyes.

Relaxing her grip on the reins, she looked about her at the glorious morning, a lingering scent of late-blooming lilacs in the air, the sky high and blue, the sun dazzling. Perhaps she would perspire before it was over. How she loved to perspire.

Ahead now, just at the end of the parkway and beyond the fence, she saw the Mermaid. Mixed feelings there. As a girl she used to ride down and talk secretly to Humphrey Hills, the little boy who'd grown up to become proprietor of the Mermaid. At that time, Humphrey was her secret excitement, her private pleasure, her sense of breaking out without shattering anything. There was the art, to break out without shattering either yourself or those around you. Over the years she had become quite skillful at it.

Now as Falstaff drew near to the end of the parkway,

she looked across the road, her black veil still in place.
On occasion, she'd caught a glimpse of Humphrey Hills
on the terrace of his inn, looking quite prosperous. Several
times in the past, she'd tried to call to him. But he never
looked up and always, a few minutes after she would appear, he would disappear, as mysteriously as he had disappeared when they had been children, one day waiting at the
side of the road for her with a nosegay of wildflowers, the
next day gone.

An ancient mystery. Slowly she shifted in her uncomfortable position and tightened her grip on the reins. But
there was no need. It was as she had guessed. Falstaff knew
exactly where they were going, and without the slightest
urging from her, he turned to the left, skirting the fence,
picking up speed, leaving the Mermaid and the old mystery
of Humphrey Hills far behind.

"Now hurry," she whispered, again leaning over the
animal's neck, confident that they were far enough from the
house to elude the careful eyes of all who might be watching.

As the horse continued to increase his speed, she saw
with visible certainty the goal before her eyes. "Hurry,
hurry, please," she begged, and dug her foot deeper into
the stirrup, giving the horse his head, already feeling the
wind on her face.

Ahead she spied the beginning of the woods, the dark
line of green behind which lay her private paradise. In her
pocket she heard the comb and bottle rattling together as
the speed of the horse increased. It was like a melody, a
peculiar refrain heralding what was to come.

At their approach to the woods, the horse, instead of
slowing to select a prudent safe course, plunged straight
ahead, crashing into the dark shadows, impervious to the
low-hanging branches which might prove hazardous for his
mistress. Quickly Harriet crouched low, clinging to the
mane, laughing outright at his daring, and breathing deeply
of the dark woods and hidden violets.

Not much farther. He knew it and she knew it. It was as
though a mighty impulse had been loosed simultaneously
in both of them. Still she clung to the mane, reins abandoned, and looked about and saw it, just ahead, the golden
meadow, hidden from all views of the road and the estate,
the place where gypsies had once encamped, where as

magical a transfiguration as was humanly possible could take place.

"Here," she called out, full-voiced, and at first shocked herself with the sound of her voice, unrestrained. Upon the instant, the horse cleared the last of the trees and ambled to a stop at the edge of the meadow.

For a moment she merely sat erect, carefully checking the surrounding, making certain they were alone. In that moment was contained the shock and forewarning of enormous possibilities. Quickly now she slid to the ground, her legs still trembling with exertion from the ride and the promise of events to come.

Then the transfiguration commenced. Methodically, deliberately, her hands moved up to the high-buttoned jacket, her fingers shaking as she separated buttons from buttonholes until finally she shook free of it and placed it to one side. Next came the shirtwaist, the mild early summer air already reaching her skin. Shortly the white blouse joined the abandoned jacket. Then it was the hat's turn, long pins removed and carefully reinserted into the fabric, veil folded neatly. At the same time, she pulled the two heavy clasps which held her hair and smiled warmly up at the sky as she felt her hair tumble freely down her back.

Boots next, seated upon the ground, like a gypsy herself, then hose, then at last pantaloons, until all that remained covering her was the thin white chemise. Slowly she stood and with wonder examined herself. She had never quite dared to remove the chemise as well. Dare she today? No. The current was strong, but caution and prudence were stronger. It made no difference. She could feel the sun well enough on her bare arms and shoulders, could see her breasts beneath the chemise. Wishes, dreams, and possibilities that had once had no other life than her own imagination lived now in reality.

Behind her, Falstaff snorted and nudged her gently as though to remind her that while she was luxuriating in her new freedom, he was still bound and girded. Warmly she laughed and nuzzled his head and quickly pulled the reins forward and removed the bit from his mouth, then darted back to his side and loosened the girdle beneath his stomach until the entire saddle fell to earth.

Suddenly he lifted his head and whinnied out his approval and ran toward the center of the meadow, his feet lifting, head lowered in a cavorting, playful mood. She laughed at him and called him back. "Not fair," she cried out. "Wait for me."

And within the instant, the beast returned to her, standing patiently as though he knew full well what came next. She had scarcely ventured to touch the strands of his mane when with one graceful leap she was pulling herself upward, legs spread this time, straddling his massive side. The sensation of his flesh against her soft inner legs was acute. The same current ran in both of them and a secret passed back and forth.

Astride him, she sat erect, entirely mistress of the situation. "Now," she whispered. And at the soft command, the horse lunged forward, no delicate pace this time, moving almost immediately to top speed while she grabbed at his mane and tightened her knees against him and gave herself fully to the power of his body.

The dark green fringe of trees passed by her in a blur. There was a kind of anguish moving through her. "Faster," she urged, feeling an unloosening of passion. Dear God, faster, please. She wanted to see nothing whole or clear. The only things that mattered were speed, power, the feel of wind on her face and in her hair, and that peculiar sensation which attended the lower part of her body where her legs parted to accommodate his massive girth.

Round and round they went, encircling the meadow at a frenzied pace and all that she saw and heard and felt overwhelmed her. She was aware of her chemise, backward-blowing in the wind, drawn up on either side to accommodate her position. The sight of her bare legs pleased her. And how sharp the sensation was becoming.

Then suddenly she bent over with a welling of desire, the sweet suffocation of anguish, everything blooming magically during this interval of dreams. Every twilight corner of her life was suddenly filled with explosions of light and warmth until at least she could bear it no longer.

Sensing his mistress's limit of endurance, old Falstaff slowed to a gallop, then a walk, then he stopped completely and nibbled new grass while she, in her extremity, slid from his back, her eyes closed. With a gasp she stretched out in the grass, unable to express even in thought what had happened to her. She did not speak but lay absolutely still, one hand covering her breast, her eyes swimming over undreamed-of things.

Shamelessly she lay, her legs still softly spread, and it astonished her to discover, as she always did, how rich was the life of her imagination and how totally removed from the real world.

The fantastic game continued for two hours, she standing now and then to remount Falstaff, then ultimately sliding off again, to lie in the grass and study her feelings and think on things, not in words, but in images, shameful images, shamelessly conceived.

At last she rose a final time, calm and silent and spent, and the restoration commenced, the clean linen withdrawn from her jacket and used to remove the moisture of sweat from her legs and neck and face. Slowly she redressed herself in the restraining garments, still astonished at how well she felt, how bearable now was the unbearable, her thoughts of James Eden and the coming engagement party, the underworld of her despair. It was simply a matter of learning to live in a world without danger or surprise, but she could do it because she would have to do it. It was expected of her. And she could do it because of her times alone in this meadow, astride that marvelous horse who out of all the creatures, human and otherwise, in her world understood her most completely.

Dressed at last, she withdrew the comb and restored her hair into a tight knot, and splashed lavender water gently about her neck to conceal the odor of human sweat. Then apologetically, gently she imprisoned old Falstaff once again in his bridle and bit, laboriously lifting the saddle and strapping it beneath him while he moaned softly and stamped at the earth.

"Next week," she whispered, in an attempt to console him, and console herself as well. Then with every defense and propriety laced rigidly into place, she pulled herself up into that prim position, knees together, and looked longingly down on the matted grass where she had recently lain with such abandon. Even though she'd been coming to her secret meadow for over a year, only now did she grasp the importance of the place. Were there meadows on Eden Point? And would there be a Falstaff for her?

No answers, and now she made haste for home, made equal haste to forget the sensations which had almost undone her. They were not negotiable where she was going, her undreamed-of things.

Long before she was ready for it, Hadley Park came into view, the rigid lines of the old estate seeming to speak in advance for the rigidity contained within.

And old Rudy was waiting for her, grinning up. "Nice ride, milady?" he queried softly.

"Very nice, Rudy, thank you." The step in place, she slipped easily from Falstaff's back and hesitated a moment for final instructions. "Brush him well, Rudy," she said, without smiling, "and give him an extra portion of hay."

The old man laughed openly. "He'll take what he wants, milady. It's his nature and nothing I could do would stop or change him."

She looked again at the handsome animal, a slight wistfulness in her eyes. Then she lowered the black veil over her face, lest the wistfulness show, and walked sedately into the cool, dark interior of Hadley Park to face her mother, her father, the dread of the impending engagement with James Eden, and any other hazards, known and unknown which were yet ahead of her.

Eden Castle
North Devon
May, 1836

The Countess Dowager of Eden Castle, the Lady Marianne, lay late abed on this glorious May morning. In her hand she held the disquieting letter from Sir Claudius Potter. It had been delivered to her a few moments earlier by Mrs. Greenbell, who was now fussing with the grate in the fireplace.

Considerate of the old woman, Marianne lifted her head. "The chill will be dissipated shortly, Mrs. Greenbell. Don't bother with a fire."

The portly woman raised up from her labors and looked puzzled toward the bed. Once the children's nursemaid, she had stayed on at Eden Castle and now served more as Marianne's companion than servant. Marianne looked lovingly in her direction. They shared the same birth year and now at sixty-seven they were well into old age together, both widowed. Although Mrs. Greenbell had had children, they were all dead, and Marianne was more than willing to share her own unruly brood.

"You said you were cold," Mrs. Greenbell stated, still looking confused.

"I'm always cold," Marianne laughed. "You should know that by now."

The two women exchanged a glance. Mrs. Greenbell moved closer with a lecture. "Some extra flesh wouldn't hurt, you know," she said, critically eyeing Marianne's frail frame.

Marianne waited out the lecture, as she'd waited them out for the last thirty years. She'd never carried much weight, saw no reason to start now. With the exception of the continuous chills, which she could date from that cold winter night nine years ago when Thomas had slipped from her, she was hale enough. That had been the day the sun had disappeared, and the nights had become merely unbearable hours to get through.

As though aware of the mood into which Marianne was slipping, Mrs. Greenbell stepped closer. "Will you be getting up and about this morning, milady? And what of breakfast? Miss Cranford is waiting—"

At the mention of the name, Marianne looked up. She disliked the thought of Miss Cranford waiting on her for anything, that officious female who had moved into the castle years ago in the company of her brother, Caleb. From Yorkshire they had come, both as hard and as cold as the moors of their birthplace. Caleb had served as tutor to the boys, and Sophia Cranford had taken over the duties of head house warden after the death of dear old Dolly Wisdom. Now that the boys were grown and Caleb's tutorial services were no longer needed, he had assumed the role of companion and business adviser to James. As though pondering an ancient mystery, Marianne brooded, on whose authority? How *had* the Cranfords managed such a discreet and skillful climb?

Out of the habit of honesty, Marianne was incapable of repressing her feelings. "The hag," she now muttered.

Mrs. Greenbell smiled. "You should see her this morning," she gossiped. "In a gown of lavender taffeta." She leaned closer. "With paint on her face."

Marianne shook her head. "Just coffee, Mrs. Greenbell, please." She looked up, almost pleading. "And would you fetch it yourself? Bring two cups, one for you." Marianne disliked asking the old woman to perform servant duties. It was a long climb four floors down to the kitchen. She might have used the bell cord beside her bed, an elaborate system of signals installed several years ago at Caleb Cranford's insistence. But if she pulled the bell cord, she knew who would appear. And she wasn't up to it. Not this morning.

Uncomplaining, Mrs. Greenbell started for the door. Again Marianne stopped her. "Was this all the post?" she inquired. "No word from Jennifer?"

Mrs. Greenbell shook her head. "There were other letters, a few for the Cranfords, two for Lord Eden—"

Marianne looked sharply up. "Lord—" She caught herself. Embarrassed, she shook her head and turned her eyes toward the morning sun spilling in through the windows. Incredibly she felt the beginning of tears. When would the name cease to have power to stir her? "Lord Eden" no longer meant Thomas. Lord Eden meant James, her younger son.

Aware of Mrs. Greenbell's close scrutiny from the door, Marianne tried to alter the expression on her face. When would she learn not to reveal herself so pitifully?

"Just coffee, Mrs. Greenbell," she smiled, lowering her eyes so the embarrassing moisture wouldn't show.

But the kind soul at the door apparently knew and understood well. "It takes time, milady. Don't be too harsh with yourself."

"But nine years, Mrs. Greenbell," she murmured. "Nine years, and still at night I think I hear him moving about in his chambers. I walk the headlands and hear his voice in the wind. I enter his sitting room and smell his fragrance, sense his presence." She drew her knees up in bed and rested her head upon them. "Nine years," she murmured, as though amazed. "When will those feelings pass?"

Slowly Mrs. Greenbell came back to the bed. "Perhaps never," she counseled. "Nor would you want the feelings to leave you forever. When a husband and wife have been as close as you and Lord Eden, there is really no such thing as separation. One might walk ahead of the other, but never a complete separation."

Marianne listened, staring sideways at the room, which blurred under the patina of her tears. "I used to pray to God that He take us together—"

"We have no right to make such a request," Mrs. Greenbell scolded lightly.

Marianne shook her head. "Then how to survive?" she queried softly.

In a rapid change of mood, Mrs. Greenbell stood up, all business. "By losing yourself in the needs of others, by keeping busy, by giving your children the love and attention they require."

Marianne closed her eyes. Oh God, but sometimes the dear woman *was* tiresome. Well, enough. She was right on one score. According to the morning letter from Sir Claudius, one child, apparently, was in need of her attention. As for the others, James now seemed to need nothing as long as he had his hounds and horses and the companionship of Caleb Cranford. And Jenny, poor Jennifer, how was Marianne to know what she needed?

Her private grief over, Marianne suddenly threw back the covers and left the bed.

In a state of some confusion, Mrs. Greenbell hovered between the bed and the door. "Do you want your coffee first, or shall I stay and help—"

"I need no help," Marianne announced, a bit sharper than she might have wished.

The old woman retreated, shaking her head. "One minute weak and weeping," she grumbled, "the next—"

Again at the door she stopped. "I beg your pardon, milady, but Lord Eden".—she stopped to clarify—"young James would like a word with you. At your convenience."

Linen in hand, Marianne dabbed at her face. "I thought he was out riding," she said, her voice muffled. "Isn't he always out riding?"

"He said he'd be back shortly before noon." A knowing smile crossed Mrs. Greenbell's face. "I think it's about his young lady and her coming visit."

Marianne lowered the linen from her face. Mixed feelings there. Harriet Powels. Lady Harriet, the shy blue-blooded female whom apparently James had chosen to move the line forward. She was due the last of June for a fortnight's visit. Her parents, Lord and Lady Powels of Hadley Park, Shropshire, were coming with her, and in the final days of the visit, Marianne assumed, an engagement would be announced. Well, perhaps it would mean grandchildren. She looked forward to grandchildren, and since Edward did not seem to be making progress in that direction, nor Jennifer, perhaps it was up to James and his shy Harriet.

She turned back to the bowl. She thought all of the plans

had been made. "Of course I'll see him," she murmured. "Let me know when he returns."

As she splashed the cold water again over her face, she heard the door behind her open, then close.

Alone. She froze for a moment over the bowl, water dripping. The room was so quiet. Bent over, her breathing caused the motion of small waves on the water. The man sat in her mind like a rock. What Mrs. Greenbell did not know and what Marianne would never tell her for fear of shocking that good Methodist countenance was that the main thrust of Marianne's longing for Thomas was physical.

Suddenly, as though in the throes of agony, she doubled over, a soft moan escaping her lips. She stumbled back to the bed and stretched out. For a moment, she was quiet, staring upward at the ornate plasterwork ceiling. Abruptly she turned on her side. In a glint of sun near the far window, she spied her orrery, the clockwork mechanism of the solar system, a miniature sun and moon revolving around the earth, a gift from William Pitch.

For the first time that morning, she found a moment's respite from her loneliness. Slowly she pulled herself across the bed, crawled off the other side, and moved toward the orrery.

It's the solar system, Marianne, the intricate movements of the sun and moon charted to the last second.

William understood. William always understood. She formed a quick resolution in her mind, to write to the man today and invite him and Jane to the engagement party next month. She realized with a wave of humor that she was even hungry to see Jane, her half-sister, William's common-law wife. The Devon air would be good for both of them. London was becoming a pestilential city. Yes, she would write to them this very day. With those old and familiar faces around her, perhaps her loneliness would abate.

Renewed with purpose, she moved hurriedly back to her dressing table. As she passed the bed, she spied Sir Claudius's crumpled letter. She'd forgotten about that. Slowly she bent over and retrieved it, took it with her to the table where the light was brighter to read again of Edward's latest offense.

Sir Claudius's prim, neat manner fairly sprawled with rage across the page. Apparently Edward was selling

again, the estates dwindling. She would have to break the
news to James. It was sure to cause a scene. And there was
a scandal of some sort, an adultery case involving a young
wife and Edward. And there was more. He'd last seen
Edward, looking very disreputable in the company of a
prostitute, fodder for his zoo on Oxford Street, the radical
Daniel Spade apparently controlling him like a puppet.

And there was his customary closing paragraph, his
fervent prayer, that God would take him before it became
his unenviable task of presiding over a lawsuit, pointing
out how very singular the case would be: the plaintiff, the
younger, legitimate son of Lord Thomas Eden; the defendant, the elder, dissipating, illegitimate son of Lord
Thomas Eden.

Finally he pledged lasting affection for the Countess
Dowager, a sentiment which caused Marianne to shudder.
Then there was his signature, as pompous and fastidious
as the man himself.

Slowly she shook her head as though still amazed by the
tangle of affairs. Well, there would be no lawsuit, at least
not while she was alive. She could handle her sons, even
the headstrong Edward. The Eden estates were vast. Perhaps, morally, some of it should be given away. There
would still be plenty for James to use for hunting. As for
the scandal of the adultery case, probably all of London
was grateful for the diversion. In her time, she'd caused
too many scandals herself ever to be shocked by anything
her son might do. As for the "zoo" on Oxford Street, as
Sir Claudius had indelicately put it, she loved Daniel Spade
as though he were her own son, agreed with his principles,
and gave his Ragged School her full support. It was a
fitting end for that cold house, its walls imbedded with
generations of Eden arrogance, to suffer now the shouts
and laughter of street children.

Good God! Quickly she left the dressing table, appalled
at her capacity for the past this morning. She flung open
her wardrobe, pleased by the sudden appearance of her
gowns. Giving in to a moment of bitchery, she remembered
Mrs. Greenbell's description of Sophia Cranford, dressed in
lavender taffeta this morning.

Then Marianne would choose pale yellow silk. For some
reason she felt a stern need to look her best. Yellow was
the color of the sun, lavender its shadow.

She dressed with care and brushed her hair back and deftly knotted it into a chignon. Then she stood back and assessed the image, the elegant yellow silk, simple, with a scooped neck and wide flaring skirt with just a hint of bustle. Not bad for an old woman, although a telltale line about her neck disturbed her. She reached for her jewelry case and withdrew a single strand of matched pearls. Extending her head forward, she joined the delicate clasp beneath her hair and raised up for another look. Better.

Where was Mrs. Greenbell with the coffee? She turned away from the pier glass, weary of preening. She had much to do today. Her correspondence, for one thing, her letter of invitation to William and Jane. And she should acknowledge Sir Claudius's hysterical letter, although she hadn't the faintest idea what to say, and she really should write a suitably stern and maternal letter to Edward, suggesting that he should stay out of other men's beds, particularly when their wives were in them. She wondered ruefully if her "maternal" letters were as great a bore to him as they were to her.

She left her bedchamber with the image of her son constantly before her and took refuge in her sitting room, once Thomas's chambers. As she heard a rap at the door, she turned as though grabbing for a lifeline. "Mrs. Greenbell," she called out, "come—" She heard the door open in her bedchamber, heard voices, or more specific, heard a single voice, the rather prim, irritatingly high-pitched, very proper voice of Sophia Cranford.

Ah, there was reality. As Marianne turned away from the window, she saw Mrs. Greenbell first, her plump face angling into a deep, unspoken apology, carrying a breakfast tray.

Then behind her appeared the woman herself, a slim, hard blade of a woman, done up indeed in lavender taffeta, her black hair drawn so tightly back there seemed to be a pull about her eyes, a little lace cap perched atop her head, and carrying in her hand the ever-present, gilt-trimmed leather notebook, an appendage of nature, according to Thomas.

Marianne ducked her head to hide a smile. Then the woman was upon her, effusive as always at the beginning of each of these encounters. The cold silence of disapproval and God alone knew what else always came later.

"Milady," Sophia murmured, bowing from the doorway.

With a vague smile Marianne returned the greeting and went to the serving table, where Mrs. Greenbell was just pouring a steaming, fragrant cup of coffee. As Marianne lifted the cup, again Mrs. Greenbell caught her eye and held it, an unspoken message passing between the two old friends, both fully aware of what it was like to be trapped by Sophia Cranford.

Marianne noticed the tray, a lovely arrangement of grapes, two rolls, the silver urn. "Wouldn't you like a cup?" she asked Mrs. Greenbell, noticing only service for one.

Pointedly Mrs. Greenbell demurred. "Miss Cranford said she had business to discuss with you. I'll come back later."

Coward, Marianne thought, as the woman hurried to the door.

Mrs. Greenbell smiled and closed the door behind her. Marianne looked awkwardly about, wondering precisely who should make the first move. The woman continued to stand as though she had a rod down her back, her fingers over-laced and resting on the notebook.

Annoyed, Marianne took her coffee to the window, determined to let the silence expand as far as necessary. She knew precisely what the problem was. Of all the people in her world, including dukes, earls, and all the social lionesses of London, Sophia Cranford was the only person alive who still was capable of making her feel like a fisherman's daughter. The realization pinched.

"You had business, I believe," she said now, coolly, from the window.

When it seemed as though the woman behind her would never speak, she did, in a most unctuous tone. "I trust milady slept well," she purred, the voice in its artificiality seeming to climb even higher.

The question was rhetorical, requiring no answer, and Marianne gave her none. Down below, just entering the castle gates on horseback, she saw her son, James, in the company of Caleb Cranford. The two were inseparable. Again she found herself wondering precisely at what point this Yorkshire brother and sister had climbed to such positions of power and influence within the castle.

Now from behind, she heard Sophia again. "It's a lovely morning, milady," she said. "May at its loveliest."

Marianne sipped her coffee and counseled herself patience. Play the game, whatever it might be. "It is indeed," she agreed, still keeping her eyes on the lovely morning and the sight of her younger son just dismounting, a slight figure of a man compared with Thomas and Edward. "I see my son is back," she commented, watching both men now, Caleb's solicitous hovering, whispering something to James, both men laughing heartily. At last she turned to face the woman waiting behind her. "Their customary morning ride, I assume?" she smiled.

Sophia nodded, as though pleased with herself. "Caleb revels in his friendship," she pronounced. "The way they carry on, I sometimes find it hard to believe eighteen years' difference in their ages; they are more like brothers."

Marianne returned to the serving table and the coffee urn. As she refilled her cup, her patience dwindled. "I believe Mrs. Greenbell said you had business."

"Yes, indeed!" In a flurry of efficiency the woman snapped open the notebook.

"Ah, here we are." Sophia now smiled, looking up from her search. Apparently she saw Marianne's close scrutiny. Her face seemed to freeze. "Anything wrong, milady?" she inquired politely.

Quickly Marianne turned away. "No, nothing at all. Please go on. What is the nature of your—"

"Well, of course, it's about the party scheduled for the last of June, for Lady Harriet Powels—"

"What about it?" Marianne asked snappishly.

Again Sophia seemed to hesitate. "Well, milady, I must know—"

The woman lifted her eyes as though in a prouder attitude. "I loathe bringing up the subject, milady, for both our sakes, but I must know how—generous Mr. Edward intends to be with us for that important occasion."

The light dawned. Money. That was the nature of her business. Appalled by the woman's tastelessness in bringing up such a subject, Marianne sat lightly in a near chair and placed the coffee cup on the table. "We have our customary allowance," she said. "No more, no less. But I should think it would be quite enough to—"

Sophia stepped forward as though gaining courage. "These are Powelses, milady," she said, pointedly, "renowned for their generosity, their country house parties—"

Marianne bristled. "Miss Cranford, we shall receive them

warmly and give them our best hospitality. Beyond that, there is no reason to discuss it further."

The reprimand won her a moment's silence. But it was only temporary. As Sophia perused the notebook, Marianne knew a rebuttal was forming.

"Then, milady," she smiled sweetly, "may I have your ear concerning the menu?"

"You have it."

"I see an eight-course meal, at least."

"What else?" Marianne murmured sarcastically, already dreading the event that was still a month away.

"First, there should be a choice of soup, clear and thick, hot and cold—"

"Why a choice?" Marianne asked, looking up.

"They will be accustomed to a choice," Sophia smiled, as though pleased by the nature of Marianne's question. "Then," she went on, taking the floor now, pacing back and forth in a rustle of lavender taffeta, referring constantly to the notebook. "Then two kinds of fish, poached turbot, say, and salmon mayonnaise would be nice. And two removes, turkey and roast lamb, perhaps might accompany several entrees, such as cutlets, vol-au-vent, fillets of leveret, or sautéed fillets of fowl. Then there might come a sorbet, and after that, the game course—"

Marianne listened and watched, her mind trying to follow the woman's words. She felt cold and malicious and very useless.

"Are you following me, milady?" Sophia asked, stopping in her rigid little back and forth movements.

"I am," Marianne murmured. "Do go on."

"Well, if you'll forgive me again, milady, this is where some expense might be involved. We've had great trouble of late acquiring game. It would be my suggestion that we have quail and ortolon shipped over from the Continent. We must also have numerous entremets, lobster salad, maraschino jelly, truffles with champagne—"

Marianne stood. "Sweet Lord, Miss Cranford, such a menu will surely kill them—"

"I assure you, milady, they are accustomed to it and shall be expecting it. So, what do you say to that?" Sophia now inquired, and Marianne hadn't the least idea what she was talking about.

Lovingly she caressed the back of the chair, Thomas's

chair, then turned to dismiss the awful woman. "I'll leave everything in your capable hands, Miss Cranford," she smiled. "I'm certain you know what to do."

The compliment seemed to please the woman. But instead of serving to dismiss her, she simply turned a page of the notebook and launched forth into another problem. "And I shall need a guest list, milady," she announced. "Invitations should have gone out last week. If you recall, I asked you for—"

Yes, Marianne recalled. "I'll have it for you this afternoon."

"And musicians. What do you—"

Marianne felt as though she were beginning to drown in the endless detail. Curtly she said, "I leave everything in your hands, Miss Cranford. Everything! Please spare me this morning. I have neither the heart nor inclination for it."

"Very well," Sophia replied, clearly pleased with the responsibility, although rather reluctantly she closed her notebook. "The funds in the household accounts may not cover the expense of the fete," she announced, straightening her shoulders. "I may have to impose upon our creditors—"

Marianne looked up. "I find that difficult to believe," she said, shocked.

"It's true, milady."

Marianne left the writing bureau and confronted the woman in the center of the room. "We are provided for handsomely," she said. "Thirty-six thousand pounds a year. I find it hard to believe that—"

But Sophia held her ground. "I keep careful books, milady. If you'd care to study them—"

It was the last thing Marianne wanted to do. Still, she didn't understand how with that vast amount of money they would have to use credit. They did little entertaining, the meals generally were simple. Her annoyance increasing, she turned away. She'd never had to discuss such matters when Thomas was alive. Then the full receipts of the estates had been put at her disposal, no questions asked. Now the receipts were gathered bimonthly by their agent in Exeter and taken directly to London, to Sir Claudius, where under Edward's direction, the sum of thirty-six thousand pounds was sent back for the running and maintenance of Eden Castle.

As though intuitively following the direction of her thoughts, Sophia moved closer. "It's a vastly unsatisfactory arrangement, milady," she quietly suggested, "the Countess Dowager receiving an allowance from her son—"

Marianne shook off the woman's closeness and moved farther away. "The property is Edward's," she said, with a calmness she did not feel, "to do with as he likes."

"And what of James?"

"What about James?"

"Is he to play the pinch-penny host to his future wife because of his brother's stingi—"

Marianne interrupted angrily. "That's enough, Miss Cranford. You are overstepping your bounds. Edward has been the heart and soul of generosity. He pays your own rather handsome salary. Now, please, never mention his name again in such tones."

The woman lowered her head, not true repentance, Marianne knew from experience, but certainly a good mask. "I offer my sincerest apologies," she murmured. "I was only trying to do my job, a difficult job under the best of circumstances."

Reluctantly Marianne agreed. "I'll write to Sir Claudius today," she offered. "You shall have the party you want —without credit."

"Thank you, milady. But again, begging your pardon, it's not *my* party. It's for James, for his future happiness. Alliance with the Powelses could mean—"

Marianne knew what it meant and did not need Sophia Cranford to point it out. James's union with the Powelses meant a degree of restored respectability to the Eden name, respectability which had been lost when Thomas Eden had married—"Is there anything else, Miss Cranford?"

"Yes, one other matter," the woman said, her voice gathering strength, as though she'd spotted Marianne's weakness. "Will Mr. Edward be present?"

Again, Marianne looked over her shoulder, impressed, in spite of herself, by the woman's persistence to pursue painful subjects. "Why?" she asked.

"I need to know who will preside? James or Edward?"

Marianne stood, confronting the woman. "Neither," she pronounced. "I intend to write today to my old friend Wil-

liam Pitch. If he can join us, he will preside. The place
of honor belongs to him."

Obviously this news did not please Sophia. The little
lace hat atop her head bobbed back and forth as she
shook her head. "I'm not certain that the Powelses—"

"Damn the Powelses," Marianne exploded. "This is my
home and I will do as I please, do you hear?"

The woman looked up, color draining out of her already
colorless face. "I am an intelligent woman, milady," she
began, her voice trembling slightly. "I understand the full
range of the English language and need no obscenity to—"

Regretful, Marianne shook her head. "I'm sorry, Miss
Cranford," she muttered. "It's just that I was beginning to
lose track of who was the guest, who the host."

For a moment, the two women stared at each other, as
though from opposite sides of the world. Sophia Cranford
spoke first, clearly reining in her offended nature. "I
shouldn't have brought the subject up this morning, milady. I can see that you are quite undone—"

"I'm not undone," Marianne protested. "I merely wish to
be mistress in my own home, a role I served well until—"
She stopped herself in time. The room felt suddenly stifling.
She relapsed into silence and again retreated to the window. The courtyard was empty save for the porters and
the gatemen. Where was James? She still had that to look
forward to.

She had hoped that her turned back and silence would
signal an end to the unpleasant confrontation. But it didn't.
Sophia merely moved up alongside her at the window, on
her face an expression of triumph. "I beg your pardon,
milady, but I suspect that the post brought bad news."

Marianne held her silence and stared rigidly down.
Sophia went on. "I'm pleased to say that the morning post
brought good news to me, a letter from Jennifer which I'd
be most happy to share."

Marianne continued to stand still, but her eyes watched
longingly as the woman removed a letter from the back of
her notebook. Even from that distance, Marianne saw and
recognized the familiar handwriting, the lovely flowering
script of her daughter. The letter appeared thick. The last
word Marianne had received was a polite note, less than
three paragraphs, some months ago. "I'm not in the habit

of reading another's mail, Miss Cranford," she said, finally wresting her eyes away from the letter.

"But I give my permission." The woman smiled sweetly. "It's a charming account of her life at Roe Head. I think it would lift your spirits considerably."

Marianne felt an ominous stinging behind her eyes. She leaned closer to the window in order to obscure her face.

When she failed to reply, Sophia retreated, as only a victor retreats, with head high, voice firm. "I'll leave it here on the table for you, milady. Perhaps later you'll change your mind." Her voice became quite light, almost happy. "The dear child is going to try very hard to make it home for her brother's engagement party. The term is over, but she had considered spending the summer there. I've tried to impress upon her how important her presence is to you, and she has promised to make every effort."

The burning in Marianne's eyes increased. How considerate of the bitch, after having spent the last twenty years successfully driving a wedge between Marianne and her daughter, now to urge a reconciliation. What had happened to Jennifer's childhood? Marianne couldn't remember. It seemed as though she and Thomas were always absent, either in London or the Continent, selfishly enjoying each other's company to the exclusion of the children. And every time that she had protested their frequent absences, Thomas had merely laughed and said, "Leave them to the Cranfords. When they reach a civilized age of eighteen, we shall introduce ourselves and welcome them to the family."

But by eighteen, it had been too late, their characters formed, with perhaps the exception of Edward, who had taken refuge in the warmth of Jack Spade's cottage. The other two had been formed by the Cranfords, Caleb and Sophia, surrogate parents, their influences strong and irrevocable on both Jennifer and James.

"Are you well, milady?" Sophia asked quietly from the table.

Marianne nodded.

"Then I'll entrust Jennifer's letter to you for your enjoyment, and leave you be."

She heard the door behind her open, then close. Quickly she turned back into the room, her eyes traveling rapidly to the table. The letter was still there, as she knew it would be. She felt battered and misshapen, as though the woman had physically assaulted her.

The school in Yorkshire had been Sophia's idea, a life of service for an intelligent young woman with few of nature's natural endowments. And Jennifer had gone effortlessly along with the idea, taking to the spartan life of schoolteacher as though she had a moral debt to pay, although Marianne knew all too well that it was *her* debt her daughter was paying. What tales Miss Cranford must have told her about her mother, Thomas Eden's whore.

No, she would not read it. This decision made by the window held until, circling the table twice, her hand went out and almost touched the letter. Finally she lifted it. It *was* thick. She stared down at the handwriting.

"Oh, Jennifer," she mourned aloud. Slowly she opened it. As her eye fell on the salutation, "My Dearest Sophia," tears crested again. Never had she been the recipient of such an affectionate greeting. Her heart ached, yet she read, hungry for news.

The letter, well written and chatty, spoke of the regimen of the school, her own duties as teacher of pianoforte, the number of girls enrolled there, how satisfying the work was and how spartan the existence. She mentioned James and Caleb, said she had received a lovely letter from Edward, and prayed for him nightly.

In the last paragraph, as though all light and warmth had been turned off, Marianne read,

Make no promises to my mother about my return in June. I should like very much to share in James's happiness, but that dismal castle holds no other joy for me save your own strong and beloved face. I know my duty, and if it's at all possible, I shall come. But out of necessity, my stay will be brief, and I must return to the work God has set for me. I think of you daily, dear Sophia, and miss you intensely. Sometimes when my loneliness seems unbearable, I must only think on you who have been like a mother to me, and I am instantly made whole again. Daily, I thank God for your presence in my life. Without you, what an empty thing it would have been—

There was more, but Marianne couldn't see the words. The tears were silent, the letter clear and painful. She

groaned softly and lowered her head until it was resting
on the bureau.

Almost at the same moment, she felt two arms about her,
heard a gentle, anxious voice inquire, "Is there anything I
can do?"

She shook her head. Mrs. Greenbell continued to hover,
clearly moved. "Please, milady," she whispered. "It serves
no purpose."

Marianne stood up, erect, sighed in a lost way, yet
smiled. "I feel a stranger here," she said, "a trespasser
almost."

"That's nonsense," scoffed Mrs. Greenbell.

"Perhaps, but it's true." She stretched out her hand to
Mrs. Greenbell, bidding her to come close. "Please never
leave me," she whispered. Then the two women were in
each other's arms, the embrace close and warm, Mrs.
Greenbell assuring her that she had no intention of leaving, that in the future she would try to spare her Sophia
Cranford. "I'll handle the old hag," she promised. "I know
her weaknesses, and she knows I know."

Marianne laughed, wiping the tears away. "Then, for
God's sake, please share them with me."

But Mrs. Greenbell merely held her at arm's length and
proceeded to straighten her hair, repair the damage that
had been done to her face. "Come, milady, have some
food. You've not touched either the fruit or the rolls."

But Marianne shook her head, her eye falling on Jennifer's letter. "Please return that to Miss Cranford," she
said quietly. "I would prefer not to lay eyes on the woman
for the rest of the day."

"Your son is waiting, milady," Mrs. Greenbell now announced.

With a conscious effort of will, Marianne crushed the
feeling of dread within her. This was James, her son, not
some stranger. "Give me a moment," she asked, "then let
him in."

"And you are sure you—"

"I'm fine."

As Mrs. Greenbell went to gather up the breakfast tray,
Marianne saw her tuck the letter inside her pocket. At that
moment, she decided to write to Jennifer that very day, a
letter as warm and as full of love as she could make it.
Perhaps it was not too late. They still were bound together

by flesh and blood, and there were a few good memories, shared memories with Thomas and the children, at Twelfth Night celebrations and special festival days. Perhaps with gentle prodding, Jennifer might remember. And forgive.

A few moments after Mrs. Greenbell had left the room, she heard a knock on the door. "Is that you, James?" she called out. "Please, come in."

The door opened and her younger son, Lord Eden, appeared, his face still ruddy from his morning ride across the moors. She was in the process of opening her arms to him, when behind him she saw Caleb Cranford, the two men moving in tandem into the room.

She withdrew her arms, refusing to share such intimacies with the man following behind her son, a taller, male version of the woman whose presence still contaminated the sitting room.

As though uncertain of himself, James started across the room and delivered a light kiss to her cheek, then stepped quickly back, a perfunctory gesture, nothing more, as though he'd been told to do so. She saw him turn immediately toward the man in the doorway as though awaiting the next command.

"Good morning, Mother," he said, politely, bobbing his head.

Then Caleb Cranford echoed the greeting. "Good morning, milady," he smiled, bowing from the waist.

"I trust you enjoyed your morning ride," she said pleasantly to James. "I saw your return a few moments ago. In which direction did you ride?"

"To the Hanging Man," James replied, standing awkwardly at the center of the room.

At thirty-five, he still looked like a little boy, with the exception of the fact that what had passed for charming passivity in the child now conveyed itself as weakness in the man.

Lightly Marianne scolded him. "That disreputable place," she smiled. "With miles of magnificent headland, I don't know why—"

"We went for the news, madam," Caleb interrupted from the door. "The pub is the only place this side of Exeter where a gentleman might avail himself of London newspapers."

Marianne looked up at the pencil-thin man, resentful

of the intrusion. "And what is happening in London that is
of such importance to—"

"A trial, madam," Caleb replied, "a most interesting
trial."

"What trial?" she demanded.

Again Caleb Cranford took over. "Surely you've been
aware of it, milady," he said. "The adultery trial concerning a Mrs. Charlotte Longford, and—"

"I don't follow gossip, Mr. Cranford," she interrupted.
"I never have. The majority opinion on any subject is always wrong. Street gossip is just that."

"This isn't gossip, milady," he persisted. "The accounts
of the trial are fact—"

"And how do they concern you?" she asked, knowing
full well what his answer would be.

He stepped further into the room, uninvited. "Regretfully Edward's name has been attached—"

"To what?"

"To the lady in question."

"But nothing has been proved," she countered.

He smiled, like his sister, with just a hint of triumph.
"Then you *do* know of the trial of which we speak."

Trapped, she tried to stay calm. "I know of it," she admitted. "What I fail to understand is your interest in it."

"Oh, not my interest, milady. I was only thinking of
James. What an embarrassment with his future in-laws
coming."

She glanced at James, saw him following the conversation like a tennis set. She'd had enough. Both Cranfords in
one morning were too much. She stepped to James's side
and lightly took his arm; he seemed to stiffen at her touch.
She ignored the unpleasant sensation and spoke softly to
the man standing a distance away. "Mr. Cranford, with
your kind permission, I'd like a word with my son alone.
You occupy most of his attention out of these chambers.
Here, I'd like to lay claim to a mother's right to privacy."
She smiled, hoping to conceal the rage she felt inside. "I'm
sure I can count on your understanding."

Apparently taken aback by the dismissal, she saw a
blush creep over his face. "My apologies, milady," he murmured.

She thought she saw a look pass between the two men,
but it was over before she could interpret it. As Caleb

started through the door, James called after him, "I won't be long, Caleb. Wait just outside for me."

Again Caleb bowed low, with a deference which verged on idiocy. "As you wish, Lord Eden," he murmured.

Marianne turned away to hide her disgust, overcome by the difference between the man who had previously worn that title and the boy who wore it now.

From behind her, she heard his voice, almost feminine in its pleading. "I wish you wouldn't speak to Caleb like that. He's very good to me. I feel a deep affection for him."

She decided to let that pass. There were other more urgent matters at hand. "This trial," she said, picking up the thread of the foolish conversation. "Is that what you wanted to see me about?"

He shook his head and sank wearily into a near chair, as though suddenly overcome with fatigue. "No, but it *is* important."

"How so?" she asked, prodding.

"Caleb says—"

"I don't care what Caleb says," she interrupted. "I want to hear your thoughts."

From his leisurely position, legs extended, he faltered. "Well, he is behaving scandalously. Caleb says—" He caught himself in time and apparently converted the thought to his own. "In my opinion, he might very well end up in prison himself. Then where would we be?"

Marianne looked at him, not totally unsympathetically. Again, the blame was her own. While Thomas was still alive, it had occurred to her to suggest that he divide the estates equally between the two boys. But it had never been done. That ancient deed, with which Thomas had regained her love, still stood as valid today as it had been thirty-seven years ago, the signing over of the castle and all the estates to the illegitimate Edward.

Her manner and attitude softened. "Don't worry, James," she counseled. "He would never do anything to hurt you. I'm confident of that. And his involvement in this sordid little matter is unimportant. If you don't trust me, believe Sir Claudius, who I'm quite certain will make every effort to keep a sharp and watchful eye."

Abruptly James sat up, as though unwittingly she had struck at the heart of the matter. "But why must someone have to keep an eye on him, Mother? And how long can we count on the watchful eyes of others?" He pushed himself forward out of the chair and began to pace restlessly. "It's an absolutely impossible situation," he muttered. He turned and confronted Marianne directly. "If I'm to take a wife, how am I to support her?" he pleaded. "On the allowance given to me by my brother?"

While Marianne did not have the solution to that problem, she had given it thought. "I plan to talk with him," she promised.

He looked at her, hopeful, then doubtful. "Poor Mother," he smiled, almost prettily, a little boy's smile which touched her. "Your neck is in the same noose by which he controls all of us."

She disliked such a sentiment. "He doesn't control us, James," she corrected. "He's been very generous in all matters."

At that, James pulled away from her nearness, casting a mistrustful look on her last words. "Generous," he scoffed. "Out of an income of over a hundred thousand pounds per annum, we are given a token handout of—"

"I'm sure he will increase it. All we need do is ask—"

The derision spread across his face. "How? On our knees? With our hats in our hands?" He hesitated, then looked directly back at her from across the room. His manner had changed, the little boy look gone. "Caleb says it cannot continue."

Oh God, it was a round-robin, all avenues of conversation commencing and ending with Caleb Cranford. Out of sorts from the splintered morning, Marianne gave voice to a harsh sentiment. "And what does Caleb have to do with it?" she demanded, half in anger. "Whatever problems exist in this family, we are quite capable of solving them without the help of either Cranford."

From where he stood about twenty feet removed, she could see the shock on his face. "How can you say that?" he demanded, his voice shaking slightly. "Sophia and Caleb Cranford have devoted their lives to this family. By your own command, Caleb keeps the household books, books on the entire estate for that matter. And without Sophia, that untrained and undisciplined nest of girls in the kitchen would run riot, and you know it." He stepped closer, as though she weren't paying the proper attention to him. "They *are* part of this family, Mother, as much as any of us, and by right of years of loyalty and devotion, I put a great deal of stock in their opinion, on all matters, as did Father, as should you."

Defeated, she sank slowly into the chair near the table. Whatever fleeting and wistful thoughts she had ever had for dismissing the Cranfords lay in a shambles about her. Her grasp on her two younger children was tenuous at best. Now it was as she had suspected. The weak glue that held them together was the Cranfords. She remained immobile and wondered if it was customary for a mother to feel such an alien in the presence of her son.

Finally, without looking at him, she asked, "And what does Mr. Cranford suggest?"

He took her hand, an affectionate and totally unexpected gesture. "I love you dearly," he confessed, his eyes seeking hers, the child again. The smile changed, grew mournful. "But you really did leave me in a topsy-turvy world."

She looked at him. Against those words she had no protection. If he sensed her vulnerability, he gave no indication of it and went on speaking. "How much better for both sides and more honorable had the estates been divided. As it is, I'm a pauper in my own home. I cannot go on forever, as Lord James Eden, taking handouts from an older brother." His voice grew hard. "I *will* not go on like that. I am thirty-five, on the verge of taking a wife, yet here I am, still dependent, still running for favors to a—"

Suddenly he stopped speaking. She knew what word had been forming on his lips. *Bastard*. She closed her eyes and lowered her head. He had spoken the truth and as always the truth was a prologue to pain. Again she asked, "And what do you suggest?"

This time he answered her bluntly. "Caleb suggests a lawsuit." As though he feared an immediate rebuttal, he hurried on. "Oh, not right away. Let me announce my engagement next month. Harriet and I are planning a Christmas wedding. Let that event transpire. Then shortly after the first of the year, I shall journey to London with my bride and confront Sir Claudius with the possibility of a discreet lawsuit." He paused. "I seek for nothing more than what is justly mine. Half of the estates, that is all. And Eden Castle. Edward will have plenty left for his Ragged School and his—assortment of friends."

She had suffered the plan to be outlined in full, had held

her tongue throughout the entire recitation, a recitation which sounded well rehearsed as though someone had coached him in the words.

Then it was her turn. She looked up. Although she was late in speaking, the words she was about to utter had been formed years ago. "There will be no lawsuit," she pronounced. "Not now, not ever, at least not until I am in my grave." Out of the corner of her eye she saw his face, the rebuttal taking form. But it was her turn to hold the floor. "There will be no lawsuit," she announced again. "And make no mistake," she added, "there is no such thing as a discreet lawsuit, not where an Eden is concerned. Out of respect for the memory of your father, there will be no lawsuit."

Having made the pronouncement, she now tried to soften it. "I have erred, James. I'm the first to admit it. And further, I will admit that the situation for you is intolerable. With that in mind, I intend to seek a private conference with Edward, at the first opportunity, and see if I can obtain privately what you plan to do publicly." Her voice softened. "Edward is your brother," she reminded him. "He bears you no ill-will. I rather imagine that he will be delighted to get rid of a portion of the responsibility."

Abruptly James stood. "He's getting rid of more than responsibility," he muttered. "If someone doesn't make a move soon, there will be nothing left of Eden."

"He's sold a little, yes," she concurred, "but—"

"A little!" he parroted. "According to Caleb, he's been averaging a thousand acres for the past four years. At that rate—"

She tried to soothe him. "There's enough, James. More than enough—"

From the window, he looked back. "Sophia said that you had received another letter from Sir Claudius this morning. Not a social letter, according to Sophia—"

She turned to face him. The outrage was there, hungry to surface. "Sophia said," she repeated, shocked. "And what right, may I ask, does Miss Cranford have to examine my mail?"

"It's delivered to her from the gatehouse," he replied, coolly. "It's her job—"

"To sort, yes," said Marianne, her voice still rising, "to

pry and poke and draw conclusions, no!" Suddenly she became aware of her emotions racing out of control. She grasped the back of the chair. "I will not have it," she cried out. "You may convey that message for me, or better still, send the woman to me and I shall inform her myself."

James now seemed to be suffering from the same lack of control. He stepped down from the window, confronting her, only the table between them. "She has your interest at heart, madam. Someone had better pay attention to what's going on."

"I've minded my affairs very well, thank you," she retorted. "I need no help from—"

"Minded your affairs very well!" he repeated. "You do nothing but mourn in this chamber and live in the past and on occasion talk to a dead man." His voice rose. "Look around you, madam, for God's sake. This place is falling apart. Can't you see? The land is being sold out from under you, the profits dwindle while your fair-haired bastard sleeps with every whore in London and hands out guineas on street corners as though they were posies—" His voice rose still higher, his face as determined to inflict pain as she'd ever seen it. "You should get down on your knees, madam, every night and thank God for the presence of the Cranfords in your life." He laughed, a harsh sound. "My God, they have done everything but breathe for you for the last thirty years. They've managed your affairs, seen to your accounts, protected you from ill-winds, and since you were too busy, they even raised your children for you."

She was incapable of thinking anymore. Without taking her eyes off his face, she moved slowly around the table until she was standing directly before him. Blindly she slapped him, a stinging blow to the side of his face.

His head fell to one side. One hand moved quickly up to the injured flesh. When he looked back at her, she saw moisture in the corners of his eyes. But he was smiling. "If that made you feel better, madam, I'm glad to have been of service."

Conscience-stricken, she moved backward as though fearful of striking him again. Her voice, when she spoke, was barely audible. "You are never," she whispered, "to speak like that to me again."

"Not speak the truth," he asked, mocking, "to my own mother?"

"Your words are not the truth," she protested.

"They are, as I see it and know it. You would have no family at all, madam, if it weren't for the Cranfords. And I warn you. Dismiss either of them and you'll lose what little family you have now. Jennifer will never come home, and I—"

The battle could not go on. She walked away hurriedly. "Leave me now. We are accomplishing nothing."

Without looking, she heard his footsteps move to the door. There he spoke again. "The matter is not closed," he warned. "Your life is over. One day, perhaps soon, you will join that old man out there in the graveyard. Pray God, you do it in time for me to salvage his property, salvage at least a shred of what was once an honorable and respected name."

"Get out," she whispered.

"I'm gone, madam," he replied lightly from the door. "It's unfortunate our meeting took this turn. I had intended to invite you to share luncheon. The Cranfords have prepared a picnic for the headlands. Seeing your present mood, I doubt if you'd appreciate the company."

She heard him pause, then heard the door close. Crumpled over the bureau, she found she could not breathe. In all that grand chamber there was not sufficient air to fill her lungs. Gasping, she raised up, and for her efforts suffered a severe pain across the top of her head, the discomfort spreading down into her shoulders, then up again into her jaws. It lasted only a moment, then almost frantically she glanced over her shoulder, as though fearful that he still was in the room with her.

But he wasn't. She was alone. She pressed her hands together, moaning almost soundlessly. Where was everyone? Mrs. Greenbell? Edward? Thomas?

Softly she slipped from the chair and went down to her knees, bent over. Was it possible that she had failed so miserably?

No answers in the quiet room. Nor did she want answers. All she desired was for the hurt to cease, for the breath to be restored to her lungs, for the sun to rise again on a world as lovely and as safe as she had enjoyed while Thomas lived.

Into her distress, a thought crept like a lifeline. Perhaps the trouble came from looking forward. Perhaps she had reached the age when Fate was trying to advise her to leave the future alone. It did not belong to her. She had no business with it. Look back. There was the safe domain, the lovely world of parties and balls and handsome, witty men and elegant ladies and glorious passionate affairs of the heart, a period beginning with May roses and ending with May jasmine.

But the mood that was upon her now was winter in its coldest shape. Then let it be spring. Abruptly she was aware of her position on the floor. What in the name of God was she doing? She was Lady Eden, the Countess Dowager of Eden Castle, with warm and dear friends who understood her and respected her and loved her.

Almost feverishly, she withdrew paper and quill. The melancholy was over. Her hand still shook, yet with flowering script, she wrote, "My dearest, dearest, William Pitch."

Standing just beyond the closed door, Caleb Cranford had waited, listening until he'd heard the resounding slap. The boy had moved too fast. Damn it! Was he totally dense?

He had no appetite for the scene that would inevitably follow, remorse and tears, and hurriedly he left his listening post, his elongated figure moving like a praying mantis down the stone corridors of Eden Castle. This unexpected emotional outburst would have to be reported immediately.

He found Sophia in the private kitchen of their first-floor apartments, putting the finishing touches on the picnic hamper that was to have been shared with both James and the Countess. As he came hurriedly into the narrow little converted room, she looked up from pouring wine from the decanter into a flagon. At first their sentences overlapped, so eager were they to communicate.

"It did not go well," Caleb commenced. "The boy moved too—"

"What happened? When I left, she was ripe—"

"They quarreled—"

"Oh God, that will serve no purpose—"

"I told him that. He seemed to want to—"

"What happened?"

As though suddenly suffering a loss of energy, Caleb sank wearily into the chair before the fireplace. He shook his head and smoothed back his long black hair. "There was a blow," he reported. Quickly he looked up to see what her reaction would be.

And equally as carefully she seemed to mask it. "Delivered by whom?" she inquired, resuming her work, meticulously cleaning the side of the decanter.

"I couldn't see, madam," he informed her. "Shortly after the meeting commenced, I was asked to leave."

She nodded as though understanding. "As was I. She seemed in ill spirits this morning."

"Then what do we do now?" he inquired, sitting up in the chair. "Should the bridge be mended?"

She did not answer right away, but continued to pack the hamper, carefully arranging the boiled eggs, the rounds of cheese, the wheat buns fresh from the oven.

Still Caleb waited, searching her face for the least sign, as he'd done since they were children, imprisoned together behind the double bars of a poverty-ridden preacher's house and the bleak, windswept moors. Even as children, they had plotted their escape. Now they were so close. "Sophia?" he murmured, leaning further up in the chair. "What should we do?"

Daintily she popped a crust of wheat bun into her mouth and smiled at him. "Do, Caleb, what shall we do?" The smile broadened. "Nothing. I despise open warfare, as you do. But in this instance, it might be the wisest course." She shrugged and came gently toward him. "It was inevitable, I'm afraid. I had hoped to postpone it until after James's engagement. But for that occasion the old woman will be decent, I'm certain of it."

She knelt before him, her eyes holding him fast, one hand gently massaging his upper leg. How he loved her when she was in this mood. "All we must do, dearest brother, is stay to our course. With or without the Countess Dowager's blessing, there *will* be a lawsuit. The fisherman's daughter can't keep the grave waiting forever. And one day, with God on our side, we shall assist Lord Eden with the running of his property."

Caleb gazed down on her strong and determined face. How calm she was, how confident, and what would he do without her. Eloquent woman, dearest sister.

With assuaging love, he gathered her to him and held her fast, detesting the need for secrecy in their passion. Where would he find a truer lover? Nowhere! Holding her close, he recalled fondly the first time they had indulged as mere children of twelve and thirteen, on a high summer day, bathing naked in a remote moorland stream, swollen by winter thaw. What had started in youthful curiosity had concluded in depths of passion that neither had dreamed possible. On that occasion they had pledged ever-lasting love, and in all the intervening years they had never betrayed one another.

"Dearest Sophia," he murmured, close to her ear, feeling himself as aroused now as he had been that first day as a boy of thirteen.

Abruptly, though with a coquettish smile, she disengaged herself from his embrace. As she straightened her apron over the lavender taffeta, she scolded softly, "There's work to be done." As she moved back to the picnic hamper, she smiled at him over her shoulder. "The boy will be along shortly, in need of comfort. We must save our energies for him."

He received her words like a necessary burden, though he left the chair and came up behind her, his hands reaching for and covering her breasts. "Then tonight?" he proposed gently.

She laughed. "Of course, tonight. Now, let me finish this and prepare yourself. By my estimation, the next knock at that door will be young James, in sore need."

Begrudgingly Caleb did as he was told. As he adjusted his coat and trousers, he continued to watch her, seeing not a sister, but a wife.

As she had predicted, a knock sounded at the door. He looked sharply up and caught her eye. "James?" he whispered.

The smile on her face hardened. She tucked a linen cloth around the top of the hamper, then looked directly at him.

"The future, dearest," she murmured. "Answer it quickly . . ."

London
May, 1836

The man was a dwarf with the rough script of the ages written on his face. Atop his left shoulder he carried a hump. His face was a scraggle of gray, unkempt beard. He was missing two fingers on one hand and three on the other. Yet he answered to the name of St. Peter. And St. Peter he was.

For a lost number of hours Edward had lain on the floor, studying the man. In the beginning he had been attended by De Quincey himself, who had brought him to this place, a pedant of a man who had spouted endless quotes in Greek and Latin, a fountain of words.

Only vaguely did Edward remember the beginning of the flight, De Quincey encountering him in the garden, inviting him to accompany him to—what had he said—cloudland? Then the stiff, awkward carriage ride, John Murrey depositing them on a strange lane named Toadley, about a block distant from the Embankment, a lane of old Elizabethan structures in various states of neglect and decay.

But with perfect confidence, De Quincey had waited until Edward's carriage had turned the corner, then he'd led the way toward one of the old mansions. There had been something so eager in his manner that Edward had succumbed.

They had picked their way across the debris of fallen statuary on the front terraces, following a darkened path which led, as well as Edward could remember, to the deserted manse.

Here the man had knocked twice on the door and shortly thereafter, St. Peter had appeared. And here he was again, bending over Edward, extending to him the keys to Paradise.

"Here, gintleman," St. Peter smiled. "Here's the last of yur wings."

As he extended the ruby-red draught, Edward eagerly took it. He thought it peculiar the way St. Peter held the glass, supported awkwardly by his remaining fingers. Then, drink. He was beginning to see too much.

St. Peter continued to hover, a friendly misshapen angel in the small darkened room. "That's the last," he repeated with a smile. "The other gintleman, he dun left. Said I was to look after yourn. And he most sartunly paid for your pleasure. But that's the last."

After Edward had drained the liquid, the old dwarf leaned close and retrieved the glass. A toothless smile was upon his face. "For a vargin, you took to it right enow," he grinned.

Edward returned the smile, leaning back on the floor, surrendering to the pleasant sensation, the lassitude in his limbs. "And where did the gentleman go?" he murmured, not really missing the flood of words, but wanting to thank him.

St. Peter straightened up, scratched intensely at his hump. "All he said was dooty calls. It's nuthin' to me, though he's a good customer, a real gintleman." He gestured with his mutilated hands to the small barren chamber. "I save this here always for him. A queer one, hisself. Time passes and I never seed him, then he appears, among such nobs like yourself. A good paying customer. True gintleman—"

Edward nodded. To everything. The bliss was spreading. Now, again, he was happy. *See-saw, Marjory Daw, sold her bed and lay on straw.* He lay back on his own straw, grinning up at St. Peter. What a glorious figure of a man, with his missing fingers and corrupted back.

Then, bowing, St. Peter left his sight.

At the height of the opium trance, his dreams were calm

and lovely. The broad swell and agitation of the storm had
subsided. The legions that had camped in his brain were
gone. His sleep was still tumultuous, but it was the splendid tumult of Paradise.

Beyond him, just out of sight, and almost beyond his
hearing or caring, he heard St. Peter again. "The last, Mr.
Gintleman. The last of your wings. Your beni-factor said
no more. Not fur now. There's those who have hurd of you
and will cum lookin'. No more, Mr. Gintleman. St. Peter
say no more."

It made no difference. With his eyes closed, Edward
smiled.

The dream soared. These sudden discoveries, flashing
upon him simultaneously, were quite sufficient to put a
summary close to all thought. For all practical purposes,
nothing mattered, not the death of William Pitch, the imprisonment of Charlotte Longford, the omnipresence of his
brother, James, the designation of bastard, not even that
softest of memories, his beloved mother.

There! What was that? A soaring rose-colored cloud. By
hurrying, he just reached out for it and was lifted, spiraling, into the heavens . . .

For three days, Daniel Spade released the classes an
hour early and sent the children, all those old enough and
wise enough in the ways of London, out onto the streets in
search of Edward.

Thus far, the concerted effort had produced nothing.
Word came back from every criminal stronghold of London that the Prince of Eden had not been seen, was indeed
nowhere about.

Now on the morning of the fourth day, Daniel, sick with
worry, called old John Murrey to his study, a large linen
pantry converted to its present use. He could not cover his
friend's absence much longer. Jane Locke had sent repeated
messengers around, requesting Edward's support at the
funeral service for William Pitch. The service had come
and gone, and still the man was missing. Now on his desk
was a scrawled message, spirited out of Newgate by one of
Edward's friends, from Charlotte Longford. The day of
punishment was drawing near. "Dear Edward, please help
if you can," she begged, even the rough parchment seeming
to bear the stench of the place. Then in the morning post,

the letter from Lady Eden. Daniel could only guess at its contents.

Sunk with distress, Daniel was not at first aware of John Murrey standing before his desk. Then he caught the whiff of stables and looked up.

"John," he began, trying for a degree of calm in his voice which he did not feel. "I want you to take me again to the place where you last saw Mr. Eden. Will you do that?"

The old man shrugged as though to say it was useless. But he went out to bring the carriage around. Daniel remained a moment longer at his desk, not at all certain he was doing the right thing. But what alternative course was there? This had never happened before, was totally without precedent. To be sure, Edward had wandered, had vanished for days at a time, into the Holy Land of Bloomsbury, down to Cheapside, but he'd always let Daniel know, either by direct word, or messenger. This time? Four days gone and not a word from Edward.

Beyond the door he spied a volunteer just passing. He summoned her, a plain, hefty woman named Matilda Davis who had fled the steel-pen factory on Newhall Street for volunteer work in Daniel's Ragged School.

"I'm afraid I must ask you to take all the classes today—"

"No bother, sir."

"I'm having John lead me over the route again." He shook his head. "We must have missed something. He may be ill—"

"I quite understand, sir." Her gentle manner was pleasing, even when she softly suggested, "Not none of us could do very long without Mr. Eden, now could we, sir?"

"No," he said, and wondered if she fully understood the extent to which they all were dependent upon the man.

Outside in the corridor, he heard the children just filing down for prayers and breakfast. "You'd better hurry along, Matilda," he urged. "Are you sure you can—"

She waved a hasty farewell, then she was gone, her voice lovingly herding the children down the steps into the banqueting hall.

As the children's voices dwindled down into the vast recesses of the house, he straightened his desk. He tucked the two personal messages for Edward inside the drawer, then stood, preparing himself for the mysterious neighborhood a distance from the Embankment, the place where Edward was last seen alive.

The staircase was empty. Beyond the broad opened front door, he saw John Murrey patiently waiting beside the carriage. Behind him he heard the children's voices sweetly raised in a morning hymn; it set a mournful mood. As he hurried down the steps, out of the corner of his eye, he saw movement, a quick darting brown something which hid just out of sight to one side of the stone steps. He considered investigating, but decided against it. He'd wasted enough time.

Daniel crawled into the carriage and watched as John pulled himself laboriously up onto the high seat. With his concentration focused in one direction, Daniel was only partially aware of a small weight apparently settling on the rear of the carriage, as though someone had swung up onto the carriage rack.

As John was about to lay the whip lightly across the horses' backs. Daniel craned his neck about, and through the small oval window behind caught a quick glimpse of a small form clinging to the back of the carriage.

"Wait up!" he shouted to John. In some irritation he climbed out of the door and strode around to the rear. "What in the—" Slowly he shook his head at the sight of a young girl clinging to the back of the carriage, her head down, ostrich-fashion, as though if she didn't see, she wouldn't be seen.

At the sound of his voice she slowly lifted her head. He did not recognize her at first. The last time he'd seen her, she'd been covered with filth, her hair hanging matted over her face, obscuring her features. Then he remembered her, the child, Elizabeth, that Edward had brought to him after his night in Newgate. She was washed and scrubbed now, and wearing a plain brown muslin dress, less a child than perhaps he had originally assessed her to be. Though her face was still pale, she stared defiantly back at him.

"Elizabeth," he scolded. "What are you doing? Breakfast has commenced. I hope you realize you're quite late—"

He extended a hand to help her, but she drew quickly back and renewed her grip on her precarious perch, made doubly precarious, he noticed now, by her mutilated hand, which could not grip at all.

The sight of the hand and the fright in her eyes caused him to alter his approach. By now John Murrey had joined him, his wrinkled face a complex expression of puzzlement and anger. "Get down with you," the old man shouted, as though the carriage were his domain and the sight of ruffians clinging to it offended him.

But the girl held her position just beyond their reach, and a moment later climbed even higher, wriggling like a monkey almost to the top. John Murrey's anger clearly vaulted. Now he extended his whip upward until the tip was touching her leg. "You heard me," he shouted, hoarsely. "Climb down or I'll climb up and pull you down."

Behind them on the pavement, Daniel was aware of several curious passers-by. The old man's shouts were attracting considerable attention. "That's enough, John," he counseled quietly. "Let me try."

Cursing, John Murrey turned away and dragged his whip through his fingers as though he were most eager to use it on the stowaway.

Daniel stepped close to the rear of the carriage until he was looking straight up. "Elizabeth," he begged, keeping his voice low and soothing. "You must come down. Classes will be starting—"

"Don't want to go to no classes," she muttered sullenly. "I want to go with you."

"Elizabeth, please," he begged softly. "I can't take you with me—"

"Why not?" she demanded.

"Where I'm going is not—"

"I know where you're going," she replied. She ceased talking and tried to renew her grip on the high upper railing. Suddenly her foot slipped. As the mutilated hand reached out for support and failed, she fell halfway down the rear of the carriage, a scraping descent which stirred a collective "Ah" from the crowd.

Before Daniel could protest, two men in corduroy jackets rushed forward and grabbed her legs and pulled her down to the pavement, their rough faces delighted with their accomplishment.

She gave a little scream and tried quickly to get to her feet again, but both men held her pinned. "That's enough," Daniel ordered, stepping forward. "Leave her alone."

"Only showin' you how to git cherries out of the tree, Guv," one man grinned.

"You can't let a piece like that go orderin' you about," the other agreed.

"I said leave her alone," Daniel repeated. Hurriedly he reached down and lifted the girl to her feet. He took her sternly by the arm and led her around to the carriage door. More to get her off the street than anything, he shoved her inside, then crawled in after her.

A few moments later as the carriage started forward, he saw a look of pleasure on her face, as though she had set a goal for herself and achieved it.

"You're going again to try to find Mr. Eden. But you've not had much luck, have you?"

"Do you think you know where he is, Elizabeth?"

"I may," she said vaguely.

He regarded her searchingly for a moment, then formed his own opinion. She knew no more than he did.

"I'm sorry, Mr. Spade," she murmured. "I didn't mean to cause no trouble. It's just that—we must find him." She leaned still closer, her young face almost sunk with earnestness. "He may need us," she concluded with devastating simplicity.

So engrossed was he in the girl's attitude and manner that Daniel was not at first aware of the carriage rolling to a halt. Not until he heard John Murrey's voice shouting down at him, "This is it, sir, this is the spot," did he look up.

Before he could speak, she was out of the carriage, standing absolutely motionless on the pavement as though listening. He followed after her and looked about at the disreputable lane. Nothing stirred, not even the trees in the stillness of morning. On either side of the street were faded old Elizabethan mansions. Many of the windows appeared to be coated by a black paste, composed of ancient soot and dampness, and every gray and crumbling exterior wore an aspect of gloom. Growing around these ancient relics was nature gone awry, swift-climbing tentacles of green vines that in some cases scaled the gray stones to the top of the towers, here and there the outline of a dead garden, jasmine and roses strangling each other, lilac bushes unattended, grown to trees.

There was all this, and nothing more, no sight or sound

of life save for the whimpering horses who stamped lightly at the pavement as though sensing the death about them.

Discouraged, Daniel made an aimless trip up and down on the pavement. He looked back at Elizabeth, who continued to stand, unmoving, in the same spot into which she'd alighted from the carriage.

Then without warning, she was running toward Number Two, a particularly large gray mansion, its front terrace cluttered with fallen statuary.

"Wait," he shouted after her, feeling a need to stay close beside her. But she would not wait and ran nimbly across the broken terrain, her feet devouring the territory as though it were familiar and she knew precisely where she was going.

Still a distance behind her, he saw her climb the steps and pound frantically on the boarded front door. "There's nothing there, Elizabeth," he called after her. "Can't you see?"

But as he was climbing the steps, he saw two of the boards give, slide to one side as though they were attached to a panel. And just beyond the door, standing in the gloomy interior, he saw an apparition of a man, a dwarf with a hunchback, his withered frame encased in a ragged black cape, his voice now raucously protesting Elizabeth's intrusion. "Wait up, you baggage," he shouted, flailing his short arms uselessly, "this here's a gintlemen's place—"

But Elizabeth would not be deterred. As she slipped from sight into the dark interior, Daniel increased his step, thinking perhaps that he should have brought help with him, of a different kind, something more substantial than a frail girl.

Now as Daniel slipped through the narrow opening, the dwarf seemed to be suffering extreme distress. He danced from one side to the other, a macabre jig on stumpy legs, still protesting the intrusion. As he focused on Daniel, he changed his approach, grew quite apologetic. "No harm, sir. My name's St. Peter and I run a respectable place. Such nobs as you can see for yourself."

Daniel stepped forward into the gloom, scarcely altered by two wall torches. There was a hideous stench to the place. Following the direction of the dwarf, Daniel ventured forward through the hall until he stood looking out over a vast room, one of the most incredible sights he'd

ever seen, barren, of all furnishings save for coffinlike
bunks and perhaps as many as seventy-five men lying about
in somnambulant states, inert figures, not quite corpses for
there was faint movement now and then as a heavy head
lifted, then turned away in apathy.

As he stared, he was then aware of Elizabeth, moving
determinedly down the rows of coffinlike bunks. In her
hand she held a candle and before each bunk she thrust
the flame forward, clearly and closely examining each
addict.

Still Daniel continued to stare, almost frozen in his
abhorrence of the waste before him. And a few moments
later when Elizabeth returned, her face lost in shadows of
defeat, he felt a peculiar relief. "Come," he whispered,
taking her arm. "We'll not find him here."

But the dwarf stepped forward and stretched out his
hand, childishly plump, and with a half-bow, he whispered,
"Is it a gintleman you're looking for?" Without waiting
for a reply, he went on, mindlessly grinning, "If so, this
here is only the first layer." The pudgy hand pointed toward the crumbling stairs. "The gintlemen gits put upstairs," he beamed. "Don't rightly know their names, don't
mind to know, but—"

Before he could finish, Elizabeth was taking the stairs
two at a time. Daniel looked back into the enormous room
filled with silent faces, then started heavily up the stairs
after Elizabeth, where he now heard a series of doors
being opened, then shut.

At the top of the landing he looked in both directions.
She was no place in sight. The corridor was dark and
airless, and lining the walls were bales of straw. "Elizabeth?" he called.

His voice echoed emptily about the walls. He looked
back. Apparently the dwarf had elected to remain behind.
But Daniel saw him, standing in the hall below, grinning
up, bobbing his head as though he approved of the
search. "In the rear room, Guv," he called up. "There's a
gintleman there, a vargin who took to it right enow. Another gintleman brung him, paid his bill, then left. Check
on that one and see if it's yourn gintleman."

At the end of the hall, encountering a dead end, he
turned again. At the opposite end, he thought he saw a
faint light which had not been there before, as though a

door had been opened. Keeping his eye on the faint illumination, he started forward. With every step, he prayed fervently, Don't let us find him here.

As he drew nearer the partially opened door, he stopped. From someplace he heard a different sound, a soft voice continuously murmuring, no words, merely syllables of comfort.

Again Daniel brushed aside the uneasy feelings within him and stepped toward the open door. Before him, in a room which more nearly resembled a stable, containing no furnishings but a mat of straw, he saw him, lying on his back, his eyes opened, though unseeing, staring fixedly up at the ceiling, his hair mussed, his clothes foul-smelling with remnants of his own sickness, his head resting in her lap, her hand continuously stroking his brow.

At Daniel's appearance, she looked up with grieved astonishment. "I was hoping it wouldn't be him," she murmured. "But here he is."

Beyond the man himself, scattered about the floor, Daniel saw the evidence of his indulgence, several flagons of wine, and close by, numerous vials, all empty, the residue of liquid still coating their sides.

Edward seemed to be stirring now, trying to lift himself from his prone position. His eyes, glazed, made a slow, deliberate circle, encompassing both Daniel and Elizabeth. At first a smile of recognition brightened his face, as struggling upward, he managed a half-suspended position, then fell back again onto Elizabeth's lap.

Quite suddenly, without warning, the smile faded. His eyes filled with tears. As Elizabeth huddled protectively over him, Daniel closed his eyes. He knew little of the addiction save for one point. Prolonged use led to one of two places, either to the grave or the madhouse. He'd heard men order it openly in pubs—"a glass of laudanum negus, warm, and without sugar." And he'd seen the effects differ from man to man, one morose and dejected, the other volatile and full of high spirits. There seemed to be two distinct periods throughout indulgence; the first, a greatly increased activity of the mind, and the second, the stupor, the descent into hazy and usually emotional abstractions.

As Daniel again assessed the scene, he felt anger rising. Heading the list of questions which surfaced out of his rage was who had led Edward here? But there were no answers, certainly not in the face of his friend, whose mouth was mutely working, as though he were trying with all his might to form words.

Unable to endure the sight, Daniel gruffly ordered Elizabeth, "Help me lift him. Let's get him out of this place."

Obediently she was on her feet, the two of them, one on each side, laboriously struggling to raise him. Finally after great effort, they had him suspended between them, Daniel taking most of the weight on his own shoulders, calling out for Elizabeth to open the door. After a few steps forward, Edward seemed aware that effort was required of him, and Daniel felt his weight lifting, at least partially assisting with his own exit.

As they approached the stairs, Daniel renewed his grip and ordered Elizabeth to run ahead and fetch John Murrey. At first she seemed loath to abandon his side, but when half in anger, half in despair, Daniel raised his voice to her, she scampered lightly down the stairs, passed the gaping, grinning dwarf, and disappeared through the boards in the door.

At the top of the stairs, Daniel tried to hold him upright, but he seemed on the verge of losing all consciousness. He slumped forward and before Daniel could grasp his arm, he slipped down two steps, Daniel breaking his fall at the last minute by reaching out and grasping his hand.

Below, the dwarf laughed. "His wings is failin'," he chirped, performing again the bizarre little dance, as though he took genuine delight in seeing a whole man fall.

Daniel ignored the jibe and hurried down the steps where, with effort, he scooped Edward into his arms and lifted him up, intent only on fleeing the place. Just as they reached the bottom of the stairs, the boards parted, letting in a blinding light of morning sun, and John Murrey appeared, being dragged by the girl.

Quickly his old eyes took in the scene before him. As his attention was drawn to the vast room filled with addicts, he breathed a quick, hoarse prayer, "God have mercy—"

"John, help," Daniel called out, trying to summon his attention to the task at hand.

"Is he hurt, sir?" John asked, taking his share of the weight, Edward now suspended between them.

"I don't think so. Hurry, let's get him out of here."

Together the two men carried him to the door, where Elizabeth had already drawn back the boards. As they angled the limp figure through the narrow opening, Daniel glanced back at the dwarf. "Do you recall the name of the man who brought him here?" he asked, making no attempt to mask the coldness in his voice.

Again the dwarf grinned. "No names here, Guv, and I don't know nuthin', not even when the wurld was made or how anybody could do it. No names. I have nuthin' to say about payin' customers." The grin broadened. "Like him there. He'll be back. They flies off and flies back." At this the dwarf dissolved into a fit of uncontrollable laughter.

Daniel listened and watched. "You'll not be seeing this one again," he shouted back. As they carried Edward toward the carriage, the last thing Daniel heard was the dwarf, still laughing, a shrill, unearthly sound.

At the carriage, he saw Elizabeth waiting, door flung open, her face still creased in concern. As they placed him inside, she slipped around to the other door and sat quickly in the seat, ready to receive him, his head again resting in her lap.

Winded from his effort, Daniel stood back as John closed the door. "If I'd a known, sir," the old man began. "I mean, that night, I had no idea—"

Daniel dismissed his apology. "It's not your fault, John. Take us home, as quickly as possible."

Inside the carriage, Daniel looked back at the gray crumbling mansion, more ominous-looking than before, now that he knew what it contained. Across from him, Elizabeth continued to cradle Edward in her arms. "Will he be all right, sir? I mean, why is he—"

With a confidence that he did not feel, Daniel tried to reassure her. "He'll be fine. He needs rest and food."

The empty words seemed to bring her comfort. She continued to stroke his brow with her injured hand, apparently uncaring now who saw it.

The shadows of the morning flitted through the carriage. Two words continued to press against Daniel's brain. *An addict.* Moving in and around those two words, like the shadows themselves, was the memory of the dwarf's parting laughter. *Once bitten, they stays bit. He'll be back.*

Edward moaned, apparently discomfited by the rocking motion of the carriage. Elizabeth leaned over him in concern.

Daniel watched, trying with all his might to crush the heavy uneasy feelings of anxiety which had arisen within him . . .

Newgate Prison

It was the night that frightened her most. Dawn was her saviour, dressing the ugly prison walls in earliest light and beginning to redden with the deep luster of a May morning.

Yet even mornings had hazards. Like now. For the last four days, the turnkeys had pushed the prisoners in the Common Cell against the wall and one by one had covered their faces with coarse brown masks, each fitted tightly over the head and down onto the shoulders, with two small slits for the eyes, one for the mouth.

As Charlotte had discovered, breathing was difficult. With the nose tightly obscured, it had to be accomplished through the mouth. After several hours of this, the lips became parched, the mouth itself useless.

Still, the anonymity comforted her. They looked alike now in their prison garb, the men in shapeless black suits, the women in black dresses with gray aprons and curiously stitched white darts covering all. Thus masked, she was no longer singled out and stared upon by the other prisoners as "the different 'un."

During the four days in which she had inhabited this wretched Common Cell, not counting the lost number of

hours in which she'd lain senseless upon the straw, her
mind rendered mute by the magistrate's harsh sentence,
she'd observed certain changes. The fatherly old turnkey
whom she had seen through terrified eyes that first night
had not been present for three days. Nor had she observed
the young turnkey, the lad who had looked upon her with
such pity.

On this the fifth morning, she noticed other changes as
well. The two ruffians who had squatted nearby in guard-
like positions were gone. In fact, looking sharply at the
line of prisoners still being masked, she saw not one familiar face. Apparently over the night, the entire Common
Cell population had changed. Only she remained.

As she made her way back to her straw in the far corner,
she sidestepped the piles of human dung left during the
night. The stench was overpowering. She felt her stomach
turn, the sour gruel from the night before rising in her
throat in a burning stream.

She collapsed onto the straw and tilted her head back
and tried to breathe deeply. But the odor was poisonous, a
combination of matter passing into decay, an accumulation
of urine-soaked straw and cabbage leaves.

During the trial she had thought that endurance would
be possible. She'd even grown accustomed to the daily
humiliation of the prosecutor, an arrogant, bewigged
gentleman who had looked at her as though she were all
the world's scourges rolled into one.

*Mrs. Longford, how many times have you committed
adultery? With whom and under what circumstances? And
isn't it true that you crossed Oxford Street, heading toward
the disreputable Ragged School, looking for more than a
way to serve?*

She groaned audibly. A faceless man passing her by
stopped and stared down. "Is it lonely you are?" he asked,
his eyes shining behind the mask.

Quickly she drew herself into a sitting position, hugged
her knees, and made herself into a tight, unresponding
knot. A moment later, the man passed, but she kept her
eyes on him.

High above on the catwalk, she saw three turnkeys
pacing. They weren't familiar. She'd never seen them before. Her eyes fell again on the huddle of male prisoners
about halfway down the cell. Their whispers continued,

their smooth brown faceless heads all turning in her direction.

The large Common Cell was as empty as she had ever seen it, less than twenty prisoners, all male except for the three old women who kept to themselves at the far end by the door. Still, she had nothing to fear as long as sunlight streamed through the high barred windows. She was safe in day.

But the silence of the room alarmed her. Usually by mid-morning the prisoners were chatting among themselves, games of chance going on here and there. Now? Nothing.

Nearby something rustled through the straw. She turned her head in that direction, forgetting for the moment the uselessness of her peripheral vision. When the rustle came again, she drew herself up to her knees and faced the spot directly. A large black rat scurried forth, darting back into the straw, then emerging again a distance away.

A soft scream escaped her lips as she drew reflexively back, her heart beating too fast. As she scrambled in the opposite direction, the male prisoners laughed, pointing their fingers in her direction.

Long minutes passed before she could still her breathing. As she took refuge in the opposite corner, she carefully kicked the straw to one side, and sat on the stone floor. She tried to draw a deep breath and turn her mind in another direction.

The distant past was relatively safe, her childhood spent in Hampstead, the youngest daughter of a fairly prosperous grocer, the pretty red silk umbrella she'd carried as a child, the holidays to Brighton, the smell of the sea, no lasting pain except the day that her small brown terrier, Dash, had been run over by a coach. Still, she had survived. The rest of it was a blur of warm sunshine and lilacs, and lovely teas and whispered secrets with her friends at the bottom of the garden, nothing, absolutely nothing preparing her for her present plight.

She even remembered the day that Samuel Longford had come to her father's house, her father's friend. Clearly he had been appreciative of the young woman who had blossomed from the little girl he had carried on his shoulders. She had not even been aware that marriage had been discussed between them. The surprising thing, even now, was that she had not particularly objected when the subject had been broached, when Mr. Longford had walked with her in the garden and kissed her for the first time. It had been like kissing Papa, warm and paternal. He had given her a handsome ruby ring and the pledge that he would spare no effort in his attempts to make her happy, that quite obviously he would die first and leave her a comfortably rich widow.

She'd agreed. What else could she have done? It was clearly what her father wanted, and at twenty-six she was well on her way to the embarrassment of spinsterhood.

Remembering all, she sat rigidly upon the floor. She had moved with Mr. Longford into the apartments above the linen shop on Oxford Street. From her bedroom window she'd seen nothing but gray and crowds of people and endless carriages and noise and confusion. How she'd missed the green of the Hampstead countryside. Then the nights—she shuddered involuntarily. Where had his courteous manners gone, his kind attitude? Alone in the chamber, he had required of her—

She doubled over, hiding her already masked face in the folds of her apron. The conditions of her memories were then such that in order to face them, she had to stand and pace lightly. The feeling of conflict was building within her. The memory of the tall fair-haired gentleman whom she'd seen only from a distance came back upon her, and while she was pacing, she felt stunned, recalling their first meeting, so innocent and businesslike.

The very existence of the atmosphere of love in the Ragged School had been a shock to her. Now the remembrance of that love mimicked her, like the moment of death in sick patients, close upon their end. It was just that she had seen him in constant activity until, one day, she had seen him silent, a look of such bereavement upon his strong face as she had never seen before. She had intended only to offer comfort. Then how had it happened that they both had found themselves in his private chambers, the need on his face entering through her eyes into her brain like a gentle intoxication, matching her own, as though they were nothing more than two blank mirrors staring at each other.

For an instant in her life, under the gentle yet passionate direction of Edward Eden, she had inhabited a moment of summer. She had never intended it to be anything else, but one moment which would fortify her for a prolonged winter.

Now the memory faded through all its stages, like departing day. Her present agony wore its way through morning, noontide, afternoon, to meet the darkness that was hurrying to swallow her. At intervals she heard, in how different a key, the men as they stirred, coughed, cleared their throats, their faces behind their masks still staring at her.

For herself, her purposes were dim. She had been permitted to scrawl one letter, and that she had sent to Edward Eden, begging him to help her if he could. No reply had come. She had not seen Mr. Longford since the last day of the trial, nor had she expected to see him. Her parents had come with condemning, embarrassed faces during her isolation of the trial, but since her exile to the Common Cell she'd had no visitors, and expected none. All she heard now was the whispering of that peculiar voice in her ear, warning her not to survive, telling her it was not worth the effort.

Exhausted, she sank back to the floor, her hands fallen limp in her lap. With a kind of abstract curiosity, she examined her right hand. How would it be done? she wondered. Would the poker be held to flame within the courtroom or be brought in from an adjoining chamber? Would she be bound or free? How would it burn? Lengthwise, or across the middle? Who would press it against her flesh? Would she endure or pass out? And what was the odor of burning flesh? And what would become of her afterwards? With an awful gluttony, her mind turned on the whole scene.

So engrossed was she that she was not at first aware of the men approaching her, stealthily on both sides. And when at last she looked up from the contemplation of her hand, she saw them as merely objects. Their attitude still did not alarm her, not even when they stepped closer, three on either side, their stained hands reaching out, as though she were a wild animal whose response could not be predicted.

When at last the threat devoured her it was too late. They were on her then, like a many-armed monster, dragging her backward away from the wall to the center of the Common Cell, someone shrieking continuously in her ear, her hands and feet flailing uselessly against their superior strength. Their long fingers dug into the flesh of her arm as one whispered close to her ear, "A harlot don't have no objection. Show us how it be dun, mistress—"

As they flattened her to ground, she saw high above her on the catwalk the three turnkeys grinning down. For several moments she kept up the struggle until at last they pinned her, two standing on her arms, the others working feverishly about her legs.

The assault launched, her eyes behind the mask closed. The sobbing mouth went slack. All the fear of what was yet to come grew, then faded. She was silent, and out of the storm, the ghost voice praised her for her surrender. It was very calm now, though for a moment longer as she passed to senselessness, she continued to hear men's threats, oaths, laughter, laments. Her arms and legs were numb. Then let the rest of her follow suit.

As she slipped deeper away, she stopped for only an instantaneous regret, that out of twenty-seven years of winter, there had been only one brief interval of summer.

No matter. Where she was going there were no such painful and arbitrary divisions. She stopped for a final contact. Her back scraped rhythmically on the stone floor. She clenched her fists and howled out her agony.

Then she ran like a madwoman from this treacherous level to a safer, deeper one.

Through the two windows, Edward watched the sunlight fall upon the bare floor. The agreeable lassitude which had attended him for a lost number of hours was over. Unfortunately he felt quite himself again.

Slowly he sat up on the pallet, trying to put the pieces of the puzzle together. He remembered with a stab of sorrow that William Pitch had died, that he had accompanied the gentleman, De Quincey, to a strange dwelling. And then—

Painfully he shook his head. After that, a blank. And how did he get from there to his chambers on Oxford Street?

It was while his head was down, eyes closed, that he heard the door softly open, heard a young girl's voice greet him quietly, "Oh, you're up, sir."

Slowly he raised his head. By the door, he saw a young woman. A stranger to him. Abruptly the pain in his head grew worse.

She was at his side then, on her knees before him. "Are you all right, sir?" she inquired earnestly.

Still with his head down, he opened his eyes and caught sight of her hands in her lap, one hand withered, with fingers missing. He'd seen that hand before. Slowly he raised his head. "Elizabeth?"

She grinned as though pleased. "The same, sir. You've had a rough go of it. Shall I fetch Mr. Spade?"

As she started to rise, he restrained her. "No, not yet. Please."

"What ails you, sir?" she asked softly. "Are you cold? Hungry? You've not taken food for ever so long. Please let me fetch—"

But again he restrained her. "In a minute, Elizabeth," he said, catching her hand and holding it. "I need—your help in other matters." Again he faltered. "I need to know, Elizabeth," he began, embarrassed. "How—did I get here?"

The light of a smile blazed across her face. "Oh, that was me and Mr. Spade," she grinned. "When you'd been missing for ever so long, Mr. Spade and me, we got the old man to take us back to that place. Mr. Spade, he didn't see or hear nothing, but I did." The smile broadened. "I heard you calling plain as the sun." She moved still closer on her knees before him. "Mr. Spade?" she went on. "He didn't know about the house. But I did. I seen dens before, the men sleeping like the dead—"

Her face was stern. "It's a bad place, sir. All the time we was lookin', I kept hoping we wouldn't find you."

Embarrassed, Edward received her words. "I agree," he murmured, "and I'm sorry to have caused trouble."

"Oh, it weren't no trouble, sir," she went on. "The trouble was when you were gone and no one knew where. Mr. Spade, he was most done in, as I was—"

"Thank you," he said simply.

The moment held, then she was talking again, telling him of that "dreadful place." So engrossed was he that he failed to hear the door open and close.

He heard Daniel's voice. "So! You're going to survive after all."

Quickly Edward turned his attention from the girl to the stern face of his friend. There was something about his stance, standing rigidly against the closed door, which suggested to Edward that he had bridges to mend. "Daniel," he smiled, extending his hand in a gesture for the man to come closer.

But Daniel refused to come forward and instead spoke with what seemed to Edward undue sharpness to the girl. "You may leave, Elizabeth," he ordered. "Fetch him some tea and a bowl of hot soup, if it isn't too troublesome to Cook."

Edward tried to object. "It isn't necessary, Daniel. I can go down."

"How?" Daniel asked. "You can scarcely sit erect, let alone—" He seemed to check himself. Again he looked sternly at the girl. "Leave us now," he commanded.

Obediently, with head bowed, she did as she was told, although she bestowed upon Edward a glorious parting smile. He tried to rise to his feet. Halfway up his knees buckled and he fell back into his sitting position. Smiling, he shook his head. "I seem to be missing bones this morning."

For a moment Daniel seemed disinclined to say anything further. The silence between them was unusual. "Please, Daniel," he begged. "I'm sorry for the trouble I caused—"

Daniel's voice was so hard and cold that Edward scarcely recognized it. "The trouble you've caused me," he began, "is nothing to the trouble you've caused yourself."

Again Edward tried to apologize, but Daniel at last stepped forward. "I wish you might have seen yourself, Edward," he said, standing directly over him. "I have never visited such a place and hope never to again." He shut his eyes as though to blot out a persistent vision. "I kept telling the girl that we would not find you there."

"I know. She—"

"She was the one who found you," Daniel went on, pacing now before the pallet. Suddenly he halted and confronted Edward with a direct question. "What in the name of God possessed you?" he demanded. "Had you no idea what you were about, no conception of the consequences?"

In spite of his regret, Edward found the strident, demanding voice irritating. "William Pitch died," he announced quietly at the first break in the torrent of words.

Instead of having the stunning effect that Edward had expected, Daniel thrust on. "I know," he announced, "a hard death for you, but did it warrant such behavior? And who led you to that place? Who was persuasive enough to lure you to that Hell?"

Edward had been expecting sympathy. The moral outrage, instead of subsiding, seemed to be increasing. Still, he tried to hold his tongue. "You're making far too much of it, Daniel. It was simply— For a short period of time, I was an opium eater. Today I am no longer such."

Apparently his words bore the patness of a quote. Again Daniel demanded, "Who was the man?"

"A fellow mourner."

"And his name?"

"Unimportant." Again Edward tried to rise to his feet. He had played the penitent long enough and was weary of the role. "You must forgive me, Daniel. I have responsibilities to attend to." He was erect now, though there was not a great deal of hope in his remaining so. By using the chest for support, then the table, he made his way to the chair by the window, counting on air to revive him.

As he sank into the chair, he was aware of Daniel watching him. Clearly the man was upset, and Edward was sorry for that. But they had seen many days together, good and evil, and they would weather this one as well. Beyond the open window, he caught sight of the second-floor apartments of Samuel Longford. There was that to attend to as well. He trusted by now that old Jawster Gray had made peace with his conscience.

Then he was aware of Daniel moving softly up behind him. "You look terrible," he said, standing at his elbow.

With a faint smile, Edward lowered his head. "Thank you."

"Do you need a physician?"

"Of course not. Some coffee and I'll be back on course." He glanced up at Daniel, saw gratefully that the expression of outrage had been replaced by something else, a most peculiar expression, not unlike pity. "Do you know, Daniel," he began, "what William Pitch's last words were to me?"

The man standing beside him was silent.

"He thanked me," Edward went on, "for sharing this life with him."

Daniel knelt beside him, the old Daniel. Edward looked at him, mystified. He was being stared at as though he were a dead man. Curious physical discomforts continued to plague him. He discovered with a shock that he was wet through with sweat, his hands trembling so that he was forced to hide them out of sight. He was aware of Daniel leaving his side and returning with a glass of water. Greedily Edward drank it, wiping the residue from his chin with the back of his hand. Now he was cold.

"You need a physician," Daniel pronounced, starting toward the door.

"No," Edward called after him. Apparently he had delivered the word in an effective tone of voice for Daniel stopped in midroom and looked back.

"Daniel, please," he smiled, clinging to the back of the chair. "Help me dress. I must look my best—"

"For what?"

Surprised at the foolish question, Edward started in a faltering pace across the room. "I must go to my Aunt Jane's of course," he said.

"For what purpose?" Daniel inquired further.

"I promised I'd assist with the arrangements," Edward murmured, and painfully he drew himself toward the wardrobe, his hands shaking as though they were palsied.

"Arrangements for what?" came the cold steady voice behind him.

Suddenly rage exploded within him. "For William's burial," he shouted, expending energy he did not have. "My God," he muttered, "have you gone senseless? The man is dead—"

"Yes," Daniel shouted back at him, "and buried. Three days ago."

Edward stared at him. Surely his wits must have wandered a little. "Three days?" he whispered. Without warning his knees buckled.

Daniel was at his side then, kneeling, cradling him. "Three days ago, Edward, it was," he whispered. "I tried to find you, oh God, how I searched. Miss Locke sent repeated messengers around. But I couldn't find you." He paused a moment. "It's over, Edward," he murmured. "You have nothing to attend to but the restoration of your own good health, and the most solemn vow you have ever made before God and man never to step foot in that direction again."

William buried? William gone? If three days had passed, then was this the fourth or the fifth? Seven in a week, and on the sixth the sentence was to take place.

Suddenly he struggled upward. He was not expert enough to solve the mystery now. "Charlotte," he whispered, again trying to run the perilous course from the floor to the wardrobe with Daniel still restraining him, dragging him back, lifting him finally and assisting him back to the pallet.

"There's time for that," he promised. "She sent word. I'll go with you tonight. Together we will try—"

Edward was only vaguely aware of Elizabeth returning, heard Daniel's command for the girl to lift his head. At his firm insistence, he obediently swallowed spoonful after spoonful of the hot soup.

A little while later he closed his eyes, his mind calm. Elizabeth was still there, bending over him, stroking his head with a cloth. And Daniel was still there.

"Edward?"

"I've promised you, Daniel," Edward murmured. "I'll not go there again. There's no need—"

But Daniel merely shook his head. "It's not that," he said quickly. He hesitated. Finally he said, "Do you remember that we have guests coming tonight? Do you think that you'll be able to—"

Guests? Edward faced him, trying again to clear the fog from his brain. So many problems intersecting simultaneously.

Quietly Daniel said, "I told you some time ago. You said that you would—"

Edward shook his head and lay back on the pillow. "I'm sorry, Daniel," he said. He was in no mood for society. "I'm afraid you must excuse me," he apologized.

He sensed Daniel's disappointment and tried belatedly to relieve it. "Who are these guests?" he asked, clearly a perfunctory question.

"Robert Owen," Daniel replied, as though the name spoke for itself.

The name meant nothing to Edward. Undoubtedly one of Daniel's radical friends. He felt resentful now that Daniel would broach such a subject. "I must go to Newgate tonight," he said forcefully. "He's your friend, not mine. I'm afraid you'll have to—"

"There are others coming and they wanted to meet you," Daniel persisted. "They're coming to see the school. Owen is interested in establishing others throughout London."

"You're the schoolmaster, Daniel. Not I. I serve no purpose here."

"That's not true."

Weary of the conversation, Edward wanted only to end it. He'd never been able to win an argument with Daniel. False acquiescence, that was the solution. "You must be doing a good job, Daniel. When other men take notice, that's always a good sign."

It worked. Daniel softened. "Without you, none of it would have been possible."

Edward quickly dismissed this for the foolishness it was. "All I did was provide you with an old house that should have been torn down years ago."

"You've done more, much more. They all want to meet you."

God, enough! With his eyes closed, Edward promised, "If I'm capable of standing upright, Daniel, I'll be there."

Apparently that was all Daniel wanted. He smiled and gently arranged the coverlet over Edward. "And later, after they have gone," he said, making a promise of his own, "we'll go together to Newgate. Charlotte will need all the sustenance we can give her."

The name alone was capable of causing pain. Edward tried not to think on the young woman who'd passed the week in the Common Cell. Charlotte needed more than their sustenance. She needed an escape route. And he intended to see that she got it.

Daniel stood then, apparently at peace. "Rest," he smiled down. "I'll leave Elizabeth with you."

A moment later Edward heard Daniel leave the room.

Then Elizabeth was there again, stroking his forehead. Edward had no great pain now. The nourishment of food had helped. There were two certainties at work in his mind: one, that he was totally unworthy of the love and care which were being carelessly heaped upon him, and two, he had to devise some way to clear the room of that love and care so that he might flee this house.

He looked up at Elizabeth and again caught her hand.

"You've wasted enough time here," he smiled. "Go and attend to your own needs. I'll sleep now."

She gave him a smile and a sigh. "I'm not wasting time, sir, and I have no needs to attend to, save yours."

Frantically his mind turned. He did not want to hurt or offend her. "Then go to your studies," he suggested. "I want to hear a quote from Wordsworth tonight."

She looked puzzled. "Who, sir?"

"Go and find out," he smiled. "Ask one of the volunteers. And tonight, tell me what you have learned."

The bewilderment on her face softened as she agreed. "I'll be back, sir."

It was a promise he eagerly received. As she stood, it occurred to him that possibly she was the only human being in his existence whom he had not wronged, or betrayed, or disappointed, or failed.

Wearily Edward turned from the confusion in his mind, his eyes closed, as though within the instant he'd dropped off to sleep. He was aware of her looking down on him, was aware a moment later of her footsteps moving across the floor. The door opened, then closed, then silence.

Then, action. He sat up, pleased to see that his body at least in part was capable of obeying the dictates of his mind. In the past, he'd always had the feeling that everything could be put to rights again. Not now. And it was this sense of urgency that accounted, in part, for his ability to stand, to make his way falteringly to the wardrobe, where he withdrew clothes, stopping now and then in his labor for balance, for breath, still hearing Daniel's words: *dead and buried, three days ago.*

The boots proved troublesome. After almost half an hour of effort, he accomplished the simple task of dressing and sat up, listening. He knew the routine of the house, the children at their books, all the volunteers, including Daniel, busily engaged. His absence would go unnoticed for a while.

Quickly he stood. The room reeled momentarily, then grew steady. Carefully he reached into his bureau for the fifteen hundred pounds. He tucked the packet of money inside his coat, then he went out the door. He would not bother with the carriage. He would walk a distance down Oxford Street and get a cab.

He took the stairs, the entrance hall, and at last was out

on the street darting between carriages, taking refuge on the opposite side and blending quickly with the foot traffic. At the end of Oxford Street he hailed a passing cab.

"Newgate," Edward called as he crawled into the narrow seat.

The driver seemed to hesitate. "Don't likes to work that end, sir," he protested. "An honest man can never tell when he'll be jumped—"

Edward shouted back, "You won't be jumped, sir, and I'll make it worth your while."

Reluctantly the cab started forward. A thousand problems presented themselves ceaselessly to Edward. Would old Jawster Gray be there? When did his watch commence? Should the escape be attempted now, in broad daylight, or under cover of darkness? And for the first time, this all-important question, where would he take her? Unless Charlotte expressed a desire to organize her own future, he would take her this very night to North Devon, to the isolation of Eden Castle. From that point on, his mother would help. Perhaps one of the larger fishing packets could spirit her across the Bristol Channel to Wales. There she would be safe.

Such a plan could not go awry. Thus relieved, he settled back into the cab, allowing his eyes to wander over the traffic outside his window.

Ahead, as they were approaching Piccadilly, he spied the Gloucester Coffee House. It was a busy establishment, all the western mails stopping there before leaving London. Having decided at that moment that it might be best to wait for night, he called out to the driver, "Stop here."

"Ain't Newgate, sir," the man shouted back.

"I'll proceed alone," Edward replied.

The area around the coffee house was so clogged with carriages that the driver had to stop a distance from the pavement. Edward paid him, then hurried into the coffee house. He spied an empty table near the window, was tempted to order negus, but changed his mind. He needed his wits about him. So he settled for coffee, hot and strong.

The harsh rays of late afternoon sun struck him in the face. Momentarily blinded, he closed his eyes and recalled the lovely, sinking feeling, the sensation of floating, the glorious dreams provided by his first indulgence in opium. Daniel had extracted the promise from him that he would not indulge again. And he wouldn't. Still, it had been most agreeable, the first time in his life that he'd felt total relief, all burdens lifted, Paradise in a single blood-red drop.

He felt his head drooping forward. He was tired, so tired. But he jerked himself upward. No sleep. Not yet. And just in time the serving girl returned with a steaming mug and he drank it eagerly, in his haste burning his tongue.

He sipped at the coffee and thought ahead to Charlotte's escape. It was only a matter of time.

The buildings of Newgate Prison formed a square, of which the four sides abutted respectively on the Old Bailey, the College of Physicians, the Sessions House, and Newgate Street. The intermediate space was divided into several paved yards, in which the prisoners took such air and exercise as could be had in such a place. These yards, with the exception of that in which prisoners under sentence of death were confined, ran parallel to Newgate Street. On the Newgate side was the main gate and office, through which prisoners entered and departed.

It was toward this gate that Edward now hurried. The hour was half past ten though there still were streaks of light in the sky. He'd walked the entire distance from the Gloucester, and in spite of having to stop several times, he felt good, his head clear.

Across the way from the main gate and the prison office, he stopped to assess the enormous structure behind whose walls human suffering knew no limitations. Edward knew it intimately enough, both as prisoner and visitor. Here was the panacea for all human woes, the red brick abyss into which men and women and children fell and from which, on occasion, they never emerged. He'd seen all aspects of it, the flogging frames, the treadmills, even the execution chamber. There had been talk of reform, much of it led by Mr. Dickens, but thus far nothing had been done.

There were two Peelers standing on either side of the office door, starched in their black uniforms with brass buttons and chimney-pot hats. Edward assumed an air of authority and walked directly past them only to be stopped by one. "You, there! Wait up."

Obediently he turned. The light was dim on the stoop.

He waited patiently as the Peeler drew near in examination. Finally a broad toothless grin broke on the sober face. "Oh, it's you, sir," the man exclaimed. "The Prince of Eden. Back for more?"

His companion drew near, apparently interested. "The gentleman, is it?" he asked. "Ain't seen you about for a few days."

Edward endured their inspection and cast a hasty glimpse through the smudged window into the office itself, where behind a broad desk he saw the night warden. He had hoped to catch a glimpse of Jawster Gray.

The first Peeler, still curious, leaned closer. "In what capacity are you here tonight, sir? Visitor or inmate?"

"Visitor," Edward replied, trying to move closer to the door.

But the second Peeler merely followed after him. "Ain't visitin' hours, your Highness," he said.

Slowly Edward reached into his pocket and withdrew two one-pound notes. Both Peelers looked shrewdly at the money in his hands.

The first one reached out and pocketed his eagerly. "I guess it won't hurt none to extend visitin' hours," he grinned.

As Edward entered the office, he heard the door close behind him. Before him, slumped behind his desk in a position of sleep, he saw the old night warden. They were alone in the barren, smelly office. A lamp burned to one side of the desk, casting a flickering shadow over the red-black brick interior.

"I beg your pardon, sir," Edward began, trying to rouse the old man. When that failed, he leaned across the desk and gave the man a solid nudge.

A moment later, sputtering, the old man lifted his head. At first he appeared indifferent to Edward's presence. Then he stiffened, his observation no longer casual. To one side of the desk Edward observed a half-empty flagon of wine. The old man continued to stare sharply up. "What is it you'll be wanting?" he demanded. "I warned that clerk the next time you should turn up it would be twice the bond."

Quickly Edward reassured him. "I've done nothing wrong, sir. I came by myself, as a visitor—"

"This ain't visitin' hours," the old man snapped. "The prisoners is all asleep."

"I'm not here to see the prisoners," Edward replied. "With your permission, I'd like to speak in private with Jawster Gray."

The name seemed to have a peculiar effect on the old man. He sank heavily back into his chair. He made a strange gesture, wiping his hands across his lips, as though there was a disagreeable taste in his mouth. Finally he muttered, "You'll not be finding him here, sir. Now, be off with you."

Puzzled, Edward stepped closer. "Could you tell me the hour of his watch, please. I'll wait if necessary."

"A long wait it will be," he muttered.

Still bewildered, Edward inquired, "He's not due tonight?"

"Oh, he's due all right, but he won't come."

"I don't understand."

The man looked sharply up. "He's passed, sir. Dead."

Edward stared down into the old face. "Dead?" he repeated.

"Fine times we're living in when a decent man takes his life into his hands just crossing the street—" Here his manner softened. He poured a glass of wine from the bottle, tipped it, and drained it in a swallow. Apparently only now did he notice the shocked look on Edward's face. "I didn't know he was a friend of yours, sir. I'm sorry to have broken the news so blunt-like—" He filled the glass again and pushed it across the desk.

Edward shook his head and stepped back, his mind momentarily motionless, all avenues closed. The old man went on talking. "Four days ago it was, sir. If I rightly remember it was the last time you was here." A Eureka smile lit his face. Soundly he slapped the side of his head. "Of course you knew him. He was on the watch that very night, wasn't he, sir?" Regretfully he shook his head. "As far as I heard, he was just leaving the White Bear on Oxford Street when one of them horse-drawn omnibuses run him to ground. We all passed the cup and gave him a decent burial. Yesterday it was. Had I known your interest in old Jawster, you'd been most welcome—"

Edward walked to one of the small windows and looked out. The two Peelers were still in place. What now? As confusion rose within him, he turned back to the night warden. "Then I must ask a favor of you," he began, returning to the desk.

Speaking of death seemed to have softened the old man. "If I can oblige, I'd be happy to, sir."

Edward looked closely down into his face. "I request the right to see Mrs. Charlotte Longford."

The name had no sooner left his lips than the old man was shaking his head again. "Quite impossible, sir."

"Why?"

"It ain't visitin' hours."

Angrily Edward leaned across the desk. "I know that," he said.

"No need to lose your temper, sir. Rules is rules."

"And I'm asking you to bend them," Edward went on.

"And blot me record? Not on your life, sir. I've put in honorable time here and I'm not going to—"

Slowly Edward reached for the packet of money in his pocket.

The night warden pushed back in his chair as though offended by the sight. "Don't try them bribes on me, sir," he warned. "I'll lock you up this very night, I will—"

Without speaking, yet holding the man fast with his eyes, Edward placed a ten-pound note on the desk near the ignored glass of wine.

"No sir," the man said sternly. "I won't be tempted, and I don't intend to sit here and—"

Twenty pounds.

"What you're doing is a crime itself, sir. I hope you realize that. All I got to do is signal them Peelers out there and—"

Thirty pounds.

"The lady won't suit you now, sir. She's quite—"

Forty pounds.

A look akin to pain crossed the old face. He pushed further back in his chair. "Leave me be, sir, and leave her be as well—"

Fifty pounds. Methodically Edward pulled the notes off until they formed an unruly heap in the center of the desk.

"What's she to you?" the old man demanded. "She's an adultress, gettin' her just deserts. A gentleman like you—"

Sixty pounds.

"Oh Gawd, sir, have a heart. Spare yourself a double shock and leave my conscience be—"

Edward's hands froze over the packet of money. A double shock? "What do you mean?" he demanded.

The man left his chair as though grateful for the opportunity to move away from temptation. "I just mean she's —done in, sir—"

"How so?"

As the pudgy little hands played with the tight collar of his jacket, a flush spread across his face. "Sometime this morning, it was," the warden said, speaking rapidly now. "My turnkeys swears they saw nothing—"

Seventy pounds.

The man groaned audibly. On diminished breath he went on. "A bunch of drunken dockmen it was who done it to her—"

Eighty pounds. Edward's hands were trembling. "Take me to her," he whispered fiercely, his eyes never leaving the man's face.

"For what purpose?" the warden shouted, perspiration covering his face, his eyes moving constantly over the pile of money on the table.

Ninety pounds.

"Sir, I beg you—"

One hundred pounds.

For a moment the tableau held, Edward still standing over the pile of notes, the warden looking down on them as though they were a cause of solemn worship. Finally he returned to the desk and commenced restacking the notes carefully, one on top of the other, his eyes never meeting Edward's face. When the notes had been reassembled, he stuffed them carefully into the pocket of his jacket. "A humanitarian gesture," he grinned, "that's what we'll call it. The lady could do with a bit of comforting."

As he reached beneath the desk and withdrew an enormous ring of keys, Edward closed his eyes in silent thanks. He had no plans now beyond seeing Charlotte. But something would happen. The money intended for Jawster had scarcely been touched. Enough remained for him to buy every turnkey and warden in Newgate if necessary.

Then the old warden was signaling to him. "Come quickly," he urged. "I can't leave the office unattended for long. Hurry!"

They left the office by the small door at the right and turned right again into a darkened passageway. About twenty yards down the corridor they came to a door composed of thick bars, through which Edward could discern a number of prisoners, all asleep on straw pallets. Beyond the door they encountered another corridor, railed off at considerable distance and formed into a kind of iron cage about five feet in height, roofed at the top. Edward had to stoop for easy passage. He looked about at the unfamiliar surroundings. He'd never been in this part of the prison before, had no idea that it even existed. Still ahead of him was the warden, the passageway leading down into a dank cellar, the stench overpowering as apparently they drew nearer to the cesspool beneath the prison.

Frantically Edward tried to remember every turn, the labyrinth growing ever more complex. At one point he called out, his voice echoing strangely in the underground caverns, "I thought she'd been assigned to the Common Cell?"

Without altering his pace, the warden replied, "Until this morning she was—"

"Why the change?"

But either the man didn't hear or refused to answer.

Then at last up ahead Edward noticed guards, the first they'd encountered since leaving the main corridor. Four of them, there were, with face masks drawn tightly over their noses, in obvious protection against the noxious fumes.

As he hurried after the warden, his agitation increased. What was she doing here? Why had she been transferred from the Common Cell, which seemed like paradise compared to these dark damp earth walls? On either side now he noticed dark, low wooden doors, windowless.

Finally he stopped. Edward saw him hold the torch close to a door as though confirming a number. For the first time, he glanced back at Edward. "It was your idea, Mr. Eden. Remember that," he said, almost apologetically.

"Why was she moved?" Edward demanded again, as the man was fumbling with the final key. "This was not part of the sentence. The Magistrate stated clearly that—"

The low door swung open.

Still maintaining a curious silence, the warden lowered his head and stepped through the door, taking the torch with him. "We have to keep them segregated, the mad ones, you know," he said, lifting the illumination higher. He turned back with a note of comfort in his voice. "If you want my opinion, she'll come out of it right enough. That hot poker tomorrow morning will bring her to her senses and she'll be right as—"

All the while the man was talking, Edward searched the small cell. Then as the warden stepped toward the center of the cell, he saw something on the far wall, a heaped something, inert, yet strangely pinned. His breath caught. Frantically he reached for the torch, ready to wrest it from the man's hand if necessary.

She was seated on the mud floor, her head erect, yet hanging at a rigid awkward angle. He thrust the torch closer, then wished profoundly that he hadn't. Around her neck was a chain tightly drawn, the ends attached to an iron ring embedded in the wall. Her arms were outstretched and pinned in similar fashion, heavy circles of iron holding each wrist rigidly to the wall. Her legs were spread in a peculiar relaxed state, the black prison dress torn completely from her shoulders, revealing bare breasts, her body falling forward, yet held upright against its own weight.

Still the light revealed more, her eyes profoundly open, but unseeing. From the right temple, there was a streak of dried blood which, passing over the cheek, lost itself under her blood-matted hair.

Slowly Edward knelt, his senses recording everything. Beneath his knee he felt the soft earth give. As his eyes became accustomed to the darkness, he saw something scurrying across her lap; looking quickly down he saw a rat scale her torn dress and disappear behind her. In a reflexive movement, he jerked her body forward, forgetting for the moment the iron rings about her neck and wrists.

"Charlotte, look at me," he pleaded. Suddenly he was aware of something else. She was cold. He leaned close to her mouth. No breath. She was dead.

Behind him he heard the warden speaking. "Most regrettable it is, sir, but I *did* warn you. In my opinion, we should do away with the Common Cell. As you well know, sir, at times we get so many crowded together, a hundred turnkeys can't keep guard. The dockmen ganged up on her, they did. Went over her good."

Without warning, caught between the talking man behind him and the dead face before him, Edward's outrage vaulted. With the speed of a madman he was on his feet with only one intent, to silence the talking mouth that was filling the already obscene air with greater obscenity.

As he whirled up and around, he hurled the torch into the far corner and reached eagerly for the man's throat. The way to stop the mouth was to crush the throat that was drawing breath.

The warden had time only to utter a single cry, then Edward was upon him, feeling the soft flabby flesh of his neck give beneath his grip. Effortlessly he wrestled the man to ground, his hands pressing, the only possible release from the horror pinned to the wall, enjoying the feel of the man's body arching beneath him. His thumbs found the Adam's apple. As he channeled the strength from his shoulders down into his thumbs, a curious hissing sound escaped through the purplish lips. The man's eyes were growing protuberant and glassy, the mouth no longer talking.

So engrossed was Edward that he failed to hear the rush of footsteps outside in the dim corridor. He was only vaguely aware of movement behind him at the door. As he turned to see who it was who had come to witness his justice, he caught only a momentary glimpse of the four masked guards.

Then without warning, something of indeterminate weight and substance was brought down across the back of his head. As his face was half raised, the side of his head took the brunt of the assault, a resounding blow which seemed mysteriously to lift him for a moment before dropping him, senseless, back to the mud floor.

Beyond the blow, he heard and felt nothing except the shrill ringing inside his head, a trickle of something wet across and down his forehead. He tried once to turn his head, but couldn't.

The mud felt cool against his cheek. Through his blurred eyes, he saw nothing. Everything turned to liquid and blended. Blessedly, nothing mattered.

At a quarter past eight, after a hectic late afternoon, Daniel sat at the end of one of the long tables in the student dining room, facing his guests, wondering what excuse he would give if Edward's absence was mentioned, as it was sure to be.

His disappearance had been reported to Daniel by Elizabeth shortly after five. Apparently she'd gone to his room to tell him something about Mr. Wordsworth. Daniel had never understood precisely what she was talking about. As the children were just coming in for the evening meal and his guests were due momentarily, he had tried to calm her as best he could with reassurances that, this time, he knew precisely where Edward was. And he did, or at least he felt certain that he did.

Now he looked up at the three gentlemen seated around the table. In honor of the occasion, the volunteers had covered one end of the student table with a small white cloth, and Matilda had placed a simple arrangement of daisies at the center. These touches had been the only concessions to the importance of the guests. His guests had eaten the same mutton and boiled potatoes that the children had eaten, and they were serving themselves from the plain crockery which was in daily use in the dining room.

Looking around, in the silence of men eating, Daniel felt that perhaps he should have gone to greater pains with the food. But then he changed his mind. This was the way he lived. And in truth his guests seemed to have no objections. That grand old reformer, Robert Owen, was eating heartily enough. Daniel smiled as he saw him sop his plate with a biscuit. It was pleasant to see such plain country manners on so great a reformer.

Accompanying him tonight was a young man from Birmingham named George Jacob Holyoake, a disciple of Owen who was undergoing some sort of training in London in order to carry the great work forward. And there was another gentleman, John Bright, about twenty-five, from Rochdale, another reformer who possessed one of the most articulate voices in speaking out against the Corn Law.

The precise purpose of these distinguished visitors in Daniel's Ragged School was still a mystery. Shortly after they had arrived about five-thirty, he had taken them on a complete inspection of the school. But still Daniel was at a loss to explain their presence.

Now, "Coffee, Mr. Owen?" he asked, seeing the portly man push back from the table and a plate so cleaned it could have gone directly to the cupboard.

The man smiled. "Yes, thank you," he said.

Across the table, John Bright was now saying something. "How long have you had occupancy here, Mr. Spade?"

"For—several years, Mr. Bright. About ten, maybe slightly more."

"It's ideal," Bright said, looking about. "The Elizabethans were certainly aware of the need for scope in a room," he added, his eye climbing up the walls to the high saddle-topped ceiling.

Robert Owen joined the conversation. "Clearly this was a private home at one time, Mr. Spade," he announced.

"Yes," Daniel concurred, "in use by the family as recently as fifteen years ago."

Robert Owen leaned forward and helped himself to more coffee. "And that family would be—"

"The Edens," Daniel said.

"Ah, yes," Owen smiled, taking the filled cup with him as he leaned back in the chair. He hesitated a moment as though carefully sorting through his thoughts. "Would it be too forward of me, Mr. Spade," he began, "to ask how it came into your possession? Please don't answer if you feel I'm—"

But Daniel laughed. "I'm not in possession of the house, Mr. Owen."

Both Bright and Owen looked pointedly at him. "I'm afraid I don't understand," Owen began. "I do see a school here, a very successful one, perhaps one of the most effective it's ever been my pleasure to visit."

As Daniel started to answer, he saw young George at the end of the table turn as though he too were interested in the reply. With the attention of all three men upon him, Daniel felt a wave of self-consciousness. "I'm here," he began, "at the generosity of Mr. Edward Eden."

It seemed a sufficient explanation, but from the manner in which they all were gazing at him, Daniel added further, "The elder son of Lord Thomas Eden."

Robert Owen nodded slowly. "I've heard of him."

It was a simple statement, but somehow Daniel had the feeling that the man had intimated more. "Does—Mr. Eden share your—enthusiasm for your work?" he asked, not looking at Daniel.

"He does," Daniel replied without hesitation. "Without him, I'm afraid, there would be no school."

Now Owen looked directly at him. "Without him, Mr. Spade," he asked pointedly, "or without his—support?"

A curious line of question, Daniel thought. "Both, Mr. Owen," he replied, for some reason feeling a little peeved.

The man nodded, apparently satisfied with Daniel's answer. From upstairs he heard the volunteers putting the children to bed. Nine o'clock. It was late. Surely the men would leave soon.

Daniel pushed his chair back from the table, trying to be a cordial host, in spite of his splintered feelings. "Is there anything else, Mr. Owen, that you care to see? The rooms below, the arrangements for—"

But the man merely shook his head. "No, Mr. Spade," he smiled. "You've been most kind to receive us. I only wish that we might have had the honor of meeting your benefactor, Mr. Eden."

"I apologize for his absence, Mr. Owen," he said. "He had planned to be here, but at the last minute he was otherwise engaged."

"I'm sorry to hear it," Owen replied. "In our movement, we have great need for men with full hearts *and* full purses."

Across the table John Bright was working diligently over his pipe. Without looking up, he asked, "Mr. Spade, what are your sources of income for the school?"

Daniel disliked this turn in the conversation. Still, he answered, "Contributions, Mr. Bright. What else?"

"From what sources?" the man persisted.

"From all sources," Daniel replied, a slight edge to his voice.

Robert Owen leaned close as though he had detected the edge and was now trying to assuage it. "These are blunt questions, Mr. Spade, admittedly, and I apologize for them. But every one of us here has the same goal in mind, the alleviation of as much human suffering as is possible within the short span granted to us by God." He stood then and began to pace behind Daniel's chair. "What we have seen here tonight does not in any way resemble the other Ragged Schools in London. This one is the ideal. The others are still struggling." He came around from behind Daniel's chair. "What we want to know, Mr. Spade, is what, in addition to your own obvious dedication, makes this school work."

So! This was the point of the meeting, a determination to establish the fountain of his blessings and perhaps to see if some of the golden water of that font couldn't be channeled in their direction.

Then it was Daniel's turn to stand. He walked a distance away from the table. He knew the need for choosing his words carefully. "Mr. Eden is very generous," he began, looking back.

"Obviously," Owen smiled.

"But," interrupted Daniel strongly, "and you may find this difficult to believe, I have never asked him for anything."

John Bright leaned forward. "Then he must be a very perceptive man to see so clearly your needs."

"He is."

Owen asked, "Is yours a friendship of long standing?"

Daniel nodded. "We grew up together on Eden Point."

"Like brothers?" Bright inquired.

Daniel hesitated, trying to catalogue in his mind the precise depth of feeling he shared with Edward Eden. "More than brothers," he replied softly, thinking of Edward's shattered relationship with his true brother.

Apparently the expression of affection had an effect on his audience of three. After a moment, Owen apologized again. "These are very personal questions, Mr. Spade. A less understanding man than yourself might consider them an affront. You have every reasonable right to toss us out, if you wish—"

Daniel smiled, his annoyance receding. "I don't wish, Mr. Owen."

"Then hear me out," the man now begged, again leaving his chair and walking steadily toward Daniel. "I have a plan," he began, "to open another Ragged School in the heart of Lambeth."

"An admirable idea," Daniel agreed. "The thought had occurred to me—"

"Then help us, Mr. Spade."

Without hesitation, Daniel agreed. "I'd be happy to," he said, "in any way."

Robert Owen stepped to one side. "I have two soldiers ready to do the work," he announced softly, and he gestured back toward the table where Bright and Holyoake were waiting.

"Then I don't understand," Daniel began. "How do you
need me?"

Again, Robert Owen seemed almost overcome with consternation. "We need you," he faltered, "as an avenue
which—might lead us to the—Eden purse."

For a moment, Daniel could only stare at the men. *As an
avenue which might lead us to the Eden purse.* He stammered, then laughed. "I'm afraid I've misrepresented myself to you, gentlemen. I am Edward Eden's friend, not—"

"And as such," Owen countered, "the beneficiary of his
generosity."

"I ask for nothing," Daniel retorted. "I thought I made
that clear."

"You did," John Bright said. "But how would it hurt to
ask? He has the means by which we can implement—"

"No, gentlemen!" Daniel pronounced, walking the length
of the table, trying to rid himself of the offensive suggestion. As he drew near to where George Holyoake sat, he
saw the young man watching him.

"Mr. Spade," the man began. "This afternoon I saw
horrors I've never seen before. As we walked along the
reeking banks of the sewer, the sun shone upon a narrow
slip of water. In the bright light it appeared the color of
strong green tea and looked as solid as black marble in
the shadows. Indeed it was more like watery mud and yet
we were assured this was the only water the wretched inhabitants had to drink."

Daniel listened closely. He knew the truth of his words.
What caught and held his attention was the eagerness in the
boy's face. For Daniel, it was like shedding seventeen years
and looking into a glass.

The boy went on, rising from his chair and coming
around the table to where Daniel stood. "As we gazed at
the pool, we saw drains and sewers emptying their filthy
contents in it, we saw a whole tier of doorless privies in the
open road, common to men and women—" He drew still
nearer to Daniel. "We heard bucket after bucket of filth
splash into it, and the limbs of the children bathing in it
seemed, by contrast white as snow. And yet as we stood
gazing at the sewer, we saw a child from one of the
galleries opposite lower a tin can with a rope and fill a
large bucket that stood beside her."

He fell silent. Daniel felt clearly the boy's anguish. "With help, Mr. Spade," the young man went on, "I could take that child and the ones bathing in the sewage and transport them to a place a short distance away and give them hope for the future. And if someone doesn't do it soon, there will be no need to do it at all."

Daniel listened, his hands shoved into his pockets. He did not deny anything that had been said. But he denied with all his heart and soul the act which had been requested of him, an act which could easily corrupt the most important relationship in his existence and make a mockery of the trust they had worked so hard and long to establish between them.

Apparently Owen saw the distress on his face. "Again, we apologize, Mr. Spade. And we'll take our leave now." Quickly he withdrew a small card from his inner pocket and handed it to Daniel. "If, after a few days, you have—anything to report, you may send the message to this number."

Daniel took the card. He felt peculiarly defeated. It had not been his work which had attracted these men to him this evening. No, the great Robert Owen and his two dedicated disciples had not been interested in that at all. Rather, Edward's purse had been the object of the evening.

The accumulated thoughts took a heavy toll. "I can't promise," he began.

"Then don't," Owen said kindly. With warm familiarity he patted Daniel's arm. "This afternoon, we happened to see in front of a lean-to, a small garden. That table linen would have covered it," he said, pointing toward the small white cloth. "Still, one dahlia raised its round red head there. Never was color so grateful to the eye."

He stepped back. "We now pin our hopes on you, Mr. Spade, as those wretched inhabitants must look to that single blossom." His voice fell. "Again we must apologize for the moral dilemma in which we have placed you. But as you well know, in the face of certain human miseries, moral dilemmas seem almost a luxury."

Again he stepped back. "Don't bother to see us out, Mr. Spade. And again, many thanks for receiving us."

At the last minute Daniel looked up. Beyond the dining room door, he saw Matilda. Apparently she'd just come down from seeing the children to bed and was now graciously showing the gentlemen to the front door.

Daniel sank heavily into a near chair. In his hand he still held the small white card. In neat and simple printing, it read, *Mr. Robert Owen—Association of All Classes of All Nations*. Then it listed a number and a street.

All Classes of All Nations. A noble thought. He closed his eyes and rested his head heavily in his hands. In his self-imposed blindness, he saw two small boys running across the headlands of Eden Point, reveling in each other's company, trusting, asking nothing of one another but companionship and mutual love.

He groaned softly and drove his fingers through his hair. What he had told the gentlemen was true. Never in his entire life-long association with Edward Eden had he ever asked for anything.

Still, the cause was just. And Robert Owen was right. The Eden fortune was vast. If only, somehow, he could bring Edward to see the need.

Attempted murder!

Sir Claudius Potter still couldn't believe it, although in spite of the rocking motion of his carriage, he held the paper in his hand and again read the words carefully: "Mr. Edward Eden has been charged with attempted murder of the night warden of Newgate and is at present being held in the—"

Sir Claudius looked out the rain-streaked window at the gray morning. The lovely green parks for which London was famed had a way of disappearing the closer a man got to Newgate and Old Bailey and the inexorable hand of Justice.

Frankly he loathed the neighborhood, loathed being summoned down here as though he were little more than a common clerk. Apparently the charge had been of such a serious nature that the magistrate had refused to do business with his clerk and had demanded the personal appearance of Sir Claudius himself.

Attempted murder!

Merely thinking on it caused Sir Claudius distress and he suffered a spasm of indigestion. He swallowed hard and made a face at the rancid taste in his mouth. Carefully he smoothed his hand over the sable-colored satin waistcoat, his fingers lingering on the white silk neck scarf. He'd dressed with care this morning. When dealing with the primitives of Newgate, a man was always slightly ahead of the game if his dress was superior. Not that he was genuinely worried about the outcome. He'd just left the old magistrate's private chambers in the Temple, and the stern old man had agreed to ignore the charges on two conditions: that Sir Claudius split his fee with him, not an uncomfortable agreement since Sir Claudius had planned to triple his fee for this service anyway; and two, that as soon as possible Edward Eden leave London for a period of at least three months.

Without hesitation, Sir Claudius had agreed to the conditions. Now all that remained was to inform the "prisoner" himself, and try to pacify the man named Daniel Spade, who apparently had discovered his friend behind bars the night before and had dragged Sir Claudius's clerk out of bed at some indecent hour. And ultimately the entire silly chain of events had led Sir Claudius to this moment and this chill and disagreeable early morning ride through the rain.

Now, weary and still suffering from indigestion, he leaned back against the velvet cushions. What sacrifices he made for the Eden family!

As Daniel pushed open the office door, he saw a small group of Peelers standing to one side. He paused on the threshold, taking the weight of their eyes.

Behind the desk, he noticed an older man, his jacket undone, his throat swathed in white bandages. It was this man who spoke in a peculiarly gruff whisper. "What is it you're wantin'?" he demanded, as though out of temper with Daniel, with his injured throat, the rain, everything.

Daniel closed the door behind him, realizing that without Sir Claudius he had no power at all. "I'm—to meet someone here," he said.

"This ain't no coffee house in Piccadilly," the old man grumbled, one hand continuously stroking his bandaged throat. "Go meet your mates elsewhere."

But Daniel held his ground. "I'm waiting for Sir Claudius Potter, Edward Eden's solicitor."

The name seemed to make an incredible impression on the old man. He gaped upward toward Daniel, an expression of angry belligerence on his old face. "Then you'll be waitin' a long time," he snapped.

Two advancing Peelers retreated. Daniel noticed sly smiles on their faces. As the tight little group enclosed upon themselves, he considered the wisdom of further talk, then decided against it. He would wait for Sir Claudius. Now carefully he moved back toward the bench beneath the smudged window and sat. Still he was conscious of all eyes upon him, the most piercing of all belonging to the old warden, who now seemed offended by the sight of Daniel seated.

"I told you," he shouted with as much force as he could muster, "it'll do no good to wait. Now, go along with—"

Suddenly the old man bent over in a seizure of coughing, both hands gripping his throat. The brief spasm left him winded and red-faced, with moisture streaming from his eyes. "Mr. Edward Eden," he pronounced in spite of his obvious distress, "ain't goin' to be leaving here for some time, I can promise you." Slowly he straightened up, making a clear effort to keep his voice down. "Tried to kill me, he did," the man muttered, "and after me being so nice to him." He shook his head. "The Prince of Eden," he pronounced sarcastically, "can stay where he is till he rots as far as I'm concerned."

Daniel listened carefully and again considered the wisdom of speaking. But at that moment through the rain-streaked window he caught sight of Sir Claudius Potter, hurrying through the rain.

Apparently one of the Peelers saw him as well. As he leaned close over the old warden, he whispered, "Here comes trouble, sir."

The warden craned his injured neck upward, the better to see. "He don't bother me none. I know the law and know the punishment for attempted murder."

At that moment the office door was pushed open and Sir Claudius appeared, drenched from the rain, his complexion, Daniel noticed, bearing a marked resemblance to the gray day. He posed on the threshold for an instant, taking a quick inventory of the plain faces which were gaping back at him. Then leaving the door wide open as though unaccustomed to attending to such trivial details himself, he strode forward, still shaking rain off his cloak and hat. He gazed imperiously down on the old warden, who, as far as Daniel could see, returned the gaze.

"I am Sir Claudius Potter," he entoned, "solicitor to Mr.

Edward Eden. I have come to effect the release of Mr. Eden."

The warden continued to look up at him with a set face.

When Sir Claudius's words failed to illicit any response, he leaned angrily forward. "I would prefer not to linger any longer than is necessary," he snapped.

"And I'm not asking you to linger at all, sir," the warden said, in his whispery voice. "Mr. Edward Eden ain't goin' anyplace, not for a good long while."

Again Daniel noticed the Peelers grinning at one another. Sir Claudius started to say something else, but then the talk within him stopped. He stepped regally back from the desk and slowly reached inside his cloak.

The old warden grinned up. "If it's money you're going after, there ain't enough in the whole world to—"

But still the hand was moving and at last it produced a single piece of parchment, neatly folded, the red seal attached and visible even from Daniel's point of view. Then it was Sir Claudius's turn to smile. As he placed the document on the desk before the warden, he said, "There might have been money, my good man. I was prepared to open my purse for you, or rather the Eden purse, in an attempt to compensate you for your—trials." The smile broadened. "But now? Nothing. Just read and follow orders. That's all that's expected of you."

A faint flush crept up the warden's face as tentatively he lifted the document and broke the seal. Apparently the order was not at all to the man's liking. "But he tried to kill me," he protested.

"And regrettably he failed." Sir Claudius smiled.

The old man stood up with such force that his chair threatened to tilt backward. "He ain't got no right," he whispered hoarsely.

Sir Claudius was now involved in inspecting a seam on one of his gloves. Without looking up, he asked quietly, "Are you questioning the authority of the magistrate?"

Daniel saw clearly the rising fury on the warden's face. He heard the Peelers whispering together. Outside he noticed that a wagon with black covering had drawn up beside the closed gates. A few spectators were now inspecting the wagon. The two drivers sitting bareheaded on the high seat waved them away with the tips of their whips.

The scene was ugly, as ugly as the scene which threatened to explode inside the office.

The warden was shouting now, apparently impervious to his injured throat. "Ah, yes," he cried, "you swells stick close together, don't you, winking at your little transgressions whilst the rest of us pass plenty of time in the yard. Attempted murder!" he shouted, jabbing his finger toward the crowd outside by the gate. "Any one of them common blokes out there would be on the gallows. But not Mr. Edward Eden, not his Prince-ship." His voice was heavy with sarcasm, his outrage taking a tremendous toll. "No," he gasped, making a mock bow from the waist, "oh no, the Prince 'a Eden gits a personally writ, specially stamped note of release from the magistrate hisself—"

"That's enough," cautioned Sir Claudius.

"Oh no, sir," the warden went on. "It ain't enough at all." Then to the waiting Peelers, he shouted, "Go fetch the royal bastard. Tell him due to some mit-i-gating circumstances having come to light, that we poor dumb ones here at Newgate has made us a dreadful error. Tell him we wronged him terrible by locking him up and tell him there ain't a mark on me throat, that the muscles is all in good order, and I'm just imagining the pain and swelling. You tell him that!" He continued to shout long after the men had disappeared through the door down the corridor.

Sir Claudius seemed to be viewing the outburst with toleration. There was an undeniable expression of smugness on his face as, reaching forward, he gingerly lifted the order, carefully refolded it, and returned it to the pocket beneath his cloak.

The gesture seemed to stir the warden to even greater fury. "That's right, Sir Claudius Potter," he sneered. "You put your little instrument away, all snug with His Majesty's seal. And when you get back to your fancy digs, you'd better lock it up in a safe place, because one day us common folk is going to come after it, and you and your kind as well, and when that day comes you can get out your fancy piece of paper and use it to wipe your ass 'cause it won't be good for nothin' else."

Before the vulgarity, Sir Claudius retreated. He drew his cloak about him, glanced in Daniel's direction, then apparently chose the opposite side of the room.

The warden, clearly suffering pain as a result of his outburst, sank heavily into his chair, both hands clasping his throat.

Opposite him, Sir Claudius maintained a silent and aloof vigil. The warden had laid his head to rest upon his desk, apparently spent. The rain tapped out a mournful rhythm against the windows. Daniel sat erect and tried to draw deep breath. He heard the footsteps while they were still a distance away, the muffled sound of boots on stone.

Only Daniel started forward and thus he was the first to greet the mournful little procession as the door was flung open and the four Peelers appeared, one in front, two behind supporting Edward between them, and one bringing up the rear, curious smiles on their faces in marked contrast to the man who slumped between his two supports, his legs dragging uselessly after him, his head limp, breathing heavily as though trying to recover from recent blows.

Inside the office, the Peelers dropped him bodily in the center of the floor. Daniel saw him sink to his knees. A wound across his head was bleeding. He knelt there before all the gaping eyes, with his hands limp at his sides, his eyes opening to Daniel with an unspoken plea for help.

Within the instant, Daniel was at his side, lifting him, leading him toward the bench by the window. Edward sat heavily and seemed at first incapable of balancing himself.

From the desk, the warden had watched it all, a look of pleasure on his face at seeing the man so undone. Now he muttered, "Get the filth out of here."

"Not so fast," Sir Claudius interrupted. "We need a signed release." He stepped back to the desk, smiling. "It wouldn't be very polite of you to set Mr. Eden free, then one hour from now arrest him again as a fugitive." As the old warden glared up at him, Sir Claudius merely smiled agreeably, one hand extended. "The release, if you please."

Daniel still hovered close to Edward. "Try to draw deep breath," he whispered. "We'll be out of here soon."

There was no response. Moreover his breathing grew so torturous that it was audible in the room. Sir Claudius looked in their direction. For a moment, Daniel thought he saw an expression of pity on the arrogant old face. Now turning to the warden, who was angrily filling out the release form, he asked, "Are all your prisoners released in such—excellent condition?"

Without looking up, the old man replied, "He's lucky to have his head still sittin' on his shoulders."

Then Sir Claudius was calling to Daniel. Apparently his signature was required as he was the party to whom the prisoner was being released. Daniel left the bench, eager to do anything that would speed their departure from this place. After affixing his signature in the appointed place, he looked back toward the bench. In his brief absence, the crowds outside the window had attracted Edward's attention. He'd half turned in an awkward position upon the bench and now appeared to be focusing on the rainy scene beyond the window.

As Daniel drew near to him, he followed the direction of his gaze. There, not fifty feet away, he saw the prison gates open, saw the crowds forced back by a sizable contingent of Peelers, two lines forming a cleared path which stretched between the gates and the back of the black wagon which had waited patiently for some time.

He saw Edward stand with effort, his eyes still fixed on the opened gates.

"Come, Edward," Daniel whispered, fearing what would shortly pass through those gates. "Come, let's—"

But Edward drew away from his touch, his hands now pressing against the windowpanes.

Daniel looked back out of the window in time to see four guards emerge through the center gate, bearing a litter between them. On the litter lay a slight figure, a gray blanket covering her face, the hem of black prison garb visible beneath the coverlet. Hurriedly the guards carried her to the back of the wagon where she was received by the two bare-headed drivers, the litter slipped beneath the black canvas.

The crowds seemed to surge forward as though insatiable, wanting a last look. Only just in time did the drivers scramble back onto their high seats and apply the whips to the horses' backs, and the wagon rattled away.

Slowly Daniel looked back at Edward. He was aware of the silence coming from behind him as apparently everyone in the small office had stopped to watch this final act. But it was Edward's face which held him.

Daniel heard him softly inquire through bruised lips, "Where are they taking her?"

Before Daniel could reply, the warden's harsh voice cut

through the suffering. "Now, where do you think, your Highness? Her folks is burying her. She's of no further use to you, or any man."

Again Edward's knees gave way. As he started downward, Daniel was there with strong support. As he grasped him about the shoulders, he looked pleadingly at Sir Claudius. "May I take him now?"

The man nodded and quickly reached for the release. Then together they guided Edward out into the rain. Above the steady downpour and the din of departing carriages, Sir Claudius shouted, "Do you have transportation?"

Daniel shook his head, his attention torn between the question and Edward's rapidly deteriorating condition.

With admirable speed, Sir Claudius hailed a passing hired chaise. Within a few moments the driver led the conveyance close to the pavement. When he saw the limp figure supported by Daniel, he kindly hopped down and assisted them with Edward, placing him inside the chaise.

As Daniel started to climb in after him, Sir Claudius restrained him for a moment. "I'm afraid it isn't quite over, Mr. Spade," he said, frowning up at the rain.

Daniel stepped back down to ground. My God, what was left?

Sir Claudius reached inside his cloak and handed him the release. "This is a very expensive piece of paper," he warned, "and it carries with it certain obligations. The magistrate wants him out of London for a period of time. I'll write to Eden Castle this afternoon and inform them that he's coming."

As Daniel pocketed the release, Sir Claudius peered into the chaise. "A good long sojourn to Eden Point might be the best thing for him. I'm sure you understand."

No, Daniel didn't understand. Almost every grief in Edward's life resided in Eden Castle, the one place on earth where his bastardy was thrust continuously before his eyes. But Daniel was in no mood to pursue the subject. If the magistrate wanted him out of London, he would do his best to follow that order.

As Daniel started to enter the chaise, he stopped for a final word. "Thank you, Sir Claudius," he said.

The expression of gratitude seemed to embarrass the man. "Well, we get paid, don't we, all of us? He's quite a handful, your friend. I would suggest that you get him immediate medical attention. Then pack him off to his mother. She brought him into this world. Let her ease his passage through it."

To that nonsense, Daniel said nothing and resumed his climb into the chaise. As they pulled away from the pavement, he saw Sir Claudius imperiously waving his private carriage forward, and he saw more, saw through the smudged windows of the prison office, the old warden carefully watching, his bandaged throat like a white banner in the gray day.

Settling opposite Edward, he allowed himself a moment to catch his breath, then leaned forward against the rocking motion and took the hand which lay limp upon the prison suit.

"Edward?" he whispered. "Can you hear me?"

But the vacancy on the face opposite him alarmed him, a clear signal that, out of choice, nothing was being received.

The rest of the ride through the wet, clogged streets of London was passed in silence so great that the faint rattling of the chaise resounded in Daniel's head. And he continued to keep a constant vigil on his friend.

A short time later as the chaise drew up before the house on Oxford Street, Daniel quickly alighted and reached back a hand to the silent man.

But there was no indication that he was either accepting or rejecting the assistance. The lips moved, but the expression did not alter. Two words fell heavily upon the air. "St. Peter," Edward whispered.

At first the name did not register, then it did. Fearful, Daniel leaned back into the chaise. "No, Edward," he protested. "It will solve nothing and only lead to—"

But the name was uttered again, stronger than before. And again Daniel objected. "Come inside, please. I'll summon a physician. You need medical—"

Suddenly a limitless anger rose on the corpselike face. He turned to Daniel with an expression so devastating that Daniel retreated. He saw again in his mind the foul-smelling opium den near the Embankment, the macabre dwarf who gleefully dispensed death in red-brown vials.

There was nothing he could do. He stepped out of the chaise and closed the door behind him. The driver was waiting on his high seat, looking expectantly down. Slowly Daniel reached into his inside pocket and withdrew coin.

He handed it up to the driver and gave him the address on Toadley Road.

The rain was yet increasing, a deluge now. As the chaise pulled away, he saw Edward turn back to the other window, his head slumped forward, the same posture of near collapse.

Daniel didn't want to think about it anymore.

As the chaise turned the corner at the end of Oxford Street, he remembered Sir Claudius's order to get him out of London. By nightfall, Edward *would* be out of London, out of this world, in fact, floating, uncharted, on the delirium of an opium cloud.

Behind him, he heard a voice calling to him from the door. He looked up to see Elizabeth poised on the top step in the rain. "Where's Mr. Eden?" she cried. "Matilda said you went to fetch him. Where—"

As Daniel drew even with her, he placed his arm about her shoulder and hurried her up the steps out of the cold rain. "He's safe, Elizabeth," he soothed. "He just needs some time to himself, that's all."

But the girl merely pulled away and went back to the large rectangular window flanking the door. "I need to wait for him, sir." Again she turned her face to the window, a determination in her small figure at least equal to the determination that Daniel had just witnessed in the carriage.

He felt dull and tired. He didn't have the heart to inform her how long her vigil might stretch, or where the object of her devotion had gone. As he started up the stairs, he looked back and saw her mutilated hand pressed against the glass. It reminded him painfully of the morning. Thank God Charlotte had escaped into death. For just an instant, Daniel begrudged Edward his temporary escape.

Quickly he smothered such thoughts and dragged himself wearily the rest of the way up the stairs. Inside his room, he stripped off his wet clothes and stretched out on the bed.

Finally, after having made him suffer anew each torment of the day, sleep obliged him to beg before it would permit him to lose consciousness . . .

Eden Castle
North Devon
June, 1836

In all her years of service to the Eden family, Sophia Cranford had never had to raise her voice in anger to James Eden. She'd raised it many times to Edward and on occasion to Jennifer, but never to James. The present Lord Eden had been a passive child, and normally he was a passive adult.

But not so this morning. At mid-June it had gone on long enough, the estrangement between the Countess Dowager and her younger son. Since that morning about a month ago when he'd provoked her to physical violence, the two had not exchanged a word, had not even shared the air of a communal room.

Now, in Sophia's opinion, it had gone on long enough. As she stood at the top of the stairs of the Great Hall, watching the shuffling reluctant progress of Lord Eden on his way to make peace with his mother, she regretted having had to raise her voice. Soberly clad in dark gray silk, she smoothed down her skirts and felt an unpleasant trembling all over, the exorbitant price one always paid when one permitted the emotions to run unchecked.

She saw him now looking back at her, the same expression she'd seen on his face throughout his entire childhood.

147

"Go along with you, James," she called out, her voice rising. "Be there by the gate when she returns."

Almost sullenly James turned away and again commenced his plodding progress across the inner courtyard. Sophia continued to watch him, bleakly wondering if, even with God's help, she could get through the days ahead. The festivities for Lady Powels and her parents had been challenge enough. Now on top of that, Edward was coming home. New weakness swept over her. Then in an incredible act of self-discipline she felt immediately strong.

Well, Edward would find a united front when he arrived, Lord Eden lovingly aligned with the Countess Dowager, an awesome alliance and a very effective one when the time came to bring suit against him. With young Lady Powels on one arm as his wife, and the Countess Dowager on his other arm, there wasn't a magistrate in the empire who would be blind to the injustice.

She noticed that he was at the gate now, apparently involved in small banter with the guardsmen. From that distance, he almost resembled the Lord of the Castle. It was only up close that the lack was so painfully apparent.

So engrossed was she in her thoughts that she was scarcely aware of Caleb coming up behind her. "A bit hard on him, weren't you?" he lightly scolded, following her gaze to the gate.

Slowly she turned. "You heard?" she inquired.

He smiled. "Only the dead failed to hear, my dear."

"There was no other way."

For a moment Caleb looked as though he might have said more, then he retreated. His hand moved down her shoulder to around her waist, his fingers pressing lightly against her breast. "I don't mean to add to your burdens," he whispered, "but it was at your feet that I learned that important lesson of subtlety."

"Dearest Caleb," she murmured, still keeping her eyes on the distant figure at the gate, "the most important lesson of subtlety is to be able to recognize when it no longer serves your purpose to be subtle."

As his hand pressed closer, she leaned back against him, her eyes closed. "Oh God, if only that old woman would die. How simple it all would be."

Caleb nodded. "She's deep in grief for William Pitch. I've heard that grief takes a heavy toll in one her age—"

"Not of her, it won't," Sophia retorted. "I do believe she's made of stone."

At the sight of a steward passing near the steps below, Sophia stepped quickly away from her brother's closeness. The steward grinned up. "Pray the weather holds, ma'am, for Mr. Eden's homecoming."

Stiffly Sophia returned the greeting. Again she was uncomfortably reminded of what she already knew, the staff's maudlin and unshakable devotion to Edward Eden. And why shouldn't they be? He filled their bellies with food and their pockets with coin.

Weakly she again leaned back against Caleb. He responded admirably with a quick warm kiss against the nape of her neck.

"Careful," she warned, in spite of her rising feelings. "There are eyes about."

"And ears," he confirmed. "Come, let's have an early luncheon, a bit of sherry, and—"

"No," she said sternly. "I must wait until I see that they're joined." Again her eyes moved back toward the castle gates where James still stood with the guardsmen, his hands shoved self-consciously into his pockets.

Caleb persisted. "She's gone to visit Lord Eden's grave. In her present state of mind, she could remain there for the entire day, as she used to do when—"

"I don't think so," Sophia interrupted. "She knows better than anyone else the importance of the festivities ahead. She has three childless children." Wryly she smiled up at her brother. "The line, dearest Caleb, remember the importance of continuity of line." The smile faded. "No," she murmured. "The old bitch will be back any moment and take over all my menus and plans as though they were her own."

She straightened herself now, attached a stray lock of hair where Caleb's kiss had fussed it loose. "You go along," she urged. "I'll join you shortly. For now I must wait. If James sees me gone, he'll bolt himself. Mother and son *will* be reunited, I swear it."

As though wanting to share her responsibilities, Caleb muttered, "The bills are mounting. I'll be in my office. Call me when you're ready."

Then he was gone. She turned from her vigil on the front gate and watched lovingly as he walked the distance across the Great Hall. The man had true stance and bearing and was far superior to her other brothers, superior even to that grim-faced old man who'd fathered them all, who had piously entoned prayers on Sunday in the little parish church at Bradford, then had crept into every available female bed in that end of Yorkshire.

She stared for a moment at the recall of her childhood, as though it were an object to be defied. She'd loathed every minute of it.

But of course the problems of the past were nothing as compared with the problems of the present, the imminent arrival of guests, William Pitch's common-law wife, old Jane Locke, and worse than that, Edward himself. She recalled Sir Claudius's last correspondence. Attempted murder! The man should be locked up. And what if he arrived, as he had in the past, with a crew of his street friends, smelling of herring and filth and onions? And what if James was unsuccessful in effecting a reconciliation with his mother?

Oh yes, the problems and complexities of life! And how much was expected of her! Perhaps years ago she should have listened to Caleb's suggestion that they emigrate, either to Australia or America. But those were barbaric places, not fit for a lady. No, Eden Castle with its line weakened by the infusion of commoner's blood, the off-spring in disarray, *that* had struck her as offering the most promising future.

As she started up the stairs, she paused again and glanced back. From that position she couldn't see James, but she knew he was there, stationed precisely where she had ordered him. Apparently for the moment, everything was under control. There were wagons due from Exeter later in the day bearing flowers and fine port. The cooking for the festivities had already started in the kitchen. She had dispatched old Mrs. Greenbell to oversee the work going on in the guest apartments. The stewards were busy in the scullery polishing silver and crystal.

Feeling as exhilarated as she'd felt all morning, she passed through the Great Hall and climbed the narrow staircase which led to their private apartments, sending her high-pitched clarion voice ahead of her, calling, "Caleb, Caleb," feeling the word deliriously in her lips, as shortly she would feel her beloved in her body.

Quickly she felt inside her pocket for the reassurance of her notebook. Afterwards she must check the endless lists, the blueprint for a future. One day, perhaps soon, she would climb the stairs to the master apartments on the third floor with the same sense of expectation, Caleb awaiting her in the elegantly carved rosewood bed.

No matter. She must wait patiently, trusting her genius, confident her plan could grow like green grass . . .

Lord James Eden, Fourteenth Baron and Sixth Earl of Eden Castle, sat on the soft clover of the headlands of Eden Point, staring gloomily out across the Bristol Channel. Where *was* she? How long did Sophia Cranford expect him to sit here, perched on the cliff like a wounded gull?

He lifted his head and stared straight upward at the high blue dazzling morning. God, how he would love to be on the moors now, riding his horse with the wind. But no, here he was, wasting the glorious morning in futile waiting to deliver an apology which he justly felt should be coming from the other direction.

Now he stretched out full-length on the soft, windblown grasses, hearing below him on the coast the fishermen of Mortemouth just coming in from the morning run. A frantic congregation of gulls were circling overhead, proclaiming the success of the catch.

With a strong surge of emotion it occurred to him how much he loved his home. "The only true Eden," his father had called it. With new pride he remembered the epithet. And with old grief he mourned for his father. How placid life had been while that great man still lived. And this thought led him irretrievably back to the troubles of the present. Surely he was the first Lord of Eden Castle ever to live on the dole of someone else. In that respect, Sophia was right. Plans must be made to alter that injustice.

Hearing voices close by, he sat up. Quickly he looked down the promenade, thinking his mother was returning. Instead the voices were coming from the opposite direction, up the cliff walk, chattering serving girls on their way to work inside the castle.

Distracted at last from his various torments, he kept his eyes pinned on the top of the walk, waiting for faces to emerge, curious to see if he recognized them. He enjoyed that aspect of life at Eden as well, the never-ending parade of fresh, robust, and willing young Devon girls, not diseased like Edward's London whores. As two bright flushed faces emerged at the top of the cliff, he wondered regretfully if this too would shortly change. Not that he wasn't fond of Harriet Powels. But there was a coldness to her which suggested she knew little of a man and his needs. As his wife, he was certain she would give him children, but little else.

Now as the two young girls caught sight of him stretched out on the grass, they stopped in their chatter. He noticed how attractively the wind blew their black serving dresses backward, outlining in breathtaking detail their young full bodies.

He sat up and called good-heartedly to them, "That's quite a climb. You'd better come and sit and catch your breath."

How sweetly they giggled together. One lifted a pretty head and called back, "If we stop to catch our breaths, my Lord, we'll catch worse from old Miss Cranford. I'm fearful we're late as it is."

James looked closer. One he recognized, the nonspeaker, a dark brooding girl he'd seen many times about the castle. The pretty blond talker he'd never seen before. "Then send your companion ahead to tell Miss Cranford you lost a heel on the climb up," he shouted. Just in case she'd misunderstood his exact wishes, he shouted again, "You, there, come! That's an order."

Again he saw the two girls whispering together. He watched closely as the issue was resolved, as begrudgingly the dark one bowed her head and went on her way.

The young girl held her position. Then slowly she started forward. As she drew near, James patted the ground directly before him, indicating where she was to sit.

Obediently she slipped to her knees. He noticed the buttons on her bodice straining against the fullness of her breasts. "A grand spot it is, milord," she blushed, "for catching your wind. Ain't nuthin' much else up here to catch, now is there?"

James laughed, finding a pleasurable release from his earlier black mood. He raised his knees and rested his arms upon them. Not to move too fast, that was the skill one needed with serving girls. Allow them a few moments' pause, to think your interests lie elsewhere. "What's your name?" he asked.

"Dorothy," she replied, modestly lowering her eyes.

"Dorothy," he repeated, as though testing the name on his memory. "Why haven't I noticed you before?"

Again she cast a furtive glance upward. "Don't rightly know, milord," she murmured. "But I've taken note of you often enough—"

For a moment, their eyes held, James trying to read what he thought was a clear invitation. He felt a tightening in his groin. Slowly his hand reached tentatively out and lightly cupped around the fullness of a breast.

Her expression, as far as he could tell, did not alter in the least. "Poor Lord Eden," she smiled sadly, sitting straighter before him as though to encourage his exploration.

Mildly distracted by her expression of pity, James felt a momentary flagging in his desire, not enough to withdraw his hand, which now had found the pleasurably hard little mound of her nipples. "Why poor?" he inquired, maintaining an air of playful fun.

She laughed quickly. "My Gawd," she went on, "the paces they're puttin' you through—your mama on one side, old Miss Cranford on the other, Mr. Edward due at the same time as your bride-to-be—" She laughed openly now. "Us in the kitchen says something turrible's goin' to happen—"

Suddenly he felt resentment that his family affairs were the subject of kitchen gossip. The smiling face before him now appeared merely impudent. With abrupt cruelty he sharply squeezed the nipple.

Reflexively the girl drew back. "Ow, sir, that hurt."

But James, on his knees now, merely followed after her as she scrambled backward. In her rapid retreat, her shoes caught on the hem of her skirt and thus self-entrapped it was a simple matter for him to climb over and pin her on her back in the grass.

Slightly breathless from the brief scuffle, he held her secure with his body, straddling her, enjoying the sensation of her futile movements beneath him. "And what else is said in the kitchen," he demanded, pinning her wrists over her head.

"Nuthin', milord," she gasped, apparently shocked at how effortlessly he had rendered her helpless.

"Nothing?" he demanded.

She shook her head. "Nuthin' of import. Now, please, milord, let me go. I'm awful late. Miss Cranford will have my hide—"

But he had no intention of letting her go. Holding both her wrists firmly with one hand, his other hand started down her bodice, separating buttons, until at last the fabric parted to reveal a thin chemise. And beneath that, nothing but the soft mounds which had attracted his attention in the first place.

She held still in her state of near-nakedness. "Not here, milord, please," she begged. "I've no real objection, but not here—"

It was a ploy and he knew it. "Why not here?" he smiled. "We're alone except for the gulls and I can assure you they won't tell."

But her protests only increased as though it had never occurred to her that harmless flirting might end like this. "Please, milord," she begged openly, her head rolling from side to side as his hand pulled down the chemise. As he lowered his lips to her breasts, she moaned, "Please, no—"

Working rapidly now he lifted himself only long enough to draw up her skirts. As he forced himself down between her legs, she howled. He felt himself swept along, her cry only feeding his ardor, unable to stop himself although he knew he should, his hand fumbling now with the front of his trousers.

"Oh Gawd, please don't," she begged over and over again as, with eyes pressed shut, she ground her head backwards into the grass.

But James was impervious to everything save the desperate need to wipe the impudence off her face and replace it with tearful, pleading submission.

Just as he was on the verge of accomplishing that goal, a strong, familiar female voice joined with the racing wind to cut through his purpose. "Let her go!" the voice commanded.

He did not need to look, not even when the voice came again, almost incoherent with anger. "Let her go, I said. This minute."

Slowly he raised himself and turned. Behind him he heard the girl scramble upward, mouthing some stupid expression of gratitude to her benefactress. With a surge of vindictive pleasure, he thought, what a fitting way to commence his apology. He listened again, with his back turned, curious as to the precise tone her lecture would take.

But when after several minutes he had heard nothing, he looked over his shoulder, surprised and a little disappointed to see her trudging back up the slight incline.

He heard, in his imagination, Sophia's voice raised in anger. *A reconciliation must be effected*— To that end, he swallowed his mortification, his damaging sense of a man reduced to a small boy, and called sharply after her, "I'm sorry, Mother—"

Then he tried to imbue his voice with a softer tone. He added, "For everything."

At last she turned to face him and as always, in spite of their differences, he was again struck by her eloquent simplicity, though he thought she looked cruelly old in the relentless light of day. He was accustomed to seeing her under the artificial and becoming light of lamp and candle. Now he saw clearly the streaks of gray in her hair, her neck flesh withered, the inevitable script of time around her eyes and mouth. He noticed something else as well, slight traces of moisture on her face which rendered him powerless.

When still she seemed disinclined to speak, he stepped up the incline toward her, trying to sort through the list of offenses for which he had to apologize. He shoved his hands into his pockets, smiling. "She seemed cooperative at first," he began. "How is a man to know when a female has changed her mind?"

Still she held him locked in a tight gaze. "From what I heard," she said, her voice faint over the wind, "she was clearly signaling her displeasure."

"And I apologize," he said. "To you, to her, to the whole damn world if necessary."

Really, he had no appetite for this at all and again turned away. To his surprise, he was aware of her presence behind him. "There is no shortage of willing ones, James," she said. "And neither is there a shortage of beds in the castle. Before we were married, your father always preferred the small room off the Buttery. He had a very comfortable couch installed there and a secure lock. In the future, consider it yours." Her voice rose with just a tinge of lightness. "Out here, you run the risk of frightening the gulls. Birds

are very graceful in their copulation. It almost resembles a
dance. I'm quite certain they would be terribly put off by
the sweating, grunting human ritual."

In a mixture of amazement and amusement he caught the
light in her eye. "I'll remember in the future," he smiled.
He hadn't realized how much he had missed her during
their silent warfare.

While she had not yet returned his smile, she seemed
willing to follow after him a short distance removed from
the place of his encounter with the young girl as though
that spot now were corrupt ground. Carefully he selected a
grassy area which afforded a breathtaking view of the
channel.

Without words, he assisted her down, and lingered a
moment to see if she was comfortable, then sat beside her,
his knees drawn up, the two of them gazing, unspeaking,
out across the blue water.

Long minutes passed before he could bring himself to
break the silence. Although he was well aware of his
numerous offenses, his mind was preoccupied with another
train of thought. "You mentioned the small room off the
Buttery," he began. "After you were married, did Father—
I mean, did he—"

A smile which spoke of faint embarrassment caused her
to duck her head. "Oh, for heaven's sake, I don't know,
James," she scolded lightly. "I didn't set a guard on him."
She shrugged and cast an exploring hand over the soft
grasses.

He noticed now a becoming blush on her cheeks. In a
way his question was not without motive. He simply wondered how a woman, transformed into a wife, felt about a
man straying.

Now he was aware of her staring at him as though she'd
seen through the question to the motive behind it. "I'm
grateful for this privacy, James," she began. She shook her
head. "Sometimes I feel as though every room in the castle
has grown invisible ears."

He knew what she had reference to. The Cranfords. The
constant and predominant source of irritation between
them. With a sigh he sent his eyes back across the channel.
"If you're so distrustful of them, Mother, why don't you
dismiss them?"

She laughed openly at the bait. "For the simple reason

that I'd lose both my son and daughter if I did, as you've pointed out before," she said.

He looked earnestly at her. "They mean you well, they really do. They are intensely loyal to our entire family and would do nothing—"

He sensed a stiffening in her and stopped speaking.

Apparently she too dismissed the unsavory subject and returned to her earlier sentiment. "At any rate," she went on, "I'm glad we're here alone."

"As am I," he smiled. Then because the feeling was so pleasant between them, he rushed on, getting the damnable apology out of the way. "And I am sorry, Mother," he murmured, "for making you so angry. It was not my intention."

Almost sternly she shook her head. "I'm as much to blame." Earnestly she returned his gaze. "I do understand, James, how difficult it must be for you."

While he appreciated her understanding, still he looked away. "It *is* a muddle, isn't it?" he commented softly.

"It's deplorable," she agreed. "I want you to know that I intend to talk to Edward, see if he would be agreeable to a more equitable arrangement."

He laughed, remembering the countless times in the past when they both had launched the subject. To no avail. "Talk all you like, Mother, but you know the outcome as well as I."

"It's different now," she said.

"How different?"

"You're to be a bridegroom."

"And do you think that will make the slightest impression on Edward?"

"I think it will." She leaned closer. "Please try to understand him, James."

He closed his eyes and rested his head upon his raised knees. With despair, he recalled a lifetime trying to understand his older brother, taller, fairer, wittier; everyone in the castle, except their father, seeming to draw nourishment from his antics and charm, while he, for the most part, was made to feel like a blight on creation.

Remembering the unfairness of his childhood, he lifted his head and murmured sarcastically, "Poor Edward."

"Yes, indeed," she agreed quickly. "James, the trouble is," she went on, speaking urgently as though her time was limited, "you see him only from your point of view."

"It's the only one available."

"No. Try seeing it from his."

"How I wish that I could," he retorted. "How comforting it would be to be able to sit here and know that everything within my sight belongs to me. The castle, the headlands, that coast, the estates, a fitting inheritance to pass on to a son, wouldn't you say?" He shook his head.

Obviously she was listening closely. When he'd finished speaking, she drew herself up. "I'm going to ask him to deed half of it to you, as a wedding gift."

Clearly she had expected an enormous reaction. When he did not respond in any way, she asked, "Did you hear, James? I said I was going to ask—"

"I heard."

"Well?"

"I wish you luck," he smiled. "For all our sakes. It's never made any difference in the past."

"I think it will now."

"Why?"

"According to Sir Claudius, Edward has gone through a period of intense suffering."

Again James looked away. "When one chooses pimps and whores and pickpockets for companions," he said to the sky, "I should think that suffering, intense or otherwise, would be the order of the day."

He sensed a kind of reserve settling over her now. "All I'm asking," she concluded quietly, "is that when he arrives, we receive him warmly, that instead of incessant warfare, we try peace for a change." He thought she was finished, but looked up in time to hear her say, "If you have no natural affection for him, try to simulate it in the glorious hope that it might become genuine. Whoever his companions may be, I know him to have a generous heart. He *will* meet you halfway. I'm certain of it."

Speech concluded. In order to keep peace between them, he nodded, all the while thinking, how futile. Was he half a Lord? Half a peer of the realm? No! Sophia and Caleb were right. As distasteful as it was, it would ultimately require a lawsuit and perhaps an unsavory trial to wrest from the bastard what was rightfully his.

Obviously she saw something in his face which she misinterpreted as acceptance. "Thank you, James," she smiled, and for the first time reached for his hand. Watching her closely, it seemed that her emotions were perilously close to the surface. Seeing her mourning clothes again, he remembered her recent loss, recalled that the news had come while they had been maintaining the angry silence between them. Now he enclosed her hand between his own. "I'm sorry," he murmured, "about William Pitch. But the man had a full and productive life. Perhaps mourning is not so much the order of the day as—"

Quickly she nodded and withdrew her hand, fumbled now for her handkerchief. "You're right, of course," she said, dabbing at tears which had appeared at the mere mention of the name. An unconvincing smile broke through the tears. "I do agree with Dr. Johnson, though, that we never do anything consciously for the last time without sadness of heart. The last letter I penned to William was on the day of his death, an invitation for them to come and share your happiness—"

In an attempt to offer her a degree of comfort, he said, "Aunt Jane will be here soon, and Sophia said she thought that Jennifer was coming—"

He saw her turn hurriedly to him. "Is it for certain?" she asked eagerly. "There was some doubt—"

He smiled. "I believe Sophia convinced her, knowing how much it would mean to you." The smile broadened. "Now, does that thoughtful gesture sound like the impulse of the enemy?"

She gave him a most peculiar look, as though he were still a child and not capable of understanding the complexities of adult relationships. He resented such an expression. Feeling that everything had been said, he started to rise.

Abruptly she restrained him. "One more thing, James," she began, as he settled back again to the ground.

"The coming festivities," she began.

"Yes?" he said quietly. "What about them?"

"The time will come when I must speak to Lord and Lady Powels about—"

She faltered. He supplied the word. "The engagement?" If he could bring this rambling to a close, there still would be time for a ride with Caleb.

"Yes. The engagement."

"What about it?"

She smiled. "Forgive the nature of the interrogation. It's

a mother's right." She looked directly at him. "Do you love her, this Harriet?"

He had not expected so blunt a question. Solemnly he tried to give her an honest answer. "I feel an affection for her—"

"Based on what?"

He felt a pinch of annoyance. "She's—suitable," he replied.

Still she waited expectantly as though he'd said nothing at all.

"She's—agreeable—"

She continued to gaze at him, her eyes unblinking.

He found his annoyance increasing. Remembering his recent incident with the serving girl, he joked, "and she's willing."

"And on these points you'll bind your life to hers forever?"

Shades of the romantic girl surfacing in the shriveled old woman. He scoffed openly. "You make it sound like a prison sentence."

"If there's nothing more in your feelings for her, it will be," she replied sternly.

Abruptly he fell to searching for the words she wanted to hear. "She has a graceful neck, auburn hair, sober eyes. She's clean, articulate, though shy—" He looked sideways at her. "I think you'll like her."

"Whether I like her or not is unimportant."

"She will produce healthy children," he added, "—something that your three offspring have thus far been unable to do."

She continued to frown at him. Then apparently as weary of the encounter as he was, she concluded, "Then you wish me to speak of banns with the Powelses?"

"Why not?" he replied hurriedly. "I rather thought that was the point of all this."

She nodded, a solemn look upon her face, as sad and preoccupied as the one she'd arrived with. He had hoped to walk back through the castle gates with her smiling, on his arm, a pretty family portrait which he was certain would please Sophia.

But apparently it was not to be. As she started to rise, he again gave her generous support. He was sorry that she had cooled toward him. And he was doubly sorry that he had been unable to fill her romantic old head with avowals of passionate love. Of course she had yet to meet Harriet. All of his encounters with the young woman in the past had been at cotillions at country house parties, and the fortnight which he'd spent at Hadley Park in Shrewsbury. Now, thinking on the shy, timid, rather stern-appearing girl, he doubted seriously if there was a single impulse in her entire personality which would in all honesty be called passionate.

He laughed openly and placed a loving arm around his mother's shoulder. "Don't worry," he soothed. "It will be a workable marriage. The Powels blood is even bluer than that of the Edens. In the marriage race, Harriet and I are the leftovers. In that respect, we were made for each other. And I promise you that she will make a good wife, and I'll try to be a good husband, and we will both try to give you suitable grandchildren."

The echo of his words sounded right upon his ears, the dutiful son giving his mother all the reassurance he was capable of giving her.

Therefore he was a little surprised and annoyed when she walked away from him without speaking, moving slowly down the long promenade which led, a distance away, back to the stone bench and the family graveyard.

"Will you lunch with me, Mother?" he called after her, remembering how in the past it had pleased her when he would forego luncheon with the Cranfords and dine with her instead.

But obviously it meant less than nothing to her today as she continued down the long walkway, her head bowed, as though, inexplicably, she was weeping again.

"Shall I accompany you, Mother?" he called again.

No answer.

"You've mourned long enough, you know," he shouted. "Please return with me to the castle—"

But still she continued on, a small figure growing smaller. He continued to watch her and thought again of Sophia's warning: "She's growing quite senseless."

Although the thought was ugly, it occurred to him that he'd rather see her dead than mindless.

Weary now of watching her, he turned away and started back toward the castle gates.

He increased his step until he was running. He was in sore need of the Cranford's company, the only two people within the realm of his society who looked upon him with proper deference and respect, who considerately reminded him daily of who he was and what was rightfully his . . .

Roe Head School
Yorkshire
June, 1836

By the light of a single candle, Jennifer Eden carefully folded the last of her garments, placed them in the valise, and laced it shut. The silence of the school echoed about her. They were all gone, the young girls to friends and families for summer holidays, the teachers, most of them off for seacoast holidays to Bridlington and Whitby, except for herself and the peculiar Miss Brontë, with whom she had shared a silent supper. All during the meal, Miss Brontë had read a book; her head dropped so far over it that her nose had nearly touched it.

Still Jennifer liked her very much. She kept to herself and afforded Jennifer the same right, unlike some of the noisy, nosy, chattering co-teachers.

Now with a rueful smile she sat heavily on the edge of her cot, thinking tonight how much she would have enjoyed some of that chattering female company, thinking how heavy Miss Brontë's silence had been during the meal, giving Jennifer time to dwell with dread on what lay ahead of her.

Slowly she reached for the opened letter resting on the near table. Here was one terror, the letter which had arrived a week ago from Daniel Spade, begging her to come to London before she returned home to Eden Point.

Not only one terror there, but many. Her brother for one. Daniel's letter hinted at an unprecedented deterioration without listing any specific cause. Not that Jennifer needed any specific listing. She'd read in the last issue of *Blackwood's Magazine* of William Pitch's death, the renowned editor of *The Bloomsbury Gazetteer*. She'd thought then how devastated Edward would be, the closest of all three children to their mother's lover.

Abruptly she sat erect, as though she somehow felt it was her responsibility to serve penance for her mother.

She stood up and took Daniel's letter nearer to the candle. Dear heavens, why had he summoned her? She was in no way equipped to deal with Edward's flagging spirit, and she loathed London with its noise and filth. Lovingly she touched her portfolio of music, packed for the dreaded journey, slightly bulky now as she'd tucked her Bible and Book of Common Prayer on top of her music.

Her hand trembled as she made a mental inventory of what was ahead of her. First, come dawn, the long chill ride in the open gig across the moors to Leeds, where for the first time she would board one of the new railways, the black monster she'd seen from a distance, belching smoke, traveling with the speed of the wind.

Reflexively, her hand crumpled Daniel's letter. Perhaps it would be God's blessing that she not survive such a trip. While she did not particularly look forward to being mangled in a railway accident, it did seem a superior fate to what was ahead of her if she survived and arrived safely at Euston Station in London. For there she would find Edward, her beloved though troubled older brother, involved in an adultery scandal. The Leeds *Mercury* had been full of accounts of the trial, had covered all aspects of it for the past month, including the ultimate death of the poor young woman.

She stared fixedly forward at the dancing candle. Surely Edward had not been involved. She knew him better than that. He was troubled, but not sinful.

As though Daniel's crumpled letter had suddenly spoken to her, she now looked sharply in that direction. As children, the three of them had played together, exploring every nook and cranny of the North Devon coast until such time as Sophia had put her foot down, claiming that two rough boys were not fit company for a young female. Then they had thrown themselves into an exciting game of cat and mouse, the three of them plotting at every turn to outwit and outmaneuver the stern woman.

And how they had succeeded, Daniel, Edward, and Jenny, climbing to the uppermost regions of Eden Castle, crouching low against the battlements while below in the inner courtyard, old Sophia had cried her lungs out.

Growing unaccountably breathless, she held rigidly still, remembering the two boys, grown young men then, while she lagged behind a mere child. In the spirit of harmless knavery they had asked her once to lift her petticoats, and in the spirit of the adoring tag-along little sister, she had obliged. At that moment, Sophia Cranford had found them.

Her face in the pale light of the candle now appeared drained of color, as though merely thinking on that certain incident, she'd suffered fresh shock. Her parents had been away as always and, as Miss Cranford had put it, the full burden of punishment descended on her shoulders. The two boys had been turned over to Caleb Cranford and, to this day, Jennifer had no idea what had been their fate. As for herself, she was taken from the nursery against Mrs. Greenbell's protestations and confined to the back room of the Cranfords' private apartments, a small windowless enclosure no larger than a closet. There, Sophia had bound her to a chair, had arranged a wooden crucifix on the table before her, and had forced her to sit for two days, denying her all food, denying her even a chamber pot, forcing her to sit in the filth of her own body waste.

Remembering the ordeal, Jennifer closed her eyes. She remembered as well Sophia's exhortation that she focus on the suffering face of Christ and pray that He remove all future temptation from her. And she remembered the most puzzling moment of all, how at the end of the two-day ordeal, sickened by the stench of her own filth, her hands numb and cold from the cord, her eyes swollen shut from weeping, when her hate for the woman was on the verge of annihilating her, Sophia Cranford had come to release her, had taken her lovingly into her arms, stench and all, and had held her throughout her tears, saying over and over again how much she loved her.

Jennifer, the child, had been incapable of understanding

the intricate emotions. All she knew was that that incident had marked the beginning of her deep involvement with Sophia Cranford, who surely loved her more than her mother did. And she also knew that that episode had marked the beginning of her fear of Daniel Spade, and all men who were not either her father or her brothers.

Drained by her memory, she sat again on the edge of the cot.

Without warning, the room went black. The candle had burned out. Frightened as though at an unusual phenomenon, she stared wide-eyed into the blackness.

In the darkness she went rapidly down upon her knees, praying, "Dear God, help me," saying the four simple words over and over again, when without warning, there was a soft knock at the door. Incapable of speech, she held still in her peculiar position and prayed now that the intruder would leave. A moment later, she saw the door pushed open, saw the light of a lamp spilling in.

At first she didn't recognize her in the shadowy darkness. Then she saw her clearly, Miss Brontë, looking like a little old woman, peering into the dark. "Are you well, Miss Eden?" Miss Brontë called softly in. "I heard an outcry—"

Struggling for control, Jennifer turned away and tried to wipe the tears from her face.

Though still squinting, the keen-eyed Charlotte apparently saw everything. With an attitude of resolution which belied her thin form, she strode into the room and removed the well-worn Bible from Jennifer's hands. "It isn't Sunday," she said. "How weary God must get, hearing our constant whinings."

Jennifer was on the verge of protesting. But something within responded to the woman's bluntness. With admirable forebearance she permitted the Bible to be taken from her hands, permitted the woman to lift her up and guide her considerately to the edge of the cot. In the splash of lamplight, their eyes met and held. Charlotte's extreme nearsightedness gave the impression that the woman was peering effortlessly into her soul. She recalled the young students saying the same thing, that as Miss Brontë tried to fill their heads with rules of grammar, she was capable of seeing the slightest mischief, even with her back turned.

"Now," Charlotte went on, with an air of dispatch, "I see you are packed. According to Miss Wooler, you are leaving tomorrow for an adventurous day which will include a ride on the railways."

Jennifer nodded.

Now curiously, Charlotte seemed ill at ease. She stepped back from the cot and peered shyly about the room. "My only regret," she said, in her funny high-pitched voice, "is that our duties with the students keep us so occupied that even at the end of a solid year together, we do not know each other." The smile broadened, though it still looked awkward on the small pinched features. "To me," she went on, "you are simply Miss Eden, Pianoforte, and coming from behind the closed doors of your classroom, I hear sounds so torturous that, on occasion, I find myself praying for the infirmity of deafness."

In spite of herself, Jennifer smiled. "On occasion I myself use two small pieces of cotton inserted lightly into each ear. Or cork works as well."

"I'll remember it in the future," Charlotte replied.

Jennifer felt the need to say something else. But she could think of nothing. In spite of the welcome distraction, the company of the funny-looking young woman with dry, frizzy hair screwed in tight curls seemed only to remind her of how soon her safe refuge here at Roe Head was coming to an end. Finally in spite of her distress, she mustered, "Will you be going home, Charlotte?"

The woman nodded. "Yes, indeed. My brother is coming in the gig for me tomorrow."

"Is it much of a journey?"

She shook her head. "Less than two hours to Haworth, across the moors."

"Are you looking forward to it?"

Charlotte lowered her head. "Yes, very much. It's always good to see my brother and sisters." She looked up, a strained expression on her face. "It would be pleasant, however, if we could stay here."

Jennifer listened closely. She knew that, unlike herself, Charlotte taught to eat, to survive, that it was her keen sense of duty to her family that made her stand apart in a single-minded drive to excel. But now she readily agreed with Charlotte's sentiment. "I don't want to leave either," she confessed. She lifted her head and drew a shuddering breath, the result of her recent tears. "I hated it here when

I first came. Now—" She glanced about. "Now," she concluded, "it seems so—safe."

"Is it so hazardous, your home?" Charlotte inquired softly.

Jennifer nodded. "It is, indeed."

For the moment she had the feeling that the woman might press for more specific details. But she didn't. Instead she slipped comfortably into the abstract. "We assign danger," she said bluntly, as though she were back in her classroom, instructing, "as we assign safety. As a child on the moors, I used to see phantoms in every mist of whirling fog." She shook her head and laughed quietly. "How peculiarly barren I've felt since I grew brave and discovered that there was nothing at the center of those whirling mists."

She paced the small area before the cot now and glanced aside at Jennifer's packed valise. With unexpected kindness she said, "Had I known you were dreading it so, you might have come home with me."

Touched, though embarrassed, Jennifer murmured, "Thank you." For an instant, she regretted that the invitation had come too late. Softly she smiled. "Be prudent about issuing the invitation next year. I may accept."

Suddenly the pinched look fell away from Charlotte's face. She beamed. "Oh, that would be lovely."

Then for some reason, she seemed embarrassed. "I'll not bother you further," she said, retrieving the lamp from the table and easing back toward the door.

Jennifer did not want her to leave and said as much. But Charlotte was insistent. "I haven't started my packing," she said. "If I'm not ready promptly at one, Branwell will be out of sorts."

At the door, she turned back with a gentle question. "Are you well now, Jennifer?"

Jennifer nodded. "Not well, but eased. Thank you for stopping by."

The simple reply seemed to please Charlotte. "In spite of what my students say, I do have sound eyes and ears and I know a human outcry when I hear one." Her light mood altered. "The saddest of sounds," she whispered. Then she was passing through the door, calling back, "You must write to me, Jennifer, and tell me about the railway ride. Tell me all about London and North Devon and the people you meet and speak with. Your letters will be most gratefully received."

Then she was gone, leaving Jennifer as she had found her, sitting alone in the dark. But it was a different darkness now, a safer darkness. Slowly Jennifer stood and prepared herself for bed, the young woman's words still inhabiting her mind. *We assign danger, and we assign safety.* Such control had never occurred to Jennifer.

Weary, yet excited, Jennifer closed her eyes and tried to sleep. But before her in the darkness, she saw a painfully clear cavalcade of the future, her brothers, Edward and James, locked in perpetual warfare, and she saw Daniel Spade, no longer a harmless boy, but in full manhood. And she saw Sophia and Caleb Cranford, trying like the saints that they were and with all their hearts to serve the disintegrating Eden family.

And she saw her mother, nodding here, bowing there, an aging coquette, her stained blood racing through Jennifer's veins, corrupting, condemning.

With some force, she pressed her head backward into the pillow. *We assign safety, we assign danger—*

Dear Lord! It was so simple and so complex, and for the time being, well beyond her . . .

London
June, 1836

For Edward, it had been enough.

Five days and nights of tranquil oblivion, floating out of touch with reality on the wings of opium, had been sufficient to dull the memory of what he had found in the dungeon cell of Newgate. It had not been enough to obliterate it. He doubted if there was enough opium in all of India to accomplish that.

But at least he could function now, and functioning he was, sitting upright, washed and shaved and in fresh garments, sitting opposite Daniel in the carriage, on their way to Euston Station to meet Jennifer.

Now he watched Daniel across from him and recalled his numerous visitations to St. Peter's establishment, bringing hot food, of which Edward had eaten little. Had Edward thanked him? He couldn't remember, and did so now. "I'm grateful, Daniel, as always."

Across the way, Daniel smiled. "That's number twenty-five, at least. And, as many times, I say no thanks are needed." He moved a hand up to smooth down the thick red hair. It seemed to Edward that Daniel had taken unprecedented pains with his grooming this evening, preparatory to meeting Jennifer. "I don't approve, Edward," he went on, suddenly sober. "But in view of the—circumstances of the last few days, I understand."

It was as close to a lecture as he'd ever come. And if that was all, Edward found it palatable. For the first time in several weeks, he felt in fairly good spirits, the pleasing opium numbness accompanying him everywhere now as St. Peter had generously shared with him the "art of the habit," had sold him twenty vials of the pure red-brown laudanum and had instructed him in the ways of consuming it wisely. Of course, Daniel knew nothing of this. It was not important that he knew. The two drops that Edward had hastily consumed in a glass of claret before they had left were working beautifully. He felt relaxed, a quiet peace inside his head only lightly tinged with the memory of tragic events.

"How long is my exile to last?" Edward asked, thinking with regret that soon the multitudinous life outside the window would be replaced with dormant heather and screeching sea gulls.

Daniel looked up out of his own thoughts. "Sir Claudius didn't say. I would imagine for the duration of the summer—"

"The duration of the—" Aghast, Edward could only gape.

Sternly Daniel reminded him, "The charge was attempted murder, Edward."

The voice, so quietly speaking, lay like something heavy on his soul. Attempted murder. Had it not been for the effective reaction of the guards, it would have been murder. Sobered by the realization, Edward again leaned back in the carriage, his eyes dully fixed now on the passing scene beyond his window.

Daniel saw the vacancy and moved to dispel it. "The change will do you good, Edward," he soothed. "You've been separated from your family long enough."

Without looking at him, Edward spoke to the window. "Others find health in the North Devon air. I find sickness."

"Then the fault is your own," Daniel scolded mildly. "It will be quite an event for the Edens, James's engagement, all of you together again for the first time since—"

"My father's death," Edward concluded for him. The two drops of laudanum were not enough. The pleasurable numbness was leaving. He stretched out a hand to the window as though for support. "Her train?" he asked disjointedly. "When is it due?"

"Nine o'clock," Daniel replied. "We've plenty of time."

Slowly Edward closed his eyes. "My mother," he began, his hands tightly interlaced between his legs. "Does she know we're coming?"

Apparently the innocent question fell reassuringly on Daniel's ear. "She does," he smiled. "Sir Claudius wrote to her."

"And who wrote to Jennifer?"

There was a pause. "I did. I thought it would be helpful if she accompanied you."

"As a nurse or a guard?"

"Neither. As your sister."

The black mood was passing in the innocent banter. The trick was to keep the mind occupied and the tongue busy. To this end, Edward leaned forward. "Is she well? Jennifer, I mean?"

Daniel shrugged, the disinterested look on his face as suspect as Edward's new calm. "I don't know," he replied. "Her letter was brief, stating simply the time of her arrival."

Abruptly Edward laughed, looking forward to seeing his sister. "We were quite a trio, weren't we, the three of us—"

Daniel returned his laugh with the warmth of a smile. "Indeed we were. The scourges of Eden, according to Sophia Cranford."

Edward's face darkened in disgust. "The bitch," he muttered. "I suppose she's still there, and Caleb as well. God, how I loathed the both of them."

Daniel tried to soften the harsh sentiment. "Theirs was a difficult task," he suggested, "with your parents away as often as they were."

Edward sat with his shoulders hunched now, as though for protection against what was ahead of him. "We've changed since we were those three scourges of Eden, haven't we, Daniel?" he mused softly.

"Not so much," Daniel replied.

The words were reassuring. Perhaps inside the high-vaulted Doric arches of Euston Station, Edward might find a moment of privacy for the purpose of reinforcing the two meager drops of laudanum. He wanted to be free of memories when he met Jennifer.

The cabs and carriages increased as they drew near to Euston Square. As John Murrey found an empty spot near the pavement, Edward reached stealthily inside his waistcoat pocket. Perhaps in the brief interim while Daniel was giving the old man instructions, Edward could successfully lift the cork and drink from the small vial. Predictably, when John Murrey had brought the carriage to a halt, Daniel in his eagerness was out the door and standing back now, waiting for Edward to follow.

"Go along," Edward called down over the shouts of the thronging crowds. "Tell John to see if he can't find a place close by and wait. She'll have trunks."

Daniel hesitated a moment. Then he advanced to the front of the carriage. As he shouted up at the old man, Edward quickly withdrew the vial and, tilting his head back, placed several drops on the tip of his tongue. With no time to spare, he hurriedly returned the cork and shoved the vial in his pocket, just as Daniel reappeared on the pavement.

"Are you coming?" Daniel called up to him.

With a quick swallow, Edward sent the slightly bitter balm on its way through his system. Heartened by the promise of relief, he stepped down from the carriage. For a moment he lost his balance. Daniel was there, offering his arm. "Would you rather wait in the carriage?" he inquired, concerned.

Edward clung to the support, all the while shaking his head. "No, of course not. I'm fine. Lead the way."

As Daniel checked the high board for arrivals, Edward stood patiently a distance behind him.

"This way," Daniel called now, extending his hand to Edward, his anticipation at seeing Jennifer clear on his face.

Following after him through the crowds, Edward thought again what a pleasing union that would be, Daniel and Jennifer. He would purchase a London house for them as a wedding present and place a generous annual income at their disposal, then sit back and bask in their love and enjoy their progeny and perhaps for the first time in his life be able to point to an accomplishment and say, "That is mine. I brought it about, and it is right and good."

Standing in the midst of the tumultuous station, with the shrieking black monster directly ahead of him belching smoke, scattering cinders, he felt enclosed by a kind of soothing novelty. It was as if in this moment, everything was memorable and worth remembering . . .

The journey was not as bad as she had feared. To be true, the black monster had reached incredible speeds. The wind had rushed past her ears, the tranquil green English countryside had been reduced to a blur.

Still, it had been very exciting, and once or twice she'd caught herself smiling back at the other passengers as, together, they had shared this most unique experience of a railway ride. And the speed! She still could not believe it, the boxlike coaches racing over the narrow tracks, approaching, on flat, level stretches, the unheard-of rate of forty miles an hour.

Now as the enormous locomotive rumbled into Euston Station, she felt giddy, as though the wild ride had robbed her of her sense of gentility and decorum.

The train was now screeching to a halt, belching great white puffs of steam. Outside her window she saw the crowds pushing dangerously close, their heads uplifted as though in admiration for the passengers who had successfully completed such a perilous journey.

Then through the crowds she saw them, those two familiar faces from her childhood.

She caught sight of Daniel first, his neck craning first one way and then the other as he searched the line of coaches. He seemed thinner from that distance, not as robust a figure as she remembered. Still, he appeared well groomed, as she knew Daniel would, neatly dressed with a broad, clean-shaven face and direct brown eyes.

Abruptly she blushed under her own close scrutiny, as though she were the one being studied. But in truth he had yet to find her and she rather liked it that way. In spite of her safe obscurity, she was incapable of sorting out her feelings. Even after her extreme punishment by Sophia Cranford, she still had nursed a secret affection for her brother's best friend. A scraped knee, a splinter wedged into the palm of her hand, or just a general sinking of her spirits always brought him running.

She smiled softly, keeping her eye on the tall man caught

in the press and pull of the crowd. How safe they all had been on those windy sunny days!

Quickly she banished her thoughts of the past as all around her she was aware of passengers preparing to alight from the train, women gathering baskets and children, men self-consciously adjusting their hats and waistcoats. As her eyes moved rapidly over the faces, she found him again, or at least found his red hair, his face turned away as apparently he motioned behind for someone to join him in the search.

Edward. As he drew even with Daniel, she saw him clearly for the first time, and gasped audibly. What had happened? There was a gauntness to his face she'd never seen before, as though he'd recently been ill. She saw Daniel draw him close, a protective gesture, as though he were someone who had to be looked after. Again, as with Daniel, she was capable of viewing Edward only as a boy. And that face had never borne such a look in his boyhood. Then he had moved with directness, had been the only one who had possessed the courage to talk back to the Cranfords, had possessed a personality of such unbending strength that even without trying, he'd won every battle, scaled every height, run the fastest, the farthest.

But now! She saw nothing in that pale demeanor that even vaguely reminded her of the boy. Dearest Edward, poor Edward, bearing the brunt of their mother's vanity, a true bastard, conceived without benefit of vows, her mother's sinful device, according to Sophia, for tricking her father into marriage.

In the aisle opposite her, she was aware of the crowds beginning to thin. The station platform was filled now with warm reunions. She could not postpone her own appearance forever. To that end, she leaned forward against the window, making herself clearly visible to anyone who might be looking from the platform.

Then suddenly Daniel spied her. Within the instant a reassuring light covered the ruddy features; he lifted one hand in a broad wave while with the other he drew Edward nearer and proceeded to point out her position on the train.

Edward too smiled and lifted a hand in greeting, though under the weight of his direct gaze, she thought again how tired he looked, how ill. With what?

Quickly she stood, grasped her portfolio beneath her arms, again adjusted her bonnet and went to meet them.

They met in the narrow door, she looking down on their faces, which now were covered with expressions of extravagant merriment. "We'd about given up on you," Daniel shouted over the crowds. "I was afraid that you—"

He broke off speaking as Edward lightly pushed him to one side and held out his arms to her. He placed his hands about her waist and swung her to ground and stood a moment holding her at arm's length, his eyes squinting at her as though his vision was impaired in some way.

"Edward," she whispered. "It's so good to see you."

Without warning, he drew her close and enclosed her in his arms. Inside his embrace, she pressed her face into his neck and realized that he had lost flesh. Disengaging herself at last, she looked directly up at him. "You look ill, Edward," she said bluntly.

He laughed openly. "And I was about to lie and tell you how lovely you look. I don't think I will now."

A little hurt by his directness, she stepped back, though managed a smile. "Why lie?" she asked lightly. "It's my best gown," she added, lifting the folds of the dark brown fabric.

Edward gave a mock shudder. "Is that what they wear in Yorkshire?"

"And what would you suggest?" she asked, standing before him as though ready and willing to be transformed.

He assessed her again, with Daniel grinning behind him, joining in the inspection. "Yellow," he murmured at last. "Yes, yellow silk to contrast your hair and cut low to reveal your breasts."

His hand had lifted as though to assist with the description of the gown. She felt heat climbing the sides of her face. And it was in this state of mind that she greeted Daniel, who was now being led forward by Edward.

When he continued to draw nearer as though he intended to embrace her as Edward had done, she quickly extended her hand. "Daniel, how good to see you."

Never had she seen such an expression on a man's face. While she had never suffered any pretensions to beauty, she felt that if, at that moment, she'd caught a glimpse of herself in a glass, she might have been beautiful. The expression of simple adoration on Daniel's face would have made her so.

But there her observations stopped as she continued to find herself held in Daniel's relentless gaze.

"Unlike you both," he murmured, "I find no fault with you. Brown becomes you, as would every color in God's rainbow."

She lowered her head for a moment's respite from the intensity in his eyes. While what he had said was not particularly intimate, it had been spoken with great intimacy.

"Thank you, Daniel," she said, at last wresting her hand free. She must make every effort to restore his light mood, for his present one terrified her. "Now, as when we were children"—she smiled up at him—"it's reassuring to know that I can count on your kindness."

Then Edward joined them again, stepping between them, placing a hand on both their shoulders. "Come," he urged, "let's leave this place. We have a reunion to attend to. Our own." He drew them close for an instant, then released them as he inquired, "Your luggage? Is it with you?"

She shook her head and looked about. "The porter took it for me. I have no idea—" She strained to see over the crowds around her. But it was impossible. Instead of decreasing, the throngs seemed to have multiplied as curiosity seekers rushed in from Euston Square to stare at the black locomotive. The costermongers had followed them and were now selling pickles and onions and herring, the whole platform resembling a picnic.

"Then come," Edward urged. "I'll send John Murrey back while we wait in the carriage."

Predictably, Daniel objected. "I'll fetch it," he offered kindly. "You two go along and wait for me in the carriage. I'll only be a minute."

Then Edward was steering her through the crowds, his arm protectively about her. She looked up several times into his face and saw that strained quality again, saw a dampness of perspiration on his forehead. It was during one of these close observations that she noticed for the first time a slight wound on his forehead, the laceration scabbed over and clearly healing, half hidden beneath his hair. The realization that his blood had recently been spilled stirred her strangely. And when halfway down the long platform, he seemed to falter and wipe his hand across his sweating brow, she took the lead, shifting her portfolio to her other arm and with her free hand grasping his arm where, beneath his black jacket, she felt him trembling.

She could see his desperate attempt to compose himself as he looked about at the traffic. Then she glanced around and saw, about fifty yards away, a carriage with an old gentleman sitting atop, waving at them with his whip.

When still Edward seemed incapable of response, she turned him in the direction of the old man and hoped for the best. As they approached, the man smiled down as though in recognition. "Are you John Murrey?" she called up.

He nodded and grinned. As he climbed awkwardly down from his high perch, she released Edward's arm and watched, concerned, as he pulled himself weakly forward into the carriage. For a moment, her attention was splintered between the strange behavior of her brother and the grinning John Murrey.

"John Murrey, I am, Miss," he pronounced, bowing. "And you must be Mr. Eden's sister."

She nodded and was on the verge of saying more when suddenly her attention was drawn to Edward inside the carriage, his head fallen back against the cushions, something pressed against his mouth, a vial of some sort which he tasted with the tip of his tongue, then hurriedly restored to the pocket of his waistcoat.

The roar of the crowd sounded fainter here. As her concern for Edward increased, she looked back in the direction they had just passed, hoping to glimpse Daniel. Nothing. Now to John Murrey she said, "I'm afraid Mr. Eden is ill. We were to wait here for Mr. Spade, but perhaps we should—"

Quickly the old man cut in. "Oh, Mr. Eden isn't ill, Miss," he grinned broadly. "Just give him a minute to catch his breath and he'll be right enough. I'll go fetch Mr. Spade, and we'll be out of here in no time."

Without giving her an opportunity to protest, he held the carriage door for her and supported her arm as she climbed up the high step. Seated anxiously opposite Edward, she called after the old man, "Hurry, please—"

Then she was aware of Edward looking at her, his head still resting against the cushions. "Don't worry, Jennifer."

With a faint accusation in her voice, she scolded lightly, "You're ill. Why didn't you tell me?"

He began to sit up now, color returning to his face. "John's right," he said quietly. "Just give me a minute and I'll be right enough."

Half angry, she again scolded, "I'll be happy to give you all the minutes I have. But you're ill. That would be apparent to—"

He leaned forward and took her hand and lightly laughed. "Don't concern yourself, Jennifer. I'm fine. Look!" He held out both his hands as though to display to her his steady nerves.

"Then what happened?" she demanded. "You were quite undone a few minutes ago. I could feel you trembling."

He laughed and eased over to join her on her side. "That place is enough to make anyone tremble, wouldn't you say? Now, tell me everything about the railway ride. Was it terrifying? Do they make a tremendous amount of noise?" He leaned still closer, a fount of curiosity. "And tell me too about that dreadful school of yours? How long do you intend to waste your life in that barren region, teaching children to make music?"

As yet he had given her no opportunity to answer any of his questions, and still he rushed on, his eye falling on the portfolio of music resting on her lap. His face seemed to brighten. "Will you play for me, as you used to?" He leaned back suddenly against the cushions, his eyes closed. "Have I ever told you how rich your music made my youth? I can hear them still, the melodies pouring forth from that old pianoforte in the corner of the Great Hall." He shook his head, the pleasure of his recall extreme. "From the courtyard it always sounded as though a sprite of magical powers had been turned loose on the keyboard." He opened his eyes and smiled warmly at her. "But it was always you, sweet Jennifer." He leaned forward again, a look of intensity on his face. "You will play for me, won't you? Promise me that you will."

She watched and listened carefully. His face, which a few minutes earlier had resembled a death mask, now seemed alive with movement. In response to his plea, she said quietly, "According to Sophia, the old pianoforte collapsed, a victim of coastal dampness."

"Then we shall buy another," he proclaimed. "The finest in all of London. Tomorrow we shall purchase it. You shall select it and we'll transport it behind us in a special wagon all the way to Eden Point."

She laughed and shook her head as though at a generous child. "Then I shall play for you," she agreed, "as long and as often as you wish."

Pleased with her response, he again leaned back, his eyes closed as though already hearing music. "It will bring pleasure to us all, Mother as well. She always complains about the castle being so silent."

Then it was Jennifer's turn to look away out of the opposite window and maintain a guarded silence. "If only we didn't have to go home," she whispered.

She was aware of nothing until he took her hand. "Please try to be kind to her, Jennifer," he pleaded. "Her allotment of time is about up. She hasn't many years left."

She permitted him to take her hand but continued to gaze off into the distance where fog encircled the gaslamps. "I try always to be kind to her," she said. "I see no reason why I should alter my behavior."

She was aware of his taut silence, as though he too wanted to say more, but realized it would only lead to grief for both of them.

Gazing out opposite windows, though still connected by their clasped hands, they sat in silence, as though both needed time to absorb the buffeting of their emotions.

She moved into a safe arena. "And what do you think of James's engagement?" she asked, wondering if he shared her difficulty in trying to imagine their brother as a bridegroom.

He shrugged. "If it suits him," he muttered. "I don't know the lady. Do you?"

"I've met her, years ago at Francis Roberts's weekend party. She seemed pleasant enough, rather pretty, shy—"

As she struggled to describe Lady Harriet Powels, she was again aware of his close scrutiny. "And what of your own future?" he inquired softly. "Do you plan to spend the rest of your life in that Yorkshire purgatory?"

She ducked her head, mildly resentful of his criticism.

"It suits me well enough," she replied, an edge to her voice.

"How could it?" he demanded bluntly. "It's unnatural."

"Why unnatural?" she asked, facing him, her resentment increasing.

"Women locked up together?" He shook his head and repeated himself. "It's unnatural."

Feeling herself growing defensive, she retorted, "Nonsense. It's a pleasant existence. It provides me with a sense of service and the companionship of good, intelligent women. I sometimes think I would be perfectly content spending the rest of my life there."

He looked at her, appalled. "I would never permit it."

"And who are you to stop me?" she demanded, a sense of play still running between them, with the heavier tone muted in the background.

Before her determined face, he retreated slightly. "I wouldn't prevent it personally," he smiled. "I'd simply pay some good man to kidnap you and take you to his bed."

"Edward!" The shock in her voice was genuine. He'd never spoken of such matters to her before.

"Oh, not just any good man," he soothed, leaning closer, the side of his leg pressed firmly against hers. "There is one good man who would gladly lay down his life for you, a noble man who would give you children and a lifetime of loyalty, and—"

"Please, Edward," she whispered firmly. "I don't want to talk about it. Not now. Not ever." She tried to move a distance away, embarrassed by the intimate nature of his words.

He leaned closer, still pursuing. "Do you know who I'm talking about?" he asked.

Rigidly she shook her head. "I beg you, Edward," she pleaded.

But he pressed on. "Daniel," he said. "I'm speaking of Daniel."

"Leave me alone," she begged.

But he wouldn't. He slid opposite her, forcing her to look at him. In those close quarters she thought she saw anger in his face, was convinced of it when he demanded impatiently, "How long do you intend to keep him waiting? He has a right to know your feelings."

In desperation, she confronted him directly. "He knows my feelings," she cried. "I have never deceived him or led him to any degree of hope or expectation." As her voice rose, the stinging behind her eyes increased. "I have no feeling for him," she declared. "No affection save that of a good friend."

Apparently her words registered. "Poor Jennifer," he mourned. "I fear you have no affection for anyone, are capable of none so long as you maintain that death-line to Sophia Cranford."

Incapable of speech, she shook her head, begging him without words to cease. Seeing her tears, he leaned back, though still pitying her. "Oh, Jennifer," he said, "how lonely you must be, and how ready is the door out of your prison—"

"I am neither lonely nor imprisoned," she wept. "Now, please, I beg you, leave me be."

This time he obeyed, as settling back into the cushions, he maintained his silence, staring glumly out the window.

As she reached frantically inside the pocket of her cloak for a handkerchief, she tried to draw a deep breath. How warm had been their reunion and how quickly he had plunged her to the depths. She remembered how often Sophia Cranford had warned her away from Edward, condemning him in the same tones as she had condemned her mother, as corrupting influences, both capable of harm. And what had he meant by the "death-line" which attached her to Sophia, strong, pure Sophia, without whom she would never have survived her childhood?

She struggled for self-control. Abruptly she felt the carriage rocking. Raising her eyes to the window, she saw Daniel hoisting her trunk upward to unseen hands. She heard him shout, "Secure it tightly, John."

Hurriedly she passed the handkerchief over her face in a desperate attempt to look normal. Opposite her she was aware of Edward, sunk into a gloomy silence.

Then Daniel was pulling himself into the carriage, his face flushed with exertion, his spirits high and intact. "What a mob!" he gasped. "Was there anyone left in Leeds? I've never seen so many trunks and—"

Abruptly he fell silent, apparently assessing the tension within the carriage. She was aware of him looking from one side to the other. Then slowly he sat beside Edward, his hands clasped between his legs, the exhilaration on his face passing into blank bewilderment.

Still moved by her recent outburst, broken by grief over the cross-purposes which ran through her life, she turned rigidly away in the opposite direction, refusing to look at either of them.

As the carriage started forward, she felt Edward's boot lightly touching the toe of her shoe. Was the contact accidental? She stole a look in his direction and met his eyes and looked away.

Then quietly into the expanding silence, Edward spoke. "We've quarreled, Daniel," he said. "Within the first hour of our reunion, we've quarreled as though we still were children."

The rest of the ride was conducted in a palatable silence, both men seated opposite her, apparently recovering from the splintered beginning and she recovering as well, gazing out the window at clamorous London, both fascinated and frightened by it, recalling how she had explored it as a little girl with her father's enormous hand wrapped protectively about her own.

On thinking of the man she glanced back at Edward, saw him slumped down in the seat, his elbow resting on the arm support. He looked fatigued, as though their quarrel had drained him of vital resources. In an attempt to alter the bleak look, she asked quietly, "Do you think we'll have time to see the museums and galleries before we leave?"

Without lifting his head, he smiled at her. "We'll make time, all the time you wish."

For some reason, Daniel protested. "Not too much, Edward. Remember, the magistrate said—" Abruptly he stopped, a flush causing his face to redden. "What I mean to say is—" he faltered. "The Countess, your mother, expects you at a—"

"We'll be there," Edward said, cutting him off. "Did I tell you?" he went on, brightening. "Jennifer and I are going to purchase a pianoforte tomorrow and take it with us back to Eden Point. You'd better come with us."

Surprised, Jennifer listened closely. She had assumed that Daniel *was* coming with them. He had been Edward's shadow for as long as she could remember. "You're not coming, Daniel?" she inquired.

He shook his head, an expression of regret on his face. "Perhaps later. The school is burgeoning. I can't just walk away and leave it in the hands of the volunteers."

"Is it going well?" Jennifer asked now, remembering Daniel's Ragged School and his devotion to it.

"Very well," he smiled. "A few days ago we had distinguished visitors. Robert Owen and John Bright—"

He studied his hands as though modesty forbade him to speak openly. "They wanted to see the school," he said quietly. "Owen was particularly curious. He had a grand scheme to establish others throughout London."

"And they will be using yours as the model?" she asked, impressed.

He shrugged. "It seems as though it's a matter of funds. But, yes, if the money can be raised—"

From his slouched position at the window, Edward spoke softly. "Why on this green earth are you worrying about funds, Daniel? Tell your Mr. Owen to establish as many schools as he wishes. The funds will be there when he needs them."

She saw clearly the surprised though warm look of gratitude on Daniel's face. Then there was a brief cloud. "I can't ask you—"

Still without looking at him, Edward cut him off. "You haven't asked. I'm simply donating." She saw a new weariness on his face. "My purpose for living is vague," he said softly. "The size of my purse is not. Establish your schools, for God's sake. Do something about that."

As he bobbed his head out the window, Jennifer followed his gaze to the scene outside where half a dozen children could be seen huddled in an open doorway. In the faint light of the streetlamp, they sat in a pitiful arrangement, the oldest holding the youngest, their hollow eyes staring out at the passing carriage.

She was aware of Daniel staring too, leaning across to their window, his face clearly reflecting what he saw. "I'll send a volunteer back as soon as we get home," he promised. "They're probably abandoned."

Jennifer listened, grateful in a way that the grim young faces had now passed from her vision. "How many children do you care for now?" she asked.

He smiled and shook his head. "Close to seventy, I

would say." He sat eagerly up. "But you shall see for yourself," he promised. "We're about home."

Jennifer began to see familiar landmarks, Oxford Circus with its fine linen establishments, then Oxford Street, that old artery of the aristocracy now a muddle of shops. Then they were before the house which in the evening light looked even more dilapidated and out of sorts than she'd remembered it.

Daniel was out of the carriage first. She watched him as he swung upward, apparently to fetch the trunk. In the quiet night and after the cessation of horses hooves on cobblestone, she heard a distant piano in the rippling lively beat of a polka.

Opposite her, she saw Edward, his eyes fixed with peculiar intensity on the linen establishment directly across the way.

Then Daniel was at the carriage door and urging her to, "Come, it's dance night. You can see the brood for yourself. If you're interested, that is," he added quickly.

She was interested and said as much. She looked back at Edward, who had not moved. "Are you coming?"

With a start he looked at her as though she had summoned him back from a great distance. "Right behind you," he said. "Is that a dance I hear?" he smiled. "Come. If you've never seen tadpoles dancing, you're in for a treat."

He led the way up the steps with Jennifer and Daniel following. A bright lamp burned in the entry hall. To one side she saw a long bench, heaped with a confusion of toys: a rocking horse on his swaying platform with red nostrils, and simple building blocks, a small reproduction of a railway locomotive, a smaller trumpet, and an assortment of rag dolls, all bearing mute evidence of loving devotion.

The piano was louder here, the tempo and rhythm of a polka clearly audible. Then it was Daniel's turn to take the lead, and after he had deposited her trunk near the bench, he pushed open the double doors which led to the banqueting hall and stood back to permit her passage.

Slowly at first she approached. Then she saw a most remarkable scene. The enormous and over-grand room which in the past had known sedate formal dinners was now awhirl with children, the tables had been pushed

back against the walls, and in an uneven and slightly
ragged circle, the children, paired, their arms raised, were
engaged in a mad, spiraling polka. They all looked so
frail and budlike, many of the younger ones already in
their nightshirts, like tiny ghosts. Near the end of the
hall she saw an old pianoforte, clearly out of tune, but
being energetically played by a volunteer, her head, indeed
her whole body keeping time.

She noticed Daniel move away from them now toward
the far wall where two volunteers presided over a bowl
of punch and a platter of sugar cookies. He was saying
something to them, pointing back toward the door. A
moment later, the older woman nodded and quickly left
the room. Jennifer knew where she was going, back to
the doorway filled with abandoned children. It was her
guess that by the time the next polka night came around,
their numbers would be swelled by at least six.

Unable to take it all in at a glance, she looked first
one way, then the other. Near the far end of the circle,
she saw a young girl break out of the formation. Her eyes
appeared fixed on the front of the hall where they stood.
She was quite thin, clearly older than the rest, her pretty
hair brushed back and tied with a white ribbon. Still she
came toward them, her face hesitant, as though uncertain
of what she was doing. She seemed to be staring at Edward, who was grinning and bobbing his head in time to
the music.

The young girl was less than five feet away from him
when he saw her at last, a warm look of recognition on
his face as he opened his arms and invited her to, "Come,
Elizabeth. How pretty you look tonight."

As though she'd waited all her life for those simple
words, the young girl slipped beneath his arm. Jennifer
noticed her hand; it appeared scarred and mutilated. And
she watched, fascinated, as Edward lifted that hand to
his lips and kissed it. Smiling, he now drew the girl close
to Jennifer. "This is Elizabeth," he said. His voice moved
rapidly into a prouder tone as he said further, "The two
of us make it a habit of finding each other. I found her
first, and on several occasions she's returned the favor and
has found me."

Jennifer hadn't the slightest idea what he was talking
about. But apparently it didn't matter as a moment later

Edward completed the introduction. "And this is Jennifer, Elizabeth, my sister. She's a schoolteacher in far-off Yorks." The young girl only hurriedly bobbed her head, then immediately turned an adoring set of eyes back to Edward.

Now Jennifer saw her abruptly motion for him to bend his head to her. As he did so, she whispered something into his ear, some message that at first produced a horrified look, then a warm, hearty laugh.

"Why not?" he exclaimed. As he shook off his cloak and handed it to Jennifer, he laughed, "Stand by to pick up the pieces. This temptress is luring me into the madness of the dance."

As he approached the circle, the younger children squealed with delight at his presence. The volunteers broke into applause and the pianist at the end of the hall craned her neck about and, beaming, proceeded to play even louder, tempo increasing.

As Jennifer folded his cloak in her arms, she watched, laughing, as the young Elizabeth arranged Edward opposite her. He towered over her, yet seemed as compliant and agreeable as a puppet.

Jennifer saw without question that everyone in the crowded room was pleased by his participation, his head bending and bobbing, his long legs lifting, literally flying about the circle now. Still she watched the pretty heads as they swirled about her, the tempo increasing until she felt herself swept up in the excitement of the music.

Then she saw Daniel beside her, lifting Edward's cloak from her arms, taking her portfolio with it, his face close, challenging her. "Shall we show them how it's done?"

Instinctively she protested. "Oh no, Daniel, I couldn't—"

"Why not?"

"I've never danced the polka in my life," she gasped.

"Neither have I," he smiled. He bobbed his head toward the room where figures large and small passed them by in a blur. "I really don't think that expertise is required. Just a certain amount of nerve and a strong constitution—"

Again she tried to protest, but he'd hear none of it. Edward's voice came now in a shout as he passed them by. "Catch us if you can," he called out, lifting the young Elizabeth literally off her feet.

"Come on," Daniel urged. "Let's behave like children. Perhaps it's safer that way."

She glanced up at him, amazed at the ability of his thoughts to follow hers. Then with a shake of her head, as though she knew that resistance was useless, she removed her bonnet and cloak and gloves and stood before him. "I'm afraid you'll have to support me the full distance. I am a true novice."

For just a moment she saw a look of extreme gratitude in his face, as though she had just expressed his fondest desire. Before she could catch her breath and long before she was ready for it, she found herself approaching the circle, Daniel's arm about her waist, their hands uplifted, a look of studious intensity in his eyes as he counted off the beats. Then he lifted her and whirled her into the circle, the room and all aspects of it blurring about her as the tempo filled her head, her feet returning to the floor long enough to execute the steps, then whirling again, her head thrown backward as she clung to him, both of them laughing now, the children urging her on with shouts, Daniel's face always before her, his strong arms guiding her through the simple maneuvers, the world and everything in it suddenly gone beautifully topsy-turvy as they defied gravity, defied old fears and new anxieties, defied everything save the madly mounting rhythm of the polka.

For Jennifer, the sensation was akin to a starving man who has grown accustomed to sustaining himself on a crust. Now she had a whole loaf and she gorged on it.

With her head thrown back, her mouth half opened, she prayed that it would never end, the color, the warmth, the music, the laughter.

Eden Castle
North Devon
Late June, 1836

For the Countess Dowager, it had been a day of welcoming. First, her half sister, Jane, had arrived about noon, looking painfully old and worn after the ordeal of William Pitch's death. Marianne had sent her directly to the guest chambers on the second floor and had instructed Mrs. Greenbell to stay with her.

Throughout the afternoon, while Jane recovered from the rigorous journey from London, Marianne had kept a constant vigil on the gate, expecting Edward and Jennifer. But as yet they had not appeared.

Now at dusk, she stood at the top of the steps of the Great Hall, eyeing the small but elegant crimson and gilt carriage just turning into the gate. One of the watchmen, stationed a distance across the moors, had ridden ahead and had informed her as to the identity of the passenger.

Sir Claudius Potter.

She closed her eyes in a brief attempt to rest them and, unseeing, smoothed down her black silk gown. Still in mourning for William, she had vowed to wear black for six weeks. Of course she would alter her wardrobe for the evening of James's engagement party, but the rest of the time, it would be black to match her heart.

191

At the carriage's rattling approach, she opened her eyes. The sun was setting. The dying day enveloped the old castle in a purple mist which was wafted in and out by the head winds off the channel. The stewards had not yet lit the torches. She wished they would. Perhaps the glowing fires would help to alter the gloom of evening. In a very real way she was tired of being sad.

Now at last the carriage door was beginning to open. She caught a glimpse of the man himself, pretentiously groomed in the latest fashion.

"Sir Claudius," she murmured, extending her hand to the man who knew her family's affairs as intimately as though they were his own.

Still engrossed in straightening himself, he gave a final tug to the blue waistcoat, removed his hat, bowed low, and took her hand. "Lady Eden," he smiled, pressing her hand to his lips.

His kiss left a disagreeable dampness. She resisted the urge to brush it away and instead said, "Welcome to Eden Castle. It's been far too long since you've graced us with your presence."

The man's pink cherubic face glowed under the sentiment. "Milady," he murmured, "if the choice were mine, I would close my London chambers and pitch a small tent outside that gate, there to bask in the sunlight of your presence."

Merciful heavens, she thought, trying to cancel the smile before it erupted on her face. He'd grown even more fulsome with age. "Come," she urged, hoping to dilute the formalities of their greeting. "You must be very tired from the journey. Your customary chambers are waiting. After a sound night's sleep, I shall look forward to hearing all about London—"

But his protest was quick. "Oh no, milady. It's the shank of the evening for me. I made an easy trip of it, stopping overnight in Exeter, taking advantage of the opportunity to confer in person with our land agent."

He stepped closer. "With your permission, milady, I would beg a private session with you tonight. There are matters of which you should be apprised. Only a brief audience," he smiled, "for all our sakes."

Apparently she had no choice. As she took his arm to mount the stairs, he saw James just coming from the Great

Hall. Close behind him followed Caleb and Sophia Cranford. Marianne stood to one side as James greeted the old solicitor, a greeting of undue extravagance, she thought, as he earnestly inquired about everything, the journey, the condition of the turnpike, the health of ailing King William, the uncertainty of the next monarch. She'd never seen him so garrulous.

"Surely the crown will not be placed on the dubious head of the young princess," he protested, leading the man upward, clearly ignoring Marianne where she stood on the stairs. "I would suggest a regent as the wisest course of action, don't you agree?"

At the top of the stairs, Marianne saw the Cranfords. Then apparently James saw them as well, and Marianne watched as he led Sir Claudius to where the brother and sister stood. "Sir Claudius," James began, "I'm certain you remember Mr. and Miss Cranford."

Apparently Sir Claudius did remember them. Marianne couldn't hear their exchange, had little desire to hear it. Instead she let her attention run in the opposite direction, toward the castle gate, still half searching for Edward and Jennifer.

"Mother, are you well?" In some embarrassment she looked quickly back, saw James beside her, the others waiting at the top of the stairs looking down.

"I'm quite well," she said lightly. "Just waiting for Sir Claudius."

"I'm ready, Marianne," he called down with a familiarity which normally would have displeased her, but now, in Sophia's presence, she permitted it, even enjoyed it.

At the top of the stairs, as she took Sir Claudius's arm, she gave Sophia a clear command. "We will be in the small library off the Great Hall," she smiled. "A bottle of sherry would be nice. Then no more interruptions."

Normally she did not permit her voice to assume such a master-servant tone when dealing with any of the staff. Now, however, she relished it and watched, amazed, as the woman withdrew the ever-present leather notebook and made a note of some sort.

Marianne laughed. "Oh, surely, Sophia, you can remember a single bottle of sherry."

The woman gazed evenly back at her. "Since I'm held

accountable for the inventory, milady, I find it helpful to keep careful books."

"I'm sure you do," Marianne murmured. As she glanced ahead through the Great Hall, she saw Mrs. Greenbell entering the room. It then occurred to her that if she were sequestered with Sir Claudius for a period of time, she would be unable to keep an eye out for Edward. And since she did not trust any of her present company, James included, she decided to appoint Mrs. Greenbell to a position of lookout.

"Excuse me, please," she murmured to Sir Claudius. "I'll only be a moment—"

Abandoning him momentarily to the company of James and the Cranfords, she signaled Mrs. Greenbell and met her in the center of the large room.

"I apologize for a request," she said, in advance, approaching the woman and placing her hand affectionately on Mrs. Greenbell's arm.

Mrs. Greenbell dismissed the apology with the warmest of smiles. "I'm here to serve you, milady," she said. "Busy days ahead."

Marianne nodded. "And Jane, how is she? I had hoped to join her this evening, if she's up to it, that is."

Sympathetically, Mrs. Greenbell shook her head. "She dozed briefly this afternoon. I took tea with her. She's still very much in mourning."

"As we all are."

For a moment both women stood with their heads down. From the doorway, Marianne heard laughter. It seemed such an odd sound, she looked up. Sir Claudius apparently was getting on very well with the Cranfords, the four of them, including James, in a close, intimate huddle.

Mrs. Greenbell followed the direction of her gaze and now commented, beneath her breath, "I see 'the necessary evil' has arrived."

Marianne smiled. Obviously Thomas's epithet for the man was common knowledge.

Mrs. Greenbell withdrew a handkerchief from her sleeve and pressed it lightly against her mouth as though to conceal her words. "They seem to be getting on very well," she murmured. "I would have thought that everything had been said in their endless correspondence."

Marianne looked up, surprised. "Whose correspondence?" she demanded. "James and Sir Claudius?"

But Mrs. Greenbell shook her head and faced in the opposite direction as though to speak with greater ease. "The Cranfords and Sir Claudius."

Marianne stared at the woman. "I—I don't understand. Why would they have occasion to—"

"Heaven only knows," Mrs. Greenbell interrupted. "But the letters fly back and forth every month, sometimes twice a month. I take them to the gate and receive them as well."

Bewildered by this new information, Marianne again glanced back toward the group standing in the doorway.

"I still don't understand," she murmured again.

"I didn't mean to upset you, milady," Mrs. Greenbell whispered. "For some reason, I thought you knew about—"

"No, I knew nothing," Marianne replied quickly, her eyes and voice level as she stared toward the door.

Then Mrs. Greenbell was there, summoning Marianne's attention back. "You had a request, milady. I don't mean to rush you, but I promised Miss Locke I'd walk with her this evening."

Concerned, Marianne brought her attention back. "Is that safe? I mean, is she—"

Mrs. Greenbell nodded. "I think a walk-about would do her good. She's been complaining of cramps in her legs, from the confinement of the journey, I'm sure." She folded her handkerchief and returned it to her sleeve. "She was hoping that you might join us."

With resolution, Marianne nodded. "And I shall, as soon as I can rid myself of that—" With an expression on her face which disguised nothing, she glanced again toward the group in the doorway. "Sir Claudius has requested a brief meeting, business undoubtedly."

She drew herself up as though for an ordeal. "I'll meet with him in the small library. You go ahead and help Jane to the courtyard. What I wanted was for you to keep your eyes open for Edward. When he arrives, I want to be notified immediately."

Mrs. Greenbell looked doubtful. "Do you think they will arrive this late, milady?"

Marianne shrugged. "I've not heard myself. It seems as though Jennifer wrote to Sophia—"

Again both women fell silent, their mutual hate for the woman binding them together.

As Marianne moved a step away, Mrs. Greenbell called softly after her, "Be careful, milady. They are masters at achieving their ends."

Marianne looked back. "So am I," she smiled. "I intend to be nothing but abundantly civil," she added. "Now go and walk with Jane if you will. Tell her where I am presently engaged, and that I'll join her later. And tell me immediately when Edward arrives."

Mrs. Greenbell nodded to all the orders. As the two women parted, Marianne tried to still the anger which washed over her. She had not realized that she would have to spend her last years locked in mortal combat with the daughter of a Yorkshire preacher.

On this grim thought she made her way slowly back to the still-chattering group, Sir Claudius holding forth again, patting his paunch beneath the peacock-blue waistcoat as though describing a memorable meal. Marianne approached the group and to her mortification was kept standing on the periphery until Sir Claudius had completed the tale of the moment.

Then, strangely, it was Sophia who recognized her first, with warmth and deference, as though after thirty years she still had not perceived Marianne's intense dislike of her. "Milady," she smiled. "Is all well with Mrs. Greenbell? Is there any way in which I can ease her duties? She hasn't been looking at all well of late. I have begged her to let me take some of her responsibilities onto my own shoulders, but—"

James spoke in an affectionate protest. "Do more, Sophia?" he exclaimed. "Impossible. You perform the duties of ten women now. I forbid you to do more. We have your own health to consider."

In just barely concealed disgust, Marianne ignored the woman as well as James. "I believe you wanted a private conference, Sir Claudius," she said, smiling. "Are you still desirous of such a meeting, or has this good company distracted you?"

Sir Claudius protested, "Oh no, milady," he smiled, taking her arm. "We must talk, I'm afraid."

Then the Cranfords and James were moving away.

James called back, "We want to hear more about the hunt in the morning, Sir Claudius. You tell a fine story—"

And Sophia bowed low. "I'll send the sherry along, milady. One glass or two? You do not generally take spirits so late in the evening."

"Two," Marianne replied, eyeing the woman as though she were a devouring flame.

When the three had disappeared down the corridor, Marianne turned back to Sir Claudius, appalled to find a look of admiration on his face. "A remarkable woman," he said, keeping his voice low. "It always fascinates me to see how, on occasion, the middle classes can produce a gem."

Belatedly he was aware that he'd said the wrong thing. "My apologies, milady," he murmured. "A witless statement for this egalitarian age. Human superiority knows no boundaries, nor should know none. All of England has had your very precise example to remind us of that truth."

In spite of his overflattering words, Marianne bowed her head. How long it had been since she'd had to defend herself for who she was and where she had come from. Lifting her head, she smiled, a bit too sweetly. "As human superiority recognizes no class structure, Sir Claudius, neither does human rascality. And England has sufficient examples to remind her of *that* truth as well."

With the air cleared, she led the way across the Great Hall to the small library which in earlier days had served as a minor reception room. As Sophia Cranford had "done over" the large library some years back, in the process rendering that once inviting room almost uninhabitable with its stiff horse-hair furnishings, potted palms, and high unreachable walls of books, Thomas had insisted that the small reception room be converted to a welcoming den with a few select and well-thumbed volumes about him.

This had been done, and over the years it had become Marianne's favorite room as well. Now before the handsome carved oak doors, Marianne stopped and waited patiently, head down, for Sir Claudius to open them for her.

At the center of the room, she stopped and said quickly, "Please have a seat, Sir Claudius. With your kind permission, I believe I will stand."

He nodded, and settled rather stiffly into a green velvet settee on the other side of the fireplace. Marianne stood with her back to the dead fire, feeling that it was a good

position, the portrait of the young Lady Eden at the height
of her beauty and power hovering over the old Lady Eden,
certainly now less beautiful and less powerful.

"You had business," she said, when at last they were
arranged.

He nodded. "But first—" He sat up straight on the settee
and commenced to fumble inside the blue waistcoat pocket.
"A small gift," he smiled, producing at last a black velvet
case.

She'd not expected this and was in no way prepared for
a response. Genuinely flustered, she could only murmur, "I
don't understand, Sir Claudius—"

But he dismissed her confusion. "What's to understand?
I had occasion, not too long ago, to be in Roger Mayboles'
and I saw it and thought how greatly you would enhance
its already considerable beauty."

He smiled. "Mind you, it isn't of the same caliber as
Lord Eden's many gifts to you from Roger's establishment,
but it is antique, certifiably sixteenth century, according to
Roger, Florentine, I believe he said."

Confused, yet touched, Marianne took the small case and
opened it. There on a bed of white satin was a pearl ring,
exquisitely designed, a filigree of gold petals, a water lily
image, the modest though perfect pearl forming the center
of the blossom.

"It's lovely," she murmured, lifting the ring from its case
and slipping it on her third finger, right hand. "A perfect
fit," she exclaimed, holding out her hand. "Look!"

Sir Claudius bobbed his head. "Considering the number
of excursions I've made in the past to Roger Maybole's on
behalf of Lord Eden, I would be remiss not to remember
the exact dimensions of your lovely fingers, your wrists,
your neck—"

There was a strange intensity in his voice and manner
now as he took her hand and drew her close, on the pretense of studying the ring. "I knew it," he smiled. "It rests
there as though it had been created for that dear hand."

Before she could protest, he tightly enclosed her hand in
his own. She felt his palms, damp and sweating, and
watched, helpless, as he lifted her hand and pressed it to
his lips.

When the kiss stretched on, longer than necessary, she
tried gently to withdraw her hand. "I thank you for your

thoughtfulness, Sir Claudius," she smiled, "and I shall always feel a fondness for the ring, and each time I look at it, I shall remember the generous giver, my husband's loyal friend."

After a brief and unsettling struggle, she retrieved her hand. He appeared to be looking at her now with great cow eyes. Bewildered by his gift as well as his attitude, she went to the window seat, feeling the need to increase the distance between them and wanting only to get on with the purpose of the meeting.

Feeling certain that he would take his cue from her, she was therefore surprised when he merely followed after her and sat close beside her, his manner still intimate and growing more so. "It has been my experience," he began, his voice low, almost breathless, "that separation by death of a loved one only increases our craving for affection."

She moved farther down the window seat. "The days pass rapidly," she said lightly. "Actually I'm kept so busy, I'm scarcely aware of loneliness."

"But it's still there, isn't it?" he persisted, his arms slipping behind her. "How do you view me?" he asked.

"As a loyal and trusted friend," she pronounced firmly. "Nothing more, I'm afraid."

But his romantic inclination seemed only to feed on her denial. "I don't believe that," he whispered. "We've gone through too much together for you not to feel—"

"I assure you, Sir Claudius," she said, forcefully, "I speak the truth." She felt a burning blush on her face, mingled with a strange surge of pride. She thought she'd fought off her last seducer years ago, Lord Sedgeworth, it had been, who'd tried to corner her in the solarium of his country house in Kent. She'd been quite skillful then at leading them on, then abruptly turning them around. Thomas had never approved of her little flirtations, but she'd always known they were innocent, so what was the harm?

However, she'd flirted in no way with Sir Claudius, had never in her wildest dreams viewed the pompous little man as anything but the family solicitor, who with great regularity increased the size of his fee. "Sir Claudius, I beg you," she pleaded now. "Release me or I'm afraid we both shall make fools of ourselves."

She caught only a glimpse of his reddened face, then at

that moment, behind her, she heard a soft knock on the door. Struggling to restore herself, she opened the door quickly, grateful to whoever it was on the other side.

"Your sherry, milady," Sophia announced after a discreet pause, as though those eagle eyes were assessing the tension in the small room. "Shall I pour?"

Without looking at her, Marianne murmured, "No, thank you. We'll manage—"

There was another pause, then she heard Sophia leave the room, heard the door close and did not at first hear retreating footsteps, as though she were lingering in the hope of hearing something.

In an attempt to give the woman nothing on which she could feed, Marianne turned to face the solemn-looking little man still sitting in a state of abandonment on the window seat. "May I serve you, Sir Claudius?" she asked lightly, as though nothing at all had transpired between them.

But the man shook his head and withdrew a lace handkerchief from his waistcoat and delicately patted his forehead.

Despite his negative response, Marianne poured a small glass of amber sherry and carried it to him. In order to speak softly, in fear that Sophia might be outside the door listening, she had to decrease the distance between them. "Here, drink," she urged tenderly. As the pitiful little man accepted the glass, she took his handkerchief from him and kindly patted his brow. "Dear Sir Claudius," she began, "you are one of my dearest and mose respected associates. You have never been anything less, and—" She paused for emphasis, then sortly added, "And you will never be anything more."

To blunt the directness of her last statement, she sat beside him. "Words cannot express how important you are to me and my family. You know our affairs as intimately as we know them, and what a terrible hindrance it would be if you withdrew your support." Again she hesitated, then went on. "As for my affection, and any craving I might experience, both, I fear, were buried with Thomas." She smiled and lightly tucked his handkerchief back into his pocket. "Now it's merely a memory, providing me with neither comfort nor torment." Her speech over, she concluded gently, "Do you understand?"

Harshly he laughed, as though to rebuke her. "Madam, I have no idea what prompted that curious outburst. I simply made you a gift of a modest ring, nothing more. I hope you did not misinterpret it as some declaration of lasting love."

Amazed, she stared up at him as he paced now before the fireplace, impressed as always by the ability of the male ego to deceive itself. Well, no matter. At least she'd put him off. Let him assume whatever defense he needed to get on with the dreary encounter and end it as soon as possible.

On that hope, she stood, assuming an air as businesslike as his own. "Then the subject at hand," she began, "if you will—"

"The subject at hand, madam," he began, his voice without margin, "is you and your somewhat disintegrating family."

She moved directly into the onslaught, with only the table between them. "I don't understand, Sir Claudius—"

"The fact is, madam," he began, only briefly glancing at her, "your elder, illegitimate, son is slowly destroying the Eden estates, valuable property which has been carefully amassed over the last six hundred years by a long line of noblemen who were dedicated to the realm and who served England well; all that is being systematically obliterated by one errant bastard who consorts with pimps and whores while the present Lord Eden is forced to occupy a position scarcely above pauper with his hand outstretched like a beggar for whatever pittance Edward chooses to drop in it. The situation has always been intolerable, madam, but now, with James approaching the honorable state of matrimony, he insists and I agree with him that he will tolerate it no longer."

As he paused for breath, she tried to clear her head of the barrage of offensive words. Never had she heard him refer openly to Edward as a bastard, in fact all his words had been alarmingly naked, as though he cared not at all for her feelings.

Strangely, his cruelty made her feel resilient. "Do go on, Sir Claudius," she invited politely.

And he did, with enthusiasm. "Then steps must be taken to alter the arrangement immediately," he said. "I'm kept well informed of the books of Eden Castle. Each year, in spite of Miss Cranford's superior juggling act, you slip deeper and deeper into debt. Were you aware of that condition, madam?"

"I knew the annual income was limited and limiting, but I thought—"

"According to my sources," he went on, interrupting, "you pay little or no attention to the business of the estates."

"I am not apprised of—"

"You should make it your business to be apprised of everything."

"Thomas always—"

"Lord Eden is dead," he said with what seemed unnecessary cruelty.

For the first time, she retreated, a fatal mistake. Sir Claudius saw her weakness and moved to exploit it. "Now," he went on with clear relish, following after her to the window seat where she'd sat wearily, head down. "Let me apprise you," he said, filling the word with sarcasm, "of your elder son's recent activities and see if you find him competent to control such a vast pool of wealth."

As he began to talk, he commenced pacing again, as though deriving both energy and pleasure from what he was saying. "He sells monthly, yes he does," he declared, "on occasion coming to my private chambers himself, foul-smelling, frequently in the company of his street friends, demanding, arrogant, ordering me about as though I were little more than a common lackey. And when he isn't selling land, he passes time either with his radical friend, Spade, who is slowly bilking him of all profits from the sales. Or he busily occupies himself with tavern brawls so he can get arrested and thrown into Newgate." He shook his head as though freshly shocked. "Twice, frequently three times in the course of a single month, my clerk is forced to pay his bond. And that expense too comes out of the estate."

She continued to listen, hearing nothing that she did not know, but finding it worse coming from Sir Claudius's condemning lips.

"But all of this, madam, is merely prelude to his last offense, the result of his involvement in the adultery case with the Longford woman." He stepped closer. "I don't think you realize how much you are in my debt concerning the successful outcome of that trial."

Successful? Marianne looked up. "I read that the young woman had died as a result of her ordeal."

"A fitting end," Sir Claudius nodded. "But in case you failed to notice, Edward's name was kept clear of it, through my efforts and my efforts alone. If the fool had had his way, he would have leapt forward and admitted complete involvement in the matter."

"Was he—involved?" she asked warily.

"Of course he was," Sir Claudius snapped. "Involved from the beginning in every way. And further, that once elegant domicile on Oxford Street has now been stripped and serves as a watering hole for every radical leader in London. They meet surreptitiously, but don't think I don't know about it."

"I thought it was a school," she protested.

"A front, madam, I assure you, merely a front." He lifted his face as though on a note of pride. "I have eyes and ears, good ones, I might add. My own as well as others'. The list of men passing in and out of those doors could one day spell ruination for this England, as we know it."

"Go on, Sir Claudius," she said. "But not about Daniel Spade and his activities, I beg you. I have no authority there, let alone influence. Tell me of my son."

"The two are inseparable, madam, both in body and philosophy. Mr. Spade manipulates Edward as though he were a master puppeteer."

She sat up, her anger increasing. "I find that hard to believe—"

"What would you say, madam, to attempted murder?"

She looked up. "I don't understand—"

He seemed eager to inform her. "The last time I was summoned to Newgate, less than a week ago, Edward had been charged with attempted murder."

"Why?" she begged. "Surely it was a false charge. Edward is incapable of—"

"Was," he corrected her. "I saw his handiwork for myself. The night warden suffered a heavily damaged throat. He could scarcely talk."

"Then there had to be a reason—"

"None," Sir Claudius cut in. "The warden had treated

him with extreme kindness, had broken all rules to permit him passage to the Longford woman's cell. You see, it was the night before the sentence was to be carried out. I suppose he had some foolish notion of helping her to escape. It wasn't necessary. The woman was dead. He was apprehended himself, imprisoned for the duration of the night. Then only because of my close professional relationship with the magistrate and a sizable bribe was I able to get the charges dropped, on one condition, that he leave London immediately and stay away for a period of several months. Now, I ask you, madam, where is he?"

"Edward?" she asked vaguely.

"Yes, Edward," he snapped. "He should have been here days ago. But James tells me he has not as yet—"

"No, he hasn't arrived," she murmured, "though I expect him any—"

"The magistrate's conditions were clear. He was to leave London immediately."

"Please, Sir Claudius," she murmured, "I cannot answer for him. You must ask him yourself."

"As I intend to," the old man replied. "It was on the strength of my reputation that he enjoys his present freedom. He may do what he likes with his own reputation, what is left of it. But he is in my debt now."

Marianne turned away to the closed window behind her and tried to push it open. Apparently it was stuck. She felt a need for air, a good strong ocean gale to cleanse the small room of the despicable man and his words. He couldn't help but see her struggle, yet made no move to assist her.

Instead he said sternly, "Then we have no choice but to wait for Edward, that is, if he comes at all."

She turned back from her futile efforts with the window, relieved that she had something positive to say, "Oh, he'll come, Sir Claudius, I can assure you of that."

"You've had word?"

Her confidence was short-lived. "No, but—"

"Then how can you be so sure?"

"Jennifer," she said. "Miss Cranford had word from Jennifer. She's coming with Edward."

The confession that she received word of her children through someone else seemed to increase his pleasure. In a tone of mock consideration, he suggested, "Well, let's leave the dreary subjects behind and discuss the sweeter ones. Is all in order for the coming festivities?"

For a moment, she had to turn her mind forcibly to the question. Then she remembered. "Lord and Lady Powels," she murmured.

"Yes," he beamed. "What a happy union that will be, two of the great houses of England united."

She remembered James's less than convincing avowal of love. "Perhaps we shouldn't push," she suggested. "It can only lead to unhappiness for—"

"But I don't understand, milady," he demanded. "According to James, it was quite settled." He moved back to where she sat. "Not an hour ago, James himself told me that first banns would be published next month."

She looked up at him and felt stupid and out of touch. "He's never told me that—" she began.

Sir Claudius's bewildered anger increased. "And what, pray tell, madam, did you think was the purpose of these festivities?"

She shook her head, her distress increasing. "I've—never met the young woman," she stammered. "I merely thought that I was—"

"And does that mean that you have not spoken to her parents?"

"We've corresponded, yes."

"On what matter?"

"On a variety of matters."

"Dowry included?"

She lowered her head. "No," she murmured. "It seemed —premature—"

Apparently shocked, Sir Claudius stepped back. "Great heavens, lady. In your younger days, you had a mind. Now, what's become of it? You are allowing Lord and Lady Powels to travel all this distance without a specific commitment?"

She felt exhausted under the ceaseless torrent of words. "I did not feel that it was my place to speak of commitments."

Still he continued to stare down on her as though she were a lesser creature. The anger which she'd detected earlier softened into a kind of brutal condescension. "Not to worry, madam," he soothed. "How unfair of us to expect you to know the ins and outs of these arrangements. I really had no idea how well Lord Eden managed for you."

Her deep resentment was still there and growing, but she simply lacked the will to express it. Before his offensive words she turned again to the closed window and contented herself with staring out into the darkened garden. She listened, struggling to hold back tears of rage.

"It's quite out of the ordinary," he was saying now, "but I will speak with the Powelses when they arrive. I'm quite certain they have been expecting a discussion of dowry and will therefore in every way be prepared for it. If you wish, madam, I'll handle everything."

She wondered if he was consciously aware of his attempt to hurt her. At this point she had ceased to care. He was right in one quarter. Thomas had covered for her, lovingly hiding all the unpolished and unknowledgeable edges. She might have married aristocracy, but she was still a fisherman's daughter.

Now she said, "Do what you like, Sir Claudius. You will anyway. You need no permission from me." She could not abide his closeness a moment longer. "Then if that's all, Sir Claudius, I beg you to excuse me. I have my sister with me, whom I've neglected long enough."

He sat alone on the window seat. "Ah, yes, Miss Locke," he pronounced, his lips mincing the name, as though to imply the weight of shame behind it. "She must be quite aged now."

"And in excellent health," Marianne smiled. "We Lockes seem to possess the gift of longevity. Now again, if you'll excuse me—"

But he didn't. "There is one more item of business, madam," he said.

She gave him an agonized look. "I can't imagine what we have failed to discuss," she said.

"The future, madam," he smiled, "merely the future and all that it entails."

"Then be quick, Sir Claudius," she commanded. "It's late and I'm very tired."

"As we both are," he concurred. "It's simply this. While neither of your sons, madam, has made a habit of communicating with you, one, at least, has taken me into his confidence and sought my advice."

"And that would be James, of course," she said.

"Yes, James," he confirmed. "I shall now apprise you of our plan. We shall see the festivities through to their hopefully successful conclusion," he began, "resulting in the engagement of Lord James Eden and Lady Harriet Powels. There will be a Christmas wedding, then next spring, Lord Eden has proposed a simple lawsuit."

She straightened up from leaning against the table.

"There will be no lawsuit, Sir Claudius," she said, on diminished breath. "Not while I live. And I warn you further, Sir Claudius, that if you attempt such a matter, I will use all the power at my disposal, which is considerable, not only to block your efforts, but in the process to discredit you as well."

She moved still closer. "I am not without friends in high places, as you so well know, men of prominence who knew and respected my husband. If you attempt a lawsuit, I will not only attend the hearing, I will speak out fully and without restraint. Whatever alliances you may have formed with certain people in my household, they should not be seriously considered, for the fact remains, it *is* my household. *They* are here because of my indulgence and my generosity. Consider that as well."

He was retreating. "I will never understand you, milady," he muttered, pushing open the door.

"I'm not yours to understand," she replied quietly. "As my solicitor, your only responsibility to me is obedience."

It was a bit harsh, but seemed to her only partial payment for his earlier humiliation of her.

But still he would not totally give in. "The hour is late, madam. We'll discuss it further when we both are in a more rational state of mind."

With a smile which bordered on the impertinent, she said, "I'm as rational as you'll ever find me, Sir Claudius." Through the opened door, she could see across the expanse of the Great Hall to the far corridor, dimly lit. Though her eyesight was weak, she could just make out the black, spidery figure of Caleb Cranford.

"I think we've said all we need to say," she concluded, turning away at last. "We both have people waiting for us. I shall look forward to seeing you at breakfast. Perhaps a morning ride would be nice. The headlands are lovely this time of year, green with June ripeness, and—"

As she looked back, she did not bother to complete her

sentence. He was gone, the doorway empty, the man himself moving rapidly across the Great Hall in a steady line toward the far corridor and the shadowy figure.

Normally she would not abide such rudeness. But she was so relieved to be rid of his presence that she went to the door and slammed it after him and stood alone in the small room, her mind struggling to assimilate all aspects of the dreadful encounter.

Attempted murder. Not Edward. He was incapable of such an act. Surely there were extenuating circumstances which Sir Claudius either was not privy to, or had simply chosen not to reveal to her.

Suddenly she felt the ring on her finger and looked down as though seeing it for the first time. As she remembered the sensation of his kiss, she rapidly stripped the ring from her finger and hurled it across the room. It disappeared into the cushions of the window seat.

London
Late June, 1836

Edward was in no rush to leave London. In spite of
the splintered beginnings of his reunion with Jennifer, he
had thoroughly enjoyed the last few days with her, the
two of them exploring London, three of them really, for
Daniel accompanied them whenever his responsibilities at
the school permitted. The hours had passed quickly and
pleasantly as Edward was becoming quite skillful in administering to himself the necessary dosage of laudanum,
the precious elixir providing him with a calmness of spirit
he had not felt since he was a boy.

Then the pinnacle yesterday, when the three of them had
gone to Masson's and purchased their finest pianoforte, a
wonder with rosewood case and inlaid ivory filigree. How
Jennifer had protested the expense even as her eyes had
shone with unprecedented light.

Now at dusk he was packed, their trunks already loaded
upon the carriage, awaiting the arrival of the pianoforte
from Masson, who'd expressed great concern that his handsome instrument would immediately be put through such
a tortuous journey. Nothing would do but that a special
wagon be hired to transport it.

209

No matter. It was a pleasant delay, a convenient post-ponement of the dreaded trip to North Devon.

As Edward waited in his second-floor chambers, he heard only the street sounds below and the distant laughter of the children in the back garden. Their common room, the ban-queting hall, had been usurped by Daniel for some sort of meeting with his friends. Jennifer was packed and in the back garden, passing the time with the volunteers and the children, her habit of schoolmistress too strong to break.

Directly beneath him, he saw a small black cab pull up to the pavement, saw three gentlemen alight and hurry beneath the eaves of the house. There had been a steady parade of men for the last half an hour entering the doors of his house.

It was none of his concern. Too often in the past, Daniel had tried to involve him in his zealous activities. And while he appreciated the nature and cause of good works, he could not in all honesty share Daniel's zeal.

Then suddenly, he heard the rattling approach of a large conveyance, not a cab again, surely. Quickly he leaned forward. Not the wagon from Masson's either, but a large private carriage into which were packed at least eight men who now, one by one, were alighting, common men as well as he could tell, scarcely able to hire such elaborate equippage.

Curious, he leaned closer as the men continued to emerge from the carriage, four, five, six, stepping down, workmen in moleskin and loosely fitted smocks, followed at last by a well-turned-out gentleman in top hat and cape, a huge man who towered over the others and who now seemed to be herding them toward the door.

Stirred to interest in spite of himself, and bored with the silent waiting, Edward held his position by the window until the top hat had disappeared beneath the eaves. Then he hurried to the door and opened it a crack. Below in the entrance hall, he heard a swell of male voices, Daniel's predominant among them as apparently he gave the large party the warmest of greetings.

There was heavy shuffling, the sound of boots moving across the floor, then the banqueting hall door was closed and Edward was left in silence, struggling to digest his curiosity.

By his estimate there must be close to fifty men in his

banqueting hall, all of whom apparently had been awaiting the arrival of the six laborers and the giant man in the top hat.

From behind the closed door, he heard the sound of muted applause. His curiosity vaulted. If he was careful he could slip in without being seen. John Murrey could inform him of the arrival of the wagon from Masson's. Jennifer was ready and at present well occupied. It might be interesting to see and hear Daniel's friends.

On that note of resolve, he reached for his cloak and drew it about his shoulders, feeling it would give him a certain disguise as though he'd come in from the street. Outside the closed banqueting hall door, he paused, listening. A man's voice, not Daniel's, was holding forth. Quietly he pushed the door open and slipped inside.

Quietly Edward joined those standing at the rear of the hall. Fortunately no one took notice of him and he was free to blend his attention with theirs, observing first the peculiar mix of the audience, some fairly well dressed, like clerks or scribblers from Fleet Street, others clearly of the lower classes, their crushed hats clutched in their hands, but all turned toward the head table and the man speaking, the giant with red hair saying something about the uniqueness of the gathering.

"—for the first time, pulling together," he shouted in an eloquent, clearly well-trained voice, "our past differences forgotten under the weight of injustice measured out to these men." He gestured broadly to the six men seated to one side. As one, they self-consciously lowered their heads.

As for the dramatic speaker, Edward felt recognition dawning. He'd seen him before, his likeness on posters, advertising radical reform. Unless he missed his guess, this was Feargus O'Conner, the radical agitator, recently exiled from his native Ireland, a most dangerous incendiary, according to *Blackwood's*. Apparently Daniel was now cultivating the madman. But mad or not, he was a most effective speaker, captivating one and all, including Edward, who listened closely.

"And it is with no sense of pride, gentlemen," O'Conner was saying now, "but rather with profound shame that I present to you these men, as much victims as though they had individually mounted the steps of Newgate and presented their necks to the hangman, men whose lives have been ruined, whose futures are as dim as their pasts—"

Then with head upraised, arms outstretched, he announced, "Gentlemen, I give you the Tolpuddle Martyrs."

As the hall erupted in hearty applause, Edward again craned his neck forward. Tolpuddle Martyrs. He remembered the case, in fact he'd had it forced upon his attention by an indignant Daniel, when had it been—three, four years ago? Even William Pitch had written a condemnatory editorial, championing the lost cause of the six laborers from that Dorsetshire village of curious name who had been sentenced to deportation for the technical offense of "administering unlawful oaths" to members of their small union. The government, frightened by unionist activities, had imposed oppressive measures, and had sentenced them to exile in New South Wales. That was the last Edward had heard of them.

Again a hearty cheer rose from the crowd. Daniel appeared red-faced. He stepped back from the podium and motioned for one of the six men to come forward.

At first the man seemed hesitant. Clearly the youngest of the six, he looked almost pleadingly at the other five as though begging them to relieve him of this duty. But when no relief was forthcoming, he stood awkwardly and adjusted his plain worn brown jacket, then slowly, with Daniel's assistance, he came forward until he stood behind the podium.

The hall fell into a taut silence, all faces upturned in his direction. Edward felt a wave of sympathy for him. Obviously he was not a talking man. Still mauling his well-crushed hat, he bobbed his head. "I ain't much of a man with words," he began, "an', even if I was, I don't rightly know what it is you're wantin' to hear—"

In between the man's lengthy pauses, Edward could hear the children laughing in the garden.

The man finally went on, still kneading the crushed hat. "We're back, as you can see, safe, and maybe not quite as sound as we was 'fore we was sent off. A few of us, right enough, is bitter, feelin' we ain't done nuthin' to bring this down on us—"

He ducked his head. "You see, how it was, we had us a little union, not much, oh Gawd, it weren't much, just a few mates workin' together. But I guess it rightly caused alarm in high places."

Behind him, his five companions had yet to move. They appeared to be listening as closely as the rest of the audience.

"Anyways," he went on, "we found ourselves in irons one day, on a great ship, forced to leave our families behind. We ended up in New South Wales, in a prison colony." He paused and again lowered his head. "Don't rightly know if you want to hear about that or not."

A voice shouted, "Tell us everything."

The man looked up and slowly nodded. "Well, it was hard labor, it was, and a turrible climate. The work was laying roadbeds and the wardens carried whips. Ain't a one of us don't bear the mark of the whip with us, and we'll take it to our grave."

Edward closed his eyes. He wondered if the wagon from Masson's had come yet. No one would know to look for him in here. This was Daniel's domain.

For what seemed an incredibly long period of time, Daniel and O'Conner let the surly mood grow. While fascinated, Edward felt discomfort. The man who had spoken was clearly honest and poor, and his message had fallen for the most part on honest and poor ears. It was a conspicuous quality that Edward felt, the vice of wealth.

Then above the din of the angry audience he heard Feargus O'Conner shouting, his arms raised, calling for quiet and order. After several moments the crowd reluctantly obeyed, settling back onto the long benches, their faces flushed and still angry.

With the expertise of a trained speaker, O'Conner held his place behind the podium, unspeaking, until once again total silence had fallen upon the hall. His face was hard, angry, resolute, and when he spoke, his voice matched his face.

"A simple question," he began, "has been put to us tonight. Who—owns—England?" he demanded, and paused as though to let the question sink in. Then he demanded again, *"Who—owns—England?"*

Edward now saw O'Conner quickly withdraw a parchment from his inner pocket. He unfurled it and held it suspended before him, and again waited for silence. "I have here," he began, "the seed of the future." He held the parchment up. "The outline," O'Conner went on, full-voiced, "of what I propose we call The People's Charter."

Edward noticed the journalists again bent over their notebooks. *The People's Charter*. Every word of what was transpiring here would within the week appear in every newspaper in London. He thought ruefully of the reaction to such a charter, the revolutionary nature of everything that had been said here tonight, the six martyrs paraded out, designed to arouse emotions, then Feargus O'Conner stepping in to control and manipulate them. Most skillfully done, the whole thing, yet behind the skill, Edward saw clearly the cause, just, irrefutably just.

Then O'Conner was speaking again. "It's only an outline, a blueprint as it were," he shouted. "As Daniel said earlier, the great work has only begun. But let me share with you this outline. Let me test it on your ears for sound, for reason."

As O'Conner lifted the parchment, all heads seemed to crane forward. "We demand of Parliament," he began, "one, an extension of the franchise. Universal male suffrage."

As his voice continued to explode across the hall, a loud cheer went up after each item. As Edward felt the excitement grow, he grasped the door, realizing fully what was contained on that piece of parchment. They might be the seeds of the future, but they also were the seeds of revolution, which, if implemented, would alter forever the course of England.

Then Edward had seen enough and pushed open the door and welcomed the silence on the other side. He closed the door quickly and leaned against it as though bodily to contain the insurrection which was taking place inside. Daniel was no longer playing with his Ragged School. He was now—

Suddenly he heard a voice calling to him from the top of the stairs. He looked up as though summoned back to the reality of the moment. It was Jennifer, her bonnet in place. "Edward, is it you? We've been looking everywhere. The wagon has arrived and John Murrey says—"

All the way down the steps she talked. But as she drew even with him, she fell silent. "Were you in there?" she asked, in mild alarm. "What's going on? The noise fright-

ened the younger children. Is Daniel in there? He asked us
to call him when—"

But he merely pulled her close under his arm, lifted the
satchel from her hand, and walked slowly with her toward
the door. "Let's go home," he smiled softly, "while there is
still a home to go to."

She pulled away in minor protest. "But Daniel said—"

"Daniel is—occupied," he replied bluntly.

In a way he was pleased by the look of disappointment
in her face.

Then Edward saw it, the enormous wagon with the tiny
oval of Masson's printed neatly on the side, four horses
under harness and two relief horses bringing up the rear
and in the middle the gigantic canvas-covered lump, four
men stationed about, their hats pulled down over their
faces, all serving one purpose, to keep the grand pianoforte
rigid and secured.

It was quite a spectacle, somehow made even more
dramatic by the echo ringing in Edward's ears. *Who—owns
—England? The aristocracy.*

"Is all secure, John?" Edward shouted up.

"Aye, sir. We've been waitin.' It will be a night journey,
I fear—"

"No matter." Edward shouted back. He led Jennifer to
the carriage door and assisted her inside. Then he stole
another look at the immense wagon, transporting the expensive luxury.

*Descend, Thou, and share with us this horrid living
chaos of ignorance and hunger—*

"Is all secure there?" he shouted back to the two men
sitting atop the wagon, reins in hand.

They nodded without speaking, a sullen look in their
eyes.

"We'll make it at broken intervals," Edward called up,
hoping to remove a portion of the sullenness from their
faces. "Feel free to signal at any cause."

Again the men nodded, and again said nothing.

Quickly he swung aboard and closed the door behind
him. As the carriage started forward, he noticed Jennifer
lean forward as though hopeful that at the last minute
Daniel might appear. "He said he wanted to tell us goodbye," she murmured.

"And he would have," Edward tried to reassure her. "But he was quite busy—"

"With what?"

"A meeting."

"About the school?"

He hesitated, not altogether willing to place upon her the full meaning of what he had witnessed. "In a way," he replied softly.

She leaned forward, as though she had fully understood. "The school is very important to him, isn't it, Edward?"

He nodded, wishing the conversation would end. While he loved her dearly, his mind was still on the turmoil of all he had witnessed. "It's his life," he said simply.

She nodded and gazed out the window. "Do you know what I told him?" she asked, a faint blush visible on her cheeks in the passing light. "I told him there was no reason why I couldn't teach music here instead of at Roe Head."

He smiled, extremely pleased with her change of mind. Lovingly he reached forward and took her hand. "And I agree, and what joy it would be for both Daniel and myself to have the pleasure of your company."

The blush spread. The drawn pallor which he'd first noticed on her face was all but gone. While not beautiful, she certainly was a pleasant-looking young woman. If only he could retrieve her permanently from those cold Yorkshire moors where Sophia Cranford had sent her into exile.

"I shall hold you to that decision," he warned lightly, patting her hand, then releasing it. "And at the first opportunity I personally will assist you in penning your letter of resignation."

He thought he saw a momentary cloud on her face as he pressed her for a final resolution. He watched as she settled back into the cushions. Then he did likewise, first occupying himself with an estimate of how long the journey might take. It would stretch throughout the night and well into the next day.

Again, no matter. He welcomed the black silent interval. He needed time to assimilate what was ahead of him, as well as what was behind him.

Who—owns—England?

The traffic was dwindling, the arteries on the western edge of the city free, with easy access. As the carriage picked up speed under John Murrey's skillful hands, Edward permitted his eyes to blur. Thinking now in economic terms, financial security was necessary before one could indulge in the luxury of human decency. Even the reformers would admit to that fact.

As the thoughts continued to jostle about his head, his hand moved surreptitiously to the pocket of his waistcoat.

The vial was there. Across the way he noticed Jennifer safely lost in her own thoughts. One last excursion into the blue endlessness. Daniel and his frenzied companion would still be there when he emerged, as would Eden Castle and its wretched inhabitants, as would the awful weight of his wealth, and the mocking past. It would all be there, waiting for him.

Sensing future defeats, he tipped the vial to his lips, while the carriage wheels moving rapidly over the turnpike seemed to hammer a steady refrain,

Who—owns—England—Who—owns—England—Who— owns . . .

Eden Castle
North Devon
Late June, 1836

Though seventy-two and considered by all to be dim-witted with age, Jane Locke nonetheless had a shrewd eye and a sharp awareness of the human drama being played out around her.

On this her first morning in Eden Castle, she assessed her sister, the Countess Dowager, and made a blunt diagnosis.

"You're lost," she pronounced stiffly. "You've forgotten who you are. Come, let's walk down the cliff to Morte-mouth. William always said if the end is muddled, search for clues at the beginning."

Predictably Marianne had protested, claiming much to do, claiming Edward's imminent arrival, claiming all and nothing. But Jane had seen through her protests. As far as she could see, that was part of the problem. Marianne had nothing to do, her every duty usurped by the giraffe, Sophia Cranford. And as for Edward's "imminent arrival," the horizon, as seen from Jane's upper chambers, was clear and unbroken. Knowing her nephew as she did, she had awaited his "imminent arrival" following William's death. To no avail. She knew all too well that Edward's nature frequently permitted him to confuse "imminent" with "never."

Now, however, as she assessed her sister over a cup of breakfast tea, she announced, "We need a long walk-about, both of us. It will do us a world of good. How long has it been since you've made the cliff walk?"

For the first time in what seemed hours, Marianne looked up from her silent brooding, traces of a faint smile on her face. "Ages," she murmured. "Well before Thomas's death."

Jane faked shock. "You've not been to Mortemouth since then?"

Marianne shook her head. "Why should I?" she asked. "I spent the first half of my life trying to get out of that wretched place. Why should I spend the last half trying to get back down to it?"

"We had many friends in Mortemouth once," Jane countered lightly.

"Dead, I promise," Marianne muttered, draining her teacup. "All dead."

Now Jane felt a brief annoyance of her own. "It's a glorious June morning," she wheedled. "Surely we could find someone alive in Mortemouth."

Marianne looked askance at her. "You're really serious, aren't you? Have you forgotten how steep the cliff walk is?"

Proudly Jane lifted her black ebony walking stick with the sterling silver head. "I have three legs, and a spare in my trunk for you," she replied, undaunted.

Marianne rose slowly from the small table on which rested her untouched food. "I had thought we would walk the headland," she suggested. "It's a lovely even walk, culminating in the graveyard—"

"Good God, no," Jane shuddered. "I'll be keeping company with the dead soon enough, as we both will. For what little time is left, I prefer the company of the living, thank you."

For the first time, she thought she detected a soft look of acquiescence on her sister's face. "Mortemouth," she pronounced quizzically, as though still baffled by the proposition.

"Mortemouth," Jane confirmed with a smile. "I want to feel the cobbles beneath my feet again," she said. "I want to smell the fishermen in from their morning run. I want to touch the climbing roses on the walls, and I want to gaze once more upon that three-room cottage where I passed what surely has to be one of the most miserable childhoods on record."

Marianne looked up into her face, and for a long moment the gaze held. Then, unaccountably, Jane saw the beginning of tears. Before they could spill over to the embarrassment of both, Jane put her arms about Marianne's frail shoulders and drew her close.

A few minutes later, Marianne pulled away and dabbed at her eyes. "Then down to Mortemouth," she smiled. "It might be fun at that."

A short time later, with their bonnets and summer capes in place, they stood in a blaze of morning sun on the stairs of the Great Hall. Already Jane thought she detected a becoming flush on Marianne's pale cheeks. Yes, her prescription had been a good one.

As they were just starting down the stairs, Jane heard a strong masculine voice calling to them from the Great Hall. As they turned, they saw Caleb Cranford hurrying toward them. "Oh God, what does he want?" Jane muttered.

Marianne gave no reply, but Jane clearly felt her stiffen, as though, with the sound of his voice, a battle alarm had gone off within her. Now the man was drawing nearer, his lean, hard face and black hair completing the spider image. "I beg your pardon, milady," he said, drawing even with them on the steps and bowing obsequiously. "I was sent to see if I could be of service. My sister saw you passing through the Great Hall and wondered if—"

Jane drew herself up to her considerable height and adjusted the cerise ruffle about her neck. "If we had required your assistance, Mr. Cranford, we would have summoned it. Lady Eden and I are simply going abroad for a spell, down to Mortemouth—"

The news did not please him. "To Mortemouth, milady?" he asked archly of Marianne.

Jane saw her nod weakly, her head down, as though intimidated by the man's presence.

"May I inquire why, milady?" he asked further.

Enraged, Jane held her tongue at the man's daring and her sister's meek behavior. In the old days Marianne would never have endured such impudence. "We'll only be gone a short time, Mr. Cranford," she replied, still apparently unable to look the man in the face.

He smiled indulgently, like a father to a misbehaving child. "I'm afraid I cannot allow it, milady," he said, shaking his tiny spider's head. "The path is hazardous and unsafe. And I'm certain the populace of Mortemouth has changed. It would not be prudent—"

Then Jane could hold her tongue no longer. "Mr. Cranford," she interrupted, holding her walking stick at midpoint as though to use it as a weapon. "Her Ladyship and I are going down the cliff walk to Mortemouth this morning. I feel certain that we know the hazards better than you. And I strongly protest your interruption. Now, run along to whatever it is you do to earn your keep in Eden Castle, and I would strongly advise in the future that you obey the time-honored ritual of all servants concerning their mistresses, and that is not to approach unless summoned and not to speak until specifically invited to do so."

As they started down the stairs, she saw Marianne look backward, as though to apologize. "For God's sake," Jane whispered fiercely, "remember who you are. Keep your eyes front."

"But—"

"Eyes front," she hissed again.

They had just reached the bottom step when the man apparently recovered from his shock enough to call after them. "It's her Ladyship's welfare that I'm concerned with," he said, his voice cold now. "If you insist upon this foolishness, I cannot permit you to go unaccompanied."

Just as Jane was turning with an effective volley on her lips, Marianne stopped her. "Please," she murmured, "please, Jane, don't. No more trouble, I beg you—"

There was something so pathetically urgent in the plea that Jane had no choice but to obey. Still smoldering, she watched through narrowed eyes as Caleb Cranford summoned two uniformed stewards to his side. She continued to watch as the man whispered something to the two men. As the stewards started down the steps, she saw Caleb's triumphant smile. "You are accustomed to looking after yourself, Miss Locke," he beamed. "Her Ladyship is not."

Jane looked first at the stewards, then at Marianne, who continued to stand as though reprimanded. She glanced back up at Caleb, who stood at the top of the stairs, his hands behind his back, as though he were Lord of the

Castle. Merciful heavens, she thought sadly, how times had changed.

As they started across the inner courtyard, Jane was aware of the stewards falling into place about ten feet behind. "I never thought I'd live to see the day. Why do you permit them to stay?" she asked bluntly. "They've passed the point of usefulness to you and your children. Why don't you send them packing back to Yorkshire where they belong."

Again Marianne shushed her as they were approaching the gate and guardsmen. Jane observed quietly as Marianne spoke to them all, calling them by their first names, inquiring of one or two about wives and children. The men responded with respect, quickly drawing up the twin grilles, then standing a distance back for the ladies to pass. To one gnarled old man on the other side, Marianne made a specific request. "Samson," she began, "if my son Edward arrives in our absence, please sound the bell loudly. We're going down into Mortemouth. I can hear the summons from there."

"Aye, milady," the old man grinned. He went on, flattered that the Countess Dowager had singled him out for a personal request. "We've sent riders as far as Taunton to be on the lookout. We'll have word soon, I'm certain, of Mr. Edward's approach."

Marianne smiled, grateful, then again took Jane's arm for the slight incline which led down to the beginning of the cliff walk. Behind them trailed the two stewards, moving closer now, or so it seemed to Jane, as though their task was not only to oversee, but to overhear as well.

Bending her head into the wind, Jane felt a trace of that cunning which in the past had supplied her with what she wanted. As they drew near the beginning of the steep walk downward, she pulled away from Marianne and moved back toward the stewards. As she approached, she withdrew a small purse from her pocket. "A pound note for each of you," she announced, "if you'll stretch out in these soft grasses here and take a nap."

The two young men looked briefly at each other, then at the money being offered them.

"Two pounds apiece," Jane went on, "if you'll wait here for us and keep your mouths shut."

How easily certain obstacles were overcome. With deferential bows, they took the money and wandered a distance away, looking vaguely about as though searching for a likely spot in which to take their rest.

Her faith in servants intact, Jane returned to Marianne, who apparently was in the mood to protest everything. "You shouldn't have done that," she scolded. "They'll take your money and tell Caleb anyway."

"Then let them," Jane purred. "You can sack the lot of them and I'll help you."

As she led the way down the cliff walk, she looked back now and then at Marianne. At first it seemed as though all her energy and attention was focused on the steep descent.

But at midpoint, as Jane looked back again, she saw her sister in close examination of a clump of sea lavender, her eyes assuming a strange, faraway expression. "We used to gather armloads as children," Jane called back. "Do you remember?"

Marianne looked up and nodded. Jane noticed high color rising on her cheeks and thought, good.

A quarter of an hour later, at the bottom at last, they both paused to make repairs. Jane hastily withdrew her handkerchief and patted her brow where a sweat of exertion had broken out.

Marianne smiled. "It was your idea."

"Yes," Jane replied, taking full responsibility. "And I'm glad we've come."

As they strolled together, they said nothing. Their dim eyes sought out familiar passageways and the glories of small gardens. As they turned into the street which fronted the ocean, the foot traffic increased, causing Marianne to marvel, "It's grown. So many people."

Jane nodded and tightened her grip on her sister's arm as though to lend her support. She noticed a few faces look up, look away, then glance quickly back as though suffering belated recognition. Then mysteriously the foot traffic seemed to clear for their passage, the older men quickly removing their hats, the women all curtseying.

"We should have worn masks," Jane whispered, as she saw Marianne inclining her head in first one direction, then the other. But in spite of the increasing recognition, no one made any attempt to speak to them or stop them in any way, and they were permitted to walk the length of the street, uninterrupted, following the pavement as it veered upward into the narrow lane which they both knew by heart.

As Marianne caught sight of the cottage, she halted.

"Shall we knock," Jane suggested softly, "and ask for a cup of tea?"

"Oh, we couldn't," Marianne gasped, as though she'd taken the suggestion seriously.

As they drew even with the small cottage, Jane noticed an air of emptiness about it. She separated herself from Marianne and walked close to a crumbling white picket fence and peered over into a sadly neglected front garden. "I do believe there's no one home," she called back.

But still Marianne protested. "Come away," she whispered sternly. "They'll see you."

In spite of the protests coming from Marianne, Jane laid the broken gate to one side and stepped through to the gravel walk, always keeping a sharp eye on the small windows which flanked the front door.

But there was no sign of movement. She stuck her head through the upper half of the Dutch door. The interior was chaos, overturned chairs, a broken table, a tattered white curtain fluttering in the breeze of the opened back door. She entered the low narrow room, looking carefully about for the first reason to flee. A moment later Marianne followed after her.

They stood, unspeaking, in the ruined interior of their childhood home.

As their bleak inspection extended to the remaining two rooms, the fact of abandonment was confirmed. "It's in dreadful shape," Marianne commented, lifting her finger to a dust-covered table in the rear bedroom which once had been hers.

No longer feeling the need for either whispering or stealth, Jane gingerly righted two of the fallen chairs. Her cerise gown already soiled, she made an attempt to dust the chairs, then gave up and sat heavily, her legs spread a distance apart. "Good God," she exclaimed, looking about. "It's shrunk. Can you imagine at one time five of us existing here? Can you believe it? You, me, Russell, Father, and old Jenny Toppinger, all brushing up against each other, and hating each other in the process."

Marianne appeared in the doorway. "I hated no one,"

she smiled. "And I remember it all with a certain fondness."

"You would," Jane said, a soft sarcasm filling her voice.

But it was not the past that plagued Jane. The past was over, and as she had always been a practical woman, she realized this and was capable of dealing effortlessly with it. No, the future was the concern now, both for her sister and for herself. With William's death, she had sold the house on Great Russell Street in London. Wise enough to know that William's literary friends would not necessarily extend their friendship to her, she had packed her belongings and had now come to Eden Castle to stay. She had envisioned for herself and for Marianne, long fireside chats, resurrecting pleasantly that part of the past that was worthy of resurrection, the whole closing chapter of her life free from tension and hostility and drama. Now from the increasingly sorrowing look on her sister's face and from the memory of her encounter with the despicable Mr. Cranford, she realized with a sigh that she would have to take matters into her own hands if she was to achieve her desire for the future.

"When did you lose it?" she asked now, almost blithely, trying to shatter the room's hold on her sister.

Marianne looked sharply up. "I—beg your pardon?" she stammered. "Lose—what?"

"Your ability to control people," Jane replied without hesitation. "William said time and time again that you should have been born male. He said you would have made a brilliant general."

But Marianne seemed to grow more depressed. "William said a great deal," she murmured.

"He meant that, though," Jane persisted. "It was one of the first characteristics that attracted him to you." She stood now. As she ran a finger along a dusty sill, she longed for a greater skill of diplomacy. But she had been born blunt and apparently she would die so. "Why did you not dismiss the Cranfords years ago?" she asked now.

For an instant the confusion in Marianne's eyes mounted. "I—don't understand—" she said.

"Of course you do," Jane replied, slowly encircling the chair where she sat. "Why do they stay?" she asked again. "Why have you permitted them to stay?"

Marianne leaned back in the chair. When it seemed to

Jane that she would never speak, she spoke, her voice low. "Am I unique, Jane, or do all women find a conflict between being a wife and a mother? I looked at my children and saw need. And I looked at Thomas and I saw need."

She glanced across at Jane and announced sternly, as though it were something she should have known, "The Cranfords took over my duties with the children, and in the process, took over my children as well." She walked the short distance to the door and appeared to be gazing out at the overgrown garden. "If I were to dismiss Sophia Cranford today," she said calmly, "I would never see my daughter again. If I were to dismiss Caleb Cranford, James would go with him. As for Edward, I doubt seriously if he has any real need for any of us." She paused, then turned back to Jane. "How wise you were not to have children," she smiled.

For a moment, Jane foundered. She had wanted nothing so desperately as she had wanted children, William's children.

"And what are the Cranfords up to now?" she asked, feeling unqualified to pursue the matter of children.

Marianne shrugged, her eyes still devouring every corner of the room. "A lawsuit," she said flatly. "They have aligned themselves with Sir Claudius Potter and have convinced James that a lawsuit is the only way to recover the estates from Edward."

"Good God," Jane gasped, beginning to understand for the first time the black mood which had enveloped her sister. "And what do you intend to do about it?" she asked quietly.

Marianne shook her head. "What can I do, dear Jane? Please tell me, if you know. I've told Sir Claudius that there will be no lawsuit while I'm alive. But we all know that I am powerless to stop it."

She turned away, rubbing her arms as though she were cold in the June heat. There was silence in the small room. Only the distant bird calls sounded in the back garden.

Jane placed a hand on her sister's arm, as though again to summon her attention. "There *is* something you can do," she smiled. As Marianne looked up, Jane went on in her most persuasive tone. "You can remember who you are," she said firmly. Her voice continued to rise as though she were literally trying to send the words through the pale countenance before her. "You are Lady Eden, the Countess Dowager, widow of a peer of the realm." She stepped in front of Marianne and grasped her by the shoulders as though to shake her out of her lethargy. "There was a time when you convinced all of England of that fact. Now all you must do is convince two Yorkshire scoundrels."

Marianne returned her sister's gaze, a look of disbelief on her face. But out of that disbelief a smile emerged. "I may need daily reminders."

"And I shall be here to supply you with them."

The two women embraced. While Jane was not absolutely certain what, if anything, she had accomplished, at least, there was a semblance of peace on her sister's face.

Just as the embrace was coming to a conclusion, she felt Marianne stiffen. "Listen!" she whispered.

Obediently Jane listened and heard nothing. "What is—"

But Marianne merely shushed her and again whispered, "Listen. It's the gate bell. Don't you hear it?"

In all honesty, Jane had to confess, "No, it's probably just a buoy out at sea."

"No," Marianne smiled. "It's the gate bell, I know it. It's Edward—" She dashed back to the chair and retrieved her bonnet and was well on her way to the door before Jane could restrain her. "Marianne," she scolded her, "consider your age as well as your position. If it's Edward, he will wait. He's kept you waiting long enough."

She had not intended for her voice to be so stern, but at least her words had accomplished their purpose. The clearly agitated Marianne seemed to be making an effort to rein in her enthusiasm. Almost sedately now, she placed the bonnet on her head and carefully tied the ribbons.

Outside in the garden, the gate bell was audible even to Jane. "I hear it now," she said. "Apparently your wandering son has come home."

Marianne smiled a most radiant smile and increased her pace. But again Jane stopped her. At the gate, she pointed toward the end of the narrow lane where a fair-sized crowd of curious Mortemouth citizens had gathered. Apparently news of the Countess Dowager's presence among them had spread.

"Pay them decent respect," Jane counseled, keeping her

voice low. "It will take only a minute. In the future their allegiance could be of vast importance to you."

For a minute she saw a splintered look on Marianne's face as she was clearly torn between the frantically ringing bell and the little knot of onlookers. But again she took Jane's counsel, adjusted her summer cape, and led the way down the lane, her head erect, the same stance and attitude of her younger days, a born countess. Let the Cranfords confront *that,* Jane thought, pleased with herself.

As they drew near, the crowd parted, the men swiftly removing their hats. Graciously Marianne greeted them, speaking aloud on occasion and at other times merely bobbing her head. Once through the small crowd, she seemed determined again to increase her step. But again Jane drew near and restrained her. "It will do no good to arrive in the inner courtyard breathless and undone. Your son will wait, I promise."

As they drew near the bottom of the cliff staircase, the ringing of the bell became even more frantic. Starting the steep ascent, Jane took the lead, reaching back for Marianne's hand, the two of them leaning laboriously into the ascent, wind increasing, the expression on Marianne's face one of effort coupled with boundless joy.

At the top of the walk the two old women stopped for breath. Jane faced Marianne, whose eyes still bore the look of unbearable anticipation. "Now," she pronounced, "let's see you." Quickly she reached down and made an attempt to brush the dust from the hem of the black gown. She adjusted her sister's bonnet, which had become askew during the climb up.

Marianne stood immobile and docile before her, permitting the minor adjustments. Suddenly her eyes froze on something, an incredible light on her face. Jane looked ahead, and saw him as well. Apparently he'd alighted from his carriage inside the inner courtyard, had found his welcoming committee lacking, and had come in search of his mother.

For a moment, she felt Marianne pause beside her as though the mere sight of him had left her paralyzed with joy. Even from that distance, Jane could see his face, handsome still, in spite of his reputation for dissipation, his long fair hair blowing in the wind, his jacket opened, the best of Thomas Eden, the best of Marianne, combined in one burst of creativity, the whole magnificent effort a mockery for the lack of legitimate vows.

Jane was aware of the guardsmen watching, and there were a few stewards peering through the gate.

Then slowly Edward lifted his arms and opened them wide, a shelter of vast and welcoming proportions, promising protection.

Marianne whispered his name, "Edward," then she was moving, and he was moving, arms still outstretched, slowly at first, then both increasing in speed until at last, the reunion itself, his broad shoulders enveloping her so completely that for a moment it seemed to Jane as though he had devoured her.

Strangely Jane felt her eyes blur and looked quickly away. The whole encounter had a peculiar aspect to it, more like a young woman running to greet her lover than an aging mother going forward to greet a son.

Again Jane glanced back at the prolonged embrace, the two of them apparently content merely to stand in one another's arms. She watched a moment longer, then again averted her face and looked out across the channel. The wind was picking up, causing a ruffle of white caps.

Would the embrace never end?

She remained silent in mild dismay, divided between shock at her sister's wantonness and surprise at her nephew's show of warmth, not exactly knowing who in this moment was the madder of the two, the mother who received her son in that manner, or the son who greeted his mother in that manner.

Enough, Jane thought sternly, sensing eyes peering out of every window of the castle.

But obviously the two at the top of the incline, locked in each other's arms, disagreed.

It seemed only a moment that Marianne had confused her son's arms for those of her dead husband. No more.

Then she held him at arm's length and studied his face and saw it changed, older, more sorrowing.

He was treating her to the same close scrutiny. "As lovely as ever, Lady Eden," he smiled, inclining his head. Then he caught sight of her soiled gown. "You've been down to Mortemouth," he commented softly.

"Jane's idea," she smiled, motioning to the old woman waiting a distance away.

Gently he broke away and moved toward Jane. Marianne saw him greet her warmly and gallantly extend his arm to her and together the two of them rejoined her.

As they drew near, Marianne heard Jane scolding. "That was quite a greeting," she grumbled. "Enough to keep the servants gossiping for weeks—"

Marianne laughed. "A mother and son have certain privileges."

"Indeed they do," Edward concurred. As he moved between them, they each took an arm and began slowly to make their way toward the castle gate.

"Was it a hard journey?" Marianne asked.

"It was," he said, after what seemed a long pause, as though at first he'd not heard the question. "Jennifer's with me, you know," he added.

She nodded, silently bracing herself for the reunion with her daughter.

Edward spoke on. "It occurred to us while we were in London that Eden Castle lacked a pianoforte. So we brought one with us. Masson's finest, I might add, though it slowed us considerably."

"A pianoforte," Jane exclaimed. "How lovely! It's been years since I've heard Jennifer play."

Edward smiled, as though pleased that someone shared his sentiments. As for Marianne, her attention had already been drawn through the castle gates and into the inner courtyard where she spied first the enormous wagon with the cumbersome lump, clearly the new pianoforte. Then she saw the tight little knot of people standing on the steps leading up to the Great Hall, talking animatedly among themselves until at last, apparently spying the three passing through the castle gates, they all fell silent.

In spite of Jane's recent efforts to bolster her courage, Marianne felt a compulsion to run. It was never an easy task to face one's failures.

Edward didn't seem to notice, but apparently Jane did and now she caught Marianne's eye and with a massive and stern expression indicated that she was to stand erect.

You are Marianne, Lady Eden, the Countess Dowager of—

Abruptly Marianne withdrew her arm from Edward's.

Under her sister's merciless gaze she had received the message. She walked alone now, the other two following after her.

Sustained by Edward's warm embrace, more convinced than ever that the Eden fortune was in the proper hands and would stay there, she drew far ahead of Edward and Jane, her eyes focused on the young woman in the plain brown traveling suit, looking twice her age, Marianne thought, looking as withdrawn and secluded as Sophia Cranford, who stood protectively beside her.

Armed with Edward's recent expression of love, she felt a surplus of love to give, and while she was still a few steps away, she opened her arms, calling out warmly, "Jennifer," then quickly closing them again when it became apparent that the girl had no intention of coming to her.

Instead, as she drew near the stairs, Jennifer stepped politely down and extended her gloved hand. "Milady," she murmured.

With grace, Marianne endured the slight. "It's good to see you again," she said softly. "I must confess I spend a great deal of time worrying about you in cold Yorks."

"The cold differs little from Devon cold," Jennifer replied courteously. "And I apologize for not writing. My duties keep me very busy."

For the moment, Marianne allowed her eyes to wander up to the grinning Sophia, who always seemed to receive a letter a month from Jennifer. Then behind Sophia, she saw Sir Claudius, his soft pink face sobered, his eyes seeming to rest suspiciously on Edward. She noticed for the first time that Caleb was missing, as was James. "Where is—"

Immediately Sophia interrupted, as though reading her mind. "Caleb has gone to fetch him, milady," she said primly.

The traffic on the stairs was quite heavy as the stewards rushed up and down with the trunks. Behind Edward's carriage, Marianne noticed four men standing near the new pianoforte. Hoping to elicit at least a faint light from Jennifer's face, Marianne moved to one side, nearer to her daughter. "Edward tells me that you have promised to play for us, has even provided you with a magnificent—"

"I did not ask for it, milady," the young woman said, a curtness to her voice.

"No, of course not," Marianne murmured. "I didn't mean to imply that you—"

She broke off, her futile efforts taking a toll. For a moment a confused silence settled on the group as the stewards, with continuous apology, moved back and forth. Marianne glanced over her shoulder toward Edward. He appeared as dejected as she felt. He leaned heavily against the door of his carriage as though loath to lose contact with it.

What in God's name were they standing about for? "Let's move inside, please," she suggested. "There's no reason—"

But again Sophia interrupted her. "We're waiting for James," she smiled. "He's in the stables. As I said, Caleb has gone to fetch—"

Then Marianne heard Jane's voice. "Miss Cranford," she said, moving forward, striking the gravel with her walking stick. "Lady Eden wishes to retire inside. Would you be so good as to lead the way?"

The tall angular woman gaped at Jane. Marianne saw two dots of color rising on her cheeks. "I thought, out of courtesy," she snapped, "it would be best—"

"You're not paid to think, Miss Cranford," Jane smiled, starting up the stairs now, pausing a moment to kiss Jennifer lightly on the cheek. "You look terrible," she said bluntly to the girl. "You need some Devon sun." Then she was on her way again, tapping out with her walking stick her forward progress up the stairs.

Lacking her sister's appetite for tension, Marianne glanced back at Edward, saw a half smile on his face as, still leaning against his carriage, he shook his head. Then Marianne heard Sophia's high-pitched voice. "Here he comes," she proclaimed.

As Marianne glanced up at the shrill announcement, she saw all eyes following the course of Sophia's extended hand. Marianne knew who it was without looking, but she looked anyway along the sandy tracks that led into the inner courtyard from the stables. She had hoped to postpone the meeting, at least until after dinner, after Edward had had a chance to rest, and she'd had a chance to talk with him.

But apparently it was not to be. With fixed eyes she watched along with the rest as the distant figure appeared at the far end of the courtyard. She noticed that he wore his blacksmithing apron. Obviously he'd been attending his horses. Although there were four trained blacksmiths at the Eden stables, nothing brought James greater pleasure than to preside over the forge himself.

Behind him, she saw Caleb Cranford, his rigid figure in curious contrast to James's slouched one. The tall Yorkshireman seemed to be herding her son along the path, as though, at the first sign of retreat, he was there to change his mind.

The man in the black apron was drawing nearer, his head still down, his step slow and uneven as he fumbled now with heavy gloves. Then he made an attempt to straighten his long dark hair and again commenced forward motion, moving not toward Edward, who had stepped forward to greet him, but rather toward Jennifer, who stood halfway up the stairs.

"Jennifer," he smiled, taking a step upward, then extending his hand which, as far as Marianne could tell, her daughter took eagerly and came down the steps and into her brother's arms for a quick embrace.

Smiling, he held her back. "I'm in no fit condition, I'm afraid," he apologized.

Jennifer looked with what seemed to be genuine affection upon her brother. "I've missed you, James," she smiled.

"You look splendid. The school must agree with you. You must tell me all about it. The only word we receive is secondhand, through Sophia's letters—"

Throughout this exchange Marianne looked at Edward, who stood, head down, both hands shoved in his pockets, all his considerable attention apparently focused on moving small pieces of gravel about with the toe of his boot. He had to be aware of the slight.

Then the light banter at the steps ceased. All about the gathered company was a new tension, as though something of great import was about to happen. Then James was standing before his brother, apparently amused by Edward's preoccupation with gravel.

"Edward, welcome home," James said, kindly enough.

Edward looked up, as though surprised by both the voice and the sentiment. He seemed to be having difficulty bringing James into focus. Say something, Marianne thought quickly, say something back to him, kind and unimportant.

And Edward did. He extended his hand and as James took it, Edward murmured, "I fear we've interrupted important work." He smiled, gesturing toward the smithing apron.

"No, not at all," James reassured him. "There are always small jobs to be done, and countless men who can do them better than I can. Still—" He paused and shrugged, as though for a moment calling to account his own worth.

Now James caught sight of the enormous wagon, the four men still poised beside the canvas-covered lump. "What prize have you brought from London?" he inquired, moving around Edward, walking toward the wagon.

At his approach, all four men bobbed their heads, as though in recognition of the Lord of the Castle in spite of his smithing apron.

Edward followed after him and shouted up, "Unveil it. Let's see if Masson's worries were groundless."

The four men scrambled upward, each to their corners and commenced untying the ropes. All heads swiveled in that direction as the men released the canvas covering and drew it back. A low murmur of appreciation arose from the company as all stared in admiration at the handsome instrument. Clearly it had made the journey safely and intact.

"I bought it for Jenny," Edward explained. "She's promised to give us several concerts, haven't you?" he called back to the young woman on the steps.

The sudden shift of attention brought a blush to her cheeks. "If you wish," she murmured and seemed to push closer to Sophia as though for protection.

Edward was now calling instructions up to the men, telling them where to place the instrument. As Edward grew more expansive, something seemed to have sobered James. He withdrew several steps from the activity around the wagon and continued to eye the grand pianoforte as though assessing its cost.

If Edward saw the expression, he gave no indication of it and merely followed after James, his manner still light. "I had ulterior motives as well," he said, his voice low, but loud enough for Marianne to hear. "I've been trying to coax

Jenny not to go back to that Yorkshire prison. I thought perhaps if she had a pianoforte—"

But James stiffened and interrupted. "I was under the impression that she enjoyed teaching—"

"Enjoyed it," Edward exclaimed. "Being shut up and cut off with only women and screaming children for company." He leaned closer, his voice very low now. "Yours may not be the only wedding in the coming year. Daniel Spade may have plans for Jenny. They get on very well."

Clearly appalled, James withdrew another step. "Daniel Spade?" he repeated. "Surely you're not suggesting that Jenny—"

Although Marianne was certain that no one was overhearing the conversation but herself, she took steps to end it. Moving between her two sons, she counseled quietly, "Jenny is quite capable of plotting her own future." To Edward she smiled, "The piano is lovely, a welcome gift." To James she suggested, "Why don't you have Caleb select several good wines for dinner tonight. I think we should have a family celebration before the other guests descend next week."

With both men momentarily defused, she lifted her voice and spoke now to those waiting on the steps. "Sophia, would you be so kind as to see Jennifer to her chambers. I know she must be tired. And Jane, please escort Sir Claudius to the library for a glass of sherry before lunch. There's absolutely no need for us to stand about in this heat."

As the company made tentative motions to disperse, she looked again at Edward and James, took both their arms, and drew them close. "I can't tell you," she began softly, "how much it means to me to have you both home. The coming days will be busy and filled with duties, but for now, we are all together and at peace, and for that, I'm grateful."

Her mood seemed to spread to her two sons. Edward kissed her lightly on the cheek. Then to James, he said with great warmth, "Forgive my rudeness. I haven't yet congratulated you. I look forward to meeting your future wife."

James smiled. "She'll be a good addition to the family, and I'm certain she will produce sons." Then hastily he added, "If you'll excuse me now, I must finish in the stables."

With that he was gone. Edward continued to stare after him. "Were we just then talking about a wife or a brood sow?" he asked softly.

Rising partially to James's defense, Marianne said, "He seems to feel his duty keenly to produce an heir."

"Do you know the lady?" Edward asked, still watching his brother.

"I know the family, of course," Marianne said. "I've never met Harriet."

"I hope she is fully aware of the purpose behind her entry into this family," Edward commented as though feeling pity for the young woman whose first duty would be to reproduce.

"I'm sure she is," Marianne smiled. Again she took Edward's arm and tried to turn him from the diminishing figure at the end of the path. "Come, let me take you to your chambers. If you like, we can lunch there alone. I must speak with you."

He detected the tension behind her words. "How long has Sir Claudius been here?" he asked pointedly.

"Long enough."

"Then, in that case, I plead guilty to everything."

"Come, Edward," she urged. "The heat is dreadful. Let's retire."

Gently but steadily she guided him up the steps. On his brow she noticed beads of perspiration in which his hair had gotten caught and now lay plastered on his forehead. His face appeared suddenly to have gone white.

As they entered the cool shadows of the Great Hall, she saw three curious serving girls peering out, excited at the increased traffic passing through the castle. As she drew near, they started to retreat. She called sharply, "Bring a pitcher of lavender water and clean linens to my third-floor chambers. And be quick."

As the girls disappeared, she turned her attention back to Edward. He appeared to be breathing heavily now, and his weight upon her had increased as though his legs were giving way. "Edward, what is it?" she whispered in concern.

At that moment Sophia Cranford appeared in the far corridor door. On seeing his colorless face, she stepped forward, a mask of concern imperfectly hiding her curiosity. "Is he ill?" she asked. "He seemed well enough when we left him."

"He's merely fatigued," Marianne replied, trying to walk erect and thus conceal the full extent of Edward's mysterious weakness.

"Shall I call for Caleb?" Sophia asked primly.

"No!" Marianne's reply was sharp. "He'll be fine. He simply needs a moment to rest." As she guided Edward past the gaping woman, she called back, "We'll lunch alone in my chambers. I'm certain the others will understand. Please send Mrs. Greenbell with a tray."

Although Marianne had dreaded the three flights of stairs, she was relieved to see that Edward apparently had recovered a portion of his strength. He grasped the handrailing and laboriously pulled himself up.

Breathing heavily from exertion and undone with concern, she led him slowly to the third-floor corridor, the stone walls of the castle now serving as his support. As they drew near his customary chambers, only a short distance from hers, he pulled free of her support. "Leave me, please," he begged in a hoarse whisper. "You were right. I—need a moment—alone."

She started to protest, but changed her mind. As she pushed open the door which led into his chambers, she stepped back. "I'll be down the hall if you need me," she reminded him.

Quietly she closed the door. As she stood alone in the corridor, her mind turned. She'd seen the ravages of the Dreaded Disease, and knew that Edward exercised no discrimination in his choice of companions. But surely not that. Oh God, please not that. What a trump card for the Cranfords, to drag a diseased Edward into court.

But it wasn't that. She was certain. Then what?

Hadley Park
Shrewsbury
Shropshire
June 29, 1836

At dawn on the morning of June 29, an entourage of five carriages left Hadley Park outside Shrewsbury heading in a southwesterly direction toward Eden Castle on the North Devonshire coast. Now with the first rosy signs of sun creeping over the Shropshire hills, Harriet sat well over on her side of the carriage and gazed bleakly out the window. So! The dreaded journey was under way at last.

Beyond the carriage window, Harriet took careful and loving note of the Shropshire landscape, the rolling green meadows dotted with sheep, a soft morning fog just burning off, leaving tints of primrose pink where the sun poked through. She shivered slightly in the morning chill.

Seated opposite her was her mother, who apparently had seen the trembling. "Draw your cloak about you, Harriet," she commanded. "It will serve no purpose to arrive sniffling."

Harriet did as she was told and wondered sadly if it would serve any purpose to arrive at all. Not that she had anything against James Eden. At recent country house parties, they had passed fairly enjoyable intervals together. In the past he had required nothing of her but a ready ear, or at least the pretense of a ready ear.

239

She knew all too well, however, what had drawn them together, had led their families into tentative discussions concerning a union. Both she and James were leftovers. Everyone else in their circle had been spoken for long ago.

So they were to be joined like two machines, the male machine penetrating the female machine and leaving a seed, and out of her womb the future would emerge, and her only purpose for drawing breath would have been fulfilled.

The thought hurt. It was like being born to nothing, her father eyeing her even now as though she were one of his prize ewes on her way to the breeding sheds.

Beyond her window, she saw the end of the parkland, the narrow turnpike and, across the road, the Mermaid Inn. She thought of Humphrey Hills, the little boy with whom she had played as a child. Humphrey had loved her. She might have married him if custom had permitted. The wife of an innkeeper? Why not? How would it differ from being the wife of a lord? But of course custom had not permitted it.

Opposite her in the rocking carriage her parents' faces bobbed back and forth before her vision. She loved them both very much and was only sorry that she had so vastly disappointed them.

She looked away and closed her eyes, recalling the conversation she'd overheard between her parents recently concerning her ability to breed. "A fine full figure," her father had said. She had blushed then and blushed now, surprised that he had noticed. She was too tall, her mother had said, men preferring them small and dainty. But her breasts were good, they both had agreed, and her hips sturdy. She had never known an illness, another plus.

Thus Harriet had overheard them outside the morning room, discussing and cataloguing her various attributes, expressing in the end complete bafflement at her persistent single status. "She simply does nothing to encourage them," her mother had despaired. "She treats them one and all like—idiots," and the word had come out an obscenity. Her mother had concluded the discussion with her customary scolding, blaming her father for not permitting them, years ago, to take a London house where "the girl" might have learned a woman's wiles, blaming him too for that continuous line of German tutors who had filled her head with Greek and Latin and mathematics, all totally useless in the marriage race.

As they turned the corner heading toward the turnpike to Worcester, she saw the trailing entourage of the other four carriages, the second filled with servants, the third and fourth given over entirely to trunks, the fifth filled with her father's sturdiest guardsmen to look after the horses, repair the carriages, and watch out for highwaymen. Their itinerary consisted of Worcester, Cheltenham, Gloucester, a night's rest with their good friends the Berkeleys at Berkeley Castle, then Bristol, Cheddar, Taunton, Barnstaple, and Eden. If all went well, they were scheduled to arrive early in the evening on the following night.

If all went well—

As they passed through the village of Much Wenlock, the carriages resumed speed, the wheels of the rough terrain beating out a curious tune. Why did her mother persist in looking at her like that, as though she were an object of consummate pity? She wished now that she'd taken her private carriage and ridden behind. It had been discussed in the event that Harriet had wanted to extend her visit with the Edens.

But her father had said no, said they all could learn as much as they needed to know about the Edens in the official visit. She knew, although her father had never expressed this openly to her, that he had reservations about the union. The Eden blood was slightly tainted with the influx of common blood, the present Lady Eden having been the object of much scandal before she had married Lord Thomas Eden. The younger Eden son had been mentioned as a possible suitor years ago, but her father had discounted it then. Only desperation had now driven him back to the Edens. *The girl must bear fruit.*

If Harriet remembered correctly, there was an elder son as well. A bastard. James had mentioned him once in passing, the man apparently an embarrassment to the entire family, living scandalously in London.

The sky overhead was a blue endlessness. She sent her eyes there now and wished with all her heart that she was back riding Falstaff to their secret meadow, or reading by her little rounded turret window which gave such a splendid view of the Shropshire Hills. But to what end? She couldn't very well become a recluse at twenty-five, although that was her natural inclination.

If only she were capable of defining love. There had been Humphrey Hills, but that had been companionship more than love. And she had known one infatuation, safely platonic and from a distance, a fourteen-year-old schoolgirl infatuation with her German tutor, Herr Swartz. He'd been thrice her age, but she'd felt an unprecedented stirring in his presence as he'd read to her from Homer. She'd written a love poem to him and had carelessly left it about on her dressing table. Apparently someone had found it, and a short time after that, Herr Swartz had been dismissed.

Now in the cold light of growing older, she did not look forward to life without a definition of love. But as her mother had sternly pointed out, love had little to do with it.

Across the way, she heard her father speaking. He was listing as usual his projections of possible catastrophes. It was a sport with him, quite probably because it upset her mother so.

"Not an easy journey, this," he muttered, "particularly dangerous in early summer after spring thaw. My God, when I think on it. Two rivers to ford, the current capable of washing us away. That axle on the second carriage is weak, might break at any moment and send the horses down upon us. Did I tell you, there's a lame horse in the fourth team? Sorely lame. Could unbalance the others and cause a collision. And that stretch of road between Berkeley and Taunton? Particularly bad, or so I've heard, ruts as high as the carriage floor. We could be ripped in half—"

With her eyes closed, Harriet listened. Dear God, she prayed, just let any one of them happen . . .

But nothing happened.

In fact, to the contrary, the journey was placid and uneventful. And in the late afternoon of the following day, after a pleasant interval at Berkeley Castle during which time the Berkeleys had more than filled her parents' ears concerning the Edens, she caught her first glimpse of the stark outline of Eden Castle, black in silhouette against the red sunset. She sat up, resolved to meet her responsibilities.

During the journey, something had passed from her, something which was above both happiness and grief, that something being her girlhood vision of romantic love. She had only duty ahead of her now and she divined without fear that she would become yet more lonely, that from now on she was a force enclosed within herself.

Then she heard shouting outside the carriage, saw an escort of Eden watchmen on horseback, each carrying a blazing torch. Opposite her, she saw her mother nervously adjusting her person.

And her father was there, peering excitedly out of the window at the escort. "Fine horses, those," he said, clearly making a value judgment of some sort.

As they approached the central gate, the carriages slowed for entry, and in that moment Harriet caught her first glimpse of the inner courtyard, festooned with hanging lanterns, while atop the walls of the castle watchmen stood at close intervals with lit torches, a colorful spectacle, culminating at the broad expanse of stairs which apparently led up into a Great Hall.

In the carriage's slow progress around the courtyard, Harriet leaned close to the window for a better look at what might well be her future home. There was a roughness to the castle, quite alien to her after the classical elegance of Hadley Park, something almost overly dramatic about the high stone walls, purple and gold-appearing in the mix of diffused sunset. It was vast as well, she decided, looking up at the high battlements, clearly designed as a fortress, a lonely outpost to withstand any ancient enemy who foolishly thought they could enter England by the channel.

Seeing it thus in an imaginative blur of past and present, Harriet felt mildly intimidated. Would it ever be possible to be mistress of such a place? The carriage was slowing even more, preparatory to stopping at the foot of the Great Hall stairs, where a considerable crowd of people had gathered.

"Straighten yourself," her mother whispered sharply. "Your bonnet is askew."

Harriet did as she was told. Poor Mama, she thought. How troublesome it must be to have an unmarriageable daughter. Seeing her mother's tense face, Harriet again vowed to do her best to snare Lord Eden and endure him for the rest of her life. If she were truly fertile, perhaps once in a communal bed would be enough.

Then with a rattle, the carriages came to a halt. Outside

the window she caught a glimpse of the silent group of people, all faces turned toward the lead carriage. Stewards bearing lanterns lined the steps and in this faltering light she caught sight of James, the one familiar face, yet not familiar. In a sudden panic, she realized she'd not remembered him being so short. At the Carlyles' Christmas masque only last season, he'd not appeared so short. When she alighted the carriage, would she be taller than he?

Her father alighted first, leaning heavily on the stewards for support, his old joints clearly stiff from the journey. Once down, he turned back and extended a hand to her mother. Still inside the carriage, Harriet saw a frail old woman step forward, as bejeweled as her mother. It must be the Countess Dowager, the notorious Lady Marianne. To Harriet she looked neither scandalous nor notorious, merely frail and tired and perhaps a little unhappy.

So fascinated was she by the appearance of Lady Eden that Harriet failed to notice James smiling at her from the door of the carriage. Now he gave her a somewhat stiff bow and extended his hand to her. "Don't be afraid," he whispered. "I assure you we are harmless."

She returned his smile and permitted him to lead her down from the carriage until they were standing side by side on the ground. She was not taller than he, thank God. As tall, but no taller. She sternly scolded herself for such vanities and looked up to see the Countess Dowager moving slowly toward her parents.

The greeting was warm, her voice extraordinarily musical as she welcomed them to Eden Castle, trusting they had had a safe journey, recalling graciously the beauty of Shropshire as she'd seen it on a visit with the late Lord Eden.

Her mother, Harriet noticed, seemed to be having difficulty lifting her eyes from the dazzling diamonds gracing Lady Eden's throat. Finally she did though and returned the greeting with admirable warmth, apparently unable, as Harriet had been, to see any traces of the fisherman's daughter in this elegant face and voice.

Then it was her father's turn, Lady Eden seeming to act with even greater warmth, as though in her passage through life, the male of the species had always been of sharper interest to her. As she launched forth into an impressive and informed discussion of woolens and process manufac-

turing, Harriet waited beside James, feeling like a prize hog
on the block. She noticed other faces in the silent group
focusing on *her* rather than on her father. She felt like
shouting at them, Yes, I'll breed well. And in an attempt
to gain some relief from the gaping faces, she lifted her eyes
to the top of the Great Hall stairs, allowing her vision to
skim over the staring heads and up the line of stewards
bearing lanterns to—

With a quick glance she looked up, then looked away.
She had hoped for an empty space which would be incapable of staring back at her, but she had yet to find it,
for at the top of the stairs, she saw a man, a tall man with
fair hair. Unlike the others, this man wore casual dress,
coatless, his shirtwaist opened at the neck. He leaned with
one shoulder against the stone archway which led into the
Great Hall, one booted leg crossed and propped up before
the other one, his arms crossed on his chest, a peculiar
expression on his strong face as though while he was interested in the arrival, it was only a clinical interest, as
though confident that nothing would be required of him,
and grateful that it was so.

Quickly Harriet lowered her head, embarrassed to have
looked directly at him. She fell into a brief examination of
her gloves while to one side her father and Lady Eden were
apparently getting on famously. Beside her James restlessly
shifted his weight. An old man was now stepping out of
the little knot of people, looking quite dandified in his
scarlet satin waistcoat. Meticulously he extended a hand to
her mother as Lady Eden presided over the introductions.
"Lady Powels," she smiled, "may I present Sir Claudius
Potter. Since Lord Eden's death," she added, graciously,
"my right hand and, on occasion, my left as well."

The old man made an obsequious bow and took her
mother's hand. Harriet could not hear what was being
said, indeed had little interest in it. Apparently the intro-
ductory ritual was to be formal, all tedious custom to be
observed. Certainly without meaning to, she let her eyes
move slowly back up to the top of the stairs.

He was still there, his gaze focused rigidly upon her.
Even though his face was largely in shadow, she thought
she could see the light of a smile in his eyes. He seemed
excluded, standing alone at the top of the stairs, though in

truth the exclusion seemed not to bother him. She wondered who he might be. Not a servant certainly.

Again she felt a blush of embarrassment at the intensity of his gaze and lowered her eyes in time to see Lady Eden approaching her, the magnetic warmth of that smile now aimed in her direction.

Feeling no need for a formal introduction, greeting her as warmly as though she'd known her forever, Lady Eden embraced her lightly, and called her by name. "Harriet," she murmured, "how I've looked forward to this moment."

Confronted with such a generous and hospitable spirit, Harriet responded generously, "And I, too, Lady Eden."

For a moment, the woman seemed to be silently assessing her. Apparently she found something that pleased her for now she patted Harriet's hand warmly. "I know we shall get on beautifully," she said. "How pleasant it will be to have young people again at Eden Castle."

Then with gentle and diplomatic skill, Lady Eden arranged a reception line, guiding Harriet close to where her mother and father stood, inserting James between them while she took up a position to Harriet's right. As everyone was taking their appointed place, Harriet again looked up toward the top of the stairs. Still there. Unmoved. He might have been a statue. *Who was he?*

Then Lady Eden was saying, "I would like to present my sister, Miss Jane Locke—"

Harriet's attention was drawn back to a tall angular old woman now standing before her in a brilliant cerise gown, cut a little out of fashion but becoming nonetheless. The Berkeleys had spoken this name as well. Again Harriet found the tales hard to believe. The old woman standing before her now looked only slightly less elegant and serene than Lady Eden herself.

"So you're Harriet," she pronounced somewhat bluntly. Before Harriet could respond, she rushed on. "Well, I hope you brought your dancing legs. There's five nights of balls ahead of you." There was a gruffness about the old woman, reminiscent of Harriet's father. Age had been less kind to her than it had been to Lady Eden.

Now Harriet smiled pleasantly. "I love to dance," she said, "though I'm not very good at it. Still, I look forward to the festivities."

Jane Locke started to respond, but Lady Eden apparently

applied delicate pressure to her arm and moved her along to make room for Sir Claudius Potter.

Here was an inspecting face if she ever saw one, the old man almost lasciviously viewing her.

She did not like him and delivered her greeting quickly, leaving Sir Claudius to Lady Eden while on the other side a pleasant-faced, grandmotherly type was engaged in earnest conversation with her mother. Clearly there would be a pause. She was acutely aware of James standing stiffly beside her as though still at attention. She considered speaking to him, but she could think of nothing to say.

At the same moment, he apparently felt the same need and asked politely, "How was the journey?"

"Very calm, thank you," she replied.

"No difficulty?"

"No. None at all."

"Good. Very good."

Silence.

She looked back up at the top of the stairs. Perhaps it *was* a statue. As far as she could tell, the man had not altered his stance in any way. How would it hurt to inquire about his identity? Obviously she was going to meet everyone sooner or later, and the man's distant involvement in the affairs of the moment greatly appealed to her and even caused a flare of envy. How pleasant merely to stand and watch with nothing required of you.

She leaned close to James. "Who is—"

But at that moment the old woman with the kind, grandmotherly face was now approaching. Lady Eden stepped forward as though this introduction would require something special. "And this is Mrs. Greenbell. If you're ever in need of anything, from a ready and understanding ear to a hot water bottle, this sainted soul is the one you should call for."

Harriet returned her smile and felt instantly a very positive and good relationship with the woman.

Again the line seemed stalled in the vicinity of her mother and father. A rather sad-faced young woman stood before them now, listening attentively to something her mother was saying. Harriet watched them, envious of her mother's ability to speak with ease. Harriet had never seen her at a loss for words. Of course those words were generally empty, but nonetheless they were words, capable of filling a silence. And since the one around her was now deepening to an oceanic depth, she tried to clear her mind of all superfluous concerns and addressed James directly.

"Eden is lovely," she murmured.

He nodded. "It is," and looked vaguely about at the castle walls. "I suppose in a way," he added, "it's seen better days. We try to keep it modern and up to date—" He shrugged. "There's only so much you can do with it."

It was Harriet's turn to nod. Oh God, now what? She noticed the old man, Sir Claudius Potter, climbing laboriously up the stairs. He stopped by the man in shadow, leaning against the wall, and said a few words.

In her desperate need for distraction, Harriet watched. The old man might as well have been addressing a post. There was no response. She thought she detected an angry look on the old face, and continued to watch, fascinated, as the old man strode rapidly past the leaning statue.

It occurred to her that if the man was a servant, he would have moved immediately at Sir Claudius's command. But still there was no movement. She wished she could get a closer glimpse of his face.

Now her mother's chatter was coming to an end, the line moving again, the young woman extending her hand to Harriet's father. Harriet watched her closely and noticed a painful timidity about her. In fact on almost every face that Harriet had met, there was an expression of personal sorrow. The sea air may well have provided them all with long lives, but the quality of those lives was sadly questionable.

For just an instant, Harriet had a glimpse of herself fifty years from now, standing on this same spot, perhaps welcoming a young lady to whom her unborn son was engaged. Between that point and where she now stood stretched long black miles, unbroken even by occasional intervals of joy, condemned to a loveless marriage, although there was always the possibility that love might come later, as her mother had assured her it frequently did. But if it didn't—

She tried to stand a bit straighter and draw deep breath. Lady Eden was saying, "And this is my daughter, Jennifer, Lady Powels—"

Grateful to leave all bleak thoughts behind, Harriet took the small hand extended to her. "Jennifer," she murmured.

The girl was probably very close to her own age yet her left hand bore no ring. Apparently the Edens had seen fit to leave her alone to enjoy her spinsterhood.

"Welcome to Eden Castle," Jennifer whispered, her timidity so painful she could scarcely lift her eyes to Harriet.

"Thank you, Jennifer," Harriet responded, vowing to herself to be very kind to the young woman. "Perhaps we might go for a walk tomorrow," Harriet boldly suggested. "I'd like very much to see all of Eden, with you specifically as my guide."

Unfortunately the request had an adverse effect. A burning flush crept up the pale cheeks and she looked continuously over her shoulder at the tall thin woman just coming up behind her.

This same woman had overheard Harriet's request and now answered for her. "Jennifer has not been feeling well of late," she pronounced, stroking a notebook in her hand. "But I assure you, we will find you a competent guide elsewhere." The stern face brightened. "James here, perhaps. He would be an appropriate guide."

At this, James rallied from his lethargy and for the first time took over the chores of introduction himself. "Harriet, I would like for you to meet Sophia Cranford."

Harriet waited for further explication and when none seemed forthcoming, she extended her hand to the woman. In a quick gesture the notebook was shifted to the opposite hand and the two women met. "Forgive my intrusion into your conversation with Jennifer," Miss Cranford now murmured. She leaned close as though for a confidence. "The child is not ill, but neither is she well. She is not, by her own choosing, of the idle class. She works very hard during the winter at a school for the daughters of the clergy in Yorkshire."

A man who appeared to be a male version of Sophia Cranford was approaching Harriet now. Miss Cranford did the honors. Reaching for his arm, but stopping short of contact, she smiled, "Permit me, Lady Powels, to present my brother, Caleb Cranford."

The man, she noticed, was slim to the point of emaciation. And in that moment, Harriet observed something else, a feeling of disquietude emanating from Lady Eden, who continued to stand on her right and who had been totally passed over in this latest flurry of introductions. Fairly skillful at recognizing a battlefield when she saw one, Harriet was now convinced that she was standing squarely in the middle of one.

Then Miss Cranford was there again, filling the silence. "I've assigned quarters in the servants' hall to your attendants," she said, suddenly adopting a manner of efficiency. She flipped open the small notebook and withdrew a single sheet of paper. "Here are the numbers," she explained further. "In your chambers, you will notice a system of bells. The numbers there correspond with these rooms. If you desire a specific service, ring the appropriate bell and the attendant will appear."

The woman looked very pleased after her little speech. It struck Harriet as absurd. At Hadley Park, her servants did not need bells to summon them. They knew what Harriet needed and when she needed it. Beyond that, they were free agents, able to come and go as they pleased.

Harriet murmured thank you to the woman and tucked the paper inside her glove and looked with pleasure to see that the line was over. The staff of the castle still stood at rigid attention, a rather large staff, she thought, her conservative guess was over sixty. But then she remembered the coming festivities, the guests who would be arriving over the next few days, all coming to honor James and—

Suddenly she felt weak as though burdened with unnecessary baggage. She looked to one side, to where Lady Eden had withdrawn in close company with Mrs. Greenbell.

In the opposite direction, she saw her parents, her father giving orders to the coachmen who had driven the carriages. And at the top of the Great Hall steps, the man was still standing.

Then, to her amazement, he smiled directly at her. The others standing about noticed the focus of her attention, and all heads swiveled upward. Lady Eden stepped forward, murmuring, "How thoughtless of me—"

But if she said anything else, Harriet did not hear it. Her full attention was given over to the man who was just pushing away from the wall. He stood erect at the top of the stairs, and she saw his face for the first time, a rich, though mildly weary face with strong features, his hair, fair, shoulder-length, a bit ruffled as though he'd recently driven his hands through it, his casual dress now even more singular, surrounded as she was by fancy dress.

Now, as though perfectly willing to stand as long as necessary for everyone to look their fill, he lifted his head. Then slowly he started down the stairs at an easy gait, his eyes still focused with embarrassing intensity upon her, walking straight toward her as though he were on a confidential mission.

Under the intensity of his gaze and the steadfastness of his approach, Harriet felt a peculiar agitation.

As he continued to bear down upon her, she was aware of the others moving back. Whatever the force was, she was obviously destined to meet it alone. Still he came, bearing himself handsomely from his lonely position until at last he stood directly before her.

She managed a smile and wondered frantically why in the name of God someone didn't speak. As he looked down on her, she found that she had neither the will nor the energy to stir. Immoderate emotion continued to plague her and when she thought she was incapable of enduring another moment, he spoke.

"I am Edward Eden," he said, his voice soft in its simplicity.

Before she could respond, Lady Eden was at her side, murmuring apologies to both of them. "I'm sorry, Edward," she whispered. "I really didn't see you there at the top of the stairs." Her voice lifted, her manner became more formal as she said, "This is my elder son, Edward Eden." Then as though by way of explaining the awkward oversight, she added, "We see so little of him. He spends most of his time in London."

Harriet nodded, her eyes still caught and held by the intensity of his gaze. So! This was the illegitimate son. Surely never before in the history of mankind had illegitimacy produced such remarkable features.

Blushing from the daring of her thoughts, she returned the greeting. "Mr. Eden," she said. Then, curiously, she felt words forming. "And how is London these days?" she asked quietly, a little amazed at what she was doing. "I'm afraid we rustics seldom attempt the journey. Between the hazards of the road and the promised hazards of London, we stay among our sheep where it's safe and—"

"Dull?" he smiled, completing her thought with an impudent insertion of his own.

In spite of the impudence she laughed. "Perhaps. Though there are times when the weekly newspapers bring me quite enough of that great city."

"You should never pay the slightest attention to journalists, Miss Powels," he continued, still standing erect before her. "Though I live in the city and love it, I scarcely recognize it after certain scribblers have finished with it."

"Is there such a distortion? I thought all journalists were pledged to the truth."

"To *their* truth, yes, of course," he conceded. "But the wise man, or woman," he added pointedly, "comes and judges for herself."

As the others apparently were willing to stand and watch, Harriet was is no hurry to end the conversation. The lovely late June dusk had begun to spin a pink web about the inner courtyard. "Tell me what you do in London, Mr. Eden," she asked lightly.

He answered as rapidly as though he'd known her question in advance. "I do very little, Miss Powels," he smiled. "I don't have to." This was said simply, as though out of the habit of honesty. He stepped back and gestured in a southeasterly direction. "Do you remember the town of Taunton?" he inquired politely. "You must have passed through it mid-afternoon."

She nodded.

"When you left that thriving village," he went on, "you were on Eden land. You traveled across it for most of the afternoon."

She saw her father step close with interest. "Tenanted, I assume?"

"For the most part, yes. We do have sheep, nothing to compare to your herds, I'm sure—"

She saw her father smile, as though he'd made a point.

Edward Eden went on. "But of course, unlike you, we have in addition to the land on one side, the ocean on the other. It provides a rich bounty."

Harriet found herself wishing that her father had stayed out of it. It was graceless to speak so soon on such matters. Then too, he had drawn off the bulk of Mr. Eden's attention. She was a little shocked to realize that she felt it as a privation.

Lady Eden was beside her now. "How thoughtless of us," she apologized, "to keep you standing about for so long. I'll have a steward take you to your chambers."

But at that moment, Sophia Cranford interceded. "I will take her, milady," she said forcefully, "and Lord and Lady Powels as well. Now, come along, all of you."

Then they were moving up the stairs, her mother chatting with Sophia Cranford, while, behind, Lady Eden held her position as though perfectly willing to let someone else take the lead. She saw her father following after the small procession, his discussion with Edward Eden apparently concluded.

They were moving through the Great Hall now, a few servants standing at attention as they passed. At that moment, she heard light footsteps behind them and turned to see Jennifer following alone a distance behind.

Happy at her appearance, Harriet drew lightly away from James and waited for the young woman to catch up. But the girl merely stopped a distance away and without raising her eyes murmured, "If you'd care to walk tomorrow, Miss Powels, I'd be happy to escort you—"

Pleased, Harriet walked back to where the young woman stood. "I beg you," she smiled, "let's not be so formal. Harriet, and may I call you Jennifer?"

Still without looking up, Jennifer nodded her head. "If you'll excuse me now," she whispered, and within the moment she was gone, like a frightened animal, slipping out of sight down one of the corridors which led off the Great Hall.

Harriet looked back at James, who was still watching. "She seems very nice, your sister."

He nodded. "We don't see much of her. Like Edward, she's gone most of the year. I seem to be the only stay-at-home."

He took her arm again and as they hurried to catch up with the others, Harriet looked about at the bleak surroundings. It seemed such a dank cold place, this castle, quite a contrast after the light, sunny, high-ceilinged halls of Hadley Park. She tried to imagine passing a childhood here and shuddered lightly.

Still ascending after a small landing, she felt the air grow damp and cool upon her face. Ahead, she saw her mother clearly growing winded from the climb while Sophia Cranford moved straight ahead, undaunted. Her father seemed to be keeping pace, although he too turned, looking at one wall, then the other, in clear disdain.

Harriet felt a menacing dip in her spirits as she tried to envision herself moving through these corridors for the rest of her life.

Then before a small arched wooden door, the grim little parade came to a halt. "These will be your apartments, Miss Powels." Sophia Cranford pushed open the door and Harriet caught a glimpse of the interior, dark and shadowy. As she started across the threshold, Miss Cranford ordered James to "Keep her company until I return. Then we must leave our weary guests alone for an interval."

James smiled awkwardly and stood back to allow her to pass before him into the apartments. "These chambers originally belonged to my grandmother," he said, in the manner of a tour guide. "I hope you will find them to your liking."

Harriet assured him that she would and stepped to the center of the reception room, a small stone cell graced only with a central table, two straight-backed chairs, and against one wall, her arrangement of trunks. Beyond this room she saw the sitting room, not quite as spartan with a series of rich Brussels tapestries decorating the wall, a very handsome white marble fireplace, a furl of red and blue Persian carpet beneath her feet, and a pretty arrangement of roses on a broad round table.

"They're lovely," she exclaimed, touching the flowers. On the far wall she noticed two small windows, waist high, through which she saw night. A single lamp burned on the table beside the roses. To the left on the far wall she noticed a door which must lead to sleeping chambers.

Apparently he'd taken careful note of her quick inventory and now offered, "If the rooms are not suitable, I'm certain Sophia can—"

"Oh no, they're fine," she hurried to reassure him. She looked out the small windows which gave a view of nothing save turrets and more gray stone. Rather alarmed, she looked at the single lamp and tried to imagine the room at midnight. "Another lamp, perhaps," she ventured tentatively, longing for her brightly lit chambers at Hadley Park, a round dozen bronze lamps lighting every corner.

"Of course," he agreed. "I shall see to it immediately."

As he turned to go, she called to him apologetically, "It's not necessary now," she suggested. "Later."

He stopped as though at her command. Their eyes met in the awkward silence. His moved away first. "So," he said, in a suddenly expansive mood, rubbing his hands together as though they were cold. "You're here," he added further, "and you've met the Edens." He looked back at her. "Would I be too bold to inquire as to your opinion?"

Taken off guard by the direct question, she took momentary refuge in a close inspection of the roses. "My opinion concerning what?" she asked.

He shrugged. "Everything."

The tension of the moment, the strange surroundings, her dwindling spirits all took a toll. "I'm sorry, James," she confessed. "I'm not certain what you want me to say."

His expression was angry, certainly out of sorts, as though events had gone hard for him as well. "I should think it would be apparent," he said in a businesslike manner. "Can you," he began with admirable purpose, then faltered, then tried again. "Can you, that is to say, are you able to—envision a future here?"

He was moving too fast. Embarrassed, she turned away. "Why don't we see how the days pass," she suggested. "Then perhaps later—"

But he merely stepped forward as though she had not spoken at all, a curious tension on his face. "I need an heir," he said, even more bluntly than before.

Her embarrassment now was a source of pain. She was fairly certain that James was the sort of man who would find a woman's love soothing to his ego as long as he was not obliged to return it. However, love had never been mentioned, wifely or otherwise. "Well?" he prompted, still watching her. "Surely you knew that was the point and purpose of—"

"I knew," she nodded, unable to look at him.

"Then what?"

"I need time," she whispered, almost fiercely, to the window.

To this he did not respond, but instead came up behind her. She felt first his hand on her arm, an insistent hand that was now turning her toward him.

"There's no need," he smiled. "I *am* fond of you. And I

had thought in our brief times together that you were fond of me, at least you gave me that impression."

She was so cold. But she decided that as long as she could bear the cold she would hear him out.

But steadily, moment by moment, it grew worse. Both his hands were holding her now. She saw herself in her imagination running on ice. Every few paces she fell, for her slippers would not grip the frozen terrain. And each time that she fell, the monster pursuing her watched and smiled grotesquely.

Fortunately his kiss was passionless and short-lived. He released her and stepped back. "I think we could have a good life together," he said.

She continued to stare forward. Now all that she saw was long white miles and she heard the terrible silence, and still she felt the cold.

How cold it was!

Then she heard another voice, a false, cheery, high-pitched woman's voice. "Ah, there you are, the lovebirds. I trust, Miss Powels, that you will be comfortable here. I know it's isolated, but it makes for quiet sleeping. Out of all the apartments in this wing, I do believe—"

The chirping bird voice of Miss Cranford ceased. "I say, are you well?" she inquired, coming around the table and stopping short by a few feet.

James answered for her. "She's merely tired, Sophia. We've really been very thoughtless, you know. After that long journey—"

Harriet rallied. "He's right," she murmured. "I need a bit of time to—"

"And you shall have it," Miss Cranford insisted generously. "There will be a simple dinner tonight at ten. I shall either come for you myself or send James."

Harriet smiled and tried to look grateful. Apparently her expression satisfied both, for they were moving toward the reception hall now, Sophia reminding her with pride of the system of bells and pointing to a small panel beside the archway. "It's really quite efficient. Your servants are waiting below. All you must do is summon them."

Then, blessedly, Harriet saw the heavy wooden door close. She held still for a moment longer, listening to their retreating footsteps. Then silence.

Gently she reached out and touched the table cautiously

as though she were afraid of breaking something. She tried to breathe deeply and found she was incapable of it.

Then she moved forward into activity, ripped off her gloves, and discovered the sheet of paper which Miss Cranford had given her earlier, the familiar names of her servants corresponding to certain numbers. With trembling hands, she took the chart to the bell panel beside the door and tried to hold it steady, tried to clear her eyes of tears at least to the extent that she could read.

Nelda. That would be her lady's maid, and beside her name, was that a two or a three? And there was Mary, and what was that number? A four? She couldn't see and in frustration lifted her hand and pressed wildly on all the buttons, expecting the sound of a shrill alarm, the desperate need to signal someone for help.

But the buttons merely gave beneath her shaking hands and made no sound. If the alarm was going off somewhere, she couldn't hear it. Help would not come. She was alone in this dreadful place, faced with no options, no alternatives, only the pressing weight of duty.

What was it James had said? The point and purpose of this whole affair. Of course she could go quietly home to Hadley Park and endure the condemnation of her parents and live to full spinsterhood. Her life would be saved, but she would be as dead. A few days, a few years, a lifetime are all the same when you've lost the illusion of your own worth.

Suddenly her head dropped forward against the wall, her forehead resting on the unresponsive panel of buttons. The tears ceased. One cried when there was hope.

Her eyes stared unseeing at the floor. Then this was her destination, this narrow cold cell.

Calm. Be calm . . .

During the next few days the procession of carriages passing through the castle gates was endless. Edward watched most of it from his chambers on the third floor through windows which gave a perfect view of the inner courtyard. The hanging lanterns were still in place and supplemented now by banners of all colors bearing the coats of arms of each visiting house. Each carriage seemed to require even more pomp and ritual than the one before it as trumpeteers brought out from Exeter heralded the new arrivals.

It had been like a circus, and Edward had viewed it from a safe distance, through eyes glazed by repeated draughts of opium. He'd taken no part in any of the receptions. The guests were strangers to him, old friends of his mother's and father's come to witness the ritual of continuity of line. He'd thought that by staying out of sight he was performing a service for the family. Bastardy at best was an embarrassment, something to be kept in the closet, certainly on an occasion such as this.

During his self-imposed confinement, he'd enlisted the aid of his coachman, John Murrey, and had instantly elevated him from coachman to steward. He had given him instructions that he and he alone was to see to *all* of Edward's needs. Certainly John Murrey knew of Edward's addiction and was not likely to say anything if he found his master lying dazed upon his couch. As long as Edward had to endure confinement at Eden Castle, this was a workable arrangement.

Thus he had passed the days in pleasant oblivion, and now awakened to find dark outside the windows, dramatically broken by the continuous rows of torches along the castle walls. John Murrey was bending over him, his gnarled hands trying to shake him out of his drugged lethargy. Somewhere off in the vast distance he thought he heard music.

"Mr. Eden, sir," John whispered. "Please, sir, wake up."

Reluctantly, Edward lifted his head, trying to oblige the old man and curious, though a little annoyed, to know the nature of his urgency.

Convinced that since his eyes were open, he was capable of hearing words, John Murrey stood back from the bed a respectful distance. "Beggin' your pardon, sir, but I brought your food—"

Annoyance increasing, Edward shook his head and lay back on the pillow. "No food, John," he muttered. "No food, not now."

"You must, sir," the old man pleaded. "The lady was here, your mother. She wanted to come in, sir, but I wouldn't let her. You were—" He hesitated, at a loss for words to describe the early stages of an opium trance. "You—were not suitable," he concluded.

Edward stared up. Slowly he raised himself again from the pillow. "I'm grateful, John," he muttered.

John Murrey backed away a few steps. "You won't be, sir, when you hear the rest of it," he said ominously. "I told the lady," he began, "that you would come down tonight."

Edward started to protest, but John cut him off. "It was the only way, sir," he pleaded. "She was carrying on like—" He shook his head, still pleading. "Please, sir, just long enough to let her see you."

"I'm sorry, sir," murmured John Murrey, seeing the desolate look on his face. Then stepping forward with a daring which spoke of his own discomfort, he said, "Don't know why we ever come, sir, beggin' your pardon. Don't belong here. Either of us. Back in London, that's our proper ground, back with the others who don't stand on no ritual. But here—"

He broke off suddenly and with his arms made a massive gesture of rejection. His face grew reflective. "At home in London, Cook's always nice and gentle, saying, 'Here, John, have yourself a cuppa tea,' or 'John, sit while I fetch you a pint.'" A look of genuine sadness covered the lean old face. "And the young 'uns always laughing and shouting, and Mr. Daniel keepin' things in order, yet kind—"

Edward listened carefully to the whole recitation, sharing the old man's homesickness. He steadied himself on the bedpost and joined him where he stood a short distance away. Affectionately he rested his arm on the bent shoulders and promised, "We'll go home soon, John." He stopped short of telling the man that they could not return to London. Not at least for the duration of the summer, that if they didn't pass their exile here, they would have to pass it someplace else.

As though to soften the blow of this unspoken message, he patted John on the shoulder and promised, "I'll dress now, and a bite of food might help." He stood erect as though to make good his vow. "If you said I'll be there, then I'll be there."

It was approaching midnight when at last he stood before the pier glass, shaved, dressed, and mildly fortified with a glass of claret lightly laced with laudanum. It was his intention to be back in his chambers by one o'clock, a perfunctory appearance, undoubtedly designed to display family unity.

"You look fine, sir," smiled John Murrey, making a final adjustment to the black dress jacket.

Edward received the compliment for what it was and turned away from the pier glass. "Help yourself," he said, motioning to the half-filled bottle of claret on the table. Then dreading the ordeal before him, but determined to get it over with, he headed for the door. He stopped and looked back at his chambers, old John Murrey watching anxiously. Grateful for such concern, he promised again, "We'll go home soon, John. Bear with me."

Without hesitation, the old man replied, "I'm always with you, sir. I'd be in my grave now if it weren't for you." He lifted a hand to his forehead as though in salute. "You lead. I'll follow," he grinned, revealing missing teeth.

Edward stared at him, remembering the night he'd found him, half-starved under Westminster Bridge, beaten and left for dead by a gang of river rats. How changed he was now. Not an excess of flesh, but filled out, a piece of humanity that once had been wreckage. The intensity of Edward's gaze clearly began to cause the old man embarrassment. Quickly Edward averted his eyes and turned to the door. There was a good possibility that he had just turned his back on the choicest company in all of Eden Castle.

He closed the door behind him and moved toward the end of the passage and was just in the process of taking the short hall which led to the landing when he heard voices coming up the stairs, a chattering, anxious procession, mostly female, though he thought he detected the lower registers of a man's voice.

Quickly he drew back into a small alcove. He was not ready yet to face the company, but in a way he was curious as to the nature of this procession. Then he heard Sophia Cranford's voice, unmistakable, like a curse from God. He drew farther back and felt a sort of sullen anger as it occurred to him that perhaps this chattering delegation had been sent to fetch him. He heard the voices clearer now, earnest male voices, both James and Caleb.

"Let us call the physician," he heard Caleb say over the continuous hum.

And then James, "It might be best. One can't be too careful. Fever is rampant—"

Then Sophia's voice, scolding. "Oh, for heaven's sake, James, you'll frighten the girl to death. Fever! I've never heard of anything so ridiculous."

"She just needs to lie down a bit," somebody said. "It *was* warm below, and—"

They were in the small passageway now, less than ten feet from where Edward hid. He felt stealthy and ridiculous, but any move was out of the question. He relaxed against the cool stone wall, relieved that they had not come for him. No, someone else was the focal point of their attention, someone who was ill, or who had begged off on the pretense of illness.

"Please," he heard a woman whisper. "Go back to the ball, all of you. Miss Cranford is right. I only need a—"

Then he heard Miss Cranford again. "And leave you? The guest of honor? Never. Certainly not. I'll sit with you myself—"

"It isn't necessary—"

"Or James," Sophia suggested. "Yes, James will sit with you."

The pleading voice seemed to grow unduly distraught. "No, please, I beg you. Just an interval alone—"

Listening closely, Edward thought he heard the voice break.

Then he heard another female voice, younger, timid. "I'll stay with her, ma'am. She'll be right enough, I promise you. Back at Hadley Park, milady always needs a brief respite during entertainments—"

Obviously the prolonged speech from the servant had shocked Sophia into silence. But when Miss Powels confirmed her maid's words with a final, "Please, she's right. Go back to the party, all of you," Edward heard a moment's muddled silence.

"Well, it *is* warm," Sophia agreed, half-heartedly. "I'll have a pitcher of fresh lavender water sent up."

"It isn't necessary," the young woman said.

James stayed for a final inquiry. "Are you sure?"

"I'm fine," she soothed.

The voice sounded firm and reassuring. The little company broke up, several moving back down the stairs now.

Edward held his position in the alcove. He'd heard footsteps on the stairs. He had yet to hear footsteps moving toward the east wing. Then he heard the maid, her voice concerned, "Come, milady. I'll help—"

"No, you go along as well, Nelda," the young woman insisted. "I need no help. I'll lie down for a moment and if I need you, I'll ring."

"But, milady, I said that I—"

Suddenly the well-modulated voice rose, no longer affable and compliant. "I said go along, Nelda. If I need you for anything, I'll let you know." The voice vibrated with emotion, like a survivor clinging to a single piece of wreckage.

Clearly the servant had not often heard that tone from her mistress and now beat a quick retreat. "Yes, milady," she murmured, her voice fading as she hurried down the passageway.

He heard a light flurry of footsteps on the stairs, then he heard nothing else, though by his estimate there still was someone standing less than ten feet away.

With his head pressed back against the wall of the alcove, he continued to listen. Was she going to stand there all evening?

Then he heard a first tentative step, and something else, a quick inhalation of breath, like a sob.

He heard it again, a second sharp inhalation of breath, a sound of such consummate wretchedness that he threw hazard over and leaned forward. He saw her standing in the center of the passageway, both hands clutching her mid-section as though indeed she were ill. He had never witnessed such inarticulate grief, almost childlike in its manifestation.

His instinct was to speak. But prudence intervened, and he continued to watch as now she made her way slowly down the corridor, the sobs catching in her throat. He followed a discreet distance behind.

Then just as she was approaching the door which led to the guest apartments, she seemed to lean heavily against the wall, her head flung back as though for an instant she'd been unable to draw breath. In one of the most pitiful human sounds he'd ever heard, she moaned, "Oh God, help." Then he saw her slowly collapse against the base of the wall.

Never taking his eyes off her, he advanced, sending his voice ahead. "Milady, may I—"

Again he stopped to see if there was any reaction. There wasn't. From where he stood she appeared lifeless, her face obscured by her position. He was aware of the distant music coming from the festivities below, the orchestra playing out a quadrille, the entire company apparently unaware of the guest of honor collapsed in the upper corridor.

"Milady," he whispered again, drawing nearer, feeling an increase in alarm as still she showed no signs of life or movement. He knelt beside her and lightly touched one opened hand. When there was no response, he drew her backward from her collapsed position and saw her face for the first time, pale and colorless, still wet with tears, eyes closed.

Without further hesitation he lifted her in his arms and carried her rapidly into the guest apartments, through the small sitting room, and on through to the bedchamber. There he placed her on the high, canopied bed and fetched the lamp, burning low on the table. Moving rapidly now, he stripped the long white gloves from her arms, drew a light coverlet up over the blue gown, and commenced rubbing her hand. It was cold, without response.

Frantically, he looked over his shoulder at the scattered items on the dressing table. He saw several small bottles and from that distance searched for one that resembled smelling salts.

But then he felt her hand stir, lift briefly. He saw her eyes open, then close, the head toss once upon the pillow, then hold still.

She was back, her eyes open and staring at him. He smiled and stood up from the bed in an attempt to put her at ease. But still her response was one of alarm. As she started rapidly up from the pillow, he stepped forward. "No, please. Lie still," he urged. "For a few minutes anyway."

At the sound of his voice, her eyes seemed to grow ever wider. One hand moved up to her throat.

"No need for alarm," he soothed. "I was just on my way down to lift a toast to you when I found you outside."

He hesitated, not certain how he should describe her collapsed state.

She seemed to be surveying him in bewilderment and it occurred to him that perhaps she didn't remember meeting him the night of her arrival.

"I'm Edward Eden," he smiled. "We met briefly that first night."

Then he heard her first words. "I remember," she whispered. She lifted her eyes to the canopy overhead. "What I don't remember," she went on, "is how I got here."

He considered persisting with his lie, the story that he'd simply found her in the passageway. But he changed his mind. "I can't give you details of the entire evening," he began, speaking gently. "I only saw you about fifteen minutes ago as you came up from the ball." He paused to see if the reminder was sufficient. Apparently it wasn't. "There were others with you," he continued. "They thought you were ill."

Then something registered. Her eyes closed as though she wanted to blot out the memory. "I'm—sorry," she whispered.

"Why don't you lie still for just a while," he suggested. "Would you like for me to ring for—"

She shook her head quickly. "No, please." Her hand moved back to her hair and loosened the clip. A moment later a cascade of long auburn hair slipped down about her shoulders, causing her to look younger. "It's so—warm," she murmured, and again she leaned back into the pillows.

He gazed at her, then walked rapidly to the table where he'd seen her articles of toilette. He lifted a clean linen, poured water over it from the pitcher, wrung it lightly, and returned to the bed. "If you won't let me summon help, then you must accept mine," he said, approaching the bed with the cool damp cloth.

When she registered no objection, he placed it on her forehead. "Are you feeling better?" he inquired politely.

The softest of smiles graced her features. "I've never done this before, so I'm afraid I have no gauge for my feelings." Lightly she shook her head and rearranged the damp linen to her liking. "Would you say that I fainted?" she asked, as though genuinely wanting to know.

"In my judgment, yes."

The smile on her face grew into a gentle laugh. "So that's what it's like. I had a friend when I was younger who could faint at the sound of a strong wind. I always thought she looked so appealing. I used to hold my breath, thinking I could induce a similar condition. But it never worked."

"I'd say you did something right tonight."

Again she looked up at him. The smile faded. She seemed on the verge of saying something, but apparently changed her mind. Instead she made an attempt to sit up. "I'm quite restored now," she said, her manner formal, her head bowed.

"Are you certain?"

"Yes." She tried to stand, as though to demonstrate the validity of her words. But suddenly she wavered again, both hands reaching out for support. He was there and gently helped her back to the side of the bed. "Please," he urged. "Stay still for a while longer. There's no rush."

Apparently she had no choice but to obey. As she settled again on the edge of the bed, she fingered the damp linen, her head down as though embarrassed by her weakness. "It was so close downstairs," she began, "the company large and noisy. And the meal was heavy, so much—" She broke off midsentence as though not particularly interested in her own words. She looked directly at him. "I'm really quite well. And you have been very kind. I don't want to inconvenience you any—"

"You're not inconveniencing me," he hastened to reassure her. "As I said, I was coming to toast the guest of honor. I can't very well toast her if she's not there."

Almost shyly she glanced in his direction. "There's no reason for you to stand about. Please take a chair—if you wish."

Without hesitation he dragged a large overstuffed chair from the center of the room and positioned it about four feet from the bed. He watched fascinated as her hand moved over her breasts and up to her throat. She still seemed to be suffering from distress. "Do you suppose they will come looking for me?" she whispered.

"Most probably," he concurred. When he saw the bleak look on her face, he suggested, "You're not terribly pleased with us, are you?"

She looked sharply up at his words, a protest already forming. "That's not true," she said apologetically.

"Isn't it?" he persisted. "Out there"—and he inclined his head toward the corridor—"you did not resemble a gloriously happy future bride."

She looked at him as though within the moment she had grasped the meaning of his words. As her embarrassment increased, she stood, and using the bed for support, walked around it as though to put a safe distance between them. "Please," she begged softly, "let's not speak on such matters."

But he persisted. "Why were you crying?"

Rather defiantly she looked at him across the expanse of bed. "I told you. I wasn't feeling well."

"Are you going to marry James?"

Suddenly she turned away from the bed and walked rapidly to the windows on the far side of the room. Her voice when she spoke sounded as strained as it had in the corridor. "I can't understand why there are no views from these windows," she said. "We're certainly high enough and I've heard forever about the vistas of Eden. Where are they?"

He left the chair and went to her. "Are you feeling stronger?" he asked.

She nodded.

He caught her hand and turned her away from the viewless windows. "Then come," he smiled. "I'll show you vistas."

A strong protest was forming on her face. "We can't go back down," she gasped. "They'd see us and never let us pass."

Now excited by the idea in his mind, he merely led her forward. "We're not going down," he said. "We're going up." Rather melodramatically he pointed toward the ceiling. "Come! The air will do you good, do us both good. I haven't been on the battlements since I was a boy."

He could see that the idea appealed to her. He made a hasty assessment of the full-skirted ball gown, then warned, "The passage is narrow and steep. Would you care to change?"

But clearly the adventure had taken hold in her mind and she didn't want to hesitate. "No, let's hurry. They may come back."

Still holding her hand, he guided her rapidly out of the bedchamber and through the reception hall. At the door he paused, opened it a crack, and peered out in both directions. He looked back at her with a massive shushing gesture, delighted by the look of excitement on her face.

"Stay close behind," he whispered, exploiting the melodrama of the moment because it seemed to please her.

Then, still holding her hand, he hurried out into the corridor, moving east along the passageway toward the secret stairway which he and Daniel had discovered as boys, thinking it their unique find until his father had spoiled it by giving them a complete history, telling them how it had been built to accommodate Queen Elizabeth's numerous and unofficial lovers while she had been on state visits to Eden. The stairway ran the entire height of the castle, a narrow twisting passage commencing at an unobtrusive door in the east wall and culminating, through a trap door, out on the battlements.

As they stole like culprits down corridor after corridor, Edward felt the years rolling back. He was a boy again, running with Daniel to one of their secret places. In his growing excitement he felt a peculiar increase in the effects of the opium in his system. Every sound of their footsteps was recorded distinctly in his ear, and since he had been thinking on Daniel, he thought he heard his voice.

Edward turned sharply and looked back. Harriet was still behind him, her once pale cheeks now flushed with excitement. "What is it?" she whispered.

"Nothing," he murmured, realizing that it was merely the effects of opium, altering the bonds of both space and time.

"You're not lost, are you?"

Returning to himself, he offered reassurance which sounded strangely like the younger Edward. "Lost?" he laughed. "In my own castle? Come, it's not much farther."

Although they were well past the inhabited areas of the castle, still Edward led the way with an air of stealth, guiding her carefully up a series of stone steps, brushing cobwebs out of their path as the corridor narrowed and grew darker. Only then did it occur to him that he should have brought a lantern. But in the next minute he was pleased that he hadn't. What he felt coming from her was not fear, but rather an almost shining sense of daring, as though she had lived too long within the safe confines of decorum and good sense.

Then it was before them, the small door which led to the narrow secret stairway. "I'll go first," he whispered. "Put your arms about my waist."

She did as she was told. He anchored her crossed arms with one hand and pulled the door open. "If I recall," he murmured, "there is one steep step up here, then the stairway itself."

And it was so, and slowly he led her into the black artery, feeling her arms tighten about his waist, yet she was willing to follow him. "Are you well?" he whispered, though whispering was no longer necessary.

"Yes."

"I don't remember it being so dark."

But if she heard, she gave no reply and continued to follow stumbling now and then, but always holding tightly to him.

Then at last they had reached the heights. Lifting his hands, he felt the trap door. When it didn't give with his first effort, he tried again, stepping farther up and putting his shoulder into it. For an instant he wondered if it had been secured in some fashion. But then he heard an encouraging scrape, felt the ancient barrier give, and a moment later he lifted it, resting its full weight on his shoulders.

First came the wind, the incredible gale force that he remembered as a boy, a whirlpool alliance of channel breezes and ocean currents blending and buffeting the top of the castle in a continuous assault. Alone at the top, he glanced about, lifted his head to the wind as though it were medicinal, then quickly extended a hand back to her where she still waited patiently on the darkened stairway.

He watched her face carefully as he led her up. Vision was simple with the full moon and cloudless heavens. She returned his glance with a degree of apprehension, then cleared the stairway. She took the first slap of wind and seemed to recoil from it as though she'd not been expecting it, then lifted her head and closed her eyes as though to receive it again, this time with pleasure.

She said nothing, nor did he as they walked slowly around the battlements, something on her face which suggested that she was not quite believing what she was seeing, as though she had stumbled into a dream made up of unearthly vistas.

He closed his eyes briefly, then opened them and saw her walking a distance away, her long hair free and unencumbered, blowing back in the wind. She walked to the end of the battlements, gazing out over the channel as he had done, then leaned out as though to see the castle below.

Without wanting to alarm her, he called out, "Be careful."

He held his position and watched as she encircled the entire area twice, leaning out in spite of his warning now and then as though to check her position with earth below. There was something childlike about her, an excitement which bore no resemblance to her earlier state. Then at last she returned to where he stood, her hair quite undone and streaming about her face. "And you prefer London to this?" she asked, lifting her voice over the wind.

He smiled. "There's more to Eden than this secluded battlement," he said, a mild warning in his voice.

She looked at him and slowly nodded, as though again fully understanding his words. Still, "It's beautiful," she went on, "so different from—"

But the wind took her words and lifted them and blew them away and he couldn't hear. He remembered the protection of a large chimney near the opposite edge of the battlement, the spot where he and Daniel had planned their strategies.

"Come," he suggested, leading her into the narrow opening. "At least we won't have to shout here."

The closeness of the confinement was pleasing. He saw her leaning against the chimney and looking upward at the night sky. "I must say," he smiled, "you look totally restored."

"I am," she replied. She seemed to suffer a slight self-consciousness, then added, "Thank you, Edward, for bringing me here."

The fact that she had addressed him with familiarity was not lost on him. "I would come here every day," she murmured, "if I resided at Eden.".

"Will you?" he asked quietly. "Reside at Eden, I mean?"

She glanced at him, no longer embarrassed as she had appeared below in her chambers. Now her expression was one of resignation. "I suspect that plans of that nature are being laid."

"And is it your desire?"

"I don't think I have much voice in the matter."

"Why not?"

For an instant he saw the gloom on her face even though

she was staring silently out to sea. She was not, as he had expected she would be, the empty-headed, cold-natured, pampered daughter of a peer of the realm. There was the suggestion about her of unmined riches.

So intent was his scrutiny of her that only now did he realize that she was returning his gaze.

"Why have you not joined the company for the last few days?" she asked, displaying a bluntness which at least matched his own.

He laughed and shook his head. "I know none of the guests," he offered lamely. "I felt out of place—"

"Sophia Cranford said you were ill."

"Ill?" he repeated. "She'd like that very much, but I assure you, I'm not ill—"

"Why did you hold back that night we arrived? You were the last to come forward in greeting, yet it's your castle."

"You were not my guest," he replied, finding her questions interesting.

"Still you stood very much apart," she persisted.

"I am apart," he said. "As I told you, I spend most of my time in London."

"Why?"

"It suits me." He was aware suddenly of a strong acceleration of his pulse. She had shifted her position, had bent over as though in examination of something at her feet.

"Look," she smiled.

He lowered his eyes to where, below her skirts, he saw bare feet. "What in—" He started forward.

She laughed. "I lost my slippers on the stairway."

He started to bend down and only at the last moment caught himself. She saw his unease. "It's quite all right," she said. "I can retrieve them later."

He continued to stare down at the small white naked foot. Then she lowered her gown and stood erect again. She seemed totally at ease now, the grief which earlier had plagued her completely gone. "Does it get very cold here?" she asked lightly, her mind obviously turning at random.

"In winter, yes," he replied, still amazed at the tumultuous feelings the sight of those bare feet had aroused within him. "A damp cold," he went on, "and on occasion, snow."

"I dislike winter," she said, as though it were an innate failing. "I remember being forced to take walks in winter. It always seemed so dreadful and unnecessary, coming home in the raw twilight with nipped fingers and toes—"

He watched her carefully, not clearly listening to what she was saying, concentrating instead on the play of moonlight upon her face, the way one side of that lovely cameo would appear first lit, then in shadow. Then softly she said, "If I don't have to think very much on what's ahead, I may come to reside at Eden Castle."

He saw it again, the desperation on her face. It occurred to him that it would be more considerate to divert her attention to something else.

But he didn't. With a full awareness of what he was doing, he said, "You're not a pawn, you know. Your life is your own."

She looked at him as though shocked by his idiocy. "Clearly you are not a woman," she smiled.

"Meaning?"

"Meaning that you are able to entertain such luxurious thoughts as self-determination."

"And you are not?"

She looked at him with a timid glance. "I serve no purpose, fulfill no destiny other than reproduction."

"That's nonsense."

"I wish it were." Suddenly she pressed her head back against the chimney, her eyes closed. "Oh God, let's not talk of it," she begged. The despair lasted only a moment. "Tell me of yourself," she asked quietly. "How do you pass your days in London?"

When he failed to answer, she prodded gently. "You must do something. I thought I was the only one who existed in a vacuum."

"We—have a school," he began, trying to rally his wits about him. "A Ragged School, they call it." He shook his head. "I have little to do with it. It's simply established in my house. Daniel runs it. Daniel Spade."

"A good friend?" she inquired.

"The best," he replied. "We grew up together. Here at Eden." He looked about him. "The last time I stood here, I was with Daniel."

She seemed to be listening closely. She surprised him

then by asking almost blithely, "Why have you never married?"

While it was a simple question, it was not so simply answered. "I've never met anyone who would have me," he smiled.

"I don't believe that."

"It's true."

"Is it because of your illegitimacy?" she asked, again painfully blunt. "Bastards marry," she said simply. "I'm sure you know women."

He nodded, fascinated by their game of truthfulness. It was as though neither of them seemed inclined to censor any thought, no matter how painful or scandalous. If it was a game, and he was certain it was, he decided to play it willingly. Now in an attempt to shock her, he said, "I know prostitutes for the most part. There's a young girl now, living in the house in London. Elizabeth is her name."

"Where did you meet her?" she asked, apparently not shocked in the least.

He felt a moment's unease. How glibly they were speaking of unspeakable things. "In Newgate," he replied, monitoring her reaction. But again he saw nothing. It was as though this sheltered blueblood was beyond being shocked.

"The prison?" she inquired casually.

"The prison."

"And what were you doing there?"

"I was under arrest."

"On what charge?"

"For public brawling."

"And you met Elizabeth there?"

Again he nodded, unable to account for her remorseless interest in such sordid matters. Under normal conditions and in polite circumstances, they ought to have been discussing a comparison of Shropshire hunts and Devon hunts, the Christmas cotillion, the state of King William's health, the pros and cons of the German influence on the young Victoria.

"Did she offer herself to you?" she asked then, the shadows completely gone from her face.

Incredibly he was the one who suffered embarrassment. Still he replied honestly, intent on playing the game. "She did," he replied, amazed at the face opposite him.

"And did you have her?"

He shook his head.

"And why not?" she persisted.

"She's scarcely a child," he murmured. "Very young."

"So you took her home?"

He nodded.

She seemed to be listening with incredible intensity, as though her fascination knew no bounds. She stood erect before him now, no longer leaning against the chimney. A curious resolution seemed to settle on her face. Then he heard her voice again, speaking dangerous words. "Did you know the adulteress, Charlotte Longford?"

Suddenly there churned inside his head a memory. He turned away, taking refuge for the moment in the nimble beams of bright light playing about the night sky.

"I'm sorry," she murmured. "But we do receive newsprint in the Midlands. The account of the trial was carried in full. Your house was mentioned. I believe she worked there as a volunteer—"

Still he made no response. The game of truthfulness had gone too far. Her inquiries were tactless.

"Did you know her?" she persisted, moving up close beside him.

He nodded, trying to ignore the wound, those prevailing memories of guilt.

"Did you make love to her?"

Suddenly he turned on her. "Why are you asking these questions?" he demanded.

"I have no right," she agreed.

"No."

Then in spite of their mutual agreement on the impropriety of her words, she asked, with a slight though all-important variation, "Did you love her?"

Now she appeared before him like a tormentor. The memories and images were as fresh as though they had just occurred. He saw the rat scrambling up the prison garb, then disappearing behind her back. He saw himself try to pull her forward, saw the grotesque angle of her neck and head as she remained in spite of death, pinned to the wall.

As these images returned to him, he looked back at Harriet, perplexed. "Why?"

"Ahead of me is a lifetime of lies," she said simply. "I can play the role, I really can," she exclaimed with grieved astonishment. "I'll work my way through the years, obedient and docile, if only I can have a *now*, one perfect, honest now."

Her cheeks seemed to grow pale as though she belatedly suffered from her own daring. "I know nothing and have no time to learn," she went on softly. "You've known both passion and grief in abundance. Please share them with me. I shall feed on them for the rest of my life and—"

She didn't finish her thought, but turned away. He had never heard such a plea, or had it been a confession? He stretched out his hand for her arm and touched it, gently turned her toward him. As he drew her still closer, he imagined her feet white and naked near his boots. She lifted her hand to his face and with two fingers traced the angle of his jaw, culminating in a light caress of his lips.

The moonlight vanished from her face as the shadow of his head replaced it. He moved at first with a certain tentativeness, still bewildered by her. He heard again her words, "I'll work my way through the years, obedient and docile—" She spoke nonsense and later he intended to tell her so.

But for this moment he felt no need for words. He bent his head and touched her lips with his, found them open and receptive, and drew her still closer, pinning her to him in an embrace as though he intended to pull her through him. As his tongue explored her mouth, he was aware of her arms about him, the press of her body against his.

As the kiss ended, they looked at each other as though mutually shocked by the degree of their passion. There still was a lingering look of sadness on her face. But with a conscious effort of will, he dismissed it.

Again he felt her hand on his face, her fingertips tracing his jaw. "I'm memorizing it," she whispered, "against the day when it will be gone from me."

"I will never be gone from you," he vowed, gathering her to him.

"No," she agreed, in the last moment before their lips met again, this embrace even more violent than the last. He had the feeling of fast-gathering tumults. His hands on her back moved down to the softness of her hips. In spite of the skirts, he felt the contours of her legs. "Come to me," he whispered as the kiss ended.

"I will," she promised. "Though not here, not now."

"When?"

She drew away from him, her voice manifesting a peculiar disciplined quality. "Our perfect now will last five days," she said, looking back at him, as though reining in her own feelings.

He watched her closely and thought her the most beautiful creature he'd ever seen. He was certain she felt as he did. Then why talk of a limited now? Of course they had the others to contend with, but the announcement could be made quietly, swiftly, and then they would leave immediately, not for London, not for a while. Perhaps Scotland, a Highland cottage, isolated, where at leisure and in seclusion, they could learn what had occurred in the years before this night.

As he plotted their future in one direction, he heard her still speaking of a limited bliss. "Five days," she repeated, her voice strangely calm. "We'll make a bargain on it. I would like to walk with you, to feel you at my side. And we will ride one day, across the moors, so that I may see you on horseback, and one day we shall explore the beach together to chart one another against swelling space—" Her voice dropped even lower. "And one day you will make love to me—"

For a moment, she seemed incapable of further speech. He stepped forward and took her hand and the contact seemed to give her strength.

She looked up at him and her manner changed again, grew light and calm. "I'd be most grateful, Edward, if you would do all this for me. Is it asking too much?"

He didn't know whether to laugh or scold her. He'd never heard a love plotted with such dispassionate precision. "And afterwards?" he asked, moving closer, incapable of keeping distance between them.

She permitted the embrace though not as generously as before. "Afterwards," she smiled. "The engagement will be announced, and within the year I'll become Lady Eden."

The wind had blown clouds up and these clouds now obscured the moon. With the light gone, he could not see her face. But he thought her words absurd and said as much.

"No," she protested. "We shall not pursue it beyond five days."

"I won't permit it," he argued, feeling her motionless in his arms.

"You'll have no choice," she said.

"But you don't love him."

"Of course not. But everyone will be pleased and I'll do my best to be a good wife." Then again she commenced that peculiar scrutiny of his face.

Now the gesture annoyed him. Angrily he caught her hand and drew it away, held it rigid against his chest. "You're speaking nonsense, you know."

If she noted his anger, she gave no indication of it. "Five days, Edward," she whispered. "Please give me five days—"

He considered it further, but changed his mind. The five days would not be constant. There would be endless interruptions, a need for deception and stealth. But since he could not for the moment dissuade her from her foolishness, he would give her the five days, then take her away for eternity.

In answer to her request for five days, he nodded and drew her close. His whole consciousness was concentrated on the perception of those points where their bodies touched, her legs between his, her hips and breasts pressing against him, her head against his shoulder. "You cannot plot or plan the course of love," he warned her gently.

"When there's no time, there is no choice," she replied. "I'm far richer now than I was an hour ago."

"Why were you crying downstairs in the corridor?" he asked. "Why did you leave the company?"

"In search of you."

"You might have asked for me."

"Or someone like you."

He felt a brief stab to his pride. "Then anyone would have served?" he asked.

"Oh no," she smiled, looking up.

And again at the sight of her face, a desire came over him, the beauty and mysterious power of love. He shook his head, bewildered by this most peculiar situation. In a kind of bemused detachment, he asked, "And how do we meet during the five days? The events of every day are plotted. How shall we—"

She shook her head. "Not every hour. The period following luncheon is free. The ladies rest, the gentlemen ride or gamble."

"And where shall I find you?"

"At your side. Just look. I'll be there. And I shall claim fatigue every night and retire early, like tonight." She lowered her head. "On the last night—"

"There will be no last night," he said sternly.

"I'm afraid there will be, but neither of us shall mind. At the conclusion of that night, we shall be fortified."

"You perhaps," he protested. "Not me." He bent his head low and kissed her again. In clear longing she leaned into his arms, her hands on the back of his head, guiding his face into the softness of her breast. With his tongue, he tasted her flesh.

"Not now," she murmured. "The memories must be in order. Sixty years from now I want to be able to stand on this spot and recall it all in sequence. Otherwise it will grow muddled in my head and I shall lose it."

He watched her for a moment, as she moved back into the full force of the wind, then followed after her, unable to decide whether her clinical plotting was a kind of madness or superior fortitude. No matter. Before these five days ended, she would know, as he knew, that the engagement ball would never take place, or if it did, it would be without the guest of honor. He'd not thought before in terms of marriage, but now he did, a simple ceremony performed in Edinburgh. He would not, could not sacrifice her reputation.

He came up softly behind her where she stood at the edge of the battlement, gazing out over the channel. He slipped his arms around her waist and felt a pleasing sensation as she leaned back against him. He bent his head low, whispering close to her ear. "Are you cold?"

"A little."

"What are you thinking about?"

"How dark the water is and how deep."

"It poses no threat to you."

Suddenly she looked back at him. "Did Charlotte Longford die?"

Again the bluntness of her question caught him off guard. Residual pain there. Old grief. Slowly he nodded.

Now she seemed to be the one offering comfort. "I'm sorry for you," she said softly, "but not for her. She merely

fulfilled her destiny. Before it's over, we'll all do as she did.
We'll all go, senseless, to our destinies."

Again her words were absurd, her manner almost frightening. He drew her close and tasted the salt of tears, as
though he felt keenly the tragedy of Charlotte Longford,
the presence of some sort of an abyss.

With passionate sternness he vowed he would not permit
it to happen again. This woman would not suffer because
of him. There would be no abstract and coldly clinical
"perfect now." They had found each other in despair in a
darkened corridor, but the rest of their days would be
passed in the full freedom of light.

Though the kiss had ended, he continued to hold her.
There would be no abyss for either of them. He would see
to it.

He would see to it . . .

"She *does* seem to suffer endless headaches, doesn't
she?" whispered Mrs. Greenbell as she served Marianne
her coffee from the heavily laden buffet in the Banqueting
Hall.

Marianne took the cup with a smile and lightly shook her
head, indicating silence. There was talk enough at the far
end of the long table where the stragglers and late sleepers
of the company were enjoying a lavish breakfast.

Although there were chairs enough at table to accommodate sixty, less than ten lingered over coffee and at the
buffet. The rest of the company had already dispersed for
various morning activities, some riding out across the
moors, others walking the headlands in an attempt to clear
their systems of too much food and drink and too little
sleep.

Marianne felt the heaviness herself, a heaviness made
complicated by the almost constant absence during the last
four days of the guest of honor, Harriet Powels. What a
variety of ailments the young woman had laid claim to!
And always, after her softly spoken apology and after she
had fled the room, her poor bewildered parents had taken
up the refrain.

"Never known a day's sickness in her life," Lord Powels
pronounced now, eating heartily in spite of his distress, as
he had done at every meal. Clearly he was a man who
enjoyed his food.

His wife was not faring so well. Marianne watched closely as the delicate woman fanned herself with a white lace
handkerchief, still eyeing the central arch through which
Harriet had just fled. "She refuses a physician," Lady
Powels murmured. "I don't understand. I really don't."

To her right sat Lady Carlisle, who tried to comfort her.
"Nerves, my dear, female nerves. Brides have suffered
thusly since time immemorial. No cause for alarm, I assure
you. Don't you agree, Lady Eden?"

Marianne smiled and nodded and again took refuge behind her cup. The feeling persisted that she and all of
them were sitting in the eye of a storm. The only difference
was that she knew it and they didn't. And regarding the
young woman with the "shy and sensitive nature," what
Marianne had seen of her three days earlier had been
neither shy nor sensitive.

At the far end of the table, she saw Sir Claudius just
taking a chair. Following behind him was a steward with
a prudently filled platter, dry toast, a small arrangement
of summer fruit. Apparently he'd fully recovered from the
earlier madness of his amorous advances toward her.

Then she heard his familiar voice. "With all apologies,
milady, but you are looking very weary." His voice, coming from the end of the table, dragged every eye with him.

With a smile she took in the gaping faces. "We are all
fossils here, Sir Claudius, fit only to sip coffee and comment on the aging process as it appears in others."

Her gentle humor was rewarded with brief laughter. Sir
Claudius nodded his head as though accepting the rebuke.
"Milady," he smiled, wiping his fingers on his napkin.
"The comment was not intended as criticism, merely observation." Now he folded the napkin into a meticulous
square. "I agree," he went on. "Let the others ride and
race the wind. For myself I would be most content if you
would join me in the library and permit me the honor of
reading to you."

The fact that there were a dozen others eavesdropping
on his proposal seemed not to bother him at all. "I've
been told," he smiled, leaning back in his chair, "that I
have a pleasant voice, and I've come armed with the
latest popular London fiction, a new series by the scrib-
bler Dickens, called *Pickwick Papers*." He continued to
stare in her direction as though impervious to the numerous

sets of listening ears. "The middle classes seem to dote on the man," he concluded. "Perhaps, together, we can discover why."

Apparently the suggestion held great appeal for Lady Carlisle. She sat up, adjusting the froth of lace at her wrists. "Is your recitation open to the public, Sir Claudius? I can't think of a more charming manner in which to pass the morning."

Others joined in, a genteel though clamoring chorus of old people desperate for some new and innovative way to pass the endless hours.

If Sir Claudius was disappointed that Marianne's attention would not be his alone, he gave no indication of it. Now like an overworked schoolmaster, he urged the others to hurry along with their breakfasts while he went to his chambers to fetch the man, Dickens. "We shall regroup in half an hour in the library," he announced sternly from the door.

His private invitation to Marianne clearly forgotten, he left the room. Then at the door she spied a curious duo, her sister Jane in the company of Sophia Cranford. The annoyance on her sister's old face was apparent. Clearly, at some point between her chambers and the Banqueting Hall she had been ambushed.

At her sister's slow approach, Marianne stood, lightly kissed her and whispered good-humoredly, "A woman is judged by the company she keeps."

Jane lifted her walking stick as though she intended to give Marianne a sharp rap for her impudence. "Like a vulture, she was lying in wait for me just beyond the Great Hall." Now, in a quick change of mood, she glanced toward the buffet. "I'm starved," she announced. "Did the gluttons leave a shred?"

As Jane turned her attention to the buffet, Marianne glanced back toward the door. Only Lady Powels remained, in a close huddle with Sophia, clearly giving her the latest bulletin on her daughter's deteriorating health. Marianne knew that Sophia would not take kindly to the news.

And she didn't. At that moment, Marianne saw Sophia step back, the ever-present notebook pressed against her breast as though the shock were too much. "Well, it's clear, Lady Powels. She must see a physician."

From where she sat, Marianne saw the stricken look on Lady Powels's face. This was neither the time nor the place to speak of such matters and even if it were, Sophia was totally lacking in all authority to do so. My God, but the woman was a continuous embarrassment.

Now Marianne sat up straight and literally hurled her voice in the direction of the offender. "It is a matter of no great consequence, Miss Cranford, I assure you. If we summoned a physician for every headache this morning in Eden Castle, there wouldn't be a medical man left in the entire West Country."

The look of gratitude coming from Lady Powels was incredible, reinforcing Marianne's suspicion that this unmarried daughter must be weighing upon her. Sophia retreated with a subtle challenge. "I do hope you are right, milady."

Lady Powels hastened to reassure her. "She'll be in the company tonight, I promise."

Now as though to break up the awkward little confrontation at the door, Marianne called cheerily, "You'd better hurry along, Lady Powels. Sir Claudius is an excellent reader and Dickens quite the rage."

Again the woman gave her a look of warm gratitude and departed, leaving Sophia standing alone and looking quite useless in the doorway.

Marianne watched as the tall woman made her way to the sideboard, quickly poured herself a cup of coffee, and sat a distance removed from Marianne. "I'm certain you agree, Lady Eden," she began, never taking her eyes off the shimmering coffee, "that the girl's repeated absences *are* mysterious."

"I'm not sure I do agree," replied Marianne. "It may be as Lady Powels has suggested, that her shy and retiring nature is simply not designed for—"

"Shy and retiring!" harrumphed Jane, settling into a chair between the two women, then leaning to one side to permit the steward to place her heaping platter before her. "Miss Harriet Powels has struck me as being many things, but never shy and retiring."

"How *does* she strike you, Miss Locke?" Sophia asked.

Without looking up from the obvious enjoyment of her breakfast platter, Jane mumbled with mouth half full,

"Passed over for one thing, a bit desperate, not for her-self, but for her family—"

Clearly Sophia was listening. "Go on," she urged.

But Marianne interceded firmly. "Please, both of you," she scolded lightly. "I see neither the reason nor the cause for discussing one of our guests in such a manner."

But predictably Sophia would not be deterred. "Miss Powels has exalted hopes of becoming much more than a guest of Eden Castle. We have James's future to con-sider. If there is even the slightest suspicion of—trouble—that alone should provide you with both reason and cause."

Marianne nodded. "I couldn't agree with you more, Sophia," she smiled. "But I see no suspicion of trouble, do you? Harriet is intelligent, well-spoken, and quite love-ly in her own way. If the union does indeed take place, James has every reason to consider himself fortunate."

But after a dainty sip at her coffee, Sophia sent forth new barrages of doubt. "Then why these repeated absences from a celebration which is primarily in her honor?" she asked.

"Perhaps she's bored," Jane muttered, piling eggs onto a square of toast.

Marianne ignored the remark. "I'm not certain that it's our place to account for it, Miss Cranford. She may be suffering from some minor physical complaint."

"Then a physician should be summoned immediately."

"No, I don't think that's necessary," Marianne coun-tered. Weary with effort and feeling that the woman had made her point and perhaps won the debate, she concluded simply, "Her mother has promised us her presence this evening. Let's await that moment and treat her, even in our thoughts, with understanding."

Sophia returned her cup to the saucer without so much as a scrape, and keeping her eye on both cup and saucer, asked quietly, "Has Edward made a decision on James's rightful inheritance?"

Marianne leaned forward, her hands searching for some diversion on the cluttered table. She found it in her nap-kin, which she commenced folding as though it were a most pressing task. "Such a subject is not appropriate here, Sophia," she murmured.

"With all due respect, milady, I disagree," Sophia replied.

Jane's fork fell ominously quiet over her plate.

Sophia shifted in her chair. "You see, milady," she went on, "James must know what he possesses before he can make a good marriage—with anyone. Indeed, as you know, in the past it has been his one stumbling block to unions which were far more advantageous than the present proposed one. He, of course, does not wish his brother harm. He is quite prepared to care for him, seeing to all his—appetites, giving him the shelter and protection of the castle for as long as his—illness requires."

Marianne looked sharply up. "Illness?" she repeated, stunned. "What illness?"

All activity over Jane's breakfast platter had ceased. Even the waiting stewards seemed to be listening.

Again Marianne demanded, "What *are* you talking about, Sophia? Illness? Edward ill?" She gave a brief laugh which she did not feel. "Why, I've never seen him looking better. Tired, perhaps, as we all are, but—ill?"

Sophia spoke with mock consideration. "As it is not a pleasant illness, milady, neither is it a pleasant subject." Now she looked, perplexed, at Marianne. "But surely, milady, it comes as no surprise to you. You, more than any of us, have observed Edward close at hand. Surely you've seen—"

At last Jane found her voice and the will to use it. "Seen what?" she demanded.

"The—symptoms," Sophia replied, casting a wary eye over her shoulder at the stewards, standing rigidly at attention. Now she raised her voice in their direction. "Run along, all of you," she commanded with a brief wave of her hand. "I'll summon you when we're through here."

Marianne watched and listened and felt reduced to the status of guest in her own home. Edward ill? Those two words made a continuous assault on her brain. The stewards had left the room. Why didn't Sophia speak?

Then she did. She turned in her chair, new color on her face, as though her blood were warming to the subject at hand. "The symptoms are clear," she said.

"What symptoms?" Jane demanded.

"The symptoms," Sophia went on, "of an—addict."

For an instant it was as though neither Jane nor Marianne had heard correctly. "A—what?" Jane demanded again.

"An addict," Sophia repeated. "Rather advanced, too, in my opinion," she added. "My sources tell me he requires a considerable amount every day—"

"A considerable amount of what?" Marianne asked.

"Opium," the woman said without hesitation. And when apparently the fog in Marianne's head still did not lift, Sophia said it again, more bluntly than before, "Opium, milady. I fear that your son is an opium addict."

Curiously the words had no effect of real devastation on Marianne for she simply did not believe them. Then too at that precise moment, Jane's toneless laughter rang out over the empty table, a reassuring sound in the face of Sophia's tragic expression.

"Good Lord," Jane gasped, as though in the throes of great amusement. "Laudanum, Sophia? Are you serious? All of England takes laudanum in one form or another. My traveling cases are filled with it. My old London physician prescribes it for a rainy day. Good Lord," she repeated, dabbing at the corners of her eyes, as though still helplessly caught in the throes of amusement. "You make it sound so horrific. Every babe who has ever sucked a mother's tit has partaken of laudanum. William used to say it was what made us such a placid, good-natured people."

Sophia sat up, her face stern, more than ready to meet the challenge. "I beg to disagree with you, Miss Locke. The potions of which you speak *are* readily available to the general populace. But they are also diluted with other elixirs which render them harmless on the face of it." Marianne listened closely. "But Edward's addiction is of quite a different nature, I fear. He consumes it pure, raw, dissolved in alcohol, and worse, his system now demands it." Her head bowed, her voice fell. "Unfortunately I've had experience with such addiction. In Yorkshire it was a common plague among the miners." She shook her head as though in genuine commiseration. "After prolonged use, their effectiveness as men, indeed as human beings is over. They generally retreat to a den, finding greater solace in their dreams and hallucinations than in God's world around them. And at some point, their pleasures become negative, their cravings savage." She ceased talking and looked directly at Marianne. "Ultimately, of course, it annihilates them," she concluded, a look of triumph on her face.

Marianne felt her heart beating too fast. She *had* observed something changed in Edward, at times a mysterious weakness which she attributed to fatigue. And she'd noticed too a new gauntness in his usually robust face.

Sophia moved in closer to the table. "I'm truly sorry, milady, to have to be the bearer of these tidings. With God as my witness, I thought you knew. It's common talk in the kitchen."

"Who?" Marianne demanded, still not willing to believe and not totally willing to disbelieve.

"Edward's manservant," Sophia replied without hesitation. "John Murrey, I believe, is his name. He supplies him, then sits with him through the horrible affliction." Sophia sat back, as though delivered. Slowly she shook her head. "Surely, milady, if you've not been bewildered by young Lady Powels's absence, you cannot have failed to have noticed your son's absence as well."

In the throes of distress, Marianne looked about at the cluttered table. She was unable still to face the truth of what she'd been told. That Edward had indulged, she had no doubt. But an addict?

Now she noticed Jane maintaining a strange silence, as though she too was involved in putting pieces of the puzzle together. But looming large was one predominant horror—how vulnerable Edward would be now to the assaults of James and the Cranfords. What a simple case, the legitimate second son contesting his birthright in a court of law against an addict.

"Oh dear God," she moaned audibly, resting her elbows on the table and concealing her face behind her hands.

The silence held, the other two apparently rendered mute by her clear distress.

She heard movement then, as though someone were pushing gently back in a chair. Then she heard that voice again, the same voice that had brought her nothing but grief throughout their long association.

"Milady," Sophia began, "again my apologies for bringing you such tragic news. But I'm glad I did, for now you know the urgent nature of the many problems at hand—"

Still Marianne did not look up.

Jane sat up straighter. "It has been my experience," she said, almost sweetly, to the table, "that a house warden's only legitimate domain is the kitchen and the scullery. How effortlessly, Miss Cranford, do you step into spheres that are none of your concern."

Marianne saw the flush on Sophia's face deepen. But with admirable control, she maintained her position, standing behind the chair now, talking down to both Jane and Marianne.

"My position in this household is not an ordinary one, Miss Locke," she pronounced in a low voice. "I've given long years of service to this family, as has my brother, almost our entire adult lives. We have raised the three heirs and, with Lady Eden's kind indulgence, we now take full credit for what they are."

With a wave of black amusement, Marianne thought, Take credit. Take full credit for Jennifer in her late twenties, a terrified, repressed spinster; for James, weak beyond description, with little wit and less backbone. And Edward? An addict apparently in the process of destroying his life, for which Marianne had once had such rich and limitless hopes.

Throughout these thoughts, Sophia had never ceased talking and was now saying, "But I can't do it alone. I find myself in that most unfortunate position of great responsibility and no authority." Carefully she stepped back from the chair as though the better to display her martyrdom. "There are vast problems afoot in this castle this morning, problems which, perhaps, suffering the wrong solution, could spell the end to the Eden line. And yet— What must I do now? I must go attend to the waiting stewards, must see that the consommé for luncheon is of the proper clarity, must see that the pâté is seasoned properly, and the wine chilled, and the flowers fresh in all of the chambers—"

Her eyes closed as though in consummate fatigue. With a slight shake of her head, she opened them again, resolution on her face. "So, now, milady, I'll assume my rightful and limited duties if you'll assume yours. Your sons, both of them, are on the verge of destroying themselves. See to it, milady, I beg you."

And with that brief though impressive conclusion, she

walked the full length of the table, head erect like some put-upon queen who has had the misfortune of being set down among witless and unruly subjects, and left the room.

Both Jane and Marianne watched the grand exit.

"I would give anything," Jane began, her voice firm though scarcely audible, "up to and including my modest fortune and my good right arm, if Thomas could have heard that little outburst."

In spite of her gloomy mood, Marianne smiled. Jane's thought had not been precisely her own. Nonetheless it stirred her. Oh yes. *Thomas.*

Then Jane was speaking again. "You cannot permit it to go on, Marianne," she scolded, rising laboriously from her chair.

Grasping the edge of the table for support, as Jane had done, Marianne stood. For a moment she felt light-headed.

Jane saw the weakness and misinterpreted it. "You've only yourself to blame," she scolded, "for permitting that woman ever to gain the upper hand."

But Marianne's thoughts were elsewhere. "Do you have morning plans, Jane?"

Jane craned her neck forward as though the better to comprehend the curious question. "None that amount to anything save the killing of time."

"Then walk with me," Marianne requested, still suffering an intense longing.

"Walk?" Jane echoed. "I should think you would have—"

"Please," Marianne begged, looking directly at her. "Just a brief stroll. To the graveyard."

"Of course I'll walk with you," Jane murmured, as though at last she had perceived Marianne's exact need.

Clinging together as though against the vicissitudes of an unseen storm, they made their way out of the Banqueting Hall, through the Great Hall, past the army of stewards who were hanging bowers of summer flowers for the evening ball, on out to the steps of the Great Hall where a mild June sun greeted them.

Without being consciously aware of it, Marianne must have leaned heavily against Jane, causing her sister to lend her the support of both arms. "Are you well?" Jane demanded, looking sharply at her.

Marianne nodded.

As they passed behind the great hulk of the castle itself, the sun was obliterated, and they found themselves in shadow, the earth beneath their feet soft and spongy where the dampness held year around without the drying rays of the sun.

"Wouldn't it be lovely," Marianne said softly as they walked, "if we were permitted to choose the day on which we wished to die?"

And that was all she said, but she was aware of Jane looking at her in bewilderment, in concern.

Something more was wrong, of that Jane was certain. As though Sophia Cranford's cruel little announcement concerning Edward hadn't been enough, Jane knew that her sister was suffering from some other, as yet unknown crisis.

As they walked together through the muddy dampness behind the castle, Jane tried to read her sister's face, tried to understand her curious remark about choosing the day on which to die, and considered pressing her for elaboration.

But as they emerged once again into the sun of the formal gardens, she changed her mind. Marianne was leading her into that grim tree-shaded graveyard at the extreme edge of the castle wall, the hallowed ground where Edens had been buried since the tenth century. As with visibly trembling hands, Marianne released the latch on the gate, Jane remembered grimly the number of times she had taken part in funeral processions which had led to this place.

But without a doubt, the most sorrowful of all had been the impressive funeral cortege in the spring of 1826, when a respected contingent of peers of the realm had walked along this same path, bearing the body of Lord Thomas Eden.

Jane closed the gate quietly behind her and continued to watch her sister, noting the manner in which she used the smaller tombstones for support as she made her way toward the large glistening marble block beneath which rested her life. Quickly Jane turned away. The moment was too intimate, even for sisterly observation.

She decided she would give Marianne five minutes. Then

she would insist that they return to her apartments where they would be well advised to turn their thoughts, in a practical way, to the problems at hand.

Well then, enough. Marianne had communed with the dead for far longer than was either necessary or healthy. It was time that she set herself to more practical solutions. But as Jane glanced back again at the sorrowful tableau, she discovered with a start that she lacked the courage to interrupt so mysterious and intimate an encounter.

Looking down again, she spied her father's grave, and there, slightly to the right, poor dear Russell. And a short distance beyond that, Jenny and Dolly. She had no intention of kneeling before them all. But if she could find an equitable space midway between, she would run the risk of soiling her gown and get on her knees as Marianne had done and pay her respects.

As she lowered herself painfully to her knees, she looked about with a disturbing thought. Where would they plant her when the time came? Probably in the precise area where she now was kneeling.

Quiet! There was so much quiet around her that the image of the grave doubled. Only the bird sounds could be heard and even their normally cheery chirping seemed diminished in this dreadful place.

Quiet.

Then softly into this quiet, she heard another sound. Still on her knees, she held her position, then looked up, thinking that perhaps Marianne was at last stirring.

But when she glanced over the tops of the tombs, she saw her sister still sunk against Thomas's grave, her position the same. Yet there it was again, footsteps, clearly footsteps on gravel.

Again she raised her head and looked in all directions. There, moving along the narrow gravel path which led from the east door of the castle, she saw two figures. Her immediate conclusion was that it was simply two guests, wandering far afield.

She was in the process of lowering her head when suddenly, sharply, she looked back up, her attention riveted on some aspect of recognition. Throughout the entire and laborious fortnight of banqueting and dancing she had stood in silent admiration of one aspect of Harriet Powels. And that was her dazzling, beautiful auburn hair.

Now here was that same glorious mane of fair hair, scandalously loosened and hanging free down the young woman's back, her face still obscured as she hurried along the pathway, clinging, as a vine clings to the wall, to—

Oh sweet God! Jane froze in her prayerful position, her mind far removed from prayer, as she watched the two hurry down the walk like culprits, heading toward the far gate. From Jane's position, she saw her sister's head raise slightly as the two continued their furtive passage around the edge of the graveyard.

Still both Jane and Marianne watched, transfixed, as in their approach to the wooden door, he drew her back suddenly and into his arms, where upon the instant her face lifted and their lips met in a kiss so passionate as to suggest that all their emotional faculties had been focused on the union of lips.

After the embrace they clung to one another for a moment. A moment later, Edward pushed open the wooden door and guided her through it, then followed after her. The door was closed and the graveyard was as it once had been.

Jane stared fixedly at the closed door, then pressed her eyes shut and shook her head as though perhaps she simply had seen an apparition. Good God! What was to happen now? Was an engagement to be announced between Harriet Powels and Edward? Or would they simply take their obvious passion and flee, leaving Marianne to make amends and apologies. *I am sorry, Lord Powels, but my bastard son seems to have abducted your daughter. I thank you all for attending this futile occasion. Dear James, you must try to understand your brother—*

There was a phantasmagoric quality to Jane's thoughts, as though she were spinning the specifics of a nightmare for her own amusement. But then, looking up, she saw Marianne turn and look directly at her.

"Dear God," Jane muttered again, her eyes never leaving her sister's face. With a wave of sympathy, Jane thought that Marianne looked freshly injured somehow. She knelt there, her eyes still fixed upon Jane, as though hopeful that her sister would communicate a solution.

But Jane had no solution. She tried to return her sister's awful gaze with steady eyes, but could not. They were, as

William was fond of saying, "surrounded by a horror of great darkness, on an ocean of counterfeit infinity."

Peculiar! William had uttered that quote on an average of three times per week every week for over fifty years that she had lived with him.

Until now, she'd not had the slightest idea what it meant.

He marveled at and worshipped everything.

From the crown of her thick and luxurious hair to the small white toes and all the rich and varied and partially explored territory in between, he marveled at and worshipped simply everything.

Now as they hurried across the headlands, having again successfully escaped from all the watching eyes in the castle, he drew even with her and considered reopening the one subject which had marred the four most blissful days of his life. Then it occurred to him that *he* was always the one to bring up the subject, and while their discussions were usually gentle, they always left her saddened, their passion tempered.

So quickly he decided against raising the subject again. Not now. They had the whole glorious day ahead of them, the seclusion of the little green glen toward which they were hurrying, magnificent in its isolation.

Trailing a step behind, he continued to watch her, recalling how pleased he had been by her appearance when they'd met at the secret stairway, that crown of hair undone as though in mute signal of the state of her emotions. Her gown was dark brown and plain, loosely fitted as a servant's, clearly no corsets.

Quickly now he reached out and caught her arm and turned her toward him, as though to reconfirm the expression on her face. "I just wanted to see for myself," he said. "At times when we're apart, you seem like an apparition."

She laughed and reached a hand up and tenderly pushed back a strand of his hair. "Dearest Edward," she murmured, "I may be many things, but I am *not* an apparition."

The face, the eyes, the smile, the manner, all were irresistible and again he drew her forward into his arms and clasped her to him with such force that momentarily she lost her balance. In the process of supporting her, his hand brushed across her breast.

For a moment, she looked at him with brief timidity. Then as though making a conscious effort of will, she lifted his hand, kissed it lightly, and placed it over her breast and held it there.

The exploration was brief but powerful. As she stepped away, he saw her face turn deeper crimson and knew that his suspicions were true, that she'd never known a man. "We've only this one day," she announced, that peculiar rigidity in her voice as though she was still clinging to her concept of a perfect now.

As his arm encircled her waist and they again proceeded into the strong westerly winds of the headland, he felt a menacing dip in his spirits. Surely she'd abandoned such nonsense by now. The thought of separating from her was intolerable. In their few days together he'd found in her sheltering beauty a strength he'd never dreamed possible. The past and all its potent nightmares had simply receded, sorrows certainly never forgotten, but now made bearable in her unique and precious love.

He had laid a few plans, had instructed old John Murrey to have his carriage ready at nightfall. It was his intention that they slip away while the others were at dinner, flee north to Scotland. They would be married in Edinburgh and would remain there until the scandal had subsided, the bruised feelings had been assuaged. Then after a period of time, they would return and be forgiven, of that he was certain. How could anyone, even James, hold him responsible for such happiness? And to further ease whatever ill-feelings still were at large, he would equitably divide the estates, half in James's name, half in his. And Eden would once again live up to her name. Unified with his brother, with Harriet at his side, he would at last face the future as whole, as healed as he'd ever been in his life.

For a moment, such illusions of happiness almost overwhelmed him. "Not far," he whispered in her ear, guiding her down the narrow path which led to a forest glade and then to the hidden glen cut square and obscured by thick foliage, the same impenetrable spot where he and Daniel had played Robin Hood as boys. The childhood spot had satisfied abundantly all his childhood fantasies.

Now, he thought, it would satisfy him as an adult as well, though there were no fantasies this time. His dream was moving beside him, a thing of substance.

He scooped up an armful of trailing vines to permit her easy passage. "It was the only place where Daniel and I were totally safe from the Cranfords."

"Daniel Spade," she said, as though confirming in her mind the identity of the man about whom Edward had spoken so often and so lovingly. "How fortunate you are to have so constant a friend."

There it was again, that painful longing in her voice, as though a good and trusted friend was a wealth beyond her wildest imaginings. He thought that perhaps here was the basis of his love for her. How had she survived on the Shropshire estate? Had there been no one to soothe her, to dream with her? Had she literally passed all her days in splendid and annihilating isolation?

Then he took the lead for the last assault, angled his body into the thick vines, and there it was, as isolated and as emerald green as he remembered it, a natural chamber, its walls formed on four sides by a thick hedge of willow and elder and low-growing wild rose bushes, its floor a solid carpet of mossy green.

Without a word, he motioned her through, then let the weight of the vines fall back into place, a unique chamber door. The passing years had enhanced the magical place, had made it doubly secure.

He noticed her now stepping around the edge of the glen, her head turning at all angles as though she were assessing chambers at a public inn. From the far side, she lifted her hair as though to cool her neck and asked, "No one comes here?"

He smiled. "No one but birds and a squirrel now and then and perhaps a rabbit."

"No hunters?"

"Nothing to hunt. The larger game is in the opposite direction, toward the moors."

She seemed to be listening carefully, one hand still suspended at the back of her neck, supporting her hair. Then all at once she let it drop and simultaneously lifted her face heavenward as though the weight of hair had dragged her head backward. He saw her eyes close, saw a look of peace on her face, as though she'd doubted the existence of such a place.

Watching her, Edward wondered bleakly if he'd never find the courage or the will to move. His eyes continued to feed on her. He realized now what it was that was so entrancing. In the past, he'd always seen her groomed, hair up and pulled smoothly back, corseted and bejeweled, a "picture" for appreciation, but never touching. Now in the soft abandon of that plain gown, the loosened hair, all aspects of that same picture seemed to invite touching.

As though summoning himself out of a trance, he pulled off his jacket and placed it on the ground near the trunk of a tree. She saw the considerate gesture and seemed touched by it, though she laughed softly, "Edward, this dress needs no protection."

"I was thinking of comfort."

"And I need no comfort," she replied, her eyes meeting his. "I suffer from a lifetime of comfort and foresee no discernible change in the future." She held her ground about six feet from where he stood, her eyes pleading. "No comfort, Edward, please."

In addition to the pleading, he saw something else, a determination which seemed to flag now and then, and new pleading as though she were begging him not to let her lose her nerve.

Now both stood and stared wordlessly at the spread coat. He found her mixture of tentativeness and determination moving and decided to let her take the lead, move at whatever pace she wished. He would follow, at least for the time being.

Then softly, she asked a strange, unsettling question. Never lifting her eyes, she asked, "Will you forgive me?"

He looked at her, certain he'd not heard correctly. "Will I—"

Although he tried to speak again, she interrupted him with just a step in his direction. "How skillful are you at pretending?" she inquired.

He smiled. "Very skillful. I've done it all my life."

This seemed to please her. "Then all I have to do is simply tell you that you are no longer Edward Eden?" she asked, the earnest entreaty still on her face.

"Agreed," he laughed. "Only too willingly. But who am I to be?"

"Be anyone you like," she said, her mood brightening, as though she were a child, plotting a game.

"I shall be a gypsy," she announced. "A band camps occasionally in the far corner of Hadley Park. As a child, I used to see their wagons and the smoke from their fires. I always wanted to go and see them, but I was—forbidden."

The manner in which she said this led Edward to confirm the suspicion in his heart. He wondered sadly how often that harsh word, "forbidden," had been applied to her instincts. He was silent for a moment, then he said quietly, "Don't be afraid."

Slowly she looked up at him. "I won't be afraid," she whispered, "if I can be someone else."

In that instant the charade became clear to him. He knew what he must do, the role he would have to play. And he resented neither. Assuming his new role, his tone grew suddenly harsh. "And who do you fancy yourself, gypsy?" he demanded, stepping toward her, encircling her. "A lady? Is that what you think you are, a fine lady? If so, then you give yourself airs."

Behind her, he waited to be absolutely certain that he had not misread her. With her back to him, he was unable to see her face.

Then slowly she turned, "I am not a lady," she whispered fiercely. "I am a whore, a gypsy whore," and suddenly she reached out for his arm.

He was amazed at the strength in her hand as she led him to the center of the glen, arranged him in a manner which apparently suited her. Then she stepped back and commanded full-voice, "Take off your shirt."

He looked at her, saw the sudden hardness in her face, then obliged. As his fingers moved down the buttons, he never once lifted his eyes from her changed face, the flush increasing as he shrugged the garment off his shoulders.

She seemed to be studying him then, her hands, he noticed, kneading the fabric of her skirt. Slowly she encircled him once, then twice, her fingers reaching out for his flesh, brushing lightly across the hair on his chest, then lower across his belly. "How many whores have you known?" she asked casually, disappearing from his view as again she passed behind him.

The game was on. "Hundreds," he lied, without hesitation.

"Did you undress before them?"

"Always."

"Did it—please them?"

"It must have."

Silence. He continued to stand, wondering how long the charade would last, fearful that her new and totally foreign role would slip from her grasp and leave her even more vulnerable than ever. He felt her fingertips lightly tracing the path of his spine and felt the hair on his arms stiffen, a knot form in his groin. Again he sternly counseled himself patience. It was her game, her rules.

Then softly behind him, he heard her voice again, the breathlessness increasing. "Take off—your trousers."

A brief smile crossed his face and within the moment, he leaned forward to do as he had been ordered, the boots first, each removed with a tug, then hurled a distance away, then the belt of his breeches, then two rows of buttons, easing the tightness down over his calves, wishing he could look upon her, but holding his position.

He hurled the breeches after his boots and shirt, then stood erect, thinking with humor of Eden Castle, a scant mile away, the stifling propriety, those good people not even aware of the "gypsies" in their glen.

Well, then, here he stood as God had made him. Would she be content forever with his spine and the backs of his legs? When after several long moments, she seemed disinclined to either speech or action, he called with mock gruffness over his shoulder, "Well, whore, what do you want of me now?"

Still it seemed as though all life, all movement within the glen had come to a standstill. He was tempted to glance over his shoulder in an attempt to see her face, but decided against it. "Are you there?" he asked. "Have I disappointed you? It's as God made me. If you have complaints, take them to Him. He's—"

Then as though to hush him, he felt her close behind him, felt her arms go about his waist, a backward embrace, only her hands visible and locked before him, clearly trembling.

"You do not disappoint me," she whispered. "I see no need for haste—"

Again he was tempted to take the lead, to draw her boldly before him, let her see the visible proof of his need and desire which at that moment threatened to bring him to his knees.

"Oh God, gypsy, how you torture me," he murmured. "Does it bring you delight to do so?"

At the moment when he felt he could not endure a moment longer, he was forced to endure a double agony, not only the sweet sensation of her pressed against his back, but now he noticed those trembling hands begin to move downward in a slow descent over his lower abdomen.

The earth on which he was standing seemed to sway dangerously. Her fingers explored his body as though they had eyes, up, then back again, stopping now and then as though to assess the texture, a sensation as overwhelming as any Edward had ever experienced. She was using her hands like a trained mistress, encompassing him, lifting him, apparently content with limited sensate pleasure for her eyes had yet to see, her face still buried in the small of his back.

Under the duress of the moment, Edward broke out of the charade. "Sweet God, take pity," he whispered.

Then abruptly she released him and stood back a distance and issued the invitation that he longed to hear. "Turn, sir, and look upon me as God created me."

He had never experienced such a turbulence of emotion, had never set about the act with such deliberation. Before turning he felt childlike, felt that this was as Adam and Eve must have discovered each other, with deliberateness and innocence.

He turned. She received his eyes, then slowly her hands started the long, tortuous path down the front of her gown, buttons released, one after another, an endless row which in his anticipation seemed to grow longer. Before she reached the end, the top part of her gown fell loose from her shoulders, revealing her breasts, lovelier in reality than he had imagined.

It was while he was still concentrating on her breasts that the gown fell away into a soft brown circle about her feet. As she stooped to lift it, she removed her slippers, and as though mimicking him, tossed all to one side, a small heap now of abandoned garments, hers blending with his.

"Do I resemble your whores, sir?" she asked.

"Not in the least," he replied, unable to take his eyes off her, a lovely Grecian statue come miraculously to life, alabaster shoulders sloping from graceful neck to graceful arms, those breasts as perfectly molded as though sculptors had just formed them, tapered waist, the slight ridge of ribs visible on either side, the full hips curving in semi-circles around the belly, that darker mound, then long shapely legs, one turned in as though innately aware of this new vulnerability.

Now it was her turn to endure his close scrutiny, and glancing back at her face, he observed that she was enduring admirably, the faint flush of embarrassment gone from her cheeks, though her eyes were still down, demurely fastened on her bare feet. With a soft laugh, she informed him, "I may not resemble your whores, sir, but I assure you I feel like them."

The terrible feelings of desire had returned. For a moment they'd grown subdued in the excess of beauty before him. But now, having looked and catalogued all aspects of her, he found his attention focused on that part which remained hidden. He doubted seriously his ability to merely stand and look much longer.

"May I take the lead?" he inquired softly. "Will you trust me?"

"Take what you wish," she countered. "But take it as you would from a whore, for there are no ladies present in this arena."

He started to protest her last words, but decided against it. In the beauty of their surroundings, in the honesty with which they stood before each other, words seemed to have no place. Yet still he hesitated, wondering for the first time in his life, if he could perform adequately. In the past, all his encounters had been with women who knew what to expect. Even dear Charlotte had known a husband. Now he knew that he stood before a virgin, a virginity made complex by his realization that she was trying so hard to deny it, and made doubly complex by his love for her.

For just a moment it occurred to him that perhaps he shouldn't have led her here, that perhaps they should have waited until they had fled Eden, waited for the wedding ceremony in Edinburgh.

But something about her now suggested that there would be no waiting, that indeed she'd waited long enough. "Please," she whispered, as though suffering as he had suffered earlier. "Teach me so that I may know what's at the core of this world." She stepped toward him. "The time is so short."

Time so short! God, how the words cut into him, reminding him in spite of everything that she still was clinging to her foolish notion of a perfect now, five days of bliss before she entered the prison of the future.

Then this must be perfect. And with that in mind, he lifted his hand to her, inviting her to place hers atop it and in the fashion of a splendid promenade he began walking with her in a slow deliberate manner around the glen, their eyes locked on each other and holding fast.

After two such circles, which he'd executed for the sole purpose of letting her adjust to her nakedness and his as well, he paused, looked closely into her face to see if he saw the slightest sign of failing nerves. He didn't.

Then gently he led her to the center of the glen, released her hand, and lay flat on his back, taking the weight of her surprised eyes. "Come," he invited, extending a hand upward.

Without hesitation, though clearly bewildered, she did as she was told until she was standing beside him, looking down. Still not speaking, never lifting his eyes from her face, he guided her forward until she was straddling him, then drew her down until she was kneeling over him. The first sensation of those smooth white legs parting over him caused him to press his head backward and close his eyes. He had consciously selected his position, afraid that the classic stance of domination and submission might alarm her. Lead her gently, he counseled himself, in spite of the blood racing through his body. Let her control it, gauge it, judge it as she wishes, take as much or as little.

This she did. She drew herself forward, stopping short for a moment, then lifting herself and with gentle guidance from him, received him, tentatively at first, still supporting her body, her eyes closed, head thrown back.

His hands were on her hips, still allowing her to gauge and control the penetration. He felt himself going deeper and deeper into that warm country, the sensation spreading to all parts of his body, though still in control.

Then abruptly she removed her hands from his chest
and with a short sharp cry took all of him, her mouth open
as though in imitation of her body, her knees wide spread,
her hands braced behind her as though to support her in
this new sensation.

Still in control, his hands moved up from her hips to her
breasts. Starting at her nipples and using the tips of his
fingers, he made gentle round circles, ever-enlarging. He
saw her body beautifully arched before him, connected to
him at the base.

She shifted upon him in subtle movements as though to
test the sensation. The sight of her before him in the throes
of such enjoyment made him impatient to complete the act.
But again and with the strictest of self-control, he took his
cue from her, watched closely all angles of her face, certain
that before long she would require more.

And she did. A few moments later, the slight turnings of
her body had become writhings, her mouth continuously
open. Then at last he took the lead with a sense of no
turning back, rolled her gently onto her back, angled his
body downward between her legs and commenced exploring that dark canal to its very limit.

At first he was afraid he'd moved too rapidly as he
caught sight of her face beneath him, her eyes distended
as though shocked by his sudden violence. But as he continued, he felt her hips lifting, her body joining the rhythm,
and when his mouth closed about her breast, he felt her
arms go around his back and lock him to her.

Still acceleration, deeper, harder, her hands on his buttocks as though to hold him inside her, her legs lifting in
an attempt to receive more of him, her head thrashing
from side to side as the moment drew nearer.

Then without warning she gave one sharp cry, followed
by a series of low reflexive moans. He felt her fingernails
on his back as she clung to him as though in fear of falling. He permitted his own release as together they held
each other for protection against the cataclysmic upheaval
taking place in their bodies.

Edward had never experienced such a sensation, a slow
hot shooting forward of such strength and duration that
for a moment he felt as though his entire body would be
consumed. Even after the peak of ecstasy had been reached,

they continued to lie together, their bodies still locked and shuddering.

He raised himself and looked down upon her and saw something alarming in her pale face, eyes still closed, her forehead glistening with perspiration. He leaned forward and gently kissed her.

Her eyes opened then, though focused on no specific detail. There was moisture at the corners of the dark lashes, as though the experience had taken her to sublimity, then deposited her on the other side of despair. He felt his own emotions dangerously close to the surface and wanted to speak of his terrible love for her.

But apparently she was not in the mood for words and merely caressed his face, the mysterious grief in her eyes increasing until at last she lowered his head gently onto her breasts as though she did not want him to see the grief or the tears.

For an unaccountable number of minutes they lay thus. He felt her arms across his back holding him close, renewing their grasp now and then as though fearful that he might slip away.

Predictably, locked in the mutual embrace, it was only a matter of time before their passions surfaced again, still unsatiated, a more deliberate progression this time, both of them working to postpone the explosion as long as possible, each providing the other with the greatest possible stimulation, using hands and lips, pressure and sudden lack of pressure in skillful and gratifying ways. As the summit was approached, again the silence was broken with soft moans and cries to God, the instruments of their satisfaction simple and complex, their own bodies, their own hungers, their mutual love.

The pale green edge of the glen was turning black with late afternoon shadow when sorrowfully, begrudgingly, their bodies surrendered for the first time in long hours. As Edward lifted himself to one side, he looked down on her, her legs still spread, her arms outflung, the look of grief still there, not in the least abated.

He knelt beside her and with his fingertips wiped the moisture from her forehead. "My dearest love," he whispered. Having been one with her for so long, the space between them seemed to swell. This disturbed him and caused him to speak with a force and bluntness which he instantly regretted. "Come," he ordered, rising to his knees, "we must leave here."

She looked up at him. "Why?" she asked. "It's early yet."

"Not just these woods," he added quickly. "We must leave Eden. Tonight. As soon as you can prepare your luggage."

He thought he detected a look of pleasure on her face as her hand with great and moving familiarity wandered gently over his chest and toward that part of him which obviously had brought her abundant pleasure. Dangerous sensations there. As the look of pleasure on her face broadened into almost coquettish delight, as her hand found its destination, he drew back and tried to look sternly down on her, though it was difficult, so difficult.

Slowly, as though to a beautiful child, he repeated, "We must leave here, Harriet. Tonight. We must put as much distance as possible between us and this place—"

Denied him, she withdrew her hand and stretched, her legs extended, her hands cupped about her breasts, eyes closed as though reliving in memory the recent sensations. "I don't know what you're talking about, Edward," she murmured sleepily.

He moved closer and held her face between his hands, forced her to look at him. "I'm talking about leaving here immediately in my carriage and traveling as far tonight as the horses will endure. I'm talking about Edinburgh, possibly four days hence, and a wedding ceremony after which you will be my wife."

Her attention was his now, clearly his, her eyes focused and unblinking. "And then?" she whispered.

The inexplicable expression of grief had returned to her eyes. But he ignored it and talked on. "And then," he concluded, "a life together, for all time—"

"Where?" she interrupted, as though challenging him.

"Wherever you wish," he smiled. "Scotland, Shropshire, London, here."

"Here?" she questioned. "I shouldn't think we would be terribly welcomed here."

"Perhaps not at first," he agreed. "But they will come around. In time. You'll see."

"My engagement was to have been announced tonight,"

she mused, her hands now seeking again on their own, and finding.

"There will be no engagement announcement," he said sternly, aware of her hands between his legs, stroking. He'd intended to say more, but with the softest of smiles, she straddled him again, angled their bodies together, and locked herself into place.

All hope of talk was merely a delusion. Joined again as one, her legs tightening around his back, he stood with her, his hands supporting her buttocks. In a soft expulsion of air, he lifted her head upward, her arms tightly laced behind his neck. And still holding her rigidly to him, he commenced turning in a rapid whirl, around and around, the centrifugal force centering on that point where their bodies were joined.

On this day of new and profound sensations, this apparently was yet another, as at the height of the whirlwind he felt her legs tighten, saw her mouth open, her breath coming in short spasms. As the whirl subsided, he felt her fall limp against his chest, her legs in descent, touching ground, though still she clung to him.

He supported her until she had recovered, then urged, "Please, I beg you, we must hurry."

Slowly she disengaged herself from his arms. Without looking at him, she walked the short distance to her garments and commenced shaking out the gown. In a way he thought her lack of response strange and in another way, quite normal. She must be approaching exhaustion. At least she'd not contradicted or denied his words as she had done so often during the last few days. Obviously his plan had worked. Their time here together had won his case for him.

Quickly they dressed as though someone had called to them. She finished first, not having the complication of breeches and boots. As he adjusted his shirt, he watched her stare down at the spot where they first had lain, the grasses softly matted by the weight of their bodies. He was unable to see her face, but it wasn't necessary. He saw one hand reach down, smoothing the grasses as though now the spot was sacred.

Slowly he walked to where she knelt and lifted her up. To his distress he saw that she was weeping.

For a moment she looked directly at him as though wanting him to see her grief. Then amazingly her mood

changed again in spite of her tears. She laughed and with
the back of her hand made an attempt to dry her eyes.
"There are many kinds of tears, Edward," she whispered.
"These happen to be the good kind."

His instinct was to question her further, but at that
moment she raised her head and kissed him with such
sweetness, such tenderness that he felt himself wordless.
Then "Thank you, Edward," she smiled, the tears seeming
to diminish. "I have never known such happiness, and if
I never know it again, still I consider myself fortunate."

In the warmth of her love, he was only capable of
treating the words singly. *I-have-never-known-such-happi-
ness.* Then that was enough. And after he had clasped her
to him in a final embrace, he urged again, "Come. We
must hurry." Beyond the density of the glen he saw the
blazing red twilight, knew that probably within the hour
the guests would begin to stir themselves out of their late
afternoon lethargy. The time was short. There was so
much to do.

As he hurried her toward the hanging vines and beyond,
he spoke incessantly, working out aloud for her benefit
as well as his the specific details of their escape. "Take
only what you need," he advised. "You can purchase more
later, in Edinburgh, London, wherever. And I would advise
that you pack without the assistance of your maid. Undoubtedly there's a bond of loyalty there. But she might be
tempted to speak to your parents. Do you understand?"

All her concentration seemed to be focused on their passage through the thick underbrush. But she seemed to be
listening and he was certain he saw her nod now and then.

"Also," he went on, simultaneously trying to clear a
path for her as well as plot their future, "I think it would
be wise if John Murrey parked the carriage outside the
east wall of the castle. The watchmen will be busy at the
front gate. I'll have John leave immediately on the pretext
of exercising the horses. As soon as you are ready, come
to the east wall, through the graveyard, and I'll be waiting.
Do you understand?"

At that instant a low-hanging branch caught in her hair.
With a soft cry, she drew back and dislodged it, her face
obscured in shadows. He considered again seeking her confirmation, then decided against it. She seemed to be suffer-

ing intensely now from the difficult passage, her hands constantly outreaching against rude branches.

Finally ahead, he saw the clearing of the headlands.

With his arm protectively about her, he hurried her forward across the headlands, his attention divided between the castle and her silent demeanor. He considered granting her an interval of an hour's rest, but decided against it. They must move quickly or surely they would be found out. It was his intention to leave a letter, a diplomatic plea for understanding and forgiveness.

So engrossed was he in his thoughts and plans that he was unaware of the fast pace he had set, was unaware of her lagging behind. Abruptly he stopped. "I'm sorry," he murmured. "Let me carry you. It isn't much farther—"

But as he bent to scoop her in his arms, she protested vigorously. "No, please, don't. What a sight that would be," she smiled, "the fiancée of one brother returning in the arms of the other."

He wished she hadn't mentioned it. But of course she was right. In the eyes of the company, she did belong to James. But in *his* eyes, that was a possession which James would never claim.

She allowed him to approach, her face once again soft with love. "I shall never forget this day," she whispered, "or that spot."

"Nor I," he smiled. "Fifty years hence," he promised, "when we are old we shall have our anniversary dinner there in that glen, just the two of us."

She returned his smile. "And we shall mark the spot with a small commemorative stone, and on it shall be carved the words, 'The True Eden.'"

Her laugh, like music, reassured him, though still it reminded him that carved stones fifty years hence had nothing to do with the problems at hand. As he hurried her toward the castle wall and the low wooden door, he asked earnestly, "Do you understand?"

Before she stooped to pass through the door, she looked up at him. For a moment he thought she would never speak, but at last she nodded. "I understand everything," she said.

Maintaining silence, they moved rapidly toward the east door and with a mutual sense of relief slipped quickly into the safe darkness of the passage. He could hear her moving a step or two ahead of him, her sense of direction steady as now she led the way up the secret stairway until at last she stood before the door which opened out onto the third floor corridor and the ultimate safety of her chambers.

Here she stopped and leaned against this last barrier as though beyond this spot their separation would be unendurable. Secure in this last temporary isolation, he grasped her to him. And she responded as though all he had to do was suggest it and she would gladly retrace her steps and return with him to the glen. In the semi-darkness he could not see her face, but he knew that she was weeping again.

"No need," he soothed, kissing her eyes, tasting the salt of tears. "Do you have doubts?" he inquired softly.

She shook her head.

"Then no need for tears," he comforted. "In an hour, perhaps less, we'll be together again, never to be separated, I swear it."

She seemed to grow quiet, then without warning, she slipped from his arms, threw open the door, and ran down the corridor toward her chambers. He started to call after her, but changed his mind. It would only further delay their departure. Yet he continued to watch her until she slipped into the privacy of her apartments and closed the door behind her.

With the sensation of her lips still on his, he closed the passage door and started slowly down the corridor, keeping his eye on her closed door. They were both safe now.

At the end of the corridor, just as he was in the process of turning the corner, he stopped, feeling a peculiar heat on the back of his neck. He fought it for a moment, then gave in to the sensation of eyes upon him. Looking rapidly over his shoulder, he spied a small figure clad in mussed dark brown standing by the door at the far end.

Her. From that distance he could not read her expression. He saw her merely clinging to the door. He stepped forward and with a broad gesture threw her a kiss the length of the vast hall. Whether she received it or not, he was unable to tell. But a moment later he saw her bow her head against the door, then she slipped from his sight.

In her inexplicable appearance, he felt all his senses as though wrapped in sleep. The only clear sensation was terror. He'd felt such bliss and now in her sudden absence, he felt only pain.

With resolve he dismissed his feelings. Their love was shared, of that he was certain. Even if they were not permitted to leave gracefully, nonetheless they *would* leave. He dreaded a scene for her sake and would make every effort to avoid one. But no one would keep them apart. What healing powers they had discovered. He stood in a better world now.

Then hurry! There was so much to do. Silence his fears in movement. And he took the stairs running, as though to outrace the fiends which plagued him.

Something was amiss, of that Sir Claudius was certain.

Precisely what it was, he had no idea. But he was a man of keen sensitivity, and in spite of the elegantly decorated Banqueting Hall, the garlands of flowers, the crystal chandeliers ablaze with thousands of candles, the coiffured ladies and gentlemen, the black-coated stewards now filing past bearing silver trays laden with delicacies—there, a three-tiered game mousse, and there, a magnificent Galantine de Dinde à la Volière, and there, a mounded lobster salad, and there, a chafing dish filled with truffles in champagne—in spite of all this prodigious elegance and plenty, something was amiss.

As Sir Claudius straightened his white dress shirt front and prepared himself for the gluttony ahead, he thought with a wave of concern that the something amiss might have to do with Lady Eden's red and swollen eyes. As Sir Claudius sat to her immediate left, he was in a perfect position to see. Although she was beautifully gowned in royal blue silk, she looked aggrieved somehow, her manner not at all that of the proud mother on the verge of welcoming a handsome and superbly qualified daughter-in-law to the bosom of the family.

In fact, though they had been seated at table for over a quarter of an hour, had already lifted their glasses in toast to the occasion, Lady Eden had not once lifted her eyes from her wine glass. He'd seldom seen her so subdued and sorrowful. And in spite of her recent rejection of him, he still was very fond of her. They'd been through far too much together to let one small rejection splinter their relationship. If he couldn't get into her bed, he'd have to be

content with getting into her purse. But no matter. He'd
do it with grace and dignity.

Now, midway down the enormous table, he saw Lord
Carlisle stand, his bald head glittering under the illumination of the chandeliers. A pompous ass, really, Sir Claudius
thought, a political charlatan who toyed with the Whigs
as a cat toyed with a mouse, fashionable sport perhaps
half a century ago, but no longer, not with the dangerous
radicals afoot and gaining power.

What *was* the old man saying, Sir Claudius wondered,
trying to hear over the chattering females to his right. Ah,
there it was. A toast to—the Princess Victoria? Bad taste,
that. Extremely bad taste with the old king still alive. Lord
Carlisle was playing with fire.

The toast over, Sir Claudius sent his attention back to
Lady Eden. Something *was* amiss. It broke his heart to
see her so downcast and preoccupied. Even her half-sister,
Miss Jane Locke, customarily a common talking machine,
also seemed subdued, as though a glass jar had fallen over
both of them.

As the chatter and laughter increased at the opposite end
of the table, Sir Claudius sent his attention in that direction, determined to put together the clues of the something
amiss.

James was there, presiding at the head, in his proper
place as Lord Eden. He seemed to be in close conversation
with Lord Powels, as close, that is, as the empty chair
between them would permit.

Ah-ha! Had he hit upon something? The bride-to-be
absent again and on the very night when her engagement
was to be announced? Had something gone awry there?
No, it was unthinkable. Lady Eden would not permit the
festivities to go this far without being certain of the dramatic climax, the union of two of England's great families.

"Yes, please." Sir Claudius spoke aloud to the steward
bending over with twin platters laden with poached turbot
and salmon mayonnaise. Another steward, white-gloved,
stepped forward and spooned two generous servings onto
his plate. The gluttony was under way.

With his fork raised, Sir Claudius was about to plunge
in when suddenly he thought of Edward. Discreetly he
sent his eyes the length of the table, then back again.

Missing! Peculiar, yet not so peculiar. Edward set his

own timetable and the rest of the world be damned. Still, out of courtesy for the occasion, the man might have put in an appearance.

Well, enough for now. The salmon mayonnaise looked delicious. Opposite him and about four seats down, he caught Sophia Cranford's eye. In a subtle gesture, he touched his hand to his forehead in salute, his way of paying compliment to the woman's prodigious efforts which were clearly displayed all about him.

Feeling a little envious now, Sir Claudius heard the laughter rise at the opposite end of the table, the company beginning to relax under the soothing influence of good food and wine. Only his end of the table still appeared sunk in gloom. My Lord, what a funeral here, he thought. A prenuptial feast at one end, a wake at the other.

Opposite him and midway down, seated between Caleb and Sophia Cranford, he noticed Jennifer. She looked, as always, like a hunted animal. Good heavens! Sir Claudius never thought it possible for nature to be so capricious, three such lackluster offspring emerging from two people who in their heyday had literally dazzled all of England.

Well, certainly there were no answers, and as his plate was empty and he had no immediate occupation either for his mouth or his hands, he straightened himself in his chair, dabbed his linen against his lips, and decided to make an attempt to break the wall of Marianne's silence.

"Milady," he began softly, lightly touching her right hand, which lay limp upon white linen. "Forgive me for intruding, but I fear your mood does not match the occasion."

Sweet God, was it his imagination or had the entire company fallen silent, all eyes and ears now focused on his end of the table?

Slowly Marianne looked up, her eyes still red as though recently she had shed tears.

Just when the silence and the waiting were on the verge of becoming embarrassing, she spoke, a faint smile warming her cold features. "You're not intruding, Sir Claudius," she murmured, "and if my expression alarmed you, I apologize." Now she raised her voice as though addressing the entire company. "In truth, I was merely enjoying a moment of private contemplation. You must forgive me if I lapse into brooding. Quite naturally my mind and heart go out to those—missing—"

For an instant Sir Claudius thought she'd made reference to the two empty chairs. But then he knew she was referring to another, to Thomas.

Sensing the tribute, the entire company fell silent. "To Thomas," she toasted intimately, "to—my Lord." Solemnly the company rose, glasses in hand, to join the toast.

While it was touching, it couldn't go on or else the entire evening would simply drown in old grief. Now in the far corner of the hall next to the stairs, Sir Claudius saw the musicians entering. Just in time, he thought.

But before they started, he had a toast of his own. "Your attention a moment longer," he announced, appalled at how high and womanlike his voice sounded. "For this glorious fortnight on a spot of earth aptly named," he commenced, "I lift my glass to the Countess Dowager, to that ray of sunshine which has warmed all our lives, to Lady Eden, to Marianne—"

A welcoming shout of "Hear! Hear!" rose about him, though as he lifted his glass to his lips, he noted several of the company who did not—Jennifer for one, who simply stood before her place. And Sophia Cranford, who took one rapid sip, then left the table and hurried toward the gathering musicians.

Well, so be it. He couldn't mend all bridges at once. The others responded warmly and the look of pleasure on Marianne's face was reward enough. Perhaps now she would have done with her ghosts and play her role properly.

As Sir Claudius settled back into his chair, she leaned over. "How thoughtful of you," she whispered.

"Thoughtfulness had nothing to do with it, milady," he countered gallantly. "I meant every word." He took her hand and kissed it, pleased to hear voices around him rise again, everyone talking, helping themselves to the intermediate course of cheese, butter, raw celery, the stewards moving about the table in a blur now, trying to remove the first plates and reset with fresh china and glasses. From the far corner he heard the first strains from the musicians, a gentle selection, unidentifiable and a perfect aid to good digestion.

Sir Claudius felt satisfied with himself. Single-handedly

he had moved the party forward, though not cured it of course. It still lay about him like an invalid, something amiss, something terribly amiss. But at least death had been stayed for a while.

He noticed Marianne taking a generous portion of cheese onto her plate and two leafy spears of celery. And of course he couldn't help but notice the warmth of her smile as she asked him a direct and thoughtful question.

"And your reading, Sir Claudius?" she inquired. "How did your reading go this morning?"

Before he could answer, Lady Carlisle at mid-table answered for him. "Simply splendid, Lady Eden," she smiled, leaning forward in an attempt to project her voice over the distance. "I really think Sir Claudius missed his calling. He should have been an actor on the stage. He positively brought Mr. Dickens to life."

Modestly Sir Claudius shook his head and raised a hand.

From the company came a peculiar crunching sound as all munched on the cleansing second course. Then, at mid-table, Sir Claudius saw the craning neck of Sophia Cranford. She seemed to be rigidly focused on the massive arched doorway which led out to the corridor beyond. Clearly the absence of someone was beginning to weigh on her.

Through the clutter of stewards he saw her lean across the ever-silent Jennifer and whisper something to Caleb. He watched Caleb's stern eyes move toward the empty doorway, then saw the man nod as though in agreement. A moment later, he saw Sophia leave her chair, and move down the long line of chairs until she stood directly behind Lady Powels.

Sir Claudius watched the whole little drama with a keen eye trained for such things. He'd not passed a lifetime in the law for nothing. And a few moments later, he saw Sophia assist Lady Powels to her feet, withdraw her chair, and walk with her to the doorway, their two heads bent in close conversation.

At the bottom of the short flight of stairs, Sophia abandoned her and left her to make the next ascent alone, which the woman did, looking strangely limp somehow, her russet-colored taffeta gown accenting the whiteness of her face.

A short time later, Sophia returned to the table, after first stopping by the musicians and whispering further instructions. Almost instantly the music changed, the pace and tone accelerated, a mazurka of sorts, as though to cover and hopefully drown out the something amiss.

Sir Claudius breathed deeply, as though for several long moments he had forgotten to breathe at all. As he lifted his fork and aimed it toward the galantine, he suddenly noticed the three women around him, Marianne, Jane Locke, and Mrs. Greenbell, their faces riveted on the empty staircase, clearly signaling that they too had observed the whole little drama.

As his curiosity vaulted, he again considered offering comment and again changed his mind. He had the most pronounced feeling, as he frequently did in Old Bailey, that the final act would be played out soon enough. And on that note, he held out his tongue and placed upon it a gratifying forkful of turkey galantine.

All along both sides of the table he now heard voices rising as though in competition with the swelling music. The army of stewards moved up and down as though in an attempt to keep pace with both the music and the voices; the third remove, a roast of beef, was now being presented to him even before he had savored the galantine.

As though helpless to alter the chaos, he saw Marianne lean forward, contributing to it as she attempted to launch into a conversation with Lady Carlisle halfway down the table. As the din rose, Sir Claudius felt his eardrums on the verge of exploding. What had happened to this curious dinner party which only a short time before had appeared to be in death throes? Still the music swelled, amplified to an unbearable extent.

Sir Claudius took refuge behind his napkin for a moment's respite, his eyes closed.

It was while his eyes were closed that he heard the musicians halt suddenly in their frenzied rendition of the nameless mazurka. For several moments voices persisted, unaware that the support of music had ceased. He heard a fringe of residual laughter, all voices mysteriously fading now, the sudden silence after the din almost ghostly, as though the same power source for all had been abruptly switched off.

Slowly Sir Claudius lowered his napkin, caught sight

first of Marianne, her hands forming two rigid fists upon
the table. In variation, her demeanor was repeated the
length of the table, no sound now, all heads turning slowly
toward the arched doorway.

He saw first Lady Powels scurry down the steps, her
head bowed as she took her place at table. As she sat
quickly, she raised a pale face to Sophia Cranford. Sir
Claudius thought he saw her nod, but he couldn't be certain. All he knew was that the once frenzied party had
come to a halt. All eyes were focused on the empty archway.

As this contrasting scene unrolled, Sir Claudius again
felt ill at ease. The change had been too stark. Had the
entire company gone berserk? Or did everyone know
something he didn't?

Since the latter was not possible, Sir Claudius settled
on the possibility of the former and joined the others in
their irrational interest of the empty archway.

Seated at the far end of the table, his vision was blocked
by a number of craning heads, the women mostly, straining to see the nothing that there was to be seen.

Then the nothing turned into a something, an apparition
in white satin, appearing suddenly in the door, the guest
of honor herself, Harriet Powels. He heard a quick intake
of breath from the company. Next to him he saw Marianne
crumple softly forward, resting her head in her hands as
though she were giving a fervent prayer. Then slowly she
lifted her eyes and joined the rest of her guests in an almost savage scrutiny of the young woman.

With no other alternative open to him, Sir Claudius
joined them, although in truth he was still baffled. The
young lady had appeared late many times before and had
not appeared at all almost as frequently. Clearly she was
the sort of female who did only what she chose and when
she chose, not a very creditable qualification for a wife.

Now he noticed that the strangeness, instead of diminishing, was only increasing as the young woman maintained
her pose in the archway, standing rigid, as though more
than willing to take their judgment upon her shoulders,
concealed shoulders, he observed now, in curious opposition to the fashion of the day, the white satin gown almost
prim in its severity, all flesh save her hands and face

tightly covered, a virginal, cold apparition, the gown in spite of its rich fabric resembling a nun's habit.

Again, not a very promising omen for James. The dress somehow defied her femininity and left her resembling a scaled dead fish. With a silent wave of bawdy humor, the thought occurred to Sir Claudius that the girl had probably never been touched by any man save her father, a tight virgin and likely to remain so. Poor James, he thought again, his thoughts running ahead to the incongruity of a wedding night with such a creature.

Well, good heavens, was she simply going to stand there all evening? Now Sir Claudius began to grow nervous for her. She was presenting herself to them relentlessly, as though she were a prisoner in the dock. Would no one go to her? Would no one end the brutal inspection?

Ah, thank God. At the last minute, he saw Sophia Cranford lean forward and whisper something to James, saw the slight, shy man stand tentatively and step toward his bride-to-be, covering the twenty feet which separated them at a funereal pace which matched the glazed remote look on Harriet's face.

Something *was* amiss, Sir Claudius thought again. Now all faces seemed to be magnetized by the silent young woman who sat stiffly in her chair, her back straight, her hands laced primly in her lap.

Finally, blessedly, he saw Sophia Cranford lift her hand in signal for the musicians. And a moment later the music commenced, softer now, more melancholy, or was it simply Sir Claudius's imagination, the appearance of the girl affecting merely everything? With relief he heard the company beginning to chat softly among themselves, the stewards moving back and forth with the fourth remove. The party was at least partially reviving except for Lady Eden, whose face mirrored the young woman's as though these two shared a secret knowledge.

Alarmed by what he saw, Sir Claudius leaned close. "Marianne, I beg you," he whispered. "It will pass. Remember yourself as a young bride."

The words seemed only to depress her further. He leaned still closer to deliver comfort when suddenly above the muted talk he heard a new sound, men's voices raised, out of sight, coming from the direction of the Great Hall.

He saw Marianne's eyes flash upward, a mysterious look of recognition as though she'd been expecting the voices.

Wearily, Sir Claudius closed his eyes. No more. Please. The drama of the evening had been quite enough, thank you. But apparently there still was the final act to be played out. Fate obviously was impervious to the toleration of the company.

They *were* men's voices, he heard them clearly now, one old, subservient, several younger ones, protesting, and predominant among them, one strong, outraged, and very familiar.

A moment later, looking up, Sir Claudius saw the doorway filled for the second time that evening, no silent apparition in white satin now, but an angry, flushed Edward Eden, dragging behind him his old manservant and three protesting watchmen, their hands outsearching in futile restraint.

Catching sight of the company, the watchmen fell back, as though belatedly aware that they had penetrated beyond their legitimate territory.

But not Edward. Coming upon the company and the elegant banqueting table, he halted only momentarily, his eyes seeming to take in the faces that stared back at him. He paused in the door and completed his inspection, his eyes lingering in painful scrutiny of one, the young woman, who sat with new rigidity.

Now he saw Edward draw himself up as though aware of his position as spectacle in the doorway. For the first time, Sir Claudius noted his garb, traveling clothes, dark gray, a lighter gray cape swinging from his shoulders. Even as he spoke, his eyes held rigid on the young woman, who continued to be the only guest at table who apparently felt neither the compulsion nor the curiosity to look up.

"I beg your pardon," Edward pronounced now, his voice low, though clearly audible as though he were exerting an effort of will. "My apologies for being tardy on this occasion. I had an—appointment," he added, his voice seeming to catch on the last word, his eyes still resting embarrassingly on the young woman. "But since the party failed to appear, I thought it best if I came to fetch her."

Her? What *was* the foolish man talking about? Sir Claudius glanced at Marianne, saw her face white. Down the

way, he saw Sophia Cranford start from her chair, saw a
quick restraining gesture come from Caleb.

Edward started down the steps, eluding altogether one
final and restraining hand from old John Murrey, the
servant succeeding only in jerking Edward's cape from
his shoulders, Edward continuing, undaunted, to the table,
where he stood directly behind James, who sat half turned
in his chair as though ready to defend himself as soon
as he could identify the threat.

But in truth there was nothing threatening on Edward's
face. To the contrary it bore the softest expression of repentance and the voice followed suit, as extending a hand
to his brother, he almost begged, "Forgive me, James. I
had no intention of it happening like this."

But James, clearly as bewildered as everyone else, merely
gaped up at him, his mouth open in an imbecilic expression. "No need to apologize," he faltered. "I'm certain you
can catch up with us. There's your chair waiting, and—"

In a rather limp gesture, he motioned toward Edward's
vacant chair. He might have said more except that Edward's apology now took the shape of a mildly sorrowing
smile. "I've not come for dinner, James," he said.

Heads up and down the table were turning about in
nervous confusion. The musicians had ceased playing altogether. The stewards looked discreetly away from the
confrontation at the head of the table.

James stood then, apparently making an effort at understanding. "Then what?" he asked, taking one step forward,
shortening the distance between them.

For the first time, Edward seemed to be the one who
hesitated. The angle of his vision continuously slanted
downward on the young woman whose frozen exterior
now seemed altered in that her mouth was slightly open
as though she were having difficulty in breathing. Still the
tableau held, James waiting patiently for an explanation,
Edward looking hopefully at Harriet Powels, as though
he expected her to speak on his behalf.

And when she didn't, Edward stepped forward and with
great intimacy placed his arm about her shoulder and
bent close as though to speak. Sir Claudius heard again
that intake of air as the shock of such a gesture registered
with the guests. But of far greater impact was the reaction
of the woman herself who, at his touch, drew rapidly to

one side, a moan escaping her lips as though his touch were hot, or had caused pain.

Sir Claudius was in a perfect position to see Edward's face. In all the many years of his vast and usually repellent association with the Prince of Eden, he'd never seen such an expression on that normally self-assured face, a horribly raw look as though the man were being broken in half.

And when again, as though disbelieving, Edward reached forward and touched the woman, and when again she moaned even more pitifully than before, Sir Claudius saw James stir himself out of his lethargy and into a kind of zealous chivalry, as stepping forward, he made the foolish mistake of coming between Edward and his agony.

James drew himself up to his poor height. "I beg your pardon, sir," he pronounced artificially, as though he were delivering words from a play script.

For the moment, the confrontation held, James, one hand upraised as though physically to prohibit Edward from moving closer, and Edward himself, giving them all the benefit of his face with its confused, embattled expression.

Then abruptly there was movement at the head of the table, Edward trying to step around James's restraining hand, the movement provoking another outcry from the young woman, as though again she had been touched.

At that point James's latent chivalry vaulted. "Edward," he pronounced, "the lady is making it clear. She does not desire your company." Then he placed both hands on his brother's shoulders and pushed him back. "I must ask you to—"

But whatever the nature of James's request, it was never voiced, for suddenly the fatigue and pain on Edward's face blended. He looked down as though in surprise at James's restraining hands and apparently the sight of those hands set the winds of inspiration blowing.

He started forward and again James restrained him and in that moment, all the civilized propriety of the occasion fell away. In one fluid and incredibly swift movement, Edward drew back his fist and angling his full body weight into his shoulder, delivered a stunning blow to the side of James's jaw, a blow of such force that it sent the man reeling backward onto the table, scattering cutlery, crystal,

and filled plates in all directions, women screaming now,
pushing back in their chairs, a few of the gentlemen starting forward, their attention divided between the unconscious James spread indecorously on the table before them
and the clearly deranged Edward, whose face shone with
two brick-red spots and whose body was still angled and
ready as though willing to take on all comers.

And when a moment later, a glassy-eyed James seemed
to revive and lift a wobbly head and make a futile effort
to propel himself off the table, and when Edward stepped
forward and grabbed him by his jacket as though to aid
him to his feet so that he might knock him senseless again,
there was a sudden sharp outcry to Sir Claudius's left,
Marianne on her feet, at last stirred to action by the barbaric sight of one son beating the other senseless. As Edward renewed his grip on his still-wobbly brother and when
it became apparent to all that he was prepared to deliver
another blow, Marianne cried out to the gaping watchmen,
"Restrain him, please restrain him—"

Clearly it was the command they had been waiting for
as with admirable speed they were down the steps, their
triple strengths tearing Edward loose from the confrontation, enduring quite a struggle with him as the outrage of
one seemed superior to the strength of three.

As the area beyond the head of the table became a hissing arena of oaths and curses and shouts, Sir Claudius felt
a warmth on his face. Scandalous! The ruined table was
pitiful to behold, the guests terrified, the spilled wine,
the broken crystal, the bouquets of flowers scattered about
amidst the garbage of food, a yellow smear of butter on
the back of James's coat, James himself still in a dazed
state, dabbing at the small stream of blood which slipped
down the side of his mouth.

But the tempest was not over, far from it. With a watchman restraining each arm, Edward continued to strain futilely against his captors, his body arching, his person
undone, his waistcoat askew, sleeve torn, as energy and
strength persisted. Old John Murrey hovered a safe distance behind, a look of disaster on his face.

Marianne, still standing, found her voice again and the
will to use it. "Take him to his chambers," she commanded,
"and lock him in."

The command seemed to work an even greater pain on

Edward, although for a moment he returned his mother's gaze with the hypnotic effect of accusing eyes, as a snake's stare holds a bird. But when the watchmen with their superior strength jerked him about, twisting his arms completely behind him in the process and half led, half dragged him away, the struggle was on again. The third watchman joined them midway up the stairs and grabbed Edward by the feet, thus rendering him totally helpless. The last glimpse that Sir Claudius had of the Prince of Eden was an unceremonious one, the man being hauled face down from the Banqueting Hall.

For a few moments thereafter, the entire company sat in their awkward positions, motionless with horror. In the distance could be heard cries of outrage and protest. Old John Murrey remained a moment longer, his head bowed in consummate embarrassment, his hands kneading the gray cape. "Milady," he murmured to Marianne. "May I—see to him?"

Looking up, Sir Claudius saw silent tears streaming down Marianne's face. "See to him," she whispered.

The old man bobbed his head and hurried up the stairs as fast as his age and the weight of emotion would permit.

Silence again. Sir Claudius expected the motionless guests to stir, Marianne certainly to dismiss them, *someone* to take charge of the shambles which once had been an elegant table.

But when no one did, he looked back at Marianne, whose attention now seemed mysteriously riveted on a spot halfway down the table. She was looking at her daughter, Jennifer, who was returning her mother's gaze with eyes level and cold, a steady light of hate passing from the young woman to the older one. And even while Sir Claudius was watching, he saw Jennifer stand up at the table and push her chair back, her voice as level as her eyes as she said to Marianne, "You had no right, Lady—"

Marianne started to reply, but she was not given that opportunity as Jennifer continued backing away from the table. "Haven't you caused him enough grief?" she whispered. "Did you have to humiliate him in that fashion?"

She might have said more but her voice broke and she ran from the Banqueting Hall.

Now there was movement, a few heads lifting to see

how Marianne would take this public indictment from
her daughter. Across the table, Sir Claudius saw Jane
Locke and an ashen-faced Mrs. Greenbell, who quickly
surrounded her and gave her the support she needed, the
bulk of both women obscuring the frail broken figure of
the Countess Dowager.

Gently and with apologies to no one they led her from
the room by the opposite door.

Good God, enough, thought Sir Claudius angrily. Someone would have to take charge, and since both Cranfords
seemed unwilling, and poor stunned James unable, then it
would have to be he.

Clearing his throat, he pushed away from the table.
"Ladies and gentlemen," he began. "May I kindly suggest
that we retire for the night. The evening has been unfortunate, for all of us, but most unfortunate for this family
who has so graciously embraced us with hospitality— Let
me kindly suggest that we—withhold our judgment, extend
our understanding, and—retire for the evening."

There! That was good. Then why was no one moving?
Well, he would simply have to try again. As he opened
his mouth, he saw at last faint movement, coming from a
most surprising figure, perhaps the central reason for the
entire disastrous evening, the young woman who resembled
a statue.

Now this slim figure stood and by her stirring seemed to
stir a few of those around her, James for one, who extended a hand which was so coldly ignored that he instantly withdrew it.

But for all the splintered emotions around her, Miss Harriet Powels seemed as possessed, as unruffled as though
she were indeed made of marble.

Yet as she approached the bottom step, her hands suddenly moved out on either side as though to steady the
air about her, and in the next moment she collapsed in a
soft white heap, her face as white as her gown.

Her mother screamed, then both father and mother were
on their feet running toward their fallen daughter, who
apparently had at last succumbed to the events of the evening. With the assistance of a steward, Lord Powels lifted
his daughter in his arms, her mother weeping openly now,
trying to stroke the white unconscious face, as again the
company was treated to an exit of undistilled agony.

Sir Claudius realized that he was still standing, and began to feel weak himself. As he slowly sank down into his chair, he saw Lord Salisbury rise and place a protective arm about Lady Salisbury and lead her from the room. A moment later, others blessedly followed suit, many of the women weeping quietly, the expressions of the gentlemen mirroring his own. For the first time since he'd known Sophia Cranford, even that strong woman seemed destitute and leaned heavily on Caleb's arm, stopping briefly at the head of the table to examine James's wound, then taking him with them to their private chambers.

A few minutes later, Sir Claudius looked up to see the vast room empty, the stewards standing at attention in a rigid line, their faces expressionless, betraying none of the heated emotions of the guests.

At that moment, the memories of events conspired against him and he afforded himself the crude luxury of placing his elbows on the table and resting his head on the indecorous perch.

Into his quiet distress came the cracked voice of an old steward. "Begging your pardon, milord," he murmured politely, "but shall we clear now?"

On a wave of self-pity, Sir Claudius glared up at the old man. "What do you think?" he snapped and stood and walked across the Banqueting Hall, heading toward his own chambers and the comfort of a full decanter of brandy.

Something *had* been amiss. And hell-gate was on the verge of opening even wider.

Frightened, Jennifer looked at the grim walls and endless steps which led up to the third-floor corridor and Edward's private chambers. She glanced nervously over her shoulder to see if anyone had dared to follow her out of that horrible room. They hadn't, and with new outrage she began to climb the stairs.

Finally she reached the third-floor corridor, and a distance beyond, she saw Edward's chambers, the door closed and bolted, the three watchmen standing firm, their eyes like those of a mastiff confronting a cat.

Before them, Jennifer halted. Winded from her rapid climb and her weight of emotions, she turned her head away, the better to address them. "I command you to let me pass," she said, her weak voice betraying her false courage.

They merely looked down on her. "Can't," one grinned.

The second one suggested kindly, "You don't want to go in there, milady. Your brother's stark raving mad, he is. Let him—"

She faced them now, her face rigid, and forced herself to speak a certain name. "Then I shall simply have to return to the Banqueting Hall and inform my mother that I cannot fulfill her errand because I was denied passage by her watchmen."

For a moment, the three men continued to stare down on her, their very glances rendering her inferior. Finally, although he shook his head disapprovingly, one of the men stepped to one side and threw the bolt on the door. "Milady," he muttered, bowing low, and with a sweeping gesture indicated the clear passage.

She lifted her head and stepped forward. She pushed open the door. The room was dark, only a small candle burning on the center table, its faint illumination casting a dim light.

"Edward?" she whispered softly, moving a step farther into the room. While there was no reaction from the figure on the bed, she saw the one slumped in the chair look up, saw in the dim light the emaciated face of John Murrey.

"Milady," he whispered, as though someone were sleeping or ill. "You oughtn't to be here, you really shouldn't. Please go along with you. Ain't nothing that you can—"

But even as he spoke, she started to shake her head in rebuttal. She'd made it successfully past the three men outside the door. Compared to them, John Murrey was nothing.

Without speaking, she lifted the candle from the table and carried it to the bed. Looking down, she gasped, "Oh my God," and lowered the candle for a closer examination of the incredible sight, her brother lying on his back, his shirtwaist completely undone by the recent struggle, his head without benefit of pillow, his arms drawn over his head and secured to the bedposts with pieces of leather, restrained like a madman, though in truth there was nothing about him now in need of restraint. She saw his eyes open, though unfocused, fixed on some spot on the darkened ceiling, the rest of his body lying limp.

If shock and pity had been her first reactions, anger followed fast behind as she looked accusingly at the old man who stood opposite her at the bed. "John, how could you let them do this?" she demanded.

In a burst of energy he sprang to his own defense. "And how was I to stop them, milady?" he protested.

Quickly she placed the candle on the near table and commenced pulling at the leather straps twisted tightly about his wrists.

Now it was John Murrey who protested. "Milady, they said not to—"

But she looked sharply up at him and commanded, "Tend to his other hand."

Finally he fell to work on the bonds and a few minutes later Jennifer jerked free a strip of leather and hurled it into the shadows. John Murrey pulled his side free and dropped it wearily on the floor.

In a hard way, Jennifer wished she'd left him bound, wished her mother might have seen him thus, the result of her own handiwork. If that selfish, vain woman wished him destroyed, why had she even bothered to give him life? For that matter, why had she bothered to give any of them life?

Recovered from her weakness, made strong by hate, she looked down to see Edward moving. Gently she reached out a hand and touched his hair. "I'm—sorry," she said.

He lifted his head and looked directly at her as though seeing her for the first time. "Jennifer?" he questioned, as though in his distracted state he was uncertain of her identity.

She smiled, glad that she had followed after him. Now again anger moved across her. "They had no right—" she began.

Incredibly the faint light of a smile crossed his face. "Oh, they had every right," he disagreed. "I would have killed him."

While Jennifer, in the past, had enjoyed a degree of skill in bringing comfort to young girls, she found herself totally at a loss for words. All she could think of was a blunt and impertinent question. "Did you—" she began, faltering once. "Did you—love her?"

At first she thought he hadn't heard. There was no discernible change in his posture. And when a moment later, having received no answer, she was on the verge of asking it again, he suddenly thrust himself forward, moving rapidly away from her hand and the question.

"I'm—sorry, Edward," she apologized. "I shouldn't have asked. It was none of my—"

The silence in the room was heavy. Embarrassed, she considered leaving. But where would she go? Back down to the Banqueting Hall and the repellent presence of her mother? To the Cranfords' sitting room and be reminded again of everything that she was not. No! She must start moving away from the Cranfords. It was time. Past time. Then where? To the loneliness of her childhood chambers filled with dead china dolls and memories more painful than her present awkward position?

Lost in her own uncertainty, she did not at first see Edward looking at her. He seemed to stare at her as though he were reaching a hard decision. Then he requested, "Jennifer, would you leave us now. Please."

The dreaded words, so kindly spoken, had a disastrous effect on her. In her own defense she stood a little straighter. "I—came to look after you," she smiled.

"And I'm grateful. But John is here. I need no—"

"John is your servant," she protested, hearing the fear in her voice and hating it. "I'm your sister—"

Standing by the door, the old man inquired with bowed head, "Shall I take my leave, sir?"

"No," came the firm voice from the shadows. Then the voice softened. "Please, Jennifer, leave me for now."

The words struck heavily against her. For a moment she tried to digest her dismissal. Intent upon her dilemma, she never noticed the shadow come from behind her, and it was with surprise that she felt a hand on her arm.

Through a blur of tears she looked up into his face. At the very instant she thought she had been banished, she found herself welcomed back into his love.

Inside his arms, she wept quietly. He held her, murmuring, "Poor Jennifer," as though *she* were the one who had been dragged up the stairs like a common criminal and placed under guard.

A moment later her tears abated, and he released her

and walked slowly back to the bed and sat heavily, his hands clasped between his legs.

She watched him, wondering if, in spite of their recent closeness, she still was under orders to leave. But then came the reprieve she'd been waiting for. "Stay if you wish," he muttered, not looking at her. "Stay as long as you wish. I could not possibly send you to that death outside the door."

She nodded. As she settled into a chair on the far side of the table, she saw Edward give an unspoken signal of some kind to John Murrey, saw the old man hesitate a moment, then saw him start forward toward the decanter of claret on the table and a single glass.

Jennifer watched carefully as he half filled the glass, then went to the wardrobe, unlocked it, and withdrew a small square-cut bottle from a heavy leather valise. The old man seemed to gaze upon it, an extraordinary expression on his face. She saw him look back at Edward, then slowly go toward the table and the half-filled glass of claret.

She knew what it was. Sweet God, hadn't she heard the Cranfords whisper of his addiction? As John Murrey poured a small amount into the claret, she whispered urgently, "No, Edward, please—"

He did not look at her, and his voice bore no trace of the tenderness he'd recently offered her. "I warn you, lady," he said, "keep still or leave. I offer you sanctuary in exchange for silence."

Reprimanded, she sat back, though continuing to watch, horrified, as apparently the moderate dosage offered by John Murrey did not please him. Reaching out, he relieved the old man of the small bottle and poured an even half of the contents into the claret.

She watched, silently grieving, as he lifted the glass, tilted it gently from side to side, his gaze focused on the dark crimson mix.

Apparently when the blend was to his satisfaction, he lifted it upward. "An elixir," he smiled, "to heal all anger and bring forgetfulness."

As he tilted his head back and commenced to drink, Jennifer closed her eyes. A few seconds later she looked back. She saw then that she was the only one watching. John Murrey had gone back around to the far side of the bed, had arranged a chair in close proximity, and had now sunk into it, assuming a vigilant position, as though he'd performed this role many times before and thus knew precisely what to do.

She had no idea what to expect, but somehow expected more than what was happening, Edward loosening his boots now, almost lethargically pulling them off, his hands moving heavily about. A few minutes later he was asleep.

Again her eyes blurred. "How long will he sleep thus?" she asked, without looking at John Murrey.

"He'll be—senseless the better part of the night," the old man replied.

Senseless? A strange way to describe sleep. Well, then, she might as well make herself comfortable. She went to the table and drew the chair close. In the final moments before she rested her head on the table, she thought how peaceful he looked.

If this was addiction, perhaps it was a state greatly to be desired.

What she heard first was merely a restlessness. She had no sense of time and thus was unable to determine how long she'd been asleep. Raising her head to the new sound coming from the bed, she noticed the lamps had burned low. Yet beyond the windows there was not a trace of dawn.

There was the sound again, a faint moan and stirring. She looked toward the bed, to see at first only a gentle thrashing, as an invalid feeling the discomfort of a high fever. But it wasn't Edward who alarmed her as much as it was John Murrey. The old man stood over the bed, his eyes alert.

"What is it, John?" she whispered.

He looked sharply up at her. "Go back to sleep, milady," he said, "or better, leave us."

She looked toward the bed again, her attention splintered between John Murrey and Edward. The moans had increased and the restlessness as well. From where she sat, she saw his face contorted.

No sooner had she stood than a full-blown piercing cry left his lips. At the same time, his head jerked backward against the pillow. The violent trembling had spread over his entire body now, his legs drawing sharply up, then shooting out rigid again.

Fully awake and terrified by what she saw, she started toward the bed. "John, what is—"

But again the old man stopped her, a tone of pleading in his voice. "I beg you, milady, leave us. If you feel any love for him, please leave."

Now John Murrey tried to wrench Edward's hands away from his face, where his fingers were digging into his eyes, as though in an attempt to remove those instruments of sight.

With dogged persistence, John Murrey restrained him, the two men angled sideways across the bed. And when a moment later, Edward gave one mighty wrenching upward and with inhuman strength almost dislodged the man astride him, Jennifer drew back out of empathy for the wretched creature and ran from the room.

Outside in the darkened corridor, she closed the door, then leaned against it. In her heart was a dark knowledge. The Cranfords had been right. He could not survive many such nightmares, though death seemed to her a rich blessing in comparison with what she had just witnessed.

Suddenly she heard footsteps. Looking up, she expected to see one of the watchmen who perhaps had been dozing a distance away and had heard Edward's cries. She saw nothing at first, but as she was making an attempt to wipe the tears from her eyes she saw two figures approaching.

She was on the verge of calling out for identification when she saw one figure step forward. The identity was clear now.

As she turned her back, the shadowy figure spoke her name in a voice which betrayed recent weeping. "Jennifer, please."

Without looking, Jennifer replied, "Yes, milady?" leaving the burden of exchange on her mother.

In the quiet interval she continued to hear Edward's agony and now she made a quick resolve. She would not permit either of them to cross the threshold. She would not subject Edward to that humiliation.

Thus resolved and feeling stronger, she leaned in toward the door and was just pushing it open when again she heard her mother's voice behind her, closer now. "Please, Jennifer, wait," she begged.

Obediently Jennifer waited. "What is it, milady?" she demanded. "I'm needed inside."

There was a moment's pause, then she heard the hated voice again. "I heard cries," Lady Eden began.

She might have said more, but at that, Jennifer turned, saw her mother clearly now, reduced somehow by the simple dressing gown, her legendary beauty gone altogether.

"Of course you heard cries, milady," Jennifer replied, knowing that it hurt the old woman not to be called mother. "Why not cries? They are most fitting in these old castle walls. I've heard cries of one kind or another since the day I was born. I'm not at all certain why you are now surprised by them."

She thought she saw her mother give in to a subtle collapse. With Mrs. Greenbell's help, she stood erect and took a step forward. "Edward," she pleaded. "Give me news of Edward."

"Surely you can hear, milady. Listen!" And there it was again, the continuous moans, punctuated now and then by an outcry. "I've no news to give you," she went on. "I found him bound to his bed, on your orders, I assume. I released him, then watched as he prepared a potion for himself. He drank it quickly, enjoyed a brief sleep. Then the poison took effect." She looked at her mother. "He's an addict, you know."

Her voice sounded loud in the still corridor. Before her, her mother's head was bowed again. Mrs. Greenbell's dark figure hovered continuously over her and Jennifer now heard her whispered suggestion that Lady Eden return to her chambers.

"I agree with Mrs. Greenbell," Jennifer said. "There's nothing to be done here. John Murrey is with him." She paused and repeated herself. "So there's nothing more you can do, milady. You've done quite enough."

At that, she saw her mother's face lift, saw one frail hand press against her lips as a sob escaped. Quickly Mrs. Greenbell wrapped her arms around the weeping woman and turned her about.

Jennifer held her position and watched as the old women made their way slowly back down the corridor. At the moment they disappeared from her sight, she experienced a curious emotion, regret perhaps.

Then quickly she turned back into the room and held her position by the door, transfixed by the sight before her, Edward knotted now into one tight ball on the muss of blood-stained bed linens, his knees drawn up, his arms wrapped about his body, his eyes open and fixed on nothing.

Hesitantly she stepped toward the bed, keeping her eyes on Edward's apparently conscious face. "Is he asleep?" she whispered.

With effort, John Murrey stepped away from the bed and sank heavily into his chair. He shook his head. "Not asleep, milady," he said hoarsely. "Not awake, either, but at least he's quiet." With that, the white head fell backward against the chair, his eyes closed.

Timidly Jennifer approached the bed and the curled lifeless figure of her brother.

With some effort she dragged a chair from the center of the room and positioned it close to the bed. She maintained a constant vigil, lifting his hand once and pressing it to her lips, wondering at the demons and fiends who had caused him such agony.

The following morning, Edward awakened first to find Jennifer asleep on one side of the bed and old John Murrey asleep on the other, a mismatched pair of guardian angels if he'd ever seen them, though at the moment his attention was drawn to the window, to the rude noise which had disturbed his hard-earned sleep.

Leaving the bed slowly, his muscles clearly objecting to movement after what he'd put them through the night before, he made his way to the window, shielded his eyes against the morning sun, and looked down to see a continuous procession of departing carriages. Obviously the events of the night before had been too much for these noblemen. He watched carefully for the Powelses' entourage and not seeing it, he dared to let his hope vault. Perhaps she was still in the castle, perhaps she would grant him an audience. Perhaps—

But at that moment the large amount of opium still in his system caused him to suffer uncomfortable nausea. He made it as far as the table, feeling certain he could make it back to his bed, not wishing to disturb the two who obviously had sacrificed much on his behalf.

The nausea increased. He felt a cold sweat on his forehead. His breath seemed to be blocked in his lungs. A suf-

focating sensation was his last awareness, that, and the
table rising up to meet him.

When he fully awakened again, he was back in his bed.
It was raining outside his window and the room was dim
with evening light. Jennifer was beside him and it was
she who told him of the events of the day; the curious
brunch at mid-morning with less than a dozen guests present; their mother, ill-looking and dressed in severe black,
on the arm of Lord Powels, announcing in a voice which
was scarcely audible the coming union of their two families; then all the guests disappearing, the Powelses taking
their mysteriously ill daughter home to recover, to publish
the banns and to set a nuptial date. James had left immediately with Caleb Cranford on horseback for a day-long
ride across the wet moors; everyone absent from the reception halls save the servants; the whole castle locked into
a gloomy cold silence.

Edward listened closely and noticed how suddenly Jennifer paled and then blushed. He wanted to reassure her
but found he could not speak. His memories turned constantly back to Harriet, to the perfect now they had shared
together. He had thought his love had made a difference.
But obviously the engagement had been announced, the
wedding would take place.

"Edward, please don't," Jennifer whispered, apparently
seeing his grief. He looked up at her in the soft light of
the rainy evening. A curious thought entered his head and
he voiced it. "You really should go to Daniel, you know,"
he whispered. "He loves you very much."

But the words, instead of pleasing her, seemed only
to cause her pain. He saw her quickly turn away in the
chair, hiding her face from him. Seeing her repudiation
and still suffering from his own, he raised his voice and
called for John Murrey, who could provide him with at
least a limited escape from this gloomy hell.

Thus the pattern was established and thus it held through
all the long dreary rainy months of summer. From the
night of the chaotic engagement banquet in late June until
well into September, not once did the residents of Eden
Castle gather for a common meal. To the distress of
the staff, which had now shrunk back to its normal size,

each member of the family demanded private menus served in all corners of the castle.

By unspoken signals, they each seemed to know when the corridors would be free for passage without running the risk of encountering one another, although in truth there was little passage save for that of the servants, who were kept running at all hours of the day and night, carrying warm milk up to Lady Eden, endless bottles of claret up to Mr. Eden, hearty six-course meals to Lord Eden, who alone seemed to have retained his good appetite, and mainly soft boiled foods to the Cranfords' rooms, where at least for the time being, Sophia Cranford seemed to have gone into hiding, appearing only when necessary to deal with the agent from Exeter.

But of course, as all the older servants knew, this family had never known good days, had known only evil and less evil. Still, this was the worst, this wet, gloomy, miserable summer when no one met and no one spoke, where no foot moved for fear of making a false step.

In the pre-dawn hours of September 23, Jennifer slowly raised her head from off the cot to see if Edward was still sleeping. He was. The night, thank God, had been peaceful. In fact they had not had to use those hideous leather straps which had become permanent fixtures on the bedposts for several weeks.

Edward had told her repeatedly that ultimately the violent nightmares would abate. And apparently they had. Further he had told her not to worry when he entered the "abyss of divine enjoyment." In spite of how he might look, how ferociously he might rage, he had assured her time and time again that the pleasure far outweighed the pain. She'd not believed him then, nor did she believe him now, but at least he gave the appearance of peace.

Carefully now she sat up on her cot beneath the window and surveyed the wreckage of the chamber. There on the opposite side of the room was John Murrey. How well she knew him now, that toothless wonder of loyalty and blind devotion. The fact that they were sharing the room communally had at first appalled her. In the beginning she'd used the cot only for brief afternoon naps. But for the last several weeks she passed nights here as well, generally slipping out in pre-dawn hours when she could be assured that the corridors would be empty. Then she'd go to her chambers to bathe, brush her hair, slip on a fresh dress and return, ready to face another day, relieving John Murrey, sitting with Edward. Sometimes the two of them passed the entire day without words as, helpless, she watched his illness increase.

Quietly now she rose from the cot and walked slowly to the bed on which he was sleeping. She looked down. Once she had thought this unique older brother to be the tallest, strongest man she'd ever known.

Now? He looked shrunken. His eyes, when awake or asleep, stared out of dark purple shadows. His lips closed more thinly than before and his whole face was gaunt. She'd considered writing to Daniel Spade, but had always dismissed the notion. For one thing, she wasn't certain that Daniel Spade and London were the proper solution. Daniel Spade had known of his growing addiction long before she had and apparently had done nothing to curb it.

Then what? She continued to stare down on her sleeping brother, trying to sort through all the dimensions of what was ahead for him. With her gone, there was nothing ahead for him but increased dosage, increased lethargy, addle-headedness, and eventually death. And at the heart of the tragic dilemma was the greater mystery, the unanswerable question which on occasion he'd tried to answer for her and failed. Why? Why any of it?

Then why leave him? If she was to depart in a fortnight, he would leave with her. She needed an escort. The air in Yorkshire would be crisp and cool by now, the change of scene and clime bracing and health-giving. Perhaps she could talk Miss Wooler into leasing to him one of the apartments near the back of the red brick school. At least for a while, until his routine was altered, his habit broken.

As the plan evolved, she held rigidly still. Of course he might refuse. But at least she could try. Whatever sorrow had set him on his present course, she felt certain that the true source of that sorrow resided in Eden Castle. It certainly did for her. Why would it be different for him?

No! She had to take him away. But she would have to go about it with great diplomacy, perhaps appealing to him from the position of her own need, her dread of making the long journey alone. She felt certain that the drug had done nothing to alter his basic kindness. She'd served him well over the last few months. Now perhaps she could appeal to him for help.

She would try. And on that note of hope, she slipped quietly from the room.

A soft awakening.

He enjoyed the soft awakenings when at first his mind refused to create the bridge across which his unconscious would march from the glories of the night to the harsh realities of day.

Thus it was with him now, as he opened his eyes, sensing someone staring down on him, but seeing nothing but a pink-tinged fog, every object in the room softly blurred. My God, how glorious the night had been. Yet a single night only?

Sitting upright, he rubbed his eyes and discovered that he received no sensation of rubbing his eyes. There seemed to be a pressure on his face, but the sensation went unrecorded. For a moment he stared at his hands as though they belonged to someone else, as indeed they did, those soiled unkempt extremities of himself. Surely it had not been those hands which had embraced Harriet.

Foolhardy, that, giving in to that memory! But once the wall was breached, other memories came down upon him, the quickness of her steps as she'd hurried down the secret stairway, the dazzling lights in her hair as she'd stepped out into first light, her curious strength even at the moment of complete submission, her face, her eyes, her voice—

For too long, he gave in to this self-induced torture which caused the mussed room to reverberate around him. Oh God, the bridge had been built, stronger than he'd ever built it before. At the end lay murderers in waiting, armed with knife-sharp memories.

And there were others: there, Charlotte Longford; and there, Jawster Gray; and there, thousands of homeless children all running toward him; and there his mother weeping; and Harriet, robed in white, laughing at him; the tempest of human faces still coming, always coming, closer, closer. He wanted—what? To leave this place, these chambers, these cold castle walls imbedded with misery. He wanted—what? Not London, not yet, though he hungered for Daniel Spade's strong face.

Then where? Again he closed his eyes and walked

further across the bridge and in his imagination almost
stumbled over a man who lay sprawled in his path, his
clothes dirty, vermin crawling over the back of his withered
neck, his outstretched hands revealing his fingernails like
yellowed claws. Who was this senseless creature and how
did he come to be here? With a nudge of his foot, Edward
rolled him over and saw himself.

The sight did not shock him. He'd known the identity of
the man from the beginning, knew precisely the path he
was taking. But now he felt only resentment of the waste,
double resentment of the weakness. Perhaps it was not too
late. All he needed was a course of action, a movement
away from here until he could take himself in hand, make
an attempt to cleanse his system and, more important,
cleanse his mind of all memories.

Yet even at that moment he still saw her as he'd seen her
that first night high atop the battlements, the channel
breezes blowing her gown, her eyes fixed upon his face
with an intensity he'd never seen before.

No more! Sternly he sent the memory away. Perhaps he
could talk old John Murrey into shaving him this morning.
Then he'd sit with Jennifer beside the window and count
the sea gulls and watch the small packets navigating the
channel. Dear Jennifer. How he was going to miss her.
What solace she had brought him during—

There abruptly his thoughts stopped. Not here, not
London. Then perhaps— His head lifted at the thought.
Yorkshire. Of course, he did not want to impose anymore
on Jennifer. And there was always the possibility that she'd
had enough of him and viewed him as nothing more than
an albatross. Perhaps he shouldn't.

Yet a moment later when he heard the door open, he
lifted his head and saw her standing there, clean, brushed,
her face shining like hope. Peculiar, he'd seen her before
standing thus and she'd never struck him as so lovely.

"Are you awake?" she called softly.

"I'm awake," he said, trying to give his voice a firmness
as though to signal to her that the sickness was over, that
no longer would he be a burden to her.

Slowly he rolled from his side onto his back and stared
fixedly at the ceiling. "It's—over," he said. "I swear it."

At first she obviously did not understand and continued
to stare down on him. He began to speak again, fearful

of losing the thread of what he had to say. "No more," he began simply. "I did not intend for it to go like this. In the beginning it was just—" He tried to remember the beginning, the night of William Pitch's death.

He looked up to see her listening closely, and the next minute she was seated beside him on the bed, her head pressed against his chest. He held her close, one hand smoothing back her hair. "How can I ever repay you?" he whispered. "I always knew your presence. In the blackest pit. I somehow could always see your eyes."

She raised up, the light of hope on her face. "Are you certain, Edward?" she begged as though in need of reassurance.

"I swear it," he replied emphatically. His mood changed now as though he were weary of gloom. "As a matter of fact," he began, "I was just thinking—"

"You can't go back to London," she interrupted.

Solemnly he nodded. "You're right."

She moved closer to him. "And you can't stay here."

Of course she was right. He couldn't stay here. He looked up at her, as though baffled by all the closed doors. "Then where?" he asked, seeing the answer already forming on her face.

"You'll come with me," she said, firmly, standing up from the edge of the bed, as though ready to do battle with any rebuttal he might offer.

But he offered none and watched and listened with a grateful heart as she laid plans which, somehow, in their firmness suggested that they had been made some time ago. "I must report by the end of September," she began. "Since it's a journey of some distance, we should leave within the week. I'll need an escort and you shall be it. We'll take your carriage and John Murrey can drive and—" As she talked on, he watched, fascinated. He thought again of Daniel Spade and his deep love for her. If only—

She was standing directly over him now, that face which earlier had been hesitant now covered with a glowing radiance. "Miss Wooler has several apartments at the rear of the school where she lets parents reside on Visitor's Day. I'm sure we can talk her into—"

He'd not considered that, not permanent residence. It was his intention only to make the journey with her, see her settled, see firsthand the life against which Daniel had to compete, then return to London, stopping by Shrewsbury, by Hadley Park, in the hope of gaining an audience with—

The thought had come upon him like a thief in the night and caught him unaware. *To stop by Hadley Park and gain an audience with—* While Jennifer talked on about the glorious future, Edward found himself still sunk in the past.

"Edward?" The concerned voice belonged to Jennifer, who apparently had seen the new gloom in his face. "You are—in agreement, aren't you?"

Wearily he tried to drag himself up out of the abyss. "In complete agreement," he smiled. "I can think of nothing that would suit me more."

The expression of victory on her face was a fitting reward. Again she embraced him lightly and seemed to grow more excited, talking now of plans for the journey, how pleasant the interval abroad would be with him.

In a desperate attempt to throw off memory, Edward tried to match her enthusiasm. He pushed back the coverlet and sat up on the bed, forcing himself into a good humor. "Then we must make preparations," he announced. "Old John there must be awakened, the carriage overhauled, new axles—" As though to carry out his own counsel, he stepped down to the floor and took two steps toward his sleeping friend when suddenly the room commenced to whirl about him. The last sound he heard was Jennifer's cry as he collapsed midway between his bed and John Murrey's chair.

When he came to, John Murrey was bending over him, trying to lift him. And Jennifer was on the other side, lightly scolding. "You're weakened, Edward. It will take time—"

Suddenly he disliked being viewed as though he were some unaccountable specimen. "Then, food, I suppose," he said weakly, wanting only to disband the morbid little gathering. "And look to the carriage, John," he added. "See that it's sturdy. We're accompanying Jennifer to Yorkshire—"

After John Murrey had left the room, Edward opened his eyes to see Jennifer still there, alarm on her face. "Will you be able to travel, Edward?" she asked gravely.

"I'll be ready," he smiled. "I promise."

"Then I'll leave you for a while and return with an enormous breakfast, every bite of which I shall feed you myself."

He had thought to say something else, but before he could stop her, she was out of the room, the sound of her footsteps diminishing down the corridor.

He lay still. Perhaps it couldn't be accomplished. The system had grown accustomed to its safe delirium. Perhaps it would object to a sudden and complete absence—

Slowly he opened his eyes to the realization that he was alone, that both his guardian angels had departed and left him with the cabinet there, less than six feet away, and behind that small door were the dancing streamers, the eternal and delirious misery, the deep sighings of the poppy.

His throat went dry at the thought. Six short steps at best to oblivion. Slowly he turned his head in that direction as though he'd already accomplished the distance. He raised himself on one elbow. The room and all the objects in it remained steady.

As he swung his legs over the side of the bed, he saw them clearly for the first time and stared incredulously down. They were not his limbs, not those pale wasted specimens. No wonder they refused to support him. There was not enough flesh there to support a child. His mind could not put thoughts together and merely passed individual words through his consciousness. *Breakfast—Hadley Park—Four steps—*

He moved forward, left the support of the table, his hands ever outreaching. One step, then two, the cabinet coming closer, three steps, the surface of the floor like water, threatening to wash over him.

He devoted what little energy he had to angling himself around to the front of the cabinet. His hand reached for the small knob and pulled it open. There it was, the temple of his need.

His right hand lifted toward the square-cut vial, gleaming as though at its core was heat. The glass itself felt cool to his touch. He grasped it firmly and with his teeth removed the small cork and spat it out. With the vial clutched in his hand, he was in the process of lifting his head when suddenly on the top shelf of the cabinet, his eyes fell on a reflecting mirror.

The face stared back at him. It was the image of a madman, or a dead one, the hair long, twisted, streaked with
new gray, the eyes less visible than the fields of dark
shadows into which they were sunk, the tint of the skin
yellowed, the mouth open, listless, a monstrous face, detail-
ing every step and twist of the dishonored past, a fool's
face that did not know its state of death and thus still
moved, aping the expression of a living man.

With one motion he lifted the vial to drink, saw the de-
cayed fool do likewise, and on a last effort of will, instead
of drinking, hurled the vial toward the reflection, heard the
shattering of glass at the double destruction.

His limited energy totally exhausted, he sank to the floor
to deal with the need, expecting to find comfort in his self-
denial, but finding nothing but cold stone floor, the craving
still with him and growing.

Exhausted, he pressed his forehead on the floor. Had he
the strength for life? Or the appetite? Could he wage this
battle and win it?

The reply came softly and settled over his numbed limbs.
He must, or he was nothing.

On the next to the last Saturday of one of the most
glorious Septembers that had ever graced the North Devon
coast, the Countess Dowager, Lady Marianne, broke out of
her prison of silence and seclusion. Against the stern
advice of both her sister and Mrs. Greenbell she broke out,
arising before dawn and dressing herself in one of the plain
black gowns left over from Thomas's mourning.

She was tired of self-imposed imprisonment, and she
knew all too well what day this was, who was departing,
and why. It might be, as Jane had testily suggested the
night before, merely another encounter of humiliation. But
in a way, even that curse would be a comfort after the
death of a summer, proof at least of life and a capacity to
feel.

All Marianne wanted to do was tell her children goodbye. Was there anything so unusual in that? And certainly
they'd made no attempt to keep their departure a secret.
For the last week, the entire castle had buzzed with the
news.

Then three days ago, there had been the parade of
stewards bringing the trunks up from the storeroom. No,

a departure was clearly at hand and Marianne intended to
be there. Whatever had happened the night of the engagement party, it was over now, the young lady and James
safely betrothed. All that remained was to fix the date and
for that they were awaiting word from Shropshire. In her
one and only communication from Lady Powels, she'd
learned that Harriet's mysterious illness was persisting, and
until they could discover the cause and effect a cure, the
physician had prescribed isolation.

So be it. For now, *this* isolation must end and thus she
would end it. Off in the distance she heard voices. Holding
herself erect, she moved with good speed out of the room
to the top of the stairs and started down.

Now beyond her she saw the opened arched door which
led from the Great Hall to the steps. And there near the
bottom of the steps was Edward's carriage.

She felt the excitement of the journey everywhere.

She closed her eyes, remembering the same excitement as
when she and Thomas had journeyed to London, to everywhere. Then a voice was speaking to her, an old voice, un-
schooled, yet full of courtesy. "Milady, I'd hoped to see
you, to thank you for your kindness to me—"

Quickly she opened her eyes and brought into focus the
old face of John Murrey. "It was my pleasure, John," she
smiled.

John Murrey appeared to blush. In his hand was a soft
crushed hat which he kneaded constantly. In an attempt to
put him at ease, Marianne added, "And I have cause to
thank you as well, John, for your obvious devotion to my
son."

"He's my master," he replied simply. "Course he don't
like to hear me say that, but that's what he is right enough.
When a man gives you your life, I figure you owe him
something in return."

"Then I'm grateful," she smiled. She looked beyond John
Murrey into the Great Hall. "Will—he be coming soon?"
she asked.

John Murrey nodded. "He's on the way, milady, with
Miss Jennifer." Abruptly the hands stopped kneading the
old hat. "Be warned, milady," he said. "He's been ill."

She watched as the old man hurried down the steps.
Then she heard movement, coming from the direction of

the Great Hall, slow steps as though someone was walking with great difficulty.

For a time the heavy shadows falling in the center of the Great Hall obscured the two, their heads bent in apparent effort, their arms about each other in support. Once while they were still a distance away, she saw them stop, still not aware of her, Edward's head heavily hanging down, Jennifer beside him. Marianne heard her strong encouragement, "Only a few steps further."

At the moment that he lifted his head to reassure Jennifer, he caught sight of Marianne.

She returned their gaze. As she caught a clear glimpse of her son's once beautiful face, the world fell into silence.

The frozen moment of recognition over, she saw the change on Jennifer's face from warm support to guarded suspicion. The two of them were moving again, Jennifer's support as firm as ever, though now she was whispering something to him.

What it was Marianne had no idea, but she noticed a kind of renewed strength in Edward's movements, as though he were exerting all his strength in putting on a good show for her. They stopped less than ten feet from her.

As though in self-punishment, Marianne forced herself to focus upon Jennifer. When she spoke, her voice was as soft as the still September morning. "I had word that you were leaving," she began, looking only at Jennifer. She gave a light laugh in an attempt to alter the tension. "It seems as though you just arrived."

Jennifer returned her gaze. "I have passed the summer here, milady," she said with merciless politeness. "Now I have to return. I have students waiting for me."

"Of course," Marianne murmured hurriedly. She saw Edward reach out for the hand railing on the opposite side of the steps, thus relieving Jennifer of his weight. As though to rest her eyes from such devastation, Marianne looked back at Jennifer. "Have a safe journey," she smiled. "I shall keep your beautiful pianoforte safe and in good condition until your return."

Jennifer didn't seem to know how to respond to this. She ducked her head and Marianne thought, how young she looks. And when the young woman seemed incapable of saying anything further, Marianne added, "I apologize for

the summer, Jennifer. I'm certain it wasn't an ideal holiday
for you."

Then something cold crossed that young face. "It was
quite a traditional summer, milady, reminiscent of my childhood. I assure you, misery becomes the place. I felt quite at
home."

Marianne watched her daughter's hands lift and twist a
pair of black traveling gloves. Jennifer went on, as though
gathering courage. "At least this summer was not a total
loss. I've enjoyed a warm and gratifying reunion with my
elder brother."

"And for that, I'm grateful," Marianne nodded.

"Well then," Jennifer concluded. "I shall take my leave."
It was after she'd started down the stairs that Marianne
heard her call back, "Stay well, madam. You look tired."

Marianne felt exhausted, as though she'd just fought and
lost a battle. She knew that Edward was waiting, but for a
moment she did not dare to advance.

But when she heard his voice, and when she saw him
standing with both arms opened, she went, with disgraceful
affection, her eyes nearly blind with tears.

The embrace lasted for several moments. As he became
aware of her tears, he disengaged her. "No need," he
whispered kindly, his face, in spite of the wreckage, warm
with compassion.

"No need?" she repeated incredulously. "Dear God, how
can you say that?"

"Because it's true," he countered lightly. "Because the
summer is over. *All* aspects of the summer," he added
pointedly. "If the truth were known, I think we've all enjoyed our martyrdom."

Like Thomas, Edward had the ability to lift her out of
grief and into a kind of defensive anger. "The summer has
been nothing more than a variety of death," she said.
"Look at you. You—"

"I do owe you an apology," he was saying now. "It was
not my intention for events to go as they did." In a self-
deprecating manner, he added, "It is never my intention for
events to go as they do. But I assure you, I will cause no
more grief, not to others, not to myself. It is my intention
to escort Jennifer to Yorkshire, then return as soon as
possible to London." He smiled. "I'm quite certain that by
now Daniel is convinced I've fallen off the edge of the

world." He seemed to become very reflective. "What an extraordinary thing the well of memory is," he murmured, and she saw again the depths of his desolation.

Even as he spoke of the well of memory, he seemed to have fallen into it. And Marianne too remembered the scenes from early summer, Edward and Harriet slipping out of the castle, daring in their escapes.

She felt a question forming. "Did you love her so much?" she whispered.

In his eyes, she had her reply.

"And did she return your love?" she pressed on.

"I thought she did," he murmured. "She led me to believe so."

"Then what happened?" she asked, as though it were her maternal right to question him thus.

All at once the memory lifted from his face. The gloom was instantly converted into a kind of bemused irony. "I've passed the summer, madam, in search of that answer. Now," he whispered, "all that remains is that I learn to live with the unanswered question."

"Will you return here before you go back to London?" she asked.

He shook his head. "I think not. I've been away far too long. Daniel needs me."

She thought this declaration a bit absurd. While she was fond of Daniel Spade, in his relationship with her son, she knew very well who needed whom. "Is he well?" she asked quickly as though to squelch the judgment.

"When I left, yes," Edward replied. "I suspect he's plotting revolution," he added, smiling. "It seems the fashionable thing to do now."

Marianne felt mild shock. She remembered a gentle young red-haired boy who would pass the slaughterhouse in a wide arc to avoid hearing the squealing animals. "Revolution?" she repeated. "And who is he revolting against?"

Without hesitation, though still smiling, Edward replied, "You, I imagine, and perhaps me. The poor weigh heavily against him. And rightly so. They have become for him a kind of religion."

"Is he serious?"

"Oh, deadly serious," Edward replied.

"And what is your part in all this?"

Again without hesitation, Edward looked down on her and replied simply, "I love him."

Coming from the carriage, she heard a firm voice. "Edward, my apologies, but we must hurry. The first interval is a full day's distance—"

At the sound of Jennifer's voice, neither Edward nor Marianne looked toward the carriage. But rather their eyes met, a hundred unspoken messages passing back and forth.

"I scarcely feel as though you've been here at all," she murmured quickly.

"I've been here," he smiled.

Beyond his head, she saw a detached mass of early morning clouds. "Rain this afternoon," she said vaguely, "but I think you'll escape it."

"The carriage is tight and warm, John Murrey a skillful driver."

"Will you write?"

"As often as I can."

"Any word will do."

"I promise."

"Are you strong enough for the journey?"

"I am, and Jennifer has promised me the healing airs of Yorkshire."

"Dampness that kills, or so I've heard."

"No matter."

"It matters to me."

At precisely the same moment, they exhausted their supply of small, meaningless words. "Oh, my dearest," she gasped.

She was in his arms, grasping him as though she were drowning and he were the lifeline.

He responded, drawing her close, his face buried in her neck, his voice muffled as he whispered over and over again, "I'm sorry, I'm sorry," a regret so enormous as to encompass the world and everyone in it.

Without another word, he kissed her lightly on the cheek and tore himself away. John Murrey hurried up the steps to his side, offered him his support, and together they made their way slowly down the steps.

Marianne lifted her head and maintained a pose of perfect control as she watched John Murrey climb laboriously atop his high perch, affix the worn hat on his head, reach for the reins, and with a soft shout bring them down over the horses' backs.

She even managed to wave as the carriage rattled slowly forward, although no one waved back. She noticed a few curious servants peering around the wooden door which led downward into the kitchen and the watchmen on the wall staring down on the departing carriage. She was still watching as the guardsmen drew up the twin grilles and continued to watch as the carriage moved slowly through the gatehouse and out beyond to the wide and open moors.

Dear God, keep him safe.

They were well beyond Exmoor, beyond Cheddar and Bristol even, at a point of midafternoon, just approaching the green valley which led into old Bath when Edward spoke for the first time. Then what he said, with his eyes fixed on the view beyond the window was, "The countryside is lovely."

In the quiet of the carriage Jennifer let her eyes fall on her once handsome brother. "The Bastard Eden," she'd heard him called by witless villagers in Mortemouth. She remembered now how she had questioned Sophia Cranford about the word, had received at first nothing in the way of response. It had been later, inside Sophia's private apartments that Jennifer had found herself upon the "learning chair," her young mind already safely past the unknown word, but now reminded of it again in a grim way—*Lust out of wedlock, without God's blessing, the cursed parents cursing the son.* But worst of all, *Edward does not belong, has no right to the name of Eden, is doomed from his first breath to his last.*

Jennifer shivered at the thought. Then she had believed Sophia and for a period of time had avoided Edward, fearful that bastardy was a contagion. Now? No, or course not. *The child is innocent of the sins of the father.*

Still there was one point of belief. *Doomed from his first breath to his last.* That had the ring of truth to it. And there was the proof, sitting opposite her, as sunk as he had been since early morning, a peculiar look of continuous effort on his face.

Now as the carriage approached Bath, she heard John Murrey shouting at the horses in an attempt to keep them in line in the rapidly increasing traffic. She knew that it was John's plan to make it at least as far as Gloucester before stopping for the night. Now, seeing in the distance the beautiful hills and valleys of Bath, it occurred to her that perhaps, for Edward's sake, they should stop early. Perhaps there was a chance she could persuade him to partake of the warm, health-giving mineral waters. Then after dinner they could stroll the Crescent and take the evening air, his mood improved with the knowledge of a world beyond Eden.

As the idea gained momentum in her head, she again assessed her silent, staring brother. "Edward," she said, softly, trying to enter his privacy as gracefully as possible. "It's just occurred to me that perhaps we should lodge in Bath for the evening. We could—"

"The afternoon is young yet," he interrupted. "We would lose good daylight hours. I believe John said Gloucester."

It had not been a reprimand, merely a quiet suggestion that they adhere to their schedule. "I just thought the waters might be good for you," she murmured, settling back into her corner.

For the first time, he looked directly at her. "You are my medicine," he smiled. "I need no waters, just your loving company."

She returned the smile. "You have it, Edward, as you shall always have it."

Bath abandoned, she leaned her head back against the cushions, certain that the matter was closed and again it was time for silence. Thus she felt a slight shock when a few moments later she heard his voice again.

"And our mother?" he queried gently. "Surely there is enough affection in that vast reservoir beneath your breast to give a portion to her who is in such sore need."

She'd not expected this. "I don't know what you mean," she said.

"I mean," he persisted, "that you are a daughter and that you have a mother who is dying for lack of affection."

She looked directly at him. "Our mother may be dying," she said, firmly, "but I doubt seriously if it's from lack of affection. She's had that in sinful amounts all her life."

She was acutely aware of Edward still looking at her. His voice when he spoke was laced with kindness. "Why do you hate her so?"

By way of answering, she simply asked another question. "Why do you love her?"

"She's our mother."

"And what is that supposed to mean?" she demanded, amazed at how rapidly he had brought her to the edge of anger. "We slipped from her womb to be sure, we share her blood, but that's scarcely motherhood."

She was aware of his intense interest. "I am amazed to hear you speak thus," he began.

"And I am equally amazed," she replied. "Tell me the source and reason for your affection for her, you, of all of us. Because of her, you carry a cross that neither James nor I can even begin to understand. And yet you praise her, you—"

"She was not the cause of my bastardy, you know that. She thought the union was legal. It was—"

"I know who it was," she interrupted angrily, wishing only to end the conversation.

"It was trickery," he went on, "at the hands of—"

"The trickery, Edward, I suspect, started long before the day of your birth."

There was amazement in his voice. "You believe there was never any love between them?" he asked.

"Oh indeed, there was love. Her love of his money."

"Oh Jennifer, no, that's not true," he protested. "With thoughts like that you do yourself a greater injustice than you do her. What happened thirty, forty years ago is a matter of monumental unimportance. Can't you see that? They lived their lives to the best of their abilities and it's not for you or I or anyone to stand in judgment of them."

"God?" she asked bluntly. "Are you counting Him out as well?"

"Of course not," he smiled. "But even God, I suspect, will be far more merciful than you." He gazed into her face. "She loves you so very much," he said simply, and that simplicity almost disarmed her.

She disliked intensely both the subject and the weight of his attention, and with unprecedented vigor now took steps to relieve herself of both. "This really is a dreary matter, Edward," she said firmly. "I recognize the lady whom you embraced so warmly this morning as my mother. Nothing more. I give her respect and, whenever possible, obedience.

But I know, perhaps better than you who she is and what she is."

She was silent a moment and turned away, disturbed by what she was going to say. "I see not a mother, not even a decent woman, but a whore—"

Suddenly he leaned sharply forward on the edge of his seat. "Then you have a remarkably flawed vision," he pronounced. "I can only assume that someone has assisted you with your vision. Do I speak the truth?"

She pressed back against the cushions. "I don't know what you're talking about, Edward."

"Who has turned you against her?" he demanded again.

"No one has turned me against her. No one had to. You remember our childhood. Or perhaps yours was different. But every time I went in search of her, I found Sophia Cranford."

At that moment he brought his fist down against his knee. "Damn Sophia Cranford," he shouted, as though all at once a truth had been confirmed for him.

In an attempt to pacify him, she took a stern hold on her own feelings. "Yes," she murmured. "I wouldn't have said that at the beginning of the summer, but I will now. Damn Sophia Cranford. She has become mean and scheming."

"Become!" Edward parroted. "She was born thus, a true bitch who has left her mark on each of us. But on you, more than anyone." Slowly he shook his head, anger receding, a look of pity on his face. "Dear God, Jennifer," he pleaded, "look at yourself. Where I should see the soft loving angles of a woman, I see only harsh imprisoning piety. Where I should see a daughter radiant with love for her mother, perhaps in anticipation of the day when she herself would know motherhood, I see the cold, barbed exterior of a schoolmistress, a spinster in the making, a woman denying her very self."

Under the barrage of his words falling heavily upon her, she looked away beyond the window and saw the dirty edges of the city, the hovels which passed for homes, a one-legged beggar, a crying child, a hollow-eyed old woman. With what mysterious speed the world had gone suddenly ugly.

Seeing her distress, Edward slid over to her side and in a gesture both warm and forceful took her in his arms, murmuring her name over and over again, begging her forgiveness.

Thus they sat until the carriage was well out again into open country.

At some point at the approach of night, he lifted his feet and rested them on the seat opposite them and sank back into the cushions, taking her with him, never abandoning her.

From inside his embrace, she stared blankly out at the evening beyond the carriage window. What if she were wrong? In everything? What if—

"Edward?" she whispered, speaking the first word in over two hours. "What if I—" She faltered and tried again. "What if I wanted to start fresh? What—would I do?"

There was a pause. Then he drew her yet closer. She felt his cheek resting atop her head. His voice when he spoke was extraordinarily close. "Write a letter," he whispered. "Addressed to—her, not Sophia Cranford. Take that one small step. Write her a letter."

She nodded. That she could do, and that she would do.

Gloucester, then, the three of them approaching exhaustion. As John Murrey bedded down the horses, Edward acquired adjoining rooms at the Monmouth Inn. After a simple meal served in their chambers, they retired, John Murrey and Edward to one apartment, Jennifer to another.

She had planned to lie in dark silence and think for a while on the events of the day. But fatigue defeated her and no sooner had her head touched the pillow than sleep overtook her, a pleasurable refreshing sleep, the sense of an old wound healing.

The rest of the journey was placid, the painful subject of their mother never mentioned again. Edward seemed to sink back into the silence which had imprisoned him on the first day, a silence which seemed to grow deeper at evening of the second day when they had stopped for the night in the little village of Lichfield. There was only one inn, a crude country dwelling with small narrow cells and leaking roof.

He'd excused himself from dinner, claiming a need to stretch his legs. Later, Jennifer fetched her shawl and slipped out into the dwindling dusk, searching the narrow rutted road in both directions.

Then she had seen him at the far end of the road, staring up at a road sign. As she'd gone to meet him, he'd seen her and turned away from the sign, but not before she'd drawn close enough to catch a glimpse of it, one word only atop a small painted arrow which pointed down the narrow lane.

Shrewsbury.

The arrow pointed to Shropshire, toward Hadley Park, the seat of the Powels family, the present location of Harriet Powels.

He said nothing and neither did she. He simply returned her to her room, then he had joined old John Murrey for a glass before bed. And predictably the glass had turned into a bottle, then another, and finally a third, so that on the following morning their departure had been delayed somewhat, the slightly bleary-eyed Edward finally crawling into the carriage, a clear look of discomfort on his face as with every jolt of the carriage, he held his head.

She felt sorry for him, but was grateful for one small blessing. According to John Murrey, the drinks had been clean. No laudanum had been requested and none had been provided.

While clearly he was suffering, he was not drugged, although, forced to witness his silent suffering during the two remaining days of the journey, Jennifer found herself sometimes wishing that he had been drugged.

Doomed from his first breath to his last.

Perhaps in one area, Sophia Cranford had been right.

At noon on the fourth day, after a delay at the blacksmith's in Wakefield for the purpose of reshoeing a lame horse, Edward looked up with blessed relief at Jennifer's announcement, "We're almost there!"

Now after four days of this endless journey, his brain felt loose, his body stiff, his throat parched, and his eyes blind to every image save one, that small black arrow pointing toward Shropshire. As he sensed Jennifer's mounting enthusiasm, he vowed to himself to see her safely settled, then depart, as soon as possible. He was not fit company. The need within him was as pressing as ever, his abstinence merely a token gesture. Perhaps he was going about it in the wrong manner. At any rate he must return to London as soon as possible, there either to seek something or destroy something. He had no idea which.

Across the way, he saw Jennifer's delighted face as she beheld familiar territory. There too was regret. He'd been harsh with her. She'd suffered enough, had a lifetime of suffering ahead without his contribution.

But obviously such thoughts were very far from Jennifer's mind as again adjusting her bonnet, she pointed, "There it is, Edward. There's Roe Head."

He lifted his eyes to an easy slope where he saw an old and spacious building set behind gates at the end of a long and narrow lane.

As John Murrey slowed the horses to take the curving driveway, Edward thought ruefully that it resembled a nunnery. On the circular drive immediately fronting the building was a small crush of conveyances. Beyond the window, Edward saw a group of females in close huddle, obviously greeting each other in warm reunion. As John Murrey brought their carriage to a halt, Edward again vowed to himself to unload the trunks and leave as soon as possible. He might have volunteered to deliver Jennifer to purgatory, but he had no appetite to see her settle into it.

Outside the window, he saw John Murrey climb down from his perch. As the old man appeared outside the carriage door, Edward called, "Well done. Our thanks to you for a safe journey."

Jennifer echoed his sentiment and was on the verge of saying more when suddenly Edward saw her face brighten with the light of recognition. "Charlotte," she whispered softly, and before he could stop her, she was out the door and running toward a small red-haired woman who was just herself climbing down from a two-wheeled gig.

As the two women fell into close conversation, Edward wearily dragged himself out of the carriage and leaned against it. Stretching slightly, he noticed for the first time a gentleman standing upright in the two-wheeled gig, looking equally as nervous and out of place. The man had a large beaked nose similar to that of the peculiar woman with whom Jennifer was chatting.

"What now, sir?" John Murrey whispered beside him.

Still watching the scene by the gig, Edward muttered, "Unload and leave as soon as possible."

Edward held his position close by the carriage, still waiting for Jennifer to return with further instructions. Counting small blessings, he thought that at least he was not in such a prominent position as the poor gentleman still standing awkwardly upright in the gig.

Then to his mild horror, he saw the young woman reach up toward the gentleman as though to assist him to ground and in the next minute, these three, Jennifer, the lady, and the gentleman, were walking toward him.

Nothing to do but greet them since obviously that was Jennifer's intention in dragging them in his direction. "Edward," she called out now, one hand outreaching for his arm. "Give me the pleasure of presenting you to a dear friend—"

He pushed off from the support of the carriage and tried to stand erect as Jennifer intoned, "Miss Charlotte Brontë, my brother, Mr. Edward Eden."

Edward focused all of his attention on the shy creature who stood before him. "Miss Brontë," he said, his voice low as though fearful of frightening her. "I'm honored always to meet a person who shares such a large portion of my sister's life."

"Mr. Eden, my pleasure," she murmured. And apparently that was that.

Edward was on the verge of speaking again when a complete sentence left the sparrow's mouth. "Mr. Eden," she pronounced, in a high-pitched voice, "may I present my brother, Mr. Branwell Brontë whom, I'm certain, feels as ill at ease and as out of place as yourself."

Caught between her unexpected perception and the introduction itself, Edward smiled. "Mr. Brontë," he pronounced, extending a firm hand. "My pleasure, I assure you, and my congratulations on training your sister to travel so light." He nodded toward the two-wheeled gig, scarcely weighted with the presence of a single dark green trunk.

Mr. Brontë at first did not seem to understand. "I did not train my sister, Mr. Eden," he said, the same primness of pronunciation in his speech as in his sister's. "I would not attempt such an undertaking."

At first Edward thought it was an attempt at humor, but not one face about him was smiling.

"We live only a short distance away," Mr. Brontë went

on, "in the village of Haworth. My sister is not bound here by distance as are some of the young ladies."

To this rather pedantic reply, Edward nodded with due seriousness. "I thought as much when I observed your gig, sir," he said, smiling. "I'm afraid it would have been a casualty on the first leg of our journey."

"And where is your source, sir?" Mr. Brontë inquired, both his voice and speech revealing a certain archaic quality, as though his tutor had been old and harsh.

"My source," Edward replied, trying to hide a smile, "is Eden, North Devon. Just on the channel. Near Exeter." He continued to add qualifications, hoping that at least one would make a difference. None did. And when again all conversation threatened to die, Edward made a single request. "Jennifer, if you would be so kind as to direct John Murrey to your chambers, we can clear the pavement and make room for others."

Jennifer caught his mood and hurled herself admirably into the task at hand. "This way, John," she called out.

As John started forward with a large trunk, Edward was fearful that he would simply be left alone with the strange Brontës. But Jennifer at the last minute slipped her arm through Miss Brontë's and led her forward.

Edward's head was pounding from the effort of the social exchange. He closed his eyes a moment, feeling an uncomfortable warmth in the cool Yorkshire afternoon.

When he opened his eyes again, he discovered to his dismay that Mr. Brontë was still there, silently regarding him. "Are you well, Mr. Eden?" he inquired.

Laughing in an attempt to hide his weakness, Edward replied, "Quite well, sir, thank you. The journey was long. We are taught in school how limited in scope is our island country. I might suggest that our geographers attempt to traverse its length in a coach and four."

By his own assessment he thought he was doing well enough. But the man merely continued to stare at him.

The silence struck Edward as oppressive. My God, he owed the man nothing, would never see him again after today. "If you'll excuse me, sir. I must attend to my sister's needs and return to the road."

"Your destination, sir?" Mr. Brontë inquired.

It was none of his damn business. Still Edward replied, "London, sir."

"Then you have another great journey ahead of you."

"I do indeed."

Edward was in the process of passing the man by when suddenly Mr. Brontë asked a peculiar question. "Are you—prepared, sir?" he inquired. A slight wind ruffled his already blown hair, giving him a mildly demented look.

"Prepared?" Edward asked, looking back.

But the man seemed disinclined to explain himself. Instead he gave Edward a knowing look of recognition.

Well, he had the clear advantage for Edward hadn't the slightest idea what he was talking about.

Feeling helpless, Edward stood to one side and watched John Murrey deftly hoist the second trunk up onto his back and move with it toward the front door where Jennifer was just emerging with an old woman in tow.

Another introduction. The red-haired Mr. Brontë still was watching him closely. The two women were upon him now, Jennifer calling out, "Edward, come. It gives me great pleasure to present to you Miss Margaret Wooler, headmistress of Roe Head."

"Mr. Eden, my pleasure," the woman smiled. She was short, stout, and wore a white woolen dress. Her voice was fluent and sweet.

Then he was aware of Jennifer at his side, lending him support. "My brother has not been well, Miss Wooler, and the journey was long. Might we—"

"Of course," the old woman quickly replied. "How rude of me. This way, please."

Then they were moving after the old woman, Edward more or less on his own strength, though Jennifer was still close beside him.

Inside the school, Edward's head began to clear. He saw mellow oak paneling, bow windows, deep window seats, and curiously winding passages which appeared to lead off in all directions. With Miss Wooler still leading them, he found himself at last in what appeared to be a formal parlor-sitting room, heavily cluttered with bric-a-brac.

"May I offer you tea, Mr. Eden," Miss Wooler now inquired, "or perhaps a bit of sherry?"

He shook his head. "I'm quite recovered, Miss Wooler, and grateful for your kindness."

"Nonsense," the old woman countered, settling opposite him. "I've truly looked forward to meeting you. How fond we are of Jennifer. In every sense of the word, she brings music into our lives."

He smiled in agreement. "I'm afraid I would be quite lost without her." He noted the blush on Jennifer's face as she stood behind Miss Wooler's chair. In the brief interplay, Edward glimpsed what he thought might be an explanation for his sister's attachment to this dreary place. Miss Wooler. It occurred to him that in the stern yet loving kindness of Miss Wooler, Jennifer had found the mother she'd never had.

Now Miss Wooler was speaking again, and with effort, Edward summoned his attention back to the conversation at hand. He really was becoming addle-headed.

"And Jennifer tells me we will be honored with your presence for a while," the old woman said. "What a treat that will be."

Again he closed his eyes. My God, but he was weary. He'd hoped to talk to Jennifer in private about the matter. But between the mad Brontës outside and Miss Wooler before him, he had the feeling that his chances of talking to Jennifer alone were nil. Then it might as well be now.

Although he was addressing Miss Wooler, he found himself looking at Jennifer. "I'm afraid not, Miss Wooler," he began, leaning forward in the chair. "We discussed such an arrangement, I'll admit, and I can never express my gratitude for your offer of hospitality." If there was the slightest change on Jennifer's face, he was unable to discern it. "But the truth is," he went on, "I've been a truant from my own duties and responsibilities for three months. So with your kind understanding, I must take my leave."

Still Jennifer's face was unmoved. It was Miss Wooler who expressed deep regret. "I am sorry to hear it, Mr. Eden, for selfish reasons. All the ladies would have enjoyed your presence among us."

For a moment he met his sister's eyes and forced them to stay with him. When she looked away, he stood, some instinct warning him to take his leave quickly.

To that end, he warmly grasped Miss Wooler's hand and held it between his own. "My dear lady, I thank you for your kindness. Now when I think of Jennifer," he went on, "I shall have a proper setting in which to place her, a setting of warmth and love."

Now he moved toward the door, held it open for Jennifer, and with his arm lightly about her waist hurried her down the hall toward the rectangle of gray afternoon light beyond the front door.

Jennifer was maintaining an ominous silence. As they stepped through the door onto the porch, he saw with sinking heart the Brontës standing beside the gig. Apparently leave-taking was the order of the day. He had mentally prepared himself for another awkward encounter and was thus surprised when Jennifer, still grim-faced, led him directly past the gig and the two gaping Brontës without a word to either.

Alone at last, Edward was in the process of offering comfort when suddenly Jennifer turned on him, her face as white and angry as he'd ever seen it.

"You promised," she whispered, as though in spite of her emotions, she knew the wisdom of keeping her voice down.

"I did not promise," he gently corrected her.

"And what will you do in London?" she demanded, her voice rising slightly. "Who is there to look after you? Will the pattern be altered, or simply reinforced?"

"Daniel is there," he said simply.

"And you expect his assistance?"

"He's given it to me in the past."

Suddenly her anger vaulted. "Dear God, Edward, can't you see how Daniel is using you?"

For just an instant, he felt a flare of anger. He lowered his head in an attempt to try a fresh approach. "Jennifer, look at me," he begged. "Now tell me truthfully, can you see me passing time in this establishment? Can you see me partaking of afternoon tea with Miss Wooler? Serving as dinner companion to Miss Brontë?"

"She's brilliant," Jennifer interrupted defensively.

"I'm not doubting her brilliance," Edward said quickly. "I'm merely doubting my ability to—"

In an attempt to break the mood, he drew her close and took her in his arms, and for the second time in their four days together, she gave in to tears.

"I love you so much," she whispered.

"And I, you."

"Please," she went on, grasping him tightly. "I beg you. Look to yourself."

"It is my intention to do so."

"And promise me that if you look up one day and have need of a sister, you'll send for me."

It could not go on, neither for him nor for her. Then she stepped up, and lightly kissed his cheek, slipped from his arms, and ran toward the door to Miss Wooler's establishment.

The pavement where he stood was deserted in all directions save for the tentative approach of John Murrey, who had just emerged from behind the carriage. "Then is it London, sir?" he inquired, a crispness in his voice as though nothing had happened.

Edward nodded. With John's assistance he dragged himself upward into the carriage, his eye immediately falling on the place she had occupied for the last four days.

He would miss her enormously. As the carriage started forward, he turned in the seat and caught a last glimpse of Miss Wooler's school. Blessedly he saw nothing but an unfocused whirl of red brick and closed windows and shut doors.

As the carriage picked up momentum, it occurred to him that he and John Murrey had had no conference concerning itinerary from this point onward. Perhaps he should signal to John and have him bring the horses up and confer on places of intervals.

But he changed his mind. For now, it rather appealed to him, the thought of wandering about the Yorkshire moors. No harm. They were expected no place.

Suddenly the weight of a vague future pressed solidly down about him. My God, but his throat was parched, his appetite for the divine repose of opium as acute as ever. What harm? And what virtue, abstinence?

He closed his eyes. The empty landscape outside the window lay like a weight upon him. Annoyed, he became aware of the carriage slowing, John Murrey no doubt lounging atop his high seat, unaware of the need inside the carriage.

Edward opened his eyes. Yes, the speed had been broken. The horses were scarcely strolling now. A man might walk as fast. In growing need, he pulled down the window and shouted, "What is it? Why the—"

From atop the carriage, John Murrey called back, "Trouble, sir. Up ahead. On the other side. Look for yourself."

He slid rapidly across the seat, lowered the opposite window, and leaned out. There up ahead in the dying light of day he saw a conveyance tilted crazily off the road, two-wheeled, one upraised in the air, the other imbedded in the soft loam of the embankment. The driver, in an attempt to extricate the gig, had guided his horse out onto the road and was now attempting to attach the harness at that insane angle, the animal protesting, rearing back on its hindlegs, the hapless driver appearing to do a crazy jig about the horse.

Edward looked closer, some element of recognition dawning in the dim light. The man was hatless and Edward observed a massive shock of unkempt red hair. As he drew even with John Murrey, who was just crawling down, he heard his old friend mutter, "It's him, Mr. Eden, the gentleman you just met back at—"

It *was* him. Mr. Brontë of the strange questions and strange looks. As the absurd spectacle continued, Edward felt his anger soften into amusement. He'd not thought the man so full of energy, but also he'd thought him more intelligent.

As the horse continued to object to the cutting bridle, it occurred to Edward that the idiot was in real danger. Again and again the horse reared back, then fell, stamping to earth. John Murrey leaned close with an opinion. "He's goin' to get himself killed, sir."

"Then perhaps we'd better stop him," he muttered. As they started forward, John Murrey took the lead by several steps, his whip in hand. He shouted ahead, "T'ain't the way to do it—"

At that moment, Mr. Brontë took his attention off his spinning horse and looked up the darkening road. In the next instant the horse took advantage of his faltering attention to pull loose. She shook her massive head, darting wildly to the far side of the road, and started down the steep incline.

"Now look what you've done," Mr. Brontë shouted back at the two approaching figures. "I'll never retrieve—"

Then apparently recognition struck him as well. He wiped his sweating forehead and squinted through his spectacles. In his excited state, his voice cracked, "Mr. Eden, is it?" he faltered.

Drawing nearer, Edward smiled and nodded. "I'd not

expected to meet you again so soon and certainly not under such distressing circumstances."

At first Mr. Brontë seemed more than willing to return the handshake, but at the last minute seemed to change his mind. "I think you might want to reconsider," he apologized, holding up for Edward's inspection a mud-covered hand.

Edward observed now that the man's entire right side was covered with drying mud and there on the side of his forehead was a small laceration. Edward stepped closer. "You've had quite a tumble, I see. Are you in one piece?"

The man quickly bobbed his head and fell into a hurried restoration of himself. "The horse bolted," he said simply, brushing mud from his shoulder.

As he continued in his attempts to restore himself, Edward withdrew his handkerchief and handed it over. "There's a cut on your head."

Quickly the man raised a hand to the injured area as though just aware of it. "Good God," he muttered. "I'm really most grateful," he added, taking the handkerchief, "for both your propitious appearance on this treacherous road as well as for your assistance."

Edward laughed. "I haven't done much yet in the way of assistance, but let's take a look." As he turned his attention to the up-ended gig, he noticed that John Murrey was there ahead of him, his trained eye already assessing the damage.

"Axle's broke, sir," was his first diagnosis, and as though that weren't bad enough, the old man slid down into the ditch and called out further bad news. "The side's caved in, sir. Even if we drag it out, it ain't going nowhere."

Staring down into the ditch, gloomy with dusk, Edward felt a sinking of spirit. Now what? He couldn't simply abandon the man on this lonely stretch of road with a ruined gig and straying horse. Behind him he was aware of Mr. Brontë waiting silently.

"Well, then," Edward said, turning toward the waiting man, who was still dabbing at his forehead. "I'm afraid you're totally dependent upon us, Mr. Brontë. I offer you the security of my carriage and if you'll give us your destination, we shall be on our way."

In the twilight he saw the man's hesitancy. "I can't impose to that extent, Mr. Eden," he replied.

"Nonsense," Edward countered. "You have no choice.

And besides, you said that your home was not very distant."

"I wasn't returning to Haworth," the man suddenly interjected. "I have no desire to return to Haworth."

Edward thought he detected a bitterness in his voice, as though Haworth, wherever it might be, contained threats. "Then state your destination, sir," Edward urged quickly. "I'm abroad with no pressing destination. Out of respect for the love clearly shared by our sisters, let me assist you."

Again the man looked up at Edward, indecision altering and somehow softening the madness in his eyes. "And *your* destination, sir?" he inquired softly.

Edward repeated himself. Was the man deaf? "None pressing, as I said. London ultimately. At the moment I'm free as the wind."

Both men merely gaped at one another while behind them Edward was aware of John Murrey waiting beside the ruined gig.

"Well then," Mr. Brontë said finally. "May I suggest an interim step? Ahead," he began slowly, "at about two hours' distance is the village of Skipton. May I suggest that we make there for the night? There's a good inn with decent food and clean beds. With your kind permission, I shall impose upon you to that extent."

It seemed a reasonable proposal, indeed the only one, as again Edward saw the rapidly darkening countryside. It was not quite the conclusion to the day that he'd had in mind. But there was a sense of adventure to the whole thing.

The decision seemed to please Mr. Brontë immensely. Edward was about to ask John Murrey to fetch the straying horse when he saw the old man already headed in that direction. As John secured the horse to the back of the carriage, Edward stood beside the carriage door, awaiting the arrival of Mr. Brontë, who apparently had felt the need to linger over his ruined gig.

A moment later he drew near. "I am forever in your debt, sir," he murmured.

"Nonsense," Edward countered. "You'd do the same for me, or any man."

The man halted in his upward progress into the carriage. "Strange," he smiled from his half-suspended position, "the twists of Fate."

Edward nodded, and was in the process of swinging up behind Mr. Brontë when without warning the man halted again. "How fine it would be," he said, "if we could walk away from all wreckage with such ease."

In the simple statement, Edward heard grief.

As the carriage moved forward at a reduced rate of speed to accommodate the horse trotting behind, he was aware of Mr. Brontë peering closely at him. "May I return your kind concern, sir?" he asked. "Are *you* well?"

"Merely tired," Edward said, wanting now only to dismiss the strange man and his close scrutiny. "Merely road-weary, that's all, Mr. Brontë."

The man persisted. "Begging your forgiveness, Mr. Eden," he began. "But now, as with the first time I saw you, I have the feeling that I am gazing into a mirror."

Then the man disarmed him with a single question. "You are an opium user, aren't you, Mr. Eden?"

For several minutes, there was no sound within the carriage save for the rattle of wheels on packed earth. Apparently Mr. Brontë saw his apprehension and moved to dispel it. "No need for alarm," he smiled. "We're members of the same brotherhood, you and I. Better than Free Masons, actually. No secret word or handshake." His amusement faded rapidly. "Merely something in the eyes," he concluded.

Edward's first inclination was to move away from the discovery. "I've indulged, yes," he agreed. "But I'm in a period of abstinence now."

Softly Mr. Brontë broke in. "You're in a period of hell now, Mr. Eden."

"You, sir?" Edward began hesitantly. "Do you indulge?"

Mr. Brontë laughed openly. "At one time, I consumed it like air. And I suffered." He lowered his head. "Now, I regulate it. No harm is there in an unarmed man arming himself?"

Was the question rhetorical? Edward had no idea. To "regulate it," his very thought.

Mr. Brontë looked at him. Slowly he lifted his portfolio and sent one hand down into the bottom of the bag and in the next minute withdrew a small slim vial. "Do you recall the question I put to you back at Roe Head, Mr. Eden?" he asked. "I believe I inquired whether or not you were prepared for this journey?"

Edward remembered, his eyes fixed on the vial.

"Well, at that time, I'm afraid you would have had to answer no. But now, because of your kindness to me, you can answer yes."

He thrust the vial upward into the air. Incredible the speed with which Edward's eyes followed it.

At first Edward merely smiled, dwelling with great affection upon Fate. Then mysteriously the smile grew to a soft laugh. Amazed, he heard it in echo across the way, Mr. Brontë warmly sharing both his relief as well as his anticipation, the short laugh growing, first from one side of the carriage, then the other, increasing, as though they'd just shared a rich joke, still increasing, irrationally, their eyes focused upward on the vial, their heads now pressed back against the cushions, Edward laughing as heartily as he'd laughed in months and his companion joining in until the carriage at times seemed inadequate to contain their frenzy of laughter.

As he saw his new friend lift the vial ever higher as though extending it for blessings to Heaven, he dissolved again into helpless laughter and was only vaguely aware of the carriage veering to the left of the twin road signs outside his window: Skipton to the left, London to the right.

What matter? No matter!

The carriage picked up speed, a small black dot in the vast emptiness of the Yorkshire moors while inside above the clatter of hooves and the rattle of wheels came the incongruous, hilarious, yet mysteriously senseless sound of two men laughing.

London
December, 1836

In the light of a single candle Daniel Spade sat in the chill office and stared in despair at the pile of debts before him on the desk.

It could not go on much longer. The volunteer money had long since been exhausted. The teachers had received no pay for two months. The monies he had received from Edward last spring had been disbursed to impatient creditors. There would be no more coal delivery. Only that week he'd closed off the upper floors of the house and had moved all the children to the banqueting hall, where from now on they would study, sleep, and eat communally. For the young it had been an adventure. For Daniel it was a crisis approaching tragedy.

Weary and shivering, he leaned his head forward. It was truly baffling and without precedent. Never before had Edward abandoned him thus. And now the tragedy was that not just Daniel had been abandoned, but seventy-eight children had been abandoned as well.

In a surge of anger Daniel pushed away from the desk and paced rapidly. Something was wrong. Why didn't he answer Daniel's letters? My God, how many he had sent to Eden Point, all unanswered. His rapid pacing diminished as he took note of the empty room. Everything sold, for what little it could bring. He'd even approached his Chartist friends for help, but what a futile exercise that had been. Their own coffers were pitiably low, and revolutions, as Feargus O'Conner had pointed out, required a sacrifice of both blood and money.

"Then what?" he asked the darkened cold room and stood still for a moment as though expecting a reply.

But none came and slowly he returned to the mussed desk, spying among the clutter of unpaid bills and terse letter he'd received that very day from Sir Claudius Potter.

He lifted the paper to the light of the candle and reread the harsh words. "Under no power am I authorized to support your dubious undertaking—" "Look to your own responsibilities, or you will find yourself in debtor's prison—" "—the entire Eden estates are facing radical litigation—"

That last was puzzling: "—facing radical litigation—"

Bewildered, he let the letter drop from his hands. Coming from downstairs, he heard the hum of children's voices. How to feed and clothe them? How to love them and give them a sense of their own worth and dignity? How, in short, to give them back their lives?

It was a heavy storm that raged within him, so heavy that at first he did not hear the faint knock at the door. Dragging his head upward, he saw Elizabeth. "I was sent to fetch you, sir," she began timidly. "The soup is hot and we were hoping—"

Now she stood erect, her hair brushed and gleaming, her dark blue gown simply cut. The younger students called her the "pocket girl" because every dress she sewed boasted a large pocket in which she could hide her ruined hand. And she was quick, so quick.

If she objected in any way to Daniel's close inspection, she gave no indication of it. "Poor Mr. Spade," she said. "How tired and cold you look."

The sentiment almost undid him. "Neither cold nor tired, Elizabeth," he smiled. "Not in your presence."

For a moment she seemed to be regarding him with new interest. "Tell me honestly, sir," she asked. "Will we ever see him again? Mr. Eden, I mean?"

"Of course we shall see him, Elizabeth. One cannot lose a man like Edward Eden. For a while he has been attending to interests elsewhere, but I promise you, he will return."

He had no way of knowing whether she believed him or not. "Run along, Elizabeth. You have my soup for me and leave me alone to write some letters so that one day soon you will look up and there he'll be. How does that suit you?"

According to the smile on her face, it suited her fine. "I'm grateful, Mr. Spade," she beamed. "You write your letters and I'll post them this night."

As she hurried to the door, Daniel waved her on her way. "Not necessary, Elizabeth. I'll do it myself. Help the volunteers with the little ones. I'm told you have a way with them."

At the door she blushed under the compliment. "All I do is hold them and rock them, like Mr. Eden did to me, sir." She gave a cheery wave and slipped through the door.

Hold them and rock them, like Mr. Eden.

Damn! Why didn't he answer the letters? Had he completely forgotten the house on Oxford Street and its vulnerable inhabitants? Again Daniel stared at the desk. Then with angry resolve he withdrew a sheet of paper from the drawer, moved the candle closer, and held his pen suspended.

He would try a new approach, one born of desperation.

He stared down at the blank page and in his mind's eye saw a familiar face. He had sensed a fondness there once, indeed a protectorate. Perhaps age and distance had not altered those positive feelings.

He closed his eyes to rest them. Then with care, he dipped the pen into ink, shook it once, and wrote,

"My Dearest Lady Eden . . ."

Eden Castle
January, 1837

With the tip of a solitary finger, Marianne knocked the little golden orb of the sun off its path as it revolved slowly around the earth. For an instant, the brass ball bobbed crazily through the cosmos.

Seated opposite her in the third-floor morning room, at a table spread with the remains of breakfast, was her sister, Jane, peering over her spectacles. "Well, for heaven's sake," she snapped, "don't take it out on William's orrery." She reached for a golden buttery croissant and angled it into her mouth.

Marianne watched the gluttony. "Then who am I to take it out on?" she demanded. She steadied the miniature sun, set it back on its path, and rose slowly from her chair.

Behind her at the table, she left her sister's scolding face and Daniel Spade's plaintive letter, and James's mystified correspondence concerning what he'd found in Shropshire. Sweet heaven, was there no end to it?

From the window which let in the half-light of the cold January morning, she looked back at Daniel's letter. "You know what it means, don't you?" she demanded of Jane. "It means quite simply that someone in the castle has been receiving Edward's mail and pocketing it."

"It means more than someone has been pocketing Edward's letters," her old sister pronounced. "It means that if Edward is not here and Edward is not in London, where is Edward?"

Slowly Marianne lifted her head. "He left with Jennifer," she murmured stupidly.

"Of course he left with Jennifer," Jane replied, "but that was five months ago."

Quickly Marianne nodded, as though at least to give the appearance of rationality. "He might have elected to stay in Yorkshire," she offered.

"For whatever reason?" Jane inquired pointedly.

"I don't know, I don't know!" Was that her voice, as strident as a schoolgirl's? Marianne bowed her head and closed her eyes.

From across the room, she heard Jane again. "And what do you make of the news from Shropshire?"

"What am I to make of it?" Marianne leaned close to the fire to warm her hands. "What do you suppose is the nature of the young woman's mysterious illness? James only states that he was denied all access to her, indeed never saw her."

Jane shrugged and appeared to be rereading the letter, postmarked Shrewsbury and dated three weeks earlier. "Fever, I suppose," she muttered. "That would at least be contagious, thus warranting isolation."

Behind Marianne, the whistling of wind at the window seemed to be making her head throb painfully. Then there was the other problem. Poor Daniel Spade's letter, which led to the most painful mystery of all—Edward's whereabouts.

"Do you suppose that—harm has befallen him?" she asked softly, then pressed the tips of her fingers to her lips as though belatedly to halt the words.

Jane peered at her over the tops of her spectacles. "Harm? No! Not Edward. I think we must set about to find him, though, as soon as possible."

Her patience dwindling, Marianne asked sharply, "And how do you propose that we do that?"

"Simple," Jane replied. "We must write immediately to the person who saw him last."

"Jennifer?"

"Who else?"

While Marianne was contemplating with dread the chore

of writing to her unresponding daughter, Jane went on. "And furthermore, I think we must have an immediate conference with the individual who handles all incoming and outgoing mail for the castle. If it hadn't been for Mrs. Greenbell's propitious appearance at the gate when the post arrived, we might not have received these," and she gestured toward the scattered letters.

Appalled by the suggestion, Marianne leaned sharply forward. "Oh no, Jane. Please." She heard the begging quality in her voice and hated it, but not as much as she hated the proposed confrontation. "It would serve no purpose," she added weakly.

"Then let me handle it," Jane offered, as though she were looking forward to the encounter.

Marianne started to protest again, but knew it was useless, and a few seconds later, she heard Jane's voice raised in a command to the serving girls outside the door: "Fetch Miss Cranford here immediately. Tell her Lady Eden wishes to speak with her."

Apparently Jane saw the consternation in Marianne's face and tried now to ease it. "Don't worry," she soothed, coming back to her chair. "I'll be here, and I'll do the talking."

It seemed cold comfort to Marianne and she signaled as much by taking refuge by the windows, where she felt the cold blast of January wind and found that chill strangely reviving. The terrible hurt in her head was persisting, her jaws closed upon each other tighter and tighter until she thought she could no longer open them. The pain spread down her neck and seemed to settle in her left shoulder.

At that moment a knock came at the door. Marianne pressed her hands against her head, which seemed on the verge of exploding, and with an effort of will she turned away in an attempt to regain control.

The knock came again. "Let her in," Marianne commanded.

She heard the door open. Quickly she moved down to the white marble fireplace, her hands trembling, clasped behind her. She looked up to see Jane step back from the opened door, and saw the woman herself sweep in. Her nemesis. Sophia Cranford.

"You summoned me, milady?"

Drawing deep breath, Marianne managed, "I did, indeed,

Miss Cranford." She gestured toward the scattered letters on the table. "The morning post," she went on, "brought us distressing news."

"I'm sorry to hear it, milady," Sophia replied.

"One letter," Marianne continued, "was from Daniel Spade. He mentioned several letters which he had sent here addressed to Edward. Would you have any knowledge of those letters?"

If she had expected to catch the woman in an embarrassment, she was sadly mistaken. Without hesitation, Sophia smiled. "Of course, milady. They are in my writing bureau, held for safekeeping until Mr. Edward's return."

Taken somewhat aback by the ease in the woman's face, Marianne momentarily faltered. Beyond Sophia's unblinking eyes, she saw Jane, standing as rigid as a statue. "Don't you think?" Marianne began again, "that it would have been better to forward the correspondence to him?"

"Where, milady?" Sophia inquired. "Of course I would have forwarded them if I'd known where. If you know, please tell me and I will do it immediately."

Marianne turned away. "Well, it's quite apparent, Miss Cranford, that he's still with Jennifer in Yorkshire."

"I beg your pardon, milady," Sophia cut in, "but it's not apparent at all. I've had letters from Jennifer. She makes not one mention of Edward—"

"Would she be likely to mention Edward? To you?" Marianne asked pointedly.

But again the woman seemed imperturbable. She merely smiled and reached into the pocket of her dress and withdrew a letter. "Here, milady," she smiled. "Please read for yourself. This is from Jennifer, arriving only last week—"

Marianne had no desire to read the warm, chatty letter from her daughter addressed to another woman. Still, she was interested in her daughter's words, if for no other reason than to try to determine if Edward was with her.

Sophia stepped forward and extended the letter. "Please, milady, read for yourself. If you find between the lines the slightest hint that Edward is now residing in Yorkshire, then Mr. Spade's letters will be forwarded to Roe Head before the end of the day."

Faced with no alternative but to read, Marianne took the letter and withdrew back to the fire. Hurriedly she read, a brief, rather stilted account of a stoic existence, the students' constant clamor for help, the endless exercise books to correct, the difficult winter. Peculiar. There was a different tone to it from letters which Sophia had shared with her in the past.

In a reflective action, she turned the envelope over. Her eyes, dimmed by age and illness, could not at first bring the address into focus. Then they did. The storm was no longer raging safely beyond the window. The storm was within her, and the hand that held the letter was trembling so that it appeared palsied. "This," she began on diminished breath, "is addressed to—me."

For the first time she saw those stern features before her alter. "To—you, milady?" she repeated.

Marianne thrust the letter forward. "Read for yourself, Miss Cranford," she commanded, "then tell me how long you have been in the habit of opening another's mail."

Then at last, Jane moved down into the confrontation, taking the letter from Sophia, studying the address for herself, then angrily hurling it onto the table.

Now Sophia Cranford was in the awkward position of having to address both of them at once. "I swear, milady," she stammered. "It was an accident. I recognized the handwriting, and—assumed it was for me."

"Assumed?" Marianne repeated, her anger full-blown now.

"The post *does* come in quite a rush, milady, the staff, everyone impatient. I assure you it was quite an honest error. You must admit the incident is without precedent."

But Marianne was in no mood to admit anything. With pleasure she watched the disintegration before her, Sophia's left hand now digging at something inside her pocket, the veins in her neck protruding, a predator turned prey.

Quickly Marianne retrieved Jennifer's letter from the table and studied the envelope. *Lady Eden, Eden Point, North Devon.* Briefly she closed her eyes. How often she had dreamed of such a letter. True, the words were impersonal, the message distant. Still, it was a start that had almost been denied her.

Holding the letter to her breast now as though it were an injured child, she tried to draw a deep breath. Sophia's talking mouth had at last fallen silent, the woman as undone as Marianne had ever seen her.

Calmly Marianne said, "Your services, Miss Cranford,

are no longer needed here. I will give both you and your brother a fortnight to make other arrangements. But at the end of that time, I want you gone. Is that clear?"

Something was stirring on Sophia's face. "I've—offered my apologies, milady—"

"And they have not been accepted," Marianne countered. "Your service here is over. Need I make it any clearer?"

The strain on the face before her was almost unbearable to watch. The woman *was* defeated, that was clear.

But at the very moment that Marianne was claiming victory, she saw Sophia lift her head, a new expression on her face. "I do not take my orders from you, Lady Eden," she smiled, in spite of her trembling chin. "Lord Eden should return by the end of this week. He will decide the matter."

"Lord Eden?" she parroted. "Lord Eden takes orders from *me*," she said. "I have run this castle since the day of my husband's death and intend to go on doing so until the moment of my death."

The woman appeared to be on the verge of interrupting, but Marianne didn't give her a chance. The pain in her head was increasing, her throat and the lining of her mouth mysteriously dry. She reached out for support to the table and curiously felt no sensation of wood beneath her fingers.

The encounter must end. "I repeat myself, Miss Cranford," she said. "Your services are no longer required. From now on, I shall see to the post myself. You will bring Edward's letters to me immediately. Then I suggest you start making arrangements for your departure."

Something was causing a constriction in her throat. In an attempt to hide her weakness, she moved toward the window, stumbling slightly on the elevation. My God, why didn't the woman leave? What was there left to be said?

Then she heard it again, that persistent, arrogant voice. "I shall deliver the letters to you, milady, and to be relieved of the dispersal of the post is a pleasure. But I will make no arrangements for departure until I hear the command from Lord Eden's lips."

Suddenly Marianne turned in a rage, still unable to understand how she could be destroyed by such a woman. The pain inside her head was increasing. "It is my desire, Miss Cranford, never to lay eyes on you again," she said, turning away to the window.

She heard retreating footsteps behind her and might have felt relief had it not been for the sharp, needlelike numbness which was now invading her right arm. Although she was pressing the flesh of the arm against the windowpane, she felt nothing. She clung to the sill with her good left hand, her brain becoming as benumbed as her arm.

There was something she had to do. What? Was that the door closing? Was she alone? And who was pawing at her? With surprise she turned and looked into Jane's face, wearing an expression of undue concern. Curious. Jane's hand was resting on that dead right arm and still Marianne felt nothing.

"Come," Jane urged softly. "Come, you must lie down."

Lie down? Why on earth would she want to do that when there was such pressing business? Had she spoken that aloud or merely thought it? Was her mouth as dead as her arm?

"Jane—"

"I'm here, Marianne. Come."

"No." Although she was aware of Jane trying to guide her toward the bedchamber, there was a more urgent destination. She looked around the familiar room. There she spied it, her writing bureau. "Letter," she whispered. "Write—" *What was the matter with her? Why couldn't she form a complete sentence?*

"Later," whispered Jane, still trying to guide her toward the bed.

Marianne closed her eyes and tried to clear her brain. "Letter," she repeated, with effort, "—to—Jennifer—"

But when Jane still insisted on guiding her toward the bed, Marianne pulled away from her support and fell, stumbling toward the bureau.

"All right, Marianne," Jane soothed, coming up rapidly behind her. "We'll write to Jennifer now."

Relieved, Marianne permitted Jane to lift her and lead her back to the center of the room where she lowered herself into Thomas's chair. She saw her sister looking down on her, a most strange expression on her face.

"Letter," Marianne began again, cursing her sluggish brain and lips and dead arm.

Slowly Jane knelt before her. "Yes, letter," she repeated as though to a slow-witted child. *Then why isn't she fetching the paper?* Marianne thought angrily. *And why couldn't she order her to do so? The words were in her mind. Why couldn't she form them with her lips and tongue?*

Oh God, help, a voice screamed within her.

But there was no sound. And nothing moved. And she heard nothing but the wind and snow against the window.

"Letter—" she mumbled again, her tongue thick.

"Yes, letter," Jane repeated, holding her dead hand.

Roe Head
Yorkshire
February, 1837

Although the bimonthly mail packet had been delivered to Miss Wooler's narrow cramped office early that morning, it was after eleven o'clock that evening before Jennifer was free to turn her mind to such matters. And even then, after the rigors of the day, her thoughts did not move toward the mail, but rather toward the simple task of dragging herself up to her third-floor cell and the comfort of her cot.

Now, lamp in hand, she paused at the foot of the long flight of stairs and gazed upward. Her neck and back ached from bending over the keyboard, and somewhere near the core of her brain was the monotonously maddening rhythm of a metronome.

As she was just turning the corner of the first landing, she heard a voice, coming from the hall below. It surprised her. She'd thought she was the only one up.

But as she looked back down into the front entrance hall, she saw Miss Brontë. "Charlotte," she smiled, keeping her voice down in consideration of the sleeping rooms on either side of the hall. "Did you call?"

The woman looked as weary as Jennifer felt. Now in that

375

high, almost childlike voice, she called up, "I beg your pardon, Jennifer, but—did you collect your mail?"

Mail? Great heavens. She'd completely forgotten. "I'll fetch it in the morning, Charlotte," she called down and started again around the newelpost toward the second flight of stairs.

But she heard the voice again. "I think you'd be well advised to collect it now, Jennifer." Then as though aware that she was behaving out of character, Charlotte quietly added, "I promised Miss Wooler that I'd see all the mail dispatched."

Well, there was nothing to do but retrace her steps down, retrieve what she knew would be waiting for her, one primly printed letter from Sophia Cranford.

She held forth her lamp to light the dim passage beneath the stairs, and ultimately found herself in Miss Wooler's cramped office. On the cluttered desk she placed her lamp to one side and sent her eyes across the muss of papers.

Only at the last minute, on the right-hand side of the desk, she spied it, a rather large square envelope with her name and designation on it. She picked it up to examine it and did not recognize the handwriting, although on the back she saw the hardened wax with the Eden seal impressed upon it. She held the letter a moment longer and was just reaching out to retrieve her lamp when she spied a larger packet which had been resting beneath her letter. Quite large it was and of heavy parchment; the packet seemed filled with smaller letters.

Curious, she drew the lamp closer and read the inscription. *To Be Delivered to Mr. Edward Eden, in Residence at Roe Head.*

To Mr. Edward—

Hurriedly she drew up a straight-backed chair, brought the lamp closer, placed the large envelope on the desk, and with her finger broke the seal on the small one. Perhaps the answer lay inside.

After she'd read the opening paragraph, she turned over the three sheets of paper to the conclusion. Miss Jane Locke? Her old aunt? She'd never received a letter from Jane Locke in her entire life.

She stared a moment at the signature, then turned back to the beginning. It seemed that her mother had suffered a seizure, though Jane Locke hastened to reassure her that she was in good hands. But the bulk of the letter concerned Edward, Jane speaking insistently on how pleasant he must be finding the Yorkshire air and how delightful for Jennifer to have her brother's constant company, and if it pleased her, would she see to it that he received his correspondence which had been coming to the castle.

Finally with a sense of bewilderment, Jennifer completed the letter, the closing paragraph as mystifying as the first, a blunt insistence that Jennifer convey to Edward the family news, their mother's illness, of course, and James's temporary absence and the tragic news he'd learned in Shropshire, that his future bride, Harriet Powels, was apparently suffering from some serious illness and that the wedding had been postponed indefinitely.

Coming from behind her, from the area of the door, she heard a familiar voice. "You look desolate, Jennifer. May I help?"

She turned, surprised to see Charlotte standing there. In her hand she clasped a dark red book, a finger inserted at midpoint, as though she'd been reading.

In reply to her question, Jennifer murmured, "Distressing news. And so much of it. My mother has suffered a seizure."

"I'm very sorry," Charlotte murmured.

"It's not too serious," Jennifer hastened to add, "at least that's what I'm told." Her eyes moved back to Charlotte. "And my brother's future bride is suffering from some unknown malady. The wedding has been indefinitely postponed."

Charlotte stepped across the threshold, a look of interest in her face. "Your elder brother," she inquired politely, "the one we met?"

"No," Jennifer corrected. "Not that one. James, my younger—"

The woman nodded as though grateful for the meaningless clarification. "And the—other one?" she stammered, looking uncomfortable in her role of interrogator.

"They think he is with me," she said. "Look," and she lifted the large packet of letters. "They sent along his mail for me to deliver to him."

Now at last there was a clear expression on Charlotte's face, as though some suspicion had just been confirmed. "The missing are legion, or so it seems," she murmured. "A member of my family as well has been absent since September. I learned about it last month from my father, who is getting old and likes to be able to account for his children."

Jennifer listened carefully. "And you think there might be a connection?" she asked.

"Perhaps not," Charlotte replied. "It's Branwell," she went on. "You met him last September."

Jennifer nodded, feeling like an inspector in search of clues. "Our brothers met," she concluded, "but they left separately, yours, I think, preceding mine."

To this mental work, Charlotte nodded. But in the dim light her face seemed to go pale. "Forgive me, Jennifer," she muttered, eyes down, "but I know they share the same —affliction."

"Affliction?" Jennifer repeated.

"They are both opium eaters."

To which Jennifer hurriedly replied, "No, not Edward. He indulged the habit last summer, but he broke it. I know, Charlotte, I was there."

Then apparently the woman had nothing more to say except, "Good night, Jennifer. I only hope that all our missing will be shortly found." With that she was gone.

Jennifer continued to stare at the empty doorway. Charlotte had conceived of an alliance between Edward and her brother. But how could that have been possible?

As she hurried back through the corridor, she glanced into the front parlor and saw Charlotte reading. She considered reopening the conversation, but for what purpose? The hour was late.

There would be no rest this night, not healing rest. Before the week was out, she knew she would have to reply to Jane Locke's letter, a reply which would be as distressing to certain residents of Eden Castle as the letter from Eden had been to her.

Unlike Jane Locke's, her message would be simple and to the point. Edward was not with her in Yorkshire, had never been with her in Yorkshire save for that brief interval of one afternoon, and for now and perhaps forever, she hadn't the least idea where he might be.

Four days later, as Jennifer was instructing plump Louise Merritt in the intricacies of a Chopin Etude, she happened to glance out the narrow, rain-splattered window of the music room in the direction of the rounded driveway.

There to her surprise, she saw a two-wheeled gig, drawn by a single horse and driven by a tall, top-hatted man dressed entirely in black. He was not a tradesman, or old Doctor Bennet from Bradford, or any of the half dozen or so gentlemen who had a legitimate reason to call at Miss Wooler's school.

As the dissonance coming from the pianoforte increased, Jennifer left her chair, her curiosity piqued by the rain-soaked gentleman who was just now crawling out of the gig.

Behind her, she heard Louise Merritt falter and stop. "I'm—lost, Miss Eden," she whined. "What comes after—"

"Do the simple scales, Louise," she instructed tersely.

At that moment, beyond the music room, she heard the front bell ring. Jennifer moved quietly toward the door. She opened it a crack and peered out. One of the young serving girls was just letting the gentleman in. A moment later Miss Wooler approached the stranger, apparently received his introduction, then quickly gave Maudie instructions of some sort.

He seemed ill at ease, she thought. Then at that moment, she saw—sweet heavens! It was Charlotte. Obviously the gentleman had come to see Charlotte.

She knew she shouldn't be spying and considered closing the door. But what harm?

Jennifer watched and saw the gentleman withdraw a small envelope from inside his waistcoat and hand it to Charlotte. She appeared to study it for a moment, then slowly walked toward one of the rectangular windows which flanked the front door where obviously the light was better for her failing vision.

From behind her, coming from the pianoforte, she heard Louise complaining again. "What now, Miss Eden? I did C."

Annoyed by the distraction, Jennifer quickly instructed, "Then do D and E and F, two octaves up and two back, and no wrong notes, I beg you."

As again the torturous sounds escaped from the old pianoforte, Jennifer glanced back down the hall to where Charlotte appeared to be endlessly reading by the window.

Then Jennifer saw her refold the letter with what appeared to be unnecessary vigor. She walked back to where the gentleman was waiting, spoke to him in some manner to which he shook his head, obviously declining an invitation of some sort.

Then in a remarkably short time he was gone.

Curious, most curious. The incident over, Jennifer was on the verge of quickly closing the door when suddenly she saw Charlotte lift her head and stare directly at her, as though she knew she'd been spying all along. Jennifer had not expected so direct a look and now closed the door and leaned against it.

She'd just started back toward the pianoforte when she heard the softest of knocks on the door. She opened it and saw Charlotte standing there, the letter still in her hand.

"I apologize for disturbing you, Jennifer," she began, keeping both her voice and head down. "I've only just received a message that may interest you."

Perplexed, Jennifer gazed first at her friend, then at the letter. Now over her shoulder, she called out to Louise Merritt, "Do them all again and keep doing them until I return. I'll only be a moment." Jennifer closed the door behind her, and within the moment, Charlotte thrust the letter at her and urged her to read it.

As Jennifer took the letter, Charlotte explained further, "It was just delivered to me by my father's assistant, Mr. Weightman. He knew of my concern in the matter and brought it over direct from Haworth."

Since she seemed disinclined to say anything further, Jennifer glanced down at the rather dramatic handwriting and read the address: *Rev. Patrick Brontë, Haworth Parsonage, Yorks.*

"Your father?" Jennifer asked, looking up.

Charlotte nodded.

The opening paragraphs were effusive apologies from, in the words of the letter, a failed son. This was followed by someone's sincere hope that his unaccountable disappearance had not caused great anxiety.

Then one name alone leaped off that page, so unexpected in its appearance that Jennifer tilted the page toward the light at the end of the corridor, as though her eyes had deceived her.

The letter recounted a most incredible series of events including a broken gig, a late evening rescue by a good Samaritan named Edward Eden, a pleasant interval spent in sightseeing through Northern Yorkshire, and finally a destination in the green idylls of the Lake Country.

At least no harm had befallen him. Now she would not have to write that dreaded letter to Eden. And thank heavens, she knew where he was for on the back of the letter was a very specific address: *Dove Cottage, Westmoreland, The Lakes.*

With a sigh, she looked back at Charlotte and thanked her warmly for sharing the message and was slightly confused by the look of gloom which seemed to have settled permanently over her friend's face.

But before she could inquire into its nature, Charlotte stepped forward. "The name Dove Cottage means nothing to you?" she asked.

"No."

Charlotte retrieved the letter from her, refolded it and tucked it into her pocket. "Dove Cottage is the hideaway of several opium eaters, Hartley Coleridge—"

"Opium?" Jennifer began.

Charlotte nodded. "Quite a nest of them. Self-proclaimed, foolishly proud of their addiction." With a visible shudder, she half turned away. "Weak," she muttered, and the simple word came out a curse, "male weakness. At least we know where the prodigals are, and where they are likely to remain," she added ominously.

Jennifer started to protest her words, but could not. Her mind was now creating an image of Edward drugged, Edward suffering the nightmares, Edward refusing to eat.

As her thoughts took this black turn, she looked up, surprised to see Charlotte just disappearing around the corner at the end of the hall. For a moment, Jennifer lingered in the corridor, overcome with regret. What could she do? How could she reach him, anchored to her duties here?

Her mind raced upstairs to the packet of letters addressed to Edward which she had placed in her dresser drawer for safekeeping. Now at least she could forward those, though she wondered if they would make a particle of difference. Then a thought occurred to her, something that might disturb him enough to draw him out: news of Harriet Powels, seriously ill, perhaps dying. Even if she weren't, it would be an impressive message. If there was any news on God's earth capable of turning him about, that would be it.

Jennifer lifted her mind to the third floor, where she would soon commence a letter. With love and concern and entreaty she would commence it:

"Dearest Edward"...

Dove Cottage
The Lakes
February, 1837

The long walks had ceased. The sun had slipped behind a cloud and had not been seen since November. Brontë had taken to locking his study door in the morning and sometimes not emerging for the entire day, leaving Edward to pass long dreary periods alone.

So the idyll which had held such appeal in the beginning had, over the months, turned into a kind of limbo, Edward feeling, in what few lucid moments were left to him, that the entire world and all of its inhabitants had simply come to a halt, as he had done. Another minor note in this interval was old John Murrey. Disappointment was written on his plain gaunt features for all to see.

Now on this morning in mid-February, with a cold wind hurling itself against the loosened shutters of the cottage, Edward lay stretched out on a chaise near the dying fire, a feather comforter pulled up over his legs. He was cold all the time now. With shaking hands he pushed back his long hair, his fingers, in the process, brushing over the beard which he had grown. Within the silence of the room, he heard his own heart beating. This was the worst, morning, when there was nothing to do, when the opium was beginning to leave the system, when, comparatively speaking, the mind cleared and certain images returned, uninvited, to sit in silent judgment . . . a pale cheek, a strand of auburn hair.

He moaned and heard a new sound, horses, the hooves making a slapping sound on the wet road outside the window. He heard voices then, a man's shout, seeking the identity of the cottage, and he heard a reply, John Murrey's voice.

There now! What was that? It sounded like knocking. At that moment the door opened and John Murrey appeared, his smock wet about the shoulders, as though he'd recently stepped out into the rain. But it was his face that caught Edward's attention. No longer glum and sullen, he wore a smile of vast proportions. He appeared to be carrying something, but from that angle Edward couldn't see. "Close the door," he muttered, feeling a new chill rush in. "Was that a rider I heard outside?" he asked, closing his eyes.

"It was, sir," came the enthusiastic reply. "It most certainly was, and look what he brung."

Edward had never heard that glee in John's voice before and so could not resist opening his eyes. A leather packet of some sort was being offered him, along with a burst of explanation.

"He come all the way from Bradford," John Murrey gushed. "Said further he'd been hired by Miss Jennifer Eden to deliver this to you by hand."

Jennifer. Laboriously he pulled himself up to a sitting position.

Again the old man thrust the packet at Edward, forcing him to take it.

It was dark brown leather and rain-soaked. Jennifer had hired the rider? How had she discovered his whereabouts? And what news was so important to be delivered thus?

"Shall I open it for you, sir?" John Murrey offered. Before Edward could reply, the old man leaned over and released the binding.

"A letter," grinned John Murrey, as though it were the most remarkable object in the world.

Feeling inside the packet, Edward found others. "The world has found us," he commented quietly. He broke the seal and withdrew several pages. "My Dearest Edward," he read.

The first paragraph was painless and at least answered one of his questions. She'd learned of his whereabouts through her friend Charlotte Brontë, whose family had received recent correspondence from Branwell. How simple the solution, how circuitous the route.

John Murrey asked hopefully, "Good news, sir?"

Edward shook his head and tried to neutralize whatever expression had covered his face and again fell to reading. The second paragraph was more painful. How worried Jennifer had been, how concerned that harm had befallen him.

For her worry, Edward was profoundly sorry. And in the third paragraph there was more distress, Daniel Spade. Apparently Daniel's needs were growing acute and he'd sent several letters to Eden. And that, obviously, had been the alarm bell. Still he read on. His mother ill? Not serious, or so Jane Locke had said.

From the fireplace he heard a considerate inquiry. "Bad news, sir?"

He nodded. "I'm afraid so. Lady Eden has fallen ill."

But still there was more, a third page which commenced ominously, "But more tragic news"—he hesitated, then read on—"concerning James's happiness. He has received word that Harriet Powels is dying."

The word was so small, so simply written.

Dying.

How? And why?

Dear God! He leaned forward suddenly as though dragged bodily forward by the word itself.

"Please, sir," John Murrey begged, eager to assist in some way.

Since he was incapable of speech and old John Murrey curious, he merely thrust the page at him.

Still Edward continued to sit on the side of the chaise, the image of her pressing relentlessly upon him. Then without warning, as though the words had come from someone outside him, he said, "We are leaving here."

"When, sir?"

"As soon as possible," Edward replied. At that moment his vision blurred, everything in the room assuming a double image. But if John Murrey saw his weakness, he gave no indication of it.

Instead he announced, "Then I shall ready the carriage

immediately," and started toward the door. He called back. "I'll attend to the trunks when I've finished, sir. I propose we be on the road by afternoon."

Edward listened and nodded. The retreat had come to an end.

Dying. The miserable word would not leave him alone. He could not imagine her in any mood but the one in which they had shared the glen.

Under the duress of great urgency, he tried to stand but his legs buckled and he fell back onto the chaise. Breathless, he tried to slow his pulse. He must try again. He had done it once. It could be done. For the first time in a long time he felt a strong desire to be whole, not weak.

Again he lifted himself off the chaise and this time stood erect and smiled at his own weakness and spoke cool terse words to it, though he was alone and there was no one present to hear.

Hadley Park
Shropshire
March, 1837

Her name was Sigfried Halmer. She was from Stockholm and now stood looking out of the narrow fourth-floor
window of the elegant mid-Georgian estate known as
Hadley Park.

She'd not seen much of it close hand, thanks to her
charge, who lay behind her, silent and swollen, on the bed.
Of course in the first two weeks of confinement, she'd been
granted considerable freedom, had enjoyed walking down
to the Mermaid, where she'd met that interesting gentleman
Humphrey Hills. With what miraculous ease they had
met, talked, laid their plot, profitable for her, satisfying for
him. "A fitting end," the man had said, gleefully, "for the
brat to grow up, a servant, in the shadow of Hadley Park."

Quickly she glanced at the woman on the bed, as though
fearful that her thoughts had been audible. At fifty-two
Sigfried was thick-waisted and getting thicker. She'd been
hired out of Stockholm by Lord Powels himself. Sigfried
had answered the advertisement in the Stockholm paper.
The requirements had been clearly listed. One, a knowledge
of medicine and midwifery. Two, a willingness to sign an
agreement to the effect that as soon as the job was com-

387

pleted, she'd return to Stockholm and never again set foot
in England. Three, she'd take the infant with her and sell
it in Stockholm. Four, no knowledge or skill in the English
language. The fee, five thousand pounds!

Sigfried leaned closer to the window and pressed her face
against the cool glass. Five thousand pounds! The thought
warmed her. Of course, she'd signed a ready yes to all requirements, lying on the fourth for she did indeed have a
limited knowledge of English. But she'd maintained her
deception well enough over the last eight months.

Slowly she lifted her face from the window and looked
over her shoulder at the lumpen woman. A strange one,
that! Sigfried thought she had seen all kinds, but never
in her life had she seen the likes of the young woman
behind her. Was she asleep? It was impossible to tell.
Sigfried knew from the dreary experience of the last eight
months that the young woman could lie on the bed for
hours with her eyes closed and not be asleep.

Now she stepped closer to the bed, a plain iron frame
cot with a piece of muslin thrown over the bare mattress,
a place of rest as crude and uncomfortable as the entire
dreary chamber.

On the far wall was a large brick chimney which emitted
sufficient heat as long as the fire was kept stoked on the
floor below. There were several large trunks on the opposite wall which had been draped and now served as a
partition, separating Sigfried's bed and washstand from
the large common room. Meals were left outside the door
on a tray, their arrival signaled by a soft knock. The same
ritual was observed with fresh water, clean linens, chamber
pots.

For eight months both had lived in this furtive manner,
seeing no one but each other and maintaining this un-
godly silence. To be sure, Sigfried had heard the young
woman speak on two or three occasions, but she'd been
talking in her sleep and the words had been muddled.

Sigfried smiled, surveying the young woman, peculiarly
pleased by her plight, her clear humiliation. *Lady* Harriet
Powels, or so she'd been introduced by Lord Powels.
Sigfried wasn't stupid. She knew precisely what had happened. The eligible and titled lady had been betrothed to
an eligible and titled gentleman, yet at some point, early

on, she'd opened her legs to another. Now, disgraced, she must be kept out of sight until the seed, full-term, slipped out. Then with careful intake of food, the young lady would regain her virginal figure, mysteriously recover from an even more mysterious illness, and rejoin her intended, only slightly worse for wear.

As for Sigfried, she would take the excess baggage down to the Mermaid and Humphrey Hills, who already had paid one thousand pounds for their little plot, and would pay an additional thousand if she managed to deliver a whole healthy infant.

At that instant, the young woman groaned. The hands which had been resting on her breasts moved downward, clutching at her belly. Though alert, Sigfried held her position. Amused by the silent agony on the bed, she smiled. Interesting, how they all suffered alike, rich and poor, lady and whore.

A game occurred to her then to relieve the boredom and the waiting, to see how long the Queen of Silence could hold out before crying aloud for help. If birth were truly imminent, it was Sigfried's guess that at most the stubborn young woman would last three hours, perhaps four. But as soon as the brat's head shifted and began to press down on vital organs, as soon as her bones began to feel as though they would crack and split with the upheaval of birth, as soon as the water burst and the high-born fastidious woman had the sense of soiling herself, then Sigfried knew from experience those prim lips would utter an entreaty, and the weeping would start, then the moans, and ultimately the screams.

Roughly Sigfried drew back the coverlet and lifted the nightdress. With her hands cold from the window, she clamped down on the protruding lump, causing the young woman to press backward on the cot, her hands covering first her eyes as though to prohibit sight, then her mouth as though to prevent outcry.

So! Sigfried smiled. The pretty wanted neither to see nor to speak. Well, there was time yet. The lump was shifting, that was clear, though the fluid in which it was floating was still intact. A good sign. The birth would not be easy. Hours yet ahead.

As she stood up from her examination, Sigfried saw the

young woman shivering. Silent tears were streaming from the corners of her eyes. The grotesque body lay naked on the iron cot, the nightshirt pushed up to her neck revealing blue veins in her swollen breasts. Sigfried smiled again. If only the young woman's intended were here now. What a pleasurable scene that would be.

Hurriedly Sigfried fetched a stack of linens from atop one of the upturned trunks and placed them on the table beside the cot. While she wanted to hear the young woman speak, she knew she must not allow screams to go on too long.

Moving more leisurely now, Sigfried went into the small cubicle where she slept and fetched her valise containing the necessary instruments. She returned and placed them on the table alongside the linens.

Then, feeling a kind of excitement, she drew a chair close beside the cot and commenced tearing the linens into strips of appropriate lengths; there must be gags for the mouth, longer double strips to tie about each ankle, binding strips to secure the wrists to the iron frame, the large pieces to accommodate the filth of the birth, and enough left over for swaddling for the brat.

As Sigfried saw one hand begin to push down the nightshirt as though to cover her nakedness, she leaned quickly forward and angrily pushed it back, shaking her head. The ugliness must be closely watched. Now Sigfried thought she saw two faint circles of color on the pale face as though she were mortified to be so openly laid bare.

Good! And again Sigfried smiled, determined to humiliate her beyond measure, as *she* had known a lifetime of humiliation. Indeed, thinking upon it, how did they differ? One was an old whore, the other a young one.

Suddenly, with brute force, Sigfried ripped a long strip of muslin in half. The girl's eyes widened at the tearing sound, as though at that moment she knew precisely what was ahead of her.

Good again! With a certain lightness, Sigfried smiled. It was nice to realize that for ever more she would be permanently etched in the young woman's memory. However rich and fine a lady she might become, there would always be private dark moments when she would remember this room and Sigfried's face.

A gleam of pleasure blazed in Sigfried's eyes. It was nice to know she would be remembered.

In the beginning it had been merely a matter of retaining her sanity. Now for Harriet Powels, lying on the iron cot in her extremity, she wondered quite seriously if that sanity was worth retaining.

The spasm of pain was receding. But she was cold. Why wouldn't the woman cover her? And why did she stare so cruelly down?

Eight months ago, she'd not thought it possible to live in such isolation. She still remembered the confrontation with her parents when she'd informed them of her predicament, her mother's weeping rage, her father's anger as he'd tried to bully a name out of her. But she'd held her silence then, as she'd held it throughout her confinement.

As for herself, although she'd never spoken the name aloud, she'd thought it often enough. *Edward*. Why hadn't he believed her? Why hadn't he been content with a limited paradise? They had shared more in five short days than they'd had a right to expect. Even her present condition made a kind of sense, a reasonable price to pay for five perfect days. What she had not anticipated had been the wrath of her parents.

She'd seen neither of them during her imprisonment, and at first had had little desire to see them. The months had passed calmly with the old foreigner. There was a small side balcony off the storage attic where at night she was permitted to exercise and take fresh air. For the rest of it, her needs had been attended to, and she'd passed the days in needlepoint. And books. Endless books. She'd let in as much of the world as she could handle, so that in a way her isolation had not been too difficult.

Now in spite of the staring hard eyes of the old foreigner, Harriet smiled. The final upheaval was imminent. Then let it come. With every wave of agony she would erase her sin. As for the burden she was carrying, her father's plan was for the best. It had no place here, did not belong. The old woman, according to Harriet's father, had promised to find it a suitable place.

Then she would meet her responsibilities as it had always been her intention to do, would fulfill her destiny and fulfill her parents' dream as well, and settle into Eden

Castle, her name unblemished. And because of this, it was her private vow never to lay eyes on the weight shifting in her belly, to blindfold herself and cover her ears lest she hear a birth cry that would cause her to weaken her resolve. After her crucible was over, she would appear again miraculously recovered from a contagious illness.

She closed her eyes. The weight was shifting again. Another spasm, this one longer, her spine aching in her effort to assimilate it, the old woman still grinning down on her.

It could be endured. It must be endured with no outcry. God had been generous enough to let her know love. There had been a man, a miracle of a man. She had known him, enjoyed him, and would, forever after, know what the poets meant when they spoke the word. Love.

The spasm was passing. She was aware of the old woman standing over her, aware of hands cold as winter probing inside her, heard the woman's grunts and unintelligible mutterings in a foreign tongue. Then Harriet was aware of something else, of the old woman tying long strips of muslin about each of her ankles, drawing her legs apart and knotting the strands beneath the iron frame of the cot.

Harriet started to protest, but decided no. This too was part of the bargain, the shame and embarrassment, her helplessness in the face of her coming ordeal.

The old woman moved up to her arms and smiled down on Harriet and muttered something as she removed the nightdress altogether and commenced tying similar strips about her wrists. Then with what seemed unnecessary force she drew Harriet's arms over her head and secured her wrists to the iron frame.

Thus naked and bound, Harriet watched as the woman arranged mysterious instruments on the table beside the bed, her worn fingers stopping now and then to caress one as though she were particularly fond of it.

At that moment a grinding pain cut down across Harriet's belly, and as her body arched upward, she felt her legs pull against the muslin strips. A scream was rising in her throat. But she halted it before it passed her lips. The last thing she saw was the old woman's face, a look of anger as though Harriet had offended her by not screaming aloud.

The woman was muttering something, but Harriet

couldn't understand. Darkness soon swallowed the ugly room and the woman's angry eyes. And for some time, there was visible in the darkness only one image, the deep music of his voice, the tenderness of his touch.

Her last hope was that he had recovered, for she had every intention of doing so.

The Mermaid was a comfortable country inn located on the Shropshire-Wales turnpike. Directly across the road from the inn was an elegant black iron gate beyond which stretched the circuitous road which led to Hadley Park.

The inn had not always been a public house. Constructed in the early seventeen hundreds, its original purpose was to serve as barracks for the army of artisans and masons who were engaged in the awesome task of creating Hadley Park.

After the estate had been completed, the army of workmen departed, leaving the annex at the end of the parkland abandoned until 1790, when an enterprising Shropshireman named Simon Hills bought it and converted it into a country inn for travelers journeying between England and Wales. He made vast improvements, refurbishing the private chambers, terracing the front gardens and placing an arrangement of wooden benches about under the soft yew trees so that road-weary travelers might gaze across at the pastoral elegance of Hadley Park.

When Hills died in 1829, he left a remarkably thriving enterprise to his only son, Humphrey, who was not quite as enterprising as his father, yet cunning and troubled in his own way. Unmarried at thirty and likely to remain so, Humphrey was a slight man with a physique which more accurately resembled a young boy's than a middle-aged man's. He had had a sickly youth, plagued constantly by pleurisy and congestion, although he was in fairly good health now. At thirty, he was semi-bald, an unfortunate trait he'd inherited from his mother's family, with only a slight rim of red hair still clinging to his small round head.

But of greater importance than his physical appearance was what people in the area generally referred to as his "attitude." Having grown up in the shadow of Hadley Park, the estate and its inhabitants had become for him a kind of nemesis. Humphrey was capable of telling any passing stranger the complete history of each descendant, an incredible biographical knowledge, as though knowledge alone might somehow gain him access to that rich distant world.

Thus it was that as a boy, Humphrey, on his knees, scrubbing the red brick terrace with the acid of lye soap burning his hands, had been forced to look across the road at how others lived, a world so near, yet so remote.

Before Lord Powels had fenced the entire parkland, the little girl, Harriet Powels, had on occasion ridden her pony to the edge of the road, and more than once, Humphrey had seen her, had watched with infinite longing as she'd raced the pony back and forth, her long hair flying over the collar of her little blue velvet riding suit. And once, as he had been cutting weeds in the gulley, she'd ridden so close to him he could hear her breathing. And when with sweat dripping from his face, he'd dared to look up, he'd seen such a devastating expression of pity in her pretty face that he'd lowered his head and wished with all his heart that he were dead and not an object of her pity.

She'd returned to that same spot several days thereafter, as though hoping to find him again, and she always did, and for three months of that incredibly beautiful summer, Humphrey had learned to ignore the look of pity in her eye, and their conversation had been enjoyable.

Although only fourteen at the time, Humphrey knew he was in love, and gave in to rare fantasies, imagining himself crossing that road and entering those handsome gates as a legitimate suitor for the hand and affection of Lady Harriet Powels.

But one day as he was dressing to go out and cut weeds again, his father had taken him by surprise, had come up behind him in his dank small room off the cellar beneath the inn, had bound his wrists to the bedposts and with a horse whip had given him fifteen lashes across his back, had given him a lecture with each lash, the words more painful than the cutting sting of the whip, informing him that he was nothing, had been born nothing, and would remain nothing, that he was never to go near that side of the road again, and was certainly never to speak to the young lady, or else old Simon would wash his tongue with the same lye soap that burned his hands and left them bleeding.

The young Humphrey had endured the beating, but something important had died within him that day, and worse than the death was the birth of a new quality, a negative force brought to life in the last sparks of reason. There were those who claimed that that was the day he formed his "attitude," and while he was a dutiful son for the rest of old Simon's life, it was a subdued and savage duty. And on Simon's death, Humphrey shunned the black of mourning, shed his worker's apron for the last time, arrayed himself in pink satin waistcoat and amber cutaways, and from then on always dressed as though he were a fine gentleman rather than the proprietor of an inn.

It was his custom every night at dinner to join his guests, to sit alone at a table near the window, watching the servants for the slightest infraction, overseeing the entire comfortable wood-paneled room. In quiet moments he could be seen gazing mutely out the window at the grand estate of Hadley Park, his eyes empty, as though something were mauling him from within.

There it was that he sat on this cold night in March, the public reception rooms of his inn not as filled as he would like them to be, but the lack was understandable. Only the most urgent of journeys would take a man out in March in this part of England. From where he sat at his window table, he could see a crusty residue of new snow blowing over yesterday's brown mush, covering the redbrick terrace.

He leaned back in his chair and pushed away the remains of a beefsteak. Near his hand was a cut-glass decanter filled with his favorite port. As he poured a glass, he thought how richly satisfied he felt this night. In a month or so the turnpike would be clogged with travelers, his rooms filled to overflowing, the coin in his coffers mounting.

But there was something else this night which added to his quiet joy. Slowly he turned in his chair and gazed through the falling snow at the distant yellow windows of Hadley Park. Only one window interested him and there it was, near the very top of the grand estate, on the fourth floor, that single glow like a beacon shining. With a sly smile he brought the port to his lips and sipped. He wondered how it was going, Lady Powels's ordeal, and better still, he wondered when the prize would be delivered to him.

Oh God, he could scarcely contain himself. Of course for

a time he would have to give the brat over to the serving
women in the kitchen, and a wet-nurse would have to be
found. But the seed would grow, would become his "boy,"
and the old foreigner had assured him that it was a male; it
was riding high in that high-born belly, always a sure
sign, or so she'd said.

Oh Jesus, what sweet revenge! And what matter the
father? The Powels blood was blue enough and it was
Humphrey's intention to take that blue blood and turn it
bright common red with the same inhuman and back-
breaking labor that had been his birthright.

But the greatest scheme was to raise the boy to about
seven, then one serene day, cross the road, bastard in hand,
and confront Lady Harriet with her own flesh in a cunning
blackmail. What splendid justice, he thought, twisting in
his chair, the family thinking the embarrassment of the
illegitimate birth safely removed to Sweden while all the
time the brat had been residing beneath their very noses.

Suddenly he laughed aloud and quickly pressed his
fingers to his lips. Of course he would never let him forget
his bastard status. As soon as those young ears were old
enough to hear and perceive, Humphrey would deliver
himself of that word, would pronounce it constantly about
the boy's head, until the brand was etched on his consciousness. *Bastard.*

At that moment, an idea occurred to him, so breath-
takingly satisfying that for a moment he couldn't breathe.
A permanent brand. On the boy's chest. With the point of
a sharp knife. It could be done. While still an infant, the
ritual would be painless.

A piece of grit got in Humphrey's mouth and his teeth
grated.

He shifted abruptly in his chair and looked back out the
window where the snow was increasing. He could still
see it, that impressive hulk of Hadley Park, a few lamps
burning in the lower windows. It could be any time now,
the old Swedish woman had told him.

Any time now—

In his state of ecstatic anticipation, he did not at first
see the carriage draw up outside the window. He was only
aware of the possibility of a new guest when he heard
horses neighing.

With the natural-born instinct of a proprietor who senses

a paying guest, Humphrey sat up straight and leaned closer to the window. A handsome carriage it was, though a bit soiled.

On a note of happy anticipation, Humphrey started away from the table, hurrying through the low arched doorway which led to the outer reception hall and front door.

But as he passed a wide-eyed serving girl, he stopped, better judgment intervening. No! One sure way to annihilate any conversation he might have with the fine gentleman would be for him to appear in the reduced role of steward. Determined to play his proper role, he shouted at the retreating serving girl, "Fetch the boy! We've a late guest!"

For a few moments, Humphrey paced the long reception hall, stopping now and again to peer out the windows near the front door.

Where in the hell was that boy?

Suddenly in anger he raced to the top of the kitchen steps and shouted down, "Send up the boy!" When there was no reply coming from the basement, he grasped the hand railing and shouted again, "I'll shred his back for him, I swear it, if he doesn't—"

Then at the bottom of that dark staircase he saw the beam of a lantern, saw the flat-faced boy himself. As the boy started up the stairs, Humphrey blotted out in his imagination the dull-featured farmer's son and replaced the face with the finely drawn features of the Powels family. He saw clearly before him the unborn bastard, dependent upon him.

As the boy drew near the top of the stairs, Humphrey leveled his eyes, still seeing in his imagination the outline of the face which had caused him a lifetime of grief. Without warning he lifted his hand and delivered a stunning blow to the side of the young impudent face. The impact clearly took the boy by surprise. He emitted one sharp cry and fell a few steps backward.

He grabbed the hand railing at the last minute and, clutching his stinging cheek, he stared back at Humphrey. "Sir?" he whispered, clearly failing to understand the reason for his punishment.

Humphrey rubbed his own hand, smarting from the force of the blow. "I called for you five minutes ago," he pronounced coldly. He reached down and dragged the boy up and shoved him in the direction of the door. "We've guests," he muttered. "See to them."

He watched as again the witless boy righted himself. As he opened the door a gust of wind blew snow flurries across the floor. Humphrey hurried back to the window and stood carefully out of sight so he could not be seen from the front terrace.

Agitation mounting, Humphrey pressed closer to the window, suddenly fearful of what the boy may be saying. A wrong word, or an impudent gesture might cost him a distinguished client.

But at that moment he saw the old driver point up toward the trunks secured to the top of the carriage, saw the boy place his lantern on the snow and scramble upward.

Good lad! Apparently the Mermaid would indeed house a peer this night. Confident that all was going well outside in the cold night, Humphrey turned back toward the kitchen staircase, ready to shout again, only to find an obedient line of half a dozen serving girls, awaiting his command.

From the door he ordered, "Prepare the suite at the top of the stairs." As the girls hurried toward the central staircase he added, "And use the silk linens and the china pitcher. And lay five logs on the fire, and place a decanter of claret on the night table. Hurry!"

As the girls disappeared at the top of the stairs, Humphrey smiled. By God, let no man say to him that he was a bumpkin. He knew the requirements of class.

Then all arrangements under way, he took a moment to straighten his satin waistcoat, to lick both his forefingers and run them across his red and bushy eyebrows. Tomorrow morning, if the Fates were kind, he might share breakfast with the mysterious gentleman.

So engrossed was he in his fantasies of delights to come that only at the last minute was he aware of the curious shuffle outside the door, the old man appearing first, his face strained with effort as he supported the gentleman following behind him.

From where he stood, Humphrey's first impression was that the gentleman was ill. But once inside the reception hall, Humphrey saw him lift his head, and while he saw a face ravaged, he also saw clear and impressive evidence of breeding.

As Humphrey stepped forward to greet him, he counseled himself moderation.

"Gentlemen," he smiled, smoothing both hands down over the satin waistcoat. "Welcome to the Mermaid."

The old man stepped forward, momentarily abandoning his master. "We seek shelter, sir," he muttered.

For a moment a twinge of inadequacy swept over Humphrey. The master had not deigned to speak himself, but instead had let his man make inquiry. "The Mermaid offers you shelter," he pronounced. With a hand he motioned to the gaping boy to take the trunks upstairs. And when no one in the reception hall seemed inclined to move or speak, Humphrey side-stepped the old man and moved in the direction of the gentleman. "My name is Humphrey Hills, sir," he announced. "I am proprietor here and I am honored by your presence."

The gentleman seemed to be looking at him, but not seeing him. Humphrey moved a step closer, determined to force some sort of utterance from the gentleman. "May I offer you food, sir, or drink?"

Behind him he heard the old man cut sharply in. "We seek only warmth and rest."

Burning from the sharp retort, Humphrey glanced over his shoulder at the old man. Now assuming a hauteur of his own, he turned aside from the fruitless encounter with a rather curt announcement. "At the top of the stairs," he said. "A maid shall direct you there."

From his position near the door, Humphrey watched them both, a most curious pair, one clearly from the gutter, the other from the mountaintop, both exhibiting great fatigue.

Then an idea occurred to Humphrey. The old man had already disappeared at the top of the steps. The gentleman, facing a direct statement, would be forced to reply. "I beg your pardon, sir," Humphrey began. He hesitated at first under so direct a gaze. "Your horses, sir," he went on, "and the carriage. I'll have the boy take them around to the stables in the rear. They will be cared for."

He looked as though he might speak. At least his head lifted, but no words came out and to Humphrey's surprise and anger, he realized that he'd been ignored again.

Still smarting from the rebuff, suffering from his inability to force the arrogant man into discourse with him, Humphrey threw caution to the wind, stepped toward the newelpost, and demanded angrily, "Your name, sir." Then alarmed by his own daring, he backed away and meekly added, "For the guest book, sir. The name will be entered in the guest book."

Slowly the gentleman nodded. In his eyes fever burned, though with impressive assurance he lifted his head.

"Eden," he said softly. "Edward Eden."

The following morning, after a night as miserable as any that Edward had ever spent, he dragged himself to the narrow, diamond-shaped window glass of his second-floor lodgings in the Mermaid Inn, glanced out at the pristine landscape, and found himself blinded by the brilliance of sun on new snow.

His head ached. Each limb felt heavy and unresponding. Complete and total abstinence, as he knew all too well, was the most painful of all. Now as he pressed his forehead to cold window glass, he looked out and caught his first glimpse of Hadley Park. In silence he studied the distant elegant structure, deeply moved by his awareness of her close proximity, yet baffled as he wondered what exactly it was that he had hoped to accomplish by coming here. If James had been denied an audience with her, what chance would he have?

His head clearing, he drew his dressing robe about him and looked down at the black iron gate across the road, a fortress with two sentry boxes on either side and four guardsmen walking back and forth through the snow. No entry there without the express approval of a voice of authority coming from the estate itself.

With some effort Edward dragged a chair nearer to the window and sat heavily. Then how to reach her? Disguised? No, the idea was absurd on the face of it. And even though he might clear the gate, where, inside that pile of masonry, would he know where to look for her?

Perhaps he had yet to face the most disagreeable truth of all, that she was indeed lost to him, had been lost to him since that awful night in the Banqueting Hall.

He made a motion upward when, below, coming from the direction of the front terrace, he heard noise, feet crunching snow, a horse. He leaned forward. Below at the edge of the terrace he saw two men, one astride a horse, the other receiving an envelope of some sort. He recognized the one standing, the peculiar proprietor who had received them the night before. The man on horseback appeared to be a servant of some sort. A moment later, Edward saw the proprietor take coins from his pocket and hand them up to the servant.

Here Edward leaned closer to the window, his attention totally engaged. The servant on horseback was slowly guiding his horse back across the road where he saw the high iron gates wide open, the watchmen standing calmly to one side as the horseman rode through without interruption.

Still Edward stood by the window, concentrating now on the proprietor, who appeared to be rereading the message with great interest. Then all at once and to Edward's complete amazement he saw the little man perform a most exuberant jig. In a bizarre performance he lifted his right leg and held out his hand as though to an invisible partner and danced a few steps in one direction, then reversed legs and danced in the opposite direction. It was a most strange spectacle, the dandified little man dancing with himself on a cold snowy morning.

For several minutes Edward continued to watch by the window, until at last the man obviously came to his senses and made a hasty retreat back into the warmth of his inn. Still Edward stared down, seeing the beginning of a plan. The little proprietor had seemed eager last night to make his acquaintance. The smells of breakfast were floating up from below, and while Edward had no appetite, it occurred to him that a discourse with the man over coffee might prove profitable. The inn was in a perfect position for observing everything that went on at Hadley Park. And he had the feeling that the little proprietor had sharp eyes and would, if he could, tell a great deal.

Then if he was to play the part of the city sophisticate he must dress the role. He spied his trunk in the far corner of the room, made his way to it and lifted the lid. After some searching and discarding, he lifted out a well-tailored London suit of pale gray with pearl-colored waistcoat and gray silk neck scarf. He bathed and dressed carefully, paying attention to his grooming, a bother which he'd not done in long months.

A short time later Edward entered the dining hall and selected a small table near the window which gave him a perfect view of the iron gates across the road and the estate beyond.

A moment later he heard steps approach and turned to see a plump serving girl standing before him, the buttons on her black dress straining against the excess of flesh. "Sir?" she curtseyed prettily.

While Edward's true appetite dictated only coffee and perhaps a piece of preserved fruit, the ruse which he hoped to work upon the proprietor demanded more. "Eggs," he said, "poached, and sausages would be nice as well." He paused and sniffed broadly at the air. "And is that fresh baking I smell?"

The girl blushed and ducked her head even lower. "'Tis, sir. Cook's quite good. Both cakes and cinnamon buns, fit for angels, she makes 'em."

"Then bring me a full selection," Edward requested, "and we'll share a platter."

"Oh, I couldn't do that, sir."

"And why not?"

"Mr. Hills would have me hide, then me job," she gasped. She began to back away from the table. "I'll see to your breakfast, sir."

As the girl, still moving away, looked back, he called out, "And where is Mr. Hills this morning? I had hoped to greet him."

"He's in his office, sir. Shall I fetch him for you?"

"No," Edward answered. "Don't bother." He didn't want to be quite so obvious.

The girl still looked expectant. "Anything else, sir?"

Edward smiled, wanting very much to put her at ease. "Your name, please," he inquired softly.

Again the girl blushed. "Elizabeth, sir."

Elizabeth! With unexpected clarity the image of that other Elizabeth appeared before him. "Have you ever been to London, Elizabeth?" he asked now, knowing what the answer would be.

She looked at him as though he'd lost his senses. "London, sir?" she smiled. "Sweet Jesus, no. I've no business in London. Me Mum's here. Nothing for the likes of me in London."

He smiled at her protestations. "But no desire to see the sights?" he persisted.

"What sights?" she scoffed prettily, moving her bulky figure back through the arrangements of tables and chairs, apparently drawn into the conversation in spite of herself. "I've all the sights I care to see around here, sir," she stated with admirable confidence. "I feel best with little things, I do, if you know what I mean, sir."

Edward listened closely for two reasons: one, the girl's quiet and self-assured wisdom, and two, at some point they had been joined by a third. Edward could just see him over her bulky shoulder, the sharp features and ferret eyes of Mr. Humphrey Hills.

Mr. Hills spoke, sent his cold voice across the width of the dining hall in the sharpest of reprimands.

"Elizabeth!"

Then he was upon her, jerking her about and delivering a stinging blow to the side of her face.

As the girl reeled backward with a soft cry, Edward was on his feet. "You have no right, sir," he objected strongly. "The fault was mine. I invited her to speak."

But Hills said nothing. He followed the physical assault with a verbal one, literally driving the girl back toward the kitchen stairs, warning her that if ever again he caught her speaking to the guests, she would pay.

The girl was weeping now, still holding her injured face, and as she drew near the stairs, she bobbed her head and promised to be a good girl. Then she was gone.

Still standing before the table, Edward felt incredible anger. He considered pursuing the man and giving him the same treatment he had given to the girl. But it would have accomplished nothing, indeed would have closed the man's lips to him forever. Slowly now Edward returned to his chair, keeping a close watch on the man still looking down the kitchen stairs.

Then he was walking toward Edward, his hands behind his back, something in his attitude which suggested the harassed and overworked proprietor. "My deepest apologies, sir," he murmured, bowing his head. "I try very hard to maintain a quality establishment. For a staff I'm forced to rely on milk-maids and hay-girls, creatures more at home behind a plow than a tea service."

Still practicing self-restraint, Edward watched the manner in which the man curled his lips about each word, an affectation of speech which Edward found wholly repulsive. "I understand," Edward muttered. "Still, it was my fault. I coaxed her into speech and required her to stay. You should have delivered your blow to me. I was the offending party."

At that, the man became even more apologetic. "Never, sir," he pronounced with fervor. "You are my guest and, as such, incapable of causing offense."

My God, the man was both stupid and brutal. Again Edward smiled. "Even if I desire to engage a serving girl in conversation?"

Aware that he'd walked into his own trap, Mr. Hills gazed bewildered down on him. "I trust, sir, that for all her rudeness, the wench saw to your needs."

Edward nodded.

"And may I inquire," Hills went on, "did you sleep well? Again, with your forgiveness, you looked quite road-weary last evening."

"The chamber was comfortable."

Still fingering the back of the chair as though hungry for an invitation to sit, Hills smiled. "Have you been abroad long, sir?"

"Forever, sir, or so it seems."

Then all at once, Edward issued a brusque invitation. "Well, sit, man. Don't just hover. If you are the true owner of this place, see if you can produce coffee for us."

Edward saw a blush spread over the man's features, heard his command for coffee aimed at another serving girl who was lurking near the end of the hall. That done, he quickly slid into the chair opposite Edward, as though fearful that the invitation would be withdrawn.

Edward watched with quiet amusement as the girl deposited a coffee tray on the table between them, continued to watch as Hills waved her brusquely away and took over the serving duties himself.

The cups filled, it was Edward's turn again. "You run a comfortable inn, sir," he commented blandly. "Indeed, last evening your beacon appeared to us as a light from heaven."

The little man beamed. "It was a fierce storm, sir. Winter's worst thus far, a terrible night to be abroad—" He paused, then added, cunningly, "That is, if one had a choice."

All at once, Edward was aware that their purposes were identical, each seeking information. Now, in his most generous gift of all, he extended his hand across the table. "Edward Eden," he pronounced, "from London."

Hills responded admirably. "My pleasure, sir," and took Edward's hand.

In an attempt to clear the preliminary stalking, Edward went on. "It was my misfortune last year," he began, in storyteller fashion, "to suffer an illness, a palpitating heart," he smiled innocently. "At least that's what my physician called it. And when I'd recovered sufficiently, the blasted man prescribed a journey, a leisurely excursion, as he put it, down England's country lanes." Again Edward sipped at the coffee. "So here I am," he concluded, "on an odyssey designed to cure, but which at times has threatened to kill."

He gave a brief laugh and saw to his amazement what appeared to be genuine compassion in the man's eyes. "Well, I assure you a safe and healthy visit here, sir, and the hospitality of my inn as long as you require it."

Edward bobbed his head. "I'm most grateful."

For a moment both men sipped their coffee, eyeing each other over the rims of the cups.

In an attempt to bring the true subject closer to hand, Edward glanced out of the window at Hadley Park sitting across the road. "Tell me something of your neighbors, if you will, Mr. Hills," he suggested softly. "As long as I'm forced to make this blasted journey, I've at least tried to learn something of our country while I'm about it. If I understand correctly, Mr. Hills, you could in every sense of the word be considered native to these parts?"

"Oh yes, indeed, Mr. Eden. And my father before me and his father before him, on and on back to the beginning."

"Continuity," Edward murmured, assuming an admiring expression.

"Continuity," Hills nodded, "as good and as lasting, I might add, as thems across the road."

Edward peered at him, his mind responding to several points. For one, the mention of the estate across the road, and for another, the grammatical slippage, which perhaps indicated both involvement and knowledge. The opportunity was too great not to take advantage of it. "I have little use and less respect," Edward commented quietly, "for our noble peers. The world seems to crown them so effortlessly. For example, how many good men, like yourself, can boast a continuity of ancestry? Yet what does it gain you?

"Look at that," and the direction of his vision was clear, still focusing on the great estate, the enormous columns marching grandly from pavilion to pavilion. "Is such a structure really necessary merely to house flesh and blood? I've seen so much of want and need on this journey, Mr. Hills. And then I see—that." Somberly he shook his head. "I fear that England must look to herself," he concluded, "or else the people will look for her and in time make their own tragic adjustments."

The words might have belonged to Daniel Spade. Yet the truth was Edward's. He *had* seen much on his journey and now he did indeed look with regret on the estate across the road.

It was while he was still struggling with the peculiar sensation of the mask becoming the face that he heard Hills speak, the man's voice as intense as his own. "That don't cover one particle of it, Mr. Eden," the man muttered. "I've lived in the shadow of the Powelses all my life. I've seen and heard things no decent man could believe. I've made it my business, I have, to know all about them, and still I don't understand why I sit here and they sit there."

Edward gazed at him with mixed feelings. How painful a childhood it must have been. Then feeling that the man was truly his, Edward leaned across the table. "Tell me about them, Mr. Hills," he invited quietly. "Tell me what you have made it your business to learn."

Hills seemed to assess both Edward and his question. "I don't generally talk so openly," he protested.

"What harm?" Edward lightly countered. "I'm a mere traveler. When I leave here, you'll never see me again, though I assure you that I shall pass the word to the members of my London club. A good number of them journey frequently to Wales. I assure you that upon my return to London, they shall know of the excellence of the Mermaid."

The man beamed. "I'm most grateful, sir." Then as though an unspoken bargain had been struck, he took a long gulp of the lukewarm coffee. "Well then, sir, let me tell you about the local 'arees-too-crats.'" He stretched the word, mispronounced, into an obscenity and to Edward's chagrin commenced, "From Wales they come, land robbers in 1387."

He'd not expected the man to go so far back, but apparently Hills thought it necessary as he talked on, non-stop, for almost half an hour.

"And now," the man concluded, having made his way up through the centuries.

Edward sat up, newly alert. "And now?" he urged.

Hills gazed at him with delight. "There's a daughter," he pronounced simply. "Only a daughter. I knew her, you know, sir," he announced, pride in his voice.

"Knew her?" Edward repeated. Why had the man used past tense? "Why do you say 'knew her'? Is she—dead?"

"Oh no, sir, not dead," Hills reassured him. The light in his eyes seemed to glitter fiercely. "A bit worse for wear, if you understand what I mean."

No. Edward didn't understand and said as much and instantly regretted the urgency in his voice. Hills looked over at him as though in surprise. Then to Edward's relief the man apparently mistook the urgency in his voice for a depth of emotion similar to his own. "Don't worry, sir," he commented wearily. "She's as good as dead, or will be when it's over."

Concern mounting, Edward shook his head. "When what's over? What are you talking about?"

"We played together, we did," he grinned. "Right out there." Hills stared in the direction of the road, a glaze over his eyes as though seeing more than winter's snow. "I'd be cutting weeds," he mused, "and here she'd come, riding down from that grand palace on her pony. Course, I was no more than a lad myself, but I thought her the most beautiful creature I'd ever seen."

Then without warning the mood changed, grew harsh as he pronounced, "She spoke first, sir, yes she did. She looked down on me from her high perch and said how hot it must be, me working like that."

Edward took full note of the man's expression, love stamped visibly there for just an instant, then followed rapidly by an incredible degree of hate. "Bitch," the man muttered. "Bitch!" he repeated. A full minute passed before he went on. "Then one day that fence you see now went up, on Lord Powels's orders and that same day, my father came upon me with a whip and—"

He could not go on.

When Edward thought the man would not speak again, he spoke, the look of hate spiraling upward. "Do you believe in divine justice, sir?"

The direct question caught Edward off guard. He did well to nod.

"And I, too," beamed Hills, "for that pretty piece that caused me such grief has come to a sad end," he announced triumphantly.

"How so?" Edward inquired, lowering his hands beneath the table to hide their shaking.

"How so?" parroted Hills. He leaned yet closer. "You wouldn't believe the stories coming out of that place," he grinned. "Some say she's gone abroad. To which I say hell! Some say she's fallen seriously ill. To which I say hell! *I* know the truth of the situation, sir. Humphrey Hills knows. Humphrey Hills made it his business to know."

"And—what is the truth?" Edward prodded.

Incongruously the man snickered and immediately clamped both hands over his mouth as though someone were listening. With a jerk of his head he motioned for Edward to come closer. "You see that fourth-floor window there, sir?" and he indicated the estate across the road. "Near the east end, sir."

Edward found it and looked back at the man.

"Well, behind that there window is an attic storeroom, not fittin' for the grand lady who rode little ponies, now would you think, sir?"

The question required no answer and Edward gave none.

"Well, in that attic storeroom, the grand lady has been confined for eight months," Hills concluded proudly, as though everything had been solved.

But the mystery instead of being solved merely became more complex. "Why?" Edward asked, sending his eyes once again in an inspection of the distant window.

"Why?" Hills exploded in a burst of laughter. "Cause the grand lady is still a maid, sir, that's why." The laughter continued, leaving rims of moisture about the man's eyes.

"Don't you see, sir? If you was father to a grand lady without benefit of husband, and one day you took notice of her swelling belly, now, I ask you, sir, what would you do under those circumstances?" As Hills roared back in his chair, Edward stared, his eyes fixed on the demented features.

"Oh good Lord, sir," Hills gasped, holding his sides. "With all due apology, sleep must still be coating your brain." Again he leaned closer. "She's done opened her legs to some rascal, sir, and that someone left a growing seed and the Powels line has produced a rosy-cheeked bastard."

Edward rested his head in his hands and obscured his face.

"Are you well, sir?" Hills earnestly inquired.

Edward nodded and tried to make of his face a disinterested blank. "Are you—certain of this information, Hills?" he demanded, lifting his eyes.

Hills beamed. "I only just received word this morning that the bastard arrived late last night, a squawking, common brat, or so I was told."

A feeling such as Edward had never known before rose up within him. Memories passed through his mind of a green glen, of a tender, rare love. He found now that he could not look at the man. "And what—is to become of the—child?"

Then all at once the fountain of information dried up. In the peculiar silence, Edward lifted his head and saw Hills stand up from his crouched position at table, his face suddenly on guard. "Don't rightly know, sir," he concluded, moving away. "It occurs I've said enough. I've business to attend to, sir, so if you'll excuse me." And at last he turned and moved hastily across the room, his boots sending back hollow reverberations as they struck the stone floor.

Silence, though inside Edward's pounding head he heard one word.

Son. A very real possibility.

When in the next moment, he discounted the word, it came again.

Son. A probability.

His eyes, as though they possessed wills of their own, moved back to the high fourth-floor window of the estate.

Suddenly he stood up with such force that the chair clattered backward.

His son?

His brain felt battered. He had purposefully sought and received specific information. Now, dear God, what was he to do with it? If it was his son— And what of her? She would not abandon her own flesh. Yet neither could she enter into marriage with James with a bastard son in her arms. To write to her, that he must do immediately, to tell her that he knew. No, that was impossible. To tell her that her long and painful deception had been in vain, that was also impossible.

Still he stood by the window, the room behind him silent. There was no alternative left to him but to write. May she forgive him for his part and forgive herself as well.

When he finished his letter, the gray afternoon was half over. Wearily he left the bureau over which he had crouched for the better part of the day, the rejected wads of papers scattered about his feet. He had at last successfully composed one page, begging her forgiveness, requesting an audience so that together they might discuss the future of their son.

He still could not believe it and now took his disbelief to the window. Above the late afternoon horizon, above that dim yellow light burning in the fourth-floor window, a cold moon was rising. It was strange, he thought, the awesome juxtaposition of death and birth.

She should have told him. He had a right to know. How she must have suffered. Was suffering now.

His eyes closed. The hand that grasped the letter shook.

It was well past midnight. John Murrey was curled up before the dying fire in the dining hall. Gawd! What were they doing in this place? And when would Mr. Eden come to his senses and give John orders to make for London? Well, no matter. Long ago John had given up ever understanding his master. He loved him, to be sure, and if he ever asked for his right arm, John would joyfully give it. So, love and loyalty were there, but understanding? Never!

Abruptly John sat up, annoyed by his inability to get comfortable. As well as he could determine, he needed another chair or better just settle on the floor. It was the cold John hated. Gawd, but he hated the cold, had ever since that bleak winter of '28 when cold had taken everything in Tunbridge Wells, his crops, his livestock, his two pretty babes, his wife—

Half-raised in a sitting position, the old man held still, gazing hollow-eyed into the fire. Moving slowly, he left the chairs, dragging his cloak after him, and settled onto the floor directly before the fire, his thoughts filled with the past.

He'd had to wait until spring to bury them, had had to pass the rest of winter knowing what lay inside the three crude coffins in the wood shed. He'd had to fight off the small foraging animals to keep them from feeding on the carcasses and with the first thaw in April, he had dug three holes and had single-handedly dragged each coffin forward and lowered it into the ground. Then taking only the clothes he wore on his back, he'd left that place of grief and had walked to London, where he'd not expected to find life any easier. But at least, if the living wasn't easier, the dying might be. And there it was that the Prince of Eden had found him beneath the bridge, more skeleton than man.

Slowly John Murrey cast a searching eye up the length of the massive stone fireplace, as though even now, years later, seeking an explanation for why he'd bothered. What was John Murrey's life or death to him?

He sighed heavily and lay upon his side, his head cradled on one arm. The sound of wind outside the windows floated to him from afar. The entire inn was asleep, everyone but him. Perhaps in the morning, Mr. Eden would see the hopelessness of his position, his young lady locked behind iron gates, and even if she were not, she was betrothed to his brother. John must teach Mr. Eden the lesson that he himself had learned many years ago, that it served no purpose for a man to remain in a vicinity of pain.

On that note of resolve, he turned about a final time upon the hard floor, drew his cloak beneath his chin, and closed his eyes. In the twilight sleep between consciousness and unconsciousness, John thought he heard voices.

Quietly he turned his head and gazed through the forest of chair and table legs toward the entrance hall, dimly lit by two fixed lamps burning low. Between and around these obstacles he saw what appeared to be a woman's skirts. And standing opposite her, he saw the hem of a man's dressing robe.

Feeling annoyed and shivering, he raised quietly up and peered through the chairs for a better look. He might have known. It was the proprietor, Humphrey Hills.

Stirred to interest and enjoying his position of concealment, John Murrey leaned closer in examination of the female skirt, voluminous, belonging to a large woman, severely dressed in black as though for traveling. She was saying something to Hills, but John couldn't recognize one word. A foreign tongue.

Now John noticed Hills withdraw from the pocket of his dressing gown what looked like a sizable envelope. As he placed it in the gloved hand the old foreign woman smiled for the first time.

Still in hiding behind his fortress of chairs, John saw the woman stoop down and retrieve what appeared to be a large bread basket, a covering over the top, and hand it to Hills. The man received it warmly and seemed to be aware of nothing but the basket itself, uncommon interest, or so John thought, for a simple bread basket.

What a topsy-turvey place, with deliveries made at all hours of the day and night by foreigners dressed in black who lacked the good sense to speak the King's English. While he was musing thus, John looked up and to his surprise saw the woman gone. He felt a new icy blast rush across the floor as he heard the front door open, then close.

Shivering from the new blast of cold air, John might have slipped back to his place beside the fire, but at that moment a most bewildering occurrence took place in the hall. He saw that Mr. Hills had removed the covering from the top of the bread basket and was now cursing the loaves of bread, *cursing* them, "bastard." "Bastard" to loaves of bread?

John held motionless behind his chair fortress. Then he saw Hills return the covering and hurry off down the hall, moving rapidly in the direction of the kitchen staircase which led down to the rooms beneath the inn. Strange! A most strange place, John brooded.

Insomnia was a general plague that night in the Mermaid. The serving girl, Elizabeth, freezing in her narrow cot at the far end of the servants' quarters, was wide awake. Never had she been so humiliated and she intended never to be so humiliated again.

Now as she lay under the thin coverlet, her teeth chattering, she was aware of a small revolution brewing inside her head. One hand moved slowly up and touched her bruised cheek where that morning Mr. Hills had struck her. No, she would not take it any longer, although she knew what she was, a bondager, a bound woman, in Mr. Hills's employ as partial payment for her mother's debts. Her wages were one shilling a week, paid not to her, but the amount simply entered in Mr. Hills's big black ledger. In exchange for this she worked eighteen hours every day, from sunup to well after dark. Earlier that day, still smarting from Mr. Hills's blow, she had figured up that, at one shilling a week plus interest, she would be eighty-seven years old when she'd successfully paid off her mother's debt to Hills.

Staring upward at the low black ceiling, she felt an impulse to cry, but there were no tears left. She glanced about at the other sleeping females; all bondagers, from the youngest to the oldest. If she was going to do it, now was the time. The night was dark, the inn silent. If she ran all the way, she could be in Shrewsbury before dawn. There she would gather up her mother and put her in the back of the old goat cart and with Elizabeth herself pulling the yoke, perhaps they could make it to the Welsh border before Mr. Hills set pursuit after her.

Then do it! Stealthily she left the bed, taking care not to disturb those sleeping about her. She dressed hurriedly, pulling her black serving dress over her nightshirt for additional warmth. Beneath the cot, wrapped in a neat bundle, she found her shawl and the worn cloak that she'd arrived with.

In a quiet way, she said her goodbyes and moved silently down the row of cots, pausing before the door which led out into the central corridor. Here she stopped and made a quick decision to take the servants' exit.

As she reached the end of the first passage, she felt a dizziness sweep over her as though at her own daring. Where would dawn find her? Frozen beside the road? It was God's choice. She would abide by it.

Partially restored, she started forward again to the left, the narrow passage which led deeper into the subcellar.

No, not that direction. To the right, to the wooden steps and the door beyond.

Keep your wits about you.

As she was in the process of reversing her steps, she heard something. She held still, thinking perhaps that someone had already discovered her absence and had come in search of her. In fear she waited, trying to hear the sound again.

There it was! Listen! Coming from the direction of the lower cellar. But what? She turned suddenly and looked over her shoulder down the narrow steps which led to the subcellar. At the far end of the passage she saw a faint spill of light. There was the sound again, coming from that direction, a whimper, like a—

Baby.

It sounded like a babe crying. No, she was only imagining it. There was no infant here and God help it if there were. But as she pushed away from the wall, she heard it again, so clearly it could not be denied.

On this lower level there was no mistaking the sound. It *was* an infant.

Before the door she stopped, the cries so close now. Then she must help it. But as her hand moved to push open the door, instinct warned her back and she went quietly down on her knees and leveled her eye against the keyhole. An instant later, she clamped both hands over her mouth to keep from screaming aloud.

Hell's Face, that's what she'd looked into, the tiny circular hole permitting her to see a sight she wished most fervently she'd never seen, the man, Satan himself, Humphrey Hills standing before a table, and on the table, a red, naked, newborn infant, its tiny limbs flailing in the air as the madman's hand, so large that it covered the entire small body, tried to hold it still so that the other hand, grasping a knife point, might cut something across the small heaving chest.

She rose, trembling, on legs which threatened not to support her, convinced that she was back on her cot, dreaming a hideous nightmare. The infant's wails were rising higher as the knife point moved back and forth across its chest. Great God in heaven, why didn't he simply kill it?

Then suddenly she was running, her own safety secondary to the need to fetch help. It must be stopped while there was still time, and she must stop it. *Help.* She merely thought the word at first as she ran back down through the dark passage, past the servants' hall.

Then the word came out at last, a full cry, "Help!" Then came again, louder, "Help!" and yet again, tears streaming down her face as she found she could not rid her memory of that awful sight.

At the top of the stairs, she stopped for breath and drew back as she saw, emerging from the dining hall, the cadaverous old man who traveled with the gentleman. As he approached her, his face alert with concern, she discovered to her dismay that she could not at first speak.

But as the old man drew even with her and kindly offered her the support of his arm, she whispered hoarsely, "Fetch your master, please." And when at first the old man failed to understand, she said it again and then pushed past him to accomplish the errand herself.

"Wait," he shouted after her. "I'll go," and in a dead heat the two of them reached the bottom of the stairs simultaneously and were just starting up when from the top of the steps, she heard a deep familiar voice.

"What is it, John?"

She looked up to see him, the gentleman himself, just wrapping his dressing robe around him where apparently he'd been abed when he'd heard her cries. "What is it, Elizabeth?" he demanded.

She shook her head, not wanting to speak aloud the horror she had seen. Instead she pronounced only one word, "Baby—" and reached out and grasped his hand and started dragging him forward. "Hurry, sir," she begged. "Please hurry."

Then the three of them were retracing her steps, Elizabeth leading the way.

When they approached the narrow flight of stairs leading down to the subcellar, Elizabeth found herself incapable of thinking anymore. Her own escape had long since been forgotten. She stood back as the gentleman approached the door, tried the knob, and finding it locked, hurled himself against the wooden barrier, splintered the wood, and thus gained access to the room.

Standing safely outside the door, at first she heard nothing as it took him time to digest the horror. Then she heard a muttered oath and stepped to the door in time to see the gentleman lunge toward Hills, the little man's face a blank in the instant before the assault. Then under the blow delivered by the gentleman's fist she saw him reel backward into a stack of cartons, saw him sprawled, stunned, though reviving quickly, the knife still in his hand, stumbling to his feet again.

At that moment, the old man shouted at her, "Take the child!" and as she summoned herself out of her fear, she rushed forward and grabbed the infant, her eyes lingering for a moment on the tiny chest, a mass of bleeding cuts, the child's face red with the exertion of screaming, its eyes closed.

As the two men stalked each other, she quickly grasped the infant and ran with it from the room and hovered in the corridor outside, keeping her eyes pinned now on the knife, upraised in Mr. Hills's hand.

Then in a darting movement, Hills lunged forward. In a rapid reflexive action, the gentleman caught his upraised arm and smashed it against the table, then pinned it, shaking the knife loose, disarming the man and bringing him to his knees. The hatred on the detestable features now turned to cowardice as Hills pleaded, "No harm, sir. It's just the bastard—the one we was speaking of this morning—"

But the words, instead of pacifying the gentleman, seemed to bring him to greater fury. His hands were around the man's throat now, the entire weight of his body angled downward into those fingers as though he had no intention of letting go until all possible life had been squeezed out.

From where she stood in the passage with the whimpering infant, Elizabeth was unable to see Hills's face, blocked as it was by the gentleman himself. All she heard was a peculiar gurgling sound. Her next thought was, He's going to kill him. But the old man stepped quickly forward and placed a hand on the straining shoulders. She saw the gentleman look up as though just coming to his senses, then she saw him let Hills go.

She stepped to one side to see if the man was dead, then saw him groan, both his hands clasping his neck, his knees drawn up to his chest. She found the sight pleasing, God forgive her, the vicious little man who had inflicted so much pain now rolling about in the throes of agony himself.

During these few moments she noticed that the gentleman had found several pieces of rope and, with the old man's help, was tying Hills's hands behind his back and binding his ankles.

In a remarkably short time, Hills lay bound on the floor, his eyes searching upward, terrified, as though uncertain what would be done to him next. But apparently nothing more would be done. The two men drew away from him back to the door. The old man asked, "What shall we do?"

"Leave him," the gentleman cut in sharply. "Come, we must hurry."

Still grasping the infant, Elizabeth was aware of the gentleman guiding her back down the passage as though to assist her with her light burden. As they approached the servants' door, she saw several of her friends peering in concern at the activity in the corridor. The gentleman warned them quietly, "None of you are to go down to the cellar until dawn. Is that clear?"

Elizabeth saw them nod.

"No matter what you hear," he added, "you are not to go down. Promise me."

The girls nodded again, too frightened to do otherwise. Then she felt his hand again on her arm, steering her rapidly toward the steps, his tongue keeping pace with their steps as he issued a spate of orders to the old man. "Bring the carriage around, John, as quickly as possible. We're leaving here immediately. I'll pack the trunks and meet you out front. Hurry now!"

The gentleman saw him out the front door, then at last turned back to Elizabeth.

"Is he—" But he couldn't finish, and it was clearly an inquiry she couldn't answer. There had been no time to assess the damage done to the child. "I don't know, sir," she murmured. She moved to the steps and sat carefully on the lower one, placed the blanket on her lap and laid it open.

Throughout all this he held his position a few feet away as though he didn't want to see. Then she was aware of him moving closer until he was seated on the steps beside her, both of them staring down at the incredibly tiny and mutilated chest, a small trickle of blood still oozing from the cuts, the infant naked, his eyes closed, his arms and legs jerking reflexively in spasms.

Starting above the right nipple and moving to the left,

marked in charcoal, were the letters, B-A-S-T-A-R-D. The knife point had cut the B into the flesh and one leg of A.

Overcome, Elizabeth lowered her head. At some point she was aware of him, quietly taking the infant from her. She looked up to see him awkwardly supporting the tiny back and head, saw tears in his eyes as he held the child.

"Why would Mr. Hills do something like this, sir?" she asked softly. "And where did he come from? He's newborn, scarce a day old. Look!" And she pointed to the cut and knotted cord of his navel, dried birth blood still encrusted about it.

But if he had answers for any of her questions, he was incapable of delivering them.

He sat thus for ever so long, as though every sense were straining to comprehend what lay silently in his arms. Finally he relinquished him to her with a whisper, "I must get our belongings."

Left in the hall, she rewrapped the infant in the soiled blanket and with the hem tried to dab at the cuts, the peculiar B clearly visible. He was so small, she thought. And what a cruel entrance into a crueler world.

As she clasped him to her in an attempt to warm him, she thought for the first time of her own ruined plans. What chance did she have now? She was not only a runaway bondager, but she knew for certain that Humphrey Hills had seen her below. Come dawn, the other servants would release him and he would come staggering up out of his fury and track her down no matter where she went. She looked bleakly about the cold hall, her sense of doom complete, and she was still sitting there half an hour later when outside the front door she heard the sound of horses.

A few moments later the old man appeared in the doorway, his face ruddy with cold. "Where is he?" he asked quickly, taking the entrance hall running.

With a bob of her head she motioned upstairs and continued to sit while everyone else rushed about her. The old man reappeared a moment later, one trunk balanced on his shoulder, dragging the other one behind, letting it fall from step to step. Grasping the infant to her, she stood up to get out of the way and as she was turning she saw the gentleman come down the steps, warmly dressed in his heavy cloak. Midway down the steps, he called out to her, "Where are your things? Bring them quickly to the carriage. We've not much time—"

Only then did it occur to her that he was willing to take her with him. For just a moment the prospect held enormous appeal. But then she remembered her mother in Shrewsbury, helpless, sure to receive Hills's wrath if there was no one else around to receive it.

And when still she didn't move, he called again, more urgently, "Hurry, Elizabeth. We must get out of here. All of us."

"I can't go with you, sir," she whispered.

He looked at first as though he hadn't heard her. "But you can't stay here."

"I don't mean to stay here, sir," she went on. "I was— running away when I heard the—" She lowered her eyes to the infant in her arms. "It was my plan to go to Shrewsbury and get my mother and try to make it to Wales before—"

He appeared to be listening closely. "And what is there for you in Wales?" he asked.

"A new life, one would hope."

"And you prefer that to London and my protection?"

He wasn't making it very easy for her. "London's not the place for me, sir, nor for my mother. She's old and lame. She needs soft grass and quiet air—"

Suddenly the infant in her arms grew restless. There was a soft whimper. "You take him, sir," she smiled. "Wherever he came from he deserves better than this. Give *him* your protection. He needs it more."

From the doorway, the old man shouted, "All's loaded and ready, sir. Dawn soon."

But the gentleman didn't even look up. Instead he was staring down on her as though trying to understand her. Finally he reached inside his jacket, withdrew his purse, and handed her some notes.

As she took them, her eyes fell on the denominations. Easily a hundred pounds, perhaps more. At first she couldn't believe it. More money than she'd ever seen in her entire life. "No, sir, I can't—"

"Of course you can, and must," he countered forcefully. "Can you sit a horse?"

She nodded and though still in a state of shock heard him shout to the old man to unhitch one of the horses.

One hundred pounds, Dear God in heaven, a new birth, enough for a small cottage, medicine for her mother, a nest egg while she found decent honest employment. Then again he was moving her toward the door and out into the cold night.

As the old man brought one of the horses around, the gentleman took the infant from her. "On the back of this card," he said quickly, handing her a small white square, "is my name and my London address. If you ever need anything, you know where to find me."

Still unable to speak, she nodded, tucked the valuable card inside her pocket along with the money, and permitted him to assist her up onto the horse. As he placed the reins in her hands, he warned, "Don't tarry. Be on the bridge to Wales by dawn. Please."

One hundred pounds! She must say something to him, some acknowledgment of his kindness and generosity. But there were no words. Instead she reached out her hand to him, her eyes filled with tears, and he took it and pressed it in a firm clasp.

She drew up the hood of her cloak and wrapped the reins about her wrist. Though a cold wind was blowing over her, she felt with a strange excitement that one bleak chapter of her life was ending and a new promising one was beginning.

Then the horse was moving. She stole a quick glance over her shoulder, saw the gentleman watching her.

Swiftly she said the Lord's Prayer to its end and made the sign of the cross upon her breast. A miracle, all of it. A nightmare which had changed into miracle. She urged the horse to greater speed.

It was God's hand, God made manifest in the gentleman. Two had been saved that night. The infant and herself.

She would never forget him, never, as long as she lived.

With regret, he watched the girl ride off into the night. She would have found a pleasant home in Daniel Spade's school. He couldn't imagine what lay ahead for her. Obviously the gift of money had pleased her. But was she shrewd enough to know how quickly and easily the world would try to separate her from it?

There was nothing more he could do. He whispered,

"God go with you," then at last was aware of John Murrey standing at his elbow, urging their own haste. "Time's passing for us as well," the old man said. "And himself there won't go forever without a tit full of milk, so—"

Edward looked up suddenly at the old man. That had not occurred to him. "My God, John, what are we—"

"Never you mind, sir," the man soothed. "If we can keep him warm, he'll sleep for a while. Soon as we put safe distance between us and this place, we'll stop and find a wet-nurse."

Edward agreed, reassured by the calm voice. Clutching the infant to him, they made their way back to the carriage where John Murrey opened the door. Edward stood a moment, awkwardly engaged in shifting the bundle, unable to free a hand in order to pull himself up. Again he glanced helplessly at John.

Without words, the infant was transferred from arm to arm, and Edward pulled himself up, then again looked bleakly down on John. "I'm afraid, my friend, that nothing in my life has prepared me for this moment."

Still holding the baby, John Murrey grinned with pride. "Nothing to it, sir. I assure you. I had two beauties of my own—once."

Edward saw the look of pride in the old man's face sink rapidly into gloom. Hurriedly he moved to dispel it. "Then I shall count heavily on you, John." His own smile faded. "As I always seem to do."

Embarrassed by Edward's show of emotion, John Murrey became very businesslike. "If I may make a suggestion, sir—"

"Please do."

"Unbutton your coat and shirtwaist and keep the child close to your flesh. He'll survive with the warmth there until we can stop later on."

Edward started to protest. But when he saw John Murrey crawling into the carriage to help with the placement of the child, he slowly began to unbutton his garments.

"Good," the old man smiled and Edward watched, fascinated, as the old man pulled off the soiled blanket and dropped it unceremoniously out the carriage door. The sudden exposure to the cold roused the child out of his half-sleep. The small mouth flew open at the indignities being forced upon him. Edward had not thought it possible that so shrill a shriek could come from so tiny a frame. And in the instant of the babe's complete nakedness, both men stared down on him, Edward's eyes lingering on the small chest, the word scratched in charcoal still visible, the cuts no longer bleeding, but still red.

John Murrey too seemed almost overcome. "You should have killed him," he muttered.

"I almost did," Edward commented ruefully. As the child's shrieks evolved into shivering spasms of cold, John Murrey lifted him and angled the small package of flesh down through the opening in Edward's shirt, affixing him in a cradled position, then quickly buttoning the shirt up around him, restoring the jacket and cloak and finally sealing both the infant and Edward inside one of the great fur lap robes.

"Won't he suffocate?" Edward asked in alarm, trying to adjust to the sensation of wriggling flesh next to his own.

"Not likely," John soothed, backing out the carriage door. "Keep his face lightly covered. Warmth is the important thing."

Edward felt the small but persistent limbs pushing against him. And there was a new and disquieting sensation now. "He—feels wet," Edward whispered.

At this John Murrey laughed heartily. "You'll survive, sir. Are we ready? We've wasted quite enough time—"

Edward had never felt less ready, but his old friend was right. Perhaps the infant himself was capable of sensing danger in this place. Seated rigidly on the seat, his arms, beneath the lap rug, laced firmly about the new protuberance on his chest, Edward nodded wearily and said over the child's muffled cries, "Take us home, John, as quickly as possible."

From inside the womb of his garments, he heard the infant crying. And as the carriage started forward, Edward looked quickly out the small window on his left to the silent outline of Hadley Park. His eyes moved quickly to the high fourth-floor window. It was dark now. Apparently her ordeal was over. And for one strange moment he felt his love for her diminish, become less an agony and more a source of quiet grief.

He couldn't bring himself to believe that she had willingly given her child away. Surely she had been coerced, threatened. Yet he now remembered her cold demeanor the night of the engagement banquet. How mercilessly hard she had been, how burdened with her insane sense of duty.

The carriage commenced a rhythmic rocking and this, with Edward's body heat, combined to soothe the infant, his cries not ceasing altogether, but merely whimpers now and soft strainings. Slowly, out of curiosity, Edward pulled back the layers of covering and stole a peak downward into the cavity beneath the lap rug. That small face was becoming silent, the eyes closed, the mouth turning hungrily toward Edward's chest as though in search of a breast.

"I'm sorry," Edward whispered. "I'm afraid I'm ill equipped." He lowered the covering a bit more and saw again the injured flesh of the chest, the word itself. Quickly he wet the tip of his finger and commenced to erase the charcoal brand. The child arched upward as though eager to give him access to his chest.

The charcoal was easily removed. Of a more lasting nature was the carved B, new glistenings of blood seeping out. Edward sat bowed before the sight, his hand, massive against the small chest, taking possession of it, caressing the uninjured side, his fingers cupping about the tiny head covered with a soft cap of blond fuzz.

Though the infant was relaxing under the intoxicating effects of warmth, suddenly he opened his dark blue eyes and seemed to peer up at Edward with an open, questioning look, as though he were inquiring if all passages into life were so difficult, and would it persist or diminish, and was it standard for words to be carved on the chests of new citizens of the world?

Such an honest look caused Edward to catch his breath and again he bowed his head over the small one and clutched the infant more firmly against his chest. He could neither account for nor apologize for the tears in his eyes. If there had been any doubts before, there were none now.

This was his son.

It was a difficult journey from Shropshire to London, a trip which under normal conditions could be speedily accomplished in three to five days.

But on this occasion the Eden carriage was not traveling

under normal conditions. At John Murrey's suggestion, they followed a rather circuitous route, making for the large settlements of Lichfield, Birmingham, Coventry, and Oxford, where their chances of finding wet-nurses would be greatly improved.

Eleven days later, on a crisp bright morning near the end of March, after they'd passed the night in the outlying settlement of Barnet, with his son clasped in his arms and dressed in plain muslin shirt and doubly wrapped in two small blankets, Edward glanced out the window and saw the first spires of London.

Home! The odyssey was over. Now he was returning, greatly changed, yet with the same sense of unidentifiable grief pressing down upon him.

So be it! He would live with it. He would respond to life about him as he had never responded before, for his own sake and for the sake of his son.

Slowly he lowered his son to his lap, luxuriating in the pink face, the bright blue eyes, the skin like angel's skin. Still nameless. He'd have to correct that as soon as possible. Not his own. One Edward Eden had been enough. And not his father's. Then what?

At that moment old John Murrey shouted down, the exuberance in his voice unmistakable. "Oxford Street ahead, sir."

Edward smiled. As if he didn't know, as if he too had not been counting off the intersections. *John Murrey.* What in God's name would Edward have done without him?

John Murrey!

A name as simple and direct as the man himself. He stared down into his son's face. "It would suit you," he murmured, "and serve you well. John Murrey Eden."

Suddenly without warning, his emotions took a glorious leap upward and he laughed outright and clasped the infant to him with such force that the child objected in a soft whimper, one tiny fist flailing uselessly against Edward's face.

With a smile, Edward opened his mouth and closed his lips around the infant's fingers. The wide blue eyes became suddenly grave at the disappearance of his hand, the funny expression causing Edward to laugh even harder, a spasm of mixed emotions, for himself, for his son, for merely every living creature who had both the fortune and the misfortune to inhabit this earth.

On this cold but sunny March morning, Daniel Spade stood at the second-floor window in the house on Oxford Street and looked down in anticipation at the crowds below and silently cursed what he'd done earlier that day.

There had been a time when the fight with life had fascinated him. He'd viewed it as little more than a game with a worthy adversary. Now? The game was taking a deadly toll.

What he had done that morning was what he had done every morning for the last six weeks: send a contingent of the older boys out onto the streets to thieve as best they could, to bring the bounty back to him for the purposes of feeding the other children.

Now thinking on the harsh straits into which necessity had forced him, Daniel suddenly brought his fist up against the side of the wall and struck a resounding blow which caused the window to vibrate. Great Heavens, what was he doing? It had been his intention to lift the children off the streets and turn their faces in another direction.

Compounding his distress was another factor, the sense that he'd been abandoned by his friend. Yet that thought too caused grief, for he was not Edward's responsibility. As Feargus O'Conner constantly pointed out to him, "We won't be wanting nothing of the upper class. When the battle lines are drawn, you'll be finding us on one side, them on the other."

Of course he was right. Edward's commitment had always been at best superficial. And in the last year the Movement had changed radically under Feargus O'Conner's wild and dominating leadership. No more were the Chartist meetings conducted in gentlemanly fashion, attended by men of moderation. Now with Feargus at the wheel, they were rabble-rousing and heated, the downstairs rooms echoing with shouts of revolution. Even the vocabulary had changed: all terms of warfare now, armies, weapons, plans of attack, battle lines.

In quiet moments like this, Daniel privately wondered how it would end. He stood perfectly still at the window. Once when he was younger, he'd had such visions for the world. But what he didn't know then and what he knew now in a hard way was that visions require money.

These thoughts did terrible damage to him and again he sank back into the chair. From where he sat he could just see the end of Oxford Street before its approach to Oxford Circus. From the top of the hill near Regent Street came the sound of church bells. Noon matins.

He saw the carriage while it was still a distance away and thought of its peculiar resemblance to Edward's. But this one was different, incredibly soiled and road-weary. Besides he was not looking for carriages. He was searching for those half-dozen youthful faces whom he'd sent out earlier that morning. Pray God for their safe return.

Still that carriage was coming closer, the driver, a hunched old man whose white frothy hair blew every which way in the brisk March wind. He looked cold, Daniel thought, as worn as—

Daniel blinked and stood slowly up. That old man. If only he'd lift his head. But those were not Edward's horses. He'd never seen those—

In that instant the old man did lift his head, those familiar features clear and unmistakable—

John Murrey! My God, it was—

As the carriage drew to a halt directly before the house, Daniel continued to watch. Perhaps only John Murrey had returned. Perhaps Edward had elected to remain at Eden. Then all at once he saw something, a boot, a gray-clad leg, a shoulder, a twisted cloak. Then—oh God, a fair head, the hair mussed and unkempt, but instantly recognizable—

Edward!

Then Daniel was running, taking the stairs downward two at a time, encountering three volunteers on the steps who flattened themselves against the wall.

On the front steps he stopped, his eyes fixed on one scarcely recognizable man. Daniel's first impulse was to give a cry of alarm at the sight of his friend. He'd never dreamt such change was possible. It *was* Edward, that much was true, but an Edward he'd never seen before, an Edward who stood beside the carriage, returning his gaze, a gaunt, wasted Edward with the look of age and total exhaustion in his face.

Then Daniel was moving, his arms opened, and as he

drew close enough to see tears on his friend's face, he enclosed him in his arms. For several moments, the embrace held. Finally it was Edward who spoke first. He pulled free of Daniel's embrace and said two words, "I'm home."

Daniel nodded as though to confirm the fact.

At that moment John Murrey joined them, his own worn features slightly damp from the emotion of the reunion. "I told you I'd bring him safely back, sir," the old man grinned.

The note of pride in the old man's face was unmistakable, and Daniel encouraged it. "I'm everlastingly grateful, John. I couldn't have entrusted him to more capable hands."

Behind him now he heard a single footstep and turned to see Elizabeth approaching. Never had he seen those young features so radiant. Daniel smiled. "I told you he'd return, didn't I?"

As the girl ducked her head in modesty, Daniel noticed Edward's face. Apparently he'd failed to recognize her.

"It's Elizabeth," he whispered. "She, more than anyone else, has kept a constant vigil for your return."

Still Edward continued to stare down on her, as though disbelieving. "Elizabeth?" he repeated slowly.

"It's me, sir," she smiled. "I was so worried, but I prayed nightly and sometimes of a morning as well."

The avowal of faith seemed to have a strange effect on Edward. Then at last Daniel came to his senses. "My God," he exclaimed in a burst of energy. "There's no need for us to stand about on the pavement. Let's go inside. You must be weary and I long to hear—"

But as he reached for Edward's arm, the man drew away, clung for a moment to the carriage door, and on diminished breath announced, "I'm afraid I'm not traveling alone."

Mystified, Daniel watched as Edward crawled back into the carriage. A moment later he emerged, a small, blanketed bundle in his arms.

Elizabeth gasped. "It's a babe," and she leaned close over the tiny face, its eyes opening sleepily, then squinting shut at the bright sunlight on the pavement.

Daniel could only gape and wait for Edward's explanation.

And when he seemed disinclined to offer any explanation, Daniel smiled. "And when did you go shopping for that one?" he said, trying to lighten the moment.

But Edward continued to focus on the infant. Elizabeth was clearly beside herself as she hopped this way and that, on tiptoe, trying to get a better look. Finally she found the courage to ask softly, "Might I hold him, sir? It looks newborn, scarce—"

"He," Edward corrected her gently. "And he's two weeks, or there about—"

Daniel noticed Edward hesitate a moment, as though reluctant to relinquish his hold on the baby. Finally he eased the bundle from his arms down in Elizabeth's. She adjusted the small weight and smiled up at both of them. "He's so tiny," she whispered.

Then, the grin still on her face, she turned back toward the steps and approached the waiting volunteers in the spirit of one who has just been awarded a priceless prize.

Within the instant the females closed in around her, all their attention drawn to the infant, a cooing, clucking chorus as they gave her solid escort through the door and into the house. At that moment old John Murrey busied himself with the trunks atop the carriage and Daniel and Edward were left alone on the pavement.

Bewildered by everything he had seen, Daniel did well to shake his head. His first inclination was to question Edward at length about everything. But not here.

"Come, Edward," he urged softly, trying to lead him toward the door.

But still Edward held back, a look of amusement softening the fatigue on his face. "No questions, Daniel?" he smiled.

"Approximately a round thousand," Daniel grinned, "but not now. I'll fetch you hot water. Perhaps Cook has saved a tea leaf or two."

Edward spoke quietly. "I've brought you your youngest student, Daniel. I want you to fill his head with everything that is in yours, and fill his heart as well, and make him in your own image."

Daniel laughed. "Quite an order, I'd say."

At the top of the stairs, Edward turned to him, his face sober. "Will you do it?"

Daniel nodded quickly. "Of course I will. You know that. May I ask," Daniel continued quietly, "why your in-

terest in this particular child? If you wish I can find you
hundreds just like him, in need, with no—"

"He's my son."

Daniel blinked. "Your—"

At that moment, coming from the pavement behind
them, Daniel heard his name being shouted and looked
quickly over his shoulder to see his six young thieves
racing pell-mell through the crowded pavement.

"We done it, sir," one of the lads cried, racing up the
steps between them, dragging a heavy gunnysack behind
him.

Caught for the moment between Edward's incredible announcement and the apparently profitable excursion of
the young boys, Daniel foundered. In spite of his confusion, he counted the young culprits as they raced past them,
six in all, all safely returned. Thank God.

Inside the entrance hall, the boys proudly displayed
their stolen goods, a sack filled with potatoes, loaves of
bread, and a pocket purse containing three pounds. A few
of the volunteers hovered excitedly about, picking up the
potatoes as they rolled about on the floor.

In the excitement of the moment, Daniel forgot about
Edward. Now he looked up to see him standing in the
door, a shocked expression on his face as he demanded of
the boys, "Where did you get these things?" indicating the
loot.

The young boys drew back at the tone in Edward's
voice. One boy stammered, "It was a spilled wagon, sir,
up on Great Portland Street. We was just—"

Daniel stepped forward. "I sent them," he said, his
voice low. "We have survived for several weeks on the
fruits of their labor. And we shall eat tonight because of
their efforts." He paused. "You as well, Edward," he
concluded.

Daniel no longer felt pleasure at Edward's shocked look.
As boys, they had held nothing back, had had no secrets.
In this frame of mind, he walked to Edward and took his
arm. "Come," he suggested. "We both have stories to tell."

As they approached the stairs leading to the second-floor
chambers, Daniel felt himself warming again to the reunion. "And how did you find Eden?" he asked.

But Edward didn't respond, indeed seemed incapable of

response as though all of his energy were being channeled into the ascent up the stairs.

Who was the man laboring up the stairs beside him, who had arrived after a ten-month absence with a newborn babe in his arms whom he claimed was his son, who had looked with such clear condemnation upon stolen goods, this rich man—

But there were no ready answers, and Daniel was forced to wait, his immense love for the enigmatic man washing over him in secret sorrow.

Little did Edward know that potatoes stolen that morning at the top of Great Portland Street would be feeding him that evening. Yet there was the truth before him, in that bowl of watery potato soup resting on the crate which served as his desk.

Angrily he turned toward Daniel with the question which he'd asked in dizzying repetition throughout that long afternoon of talk. "And Sir Claudius Potter? You tried to contact him?"

And in similar repetition, Daniel nodded and repeated himself. "I tried," he muttered. "In the beginning he at least granted me an audience, if nothing else. Then about three months ago, he closed his door to me completely."

In a strict act of discipline, Edward reined in his anger. Behind him, near the fireplace, he saw Elizabeth, the baby in her arms, as he'd been all day with the exception of those times when she'd had to surrender him to the wet-nurse. A cousin of the cooks' had been found, a young woman who'd recently given birth to a dead baby. With red eyes and full breasts she'd fed the infant and had promised to stay as long as she was needed.

At that moment Elizabeth looked up at him. Those sober features relaxed into a gentle smile as though to reassure him that all was well. He turned quickly back to the up-turned crate where the bowl of watery potato soup greeted his eyes.

Somehow an apology seemed in order and Edward offered one. "I'm sorry, Daniel," he repeated again. "I had no idea."

Daniel smiled. "I tried to write," he said. "I thought you had elected to stay at Eden. I had no way of knowing you were in the Midlands, pursuing your own dream."

"Nightmare, more accurately," Edward muttered.

"Sometimes the one tends to resemble the other. They are easily mistaken."

Edward nodded. Then as though weary of the inactivity in the room, he commenced pacing. "First thing in the morning," he announced, "I'll go see Sir Claudius. The man had better have a suitable explanation."

"Don't be too hard on him," Daniel suggested quietly. "Perhaps he was simply looking out for your interests."

"My interests?" Edward parroted angrily. "My interests are your interests. He should know that by now."

Daniel looked up at him. "Are they, Edward?"

Edward heard the question and understood the doubt in his friend's face. "Perhaps once, no," he admitted. "But now, yes." He stood before Daniel. "My journey was not without benefit," he began quietly. "I would like to work alongside you."

In an attempt to lighten the mood which he himself had spun, he smiled. "I have an interest in the future now. You have the ideas," he added, pleased with Daniel's expression of hope. "And I have the money. Let's take the world by the corners and shake it a few times, and see if we can't make things come out better than before."

Daniel shook his head, as though still not believing Edward's words. "There is—so much to be done."

"And we'll do it," Edward vowed. "I promise. We'll establish Ragged Schools all over London. We'll buy additional property and staff them properly, and see to all their needs." Never had he seen such a gratifying glow on Daniel's face. "We'll have street kitchens, capable of dispensing meals, we'll establish funds for the old, for the widowed, for the ill—"

Suddenly, as though unable to absorb the torrent of words, Daniel followed after him, interrupting, "You must meet Feargus O'Conner, Edward. He's—"

"I'll meet anyone," Edward agreed, "anyone who shares our plans." He'd never felt such excitement, although in truth he'd given no thought to what he was saying. The words had simply emerged, ideas fully born.

Abruptly he stopped at mid-room. He had no idea who that other man had been, or where he had gone to, that selfish, self-indulgent man. Dear God, his future, his purpose had been here all along. It was so simple. Why had he not seen it before?

At some point he was aware of a concerned voice at his elbow. "Are you well, Edward? You look—"

"I've never been better, Daniel," he said. "A new dawn, I swear it," he added.

The quiet declaration had a profound effect upon Daniel. "Then I won't have to close the school?" he asked.

"Close it?" Edward exclaimed. "Indeed not. By the end of the month, it shall be the model on which we shall pattern the others."

With effort Daniel stepped away. "Then I shall go and inform the volunteers."

Edward watched him to the door and was still watching when he turned back with a last question. "Will you work within the Movement, Edward?"

"Why not?"

"It's considered radical."

"Radical means are called for."

"You're an Eden."

Edward smiled. "A bastard Eden. Only now do I realize the tremendous freedom that designation gives me."

There was a moment's pause. Then the door opened. A faint light caught his friend's features and from that distance, Edward saw the look of hope.

"Sleep well, Daniel," Edward called after him. "We will commence tomorrow."

Daniel nodded and closed the door behind him, leaving Edward alone with the silence, the flickering firelight casting soft shadows over Elizabeth and the baby.

He glanced in that direction, saw the love in her eyes as she kissed the tiny hand.

Was that the miracle?

Abruptly he realized that for the first time in his life, he felt truly like a rich man. The hot wind had raged itself out; its howl went silent within him. The long-deafened soul could now hear.

At ten o'clock the following morning, Sir Claudius Potter sat behind his mahogany desk and looked up into a ghost face.

My God, it *was* him. In an effort to regain his aplomb, Sir Claudius leaned back in his chair. In this position of ease, he was able to assess his mid-morning caller who had just burst in, unannounced, and who now stood before him, changed in all aspects from dark encircling hollows about his eyes to the slightly bent back, head inclined, as though strength were limited.

Sir Claudius had seen such faces before in the opium addicts who had come up before the court in Old Bailey. A terrifying thought occurred to Sir Claudius. Was the man drugged now? "Edward?" he began, as though he needed help with the identification.

The man bowed slightly. "My deepest apologies, Sir Claudius," he smiled, "for coming upon you like this."

Polite enough, Sir Claudius thought. Still on guard, Sir Claudius invited, "Well, do sit down, Edward. I must confess you were the last person I expected to see this morning."

"Why?"

Sir Claudius laughed. "According to my last reports, you've been among the missing for several months."

"And whose reports would those be?" Edward asked, seating himself at last.

"From Eden, of course," he replied lightly.

But the man was relentless. "From whom at Eden?" he asked.

The clock was ticking on the mantel across the room. "From just—everyone," Sir Claudius safely replied, his eye falling on the last letter from Sophia Cranford, delivered only a few days ago.

With his eyes down he inquired softly, "Have you heard of the distressful illness of your dear mother?"

"I've heard," Edward said. "I've had no recent word. I'd be most appreciative if you'd share it."

Quickly Sir Claudius shook his head. "I know little. She's confined to her bed. Apparently it was a seizure of some sort. She has difficulty in speaking. Her sister is there and a great comfort."

"And what else did Sophia say?" Edward inquired bluntly.

Sir Claudius felt a hot blush creep up the sides of his neck. "Yes, I receive all my news from Sophia Cranford. Apparently her hand is the only one at Eden capable of holding a pen."

Edward smiled. "Sophia Cranford will be capable of

holding a pen on Doomsday, Sir Claudius. She is God's great example of a woman with steady nerves."

Sir Claudius felt a surge of anger. "I wouldn't malign her if I were you," he snapped. "She's holding your house together for you, under most difficult circumstances."

Again Edward smiled. "Beware the servant who creates a climate of total dependency." He laughed outright now and shifted in the chair. "You bring out the best in me, Sir Claudius. I've never quoted my father on any subject, but those words are his, not mine."

"And true," Sir Claudius agreed, "though in this case I don't think they apply."

For a moment both men retreated into silence as though aware of the stalemate. Then Edward spoke first, relaxing into the chair. "And James?" he inquired. "What's he up to?"

"Distraught," Sir Claudius replied. "The year has been doubly tragic for him. His intended, the young Lady Powels, has been stricken with a mysterious illness. He's journeyed twice to Hadley Park in an attempt to see her and twice he has been denied an audience."

"Tell him to try a third time," Edward commented softly.

"I beg your pardon?"

But he merely shook his head and rose abruptly from his slumped position. "I'm grateful for this information, Sir Claudius. But for now, I've come on business."

Sir Claudius expected as much, but now had a few questions of his own. He began delicately. "Would it be rude of me, Edward, to inquire about your whereabouts for the last few months?"

The man stopped pacing. "Not rude," he said. "Irrelevant though. All that matters is that I'm back now and quite displeased with circumstances in my house on Oxford Street."

Sir Claudius looked surprised. "How so?" he asked blankly, though he knew all too well how so.

Edward stood directly before the desk. "I returned home yesterday to find what bordered on chaos. I was told that my accounts have been closed, that on your orders, my creditors had shut off all credit, and that on several occasions you refused to grant Daniel Spade even the courtesy of an audience."

Sir Claudius nodded to all the charges, feeling secure

in his position. "I thought it was in your best interests," he began, though he never had a chance to finish.

"My best interests?" repeated Edward. "You know that the inhabitants in that house are totally dependent upon me, that without my support they would starve, which, I might add, they were on the verge of doing."

Sir Claudius leaned up to meet his anger. "I doubt, Edward," he began kindly enough, "if your father had wholesale charity in mind when he deeded the estates to you. And I doubt if James—"

Again he was cut off midsentence. "What in the name of God does either my father or James have to do with it?" Edward demanded. "The estates and revenues are my own to do with as I please."

"True, but irresponsible—"

"You are not paid to pass judgment on responsibility, Sir Claudius."

"I do my best."

"Not for me, you don't." Now as though aware that anger would accomplish little, he settled heavily into the chair opposite the desk.

From where he sat, Sir Claudius could see the man's hands trembling. "Are you well, Edward?" he asked considerately.

But Edward continued to sit in silence. At last he raised his head, a look of resolution on his face. "I did not come to argue, Sir Claudius," he said quietly. "Debate is not included in our relationship." He stood up again. "I want the accounts opened immediately," he ordered. "I want all creditors informed of my return, and by four o'clock this afternoon, I want fifty thousand pounds delivered to my house on Oxford Street."

"Fifty thous—" Sir Claudius pushed back in his chair as though he had been physically assaulted. My God, the man *was* mad.

"And furthermore," Edward went on, "I would like the books for the last ten months. I assume you have them and they are in order."

Sir Claudius found for the moment that he was literally unable to speak. Fifty thousand pounds! Now on a burst of resolve he stood up. "Of course I have the books," he said. "They are always open for your inspection. And I shall most certainly honor your first two requests. But on the matter of the—"

"Fifty thousand pounds," Edward repeated, giving him no margin for discourse, "delivered this afternoon by four, if you please."

"But that's impossible."

"Nonsense," Edward countered. "I may look like a fool, Sir Claudius, and on occasion may act like one. But I'm not playing the fool now. I intend in the future to keep a steady and watchful eye on all matters concerning the estates. I would appreciate your assistance, but I don't require it." He stopped pacing and confronted the desk again. "The cash reserve is there," he smiled. "I know it."

"It was my intention to invest it."

"My intention as well, Sir Claudius. You see, we're not so far apart."

But Sir Claudius was suspicious of everything. "How?" he demanded. "Where?"

"Like all good investments," Edward replied, "in the future."

It was a vague answer. But Sir Claudius knew the unspoken specifics of Edward's reply. Now he settled back slowly into his chair. They had come to the crux, the solitary subject on which Sir Claudius might in the future base a successful lawsuit.

He leaned further back in his chair, supremely confident and spoke a single word. "Irresponsibility," he pronounced, mentally preparing his case. "There are those who contend that you are acting irresponsibly. Edward, please," he begged, "do you honestly believe that your father intended for his fortune to feed and clothe the garbage of the city of London?"

Still Edward held his silence and Sir Claudius was grateful. The point was to help the man see from another point of view. "I'm afraid, Edward, that you've allowed yourself to fall into bad company. I'm fully aware of your affection for the man Daniel Spade, but I can't help but wonder if you, in your blind way, are aware of his—reputation. Quite scandalous it is, and it has grown more scandalous in your absence. Radicals have been seen at all hours passing in and out of your house. I fear that revolutionary fires are being banked there, and you cannot, must not allow yourself to be duped by them. They are dangerous enough now, but if you throw the weight of your fortune behind them—" He shuddered involuntarily as though overcome by such a thought.

Throughout his long monologue an unusual silence reigned in the room. He kept a careful check on Edward's mood, trying and failing to discern how his words were affecting him.

"Why don't you go home, Edward," he suggested kindly, "back to Eden, to the bosom of your family who love and need you. Leave things here to me. I'll have your house cleared by the end of the week, the trash thrown out on the street where they belong. They are not your responsibility, not even Daniel Spade. He's fattened his larder long enough through the generosity of the Eden family. If you persist in your relationship with him, it will only bring you to grief. Your one, your only responsibility is to yourself, to your family, and to the perpetuation of the Eden wealth, one of the noblest fortunes in all of England. You must do nothing to jeopardize it, for if you do, you only succeed in jeopardizing yourself."

By God, but it had been an impressive speech, surely one of his best off the cuff so to speak. If only now he could gauge the effect his words had had on the man.

"Edward?" He spoke the name gently, hoping for a gentle response. He saw the man lean with both hands upon the desk and look directly down with an expression which seemed to resemble—

Pity?

Sir Claudius couldn't believe it, but there it was, a clear, unmistakable look of pity. "My apologies again, Sir Claudius," Edward said, "for disturbing you unannounced. It was not my intention to—"

He broke off and to Sir Claudius's amazement started for the door, as though the interview were over. But at the door he stopped. "It is with genuine sadness, Sir Claudius," he said, "that I terminate your relationship with my family."

Sir Claudius started slowly to his feet. Edward was dismissing him as though he were nothing more than a common clerk, as though his quarter of a century of service to the Eden family amounted to nothing. But the most unsettling fact now raging through his mind was the realization that Edward Eden had a perfect legal right to do what he was doing and Sir Claudius was powerless to stop him.

Still the man talked on. "I had hoped to have your assistance," he smiled, "as you gave it so loyally to my father and mother, but I see now that I was wrong in that assumption. I can't really believe that on any occasion, no matter how trivial, you dared to dictate to my father on the disbursement of his funds." He stepped backward. "So you leave me no alternative but to cast about for another solicitor. Please send all the books around this afternoon. I shall settle your fee with the new solicitor. And there shall be a bonus for your—loyalty."

With that, the man turned on his heels and would have departed altogether had Sir Claudius not found his tongue and the will to use it. "Wait, Edward—"

Thank God he obliged, and in the silent interim gave Sir Claudius a chance to think clearly on what he was losing. No, he could not let that rich plum slip from his grasp, not now when it was on the verge of falling squarely into his lap. How totally dependent his own comfortable standard of living was upon the Eden estates. To lose it now would be financially and spiritually disastrous.

Then he must backtrack, must apologize if necessary. He was too old to suffer the indignities of poverty and too tired to cultivate a new fortune. "Edward, please," he muttered weakly, waving the man back. "Clearly I've overstepped my boundaries and I offer my deepest apologies."

To his relief, Edward smiled warmly. "No apologies are necessary, Sir Claudius. We see things differently. It's your right as well as mine."

Sir Claudius sank back into his chair. "I shall do your bidding—in all matters," he concluded, loathing the words. "It is your right to discharge me, but I beg a second chance. Consider the memory of your father, your dear ill mother. In all modesty I know that news of my dismissal would add to her grief, and I'm certain that neither of us wants that."

For a moment Sir Claudius wasn't certain if Edward agreed with him or not. But then, "I agree, Sir Claudius," Edward said. "You know far too much about all of us to turn you loose in the world. But if our relationship is to continue, it must be on my terms. I will pay your generous fee only if you clearly understand that your role is that of solicitor, not adviser."

Meekly Sir Claudius nodded.

"And that door is never to be closed to me, as it has been closed to Daniel Spade in the past. Is that clear?"

Again, with difficulty, Sir Claudius nodded.

"And the accounts will be opened, the creditors informed of my return?"

Another nod, though he could scarcely look at the man.

"And the Eden books and fifty thousand pounds will be delivered to Oxford Street by four this afternoon?"

Oh God, could he do it? He must. "I'll do my best," he mumbled.

"I'm sure you will."

With dim eyes, Sir Claudius watched as Edward waved from the door. "Then I'll take my leave. I thank you again for your cooperation. From now on we will be working in very close concert. I trust, for both our sakes, that we'll do our best to make it as pleasant as possible."

With that he was gone, though Sir Claudius heard him call out a cheerful farewell to his clerk, commenting inanely on the glories of the morning.

Still Sir Claudius sat at his desk. With effort he tried to settle back in his chair in an attempt to digest the unpleasantness of the morning. But suddenly it occurred to him that the man would be moving across the courtyard below in a few moments, and as though he required one last chance to try to fathom the mystery of it all, he hurried to the broad windows, carefully concealing himself behind the heavy velvet drapes.

From this furtive position he looked down on the small common. Then predictably the man himself appeared, walking briskly through the bright morning sun, not a trace of weakness or addiction visible about him. With the exception of the simple clothes, it might have been Lord Thomas Eden himself, a single thrust of high Tory arrogance.

Derisively Sir Claudius shook his head. It wasn't Tory arrogance he was looking down upon, nothing so admirable as that. It wasn't even that imitation known as Whig confidence. It was worse than that. It was Radicalism, that witless amalgam of Christian charity and revolutionary zeal.

God! He could look no more, and turned back to his desk.

Then suddenly the most beneficent thought occurred to him. Why the agitation? Sweet Lord, how witless he himself had been. Why bother directing the man to the straight and narrow? Let him spend thousands, millions if necessary on his radical causes. Let his name be smeared across every page of newsprint in the kingdom. Then when the time came, and it *would* come, he would face Edward Eden in a court of law and defeat him with his irresponsibility. And judiciously he would place the vast Eden fortune in James's inept hands, and being a generous man, Sir Claudius would give the Cranfords a purse for their efforts in the whole affair and end up, as he had always planned it, with the lion's share for himself.

Abruptly he gave a gleeful little giggle. Sweet heavens, how rapidly Fate could turn her face about. Irresponsibility! How he loved the word. But now he must get to work and send a detailed letter to those steady hands at Eden Point. How pleased she would be to hear of the Prince of Eden's return, of his increasing madness, of his—irresponsibility.

"Clerk!" he shouted, pleased with the sound of authority in his voice.

"Clerk!" he cried again, doubly delighted at the sight of the terrified young man in the doorway. Before he issued his spate of orders, it occurred to him that the world naturally divided itself into two classes of men: one, the weak and witless, and two, the cunning and powerful.

There was not a doubt in his mind concerning the class to which he belonged.

Hadley Park
Shropshire
April, 1837

On occasion, Harriet Powels had trouble remembering that she was back from the dead and out of the isolation of the fourth-floor storage attic. In the first month of her hard-earned freedom, not once had either of her parents looked directly at her.

Rather, they viewed her as something to look around, or through, or avoid altogether, as her mother was doing now, bent over her needlework, in the wing chair by the far window of the morning room.

"He said that you were to wait for him here," Lady Powels murmured. "I would suggest that you obey. We both have serious reservations about your—outings—on that horse."

From the doorway, Harriet started to protest, then changed her mind. She was in no position to protest anything. And if she did, she was half afraid that her mother might look directly at her, forcing her to witness firsthand the expression of grieving embarrassment which constantly emanated from that maternal face.

Instead, she quietly removed her riding gloves, resigned to a delay, and eased into a new chair which provided her with a perfect view of the opposite wall and the painting that hung there, a lovely Italian Renaissance work entitled "Virgin and Son."

Son.

She closed her eyes. From across the length of that vast room, she heard her mother's voice, solicitous yet distant, "I trust you slept well."

"Very well, Mother. Thank you."

"That horse isn't suitable for you. I'm sure you know that."

"Why isn't he suitable, Mother? He's been suitable for years."

"He's ailing. Your father said he's not to be trusted."

For a moment, Harriet foundered, unable to see the connection between a state of health and a state of trust. At last, dragging her eyes away from the cherubic infant sitting in the Virgin's lap, Harriet stood, pacing lightly. A thought occurred to her, momentarily dampening her enthusiasm for her reunion with old Falstaff. It had been over a year since she had seen the handsome horse and shared with him their secret revelry in the meadow. But how the thought of seeing him again had sustained her. Now it occurred to her that perhaps, in the past, her parents had had her followed, had been given reports of her behavior, the scandalous manner in which she had removed her garments so that she might straddle the horse and ride him with the wind.

To be true, her father had expressed strong disapproval last night at table when Harriet had announced that she was riding today. Then she had thought it to be merely his prevailing attitude of gloom, censoring everything she did save for those quiet intervals in her room when she read.

"Must you pace like that?" her mother now scolded, still not lifting her head from her needlework.

Quickly Harriet moved back, aware that she was causing new distress. She sat in the opposite wing chair and again saw her mother lift her eyes and speak to the vacant place at her feet.

"It's really too soon, you know," Lady Powels said.

"For what?" Harriet asked.

"For—riding. For—being seen."

There it was again, that tone of complete mortification. Harriet started to lean back in her chair, then changed her mind and sat primly on the edge. "It's been a month," she said quickly. "The thought of exercise appealed." Before that bowed gray head and trembling hands, she added softly, "I can't stay in my room forever."

She saw her mother's eyes lift to the windowsill, the needlework in her lap clenched inside her fists.

As the shadows of morning sun dappled the carpet at Harriet's feet, she bowed her head and felt as though she were in an immense dream. In the wing chair she distinguished the ghostly shadow of her mother, growing uncannily larger. In the moment that her mother had lifted her eyes, Harriet had seen something in them that she'd never seen before, a quality of expression, a judgment, as though the creature before her was utterly repulsive to her.

In her eagerness to move away from such an expression, Harriet rose and her steps took her as far as the door. Now with her hand on the knob, she considered leaving, disobeying her father's command that she wait for him, and running directly to the side exit where surely by now old Rudy was trying to rein in her horse.

Only at the last minute did Harriet remember her vow not to cause them any more grief, to be the model of obedience and decorum, all still part of the price she was paying. She would wait for her father, receive his daily dosage of gloom, then she would be free to go and find her horse and together they would return to the meadow, the high sun, and that redeeming, sustaining interval of freedom.

Thus resolved, she returned to the straight-backed chair and tried to keep her eyes away from the Italian painting and the little boy. She withdrew her gloves from her pocket and commenced pulling them on, finger at a time, though it was very difficult, her hands were trembling so.

Finally she gave up altogether and sat docilely with her head bowed, eyes closed, and in order to keep her mind busy and her eyes off the painting, she tried to conjure up visions of the meadow, old Falstaff prancing and snorting, carrying her with the wind, the feel of sun on her arms, her legs astride his flanks, the sensation not unlike—

Without warning, she saw his face, the green glen. With sudden and pleasurable shock, she discovered that it was not dead and gone. Those sensations were as real

to her now as they had been over a year ago. How rich
she felt, how invulnerable to the martyrdom they were
putting her through. And if the memories were so alive
here, sitting in this stifling room, how gloriously alive
they would be atop old Falstaff.

Suddenly she clamped her lips together for fear a
sound of joy might escape and cause her mother new grief.
As she continued to sit there, the picture of docile obedience, she found it increasingly difficult to disentangle
dream from reality, and something within her urged her
not to try. Again she was aware of an important confirmation, that in spite of everything, she would survive.

At that moment she heard footsteps in the corridor outside the morning room. She sat up and made an attempt
to straighten herself. All that was rquired of her was to
endure the paternal lecture, the paternal outrage, the
paternal condemnation, and let them both, in concert,
remind her of who she was and what she had done. Then
she would be free. In eager anticipation, she stood.

She listened closely. The footsteps were drawing nearer. She waited as though at attention and heard her father
now speaking to someone on the opposite side of the door.
It was a woman's voice, she thought, vaguely recognizable.
Nelda. Her maid. Puzzled, Harriet stepped forward. She'd
dismissed Nelda for the rest of the day, had no need of
her, and preferred privacy after her time with Falstaff.
Then why—

Then the whispered voices ceased and the door opened.
The first glimpse she caught of her father was alarming,
his face as angry and wretched-appearing as she'd ever
seen it. In order to relieve herself of his face, she took
in his apparel, mussed and smelling, and there, caught
in the heels of his boots, pieces of straw, as though he'd
recently been in the stables.

At first he did not acknowledge her in any way beyond
a token glance. Then he proceeded immediately to the
center of the room and stood with his back to her, facing
her mother, some unspoken message passing between
them.

And when for several long moments, no one seemed to
feel the need to speak, Harriet stepped forward, eager to
face her daily dose of punishment and get it over with.

"You wanted to see me, Papa," she began cautiously.

Still he said nothing, did not acknowledge her in any way.

"Papa?"

Suddenly he leaned forward on the table, his arms stiffly braced, his head hanging limp between his shoulders.

Then all at once that stern head lifted, though his eyes were shut, and his voice, when he spoke, bore no resemblance to the father she once had known. "You are foolishly garbed, Lady," he said, the words seeming to choke in his throat.

Her apparel seemed a peculiar starting point for a moral lecture. "I'm riding today, Papa," she reminded him quietly.

She saw his hand then move to his side as though he were seized with a spasm. Beyond, she was still aware of her mother, silently watching.

He now strode away from the table and her closeness, the stitch in his side apparently receding. "I think not," he said, a new calmness in his voice.

"There's no harm," she countered lightly. "I feel—"

Then he turned on her, the distance of the room between them, an angry flush spreading over his face and neck. "What you feel is totally unimportant, Lady," he said, his voice low.

Calmly she waited. Let it come, all of it, like a daily purgative, alternating punishments, one day silence, the next words. Today, obviously, it was to be words.

But where were the words? Surely he'd caught his breath by now. And when she looked back, she saw him staring at her, abysmal shame in his eyes mingled with bitterness. Then the only words she heard coming from those lips were simple ones, softly spoken. "Go to your chambers," he ordered, and turned away as though he were finished with her.

"I said I was riding, as soon as—"

Now he commenced to strip off his jacket, as though the morning heat were pressing down upon him.

And when he still did not reply, she stepped closer. "Did you hear, Papa? If you are finished I—"

He turned to her. "The horse is dead," he said, so quietly that at first she was certain she hadn't heard correctly.

"I—beg your pardon?" she inquired politely, stepping to the table, one hand outreaching.

He didn't look at her, but rather repeated the message to the floor. "The horse is dead. He's been—ailing. We had to—put him down—"

Put him—

Quickly she glanced toward her mother, as though for confirmation that her ears had deceived her. But that good woman was bent rigidly over her sewing, the needle flying in and out. She looked back at her father. He too had slipped into a chair, his legs outstretched, relaxed appearing, as though at long last a score had been evened.

She felt a cry rising in her throat. But still she pinned her hopes on a slender thread. On occasion, her father had a way of mumbling, so that the message was never quite clear. "Papa, I didn't hear—"

Suddenly he was on his feet, repeating the words so she'd be bound to hear them. "The horse is dead," he shouted, that tinge of red growing on his neck. "Now get to your chambers and get out of that foolish garb. Need I make it any clearer?"

A weakness swept over her. The table was close. All she had to do was reach out for it. But she wouldn't permit herself that luxury. *Dead.*

No. She wouldn't give him that satisfaction of seeing her falter. Instead, she lifted her head and walked erect from the room, the word still following after her.

In the corridor outside, she saw her maid, Nelda, waiting a distance away, her young face creased into angles of concern. "My Lady—"

But angrily Harriet shook off her concern and sympathy and started down the long corridor in an awesome display of strength, though once the floor beneath her feet wavered and she reached quickly out to the wall for support.

Dead. The price was becoming increasingly dear. Could she pay it? She must. All the way up the stairs, she was aware of Nelda following closely behind her, her father's servant now, pleading *his* case. "The animal *was* poorly," she whispered. "He hadn't taken food in—"

Still Harriet moved forward, grasping the bannister for support, doing all her weeping invisibly, moving resolutely back to her prison.

As she drew near to the door of her apartments, she

glanced ahead and saw the dark narrow staircase which led to the fourth-floor storage attic. Once, a month ago, she had vowed to herself that she would never again in her life set foot in that grim room.

Now she cast a searching eye in that direction. A shudder crept over her. Then she was moving again, a curious lassitude settling over her limbs while behind Nelda protested vigorously, "No, my Lady. You don't want to go up there no more. Come with me. We'll—"

Who was that speaking behind her? She couldn't identify the voice and it made no difference anyway. She wanted to see again for herself that place of horror. There was always the remote possibility that it would help to alleviate the new pain which had invaded her body.

To that end, she slowly climbed the narrow staircase and pushed open the door, then closed it behind her and shut out that voice which was still pleading with her. For a moment she stood in silence in the room.

There it was before her, that cot, old linens still stacked on the near table. And there, the partitions still in place which had separated the old Swede's bed from her own. And there, still attached to the iron frame of the cot, were the strips of muslin which had held her wrists and ankles rigid.

As a soldier revisits an old battlefield in search of new meaning to meaningless pain, so Harriet methodically, deliberately took note of all aspects of her battlefield. Of purpose there was little, of meaning, none. And the only activity which even came close to raising her out of her misery was when she took up her position on the cot, first leaning forward and rebinding both her ankles to the iron frame, then stretching backward, her hands clasping the frame from behind, as though they too were bound.

Thus self-restrained, she closed her eyes as if in a hypnotic trance, welcoming the memory of pain, the memory of dead Falstaff, of the green glen, of the son lost to her forever, of Edward . . .

London
Late April, 1837

Elizabeth turned over on her bed, under the new down coverlet whose smooth hemmed edges almost touched her face. Though late, almost nine o'clock, it wasn't bedtime and she was far from sleepy.

Nearby, so close she could touch it, was the pretty new cradle, and inside was the babe. Now, as though to confirm the baby's nearness, she reached out and touched the polished rosewood, and with a shiver of delight withdrew it quickly, as though happiness, like pain, was best taken in small doses.

Fully clothed in her new dress of pale blue, she lay still beneath the coverlet, gazing up at the ceiling where the fire shadows formed images of dancing bears. Coming from the other side of the partition she heard his pen scratching.

Him!

She closed her eyes and again shivered. Was it heaven? Was this what the old priest at St. Dunstan's meant when he spoke of "the peace that passeth all understanding"? How had she been so gloriously transplanted from that dismal other life to this?

Again, in bewilderment, she looked about her and tried, in her limited way, to assess the changes. Surely they had

449

commenced on that miraculous day two weeks ago when
she'd chanced to glance out the third-floor window and
had seen the dusty carriage, had seen old John Murrey, then
had seen *him*.

Yes, that had been the start. And since then, the
changes had come so fast she could scarcely keep track of
them all. Endless deliveries had been made to the house on
Oxford Street. First the beds, not only her new one, but
beds for the children as well with real feather mattresses
and stacks of warm blankets and new linens.

And while that parade had been coming in the front
door, an equally long parade of tradesmen had been coming in the back door bringing fresh meat, white flour, sugar,
coffee, tea, eggs, sausages.

Lying still beneath the coverlet, she found herself smiling
in the semidarkness of her little partition. What was it that
he called her now, his nursemaid, and her only duties en-
tailed looking after the baby, that mysterious little bundle
who was turning rosy and fat at the nipple of the wet-nurse
in the kitchen.

For just an instant a small cloud marred her brow. His
son, or at least that's what he said, with the cuts on his
small chest, healed now. Still—where was the mother?
Had he loved her? Had she loved him? And if so, why
wasn't she here?

Well, Elizabeth knew this much. If it had been her—and
at that moment she reached out and lightly rocked the
cradle. In a way, it *was* her now.

As though to confirm her thoughts of him, she threw
back the coverlet and moved slowly to the foot of the bed,
to an angle where, leaning slightly forward, she could just
see him, sitting at his bureau, in the light of an oil lamp,
his head bent over ledger books.

For reasons she was not capable of understanding, her
eyes filled with tears. At that exact moment, to her chagrin,
he looked up from his ledger, as though summoned by the
intensity of her gaze.

"Elizabeth?" he murmured. When she didn't respond
immediately he laid down the pen and lightly folded his
hands over his work. "Is anything wrong?" he inquired
kindly.

Quickly she shook her head. She pulled the coverlet over
her and held it clasped under her chin as though taking

refuge behind it. In the expanding silence she knew she had
to speak, but all she could think of was the silliest question. "This bed, will it always be mine?"

Softly she heard his words. "The bed is yours, Elizabeth,
will always be yours."

She nodded as though to assure him that she understood,
that now he could get back to his figures and books and
she'd not bother him again.

But he didn't. Instead he leaned back in his chair and
laced his hands behind his neck and stretched as though he
were fatigued and continued to look at her.

Dear God, how she loved him. She shouldn't be staring
at him so. How was it possible that he made her feel so
beautiful when she was so ugly? How was it possible
that now, under his gaze, she felt that if she spoke, she
would be witty and quick and clever?

How were all these things possible? She had no idea,
none at all . . .

Nor did he, though Edward had found something in her
face which had stirred him deeply, even though now there
was knocking at the door and an urgent call of, "Edward,
it's me, Daniel."

The door opened and Daniel appeared, flushed and excited. "Are you ready? They are starting to arrive."

Edward nodded that he was. "Might we take a moment
first?" he asked, closing the ledger books before him and
pushing them to one side. From behind the partition he
heard his son whimper, heard soft cooing as Elizabeth
spoke to him. A moment later she emerged from behind
the partition, the baby in her arms. Cradling him close, she
said softly, "He's hungry, Mr. Eden. I'll take him to the
kitchen."

Although he was well aware of Daniel waiting, still
Edward chose to spend a minute in a personal way. He'd
been so busy of late. His moments with his son were
usually stolen, like now. "Bring him here," he asked
gently.

The weight was minimal. Still his knees felt peculiarly
weak as he held his son. Behind him he was aware of
Daniel drawing closer, reminding them both that a
christening was in order and soon. "The old priest at St.

Dunstan's could do it," he smiled, "with his namesake serving as godfather."

"And you as well," Edward added, "and Elizabeth as godmother."

He saw the expression in her face as she looked up at him. "Do—you mean it, sir?"

He nodded. "Of course I mean it. I can think of no one more qualified."

She grinned and seemed to want to say more, but instead clasped the infant to her and walked from the room with new dignity.

Both men watched. As she closed the door behind her, Daniel reminded him, "They're beginning to gather, Edward. You *will* come, won't you?"

"I promised I would," he smiled. "Indeed I look forward to it." As he commenced straightening the desk, he asked, "Tell me something about your Mr. O'Conner. You've mentioned him briefly, but I would like to know more."

Across the desk, Daniel shrugged. "He's taken the reins," he smiled. "For the first time in the history of the Movement, we have a leader."

"The right one?" Edward inquired.

"I think so."

"He's Irish?"

"Oh, indeed," Daniel laughed. "In fact, there are certain men who claim that O'Conner is first an Irish Nationalist and second an English Chartist."

"Is he?"

Daniel paused as though carefully framing his reply. "To be honest, he's both," he said. "But first and foremost he's for the people, be they Irish or English."

Edward nodded. From the scathing editorials he'd been reading in London papers, the mere name Feargus O'Conner was capable of striking fear in the bastions of management. Good! Then with the proper leadership on one hand and the Eden fortune on the other, they might just stand a chance of effecting certain desperately needed changes. How he would love to be a part of it, a kind of legacy to leave to his son.

He stood up from his chair, his enthusiasm mounting, when abruptly Daniel stopped him. "One additional word,

Edward, if I may. You might find tonight," he began, "some resistance coming from O'Conner—"

"Resistance?"

Daniel nodded. "I fear he views you as the natural enemy."

Surprised, Edward moved back, putting the desk between them. "Why?" he demanded.

"Oh, not you personally," Daniel hurriedly reassured him. "What you stand for. You are a man of great wealth. You did not earn it and therefore, according to Feargus, that makes you an—exploiter and, I'm afraid—the enemy."

Edward laughed to put him at ease. "Am I still the enemy if I choose to use that fortune in the execution of O'Conner's schemes?"

Apologetically Daniel murmured, "Of course not, not to me."

"But to Mr. O'Conner, yes?" he asked, wanting confirmation.

"I'm afraid so."

Edward hadn't counted on this. He had assumed that both he and his purse would be a welcome addition to the radicals. Now apparently he would have to go through a period of proving himself. Well, no matter. Perhaps Feargus O'Conner has already suspected the truth, that to Edward, the Movement wasn't nearly as important as the need to bring about rapid and effective change.

Since his return from Shropshire, Edward had already scouted other locations for Ragged Schools in London, had tentatively picked out half a dozen crumbling London properties that would lend themselves to his purposes, his and Daniel's. If the Irishman wanted to go along, very well. If not—

"Come, Daniel," Edward invited now, "I hear boots below. We mustn't keep Mr. O'Conner waiting and thus confirm his opinion of me as a member of the leisured class."

As he walked beside Daniel down the stairs, he caught his first sight of the men gathering in the entrance hall below, a solid crush of rough, craggy men in well-worn clothes. Edward heard a shout.

"He's coming, he's in sight."

As one, the milling men turned toward the door. Edward noticed a few of those already seated in the banqueting hall rise in their seats and look expectantly over their shoulders.

A moment later Edward heard a carriage outside roll to a stop.

Then a shout went up and as Edward glanced back to the door, he saw a remarkable figure of a man appear, surely one of the tallest men Edward had ever seen, looking even more enormous than he remembered him from that night long ago, a giant of a man, plainly dressed in worn dark brown wool, hatless, though atop his head grew thick luxurious long red hair.

"It's him," Daniel announced, his face as flushed as Edward had ever seen it.

Edward needed no identification, though Daniel gave him one anyway. "Feargus O'Conner," he whispered, his eyes abundantly pouring out a depth of feeling.

There was no question concerning whose meeting it was. Though Daniel presided, the flamboyant red-haired Feargus O'Conner dominated literally everything.

Then Daniel was introducing O'Conner in elaborate language. In spite of himself, Edward smiled. He would not have thought his friend capable of such rhetoric.

And that was the last moment of silence for, as one, the men jumped to their feet, their voices raised to a thunderous pitch of cheering, all hats waving wildly, all eyes focused on the man who, in spite of the cheers, continued to sit with his head down, his hands hanging limp between his legs.

The stormy reception lasted a full five minutes and perhaps would have gone on even longer if Daniel hadn't moved to the front of the platform, lifted both hands in a halting gesture, and finally coaxed them into a semblance of silence.

Edward continued to watch. He'd never seen such skillful manipulation of an audience before. The man seemed determined to stretch their nerves to the breaking point. And when at last silence descended, all eyes turned as one to the still bowed giant who at last was beginning to stir, his smallest movement as remarkable as Lazarus rising from the tomb.

Then all at once the man stood with sudden energy and, ignoring the convenience of the podium, walked directly to the edge of the platform as though he wanted nothing to come between his presence and their adoration.

"My friends," he began. Edward found himself leaning forward as though fearful of missing a word.

"My apologies for my late arrival. I had hoped to join you earlier, but only this day have I returned from the Black Country, a journey which has left my heart full, my body weak, and my spirit aflame."

He talked on in this vein for some time, describing in graphic detail the life of the pit people, the great northern coal fields lying around the rivers Tyne and Wear, the houses dense with swarms of people, clouded with soot and smoke, the deep darkness of the mines.

His voice fell to a whisper. "I see no point," he grieved, "in such an existence. If this is life and living, then God would be merciful to strike them all dead."

Along with the others, Edward felt himself moved by the accounts. Though the man was a powerful performer, his stories would have stood alone.

"And one night," O'Conner went on, "in a Manchester ironwork, a fitter found a barrow improperly left in his way and, in a moment of anger, he seized it with violence, supposing it to be full, but being empty, it gave way with unexpected facility and by the force of his own movement he was thrown into the furnace. The charge was within four feet of the filling hole and together with two of his comrades, we succeeded in pulling him out with little delay."

He lowered his head. Everyone waited in a state of suspended horror for the words to commence again. "The surgeon was sent for and was two hours coming to attendance. But it mattered little for of hope and help there was none." He faltered. "I held his head in my lap, bits of his flesh clung to my jacket. He retained his senses to the last and during the greater part of the hour for which his life was prolonged his voice was heard in prayer."

The words ceased.

Edward waited along with the others, hearing in the silence only the scribbling of the young reporter's pen as apparently he felt compelled to record it all.

"Later that evening," O'Conner went on, "I accompanied three of the victim's mates to his house in Coal Lane. It was our heavy burden to inform the widow. But when we arrived, we were blessedly relieved of the brutish nature of our mission, for the poor man's wife was likewise lying dead from starvation and exposure to cold." His voice became like a monotone now, as though he were filing a report. "The deceased was lying in a small heap of straw, without covering. The room was completely destitute of furnishings, firing, or food. Five young children were sitting on the bare flooring, crying from hunger and cold by the side of the mother's body.

"And there's more, my friends, the second half as important as the first. When we left the dead man's house, we took the five children up the hill to the factory owner's home. Oh, very grand it was, freshly whitewashed, with lace curtains at every window. We herded the frightened children around us as we knocked and a moment later a pert maid appeared on the other side of the door and informed us that we were to go to the rear entrance. I was about to inform that pert maid," O'Conner went on, "that we would gladly wait when behind us, just coming up the gravel, we heard a horse and rider, and turned to see the gentleman jauntily swinging a riding whip."

Now O'Conner lifted both his hands. "Quite fleshy, he was," he said, cupping his hands about his own lean belly. "Now, as we approached this fine gentleman, with the five children in tow, he seemed to ignore the children as well as the three men who were accompanying me. I alone seemed to interest him and as three stewards held his horse, he climbed down, still eyeing me with interest, and approached, smiling, his hand extended."

Here the mock amusement on O'Conner's face faded. "I did not take that hand, but instead fell to informing him of the double tragedy which only that day had descended upon the little ones. He appeared to be listening carefully. I thought I was speaking clearly. But at the end of my tale he merely patted his rounded belly and informed me that these tragedies *do* occur and there was little, if anything, he could do about them, but if I was desirous of staying for tea, he would be happy to chat with me about the Italian opera, or old King William, who would surely die any day now."

This last was delivered in a flippant manner though underlying both words and tone was a devastating sense of incredulity. Now he stood before them. "I recount it for you, my friends, as it happened. And I ask of you now, is it right?"

For an instant the direct question seemed to take them all by surprise. But finally a deep angry male voice on the far side of the hall shouted, "No!" And gradually the refrain was taken up by others.

"Shall we permit these conditions to exist?"

Again, a resounding No! which caused the floor beneath Edward's feet to vibrate.

Feargus O'Conner smiled and softly repeated, "No." He stepped closer to the edge of the platform. "Then I propose a scheme," he smiled, "a new birth, a movement so powerful as to knock all those fancy gentlemen off their horses. And it shall start here, in this very hall which in the past has housed both the crime and the criminal, this banqueting hall for the corrupt descendants of one of England's largest fortunes."

Edward stood still, newly alert.

"The past is over," O'Conner entoned now, "and I predict a new age, born here but spreading to all corners of England, a dawn in which you, the people, will sit in Parliament. And in this new dawn there will be no property of the individual. The duty of all property owners will be to share with others, and if the poor do not work less, the rich will certainly work more. This dawn will be yours," he promised. "But it will not be effortlessly achieved. We must work as we have never worked before, in the factories, persuading others, in our schools, converting the young, and in the very seat of corruption itself, Parliament."

At the end, he stood with arms outstretched as though eager to embrace a new storm of applause. And it came, as apparently he knew it would.

On one point, Edward was in total agreement with the wild-eyed Irishman. The world *was* out of kilter and becoming more so. Perhaps it was time that the Eden family paid its debt to the past, to the centuries of exploitation, and the amassing of great wealth.

With the sense of having settled a score with himself, Edward increased his applause and looked about him at the other men and felt for the first time a vague kindred spirit with them. Whatever reservations he had about

O'Conner, he would keep them to himself and try with great diligence to work with him.

The applause showed no signs of diminishing. He noticed many of the men trying to push close to the platform, hands outreaching.

When O'Conner had shaken hands with the men crowding around him, he strode though the door, Daniel at his side.

After the bulk of the crowd had pushed past him, Edward left the banqueting hall and started toward the stairs. It occurred to him that the greatest tragedy consisted of the fact that his views and O'Conner's were not that far apart. In no way had Edward disagreed with anything the man had said earlier. Starting up the stairs, he stopped and looked down toward the clogged doorway of his house. O'Conner was still there, shaking more hands, clearly enjoying the adoration of his followers, Daniel at his elbow.

A thought then came to Edward. "Mr. O'Conner," he shouted over the milling men. Instantly he felt the weight of eyes as all heads turned about. At last in the new stillness, O'Conner himself looked up. "Yes, Mr. Eden?"

Edward moved down a step. "I was interested to know," he began, forcing his eyes to stay on that strong mocking face, "what became of the five children? The ones so tragically orphaned which you spoke of earlier?"

The simple question at first seemed to fall on deaf ears. The men turned their heads toward O'Conner as though they too were interested in his response.

"Children?" O'Conner repeated.

Edward tried to explain further. "You said you found them waiting with their mother's body. What became of them?"

Clearly disarmed, the red-haired man merely shrugged and shook his head. "I—I don't remember," he faltered. "I suppose one of the pit men took them home." Now as though angry at having been caught without a ready answer, he made a strong demand of his own. "Why do you ask?" he called out.

Edward paused. "I was just curious, and concerned. I wish that you would have brought them to London. We could have accommodated them here. I fear you might have left them to an uncertain fate. With what eagerness we would have received them and tried to soften their tragic double loss."

For the first time, he heard a hush fall over the men, as though at last he might have said something they understood. Unfortunately that understanding did not extend to Feargus O'Conner.

Now Edward saw him step away from the threshold and move toward him, his voice hard, mocking, as though mindlessly he felt a compulsion to destroy. "Your charity, Mr. Eden," he said in biting tones, "moves us all." He lifted his arm, still moving toward Edward. "You want children?" he pronounced acidly. "Then I shall bring you children, wagonloads of children, all abandoned, all hungry." His voice rose in a demented tone. "You want children? Then I shall bring you children, all the children of London. Is that what you want?"

Edward waited for the infuriated voice to clear the air. Then he lowered his voice for contrast. "That's precisely what I want, Mr. O'Conner," he said. "We are at present investigating other properties and will purchase as many as necessary to accommodate them. Further, we shall staff them with paid teachers whom Daniel Spade will train and we shall not cease until we have provided a new dawn for an entire generation of English children."

He'd not planned to sermonize, yet that seemed to be the effect of his words on the staring men, all except Feargus O'Conner, whose face now bore an expression of total disbelief.

He stopped midpoint between the threshold and where Edward stood, his eyes wide and cynical. "What you've just described, Mr. Eden, requires a fortune."

"I possess a fortune, Mr. O'Conner."

"And you'd be willing to spend it in my cause?"

Edward hesitated, choosing his words carefully. "In *your* cause, Mr. O'Conner? Not necessarily. In the cause of humanity? Without hesitation."

Then there seemed to be no further reason to stay. The weight of all those eyes was beginning to wear heavily upon him. Unlike O'Conner, he was totally appalled by the spotlight. All that he longed for now was the peace of his second-floor chamber, to sit by the fire with his boots off, to listen to Elizabeth softly croon to his son. He waited a moment longer to see if there was any reason why he shouldn't take himself to that place of refuge. Finding none, Edward nodded in an unspoken goodnight and started up the stairs.

Lost in these thoughts, he was scarcely aware of Daniel's voice coming from below. It sounded strangely weak, and as Edward took the top step he looked down on his friend and saw a peculiar expression on his face, half apology, half entreaty.

But of greater interest to Edward was the fragment of the man standing next to Daniel, only one black boot visible.

Edward needed to see no more. He listened carefully as Daniel stammered, "I was—wondering, Edward, that is to say, we—were wondering, Mr. O'Conner and myself, if it isn't too late, could we, might we have a word with you?"

Still Edward focused on the black boot. No movement there, neither objection nor encouragement. Longingly Edward glanced toward his closed chamber doors. How convenient and perhaps wise it would be to say no to the two men waiting below. But as he looked back down the stairs, he saw Daniel's pleading eyes, and Edward knew better than anyone else that his friend's dream needed both a leader and a fortune.

Apparently the leader was standing beside him. Only Edward could deliver the rest of it. Well, they weren't that far apart. Perhaps a union of sorts could be consummated, but not for the sake of the Movement, or any one man.

There were greater, more pressing goals, and it was to those that Edward looked as he started back down the stairs, trying to ignore the disquieting feelings within him, the painful sense that he was being summoned only for his fortune, that all his pride and dignity and worth as a man rested on that vast portfolio of deeds and leases which his father in a moment of weakness had signed over to him when he had been a mere infant.

There was his cross and his salvation, and there too was the deep well-spring of his grief.

On one of the most dazzling June mornings in the history of man, June 20, 1837, a little knot of people left the house on Oxford Street on foot and walked through the radiant sunshine a distance of three blocks to the tiny Anglican church of St. Dunstan's. There beneath two simple stained glass windows depicting the Lost Lamb and the Prodigal Son, with rainbow colors falling on their faces, the old parish priest took the infant with the carved B on his chest, a fat three months old now, in his arms and christened him John Murrey Eden while to one side the kind-faced elderly man who had given him his name wept tears of joy.

Others in the christening party were Elizabeth, the only godmother, radiant and beaming in a newly made gown of pink silk with matching bonnet and carrying a small bouquet of pink roses which she'd gathered early that morning from the trellis at the rear of the house on Oxford Street. And Daniel Spade was there, the second godfather, who carried in his hands his christening present, a small white leather Book of Common Prayer with the infant's name engraved in gold on the cover.

And there was a third male present whom, in the midst of the quiet ceremony, Edward surveyed with modest amazement. Feargus O'Conner, the Irishman who had come close to taking up permanent residence in the house on Oxford Street and who since that first night of the Chartist meeting had never ceased to amaze Edward with the force of his personality and his single-mindedness as far as the Movement was concerned.

But for this moment, Edward wasn't thinking of the Movement. He looked lovingly at his son, who was suffering the indignities of having cold water splashed on his forehead, an offense which he was now letting the entire world know about in a sudden shriek of outrage which seemed to upset the old priest, who quickly completed his prayer and handed the squirming child back to Elizabeth's outstretched arms, where within the moment the child was made quiet by the young woman's gentle rocking.

In the final moments of the closing prayer, Edward looked about at the faces of his friends, the chilled and musty-smelling interior of the small church, his eyes finally coming to rest on his son, John Murrey Eden. And for one moment he experienced a sweeping sensation of pure joy. How faint was the past, the future little more than a remote glimmering, yet for now, he stood in the midst of friends, with his son nearby and felt a physical proximity to the Source to Whom they all were praying.

For one blessed moment, he did not see the pale and haggard faces of the children who filled his three Ragged

Schools, children with countenances like old men and women. For this moment he saw only his son, who, like the others, had been early introduced to pain and brutality. But of this Edward was certain and of this he now took a silent vow: his son, from this time on, would know nothing but love. As the prayer came to an end, and heads lifted, Edward reached forth and took his son from Elizabeth and carried him to the altar where, kneeling down, he lifted his face to the Crucifix and closed his eyes and repeated the vow to God himself.

Later that evening there was a small party for the children in honor of the special day, though the guest of honor had long since been put to bed. At Edward's suggestion, the cooks had baked white almond cakes and the three of them, Daniel, Feargus, and Edward, enjoyed standing in the corner of the banqueting hall, watching the children taste the sweet crumbly goodness.

Now it was close to midnight. The children, numbering almost one hundred and fifty, had long since been herded upstairs to bed. A few of the kitchen volunteers were still working in the banqueting hall, sweeping, gossiping about the dying King William and wondering what the young Princess Victoria would wear to her coronation.

After the last of the women had bid the men goodnight, Feargus produced from the folds of his cloak a bottle of good Irish whiskey, proclaiming, "The occasion warrants it, an adult celebration, a toast to life *and* death. Nothing better for the Movement," he'd announced further, "than the death of that inept old king."

Although Edward was loath to toast death in any quarter, and Daniel too had been less than enthusiastic, still they agreed with the blustering Irishman, sent a volunteer for three glasses, and now sat in awkward positions at one of the small benched tables designed to accommodate children. A single lamp burned low on the table before them.

Across the table, his long legs drawn up like a grasshopper, O'Conner lifted his glass in Edward's direction. "To the day and the happy occasion," he said simply. "Then to work. I've the petitions and St. Katherine's dock yet to look forward to."

Edward sat up. "Give me the petitions. I know St. Katherine's dock. I'll take them myself."

But the offer was still resting on the air when Daniel

came down with a hard "No!" Edward saw the two men exchange a glance. O'Conner muttered, "My God, man, the last thing we need is you behind bars."

Again it was clear. Of course he must remain free and protected. Who else could make the weekly trips to Sir Claudius Potter's office and return with a cash flow capable of buying property, purchasing goods, paying printing costs for pamphlets and petitions?

Now as though O'Conner sensed his plummeting spirits, he leaned forward across the table, refilled Edward's glass, and commended him on the Blackfriars Road property. "I inspected it today," he smiled. "After the christening. Quite spacious it is. What is your estimate? Two hundred children?"

Edward shook his head. "Two hundred and fifty at least," he commented without looking up.

O'Conner nodded, clearly pleased. "And Daniel informs me that you have made one additional purchase on Toadley Lane."

Edward looked sharply up, becoming resigned to the fact that anything he told Daniel eventually ended up in O'Conner's ear. "Not settled yet," he said bluntly, remembering the old opium den and what personal pleasure it would give Edward to open those locked doors to the light of sunshine. But at this point, Sir Claudius was having trouble locating the original deed, so the Toadley Lane property was still being used by the living dead.

Without warning, O'Conner leaned across the table. "Tell me, Eden, were you truly an addict?"

Edward found the direct question impertinent and the weight of memory insupportable. Still he nodded.

"How did it start?" O'Conner pressed on, apparently fascinated by the subject.

Edward was aware of Daniel stirring uncomfortably. Still he replied quietly, "It started with the death of a dear friend."

"What was it like?"

"It was like being dead and alive at the same time." He closed his eyes, remembering the nightmares, the poison which still manifested itself in his system. Yet it seemed to him in that moment that if a vial of laudanum were produced, he'd blend the elixir without hesitation into the whiskey before him.

Now as though O'Conner sensed his weakness, he smiled slyly. "Some of my men use it regularly. I have constant access to it."

Suddenly Daniel stood, his voice husky. "It's late," he announced. "No more talk."

Edward sensed his concern and smiled. "No need, Daniel. That war is over. Now we're engaged in another."

Beyond the lamplight, Edward noticed O'Conner's strong features fall into shadows. "I meant no offense, Eden, with my questions," he said kindly.

"And I took none," Edward replied.

"Then again, blessings on your son." The man lifted the whiskey and drank directly from the bottle. "Pray God, our efforts will provide him with a better world, and pray tonight for death at Windsor." He contracted his heavy brows and made a searching survey of the banqueting hall. "And we really must find another place to meet," he commented sadly. "Too cramped, this, too smelly—"

He did not finish his sentence but turned partially away as though his mind were struggling on two tracks at once. "A bitch on the throne," he mused meanly, apparently not even aware of his nonsequitur. "A German bitch at that. How England will founder! With death at Windsor, our time has truly come."

Edward watched and tried to crush the uneasy feeling which had arisen within him. The man appeared to have gone temporarily mad. Perhaps drunk. He'd consumed almost half a bottle of whiskey. Yet there was no slurring to his speech.

"Then I'm off," O'Conner shouted now, full-voiced, with a suddenness that jarred the quiet hall. At the double doors, he stopped. "Remember," he grinned. "Pray for the King's death," then he added, "for England's sake!"

With that he was gone.

They continued to sit still for several moments, their eyes fixed on the empty doorway. Finally behind him he heard Daniel's worried whisper, "What are we going to do?"

At last Edward stood. "Watch him," he suggested softly. "No more. He's still a very effective leader."

"Do you have any regrets, Edward?" Daniel asked. "I feel often that I have led you astray, cheated you of your natural role in life."

At the bottom of the stairs, Edward stopped and faced

Daniel directly. He smiled. "Is madness a contagion? I'm here because I want to be, Daniel. I'm on course for perhaps the first time, and you have put me there."

He had intended to say more, but the expression on Daniel's face so moved him that he clasped the man to him.

"To bed now," Edward concluded wearily. "We'll need at least fifty new teachers for the Blackfriars school and I count heavily on your assistance and good judgment."

The two men shook hands warmly. "Goodnight," Daniel smiled and started slowly toward the rear of the house.

Edward waited until he saw Daniel enter his own room, then quietly slipped up to his chambers, his eye falling immediately on the bed behind the partition on which Elizabeth was fast asleep.

He closed the door and stood for a moment. He felt his earlier concerns slipping away. After a brief prayer, he walked beyond the partition to his desk to the mountain of invoices and bills and plans for renovations. He should work. Elizabeth had thoughtfully left the lamp burning.

But his mind would not adjust itself to figures and debits and credits tonight. Instead he slipped into his dressing gown, turned the lamp low, and carried a chair to the edge of the partition. There he settled himself and leaned back and sat guard on the two sleeping, the finely chiseled face of his young son and the motionless beauty of Elizabeth.

The moment was too full for complete comprehension. And wisely he did not try.

Without the help of prayers for death, old King William died during the night. The cries of the newsboys in the street awakened Edward the following morning along with the mournful tolling of church bells.

He opened one sleepy eye, surprised to find himself in bed. He looked toward the partition and knew that Elizabeth was already up and dressed and in the kitchen while the wet-nurse fed his son.

Slowly he left his bed and went to the window. The dawn was dark and brooding. Workmen were already busy hanging black banners from every streetlamp. The early morning pedestrians were subdued somehow and he saw clusters of top-hatted gentlemen huddled in close conversation on the street corner. So! England would now have a queen, the young Victoria. He remembered Feargus O'Con-

ner's remarks from the night before. The man must be
watched.

Outside his door, he heard the children parading down
for morning prayers and breakfast. Even their small voices
seemed subdued. Dear God, how he loathed the presence
of death.

Then, as though to outrace the shadow of death, he
quickly washed and dressed and hurled himself into the
mountain of work on his desk.

He rubbed his hands together and picked up his pen.
Lord Shaftsbury's report first, that honorable gentleman
having sent his request over a month ago, suggesting that
all Ragged Schools be unionized so that they might arrange
plans to "assist each other."

Pen in hand, Edward commenced to write and wrote
steadily for over an hour, hearing below in the banqueting
hall the very children he was describing.

In a very real sense the future swallowed him up. His
pen moved faster across the page. In all of London, there
were now sixteen Ragged Schools. By this time next year,
there would be one hundred and sixty, and the year after
that . . .

Hadley Park
Shropshire
March, 1840

That the demanding letter should come during the last days of mourning for her mother seemed, to Harriet, most appropriate. The gloom was now all of a piece, with no discernible break at any given seam. Nor was there any longer any element of surprise in her existence. She'd known all along that the "unfinished business" at Eden Point would be finished one day.

And now there was her father, sunk in his chair in his study, his customary position since the death of her mother almost a year ago. He was coatless—there was no one to dress for now—his head and shoulders hunched over his writing bureau, lifting the letter with hands that shook, a long strand of iron-gray hair falling over his forehead.

"From the Countess Dowager," he muttered, thrusting the letter higher into the air, still keeping his back rigidly turned.

Of course, Harriet thought, and maintained her thin-lipped meekness by the door. In a way she was grateful. It was the first word he'd spoken to her in over six months.

"Do you care to read it?" he asked impatiently and shook the letter over his head.

"No," she murmured, and tried not to see him. He had suffered, was suffering, of that she was certain. She would

467

never forget his face that morning when, summoned by the maid's cry, they had found her mother dead in her sleep, the mortification gone from her face, the prim little lace nightcap askew at an almost jaunty angle, as though to inform one and all that at last she had escaped from this unpleasant world and all its accompanying embarrassments.

Strangely enough, her father's first reaction had resembled anger. Harriet had watched, helpless, as he'd lifted his frail wife into his arms and seemed to scold her for not having the courtesy of taking him with her. Then, with all the maids weeping, he had at last released her, turned to Harriet with a stricken face, and whispered, "If it were not for you, she would still be alive."

Remembering it all, Harriet bowed her head. Perhaps he had been right. Perhaps to her already burgeoning list of offenses could be added the designation of murderess.

"I think you should read it," her father continued, anger increasing. "It concerns you."

Harriet dragged her head upward from the weight of the past, resigned to the weight of the future. "I assume," she said, "that Lord Eden is getting impatient."

Abruptly her father slammed the letter down on the bureau. "He wants a wife," he pronounced and turned sharply in his chair and looked at her for the first time since she'd entered his study, a prolonged look tinged lightly with disbelief, as though confounded that any man would want the company of the creature now standing before him.

Harriet tried to relieve herself of such an expression by counting the red swirls in the Persian carpet at her feet.

Silence. Obviously his appalled amazement knew no bounds.

Finally, "Then shall I sign the agreement?" he demanded.

The red swirls were arranged in groups of three.

"Are you listening, Harriet?"

Intersecting were swirls of blues and greens.

"*Harriet!*"

His anger had lifted him out of the chair. She was aware of him standing only a few feet away. "Sign what you wish, Papa," she whispered to the carpet.

"They want the wedding to take place within the month."

Within the month. Within the month, the final setting of the sun.

"Harriet, pay attention!" His rage drew him closer until at last he took her by the shoulders and shook her violently. Not until that moment did she recall how long it had been since he had touched her.

Belatedly he seemed aware of what he'd done and stepped quickly back, his old face still buffeted by sorrow and, now, mortified.

In an attempt to put him at ease, she repeated herself: "Sign what you wish, Papa."

For a moment he seemed to founder, reaching back for the support of his chair. "It's—for the best," he muttered.

"Yes."

"They will—treat you well."

"I'm certain of it."

His eyes lifted with a grieving expression. "There is nothing for you here."

The sentiment was softly spoken, as though with a weight of regret behind it. It almost undid her. "No," she quickly agreed. "Nothing here."

"Well, then."

He turned back to the bureau, withdrew fresh stationery, and commenced writing.

Within the month.

For a moment she felt her strength failing her. The hosts of loneliness were after her. There were monstrosities in her head, images of deformed beasts, of screaming women.

Turn back? Never! And anyway, why bother? Harriet Powels was dead, a most genteel and proper death, leaving no ugly corpse to dispose of, no line of mourners or dying flowers.

This dead woman still stood upright and even watched as her father signed his name to the agreement with great flourish as though for once and all dispatching a burdensome problem.

Harriet watched until the letter was completed, then she left the study and started up the stairs to her apartments, there to pack, to prepare herself for the imminent journey to Eden Point.

She walked slowly, head down, her eyes fixed on cold marble, as though she were following a wounded animal, by the droppings of his blood.

Eden Castle
March, 1840

Sophia Cranford, garbed in her lavender best in honor of James's wedding day, paced restlessly in the cluttered confines of her private apartments. In the room beyond she heard Caleb putting the finishing touches to his grooming. Dear God, how weary she was of weak, spineless, vacillating men. And in a way, Caleb was no better than James. Indeed he'd sided with him in his stupid suggestion that they postpone the event scheduled to take place this day.

Postpone? Angrily she slapped her hands against the rustling lavender taffeta as though it too had offended her. Merciful heavens, they had come close to drowning in postponements during the last few years. First there had been the young Harriet's mysterious illness, then the King's death and the year of national mourning. Then another death, Lady Powels, Harriet's mother, and more mourning, more postponement until at last Sophia had taken matters into her own hands, had written to Lord Powels, supposedly on behalf of the senseless old Countess Dowager. And in this letter Sophia had informed Lord Powels that if a marriage did not take place by early spring, Lord James Eden would consider himself free of the promise and would look elsewhere for a wife.

Predictably that had provoked a response quick enough.

471

Apparently the old widower, sick to death of his burdensome daughter, had laid down the law. And only yesterday morning the young woman had arrived in a single carriage, looking more a prisoner than a bride in the company of two strapping male servants who had rudely deposited her with her trunks on the steps of the Great Hall.

Now merely thinking on all the circumstances gave Sophia an urge for haste. "Are you ready?" she called to the tardy Caleb. "It's approaching two. You should be down to greet the priest."

"In a moment," came the distant reply.

Merciful heavens, would he leave everything to her? Well, it would be done, she would see to it, James honorably wed to a good English name. And she didn't give a damn whether either of them desired it or not. Once they were wed, she was certain that nature would take its course. And hopefully, within the year, an heir would arrive, and hopefully also within the year, death, which had been so generously visiting others, would deign to pay a visit to Eden and take away that senseless old woman lying upstairs, the last stumbling block between Sophia and control of the Eden fortune.

Feeling a chill, she withdrew a gray shawl from the top of the cupboard—the old chapel would be cold with March dampness—and again cast a sideward glance toward the bedroom door. As she started out into the passage, on her way to greet the priest, it occurred to her that one of the first things she and Caleb should do when they came into their money was to purchase a fine carriage, finer horses, and pay a final visit to that bleak village in Yorkshire which had spawned them. Just a brief visit, of no real duration, to let the weak-spirited bastards see what had become of Parson Cranford's offspring.

As she walked down the corridor she felt something swelling in her throat and for the first time in her life felt herself on the verge of tears for no reason, no reason in the world, save happiness.

James Eden, Fourteenth Baron and Sixth Earl of Eden Point, felt completely baffled by the strange goings-on in which he was to play such an important part. Generally speaking, he disliked complications and understood them only in terms of livestock or a good racing horse.

Now as the steward began brushing back his hair, coated with oil, James felt a peculiar heaviness in his head. Quite frankly, he'd never expected to see the young woman again. It *had* been almost four years. What kind of love could be kept alive in that space and at that distance?

Seated in the chair before the glass, James closed his eyes to the fluttering hands of the steward. The most incongruous ideas were running through his mind. Once he had had a fierce desire to mount that cold lady. Once, four years ago at the engagement party, he'd been willing to play the husband. But not now. She'd arrived yesterday like a corpse loosed from its coffin, so heavily veiled that he'd failed to get even one clear look at her.

From behind him, he heard the steward murmuring, "There, sir, quite elegant looking if you ask me."

James opened his eyes. Elegant looking? He looked as though he'd fallen head first into a bucket of lard.

"Anything else, my Lord?" the steward inquired, wiping the excess oil off his hands.

Unable to look at himself in the glass, he lowered his head. "Go along with you. You've done quite enough."

The man bowed low. "Then I shall return in half an hour and escort you to the chapel."

Abruptly James's anger surfaced. "Damn it, I know the way to the chapel."

"My apologies, sir, it's just that Miss Cranford—"

"Damn Miss Cranford," James shouted further, then caught himself, as though he'd uttered pure heresy. "I'll be there," he muttered again. "Leave me alone now."

As soon as the door had closed, he reached for a square of linen and frantically commenced wiping the oil from his hair. He shifted slightly in the chair—something was pinching his neck. The fool had tied the neck scarf too tightly. The linen in his hand fell to the floor as the blank gaze took on an expression of self-pity. If his father had lived, that might have made a difference. And as for his mother—

"Oh God," he groaned audibly and found himself wishing for his sister, Jennifer. On occasion she had soothed him.

Suddenly he lifted his face from his hands as though possessed of a healing idea. Of all three children, wasn't he, James, the only one on the straight and narrow? Wasn't he the only one content to stay at Eden, where they all belonged? The thought did bring comfort, though it was short-lived, for the truth was that the worst was yet to come.

Marriage! A life commitment. Abruptly he turned away from the glass as though to turn his back on both the image and the future.

She didn't love him, he knew that. And he did not love her. Then why? *Why?* The momentum of the unanswered question lifted him to his feet and carried him halfway to the door. Where was he going? It wasn't time yet. But still the momentum carried him forward until his hand was on the knob and there he stopped, consciously aware for the first time of his destination.

A small revolution, that's what it was. Sophia and Caleb would be furious if they found out. Perhaps he could go and come without being seen.

Now with a determined step, he opened the door and moved out into the corridor. It had been months since he'd seen her. At first they all had been kept out, on strict orders from the doctors. But now the doctors had departed and no one attended her but his old Aunt Jane and the decrepit Mrs. Greenbell.

His step increasing, he realized that he wanted to see her more than life itself. If Sophia found out and was furious, let her fury rage. A son had rights of access and perhaps during the time that he had stayed away from her chambers, God had intervened, had lifted the deadly seizure and had given her back her tongue.

In his anticipation of her presence, his hands were already outreached, his mouth already whispering the name of the one person who might be able to answer some of his questions, to hold him and comfort him, to cover his forehead with cool kisses as she'd done when he was a child.

Even as he thought the name, his own painful sense of helplessness seemed to diminish. So he spoke it aloud now as he approached the door, the word evolving out of a long tortured breath, a simple word,

"Mother."

Poor Jane, Jane thought, as she sat before the fire in the sickroom. Look at her! Was this the woman who once had run one of the most notorious salons in all of London, who had served tea to Thomas Carlyle and Charles Dickens and a brilliant little man named Benjamin Disraeli?

Now? Look at her! Her gown was black, three days worn, and splattered with the remains of luncheon porridge. No more cerise. The spirit that required and supported cerise was gone. And her hair was ungroomed for a lost number of days. And her teeth pained her constantly.

Look at all of them for that matter. There opposite her at the fire, the rotund, dozing Mrs. Greenbell. Dear God, the only way they would ever know that the old woman was dead would be when her snores stopped. Well, she wasn't dead yet. The wheezing vibrations rose like minor thunder from her slack-jawed mouth. And limp in her lap was that damnable needlepoint. If she didn't die soon, the old hag would cover the entire world in needlepoint, carpet the headlands with it, drape it over the sides of Eden Point, and hang it from the dome of St. Paul's to Tower Hill.

Still Jane felt magnanimous. The old woman *was* company, could talk, unlike— Slowly her head lifted toward the grand rosewood bed.

There was the most terrible of all, her sister, her head sunken upon the pillow, her fair hair cut short for the first time in Jane's memory, butchered by the old nurse who bathed her and who suggested the alteration to keep down lice and fleas. Her eyes were open, though unseeing, fixed, as they always were, on a spot on the canopy.

The paralysis was now complete. The festering bedsores mingling with the ancient scars on her back attested to that. She was incapable of movement save with the aid of two others. She now spent her days and nights lying flat on her bed, her hands lightly clasped upon her breast, no response save for some hand signals which Jane had perfected, a tender communication in which she lifted Marianne's hand, fingers extended, and placed it in the palm of her own hand. If Marianne lifted her index finger, it meant yes. If she raised her thumb, it meant no.

Slowly, now, Jane tried to rise up from the confines of her chair, choosing to think on the few moments. Marianne clearly enjoyed her daily treat of tea and honey. And early of a morning when Jane's eyes were rested, she would read to Marianne and there too was a source of enjoyment, her sister's face glowing when fictional worlds worked out well, her eyes filling with tears when the heroine of the moment fell on hard times.

Her thoughts were wearing her out. A sharp pain lodged itself in her upper gums and cut a path through to the center of her brain. She needed brandy, though she'd never started this early in the day, and again she was on the verge of pulling herself laboriously out of her chair when suddenly the door burst open and in the dim light she saw the figure of a man.

"Who—is—" she stammered. But then she saw him clearly and recognized him in spite of his dandified clothes and his peculiar hair arrangement. "James?"

She detected a look of apprehension in his face. He seemed incapable of looking her straight in the eye. But then even as a child he'd been unable to accomplish that simple feat. "James?" she murmured, thinking how long it had been since he'd climbed the steps to this chamber. "What a pleasant surprise," she added, smiling, "and how thoughtful of you to come on such a—busy day."

She saw a vivid flush spread over his face. Effortlessly she slipped into her old manners of hospitality. "Come," she smiled, taking his arm. "It's a chill day and bridegrooms must be warm. Here, sit," she invited, offering him her own comfortable chair, and to her surprise, he did, although his position was more a nervous perch on the edge. Quickly she drew forward a straight-backed chair and placed it before him, shutting off the snoring Mrs. Greenbell.

Thus settled, the tension between them seemed to increase. "Well now," she smiled, "tell me of your plans. The wedding is today, I believe, this afternoon."

He nodded, his fingers in his lap lacing back and forth. "Yes," he repeated dully. "Rather soon now."

She nodded. "And the bride? Is Lady Harriet well? We all remember her illness." Abruptly she smiled and lifted an imaginary glass in toast. "To your persistence, James," she smiled. "How fortunate the young woman is to be so zealously loved."

She saw an angry look pass over his face. "I don't love her," he muttered.

Jane leaned forward, not shocked but pretending it. "Then why—"

"It's for the best," he said quickly, staring with dead eyes into the fire. Then mechanically, as though he were quoting someone else, he added, "Love is not necessary and may come in time."

She considered arguing and would have if she thought it would have done a particle of good. She recognized the words and even the intonation, Sophia Cranford speaking behind James's mouth. In spite of the bleak nature of her thoughts, she looked back at James and managed a smile. "I wish you well," she said, "and only regret that I won't be in attendance. Our hearts, though, go with you and your bride."

He seemed not to hear and again looked nervously about.

"Would you like to see your mother?" she asked quietly.

He glanced at her with a simple expression as though she'd just expressed the deepest desire of his heart.

"Over here," she whispered, taking his arm, already fearful for him. "Talk to her," she advised. "She does understand more than anyone knows, I think."

Leaving him to his own initiative, she watched as he moved falteringly forward.

"Take her hand," Jane urged softly. "On occasions her fingers speak."

In response to this, he glanced sharply over his shoulder as though she'd spoken nonsense.

"Her hand," she urged again. "Take it in your own." Lord have mercy, she silently prayed. Would he endure?

Then to her surprise she saw him doing as she had urged, his hand finally making contact and lifting that small dead one into his own.

Although Jane stood a distance of about ten feet from the bed, she knew she should turn away and did so at the last minute to face the fireplace and the now gaping Mrs. Greenbell, who had somehow managed to drag herself out of the depths of her noisy slumber in time to witness the encounter.

In response to the enormous question mark which was forming on Mrs. Greenbell's fleshy face, Jane merely placed a solitary finger to her lips, indicating silence. The old woman obeyed, though Jane saw her pull herself awkwardly forward in the chair, the better to see the bed.

A waste of effort, Jane thought, because a glance in that direction told her that absolutely nothing was happening by the bed. James still held her hand, but there were no words, no sounds of comfort.

Again Jane silently prayed. She was tempted to reproach him and was on the verge of doing so when suddenly from some mysterious and faraway need, James broke. The strained cord snapped, tears which perhaps had lain dormant from his youth rose up with such violence that his whole body shook. He fell on his knees beside the bed, and without warning Jane saw Marianne's body suddenly turn at a distorted angle.

Behind her, Jane heard Mrs. Greenbell utter a sharp cry as James, still clasping his mother's hand, took it with him in his collapse, clearly unmindful of her helpless state, unaware of the macabre fact that the entire palayzed body was in the process of falling over on him.

Jane couldn't tell whether James looked up first and saw what he was doing, or whether Mrs. Greenbell arrived in time to wrest Marianne's hand from him. All she knew was that with remarkable gentleness, her old companion separated the two, and concentrated her attention on drawing Marianne back to the safe center of the bed.

As for poor James, the ordeal was clearly too much. Whatever urgent need had persuaded him to climb the stairs to his mother's chambers, now that need abandoned him, and as quickly he abandoned the room, staggering to his feet, his head bowed.

Behind her at the bed, she saw Mrs. Greenbell still fussing over Marianne, saw her lean forward and clutch at her heart, as though feeling a delayed reaction to her recent exertion.

"Here now," Jane soothed, coming up beside her. "You go back to the fire. I'll stay with her."

Carefully and sadly Jane studied the face on the pillow. How much did she know? Had the paralysis extended to the brain? Did those dead, staring eyes signal total death, yet death of the worst kind, for the heart still pumped persistent life?

There were no answers, only a new and heavier silence in the room, the soft crackling of fire, the gentle beginnings of Mrs. Greenbell's snores, the sad realization that somewhere in that cold tomb of a castle, a loveless pair were being bound together for life.

Oh God, no answers to anything, and in her deepening

despair she was only vaguely aware of Marianne's face with moisture seeping from the corners of her eyes, and that one small index finger of her left hand working furiously, futilely against the cover.

On March 28, a cold, gray, snow-spitting Thursday, at three-thirty in the afternoon, Lord James Eden wed Lady Harriet Powels.

It was a grim ceremony which took place in the little fourteenth-century chapel on the second floor of Eden Castle. Sterling silver candelabra bearing twenty candles each flanked the pulpit and cast a soft rose glow over the twelve pews. Windowless, in the heart of the castle, the room was damp and smelled of old books and burned-down candles. For this occasion, no particular decoration was added, not even flowers. It was not the season for flowers.

The ceremony was performed by a young Anglican priest from Exeter, a Father Whitehead, who seemed more impressed by his surroundings than anything else. He pronounced the simple ceremony with a low voice and wandering eye, as though he were attempting to record everything so that he might report it later to his associates in Exeter.

It was all over in less than fifteen minutes, including the signing of the marriage document. There had been no nuptial kiss and the two had repeated their vows in voices so low as to be inaudible to anyone save the priest.

At the conclusion of the ceremony, when all the signing was over, the bride, her heavy veil still in place, left the chapel quickly, her lady's maid scurrying after her, and the other actors in the drama were left alone in the chapel, gazing at the empty doorway.

Then because their presence was no longer needed as witnesses, Sophia sent the servants back to their duties. She paid the young priest a handsome sum and likewise sent him on his way, uncaring that the snowstorm outside had increased.

She turned then and bestowed a loving kiss on James and urged that he look to his bride. But the groom merely shook his head and ran from the chapel, turning in the direction opposite to which his bride had disappeared, the stone floor sending back in echo the rapid clacking of his boots.

Sophia and Caleb Cranford extinguished the candles and left the chapel, quietly closing the doors behind them, as though to lock in the mood which was more accurately funereal grief than wedded bliss.

London
June, 1840

In shimmering morning sunshine, Edward sat on the
stoop of the house on Oxford Street, the long letter from
Eden in hand, and watched as old John Murrey, a doting
godfather if there ever was one, led the young John Murrey
Eden, now a robust and chubby three-year-old, on his
morning excursion to the end of Oxford Street, across to
the opposite side, then home again.

Slowly now, almost reluctantly, he reopened the letter
bearing the Eden seal which had arrived only that morning.
From Jane. He'd recognized her handwriting and now
shifted on the hard stoop, propped his arms upon his knees,
and commenced to read.

The first paragraph was Jane at her coquettish worst,
apologizing for the quality of the writing paper and be-
moaning the fact that age and a slightly palsied hand had
robbed her of her exquisite penmanship. *News of my
mother, please,* he thought impatiently.

Then the second paragraph, so harmless appearing in the
opening lines: "An occasion of some note took place at
Eden during the month of March. Your brother, finally,
after many foolish stops and starts, wed—"

Abruptly Edward's eyes stopped. There was a moment of

disbelief, that perhaps the palsied hand had written the wrong name. But then he was reading again, a secondhand description of the ceremony—Jane herself had not attended.

In all, Edward read the account three times and though there was more to the letter, he allowed the hand holding the pages to fall limp between his legs and stared, unseeing, at the pavement. So! There was a new Lady Eden. In that instant he saw her again, that one interval they had passed together.

His head dropped slightly forward under the weight of memory, regretful that his once limitless love for her was now limited in the realization that she had abandoned their son.

Edward reopened the letter and read the final paragraph, which, he discovered, to his annoyance, scarcely mentioned his mother at all. "She is as well as can be expected, we keep her comfortable. She does love her honey—"

There was a closing paragraph concerning Jane's favorite objects of hate, the Cranfords, and a rather oblique warning to Edward to be careful. There was an affectionate conclusion and her flowery signature and half a wasted page.

He stared at the blankness. Over and above the traffic noises of the street, he heard the vendors calling, the costermongers hawking their wares. A posie crone went by with flowers, announcing to all that she had for sale the same rare hybrid rose that Queen Victoria had carried in her wedding bouquet when last February she had married the German Prince.

Quickly now Edward gathered together the pages of Jane's letter as he saw, coming from his left, a miniature golden-haired sailor, running toward him, arms outstretched, his small face tilted back and laughing, old John Murrey following dutifully behind. At the last minute before he stood to scoop the child up in his arms, Edward saw, clutched in that tiny fist, the remains of a cinnamon bun. But impervious to the sticky mess he slipped his hands beneath the two small arms, crushing the letter from Eden in the process, and lifted the child, whirling, into the air.

As delighted shrieks along with cinnamon crumbs rained down on his head, he looked up into the small grinning face and found it impossible not to smile back, found it equally as impossible to take anything in life too seriously, at least for the moment. All he needed in this world was contained in the almost weightless bundle of squirming, shrieking life which he held over his head.

Suddenly overcome, he lowered his son into his arms and kissed the cinnamon-covered cheeks and was aware that the little boy was merely enduring. After a moment, Edward released him with a quick warning to stay close and looked back over his shoulder to see John Murrey grinning like a magpie.

"He led all the way, sir," the old man announced.

"A fitting epithet," Edward replied. "Pray it will be the story of his life." As he looked back at the boy, Edward noticed that he had dropped the cinnamon bun and had retrieved the crushed pages of Jane's letter. Now like a miniature reproduction of Edward himself, the boy sat on the stoop, in Edward's exact position, the pages clutched upside down in his chubby fingers, "reading."

Drawing nearer, John Murrey laughed heartily. "Monkey see, monkey do," he said. "Shall I take him in to Miss Elizabeth, sir?"

"No, leave him with me for a while," Edward suggested. "The children are still in class. I'll keep him until Elizabeth is free. Go along to the kitchen with you," he added fondly. "You've earned refreshment."

John nodded, and as he passed the boy on the stoop lovingly ruffled his hair. Edward noticed a subtle movement, the child drawing away and quickly smoothing down his hair with a characteristic expression, frowning eyes and smiling lips, so that one was never quite certain of his exact mood.

Settling beside him on the stoop, Edward fought off the impulse to take him in his arms and sat now with easy informality, two "men" passing a June morning.

"Did you have a nice walk?" he inquired softly, marveling at the dark lashes which covered the downward eyes.

No response. All the child's attention seemed to be directed at the crumpled pages in his hand.

"What did you see?" Edward prodded further. "Tell me everything."

But apparently nothing he'd seen on his walk was as

fascinating as the broken red wax seal on the back of the letter bearing the Eden coat of arms.

"What's this?" he demanded now, holding the pages up for Edward's inspection.

"A letter," Edward replied.

"No," the boy insisted. *"This,"* and with one pudgy finger pointed to the Eden seal as though put out with his father's slow wits.

Edward nodded as though at last understanding. "A coat of arms," he said, "belonging to the Eden family."

Suddenly a dazzling smile broke across the soiled cheeks. "I'm a Eden family," the child grinned.

Edward nodded. "Indeed you are. Not a family, perhaps, but a member."

The boy seemed to think on this for a moment. Then with an almost sad expression he looked back up at Edward. "What are you?" he asked soberly, clearly imitating Edward's tone of voice.

"I too am an Eden," Edward smiled.

The information seemed to please the boy and for a few moments he contemplated the pages with childish seriousness. Then all at once he looked up at Edward. "Is this Eden?" he asked, his face still serious.

Edward laughed. "No, this is London. Eden is a long way from here."

Before the child spoke again, Edward sensed the question that was coming. And it came, a mildly pouting expression on the young features. "Why are we here in London, if we live in Eden?" he demanded.

Edward shook his head. Daniel and Elizabeth both had warned him. The child was a question machine. "Because my work is here," Edward replied, hoping it would suffice.

It didn't. John turned to face him. "I want to go to Eden," he announced, his voice revealing a spoiled tone that Edward didn't care for. Elizabeth had warned him. The boy was overindulged. Still Edward couldn't quite bring himself to correct him. Instead he smiled sorrowfully and asked, "And leave me and Elizabeth and Uncle Daniel and your Grandpapa, for we must stay here. I'm afraid if you went, you'd have to go quite alone." He felt certain that this would make a difference.

But to Edward's surprise and mild shock, the child stood

on the stoop, in an attitude of complete resolution, and calmly announced, "I'll be back."

"Wait!" Edward called out, amazed to see the child toddle down the steps, apparently perfectly willing to take his chances alone on the crowded pavement. He caught up with him in a few short steps and lifted him in his arms, removing the letter from his hand, and endured his shrieks of outrage. As he carried him, flailing, back to the stoop, he saw, inside the door, the classes breaking for the morning. "There, look," he pointed out quickly in an attempt to distract the boy. "You'll have some playmates now."

With a guarded expression, the boy ceased his flailing and glanced through the door. "Don't want to play," he muttered.

"Well, then," Edward sighed. "If you are truly going to Eden Point, I'd better tell you how to get there and something about it. You might not like it, and how sad to make that long trip for nothing."

Instantly the boy settled peacefully into his arms, the defiance momentarily gone. What amazed Edward as he started up the stairs with him was that his son, with some inner wisdom, had known he was an Eden and had now demanded an explanation of his roots.

Well, then, Edward would give him one, and continued to carry him into their second-floor chambers, where he closed the door, placed John in the middle of the large bed, stretched out beside him and commenced speaking.

"It's beautiful, Eden is," he began, smiling as he noticed the little boy assume his identical position, lying on his side, one hand propping up his head, "in a part of England known as North Devon. Miles from here it is, but you'll see it one day. I promise."

The boy's interest was intense. It was as though something in that young soul had already made the connection, and all that he required of Edward was confirmation.

Later that afternoon, Edward's intention in seeking out Daniel was merely an attempt to speak privately with him on the nature of the Chartist meeting scheduled to take place that evening. He didn't think he could stand another interval of O'Conner's ranting, his systematic rejection of all the other Unionists in London, capable men who saw both the need as well as the wisdom of working by strictly constitutional methods. How often Edward had tried to persuade O'Conner to their point of view. And how often he had failed.

He had knocked twice and, receiving no answer, opened the door a crack and to his surprise saw Daniel seated, as though transfixed, at his desk, a ray of late afternoon sun falling across his hair. Before him on the desk, Edward saw a scattering of mail, all unopened save for the letter which he held in his hand.

Quietly Edward stepped into the room and closed the door behind him and continued to stand, unnoticed, for several moments. "Not bad news, I hope," he said softly.

As Daniel looked sharply up, Edward saw first a look of surprise that he was no longer alone. Then Edward took careful note of the second expression, not at all the look of a man who'd spent the entire day dealing with festering sewers and ill children. For a moment, faced with such an expression, Edward didn't speak. He'd come to talk of Radical Agitation, yet there was nothing radical on Daniel's face except what appeared to be a drenching, all-consuming look of—

Love?

Bewildered, Edward tried to make a subtle retreat. "I'm sorry I disturbed," he began. "I can—"

"No, wait," Daniel called out.

As Edward turned back into the room, he saw his friend once again eyeing the correspondence in his hand. "I—can't believe it," he whispered. Then looking up at Edward, as though wanting confirmation of what he couldn't believe, he murmured, "Look! A letter—from Jennifer, it is." He beamed. "Look," and suddenly he was on his feet, displaying for Edward's amazed inspection the heading:

Roe Head,
Bradford,
Yorks.

Edward did well to nod. Daniel took the floor, his face moving excitedly as he paced back and forth, still clutching the letter.

"I wrote some time ago," he began. "I don't believe I told you, did I?"

Edward shook his head.

"No, of course not. I—didn't think it was necessary, and I was fairly certain I'd never hear from her. It was in connection with the schools," Daniel went on. "Well, we do need teachers," he added almost defensively. "Music teachers more than anything. I've interviewed countless volunteers in search of one with mastery in pianoforte. There are none, Edward, I swear it."

"Well, go on," Edward interrupted impatiently. "What did she say?"

Daniel stopped pacing and placed the letter lovingly before him. "She didn't say no," he murmured, "and more important than that, she replied, with her own hand. Look!"

Quietly he shook his head. "Of course, it's a proper letter," he added hastily. "And she inquires after you, and tells me of her own life." His face sobered. "They suffered a fierce winter," he said. "She speaks of constant cold, of her students."

Edward watched as Daniel slipped away again, his face clearly transfixed by loving memories. "Wouldn't it be fine," he whispered to the letter, "if she came?"

The question needed no reply. Edward leaned across the desk. "Then you must write to her again," he urged, "weekly if necessary. You must keep your penmanship before her constantly, you must warm that chill of which she speaks with accounts of our life here."

At some point, Edward was aware of Daniel closely listening. "Yes," he murmured, the idea taking hold. "Yes," he agreed again with greater conviction. "She invites me to write. She does! Look!"

"Good," Edward confirmed, ready to leave him to his pleasant task. As he reached the door, he heard Daniel call after him, "My apologies, Edward. I assume you wanted to see me about something?"

From the door, Edward looked back. "No," he smiled, convinced that Radical Agitation and Parliamentary revolution were just about the farthest items from Daniel's mind. "No," he repeated again. "I just wanted to check on your well-being. I worry about you. You're so vulnerable to disease on Jacob's Island."

But Daniel was not giving a thought to disease or how he'd spent his day. He'd already fetched up a stack of new

paper from the bottom drawer and his pen now stood
poised over the page, his brow knit as though his mind
were sorting through the proper beginning.

As far as Edward could tell, Daniel wasn't even aware
when he left the room. And a moment later he found
himself in the corridor outside, head bowed, half listening
to the sound of the children in the playroom upstairs.

He smiled. Never had he felt so mysteriously filled with
thoughts of home, the result no doubt of his time with
John, and the result no doubt, too, of Daniel's news.

He hesitated a moment longer, then took the steps downward, calling out a single name.

"Elizabeth."

Roe Head
Yorkshire
February 10, 1842

Sitting alone in the front parlor of Miss Wooler's school, surrounded by her trunks, one particularly precious, Jennifer could never have explained the chain of thoughts that made her smile, but the last link in it had something to do with the absolute knowledge that she was leaving here and would never return.

Now arranging her face into a somber slant, she thought again of the shy, blushing ladies, unmarried all, who'd given her advice on the wedded state. In the beginning, she'd felt mortification. Now, only amusement, and in a way, deep pity for them.

Raising her head, she glanced beyond the curtained windows and saw the cold day. No snow yet. The coach ride from Bradford to Leeds would be safe enough. But the train was another matter. What if something should happen?

No! She couldn't bear that, and she stood quickly and walked to the window as though in an attempt to dissipate the bleak thought.

A cold draft coming through the cracks of the window caused her to shudder. Her mind raced ahead to the journey itself: Bradford to Leeds, the train to London and Euston Station, where she would be met by Edward and—

Daniel.

So simple a name to cause such a breaking storm within her. Quickly she glanced back over her shoulder to where her trunks rested, her eye falling on the small one, little more than a traveling case, in which she had safely stored his letters, those marvelous letters, over three hundred in all.

Gazing at the small traveling case which contained her heart, she felt moved. Part of her grief was her long blindness. When first he'd proclaimed his love for her, he'd informed her that it was not a matter of extravagant news. He'd merely loved her always, even from the time when they had been children together at Eden Point.

Then *she* was the one guilty of waste, the wasted hours, days, and years they might have spent together if only she'd been a different person. Well, no more. From now on, all her life, all her desires and hopes would be concentrated on this one man, still not fully understood by her, to whom she was bound by a feeling of deep love.

As she looked about at the remnants of her old life, she was horrified with herself, her utter callousness to her own past, to things and habits and people she loved, who loved her: her mother lying desperately ill, who perhaps had been fatally wounded by her indifference; to her brothers, both of whom had suffered more than she; to her dearest friend, the absent Charlotte Brontë, who perhaps more than anyone else had urged, pleaded, exhorted her to listen to her heart.

Walking slowly back from the window, her head was filled with images of Charlotte, gone now, herself launched on a new adventure, a school in Brussels and a chance at a new and better future. She'd promised Jennifer that she would write, but she'd vowed never to write a word if she had to address the letters to Roe Head. "My pen will move only for Mrs. Daniel Spade, of London," she'd smiled.

Well, write your letters, dearest Charlotte, and I promise to respond as Mrs. Daniel Spade.

The thought, so soon to be a reality, swept over her and left her breathless.

Still her agitation kept increasing until she ceased to struggle with it and now she sat with perfect exterior calm on a near chair, lifted the small traveling case into her lap, and withdrew his latest letter, the one she'd received less than a fortnight ago, the dearest one, sealing their plans, speaking of the wedding ceremony which would be performed in the banqueting hall, attended if she wished by all the children, whereupon the two of them would leave for a short journey to Eden Point to visit the ailing Countess Dowager and establish news of their marriage with all who cared to hear.

There! Listen! There it was, unmistakably carriage wheels on gravel. Quickly she returned the letter to the traveling case. At that instant, although she could not say how it happened, the front parlor was filled with women, Miss Wooler leading the way, other teachers following behind, all pressing about her, placing small gifts in her hand: sachets, lace handkerchiefs, a small red volume of Mr. Shakespeare's sonnets to read on the train.

As she felt herself being passed from arm to arm, she saw two stewards from the carriage make their way through the all-female company and hoist her trunks onto their shoulders. As one man reached for the small traveling case, she called out, "No, I'll carry that one myself. Thank you."

She saw the bewildered look on his face, but how was she to explain? Until she could hold and love the man himself, all she had of substance were his letters, and those she would never let out of her sight until she could replace them with flesh and blood.

The last arms waiting for her at the end of the walkway were Miss Wooler's. "I hate to lose a good teacher," the old woman whispered. "And I hope your young man appreciates the prize he's getting."

Jennifer smiled. "I shall think of you always, and miss you." She might have said more, but couldn't and decided to make her exit with at least a shred of dignity.

As the carriage started down the driveway, she turned rapidly in her seat for a final glimpse. Then, gone, everything was gone, Roe Head left behind, only the turnpike before her and the promise of Bradford a few miles ahead, where undoubtedly other passengers would join her.

Mrs. Daniel Spade, she thought, as she'd thought a hundred times a day every day for the last few months, since he'd first mentioned marriage. Now, under the pressure of the moment, she closed her eyes and prayed quickly for the completion of a safe journey.

As she opened her eyes, she saw that the carriage was just passing the alternate route to Haworth. And now she included Charlotte in her prayers, for a safe journey to Brussels, for a happy future for her wise and compassionate friend.

"Bradford ahead!" the coachman shouted.

Her moments of privacy would soon be over. Then let them end. Contained within her heart was enough love to embrace the whole world.

Let the strangers come. They would have to reckon with her.

London
February, 1842

From the top of the stairs, Edward shouted down at the weeping volunteers. "Get them out of here! Now! Let them wait on the pavement, but get them out of this house!"

As the second wave of children filed past him on their way down from the third-floor dormitories, he saw the fear in their small faces and realized that his tone of voice had done nothing to alleviate that fear.

Still the volunteers were moving as though they had all the time in the world. "You, there," he shouted down to a woman in the entrance hall who had collapsed on one of the benches and was now wringing her hands. "Line them up on the pavement until the omnibuses arrive and make sure their linens are covering their faces."

Finally the woman did as she was told, dabbed at her eyes and fell to directing the frightened children toward the street. Quickly he glanced toward the closed door of his chambers. What in the name of God was taking Elizabeth so long? She'd gone to pack a few things, or so she'd said. Hurriedly he cut through the line of children and knocked on the door. "Are you ready?" he shouted. "You must hurry."

Receiving no answer, he pushed open the door, angry to see her merely sitting on the bed, John beside her, his five-year-old face mirroring the horror of what was going on around him.

"What in the—" Edward began and in his own deep fear and grief could not continue.

"We've decided to stay," she announced calmly, tightening her grip on young John. "You'll need help. You can't do it all alone."

Below in the street he heard the rattling arrival of the first omnibuses. Between the bustling activity outside and the stubborn inactivity in his chamber, he momentarily foundered. Drawing deep breath in spite of the poisonous air in his house, he took her hand in his and felt it trembling.

"Please, Elizabeth," he begged. "I'm placing John's well-being in your hands. He can't stay here, you know that, and he won't go with anyone but you."

To one side, he saw his son listening.

"It will only be for a short while," Edward went on, "until the sickness passes. You'll be safe at Edgeware, the air clean. Please," he whispered, tightening his grip on her hand, "I beg you."

"I don't want to leave you," she stubbornly insisted.

"I'll be all right," he reassured her.

"Where's Edgeware?" she asked.

"At the west edge of London, a distance of about an hour, that's all. We've a new Ragged School there, and there's grass and trees. You'll like it, I know, and John as well."

"When can we return?" she asked further.

"As soon as possible."

Still she gazed into his face. "Did old John Murrey die last night?" she asked bluntly.

It had been his intention to keep this death from them. As for himself, he'd not even had time to grieve. Seven deaths within three days, all within the house, the pattern the same, the epidemic of fever and miasma which was sweeping certain sections of London. Dear God, how swiftly it moved. Nausea, diarrhea, cramps, burning fever. Somehow, foolishly, he had hoped that his house would be spared. But three days ago the old cook in the kitchen had collapsed, then five of the volunteers, then old John Murrey, and only last night—

His head lifted in the direction of Daniel's room. He must go to him, but first he must see these two safely out of harm's way. Suddenly he grasped her by the shoulders. "Elizabeth, I beg you. Take yourself and my son out of this place. Without you, I have nothing left."

His whispered entreaty had come from the heart. Apparently she understood, for the stubbornness finally melted from her face. "We're ready," she murmured and withdrew from beneath the bed a small valise.

In a rush of unspent grief he drew both of them into his embrace and prayed briefly for their safe delivery. He lifted John into his arms and thought with a wave of terror that his brow felt hotter than usual, then decided it was merely his imagination.

Speaking slowly, he gave final instruction to the boy. "You are to go with Elizabeth," he ordered, "and you are never to leave her. Is that clear?"

Solemnly John nodded.

"Now you must hurry," he urged.

As they started out into the corridor, Elizabeth looked up at him with worried eyes. "What of your sister?" she asked suddenly.

But again Edward soothed her. "I'll meet the train tonight." He managed a smile. "She'll be good medicine for Daniel. There *will* be a wedding, I promise." He knew that, for days, Elizabeth and all the volunteers had looked forward to this romantic interlude, "Mr. Spade wedded to Mr. Eden's sister." He knew further that late at night precious bits of lace had been sewn into worn collars and cuffs, the ancient passion of all women for all weddings.

Now he noticed that his words apparently had reassured her and together they waited at the top of the stairs for a place to break into the line of children. When a pause came, he took it, gently pushing her ahead of him.

Outside on the pavement, the scene was one of chaos. He'd hired three omnibuses. Thus far only two had arrived. The sky overhead had grown gray and menacing, and beyond the pavement he saw a large death wagon rattling by, a convenient disposal for the proliferating corpses.

He embraced John a final time and tried not to dwell on

the fear in his face. "More tales of Eden when you return," he smiled.

He'd thought that that would be it, but unfortunately he felt those small arms tighten around his neck. "Let me stay with you, Papa," the boy whispered. "I can help."

His only hope, Edward knew, was to arrange on his face a rigid expression. This he did and at the same time spoke sternly. "Of course you can, but I need your help more with Elizabeth." He drew his son's head down and whispered, "Who is to look after her?"

Slowly he felt the small arms relax, lowered the child until he could see his face, and blessedly saw acceptance there and a kind of pride that he was needed.

At the rear of the second omnibus he found an empty seat and assisted Elizabeth upward, tossing the valise after her.

"God go with you," he whispered.

"And with you," she smiled back. As the lumbering conveyances pulled away from the pavement, he heard her cry, "Take care of yourself."

He did not look up again until the sounds of the horses were no longer audible. As he started up the stairs, he heard another death wagon coming his way. All the bodies had been removed from his house except for John Murrey, who still lay on his bed in the little room off the kitchen.

Edward considered waving to the driver, but changed his mind. He would give his old friend a proper burial, but not now. There was no time. Daniel was waiting for him, and he hurried up the steps, and quickly closed the door behind him as though to shut out death's presence.

He stood for a moment in the empty hall, his hands and shoulders trembling with weariness. His thoughts were torn between Elizabeth and his departed son, and the arrival in a few hours of Jennifer. There had been no way to stop her from coming, no way to get word to her. Still perhaps it would work out. Daniel would rally, the fever clear.

On that note of hope, he started up the stairs, trying hard to dispel the menacing emptiness around him. Suddenly behind him he heard movement. Looking quickly back he saw an old woman, dressed in black, her head covered with a black shawl, just emerging from the kitchen steps.

"Who is there?" he called out.

When she didn't answer, he retraced his steps for a better look and recognized her as one of the dish washers, an ancient scullery maid. "You can't stay here," he said forcefully, "but the conveyances are gone."

"Meant to let 'em go," she said quietly, her old eyes glittering from beneath the black shawl.

Annoyed that she'd disobeyed his orders to clear the house, he stepped still closer. "But you must leave," he commanded, wondering if she was capable of understanding.

"Don't want to leave," she muttered.

"The house is poisonous," he shouted at her, trying to penetrate that glazed expression.

"You're here," she said simply.

He nodded sternly. "Mr. Spade is ill."

"And you'll be needin' help."

Slowly he looked down on her, his anger receding, replaced by bewilderment. "The fever is highly contagious. You could die."

"Kept the grave waitin' long enow, as it is, sir."

He found her blunt manner soothing. "What's your name?" he asked.

"Lucy, sir, jus' plain Lucy me Mum named me."

He nodded, feeling peculiarly weakened by her offer of help. She seemed passive and resigned, yet willing to face anything. Now to his surprise, she took the initiative. "Enough jawin'!" she announced. "I've lived through three fevers, sir. You'll be needin' cool water, fresh linen, and a garlic pod."

"Garlic?" he repeated.

She nodded with conviction, and moved closer with a whispered, "You see, sir, it ain't really a fever. It's an evil spirit, that's what it is, ain't it now? A turrible evil spirit that don't like garlic." She laid a finger aside her nose and nodded firmly. "You go along up to Mr. Spade. I'll be up directly."

"With—garlic?"

"With garlic."

He watched, astounded, as she disappeared down into the kitchen. Well, why not garlic, he thought wearily, and again started up the stairs.

The foul odor coming from Daniel's room greeted him at the top of the stairs. In a way he felt as though he were suffering a prolonged nightmare, that at any moment, he would awaken and find the house once again filled with children. It was the silence and the odor and the awareness of what he might find behind that closed door that frightened him.

He had been the one who'd discovered Daniel ill. Only last evening he'd come from John Murrey's deathbed to relate the sad news to Daniel and had found him huddled in a blanket, sitting on his bed, the slop jar to one side filled with his vomit, teeth chattering, and his eyes weighted with a bewildered look. He'd sat with him through the night, had watched the fever worsen, and at dawn had made the decision to evacuate the house.

Outside the closed door he paused and rested his forehead against wood. He could not in any way face the possibility of Daniel's death. Not now. He was on the verge of becoming a bridegroom and there was no Deity in Heaven who would be that cruel.

Thus reassured by irrational thoughts, he pushed open the door as he'd done thousands of times before, fully expecting to see Daniel seated at his desk, his long red hair mussed where he'd driven his fingers through it.

But as Edward stepped into the room, he saw that his friend was not seated at the desk, saw him instead lying on the bed, his dressing gown half pulled over his naked body, a putrid brown stain spreading in the area beneath his hips, the ravages of diarrhea sapping his strength, and beneath his head a vomit-soaked pillow, the head itself pressed back at a familiar angle—old John Murrey's had been in the same position—the beloved eyes closed in pain.

Edward shut the door and leaned against it. At the sound of the door closing, the head on the pillow stirred, the eyes opened, a smile of recognition crossed the face.

"Edward."

"I'm here, Daniel." Quickly he walked to the bed, his hands outreaching as though they didn't know where to commence working. Finally one rested on Daniel's forehead. The skin there felt like hot coals, and his lips were so dried they had cracked and were bleeding. As he reached into his pocket for a handkerchief to staunch the small flow of blood, he saw a new urgency on Daniel's face and decided to let the restoration go, at least for the moment.

"Jennifer?" he heard him whisper, one hand lifting.

"She arrives tonight," Edward soothed, drawing a chair close. "I'll bring her to you, I promise."

As again Daniel tried to speak, Edward considered asking him not to. The effort was painful.

But apparently Daniel would not be denied. "Look— after her," he gasped. "Tell her—"

As the effort became too much, Edward took the feverish hand in his own. "I'll tell her nothing," he smiled. "I'll leave that to you, the bridegroom."

Now he saw a faint smile on Daniel's lips. "I'd—not counted on—this," he whispered, his eyes closed. Then suddenly as though in the throes of deep anger, his head thrashed back and forth across the pillow. *"Damn,"* he muttered, tears on his face.

Edward bowed his head and pressed Daniel's hand to his lips. He felt as though he were drowning, as though he were so inextricably bound to this man that the tears on the fevered face were in reality oceans in which it would be far kinder of Fate simply to let them both sink into oblivion.

But it was not to be, for the bleeding lips moved again. He seemed to be having trouble breathing. His eyes were open and Edward saw that they were unusually bright. Words were audible now, simple direct words. "Complete the work," he whispered.

Edward nodded. "I shall, I promise."

"And thank you—for loving me."

Edward closed his eyes. Suddenly whole series of memories from their childhood filled his senses, and immediately following that a darkness covered everything. He clung even more tightly to Daniel's hand, as though literally to wrestle him from the arms of death.

He waited patiently for more words, but there were none. He saw now on Daniel's face a peculiar expression of youth. The cares were passing, the sorrows and regrets, the wasted dreams and the realized ones, all were departing from him.

Edward heard him draw three long perfectly gentle breaths. The hand suddenly clasped his own, as though, at the last moment, Death had had a change of heart. But then his head turned a final time upon the pillow. As the mouth fell grotesquely open, Edward felt as though something huge and merciless had struck him and was now threatening to drag him down.

He reached forward and lifted Daniel in his arms, tears streaming, and cradled him, buried his face in his hair and cried out in one bitter cry.

He saw all the dim light in that room shrouded in darkness and felt a portion of his soul quenched forever.

By midnight, with the help of the old woman, Edward had bathed Daniel's body, had placed fresh linen upon his bed, had gently garbed him in the white silk shirtwaist which he'd intended to wear as a bridegroom, had brushed his hair until its auburn tints were shining against the pillow, had placed candles at both his head and his feet.

Throughout all this activity, Edward had been aware of little. If the night had been hard, he knew that what remained to be done in the early hours of the morning was beyond belief. Thus he welcomed the numbness.

Shortly after one, he kissed Daniel for the last time, gave old Lucy orders to sit guard outside the door, then took brief refuge in his own chambers. The room was pitch black save for the yellow spill coming from the gaslight in the street. He wanted it dark and in the darkness made his way to the bed, then dropped on his knees in mute despair.

It seemed that in the darkness he was being watched by a cold judge who looked mockingly down on him. He closed his eyes and wept. He knew that he must spend his grief now, for in a short time he would have to face Jennifer and supply her with strength which he did not have.

There still was the element of disbelief. Daniel was not dead. If he were to go to the door now and call for him, surely he would answer. In a moment of irrationality he considered doing it, then repelled by his thoughts, he gripped the side of the bed and held his position.

What he needed now more than anything was a reason on which to place blame. And he didn't have to look very far for it. Hadn't he begged Daniel repeatedly not to go into pestilential holes like Jacob's Island? And for all his concern, hadn't Daniel laughed at him and reminded him of Feargus O'Conner's words: *Someone must soil their fingers. The rich won't. A man is not a true revolutionary until his hands are covered with filth and blood.*

Around him in the darkness stood a ghost. "Forgive me," he whispered to the power at loose in the room, and as though the bed linen was the face, he leaned over, whispering the two words over and over again.

About an hour later, he heard the night watchman outside the window call two o'clock. Jennifer's train was due at three. Slowly he rose from his crucible, clearly aware that he was merely going to another. Without bothering to light either lamp or candle he went to his wardrobe, withdrew a clean shirt, slipped into another jacket, all the while his mind racing ahead to Euston Station, to Jennifer.

He stepped out into the corridor, and the first sight that greeted him was the crouched old woman about twenty feet away, obediently sitting guard on Daniel's room.

With a conscious effort of will, he lifted his head and brushed away the apparently endless tears and walked slowly down the passage to where the old woman was seated. As he approached he smelled something peculiar, and it wasn't until he was standing directly over her that he saw the pods of garlic clutched in her hand.

Too late. "Lucy, I must leave for a short time. I'll return with my sister."

Softly the old woman moaned. "They was to have wedded," she mourned.

He nodded and found it very difficult to keep his eyes away from the closed door. "If it isn't asking too much," he went on, "would you lay a fire in my chambers? And if you can, prepare a light meal. She will have journeyed since—"

To all his requests, the old woman agreed. He reached down and patted the old hand, then hurried back through the darkness of his house. He desired only one thing, to meet Jennifer and see her through this night to dawn. Beyond that, there were no plans of any kind.

In the entrance hall, he stopped and glanced toward the kitchen steps. Somewhere beyond that black abyss, John Murrey was waiting for him as well. But there was no time now, and moving with urgency, he ran through the front door and made his way down the alley to the carriage house. He harnessed the horses himself, then pulled atop the high seat, customarily reserved for another.

Grasping the reins, he urged the horses forward through the narrow gate and out into the deserted street. A short time later, he drew up before Euston Station, abandoned the carriage to a waiting porter and, passing beneath the Grand Entrance, he caught a glimpse of the tracks. All around him he heard the cockney patter of cabmen. In the distance he heard the thundering approach of the train, saw the black engine slowly angling its enormous weight into the station shed, heard the heightened hissing of steam as the engineer applied the brakes.

Then with a sudden shrill whine the iron wheels ground to a halt. A moment later, coach doors all up and down the broad platform flew open and as the passengers spilled out there was a rush of greetings. Now he commenced to push through the crowds, trying to see over the bobbing heads, searching for one face.

He saw her, just alighting from the last coach. He stopped, taking refuge behind a near column, unable to take his eyes off her as she searched the crowds. The pertness of her bonnet, the attractive disarray of her cape, the one loose strand of hair falling gracefully across her forehead caused him to think that he'd never seen her so lovely. He noticed now that she was awkwardly trying to manipulate an armload of parcels, a small traveling case of some sort, a wicker basket, all the time her eyes moving excitedly over the push and crowd of people.

She looked straight at him and even though they still were separated by several feet, her eyes brightened. "Edward," she cried out warmly. He stepped forward and took her in his arms and held her close.

Inside the embrace, she talked happily. "Sweet heavens," she murmured, "every time I arrive here, I think I've been abandoned. Everyone seems to find who they are looking for immediately except me."

He stepped away from the embrace, though still continued to hold her by the shoulders, moved by the change which had come over her.

"Well, my goodness, Edward," she smiled, "are you just going to stare at me? And where's Daniel? Did you two get separated again? Though I wouldn't be surprised. The train was filled and it looks as though everyone has their own private welcoming committee."

As she talked, her eyes moved excitedly over the crowds. "Where is he?" she asked again. "I'll need both of you, I fear, for my luggage. Not that I brought that much. I really didn't. But as I was leaving Roe Head, the ladies surprised me with a small fete. Look," and she lifted the wicker basket for his inspection, singling out certain objects for closer inspection. "Rose potpourri," she beamed.

As long as she talked, he felt safe. When she was not looking at him, he could see her looking over his shoulder. "Where is Daniel?" she demanded now, suddenly losing interest in the contents of the basket. Still she could not refrain from looking around. Then without warning she looked straight at him. "Don't keep him from me," she whispered, still smiling. "We have years to make up and we can't afford to waste a minute."

At that moment, everything in the world seemed dark and obscure. In that immense, crowd-filled station, nothing was comprehensible.

Apparently the feeling registered clearly on his face, for in alarm, the smile gone, she stepped closer. "What is it, Edward?" she pleaded. "Are you ill?"

Suddenly he reached down for her belongings, balanced the small trunk under one arm, and with the other protectively about her shoulders guided her out of the crush of people to one of the high Doric arches where he found a small harbor of relative quiet. He placed the various bundles on the floor near his feet, then following the dictates of some instinct, rested her gently against the arch.

"No, I'm not ill, Jennifer," he began, trying not to focus on the bewilderment on her face. "But there is sickness in certain parts of London, a fever."

She nodded solemnly. "It was all the talk on the train. Many got off at Oxford, fearing contamination. We'd heard nothing of it in Yorks. Is it very bad?"

He lowered his head, unable for the moment to go on. During his silence she was patient and when he looked up again, he saw her eyes as bright as ever. "Perhaps it would be wise then," she suggested soberly, "if Daniel and I left London immediately. And you, too, Edward. The three of us could leave for Eden right away. It's foolish to take chances."

Then apparently the unthinkable entered her mind. Once again he was aware of her searching over his shoulder, still looking for one face.

He held still before her, giving her all the time she needed. The question was forming. He could see it, and in those moments of solitary suffering, it occurred to him that there was little point to this earthly life.

"Is Daniel—" She managed only those two words, then pressed her gloved hand to her lips. "Is Daniel—ill?" she whispered.

Edward was aware of a strange lightness in his head. When he did not immediately answer, she looked up at him as though suffering a sudden anger. "Is Daniel ill?" she demanded, stepping closer as though to force a response.

Finally he placed both hands on her shoulders, thinking how simple and commonplace the setting, a railway station in the early hours of the morning with costermongers bawling the price of herring.

"Daniel is dead." There were the words, gently spoken. For a moment the fact that she had received them at all was not evident, as though the message had been beyond the grasp of her intellect. In fact her head turned lightly to one side, her brow furrowed as though he'd spoken in a foreign tongue.

He began to repeat the message. "Daniel is—" Then suddenly she shook her head as though to refute the last word. He felt beneath her cloak a trembling, a seismic upheaval which seemed to start in her shoulders and spread in all directions, until he was forced to renew his grip on her.

"Jennifer, I'm so sorry," he whispered and tried to draw her into the full support of his arms. But at that moment she wrenched free with a single howl which started in the upper registers and stayed there, a high-pitched scream which in its force whirled her about and left her facing the arch, one hand upraised, the other arm wrapped about her midsection as though someone had driven a knife into her.

He stepped quickly forward, and as she slid down he caught her and lifted her in his arms, felt the dead weight of her body, saw her face drained of color, eyes closed.

Behind him he was aware of a crowd of curious onlookers who had been summoned by her scream. He turned to them and shouted, "I need assistance."

But as one the crowd began to move back, their faces clearly revealing their fear. One woman whispered, "It's the fever."

"No," Edward shouted. "Not fever. She only—"

But with the same speed with which they had gathered they now dispersed, gloved hands over their faces, their eyes fixed in horror on the lifeless woman in Edward's arms.

Angrily he shouted after them, "She's not ill, I swear it," and still cradling her in his arms, he looked down on the various bundles left on the floor. They would have to wait.

As he started off down the long platform he tried twice to engage the assistance of porters. And both times they moved away from him with rapidly retreating steps. Alone, he carried her to his carriage, placed her on the cushions, drew the lap robe over her, then closed the door and retraced his steps along the platform, gathering up the small traveling case, two large trunks, and the basket of gifts.

Throughout all this activity, he thought that perhaps it was best, at least for the time being, for her to remain unconscious, though he wished that he could blot out the resounding memory of her scream. With the last trunk loaded atop the carriage, Edward again climbed upon the high seat and brought the reins down over the horses.

A short time later, he guided the carriage into the carriage house, following the beacon of the solitary lantern he'd left burning. Quickly he unharnessed the horses and turned them loose in their stalls and at last approached the door, ready to lift her again in his arms and carry her to his chambers.

But as he approached the door, he stopped. She was sitting upright, apparently having recovered on her own from her faint. "Jennifer," he smiled and extended a hand of assistance. In the shadowy interior of the carriage house, he could not see her face. All he could clearly see was that she was clutching the small traveling case, both arms wrapped around its awkward bulk.

"Here, let me help," he said, but as he started to take the small case from her, she drew back. Now he saw her face with greater clarity, her hair mussed, the bonnet gone. But it was her face that captured and held his attention. Though she was sitting upright and her eyes were open, there was no movement in her face.

"Come, Jennifer," he pleaded again, trying to provoke a response.

She turned to him with a smile. "Take me to Daniel," she murmured, and so saying alighted from the carriage on her own and stood waiting patiently, still clasping the small box in her arms.

Grateful that she had revived and now apparently was in moderate control, he led the way, moving slowly into the house, aware of her following behind, though hearing nothing from her except an occasional soft sigh.

As they approached the second floor and Daniel's room, Edward saw old Lucy stand quickly from her place of vigil. They stopped before the closed door. "Is he here?" Jennifer whispered.

Edward nodded.

"Then put my trunks in here," she commanded. "And leave us."

Edward started to protest, then changed his mind. How wrong of him to dictate how she should spend her grief. Come morning there would be time for reason. For now, though there was something in that pale face that disturbed him, he pushed open the door, his eye immediately falling on Daniel.

He watched as she at last moved forward, heard her call out lightly, "Daniel, are you there?" Then he could watch no more. Quickly he closed the door, gave a brief order to the old woman, "Leave them alone," then hurried down the corridor to his own chambers where he found the comfort of a fire, but little else.

He'd not intended to sleep. Sleep seemed an obscenity. Yet he must have dozed, for he awakened to find a cold gray dawn outside the window, the fire burned down, and an ominous silence coming from the house. He sat up in the chair with a start and for one blessed moment knew neither who he was nor where he was. Then he remembered both and within the instant was on his feet and running. He threw open the door and gazed through the residue of sleep toward the far end of the corridor. The old woman's chair was still there, though the woman herself was nowhere in sight.

Jennifer, he thought with panic. Had she wanted something during the night and been unable to rouse assistance?

Still trying to shake off sleep, he hurried down the corridor. Surely she'd not passed the entire night in that grim room.

Although he approached the door with certain resolve, he now stopped. Listen! There was someone inside speaking. Muffled it was, but it was Jennifer.

He felt new panic. Slowly he pushed open the door.

She was lying on the bed with him, her loosed hair spread over his shoulder, on her side she was lying, the coverlet drawn over both yet revealing enough of her upper torso for Edward to see clearly that she'd changed her garments. At some point during the night she had slipped out of her dark gray traveling clothes and donned what appeared to be a white lace wedding dress. Scattered about the room in utter confusion were various other garments and what appeared to be hundreds of letters.

Edward grasped the door, unable to move through it or out of it. At that moment she saw him and raised up abruptly from Daniel's body and bestowed upon him a beautiful smile. "It's only Edward," she whispered to the dead face, "come to serve our wedding breakfast. Isn't that right, Edward?" As she clasped the coverlet to her, he noticed her hands trying to bring some order to her mussed hair. "You really should have knocked, Edward. How daring of you to burst into a wedding chamber." Then her expression softened and the fingers which earlier had smoothed her own hair now smoothed Daniel's.

"But we forgive you, don't we, Daniel? How could either of us hold a grudge on such a beautiful morning?" At that moment she left the bed gracefully, revealing bare feet and gazed sadly about at the muss on the floor. "Aren't we dreadful, Edward?" she whispered. "I tried on all my trousseau for him and he said I'd never looked lovelier." With that she commenced to scurry about the room, gathering up the scattered letters. "And then," she went on, "we read our letters to each other, every one of them, some twice," and here she ducked her head, giggling.

He saw one trembling hand coil a strand of loosened hair about her finger and she stood for a moment in the center of the room, looking blankly about, as though something had, without warning, exhausted her. In spite of her smile, there was a frightened emptiness on her face as she looked up at Edward and murmured, "It was a

lovely wedding, wasn't it, Edward? I've never seen such
a lovely wedding."

Edward closed his eyes and tried not to see anything,
though still he heard the wandering voice which seemed
to dwell in the upper registers, like a child's. With his
eyes closed, he remembered another face, as vacant, as
mysterious. *Charlotte Longford.*

Then something was pushing against him and he opened
his eyes to see Jennifer clinging to the door frame opposite him, her pale face creased into angles of concern.
"Poor Edward," she soothed, "how tired you look." She
leaned forward as though for a confidence. "Why don't
you go back to bed?" she whispered, "and leave us. After
all, we *are* married. I am Mrs. Daniel Spade."

Then Edward could listen no longer. Seeing her thus,
he closed his eyes, backed from the room, and shut the
door behind him and leaned against it.

But at that instant, he heard, coming from the other
side of the door a whispered, almost lyrical request. "Daniel, love me. I'm your wife. Please—love me—"

He pushed away from the door and ran, unseeing, toward the cold darkness of his own room.

Three days later, Edward stood on the pavement outside the house on Oxford Street and watched with dull
eyes as two hired female aides in gray capes escorted a
smiling Jennifer down the steps.

Beneath her traveling cloak, he saw that she still wore
the mussed white wedding gown. One of the aides had
tried to remove it the day before, and Jennifer had set
up such a howl of anguish that Edward had forbidden
them to go any farther.

Also they had determined during the last three difficult
days that in moments of extreme agitation the only object
which brought her immediate comfort was the traveling
case filled with Daniel's letters. Thus, again on Edward's
command, it was never to be denied her.

Waiting at the curb, he saw the new carriage, specially
outfitted with an over-wide seat which had been converted
into a chaise. Edward had hired four stewards plus the
coachman to accompany them, and had the day before,
sent a courier ahead to Eden with a letter addressed to

his brother, James, explaining as best he could what had
happened and begging him to put aside past differences
and give Jennifer all the love and understanding that she
required.

Now as he looked up, he saw her just descending the
steps, flanked on either side by the aides. With a rigid
act of self-discipline, he held himself in check. He knew
he must not do anything that would be likely to hinder
her progress. Thus at her slow smiling approach, he maintained an exterior mask of perfect calm.

"Edward," she murmured, breaking loose from the
aides' grasp, which was a gentle grasp at best. As she
went up on tiptoe to kiss him, he caught her briefly in
his arms and held her close, amazed at how fragile she
felt, as though her broken mind had somehow taken a
toll of her physical body.

Still in control of his emotions, he fell into an affectation of brotherly bluntness. "Did you remember everything?" he smiled, trying hard not to see the blankness
in her eyes.

With a light motion of her hand, she motioned to the
two women waiting. "My maids packed for me," she
smiled. Then with utter seriousness, she leaned close and
whispered, "You mustn't tell Daniel. He wouldn't approve. Maids for Mrs. Daniel Spade!" Her face suddenly
fell into a new seriousness. "You won't tell him, will you?"

Edward lifted his eyes to the sky. "No," he promised
softly. "It's only for the journey. You can't make it alone."

She took his arm and walked with him a few steps toward the carriage. "I know, but I'd not planned on making
it alone." Suddenly her face grew petulant. "I don't know
why he had to leave now. The miners are grown men. I
should think they could look after themselves."

The fantasy was hers, one she'd constructed after they
had taken Daniel's body away. She'd told Edward quite
seriously that Daniel had had to go to the Black Country
to hear the grievances of the miners, that she was to
proceed to Eden and he would meet her there for the
remainder of the honeymoon.

"It's his work," Edward now soothed, gently guiding
her toward the carriage.

At the carriage door she gave him a dazzling smile. "Of

course it is, and I stand corrected. As his wife, I must share that work, mustn't I?"

Edward did well to nod.

"And thank you," she rushed on, "for the lovely wedding, the prettiest ever I heard the guests say." Suddenly she looked disconcerted. "Where are my letters?" she demanded, looking in all directions about the pavement.

Hurriedly Edward reassured her. "They're safely inside the carriage." He opened the door and stood back so that she might see the small traveling case resting on the seat.

She looked intently at the case for a moment, as though to confirm its presence. Then she pointed to it with a solemn gesture. "That's Daniel," she smiled, her voice drifting. "I have him locked up in that case and whenever I wish, I can take him out and hold him and love him."

Edward looked away, scowling at the pavement. When he looked back, he saw the two aides assisting her into the carriage, one suggesting that she lie down on the comfortable chaise, the other drawing back the coverlet.

But apparently Jennifer had no desire to follow their suggestions. "Good heavens, I'm not sick," she protested lightly.

Edward closed the carriage door. As the two aides settled opposite Jennifer, he leaned forward with one last request. "Please look after her," he murmured. "And write to me immediately concerning conditions at Eden. If they aren't suitable, I'll want you to bring her back here."

Both women nodded. He trusted them and was certainly paying them enough. Then there was nothing more to say and slowly he stepped away from the carriage, watched closely as the stewards and coachman took their places.

At a flick of the reins, the horses started slowly forward. Quickly he turned back toward his house. Inside the entrance hall he found only stillness, though once he looked up toward the top of the stairs, thinking that Daniel had called to him.

A thought occurred to him: *The Elixir to Heal all Pain and Bring Forgetfulness to every Sorrow.*

For a few moments he stood, his eyes cast downward. So easy it would be.

"No," he whispered fiercely. "No," he said aloud, and tearing himself out of the stillness, he ran back to the door, closed and bolted it, unable to determine whether he had locked the enemy out, or locked him in.

Six weeks later, with the first warming rays of an April sun, the poisonous miasma seemed to lift from the London air. The "Curse from God," as some people called it, apparently was cancelled, though the toll had been terrible and no right-minded man who trusted in the Deity could ever believe that He had sent such tragedy.

As for Edward, he was in complete agreement with that practical-minded old statesman Lord Palmerston, who had urged the religious leaders and the populace in general to "Look to their drains."

Thus in the six weeks between Jennifer's departure and the children's return, Edward dipped deeper into his purse for a complete renovation of all his schools. He oversaw the ambitious project himself, seeking refuge in work, snuffing out the constant temptation of opium in back-breaking, round-the-clock labor.

Each school was aired, the old furnishings moved out and disposed of. The drains were opened, revealing putrescent mud, a ready poison which in many cases, including the house on Oxford Street, was found to be seeping into the water supply.

Of course this obsession with cleanliness was laughed at by most reasonable men. The radicals, including Lord Palmerston, who made the mindless connection between disease and dirt were labeled "Sanitarians," and for several weeks following the fever they were the objects of much derision and humor. Nonetheless, Edward persisted, stripped his schools, cleaned the drains, whitewashed the walls, purchased new furnishings, and feeling that it was now safe, called for the children's return.

On a mild Thursday evening near the end of April, with the hum of children's voices coming from the third-floor dormitories, after a loving reunion with his son and Elizabeth, Edward started down the stairs to the banqueting hall, to the man awaiting him.

He'd not seen him since before Daniel's death. In fact on that morning when he'd taken Daniel's body to St. Dunstan's, he'd also sent a message around to the man's lodgings in Bloomsbury, thinking that Daniel would want him in attendance at the funeral.

But there had been no response.

At the bottom of the stairs, Edward called out warmly, "Mr. O'Conner," and entered the banqueting hall, smiling at the sight of the large man, his broad frame tucked at an awkward angle beneath the low table designed for the children.

At the sound of Edward's voice, like a grasshopper scrambling, the man tried to stand in greeting. Obviously he finally despaired of ever finding a secure center of gravity and muttered, "Clearly you've spent a fortune here, Eden," bobbing his head toward the freshly renovated rooms. "Why couldn't you have spent a few bob more for a table and chair where a man can sit."

It was a mild scolding. Edward sat opposite him, smiling. "It enhances one's view of the world, Feargus, to see it from the angle of a child."

In spite of the good-humored greeting there was an unspoken weight between them. Edward considered mentioning it, to clear the air so that they could move on to other topics. But at the last moment he changed his mind. Perhaps O'Conner was one of those persons who did not seek an outlet for their sorrow.

But in the next instant, Edward saw his head bow and heard that powerful voice mutter huskily, "We are poorer men this evening, Eden, in a way which has nothing to do with coin or purse."

Edward heard and was on the verge of agreement when O'Conner went on. "Daniel Spade was a mainstay in the Movement, a trusted lieutenant."

The sentiment struck Edward as coarse. *A mainstay in the Movement!* Dear God, a man of rich and varied nature was dead, a man who— Abruptly Edward halted his thoughts. It would serve no purpose to quarrel with O'Conner on the matter of Daniel Spade's role as a human being.

"I tried to send word to you," he began. "I sent a courier. He returned with the message undelivered."

O'Conner leaned back, his eyes again moving over the cleaned banqueting hall. "I was out of the city."

"On business?"

"In part," the man replied, as though evading a direct reply. "My God, the fever was rampant. I saw no point in taking unnecessary risks."

Edward stared at him and tried to submerge certain contemptuous feelings. "Where did you go?"

"South, to Rye," came the immediate and unembarrassed response. "A good cleansing ocean breeze, medicinal in every respect." There was a swaggering affectation about him as though to suggest that all the dead were merely fools for having remained in poisonous airs.

Edward felt a rush of blood to his heart. In his mind was his last image of Daniel, lying on the bed, his head pressed back against the vomit-soaked pillow.

Again he felt that this line of conversation was not only senseless, but would render impossible any further discussions. He was aware then of the man opposite him bowing his head, both hands covering his face. "I only learned of Daniel's death upon my return to London a few days ago. I couldn't believe it." He stood now with difficulty and slammed his fist down. "My God, man, the death toll."

Suddenly he wedged himself back between the bench and table and with the tip of his finger drew a hasty outline on the surface of the table. "London," he announced.

How skillfully the man had shifted the direction of the conversation from his own cowardly flight to a vague outline of London drawn upon the table.

"Look, Eden," he commanded sharply. "Let me give you a fascinating geography lesson." On the map outline, he stabbed with his finger at certain areas which he alone could see. "There, Hyde Park. Fatalities, minimal. There, Regency Park. Fatalities, minimal. There, Mayfair. Fatalities, minimal."

As he spoke he continued to stab at various areas on the map. Edward knew what he was doing. The rich, it seemed, had not succumbed in the same vast numbers as the poor. Interesting, Edward mused, for it had never occurred to him that fever could be a political tool.

"But here," O'Conner raged on, "notice Lambeth, notice Southwark, notice Bermondsey, notice the docks."

Edward's impression of the man's lesson might have been more effective if he could only rid himself of the image of Feargus O'Conner paddling safely in the waters of the English channel.

Acting in a more subdued manner, O'Conner commenced to pace back and forth. "Why did you call me here tonight, Eden?"

The direct question roused Edward out of his grief. "I felt a need to talk."

"About what?"

"About—Daniel."

"Daniel Spade is dead," came the flat reply.

He was aware that O'Conner had stopped pacing and was now standing directly opposite him at the low table. "And what of you, Eden?" he asked.

Edward knew what he meant. Nonetheless he looked up as though seeking additional meaning. "I don't understand."

"Daniel told me once that we could count on you."

"As you can."

"In what capacity?"

"In any capacity."

"As an active participant in the Movement?"

Here Edward hesitated. "In a curious way, I've been cut in and kept out all at the same time. Now I feel a need for questions. And answers. So tell me of your Movement."

O'Conner stared down on him as though he'd asked the most ridiculous question possible. "The goals of the Movement, Mr. Eden, are quite easily explained." He drew his head up and delivered himself of a single word. "Revolution. Does that answer your question?"

Edward shook his head. "Not really. Revolution for what end?"

"For the good of the people."

"But they have unions." Edward smiled, aware that he was playing the Devil's Advocate.

"They have nothing," shouted O'Conner. "Unions!" he scoffed. "A hectic collection of old men with one hand on the Bible and the other in the workers' pockets? Forgive me, Eden, but those men represent an evil almost as great as your ancestors, for they play precisely into the hands of the upper class, unwittingly become their pawns, do their foul work for them, and in the meantime, the suffering persists, the injustice persists."

At some point Edward had commenced listening closely.

"Then what do you propose, Mr. O'Conner?"

O'Conner smiled. "Forgive me if I repeat myself, Mr. Eden. Revolution!" Then as though he sensed Edward's aversion to the word and all that it implied, he leaned eagerly across the table. "Not of the French variety," he smiled again. "A different sort of revolution will flower on British soil, and it will be fed and watered and brought to fruition by humble toilers of the British Industrial scene, an event which could well stand as among the chief contributions made by our race to the welfare of mankind."

Edward saw the man walk a distance away, where apparently he fell into a close examination of Tudor wood carving, the elegant detritus of a dead world.

Then finally O'Conner turned toward him, his face transformed. "Demonstration," he pronounced. "Not tomorrow, not perhaps even next year, not until we have successfully marshaled the entire working class of England behind us, a million strong. Oh God, imagine it, Eden, if you can." Head lifted, eyes closed, he appeared now to be rendered speechless by the vision.

"One million men," he went on, "walking silently through London's streets, a silent army, a Chartist army, marching steadfastly from Kennington Common to the Houses of Parliament, the Chartists' demands in the lead, a million men presenting those demands in a most civilized manner."

Again Edward waited, though in a new comprehension. The proposed spectacle would be very effective, unarmed men, impressive in their vast numbers, marching peacefully against that citadel of jurisprudence which thus far had denied them basic human rights.

Still O'Conner hung over the table, those broad hands kneading. "Can you see it, Eden?" he whispered, an imploring quality in his voice. "I desperately need a pair of eyes to share the vision."

Moved, Edward nodded. The man should admit need more often. "Yes, I can see it," Edward said aloud. "And I agree, it would be a most impressive spectacle."

"And effective?"

"Most effective."

"And possible?"

"And possible, though it will require massive recruitment."

On O'Conner's face, Edward saw a new expression, one almost resembling happiness. "Then—you'll help?" he asked timidly.

Edward responded immediately. With the ghost of Daniel beside him, he stood and extended his hand across the table. "It's why I summoned you here tonight."

He saw O'Conner smile. "Then neither of us has any need to mourn Daniel Spade," he said. "The Demonstration was his fondest dream, and on that glorious day, hopefully in the not too distant future, we will leave a space between us at the head of the column and we shall whisper, each in turn, 'See, Daniel, it's happening.'"

Then the moment of vision was over, O'Conner's mind apparently turning immediately to the logistics and execution of his scheme. "You spoke of recruitment," he said now. "We're already at work on it. We've divided England into twenty broad areas and intend to send lieutenants to all quarters."

Edward nodded in complete agreement.

"Such an undertaking will require funds," O'Conner said now, never taking his eyes off Edward's face.

"You shall have them."

"And clerks must be hired to keep the petitions in order as we send them back."

Again Edward nodded. "All," he smiled, "you shall have all your requests taken care of."

Then O'Conner turned away and started out into the entrance hall. "I'll be leaving for the Black Country in a few days," he called over his shoulder. "I'll see you before I go."

Alone, Edward watched until the man was out of sight. Mad? He and Daniel had both thought so once. But surely not. Overworked, easily excitable, perhaps momentarily relieved that his great dream, the Demonstration, would come true. In Daniel's name he had at last made a commitment to Daniel's cause, had pledged a large portion of his fortune, not only to the Ragged Schools, which in certain London circles were beginning to be looked upon with approval. Now he was a revolutionary, a mild one to be sure, but moving hopefully toward a changed world.

He smiled, standing alone on his darkened stoop. Strange, he didn't feel like a revolutionary. In fact he'd never felt less like a revolutionary. What he truly felt like was a doting, bourgeois father who longed with all his heart for the comfort of his son.

With that thought he lifted his head. The coming Demonstration of a million men didn't stand a chance when pitted against the awesome power of one bright-eyed, rosy-cheeked six-year-old boy.

John Murrey Eden knew who he was and of that there was no doubt. Edward took great delight in asking him, "Who are you, little boy?"

With barely concealed pride he watched as the sturdy, handsome child lifted his head and pronounced in clear tones, "My name is John Murrey Eden and my father is Edward Eden."

"He's growing spoiled," muttered Elizabeth from the door where, three days after the meeting with Feargus O'Conner, Edward was awaiting the delivery of the post. It was a ritual which Edward thoroughly enjoyed. On his orders, his son was to bring him the mail.

Now as the child scrambled into his lap, the small hand clutching thick envelopes, Edward quietly ignored the disapproving look on Elizabeth's face. As she closed the door behind her, Edward asked of the boy, "In your judgment, John, anything important?"

With adult seriousness, the child settled comfortably in Edward's arm and began meticulously to examine each letter, discounting one after another until at last he stopped, his eyes focused on one bearing the red wax seal and Eden imprint.

"This one," he announced, holding the letter up for Edward's inspection.

Edward took it from him and examined the unfamiliar penmanship. Not Jane's. Not the Cranfords'. Then remembering, the mystery was solved. He'd asked the aides to write to him concerning Jennifer.

With childish insistence, John was now demanding that he read the letter to him.

Edward agreed. "If you sit patiently while I read it first, then I'll read it to you."

Solemnly the boy agreed and nestled snugly into the crook of Edward's arm. The seal broken, Edward hugged his son to him, then lifted the letter toward the blaze of May sunshine and commenced reading the laborious hand.

"Dear Mr. Edward Eden," the letter commenced.

Regarding my word of promise to write to you here it is. Things have went well since last we spoke on the matter at hand. Journey to Eden placid and quite easeful for all concerned including Miss Jennifer who laughed at all the cows and sheep and horses. She's done well since and has fitted in well with home folks though her poor mother's ailing terrible and can't see her or speak to her, but the nicest of all is Lady Harriet, young Lady Eden, who took her right in and treated her with gentlest kindness, a lovely lady, I swear it. She had her made up some white lace gowns so we could rid her of that other one as after the journey it was done in. She likes to sit in the sunshine in her sitting room and she's there now, getting her hair brushed by Lady Harriet—

Edward closed his eyes, the letter still in hand.

"Papa? Now?" Young John had detected the pause, the closed eyes.

Edward kissed him. "In a moment," he soothed and turned his attention back to the letter, the scrawl beginning to tilt up the page.

—getting her hair brushed by Lady Harriet, and we are doing fine as well, me and Gertrude, enjoying the country air and the grandness of the place and trying to be helpful and earn our bread. There's one here who don't like us none, a Miss Cranford, but Lady Harriet says pay her no mind so we keep to ourselves and to Miss Jennifer who sends you her love and I'm saddened to speak it still talks of Mr. Daniel Spade and fetches his letters everywhere and says to one and all that he'll be coming soon and taking her away. One last thing that brings her pleasure is that pretty pianoforte which she tries to play but can't very well, though Lady Harriet is quite stern about everyone leaving her be. So all in all it's a calm season and as per promised, I and Gertrude will keep you informed.

Your Humble Servant,
Estelle Lewis

So all in all it's a calm season.

The simple phrase turned over in Edward's mind. Yet in a way it was true, the sort of calmness that follows spent grief. The woman whom he had loved, who had created this child sitting on his lap, this woman apparently now was bestowing loving kindness on Jennifer.

"Read it now, Papa?" It was John again, his face eagerly upturned.

And Edward read it, exactly as it was written, stopping only to identify the cast of characters. "Jennifer is your aunt, my sister, and she's ill. And Lady Harriet, yes, the kind lady is also your aunt, my brother's wife, and the poor old woman terribly ill is my mother, your grandmother, the Lady Marianne."

John smiled. "You've told me about her."

Indeed Edward had.

Long after the letter was read and explained with partial honesty, the two of them continued to sit together in the lengthening rays of afternoon sun, speaking of Eden and sea gulls, of cliff walks and blue water, of the headlands and the grand old castle itself, talking endlessly of a distant world which Edward could clearly see had become for John an obsession.

Eden Castle
North Devon
November, 1847

If asked what had brought about such a miraculous change in her attitude toward her bleak new life, Harriet would have replied, without hesitation, the arrival five years ago of poor wounded Jennifer Eden.

Before that unexpected occasion she had been a dead woman.

Being truly dead except for the faint beating of her heart, she had been capable of enduring anything: the cold, drafty old castle, the fawning falseness of the Cranfords, the endless winters, and on occasion even the awkward, crude attentions of her husband. Fortunately his demands in the beginning had been simple. Over five weeks had elapsed after the wedding before he'd found the nerve to come to her bed for the first time. Then he'd been mildly drunk, had made his demands, a brief uncomfortable ten minutes, no worse than bodily constipation on a cold January morning, mortifying but endurable.

Then in April of the following year, along with nature's thaw, Harriet had experienced a deeper, more significant thaw.

The messenger bearing Edward's letter to James had arrived first, and while Harriet had not been privy to its

521

exact contents, she'd been well aware of the flurry it had caused. Then three days after that the carriage had arrived. With the natural attraction of the wounded for the wounded, Harriet had thrown a shawl over her shoulders and had made the hazardous trip from her fourth-floor chambers to the steps of the Great Hall.

The day had been cold for April and she'd shivered as she'd watched the two aides alight first, had watched with greater interest as they had reached back into the carriage and had withdrawn what had appeared to be a crushed white flower. She'd still been wearing her wedding dress and how fearfully her eyes had darted across the massive front of the great castle.

Although there had been four of them on the steps that morning, both Cranfords, James, and Harriet, no one had seemed inclined to go forward in greeting, and at last, unable to endure the agony in those eyes any longer, Harriet had stepped forward, had removed the shawl about her own shoulders and had placed it about Jennifer. And out of that allegedly mad face she'd seen such a soft grateful glance.

And now? Look at her now! Harriet had time for a pleasant assessment before her appointment that was so important to others in the castle. She took a moment to survey her sitting room, a lovely rose brocade cave of warmth and comfort. How generous James had been, permitting her a free hand, allowing her to select good individual furnishings from all over the castle and arranged them to her satisfaction.

But of greater satisfaction were the two at her feet before the fire, the lovely Jennifer still clad in white—she would never wear anything but white—and, the miracle himself, one-year-old Richard, named for her dead father.

Harriet allowed the stiff needlepoint to fall into her lap and literally fed herself on the image of her son, born a year ago October, the pregnancy itself easy compared to that first hideous one, and after the mild pain, the old midwife had bent over her and placed her son in her arms and she had clung to him and remembered that someplace far away in a foreign land, she had another son, lost to her forever. But this one was here and all the unused love had rushed from her heart so that the midwife had had to scold her for fear she'd suffocate the child.

Again she looked down at the two stretched out on the fur rug before the fire. Both of them were children really, Jennifer lying on her side, cooing unintelligible words of love, and Richard responding with a dimpled smile.

Harriet smiled. What a miraculous change the infant had worked in all their lives. Jennifer had at last laid aside her traveling case of old letters. No longer did she carry them every place with her. She preferred now to carry the child and Harriet allowed it. And while Harriet couldn't in all honesty say that she loved James, he'd never given her reason not to respect him. In all ways he was attentive though undemanding.

She did not care for the Cranfords and felt uncomfortable when they discussed so openly the Eden affairs. And neither did she approve of the constant agitation which they heaped upon James, the impending lawsuit against Edward, their barbaric waiting for the Countess Dowager to die.

Edward. As she stared down on Jennifer and the baby, she thought the name again, as though testing it on her sensibilities and was pleased to feel no grief, only a pleasant residue of memories. And in that moment she experienced her greatest triumph, the realization that she had been right all along, that the plot she had constructed for her life had worked out. She was Lady Eden, and while she did not now have a great love in her life, she had known one and thus considered herself rich. She had a friend in Jennifer, she had a son and, God willing, would have more. She had wealth, position, legitimacy, and for the first time in many long years, she was at peace.

At that moment the baby whimpered, demanding to be the center of attention. Harriet watched as Jennifer scooped him quickly up into her arms and sat crosslegged before the fire, cradling him, whispering over and over again, "Baby, baby."

Harriet retrieved her needlepoint, smiling. "Not for long, I fear. He's growing. Before we know it, he'll be a man and gone from us."

Her eyes wide with worry, Jennifer asked, "Can Daniel see him when he comes? I've told him all about him. He mustn't grow too fast."

Harriet nodded. She'd long since adopted the policy that as long as Daniel was still alive for Jennifer, he'd be alive for her as well. She'd had long and bitter arguments with Sophia Cranford over the matter, Sophia believing that Jennifer would never heal so long as they permitted her to live in her fantasies. But Harriet had other theories. The world had taken a dreadful toll of Jennifer. Why not retreat into fantasies? They were by far the safest.

Deftly Harriet tied a knot, clipped it with scissors, and looked up to see Jennifer walking slowly about the sitting room, the cherubic infant gurgling placidly at the movement. The clock on the mantel said two-thirty. Time to go. Jane would be expecting them, looking forward to them.

"You'd better fetch your cloak and scarf, Jennifer," Harriet suggested now, laying the needlepoint aside. "Your mother expects us, remember?" she smiled. "The pretty room with the ill woman? Maybe Aunt Jane will have raisin cakes again today."

With childlike impetuousness, Jennifer handed the baby over to Harriet and rushed from the room.

As the hem of the white dress disappeared around the corner, Harriet hugged her son, then hurried with him into her bedchamber. No need to ring for assistance. She'd waited too long to care for a son. As she placed the baby on the bed, she gathered up the blanket and carried it to the fire. Warming it, she looked back at her child and for a moment she felt bent with loneliness for that lost son.

She closed her eyes. She could have insisted upon keeping him. No, she'd done the right thing and now it was incumbent upon her to put that child out of her mind.

Hurrying now, she reached for her cloak, drew the hood over her head, wrapped Richard in his blanket, and made her way out into the corridor where the first blast of icy air greeted her.

Estelle was there, fussing over Jennifer as Harriet had fussed with Richard. As Harriet drew near, she thought that perhaps it was a blessing that Jennifer did not recognize the ill woman as her mother. If she did recognize her, she'd never given any indication of it.

"Well, are we ready?" Harriet smiled as she approached the waiting women.

Estelle nodded, though she appeared worried. "She

seems more excited than usual, Lady Eden. Best if one of us go with you."

But Harriet shook her head. "No, it won't be necessary," she soothed.

Looking as though she was not quite convinced, Estelle shook her head. "She has something in her pocket, Lady Eden," she softly warned. "I don't know what it is and she won't show me. But you might be on the watch."

Harriet nodded. "It's nothing. I'm certain." And so saying, she took Jennifer by the arm and turned her about in the proper direction and commenced walking slowly beside her down the long corridor.

"Do you know where we're going, Jennifer?" Harriet asked softly, as they turned the corridor into another passage.

To this Jennifer nodded. "The sick woman," she murmured.

"Yes, we're going to see your mother."

"Mother," Jennifer repeated. And it seemed to Harriet that Jennifer's step increased.

Jane glanced over the once lovely tea table, then glared at the piggish old Mrs. Greenbell who'd been unable to wait. Making no attempt to disguise her anger, she scolded, "Well, it's ruined now, simply ruined."

"T'isn't," snapped Mrs. Greenbell. The old woman cast her eyes up at the scowling Jane, then lifted her cup, sipped noisily, and calmly reached for another raisin cake. Her third!

"That is enough," shouted Jane. "They will be here soon and I'll only have garbage to give them." Reaching out, she forcibly took the cake out of Mrs. Greenbell's hand and replaced it on the silver tray which earlier had held a beautiful symmetrical arrangement.

This once, just this once, Jane would have liked to have had everything pretty and proper for young Harriet. How much their visits meant to her! Even the poor senseless Jennifer was a relief, an improvement over the weeping woman who sat before the fire and the senseless drooling one behind her on the bed.

In the very next instant, Jane was ashamed of herself. Certainly no one was to blame, not old Mrs. Greenbell, who apparently viewed raisin cakes as the high point of the week, and certainly not poor Marianne, who had long since passed the limit of suffering which could be asked of any human being.

Merciful God, take her, Jane prayed as she saw the body beneath the coverlet. The once beautiful face appeared cadaverous, and on the side of the bed, she saw the ugly straps which now stretched across that frail body and held it rigidly though safely on the high bed.

The last attending physician, a young man from Exeter, said bluntly that he saw no medical reason why she should persist in living. But neither, he'd added ominously, could he find any medical reason that might cause her to die.

Looking down on her sister, Jane felt depression beginning to build. Oh, how often she had considered the kindness of the act of murder.

Still, she hadn't committed murder, and wouldn't commit this murder for one reason alone. Behind those blank eyes was an intelligence which still worked. Jane knew it in a way that no one else knew it.

As she turned away from the bed, she saw Mrs. Greenbell reaching for another raisin cake. At the same time she heard a soft knock at the door. In an attempt to control her splintering emotions, she called out a bit too harshly, "Come in, please," and looked up to see Harriet, her face baffled by the sharpness of the greeting.

"It's nothing," Jane soothed, hugging her lightly and leading her immediately to the fire for the comfort of the baby, then returning to the door where Jennifer stood waiting, her blank eyes curiously fixed on the high bed. "Come, child," Jane urged.

Quickly she relieved them of their capes and spread a thick fur rug before the fire, the baby's customary spot where all could admire him.

As Jane settled from this activity, Harriet asked softly, as though fearful of being overheard, "How is she today?"

Jane took the baby in her arms and answered briefly, almost curtly, "Same as ever." She didn't want to think about it now, not with new life in her arms.

Then to her extreme annoyance, she heard Mrs. Greenbell scolding her, "Put him on the rug. It's not fair for you to hold him."

"Old bitch," muttered Jane beneath her breath, placing the child on the rug. As she glanced over her shoulder toward the bed, she saw Jennifer standing a distance away, her eyes focused on Marianne. "Come, child," Jane called out. "Look! Raisin cakes." Her voice fell into mild sarcasm. "A few left at any rate."

The toothless old woman sitting to one side of the fire made a harrumphing noise and leaned forward and commenced waving in idiot fashion at the baby.

At that moment the child cried and Harriet smiled, "He's hungry." Quickly Jane drew up a chair close to the fire, as though to secure a good seat for this ritual. It was a poem to life, and Jane was hungry for the spectacle.

Fascinated, she watched as Harriet gently massaged her breast, the beads of rich white milk forming on her nipple, and was still watching as she lifted her son in her arms and guided his mouth to the dripping milk and heard the hungry sucking commence, his eyes closing in satisfaction.

"I wish I'd had a dozen," Jane murmured, her eyes misting over with old regret.

"Why didn't you?" Harriet asked softly.

Jane shrugged. "Ask God, for I'm sure I don't know."

"Well, they're grand, that's what they are," contributed Mrs. Greenbell. "I had two, though they're both dead now. Still, I've known mother love."

To Jane it seemed that the old woman had said this with undue meanness. Now she felt compelled to take the edge off the boast. "They're pretty enough at that age," she commented, "but when they grow up, that's a different matter. I've seen poor Marianne reduced to tears by—"

At this she looked over her shoulder and fell silent. "What in the—" Slowly she started up. She saw Jennifer bending over Marianne, placing something on her breast. As Jane hurried toward the bed, she was aware of Harriet behind her, still carrying her nursing son.

At their rapid approach, Jennifer glanced up with frightened eyes and quickly withdrew to the far side of the bed.

"What is it?" Harriet inquired.

Carefully Jane retrieved the object from Marianne's breast and examined it. "It's a small book," she murmured, bewildered.

Harriet smiled and nodded knowingly. "Just one of her most prized possessions. Read the inscription."

Still baffled, Jane opened the slender red volume—sonnets of Mr. Shakespeare, she noticed, and read the spidery handwriting on the flyleaf:

> To Miss Jennifer Eden, on the occasion of her wedding to Mr. Daniel Spade—with loving best wishes from
>
> Miss Wooler
> Roe Head, Yorks, 1842

"She meant no harm," Harriet smiled. "She just wanted to give her mother a gift, that's all." She raised her voice. "Come, Jennifer, no need to hide in the corner. How thoughtful of you."

Jane watched with mixed feelings as the senseless Jennifer re-emerged into the light of the room and took her place again beside the bed. Without a word, she reached for the book in Jane's hand and returned it to its intended place on Marianne's breast.

Jane retreated along with Harriet back to the warmth of the fire. "Do you think she knows her?" Harriet asked, readjusting her son in her arms.

"No," Jane said flatly.

"Perhaps not," Harriet agreed. And again all three women turned their attention to the beauty of the nursing infant.

Jane thought she heard a new disturbance coming from the bed, and she intended to make a check, but the baby was fretting with an air bubble and she loved to watch Harriet gently pat the tiny back. Oh yes, she should have had a dozen of them.

For some time, old Jane leaned forward in her chair, facing the fire, absolutely absorbed in the process. The joyful sound of the baby sucking was broken only by the rising snores of Mrs. Greenbell, who apparently had eaten her way into a state of complete satiation and now, warmed by the fire, had fallen instantly into a deep sleep.

Jane glanced at the old woman, then said to Harriet. "You can hear for yourself what I endure."

As Harriet wiped her breast, she smiled. "Still, she's very dear and I suspect if the truth were known, you'd be heartbroken without her."

Jane started to reply, but again fell into an adoring vigil as Harriet placed the baby, fat and filled, on the fur rug.

Jane heard her say lovingly to her son, "You wait here and be a good boy while I see your Grandmama."

Jane sighed. The pleasant part of the visit was over. Now she would be forced to endure while Harriet gave the unresponding Marianne a complete account of the baby's progress, speaking in perfectly normal tones, as though the old Countess Dowager were capable of response. In the beginning, Harriet's kind attention to Marianne had pleased Jane. Now it merely embarrassed her.

Well, nothing to do but get it over with.

As, laboriously, she turned to leave the comfort of her chair, she saw Jennifer, still beside the bed, leaning over Marianne in a peculiar position.

"Jennifer, what are—

She stopped. "Jennifer, what—" Her voice rose, then fell, and finally she screamed, *"Jennifer—"*

Still not certain what she was seeing, she took one step toward the bed. Oh dear God, it was the abundance of white more than anything, Jennifer's white dress blending with the white linen of the pillow, the white sheet, and Jennifer bent over at that macabre angle, leaning with all her weight against the pillow, and beneath the press of white pillow and white dress, Marianne's face.

Jane flew directly at the outrage, knowing in advance its significance, yet feeling the need to stop it if she could.

But she seemed incapable of rapid movement. She could never reach the bed.

Then she was aware of Harriet running past her, both hands extended.

They reached the bed simultaneously, Harriet going immediately to the far side and bodily lifting Jennifer upward, tearing the pillow from her grip and hurling it toward the foot of the bed.

"Is she—" Jane tried to ask the question, but couldn't. In the pressing crush of the pillow, the lavender lace cap had been pushed back, revealing the stiff shorn gray hair. The head itself was lying at a rigid angle, eyes open, fixed and staring. The lips were blue. Slowly Jane leaned over and pressed her cheek against the lips. Nothing.

As she lifted her eyes to Harriet she saw the young woman look toward Jennifer with an inquisitive expression. "Why?" Harriet whispered, drawing the senseless creature closer to the bed as though to display her own handiwork.

Without speaking, Jennifer tore loose from Harriet's grasp and again leaned over her dead mother. With infinite tenderness she replaced the small volume of sonnets upon her breast, then with one hand lovingly caressed the stubbly gray hair. "No more pain," she said, solemnly, shaking her head in childlike fashion. "No—more—pain," she repeated. And she repeated it still a third time, then a fourth, until it became a soft, mindless chant.

From across the bed, Harriet and Jane exchanged a glance. Murder had been done, but something else had been done as well, an act of mercy so complete that Jane could almost feel the absence of pain.

Slowly she looked back down on Marianne. Even the drawn face seemed to be acquiring new life. She heard Harriet whispering fearfully from across the bed. "What are we to do? Oh God, what are—"

Abruptly she stopped speaking as, at that moment, Jennifer leaned over the dead face and lightly kissed the lips. Then as though her work were done, she raised up and stretched; her eyes moved beyond the bed toward the tea table. The soft smile blazed into a broad one as she announced, "Raisin cakes." Both Harriet and Jane continued to watch as Jennifer left the side of the bed and went to the tea table, lifted the silver tray with half a dozen cakes on it, and took it to the fire where she knelt beside the baby and commenced to eat.

Across the bed, Jane was aware of Harriet still waiting, apparently more than willing to let her speak first. Behind her, coming from the fire, she heard Jennifer humming. It would serve no purpose to lock her in an institution. Perhaps when all was said and done, the demented woman had had more courage, more love for Marianne than anyone else in the room.

Still Harriet was waiting. Bending forward, Jane drew the coverlet up over the still face and slowly lifted her head. "Lady Eden is dead," she pronounced simply. "Only two of us know how, and I pledge to you that the knowledge will go with me to my grave. And you?"

She waited patiently for the reply. Slowly at last Harriet nodded. "It would serve no purpose to—" she began and did not finish.

But Jane did. "It would serve no purpose at all." Slowly she reached across for Harriet's hand. "Then we share a secret?" she whispered.

Finally Harriet nodded. "We—share a secret."

They both continued to look down on the dead woman. "I remember her on the occasion when she entertained Lord Horatio Nelson," Jane smiled. "She wore yellow silk, sun-colored, and there were pearls in her hair. She carried a small nosegay of violets and she broke the hearts of over three hundred gentlemen."

Jane lowered herself laboriously to her knees, found beneath the coverlet the now still hand that had held the violets. She kissed it, then pressed it to her forehead.

Behind her, coming from the fireplace, she heard the wandering voice, adding words now to the tuneless humming,

"No—more—pain—"

At four o'clock on Thursday afternoon, November 15, 1847, the Countess Dowager, Lady Marianne, wife of Lord Thomas Eden, Thirteenth Baron and Fifth Earl of Eden Point, was laid to rest in the family cemetery next to her husband and not too far from her father, Hartlow Locke.

The service was private, held in the family chapel, conducted by a priest from Exeter and attended only by family and staff. But when the cortege left the castle walls, there was a gathering of over two hundred people awaiting them, having seen the black banners flying from the turrets and having received the mournful news. They were citizens of Mortemouth for the most part, many who had known her personally, who had been direct beneficiaries of her kindness. To others, the younger ones, she was simply a legend, the young fisherman's daughter who had risen to the high rank of Lady Eden and who yet somehow never forgot who she was.

This mournful crowd was permitted to accompany the family to the graveyard where six stewards lowered the handsome coffin into the gaping hole and all remained, standing silently in place in spite of the biting Atlantic wind, while the grave-diggers heaped the earth high and patted it with what appeared to be gentle strokes carefully into place.

London
November 18, 1847

With ease Sir Claudius perceived the message behind the message. He would have to be an idiot not to understand. Still, did the Cranford woman have to be so coarse?

Marianne was dead. The morning was suited to the message, gray, overcast, chill. He felt poorer somehow.

He was feeling as weepy and as foolish as an old woman. Then to work.

There were two unpleasant tasks before him. One, he must inform Edward of his mother's death. Then he must respond to Sophia Cranford's letter with directness. He must inform her that a lawsuit at this time would be foolish. Why should they go to the trouble of running Edward to ground when he was on verge of doing that himself?

And it was plainly there for all of London to see, the man's association with declared revolutionaries, the proposed and imminent Chartist Demonstration. Dear Heaven, it was the talk of all the coffee houses and private clubs— a million men, or at least that was the rumor that Sir Claudius had heard, marching on Parliament and in the vanguard, who but Edward Eden, flanked on one side by the incendiary Feargus O'Conner and on the other by the assorted rabble who claimed a new dawn for all of mankind.

Thinking on it in this way, it was as though Sir Claudius had at last fully grasped the potential of the situation. Of course, the demonstrators would be met by troops. The Queen was young and engaged in what appeared to be an endless cycle of pregnancies. But she was not stupid. He had heard that special constables were being trained. It would probably be bloody, and for Edward, it could be fatal.

So, dear greedy Sophia, no lawsuit, no trial. Not yet. Let nature and man's foolish passions take their natural course.

To this end, he now summoned his clerk and dictated a terse yet convincing letter to the Cranfords.

As the clerk was putting the finishing touches on the letter, a dreary thought crossed Sir Claudius's mind. If the tree didn't fall soon, it would be barren of fruit. At the rate Edward was spending, there would be precious little left.

Well, at least Sir Claudius had the good sense to see that his percentage was lifted off the top intact. As for the rest of it, he could only hope that the madness reached its peak soon. With Marianne's death message still on his desk, he realized mournfully that a portion of him had died as well.

"Will that be all, sir?"

He looked slowly up into the face of his young clerk. "One additional letter," he murmured, "and this one I would like for you to deliver yourself."

"My Dear Edward," he began, "it is with sadness that I convey to you word of your dear mother's death. I have received word from Eden Castle that she died peacefully in her sleep on the Fifteenth of November, and was laid to rest beside Lord Eden." He'd started to say your father, but to a bastard those words lacked a certain accuracy.

"I send you my deepest condolences and trust that you will enter into the official period of mourning, designated by your brother, Lord Eden, to last a year from the present date."

There! It was done. "See to it immediately," he called after his departing clerk.

Now he would pray for the departed soul of Marianne. Five minutes would be quite enough, and to that end, he reached for the small hourglass on his desk, turned it over, and as the fine sand began to filter downward, he lowered his head, though he kept his eyes open lest he exceed his five-minute limit.

Quietly he prayed, "I believe in God the Father Almighty, Maker of Heaven and Earth . . ."

In spite of the dozen men, including Feargus O'Conner, who were waiting for him in the banqueting hall, it was Edward's wish that he and John go alone to the small chapel of St. Dunstan's. He knew that his son, now a sturdy ten years of age, was bewildered by the sudden change of mood which had fallen over the house on Oxford Street since that morning when Sir Claudius's clerk had delivered the sad message.

He'd fully expected O'Conner to object. In the past he'd made it clear that nothing was to interfere with the plans for the Great Demonstration.

But tonight, he seemed malleable. "A mother's death," he entoned softly, "leaves a wound on the most dauntless spirit. So, go say your prayers, Eden," he concluded. "You'll be no good to us until you do."

Edward was aware of O'Conner watching. Before him was his son, that mirror image. "Come," he smiled and placed an arm around the boy's shoulder, and thought with sadness that Marianne would never have the privilege of knowing this handsome grandson. Nor would John know her.

Under the weight of this double loss, feeling responsible, yet almost like a link between the two, he led his son out into the dark night where snow was falling on a quiet world, a quiet which persisted during the short walk, John keeping pace with him effortlessly, though clearly in a subdued mood.

As they drew near the black iron fence which guarded St. Dunstan's cemetery, Edward looked out over the snowy darkness in the direction of Daniel's grave. He still felt bitter in a way that he was alive while that rare man was dead.

"Are you warm enough?" Edward inquired.

John nodded.

In spite of the affirmative reply, Edward put his arm about the boy's shoulders. But almost imperceptibly John seemed to pull away, walk faster as though to put distance between them.

Edward watched him, momentarily puzzled. But then he might only have imagined it.

Then he saw John moving ahead of him into the chapel where the temperature varied little from that outside. The pews on either side were empty. Ahead, beyond the altar rail, he saw the plain, unadorned crucifix and its simplicity suited him. Momentarily leaving John's side, he walked the short distance to the altar and knelt.

He bowed his head and experienced a moment of confusion. What was he to say? *Thank you for taking her. Our Father Who art in heaven. In all ways is Your Word made manifest.*

God! Nothing but empty words and incoherence. Frowning, he leaned farther over the altar rail, now pressing his clasped hands to his forehead, as though to clear the fog there.

Yet nothing would come, nothing suitable to the place and the occasion. Was he so far removed from God?

With a rapid glance over his shoulder, he saw John seated midway down the center aisle, watching him.

Pushing up from his knees, Edward walked slowly back and slipped into the pew in front of him. Without looking at him, he asked softly, "Do you know why we are here?"

Without hesitation, John replied. "Because Grandmama died."

"And don't you think we should say prayers for her?"

"Why?" The question was blunt. "I never knew her."

"I wish that you had. She would have loved you so much."

"Then why didn't we go home?"

Home! It was the first time that Edward had ever heard him refer to Eden as home. Now he looked back over his shoulder and saw his son's face as stern and unhappy as he'd ever seen it.

When Edward didn't answer immediately, John went on. "You've told me for as long as I can remember that one day we will go to Eden. But we never have. For Grandmama and me, it's too late."

Bewildered, Edward could only gaze at the boy. It had

never occurred to him that the journey was so important
to him. True, he'd grown up on tales of Eden. Of course
it was quite natural that he wanted to see for himself.

"Aren't you happy here?" Edward asked quietly.

John did not answer immediately, but instead fell into
a close examination of his hands, several locks of golden
hair falling over his face in the process. Finally he shrugged,
though he refused to meet Edward's eyes.

"Look at me," Edward commanded. "I must have an
answer."

"It's not—home," he murmured, still keeping his eyes
down.

"But of course it is," Edward protested.

"Not in the way other people have homes," John countered. "Not like Eden where you lived with your father
and mother—" He broke off speaking, as though he knew
he were revealing too much of his heart.

Edward reminded him of certain inaccuracies in his
claim. "But I'm your father," he smiled, "and I'm here."

Abruptly the boy looked at him. "Is Elizabeth my
mother?"

It wasn't that Edward didn't perceive the question. And
it wasn't that he was totally surprised by it. Still, it caught
him off guard.

When after a few moments, he still had given no reply,
John answered for him. "No, she isn't," he said. "She told
me so herself."

Wearily, Edward turned back around in the pew. Dear
God, what to say? Would the greater harm be to lie or
tell the truth? And it wasn't just John that he had to
concern himself with. There was a new Lady Eden at
Eden Castle now, his brother's wife, and a new son, or
so he'd heard. In telling the truth, those three lives would
be totally disrupted. Yet in not telling the truth—

Coming from behind, he heard a gentle question. "Is
she dead?"

Edward closed his eyes. To John she was dead. To Edward she was dead, as dead as the woman they had come
here to mourn. "Yes," he said finally and in the next
breath prayed for forgiveness.

He felt John leaning over close behind him. "Tell me
about her, Papa," he whispered. "Was she like your mother? Was she beautiful? When did she die?"

"Yes, she was beautiful," Edward smiled.

"A Lady?"

"A Lady," Edward nodded.

"And when did she die?"

"Shortly after you were born."

This last seemed to sadden him. "I'm sorry for that," he mourned. Still in spite of the sorrow on the young face, there was a kind of relief, as though the weight of unanswered questions had at last been lifted.

Still uncertain what he had done, Edward turned back around in the pew. "Shall we pray then," he suggested quietly, "for both our mothers."

Now John rose without hesitation and led the way down the aisle and was already on his knees as Edward knelt beside him. No sooner had Edward closed his eyes than he heard John whispering, "What are we to say, Papa?"

Hiding a smile, Edward thought, at last, true companionship. Two fakes. Still, he whispered, "Pray that God go with their souls," he suggested, "and look after them, and always keep their memories alive in our hearts."

Although Edward thought he'd done very well, John apparently had doubts. "And that's all?"

Edward met his eyes. Wearily he suggested, "Add what you like."

"Aloud or in silence?"

"As you wish."

"Will God really hear?"

"It's rumored that He will."

Again Edward closed his eyes.

A few minutes later, there was a short, curt, "Amen," and even though his eyes were closed, Edward knew that John was standing.

"Shall we go now?" he heard him inquire as though with great dispatch he'd accomplished their purpose.

Edward nodded, speech momentarily beyond him. As they walked back out into the cold snowy evening, he again placed his arm about his son's shoulder and drew him close and this time the boy did not pull away.

Edward made a promise then. "I'll take you to Eden," he pledged, "as soon as my work is completed here. The two of us will journey to Eden. And I'll show you everything."

He'd expected an exuberant reaction from the boy. Instead John merely walked quietly beside him, apparently fascinated by footsteps in the snow.

"Did you hear?" Edward questioned.

"I heard."

"I promise I'll take you home."

Solemnly the boy nodded and with absolute confidence agreed, "I know you will, Papa."

London
April 10, 1848

The Great Day dawned cold and overcast.

At eight o'clock in the morning it was still quite dark. Edward had been up since before dawn. He'd spent the time working quietly at his desk for fear of disturbing John. Elizabeth, who now lodged down the corridor, had come for the boy a few minutes earlier to take him for breakfast and then to hand him over to his tutors. Edward had requested that she return as soon as possible. He had important matters to discuss with her.

Now in the interim of waiting, he paced back and forth in his chambers, considering all the ramifications of the day. How would it end? If only he could foresee that. April 10, 1848. How would history treat that date? The potential for disaster was enormous. He'd felt the tension in London streets for several weeks, the silent gathering of workers from all over England.

As for the opposition, they too had prepared themselves. Over the last few days, he'd observed, mingling with the workers an increase of government troops, every street corner and coffee house alive with uniforms.

Edward continued to pace, as though somehow in the quiet room he could manufacture the assurance that he needed. The trouble was that it was almost as if the nation expected violence. With the entire face of Europe in bloody and rioting change, why should England's revolution be any different?

There was no turning back now. O'Conner would come for him shortly after ten o'clock and together they would ride to Kennington Common. There Feargus O'Conner would briefly address the men. Then the silent march would commence. At this point, what would the government troops do?

He stood now gazing down from his window at the still dark pavement. Generally at this hour of the morning the street was clogged with commerce. Perhaps all had fled to places of safe retreat. Above he saw a dense blanket of gray clouds settling ominously over the still city. Too quiet. He recalled the editorialists who recently had predicted that by nightfall the Thames would be red with blood.

Dear God, no, he prayed quickly, and for the moment could find no respite from his fears. The best he could do now was to live with the anxiety and make certain inevitable preparations.

To this end, he turned back into the room, where standing by the door he saw a very pale Elizabeth, her face mirroring all his apprehensions.

"Please, sit," he invited, motioning to the chair opposite the desk.

As she obliged, he heard her say quietly, "So, it's to be today."

"Yes," he confirmed. "Is John at work?" he asked abruptly, drawing comfort from the thought of his son at his studies.

She nodded, and held his glance a moment. Then she seemed to straighten in her chair as though to move away from a dangerous line of thought. "What did you want to see me about?" she asked quietly.

He looked at her and saw the worried look on her face and abruptly changed his approach. He smiled broadly. "I only wanted to remind you of the celebration tonight," he said. "We'll be coming back here, many of us. I just wanted to be sure that there's food for all."

"All will be ready," she promised. "Cook has been working for days. You should see the pantry."

There was a pause. She looked questioningly up at him. "And that's all?"

"What else?"

She stood then in a lighter mood. "Then I must tend to a hundred other matters," she said and started toward the door.

He almost let her go, but at the last moment stopped her. "Elizabeth—"

Hurriedly he went to the desk and lifted a heavy envelope. "This is for you," he said. "Put it in a safe place among your things and there's no need even to look at it unless—"

He'd explained nothing of the letter's contents. "In the event," he began, choosing his words carefully, "that the celebration has been ill-planned, I must ask one last favor of you, that you take my son back to Eden Point. Will you do that for me?"

She was eyeing the envelope now. "There's money there," he said, "more than enough for both of you, and instructions to my brother that you too be allowed to stay in the castle, if you wish."

Quickly she shook her head. "I don't belong there," she murmured. "But I'll see to John," she promised.

"Then it's settled," he concluded, coming around from behind the desk. "Here," he said, placing the envelope in her hands at last. There was nothing more to stay for, though still she waited. He wanted nothing more in the world than to erase that look of gloom from her face.

To that end, he took her by the shoulders, then enclosed her in his arms and felt the envelope being crushed between them. He'd intended to hold her only a moment. But as he relaxed his arms, he was aware of her hand moving around his neck in a reciprocal embrace.

With his eyes closed, he rested his cheek atop her head and wondered, which was the greater force? Those half a million men gathering on Kennington Common, ready to remake the world, or that one small hand, offering comfort?

Shortly after they had left the house on Oxford Street, they began to see an increase in government troops. A strangely subdued Feargus O'Conner commented on them. "They *want* blood shed," he muttered.

"I think not," Edward said, looking out at the same scene. He saw soldiers everywhere to be sure, but they were relaxed-appearing, chatting on street corners, camping in parks with the same men they shortly would be facing on Kennington Common.

As they made their way through the city toward the river, Edward noticed an increase in traffic. From the carriage window he could see officers hurriedly drinking tea and eating breakfast, other soldiers munching biscuits, stamping their feet rhythmically while they gathered about the fires, warming themselves in the chill morning.

The officers and adjutants in command got on their horses and gave final orders to the men who remained behind and the monotonous thud of thousands of feet began. Edward saw the columns moving through the smoke and fog, an awesome sight, as though it were the government's intention to match every demonstrator with a soldier.

They were passing Westminster Bridge now. Kennington was not too far. Along the pavement outside the window, he saw the crowds increasing, the workers for whom this massive demonstration had been planned. Interspersed among them he saw uniforms, special constables who had been pressed into service, and many spectators.

"We've gathered quite an audience," Edward commented to O'Conner, slumped in the seat.

O'Conner pulled himself upright and gazed timidly through his window, his face flushed as he surveyed the chaotic scene on all sides. "If they are with us, they are welcomed," he muttered.

Then suddenly Edward heard O'Conner shout a triumphant "Look!" and leaning out the window, Edward followed the direction of his hand and glanced ahead toward the Common, and saw, not the Common, but a sea of men which seemed to grow larger even as he was watching it, perhaps not half a million men, but enough to fill the large area, with many more spilling over onto the pavements and up the embankments, men closing in around the carriage now.

Edward heard a single cry, "It's him! It's O'Conner," and the refrain was taken up by thousands of other voices which in turn relayed the message into the heart of the crowd, and all at once Edward saw a remarkable change come over the man, as though at last he'd found the narcotic which sustained him and gave him strength.

Leaving the carriage, O'Conner strode, head erect, toward the center of the mob and the flat-bed wagon waiting at the heart of the Common. As Edward emerged from the carriage, he saw a battalion of police standing at the edge of the gathering, merely watching, their passivity in peculiar contrast to the wildly shouting men. A Commissioner on horseback detached himself from the battalion and rode slowly a few yards into the crowd.

Edward thought, one man advancing. Hardly a threat. Then he hurried after O'Conner, who was moving down a small path where the men had parted to give him easy passage. Edward saw many of the men reach out to touch O'Conner and, still grasping the petition, the tall man returned their greetings. Truly he was a man fully restored.

A few moments later he'd managed to make his way to the flat-bed wagon and with one easy leap, his black cloak flying, he scaled the small height and stood erect, well above the crowds, and extended his arms as though to embrace them all.

As the roar increased, Edward made his way to the wagon and would have been content with his unobtrusive position except, at that moment, O'Conner looked down and shouted, "Come, Eden, you belong up here as well." As two strong aides grasped him by the arms, Edward felt himself lifted into the air and deposited alongside O'Conner, who suddenly raised one side of his great cloak, draped it about Edward's shoulders, and drew him close.

The gesture, clearly one of affection, was not lost on the crowds. As their voices rose again in a thunderous shout, Edward felt ill at ease, fairly certain that not one man in that mob knew precisely why they were shouting their approval of him.

When the applause and cries showed no signs of diminishing, he looked up to see a misty-eyed Feargus O'Conner, with great circumflex eyebrows, again lift his arms, though he leaned close to Edward with a whisper, "For Daniel," he murmured.

Edward nodded, though in truth he could not see Daniel enjoying this position of exhibition any more than he was. The urgency in Daniel's soul had not been for theatricals such as this, but rather in the steady, quiet, and frequently discouraging assault on human misery.

Engrossed in this special moment, Edward was only vaguely aware of the black cloak leaving his shoulders. Now as he brought himself back to the uproar and the confusion, he saw O'Conner again, standing on the edge of the wagon, his arms raised in the air, clearly signaling for order and quiet.

And when at last the quiet suited him, he slowly lowered his arms and lifted his head and shouted at top voice in an echoing tone which seemed to resound about the quietly waiting men:

"My friends, we have gathered here today to rechart the course of English history!"

As his voice rose, the men once again lifted their fists and filled the air with a roar of approval.

Then O'Conner was speaking again. "The condition of England," he went on. "That is our concern today, an England blessed with unabated bounty, thickly covered with workshops, with industrial implements, with millions of workers conceded to be the strongest, the most capable that the Earth has ever known."

This was greeted by a softer scattering of applause, not that the men disagreed, but rather that they had never thought of themselves in positive terms. Now lifting his eyes, Edward saw, just coming down Kennington Street, a regiment of quickly advancing cavalry. Peculiar, he thought, that all those horses could move silently. Of course they were still a distance away.

If O'Conner saw them he gave no indication of it, clearly caught up in his own rhetoric and the rarified mood of the occasion. "They tell us it is impossible to change the course of history. They say that it was always thus, competent men these are, too, who say these things. The Poor Law, they say, must be observed. Commercial stagnation must be expected."

As O'Conner launched forth into a heated diatribe against the Poor Law, Edward saw a second regiment of infantry, a thousand soldiers was his guess, dividing themselves into columns as the cavalry had done, half filing in one direction, half in the other, again encircling and taking up positions directly behind their companions on horseback.

As Edward watched, his disquiet increased. Surely they would not march on peacefully assembled men. God, with what ease Kennington Common could be converted into a blood bath.

Again he looked out over the men and, behind them, the troops, the darker blue uniform of the cordon of special constables, silently flanking the Chief Commissioner of Police, who sat astride his horse only a short distance away. Their plan was clear. Let the constables handle it first. If they failed, there were the troops.

Still he heard O'Conner speaking and was grateful. As long as there were words, there would be no call for action, though, as Edward heard now, those words were patently incendiary. "And now in the presence of you all," O'Conner cried, "I call the leaders of this country barbarians."

Although he was pushing his voice to its maximum capacity it showed no signs of breaking. "No blacker gulf of wretchedness," he was crying now, "has ever been created by a government for its people. Why have we been denied those enchantments, produced by the successful industry of England? Has it made *us* rich?"

In answer to the direct question came a single explosive thunderous "No!"

"Indefensible," he shouted, his arms outstretched. "To whom, then, is this wealth of England truly wealth? Not to us, the men who produce it."

It was clear that the questions were hitting their mark. The workers seemed to be pressing closer to the wagon.

"But we'll not stop here," O'Conner promised them now. "Here are our demands for a portion of that wealth which is justifiably ours." And so saying, he thrust the petition up into the air. "Here it is," he shouted again, "the new map of England where all men function and flower in equality, in a spirit of justice and brotherhood. Let it be said that on the tenth of April, 1848, Englishmen reached out and reshaped their futures and created a new world for themselves, for their sons, and for all mankind."

Then it was over. For a few moments, that vast crowd of men stood motionless, as though stunned by the vision of such a dazzling utopia. Then it came, a low roar at first, like incoming tide, perhaps a hundred voices in the beginning, then joined by others and still others until at last the sounds of the cheers struck the wagon like an inundating wave.

The men belonged to O'Conner. He could do with them what he pleased, although, at the moment, Edward observed that O'Conner seemed disinclined to do anything with them at all. Rather he stood at the edge of the wagon like a spent saviour, his head bowed, his arms hanging limp at his side, allowing the waves of adoration to roll over him.

Directly ahead of the wagon now, by about fifty yards, Edward saw the Chief Commissioner of Police slowly advancing, one man alone, urging his horse carefully through the crowds.

Still he drew nearer, a rather elderly man, though he sat excessively erect on his handsome sable horse.

Yet closer he came, his eyes fixed on Feargus O'Conner, mildness in his eyes. The man was less than ten feet now from the edge of the wagon, his face perfectly calm as he pulled up on his horse.

The men in the front ranks of the crowd pushed slowly back as though sensing a confrontation. The shouts and cries were diminishing. O'Conner seemed exhausted, yet alert, his eyes fixed rigidly on the Commissioner.

"Mr. O'Conner," the man said now, in a soft voice. "My compliments," and here incredibly he extended his hand upward across the edge of the wagon and it merely hung there for a moment, unclasped, as all eyes focused on O'Conner, who seemed completely baffled by the cordial gesture.

Around the perimeter of the crowd, Edward saw the troops still waiting. And still the hand was waiting, the morning growing colder and darker. It occurred to Edward that it must be noon or beyond, but it was almost a night sky forming above them, the heavy gray clouds beginning to pitch and roll, already dropping moisture.

At that instant the Commissioner looked up as though to confirm the unpleasantness of nature. "An unfortunate turn," he pronounced, looking truly grieved. Then heartily he insisted, "Come, man, let me take your hand. Never have I heard a more rousing speech. I predict it will be quoted for years to come."

Then at last O'Conner moved. Unfortunately he had to stoop from the height of the wagon to the lower level of the man on horseback. But stoop he did, as slowly, he clasped the still waiting hand. "I thank you, sir," Edward heard him say. Then incredibly he asked in a childlike manner, "Do you really think it will be quoted?"

"I'm certain of it," the Police Commissioner smiled. "I'll do the quoting myself, I will. Needs to be said, every last word of it."

The words of encouragement seemed to fall like healing balm on O'Conner's ears. He shook the man's hand with increasing gratitude, although at that moment he too was clearly aware of the increasing rain, many of the men pulling hoods and hats over their heads and seeming to press closer for shelter.

At last the Police Commissioner withdrew his hand and pulled the visor of his cap down over his head, his manner still sympathetic. "A bad turn," he cursed, raising his head directly into the rain. "Rotten luck, really." Then he looked at O'Conner as though a brilliant idea had just occurred to him. "*That* must be kept dry," he warned, pointing to the petition in O'Conner's hand. "Let me summon, for your convenience, several taxis. If you walk the distance from here to Westminster, the petition, as well as yourself and your men, will be drenched. A sodden committee is not a very effective one."

Edward listened closely, unable to believe his ears. The increasing rain seemed to be effortlessly quenching the revolutionary spirit.

"Come," the Commissioner coaxed. "Three taxis. I can summon them within the moment." He held out a hand as though to test the falling moisture. "It's a chill rain, and I'm afraid it's set in for the day." There was a clever combination of concern and compassion on his old face, as though he knew very well what he was doing.

But most incredible of all was O'Conner, who in turn glanced up at the spilling heavens, who looked around at his rapidly scattering men, and who at last gave the Commissioner a pleasant nod and murmured, "I'd be most grateful, for the taxis, I mean."

And with what remarkable and miraculous speed did those three conveyances appear, three black rain-soaked carriages, drawn by three black horses, all making their way through the dwindling crowd as everyone was running hurriedly for the nearest shelter.

"This way," the Commissioner shouted, leading the carriages in a circular pattern to the edge of the wagon. Within the instant the brave aides who'd taken shelter beneath the wagon scrambled out and pushed into the waiting taxis. O'Conner himself continued to stand for a moment in the now driving rain, on his face an expression of bewilderment, as though he knew that at some point he'd lost control, but was totally unable to say when or how.

He looked over his shoulder at Edward. "Eden?" he inquired. "Are you coming?"

But Edward, who had carefully charted the entire spectacle and who still couldn't believe what he had seen, did well to shake his head. He had no desire to approach Parliament in the back of a cab, and less desire to continue to associate himself with the twitching, befuddled Feargus O'Conner.

"You go on," he said quietly. "Don't keep the Commissioner waiting."

As he heard his name mentioned, the Police Commissioner looked toward Edward and lifted his hand to the visor of his hat in a small salute. "There's room for all," he shouted cordially. "No need catching an unnecessary chill."

But again Edward declined. He had conjured up many conclusions to this day. But in his wildest imagination, he had never thought of this one.

Standing alone on the wagon, Edward watched as Feargus O'Conner bent low and climbed into the lead carriage. The Police Commissioner himself, like a dutiful steward, closed the door after the "dangerous revolutionary," and with a wave of his hand and a faint smile on his old face, he gave the driver orders to proceed, at the last minute taking the lead himself in the spirit of an honor guard. As the procession passed by the waiting constables, Edward saw the Commissioner slowly shake his head, as though to inform his men that, with the help of nature, England's revolutionary fires had successfully been extinguished.

At that moment, in the distance, Edward heard sounds of the regiments disbanding. The orders came rapidly along the whole drawn-out line of columns. The calvary took the lead in columns of fours, the infantry falling in behind. In a remarkably short time, they had disappeared behind a sheet of solidly falling rain, leaving not a trace.

Less than half an hour after the conclusion of O'Conner's rousing speech, Edward found himself standing alone on the wagon, in a drenching rain, looking out over deserted Kennington Common, which only moments before had contained the efforts of four years and the revolutionary hope of all of England.

We have met here today to rechart the course of English History.

Edward could still hear the words over the steady downpour. He smiled, a stray wave of humor suddenly washing over him. Only that morning, he'd feared bloodshed, and with what melodrama he had given poor Elizabeth instructions in the event of—

He was silent for a moment, then suddenly, almost convulsively, he started laughing. The impulse came from somewhere deep inside him, so deep he could not recognize its source, yet the impulse was there and strong and he gave in to it and continued to laugh, aware of his own foolish self as spectacle, a laughing man standing alone in the middle of a wagon. Oh God, he couldn't catch his breath, yet still he laughed, his voice echoing in hollow tones around the deserted Common.

Slowly he shook his head as though still not able to believe what he had just witnessed. So much for communal effort, for vast demonstrations designed to "alter the course of history." It didn't work, Daniel, he whispered. Perhaps the only effective revolution always took place in the heart of one man. And if that were true, then let the new revolution start here, on this cold, rainswept abortive day, with a laughing fool standing alone on the bed of a wagon. Laughed out and momentarily dreamed out, Edward climbed slowly down from the wagon.

It was a long walk from Kennington Common to Oxford Street, yet he accomplished it, strangely impervious to the cold rain, still smiling now and then to himself, thinking on all that had been lost, and all that remained yet to be done.

With a stifled, sputtering sound, Sir Claudius Potter pressed his white linen handkerchief against this lips and gazed with repressed amusement at the pamphlet of caricatures open before him on his desk.

He wasn't laughing. Never in his entire life, to the best of his memory, had he ever committed the rudeness of an open laugh. But they *were* clever, these caricatures which had just arrived on London's streets this morning to be eagerly devoured by its citizens, who only now were beginning to draw deep breaths of relief after the "revolution" of last week.

Again Sir Claudius pressed the handkerchief to his lips. Take that one for example, and Sir Claudius adjusted his spectacles and again bent low over the pamphlet. Look at that, the background clearly Kennington Common, the knight on horseback with the long leash in his hand the Police Commissioner, and attached to the other end of that leash was one green baby dragon with red hair and the face of Feargus O'Conner.

And that one, the best, the central figure again O'Conner, disguised as a small boy, standing in a pouring rain, holding up an extinguished torch which the caricaturist had cleverly labeled, "England's Revolution."

With his handkerchief firmly in place, Sir Claudius quickly perused the others, a dozen in all, some emphasizing the three black taxis, others dramatizing the empty halls of Parliament and the reception table on which the Chartists' petition had been placed, ignored, and ultimately to be covered with the soothing dust of history.

Well, so much for the revolution, he thought. Now there were other matters at hand and he glanced quickly at the letter resting just beyond the cartoons, a demanding letter which he'd received only that morning from an impatient Sophia Cranford. It was clear that someone had rapidly conveyed the bad news to her, that Edward had survived the comic opera revolution, indeed was now spending the Eden fortune with even greater abandon than ever.

Slowly he adjusted his spectacles. The Cranford woman was right. Now was the time to legally take steps to remove what was left of the Eden fortune from Edward's hands and place it in the hands of Lord James Eden.

Warming to the possibilities of such a suit, Sir Claudius stared fixedly at his desk. The legal complexities were endless and unique, brother suing brother, legitimate heir turning on the bastard, one the plaintiff, one the defendant. Definitely not a jury case.

Slowly now, Sir Claudius arose from his chair, warming to the challenge. Well, then, it was up to him to find the right forum, the proper legal atmosphere so that the change could be effortlessly and painlessly brought about, painless that is for everyone but Edward.

His momentum carried him to the handsome marble fireplace where in the deep well a warming fire crackled. He stood for a moment, leaning against the mantel, his mind turning over and discarding certain possibilities. A simple hearing, yes, conducted in private offices. With his customary brilliant objectivity, Sir Claudius could present the case to a reasonable magistrate.

Here his thoughts stopped. A *reasonable* magistrate. That presented a problem. The bench was arrayed now with soft-hearted and soft-headed liberals who would clasp Edward's philanthropic activities to their breasts as a mother would a wounded child.

No! Sir Claudius must take charge here as well. He must choose the magistrate with great care. Yet, and this was where the skill came in, the choice must not be too obvious, not one of the old blueblooded magistrates like old Erskine at the club. No, not Erskine, and for many of the same reasons, not Walsh or Johnson. Then who? Who among the present magistrates could Sir Claudius count on for the right decision, all the while giving the careful impression of impartiality?

Then a name occurred to him. Sir Cedric Dalrymple, that dour Scotsman who'd arrived on the London scene about sixteen years ago, Aberdeen-born, Edinburgh-educated, "sour Cedric" the journalists called him, who had distinguished himself during the Palmerston murder case with a judgment as harsh as the Old Testament, as well as the Charlotte Longford trial.

Sir Claudius turned from the warming fire, delighted with his idea. Sir Cedric would be the man. How offended he would be by Edward's irresponsibility. How sympathetic to the dutiful younger son!

Now he must write to the Cranford woman and tell her that all was being readied for the suit and that she could rid her heart of all anxiety, for by the end of summer, at the latest, the Eden wealth would again be under the protective control of the legitimate Lord Eden.

Eden Castle
North Devon
June, 1848

When Harriet opened the door to her husband's private chambers, she felt dread. Her recent illness had taken a toll of her emotions. Now James had to excuse her from making the trip to London for the hearing. However much she prepared herself, she knew she could not go through with it.

She paused a moment, listening. She'd hoped he would be alone, but now she heard voices. She was just turning back toward the door when she heard James's voice. "Harriet, is that you?"

He seemed surprised, and why shouldn't he be? In five years of marriage, she'd never once come to his private apartments. He came to hers on occasion, and they met daily in the safe neutrality of the reception rooms. But she'd never come here before.

"I wanted to speak with you," she murmured, opening the door to speed her exit. "But I see that you are engaged, so I'll—"

"No, wait."

As she looked back, she saw his perennial expression where she was concerned, a guarded bewilderment, as though even after all these years, he still could not be

555

absolutely certain what to expect from her. "No," he smiled, drawing closer, one hand extended. "It's—fine. Is something wrong? Richard—"

Quickly Harriet shook her head, pleased as always that although there was no love between the two of them, James did adore his son. "He's fine," she said, edging out the door.

The voices which she'd overheard earlier coming from the sitting room had grown mysteriously quiet as though listening. She knew who they were and this conviction served to speed her on her way. "Later, James," she said, "it's not important. We'll speak later."

Now, "Is that you, Lady Eden?" Sophia called out, her voice changed, Harriet thought, grown lighter, almost giddy since word had arrived from Sir Claudius concerning the date for the hearing.

"I didn't mean to interrupt," Harriet called back.

"Interrupt?" exclaimed the lean, hard, old woman, drawing closer, pushing James aside as though he were an object without substance. "You could never do that, my dear," she smiled. "Come, we were just having tea and discussing our great journey to London. My goodness, it's been years since I've been to London. And it won't be all business, I promise you. Perhaps the two of us can sneak away for a look at fashions. Wouldn't that be splendid?"

Harriet had never seen the woman so garrulous. Now she felt Sophia's hand on her arm, guiding her without question into the sitting room where the scarecrow, Caleb, was on his feet, grinning as inanely as everyone else.

"Look who we found lurking in the corridor," Sophia announced, propelling Harriet toward the end of a plump sofa where before her on a low table she saw the scattered remains of tea.

Clearly there was nothing to do but see it through and wait for the first tactful moment to take her leave. As Harriet settled on the edge of the sofa, James hurriedly sat beside her. Opposite her Caleb settled back into his chair, balancing a teacup which he'd just retrieved from the table.

Sophia thrust a cup of tea at Harriet and invited her to sit back and relax. "You look—tense, my dear," she murmured as she sat in the chair opposite her brother. "Are you quite sure that you're recovered?"

Harriet nodded quickly. The miscarriage had been three

months ago. The physical discomfort had been mild, but she'd mourned the little seed and had somehow in her mind connected it with that other babe she'd lost. "I'm quite well, thank you," she said quietly to the cup of tea, and wished with all her heart that she'd kept to her own chambers, to the good quiet company of senseless Jennifer.

"Well, there will be others, I'm certain," Sophia said. "And perhaps it's just as well. If you had gone full term, the journey to London would have been quite uncomfortable for you."

Harriet looked sharply up. "If I'd gone full term, Miss Cranford, I wouldn't be making the journey to London." It embarrassed her to talk of such intimate matters before the men. Still the avenue of thought seemed to be leading in the right direction. Perhaps now was as good a time as any to inform them that she would not be making the trip to London.

"James," she began, turning to her husband, for it seemed to concern no one but him. But as she saw the expression of deep sadness on his face, she broke off. For the first time, she realized that the miscarriage had affected him as much as it had her.

Predictably Sophia rallied first. "You both need a change of air," she pronounced, setting her cup on the table. "How fortunate that events have arranged themselves as they have. In the excitement of London, I assure you, you both will regain your zest for living. Isn't that true, Caleb?"

The man nodded and continued to sip noisily at his tea. Harriet sipped her own tea, grown disagreeably cool. She gazed over the rim of the cup at the two opposite her. Somewhere deep within her the old aristocratic bonds were beginning to pinch. *They were servants. Whatever were they doing sitting here?*

She halted the thought, returned the cup to the table, and moved to ease the pinch. She stood and, taking a final glimpse at the high blue sky beyond the window, smiled warmly. "I will not be going to London, Miss Cranford. It would serve no purpose, and the hearing holds no appeal. Besides, I'm not fully recovered and feel that I would serve best by staying behind."

At last she looked at the three huddled about the sofa. As well as she could determine, no one had moved. Despite the tableau she concluded her explanation. "Jane is old, devoted, but old. I would do nothing but spend my time worrying about Richard. And Jennifer. We must remember Jennifer. The servants don't always know how to handle her. And since you, Miss Cranford, dismissed the two aides last month, I feel a great responsibility to make her life as comfortable as possible."

Still no movement. "Well, then," Harriet smiled. "I'll leave you alone. Again my apologies for interrupting. Richard and I are walking the headlands this afternoon, James. Feel free to join us if you wish."

She'd made it as far as the archway when behind her she heard Sophia stir. "Lady Eden," she called out, a portion of cordiality gone from her voice.

Harriet looked back and saw the smile again in place, though now it seemed a contemptuous smile. "I must ask you to return for a moment," Sophia went on.

"I don't wish to return, Miss Cranford," she announced. "I wish to fetch my child and take him for a walk in the warming sun. There's a constant coldness to this place. We must all take advantage of the sun."

She heard James's voice. "Harriet, I beg you," he pleaded, catching up with her at the door. "Please join us again for a few moments."

"It would serve no purpose," she said. "My mind is quite made up. I'd hoped to speak to you alone on the matter, but—"

Then Sophia was there again. "Close the door," she ordered James, "and bring your wife back."

Anger rising, Harriet started to protest. "I will not be detained, Miss Cranford. I have other things—"

"You have nothing," Sophia countered, all semblance of good will gone from her face. "Bring her back," she muttered to James, and walked away from both of them as though with utter confidence that her command would be obeyed.

Shocked by the woman's crude manner, Harriet paused to see if James would object to the treatment she was receiving. But as she looked at the bowed, slightly graying head of her husband, she saw nothing that even remotely resembled objection.

Now Harriet followed the woman back into the sitting room, certainly with no thought of cooperating, but rather to inform her of the dangerous extent to which she was overstepping her boundaries. "Miss Cranford," she began.

"Sit down," the woman interrupted.

Then anger surfaced, as raw as any that Harriet had ever felt. "I will not sit down," she said, "and I think you should know that your position here—"

"It's not my position that's under discussion," Sophia replied, turning rapidly on her. "It's quite obvious," the old woman went on, "that you understand exactly nothing."

"I understand more than you think," Harriet replied, loathing the confrontation, but determined to see it through. "I can understand and recognize a servant who—"

Again without warning the woman cut in, with what sounded like a non sequitur. "How do you think we live here, my dear?" she asked.

Momentarily thrown by the transition, Harriet faltered. "How do I think—what?"

"A simple question," Sophia said. "Surely not beyond you. How do you think we live here? Who provides us with tea and cakes?" Here she gestured toward the tray resting on the table, some dreadful look of determination in her face. "Well?" she prompted when after a few moments Harriet still had not answered.

On guard more than ever, Harriet looked over her shoulder to where James stood and saw his face filled with embarrassment. "My husband," Harriet began vaguely, "Lord Eden—"

"Your husband has nothing," Sophia cut in sharply. "We live on an allowance, my dear, all of us, including your husband, a handout as it were, from his brother, Edward, a paltry handout too, I might add."

Harriet listened, not particularly shocked, but considerably embarrassed. Never in her life had the tasteless subject of money ever been so openly discussed in her presence.

She was on the verge of saying this when Sophia took the floor again. "Lady Eden," she began, coming around the sofa, as though she knew she must retain at least a facade of decorum. "I beg your close attention. You are a comparatively new member of the Eden family. But there are some of us here who have worked for long years to see an ancient wrong made right. For your husband's sake, for your sake, and for the sake of your son, control of the

Eden fortune must be returned to the proper hands, and
that is the point of this hearing, and that is why it is so
important that you accompany us. It's your future as Lady
Eden that is at stake, as well as the future of the line."

Sophia gripped the back of the sofa as though plagued
by a painful weakness. "You mentioned my dismissal last
month of the two aides. Done with regret, I assure you.
But I found I was unable to pay their wages, and they,
quite naturally, were unwilling to stay on in a voluntary
capacity."

Harriet had not known this. She looked over at James.
"Is this true?" she asked quietly.

He nodded.

Now she had the feeling that all three were waiting for
her response. And never had she felt less capable of clear
thought. Edward was still there, in her memories. In her
confusion, she simply walked away. "And what of Edward?" she asked quietly.

At first she thought no one would answer her. In the next
instance she was aware of Sophia Cranford, hovering
close. "And how does Edward concern you? You are Lady
Eden, James's wife. Look at your priorities."

Harriet closed her eyes and leaned heavily against the
windowsill.

"A simple hearing," Sophia was saying now, "allied with
your husband and son for possession of what is rightfully
yours." She paused. Harriet felt the woman's hand again
on her arm. "What decent mother would do less?"

With her eyes still closed, Harriet tried consciously not
to think on him. She had never in her most hideous nightmares conceived of a moment when she would have to
face him again.

Suddenly she ran from the room. Someone was calling
after her, but she was in no mood for further delays. Forgetting her son, she ran through the passages of the vast
castle, longing only for an interval of privacy to test herself
against the memory, to speak his name aloud, to imagine
him in the same room with her.

A remarkably short time later, she found herself running
along the headlands, impervious to the condition of her
loosened hair and the tears streaming down her face.

Let them come. Better now than later. Drain them all so
that within the fortnight, she could stand erect beside her

husband and listen dispassionately and reveal to no one, not even herself, the hideous knowledge that lay buried within her, that she'd opened her body to her husband's brother, that she'd borne her husband's brother's child in secret, that she'd given that child away like a bundle of discarded clothes, that there was no pain, no torment, no torture devised by men for use on men that could even come close to matching the agony of conscience that she now was suffering.

London
June 18, 1848

Sprawled on his stomach in the middle of Edward's bed, his chin propped up in his hands, John Murrey Eden posed a blunt question.

"What's a bastard?"

Edward looked up from his desk, the letter from Sir Claudius announcing the hearing still in his hand. Edward pretended not to hear and fell again into a rereading of Sir Claudius's prim letter. If only he could grasp fully what it meant. A hearing, an "examination," in Sir Claudius's terms, "of the Eden assets, all parties to be present with the goal being a more equitable distribution."

Equitable distribution? Edward had been expecting a lawsuit, a court case complete with jury. At least this was what his mother had warned him of often enough. But a "hearing"?

"Papa?"

He looked up at his son, who was still waiting for a definition of bastard.

Now Edward tossed Sir Claudius's letter to one side of his desk and walked to the bed and stretched out beside John.

"A bastard," Edward began with mock solemnity, "is a

man without a father." As a definition it was too simple and leaked like a sieve. He knew that John would never abide it.

"But you had a father," the boy protested. "Grandpapa." He lifted his head and gazed at the ceiling. "This was his house."

Edward nodded, enjoying himself in spite of the awkward moment. How pleasant his life had been since the Chartist debacle of April 10. No longer did Feargus O'Conner and his men occupy all of Edward's time. O'Conner had disappeared to lick his wounded pride, though Edward had met him once since, quite by accident, outside the Reading Room of the British Museum Library, in the company of another man, a German, as well as Edward could remember, named Karl Marx. And Edward was now working in distant association with the Ragged School Union, with moderate men whose ambitions did not include remaking the entire world, but merely making the existing world better.

Now he had gloriously long intervals to spend with John, and the other children as well.

"Papa?" It was John again, dragging Edward's attention back to the puzzle at hand. "Why do they call you a bastard?" he asked with a heavy sigh as though it were exhausting work, maintaining his father's attention.

Edward smiled and ruffled the boy's hair. "There's more to it, John," he said softly.

"What more?"

"I had a father, true, but my mother and father were not married at the time of my birth."

"Does that make a difference?"

"Indeed."

"Why?"

Damn! Elizabeth was right. Perhaps he shouldn't have mentioned the word in attempting to explain to his son what was going on. "The closeness between a man and a woman that produces a child," Edward explained carefully, "must be sanctified in the eyes of God."

"Why?"

"It's Scripture."

"Just words."

"No. Law."

"Whose?"

"God's."

"Did God write the Scriptures?"

"No. He directed men."

"Men can be wrong. You've said so."

"Yes, but these were holy men."

"Who said they were holy men?"

"God."

"Who did He say it to?"

"To the men."

A look of ancient cynicism crossed John's face, followed by a mischievous grin. "Then I'm a holy man," he said with mock seriousness.

Wearily Edward smiled. "It's not my world, John. I didn't make the rules."

"You could have," John added brightly. "You can still."

"How?"

"By telling Sir Claudius Potter to jump across the Thames."

Edward laughed. "I've already done that, not in so many words, but—"

He was aware of John moving closer, those dark blue eyes alive with intelligence. "Then tell him again. You didn't ask to be born. You had nothing to do with it. Whatever your Papa gave to you is yours to keep for all time."

Edward gazed up at the young-old face. The boy's future as well was at stake.

Purposefully baiting him now, Edward posed a serious question. "Then we should attend the hearing, do you think?"

"Of course," John replied. He was on the verge of saying more when he saw the smile on his father's face. As though he were embarrassed by his own intensity, he flopped over on his back and nestled close in the crook of Edward's arm.

For a moment, Edward held him close, knowing it was not proper for father and son, but doing it anyway.

They rested thus for several moments, gazing up at the ceiling. Then Edward heard another question. "Papa?"

"Yes?"

"Am I a bastard?"

Edward closed his eyes. He could no more have prevented that question than he could have stopped the tide. "Yes," he replied, without elaboration.

"Good."

The response had been instantaneous. Slowly Edward raised up on one elbow, bewildered. "Why— good?"

John looked at him with all the confidence of youth, a confidence bordering on arrogance. "Why not good?" he grinned.

Edward returned the grin and thought of the years of agony that word had caused him. How simply his son had solved the problem. A game occurred to Edward then, a childish game which the two of them had played when John had been a very young boy. "Who are you?" Edward asked.

· Quietly the boy raised up on his elbow. His face looked strangely sobered. "My name is John Murrey Eden," he pronounced simply. "My father is Edward Eden."

In London legal circles of 1848, only the following facts were known about Sir Cedric Dalrymple: age, sixty-seven; unmarried; childless; Aberdeen-born; Edinburgh-educated. As a young law student, he'd distinguished himself at the Scots bar, had established a thriving clientele, and for some unknown reason had abandoned it sixteen years ago and had taken up residence in London. Although he fit easily enough into the encrusted tradition of the Inns, he kept to himself except in the cause of his profession, and on those rare occasions, when he appeared in the Common Hall to quietly dazzle all those privileged enough to be present with his pure, lucid and unbending interpretation of that noble complexity known as English law.

In fact, he was a man seemingly obsessed with his profession, an obsession which a decade ago had finally raised him to the bench, and this lofty elevation had lifted him directly into the status of legend. His girth, considerable, Falstaffian almost, his height, equally as impressive, and his great thick shock of white flowing hair, all were capable of striking fear in the heart of any hapless law student called to the English Bar.

This then was Sir Cedric Dalrymple, the magistrate whom Sir Claudius had connived to sit in on the hearing concerning the Eden fortune. There were barristers who wondered openly over port in the Commons why Sir Cedric was even bothering himself with such a slight case. Complex decisions were more in his line.

But that in itself was part of the mystery, and that was why on this hot, close morning of July 2, 1848, all activity in the Temple seemed to come to a standstill except for the old gardeners watering the roses in the garden of the Middle Temple.

What was it to them, the redistribution of a fortune?

After three bowls of porridge, two boiled eggs, and four cups of tea, Sir Cedric shifted his weight upon the thunder pot and tried to get his bowels to move.

All Hail to Satan, was there ever such a curse visited upon man or beast since Creation? Again he shifted his considerable weight, hiked his nightshirt higher, and tried to make himself as comfortable as possible on the thin porcelain rim.

Suddenly a rolling pain cut down through his lower abdomen; he gripped his stomach and inclined forward. On occasion, that pain was an encouraging sign, indicative of movement. He waited a moment. Now? Nothing.

Weary with effort at eight o'clock in the morning, he leaned forward again and thought what a splendid relief death would be, fairly convinced as he was that there would be no such things as bowels in Heaven.

Of course, he'd suffered thus all his life, excruciating body vapors rolling endlessly in his gut. He remembered his grandmother, that grim-faced old harridan who had raised him, telling him that the Devil resided in his bowels and unless Cedric could push him out once a day, the Devil would poison him.

Damn it! He'd have to leave it for now. He was due in his chambers in one hour. The Eden case.

Well, then, dress, he ordered himself, go and preside over the foibles of men, then return to the privacy of this room. To merely get through each day was his goal now, to retire to some country cottage where he could give in to his endless farts and gloomy temper. He was sick to death of London life. Apart from his great height and stoutness and the look of concentration in his face, Englishmen stared at Sir Cedric because they could not make out to which class he belonged. All Englishmen felt most comfortable when they could assign everyone to a proper class and generally they did not rest until that end had been accomplished.

Well, Sir Cedric had dumbfounded them this long, although he didn't know how much longer he could conceal his secret from the world.

Slowly he drew on his robe and gave small thanks for at least two blessings. One, he would not have to walk the distance to the court, and two, that damnable wig could be left on the wig stand. A sobering realization occurred to him then, the fact that after years of passing judgment, he knew that in no area of his life, in no region of his soul was he fit to pass judgment on anyone.

Outside his door he felt the first blast of the hot July sun filtering down through the arcade. As he turned the corner, heading toward his chambers on the lower level, he glanced down into the garden of the Middle Temple, always a refreshing sight with its clipped avenues of green and explosions of roses at the center. The old gardeners were at work, he noticed, men who could plunge their hands into English soil and cause miracles to happen.

Sir Cedric was just on the verge of averting his eyes when suddenly he saw a man talking to the two gardeners, his arm about the shoulders of a young boy. Taking refuge in a spot of shade close to the wall, Sir Cedric narrowed his eyes and continued to look down into the garden. There was something familiar about the man.

Sir Cedric looked closer, trying to clear the veil of age from his eyes. Then, recognition. He'd seen him last—when was it? Ten, fifteen years ago in the court of Old Bailey, the case of the adultress.

He peered closer. The gentleman did not resemble a man whose own brother was trying to relieve him of the family fortune. Nor did he resemble a radical agitator, though the papers had been filled with his name of late in connection with such causes. Before Sir Cedric turned away from his observation, he noticed that the man was changed. He did not remember him being so lean, the line of jaw quite so sharp. Over port, a few evenings ago, hadn't Sir Claudius Potter mentioned something about opium addiction?

Outside his office door he caught sight of the brass plaque which always gave him small pleasure. *Sir Cedric Dalrymple, 1832.* Then he pushed through the door and confronted his three young clerks whose flushed faces suggested that others had already arrived and the drama was on the verge of commencing.

"Is all ready?" Sir Cedric demanded, enjoying the mild look of fear in all three faces.

In answer to his question, they nodded. One elaborated, his Adam's apple bobbing nervously behind his stiff collar. "Two large tables, milord," he announced, "arranged on opposite sides of the chamber."

Sir Cedric nodded.

Then, "Fetch Mr. Eden," he commanded in a gruff voice. "You'll find him in the garden smelling the flowers. Tell him the proceedings won't take long and if he wishes to be present for the judgment, he'd better come."

Now as Sir Cedric moved toward the door which led to the inner chamber, he called back over his shoulder, "I'll need a recorder. Decide which idiot among you can hold a pen and follow after."

Then he pushed open the door and stood in the doorway, well aware of his awesome appearance and the effect it seemed to be having on the small group of people who now turned toward him with varying expressions of surprise and apprehension.

At the table nearest the door, he saw a gentleman in black, half rising from his chair where apparently he'd been in conversation with a man and a woman seated behind him. A strange pair, Sir Cedric determined, garbed similarly in black, a matched duo.

Seated to one side of the gentleman, Sir Cedric saw a young woman. She too was dressed in black. My God, was it a hearing or a funeral?

Then Sir Claudius was upon him. "Milord," he murmured, extending a bejeweled hand. Under the best of conditions, Sir Cedric was not a social man. Now he glowered at the outstretched hand and fell into a satisfying loathing of the little weasel who had burrowed his way into one of the greatest fortunes in England.

Brushing past the extended hand, Sir Cedric surveyed his chambers. Usually neat and ordered, it was now cluttered with two large tables, his own massive desk before the window, and— He looked closer. On a low table directly before his desk sat a strange object, a heavy leather case of some sort, elegantly finished with hand-tooling in a floral design.

"What is this?" Sir Cedric demanded, pointing toward the strange object.

Then Sir Claudius was behind him, whispering, "A symbol, milord, I beg your indulgence. All will become clear."

All was clear now, thought Sir Cedric, as he drew away from the man. Obviously it was to be another of Sir Claudius's theatricals. The man did not practice law as much as he "performed" it.

As Sir Cedric took his seat behind his desk, he glanced out at the waiting faces. Why the plethora of black? They resembled vultures.

"Well, then?" Sir Cedric pronounced, seating himself just in time to endure as best he could a slow seepage of air from his bowels. "What are we waiting for?"

"The—defendant," Sir Claudius simpered. "We can't proceed without—"

At that moment, the chamber door opened. One of the clerks appeared, his face flushed. "Mr. Edward Eden," he announced, and stepped quickly back from the door.

From where Sir Cedric sat, he noticed all faces at the table lift, save one. The veiled young woman continued to sit with her head bowed.

But all other faces turned toward the door where now a young boy appeared, a handsome lad of about ten or twelve, followed by the man himself.

As he appeared in the doorway, his eyes immediately fell on the near table. His inclination seemed to be to greet the persons seated there, but before he had a chance to do so, Sir Claudius was at his elbow, steering him toward the opposite table, his whispered scolding of, "You're late," clearly audible to all in the room.

From his position behind the desk, Sir Cedric watched the proceedings with growing interest. The room seemed full of tensions. In a very real, though unworthy way, Sir Cedric enjoyed the sufferings of others, and now the bulk of the suffering seemed to be coming from the table to his left.

If there was suffering coming from the table to his right, he could not discern it. The young boy seated himself and seemed to fall into a close and curious examination of his surroundings. Who he was and what he was doing here, Sir Cedric had no idea. Undoubtedly one of Mr. Eden's abandoned waifs.

As for the other, the "Prince of Eden," Sir Cedric had

heard him called, he seemed content merely to sit erect in his chair, concentrating on the large leather case.

Now Sir Cedric saw Sir Claudius align himself at a position midpoint between the two tables. How foolish of Edward Eden, Sir Cedric thought, not to have engaged his own counsel. No wonder the Eden fortune had dwindled. An idiot would have known that one man cannot fairly represent two opposing clients.

"Milord," Sir Claudius commenced, and was immediately interrupted by the door opening again, one of the young clerks appearing, tablet in hand. Quickly he took a seat near the rear of the room.

"Milord," Sir Claudius began again.

Sir Cedric nodded. "Proceed, Sir Claudius, though I'm forced to inquire, for whom are you speaking? The plaintiff or the defendant?"

The vain little man smiled. "Both, milord."

"And how is that possible?"

"It's a family matter, milord. We are all friends here. This is why we are most appreciative of your kind consideration in making the privacy of your chambers available to us."

"Then get on with the matter," Sir Cedric ordered, "although I feel compelled to warn Mr. Eden that he is not availing himself of the full measure or protection of the law."

At this, Mr. Eden looked up. "If I need defense, milord, I'm prepared, with your permission, to offer it myself."

The softly spoken announcement caused a slight rustle in the chambers.

Sir Claudius stepped forward to a position directly in front of the large leather case, and at last proceeded. "We are gathered here today, milord, with your kind permission to discuss the management of what once was one of the largest and most impressive fortunes in England. While still adequate, it has dwindled tragically under mismanagement, and unless legal steps are taken, we fear that in time it will simply—vanish."

With glazed eyes, Sir Cedric looked out over the proceedings, Sir Claudius now gesturing toward the leather case, the theatrical unfolding.

"The Eden wealth," Sir Claudius announced, "symbolically speaking, of course. Thirty years ago it was an awe-

some array of property, stocks, investments, net worth,
inestimable. Yet no more."

In an attempt to distract himself from his bowel discomfort, Sir Cedric turned his attention from what he already
knew, the facts which Sir Claudius was subtly coloring, to
what he didn't know and what was beginning to hold a
fascination for him—the man himself—Edward Eden.
Throughout Sir Claudius's interminable monologue, Eden
seemed content merely to sit erect, his eyes lifting now and
then to the symbolic representation of his own wealth. Was
it arrogance that Sir Cedric discerned in that strong face?
Certain harsh epithets were being hurled his way—irresponsible, misguided—yet as far as Sir Cedric could discern, nothing was registering.

The entire presentation lasted nearly twenty-five minutes.
The history of the Eden family was being laid out in boring
detail, the unfortunate circumstances surrounding the birth
of the defendant, though the word bastard was never
openly pronounced. There was no need. The condition
thereof had been described. Still, as far as Sir Cedric could
tell, the man himself continued to sit, unmoved.

Then, thank God, at last, the tone and timbre of a conclusion. "So it is, milord," Sir Claudius smiled, "that we
come before you today to seek your judgment on the matter
of passing control of the Eden estates from one pair of
hands to another in the hope that under new and prudent
management, the fortunes of this great and noble family
will once again flourish and stand as an effective example
of—"

Dear God, he simply couldn't listen to any more.
"Enough, Potter," he commanded at last, and blessedly,
within the instant, the fulsome old man fell silent and
bowed as though receiving a curtain call.

Now Sir Cedric raised his head. "Sir Claudius," he
began, "one simple question, if you will."

"Of course, milord, anything."

"Do you have the deed of ownership, the original document signed by Lord Thomas Eden?"

While the question seemed relevant to Sir Cedric, he
could see clearly the look of surprise and suspicion washing
over the faces before him. The young boy was whispering
something to Edward Eden, at last jarring that peculiar
man out of his remoteness.

"I do indeed, milord," Sir Claudius was saying, "although I fail to see what—"

"May I examine it?" Sir Cedric cut in, not giving a damn what Potter saw or failed to see.

He watched as Sir Claudius approached the leather case and to his surprise saw the man withdraw a folded, faded parchment. Apparently the box was not as symbolic as all had been led to believe.

Then Sir Claudius placed the parchment on his desk and continued to hover close as though only too willing to help with his interpretation of it.

"Stand back," Sir Cedric ordered with a wave of his hand. With an innate respect for old documents, he loosened the cord and gently flattened the deed of ownership upon his desk. He studied it for a moment, found everything in order, the deed signed, dated by Lord Thomas Eden, 1798, in the presence of witnesses, the Eden seal intact, the message clear. The good lord had signed everything he owned over to one Edward Hartlow Eden, then age two.

Slowly Sir Cedric lifted his eyes to where Edward Eden sat. "Do you have anything to say in your own defense, sir?" he inquired.

The man looked up at him. "I'm not absolutely certain of what I've been accused, milord. The property is mine," he added softly, "or at least I had been told so. I did not realize there were conditions to the deed of ownership."

"There are none, sir," Sir Cedric replied.

"Then while I find this meeting stimulating, I must also confess that it baffles me."

Slowly now Sir Cedric rerolled the parchment, retied the cord, though he continued to hold it in his hand. The tension was building. He could feel it. "It has been my experience," he began slowly, "that one of the most offensive acts that a man can commit is to turn his back on the wishes and desires of the dead." He stopped abruptly, not for dramatic emphasis. He needed none. But rather he wanted to avail himself of a moment's pause for judicial reconsideration. Had he been truly objective? No, of course not. Tortured by the pain in his gut and the consciousness of his own secret, how could he be? The conception that a man had of himself was all he had, and in that conception was both his curse and his salvation. Encountering contradictions along the way, all he could do was learn to live with them. And that, Edward Eden had learned to do masterfully.

Again Sir Cedric looked at him. Apparently the stigma was meaningless to him, bastard, that designation that had haunted men since the beginning of time, had indeed haunted Sir Cedric. For *that* was his secret, his own bastardy, the awareness of which had driven him all his life, had tied his gut into a knot, had caused him to deny himself all love, all softness, all hope of redemption.

Quickly he lowered his head for fear the secret was visible on his face. "The dead man's wishes are plain," he pronounced, holding up the deed of ownership. "For reasons unknown, the Eden estates were signed over to a two-year-old child. The fact that that child has now grown to manhood does not alter the deed in anyway. Thus"—and here he lifted his head as he customarily did in order to make certain that all heard and no one misunderstood—"Thus I judge in favor of the defendant, Mr. Edward Eden. This hearing is adjourned."

The scraping of his chair covered the first angry gasps coming from the table on his left. Out of the corner of his eye he was aware of faint stirrings at the table on his right. The young boy was on his feet immediately, registering his pleasure at the decision with youthful abandonment. To his left, Sir Cedric saw Potter in close huddle with Lord Eden and the two who sat behind. The only one not stirring as far as Sir Cedric could tell was the victor himself.

Then just as Sir Cedric was rounding his desk, clutching at his burning gut beneath the black robe, he saw the man stand, his voice cutting through the confusion in the chamber.

"Milord," he began, "with your permission, may I speak? Briefly, milord, I promise."

Damn! He had his fortune back. What more did he want? Reluctantly Sir Cedric returned to his desk, motioned his clerk back down into the chair, and, making no attempt to hide his displeasure, shouted, "Order!" at the turmoil taking place before him.

Slowly they obeyed, Sir Claudius easing his outraged party back into their seats, then taking a chair himself, his prim features bearing the clear expression of defeat.

What was afoot now? Sir Cedric looked toward Edward Eden. "Well?" he commanded. "Speak!"

He came slowly forward, first whispering something to the young boy, whose earlier expression of triumph had now been replaced by one of bewilderment. Hesitantly he approached the low table on which the leather case rested, as though now that he had the attention of the room, he wasn't absolutely certain what to do with it.

"The Eden wealth," Sir Cedric heard the man muse, more to himself than anyone else. Then abruptly he looked directly up at Sir Cedric, a faint smile on his face. "I make bold to trouble your Lordship," he began, laying one hand atop the leather case. "Concerning this—wealth, milord," he went on, pausing in peculiar fashion before he pronounced the word wealth, as though he had been tempted to give it another designation. "I would be less than honest if I said anything but that I have enjoyed it and spent it, and it, in return, has enjoyed and spent me. It has preceded and followed and encircled me all my life. I go to bed with its weight and privilege, and I wake up with it. And my first remembrance in this life is a soft maternal voice giving me an assessment of this—wealth and its importance. I cannot remember one day when it did not influence my life, make my decisions for me, restore a false sense of well-being to all those around me."

Sir Cedric leaned forward, suddenly interested in spite of his discomfort. "What is it that you are saying, Mr. Eden?"

But Eden gave him no reply. Instead he continued to gaze upon the leather case. The young boy, Sir Cedric noticed, was watching him in alarm and bewilderment.

Then slowly, Eden grasped the case and lifted it effortlessly into the air, as though he'd expected it to be an object of much greater weight. He stood a moment in the center of the chamber, then commenced walking slowly toward the table on the left.

At his mysterious approach all those seated about the table seemed to draw visibly back. Still he moved forward until at last he was in a position to place the leather case on the table before them.

"James," he smiled down on his bewildered brother, "you take it for a while. I'm weary of it. If I have abused it, I offer my apologies. If it abuses you, I offer my sympathy in advance." He paused here, but did not look away. "You have a wife now, and a son, or so I hear. For their sakes, I surrender all claim."

Sir Cedric could not believe it. Halfway out of his seat, he said, "The judgment was on your behalf, Mr. Eden. This is not necessary."

"The judgment was *not* on my behalf, milord," Eden said.

Suddenly the young boy was on his feet, his face angry. Some deep resentment was spilling out from behind those youthful eyes. "You have no right," he cried aloud.

Alarmed, as though the enemy had approached on the blind side, Eden looked up. "John, I—"

But at that instant, the boy stepped out from behind the table and ran for the door, not minding the clatter of his boots on the hardwood floor, nor apparently the shocked, stunned expression on Edward Eden's face.

"John—" he called again.

But the boy was gone, the door flung open against the wall, the angry footsteps diminishing down the arcade, leaving silence within the chambers.

Sir Cedric noticed Eden start toward the door, then stop, clearly a man facing complications he had not counted on. He was standing very close to Lady Eden now, so close he might have reached down and touched her shoulder.

But he didn't. Instead he glanced back toward the desk. "Do you accept my decision, milord?"

Momentarily flustered, Sir Cedric nodded. "Do you know what you are doing?"

"I know."

"Then I have no choice but to accept it."

Still Sir Cedric couldn't quite grasp what had happened. "You understand—your present position?"

Eden smiled. "I can't say that I fully understand it. But I accept it."

"Then legal steps will be taken."

"I'd be most grateful." Now Eden seemed to look about in confusion. "If you will excuse me," he murmured.

And he was gone, leaving a peculiar vacuum in the room, leaving all of them gaping after the open door, as though they too were unable to comprehend precisely what had happened.

Predictably Sir Claudius rallied first. He clamped a hand

on Lord Eden's shoulder and extended his other hand in congratulations. The two scarecrows seated behind rushed forward and embraced Lord Eden.

As for Lady Eden, she sat alone and apart from the flurry of congratulations, her eyes still fixed on the empty doorway.

Then Sir Cedric had had enough and stood rapidly and enjoyed the dampening effect his movement appeared to have on the whispering, grinning people about the table. He considered saying a last word to them, but changed his mind. What to say? Had they lost or won? Never in Sir Cedric's long legal career had he had one of his decisions overturned by the defendant himself. Yet there it was. The foolish man had given away a fortune, a decision which Sir Cedric was certain he would live to regret. Perhaps Eden was a religious fanatic, laboring under the romantic notion that it was impossible for a rich man to enter the Kingdom of Heaven.

Well, he was no longer a rich man, and Sir Cedric was certain that within a very short time the projection of Heaven would not be nearly as important to him as the realities of earth. As he swept past the table and the fawning smiles there, he thought with a wave of humor that at least something had been accomplished in that topsy-turvy morning. His gut was strangely at peace.

There were his kidneys, though, and now he moved rapidly into the outer office, passed his gaping clerks, heading for the small secluded room at the end of the passage. There he closed the door and bolted it and hurriedly drew back his robes and unbuttoned his trousers.

Ah! As his hot urine splashed down into the chamber pot, he thought, What a bloody lot of fools all men are.

He would not run far, of that Edward was certain. And indeed he caught up with him in the rose garden of Middle Temple, slouched against the brick wall, his hands shoved into his pockets, head down.

"John?" he called quietly.

The boy looked up, then turned away.

In the heat of the July noon, Edward momentarily foundered. What to say? How to explain to his son that which he himself did not understand?

It had been fatigue and a hungry desire to see what he

could do as a mere man as opposed to a mere rich man. But he'd not counted on John's reaction, or taken into consideration his deep awareness and pride in who he was.

Edward bowed his head a moment, memories of the morning still powerful. *Harriet.* He'd suspected that she might be present, but he'd not expected to feel anything. And he'd only really been aware of her at the last, standing so close to her beside the door. John himself had passed less than three feet from her. With what effort, Edward had restrained himself from informing her, "That is your son."

But of course he hadn't, and he lifted his head now and stared at his son, still turned away from him. Nearby, within easy reach, Edward spied a pink rose. He reached out and plucked it and approached quietly from behind. "A peace offering," he smiled, extending the rose around John's shoulder.

The boy looked at him, his anger reduced now to a kind of sullenness. "You had no right," he muttered.

Gently Edward disagreed. "I had every right."

"But why?"

As John faced him with the blunt question, Edward felt himself again on uncertain grounds. "Are you really suffering so?" he asked.

John made a despairing gesture, his chin still slumped against his chest. "You have nothing now."

"I want nothing," Edward countered, "except what I have always possessed." He paused. "You."

The boy looked up. "I am nothing," he said, "compared to what—"

Quickly Edward moved forward. "Poor John Nothing," he smiled.

Then John looked directly at him. His sturdy frame, already grown tall, seemed to straighten. "What will we do?" he asked.

"I don't understand."

"How will we live?"

"By our wits," Edward suggested, "by our backs, by our hands."

As far as Edward could discern now, there was not a trace of anger or sullenness in that young face. He seemed merely to be turning his attention in a most practical manner to the problems of tomorrow. "Well, never mind,"

John sighed, pushing away from the wall. "I'll think of something. For now, I think we should go home and take stock." With that, he moved past Edward and commenced walking steadily toward the street and the traffic beyond.

For a moment, Edward could only stare. He had the sensation that at some point they had exchanged roles, that John was now the father and Edward the son. "Wait!" he called after the rapidly moving figure. "Wait, John."

Hurriedly he stepped away from the wall and caught up with him on the pavement, and tried to fall into the rapid pace which the boy had set. "I assume then that you're no longer angry?" Edward inquired, breathless from his sprint, trying to find some revealing expression on that blank, strong young face.

"Anger serves no purpose," John said, keeping his eyes straight ahead. "You've said so yourself."

"Then what is it?" Edward asked.

But the boy gave no reply and continued to set a fast pace through the crowded foot traffic. At some point Edward fell behind, mystified by the transformation which had come over his son.

"John?" As Edward called out again, the boy stopped and Edward caught up with him and put his arm around his shoulder. And the boy permitted it.

Grateful, Edward thought how strange it was that with this son beside him, he didn't feel like a poor man. A whole train of fresh ideas, incoherent but interesting, stirred in his soul in connection with the events of the morning. And during that walk he thought over his whole life anew, and came to the calming conclusion that now he must live what was left of his days, dreading nothing, desiring nothing.

Eden Point
North Devon
July 28, 1848

Content to leave the sense of victory to others, Harriet sat well back in the carriage seat and watched dully the approach to Eden Castle. At last she felt a reviving sea breeze after the stifling heat of London. Opposite her, James stirred out of an endless sleep.

"Home?" he muttered, struggling upright in the seat, trying to straighten his twisted waistcoat, his eyes still sleep-gazed.

Harriet nodded. She felt broken somehow, dismal feelings which had plagued her from the onset of this obscene journey. Well, no matter. She had played her role and was now about to extract her price.

She raised up and looked over her shoulder through the small, oval-shaped rear window. The malignancies were still there in the second carriage, following them. Although they had journeyed to London in a communal carriage, Harriet had insisted that they return in two. Why not? As Sophia had pointed out, they could afford it now.

Abruptly Harriet closed her eyes. She'd known from the beginning that it would be difficult. But how impotent that word sounded now compared with what truly had transpired. For that depth of agony there were no words.

581

He'd changed, yet he was still the same. To be so close, yet so—

"My dear, are you well?"

It was James, apparently wide awake, sensing something wrong, as he'd done during the entire journey. "It wasn't—pleasant," he murmured kindly. "But we knew it wouldn't be, didn't we? At any rate, it's over."

Over! She looked sharply at him, her bewilderment surfacing in spite of all efforts to keep it hidden. "You—felt nothing?" she inquired, amazed.

He shrugged. "I said it was unpleasant. Yet it had to be done."

"Why?"

"For your sake, and our son's."

Oh dear God, she was so sick of that excuse she never wanted to hear it again. Quickly she reined in her emotions. It was not her intention to waste energy on a scene. She'd played her part in one of the most humiliating, degrading episodes in her life. Now she would demand payment.

"James," she began, her voice low, almost pleasant. "I have a request."

Hearing the tone, James looked up, as though hopeful that, at last, his difficult and moody wife would behave herself. "Anything, my dear. You've earned a treat. Name it."

A treat! It came to her then that at least a portion of her irritability was due to having been confined with James for the entire journey. Their marriage worked best with long separations.

"No treat," she smiled, "a request."

He nodded. "Name it."

"I want you to dismiss the Cranfords immediately."

For a moment he gazed at her, rapidly blinking as though he'd failed to hear. Thus for his benefit and because the words brought her pleasure, she repeated them. "I want you to dismiss the Cranfords immediately."

He stared at her as though resisting the meaning behind those simple words. "You're—joking, of course."

"No. I want them out of Eden Castle as soon as possible."

"But that's—impossible," he stammered.

"Why? Do they have some legal right to be there? We've

been fully submerged in legalities of late. Is there something about the Cranfords' position at Eden that I should know about?"

"No, of course not. It's just that—"

"Then I want them gone," she repeated, her voice less even.

She was aware of James closely watching her and equally aware of an unprecedented look of defiance in his face. "I'm afraid I can't honor your request," he pronounced at last.

"Why?"

"I have no desire to do so. Sophia and Caleb are my closest friends. I owe them a great deal."

Slowly Harriet settled back in the seat. "Then I shall leave you," she smiled pleasantly. "I shall take our son and return to Hadley Park, and you might as well say prayers for both of us because you'll never see us again."

She saw the mild look of defiance on his face change. She knew that her absence would mean little to him. But his son was another matter.

"I—don't believe you," he faltered.

"We shall be gone within the week, I swear it."

Slowly he shook his head, a clear look of pain in his eyes. "But why? I don't understand. What have the Cranfords done to you?"

"Nothing. But I can see, even if you can't, what they've done to you, and to Edward, and poor Jennifer."

"They had nothing to do with Jennifer's illness," he protested.

Harriet was on the verge of speaking further, but changed her mind. She'd promised herself not to waste energy on argument. "I want them gone," she repeated calmly, "or you'll find yourself without wife and son."

During the next few minutes he argued and raised objections of every nature. His voice became shrill and with no great effort she saw and felt his pain and was sorry for having caused it, but not sorry enough to alter her command.

As at last he fell back against the cushions in mute agony, she offered a serene suggestion: "Pay them," she said, "any amount you wish. Tell them that they are due retirement and offer them a generous purse."

"They would never take it," he snapped, glaring out the window. "They are too devoted."

At that Harriet smiled. "They are devoted," she agreed, "to their own mean and selfish ends." She leaned forward now and altered her approach. Steeling herself against sensation, she reached for his hand. "We are in the process of raising a son, James," she murmured, filling her voice with wifely concern. "God willing, there will be others. I want no influences about save those which I select." She patted the lifeless hand and abridged the last statement, "Save those which *we* select. The Cranfords are old, long past their prime. Our children deserve better."

He appeared to be listening. "They won't understand," he grieved. "They'll be deeply hurt."

"Pay them," she repeated with emphasis. "You now have control of the pursestrings. Pay them to salve their hurt."

He listened, then abruptly twisted in the seat. "I don't understand," he groaned, something petulant and childlike in his face.

With an effort of will, Harriet sent away the image of Edward which had mysteriously appeared before her. The comparison was brutal.

A few minutes later, she felt the carriage slowing for the approach to the gatehouse, heard the rattling vibrations as they moved across the double grilles.

Inside the inner courtyard, she saw, standing at the top of the Great Hall steps dear old Jane, holding young Richard in her arms. And with the sense of putting the meanness of the last few days behind her, she left the carriage even before it had come to a complete halt and ran up the stairs and threw her arms about the old woman.

In the closeness of the embrace, and with her son cooing in her ear, she looked back down on the courtyard, James apparently still seated inside the carriage, the second carriage just turning into the gatehouse.

With old Jane spilling out a hundred questions—"Tell me of London, the latest fashions, are there feathers this season, and what of the theater, did you see—?" Harriet took her son in her arms and tried to pacify Jane, and stole a final glance down on the second carriage, Sophia and Caleb just emerging, though still no sign of James.

What would he do? Would he honor and act upon her request? Would she be Lady Eden this time next week?

It was incredible, almost frightening, how little she cared.

Six days later, from her new private chambers high in the east wing, Lady Marianne's old chambers, Harriet stood at the window and watched the departure.

Stewards had been loading trunks all morning. As a going-away gift, James had given them the handsome carriage and a coachman, plus an incredible severance pay of thirty thousand pounds. No matter. Harriet would have approved of three hundred thousand pounds if that amount had been necessary.

She leaned closer to the window. James was there. Apparently he'd cancelled his customary horseback ride to the Hanging Man in honor of the occasion. Poor James. She knew he was shocked at how well the Cranfords had taken their dismissal.

And there they were, just emerging from the Great Hall, Sophia dressed elegantly in peacock blue, a gown she'd bought on their recent trip to London. And Caleb as always at her side.

As the two approached James standing by the carriage, Harriet considered averting her eyes. She could feel the intimacy of the parting even from this distance. There was a final whispered exchange, then James stepped back, his head and shoulders visibly bowed.

When the carriage started forward, she saw him raise his hand in parting, as though bereft. A few moments later he swung up onto his horse and accelerated to a rapid gallop, passing beyond the gatehouse in rapid pursuit of the carriage.

Now below, she saw the courtyard empty save for a few stewards who were cooling themselves in a patch of shade near the castle wall. The guardsmen were lowering the grilles and closing the gates. Apparently they knew, as Harriet knew, that James would ride with the carriage as far as the Hanging Man, where there would be another tearful separation, and James would stay and ease his thirst and his grief and return sometime after nightfall.

Slowly Harriet looked back into the chamber. It was hers now. She had everything: titles, wealth, complete autonomy of Eden Castle, a son and heir.

Everything. *Everything.* As she left the window, she

stopped at the edge of the Persian carpet, her left hand moving vaguely out as though for support.

All that remained for her to do now was to devise a manner in which she could learn to live with her impressive victory.

London
November, 1850

Seated atop the wagon in a cold drizzle, reins in hand, with Elizabeth and John beside him, Edward stole a final glance back at the house on Oxford Street. He'd hated to sell it, but as Elizabeth's meticulous bookkeeping had informed him, he'd had no choice.

In the beginning it had been fairly easy. Within a week of that morning when he'd ceded all claim to the Eden wealth, Edward had received word from Sir Claudius Potter that Lord James Eden very generously had signed over to Edward the deed to the house on Oxford Street plus an allotment of one hundred pounds per month.

He'd not asked for it and had considered not taking it. But there had been seventy-three children in the Ragged School on Oxford Street. And with the enrollment in his other schools already burgeoning he'd accepted both the house and the money in the name of the children, and life had proceeded, little changed from before, though considerably more spartan.

Then three months ago, while taking an early morning canter down Rotten Row, Sir Claudius Potter had urged his horse to daring speed, not taking into consideration the night's moisture still heavy on the mossy lane. The front left hoof of the horse had slipped and Sir Claudius, elegant in his black and crimson riding habit, had flown over the beast's head, his brittle old bones cracking upon impact with earth, his brittle old neck in particular. Not until the horse, uninjured, had wandered back to the stables had anyone thought to go back and look for the hapless rider.

The first month after the funeral when the allotment did not arrive, Edward had thought little of it. But in the second month, they had been forced to farm the children and the volunteers out to the other Ragged Schools, now under the protective subsidy of the Union. And only last month when Elizabeth had confronted him with a debit sheet that defied argument, he'd placed the Oxford Street property in the hands of an estate agent, had accepted his first bid of four thousand pounds, had taken one thousand pounds and had purchased a small one-story timber-frame house in the slum of Bermondsey near Jacob's Island. Of the remaining moneys, fifteen hundred pounds had gone to creditors, and the rest had been divided equally among the other seventeen Ragged Schools, a meager attempt to repay the Union for its financial aid.

Now for the past week, the three of them, Edward, Elizabeth, and John, had worked night and day whitewashing the walls of the tiny structure in Bermondsey, a spirit of fun pervading their activities despite the grim turn of affairs, all except for John, who, while cooperative, seemed to keep to himself.

Edward's purpose in purchasing the old structure was to open a "Common Kitchen." "If we can no longer fill their heads," he'd laughed, "at least we can try to fill their bellies. Perhaps that's where we should have started all along."

Now, with the exception of the natural pain associated with saying goodbye to the house that had been in his family for over three hundred years, Edward was not suffering any great loss. He had the sense at last of being perhaps where he should have always been, not straddling two worlds, but planted firmly in the one that seemed to need him most.

"Say goodbye," he suggested now to the two who were looking back with him at the house on Oxford Street.

Elizabeth, seated next to him, drew up the hood of her

worn cloak against the chill November mist. "It was always
a cold place, it was," she said lightly.

John, seated on the other side of Elizabeth, at thirteen,
more man than boy, was maintaining his usual silence.
Edward gazed at the back of his head and wished with all
his heart that he could penetrate through to the place
where thought resided.

Now Edward leaned across and lightly touched his son
on the knee. "Did you check the upstairs rooms? No need
to leave any furnishings for the wrecking crew."

John nodded. "There was nothing there. It's all in the
back of the wagon, everything that was left."

"Well, then," Edward said at last, "if no one feels the
need for parting words, we'll depart." He waited a moment
to see if anyone did. Apparently not, though long after he'd
flicked the reins and the wagon had moved slowly down
the street, Edward was aware of John, still looking back.

Apparently Elizabeth saw the concern on Edward's face
and leaned close with a whisper. "Leave him be. It's the
only home he's ever known. He'll settle in right enough."

Edward nodded and turned his attention back to the
complicated traffic. About an hour later as they approached
the low-lying area of Bermondsey, Edward looked ahead to
the small timber-frame house and saw a dozen or so men
milling about in front on the pavement, their caps pulled
low in meager protection against the rain, some stamping
their feet in an effort to keep warm.

"Our first customers," he murmured.

Elizabeth sat up, a willing soldier. "And the fire not even
started. John, fetch in firewood from the shed, then help
your father unload. At least we can let them in and keep
them warm while they're waiting."

Now for the first time during the entire dreary journey,
John spoke. "Are they really customers, Papa? Will they
be required to pay for the food which Elizabeth cooks for
them?"

"They'll pay what they can," Edward replied, guiding
the horses close to the pavement. The waiting men looked
up. A few tipped their hats. Most were old, all thin and
cadaverous.

"And if they can't pay anything?" John demanded.

"We'll feed them anyway."

"How?"

Feeling mild annoyance at the boy's difficult questions, Edward tightened his grip on the reins. One of the horses spooked, veering to the left.

As soon as he'd brought the animal under control, John was there again. "How?" he asked a second time.

Sensing the pressure of the waiting men and the chill November rain, Edward muttered vaguely, "We'll find a way," and started to jump down from the wagon.

"Find a way where?" John shouted back. "You know as well as I that all credit is closed to us, that our empty pockets are likely to be as empty tomorrow as they are today."

Stymied and laboring under a weight of confusion, Edward was on the verge of shouting at the boy again when suddenly Elizabeth stood up between them.

"Please," she begged softly. "They're watching." She waited a moment for the tempers to cool. "We have food —for a while. I lived the first sixteen years of my life under such conditions—food for a while. It isn't so difficult."

Abruptly she pushed passed Edward and swung herself down to the pavement. "If you two choose to sit here in a cold rain and bicker, that's your business. One of these gentlemen will help me with the firewood." And so saying, she turned, and within a few moments had enlisted the aid of four of the strongest men. As she led the way across the pavement, they followed dutifully behind her until at last all disappeared beneath the low door of the house.

Edward stared after them, still slightly shaken with anger. "John, I'm—" But as he turned to offer an apology, he saw that John had jumped down on the other side and was already at work loosening the ropes and canvas which held the furnishings in place. "We can always go to work, you know," Edward shouted toward the back of the wagon.

"So can they," John replied, jerking his head toward the front of the house where another small group had gathered, women this time, their heads covered with rain-soaked shawls, a few children clinging to their skirts.

Still standing atop the wagon, Edward looked first at the newly gathered crowd, then back toward John. A sudden wind gusted and threw a sheet of rain across his face. In spite of the wet cold and the activity going on about him, he felt a profound silence, as though something deeper than winter had just passed over him.

His son was right, yet he too was right, and that huddled gathering of men and women and children on his stoop, they also were right.

At that moment, he was aware of John looking up at him as though he were seeing an idiot or a fool, or both. And perhaps he was. All Edward knew for certain in that moment was that there was strength to endure everything, and that, lacking a sign from Heaven, the heart must persist. And he also knew that perhaps somewhere there was Infinite Mercy and Divine Guidance, but not here.

Here on this wretched road in Bermondsey, there was no God, not even a good imitation of Him. Here there was only Edward Eden, flawed, weak, human, cold, and now in doubt.

Yet in spite of these confusing thoughts, he jumped down from the wagon and held out his hand to the rain-drenched women and in a gentle voice urged them to go inside the house. Then he hurried to the back of the wagon and confronted John, not with words or logic, for John could defeat him there, but rather with action, hurling himself at the heavy canvas coverings where, beneath the collection of furnishings from the house on Oxford Street, was a carton of foodstuffs. It was a paltry supply and would soon be gone.

But it was a beginning, and on that Edward would gamble, acknowledging his feebleness, yet trying the best he could to lighten the burdens of others.

One half of London learned of the remarkable event which would shortly take place in their midst on the morning of June 29, 1849, when at a meeting of several gentlemen at Buckingham Palace, Prince Albert, His Royal Highness, communicated his plan for the formation of a great collection of works of Industry and Art in London to be scheduled for 1851. He also described the advantages of a site which had been selected in Hyde Park along the Serpentine at the end of Rotten Row and recommended an early application to the Crown for permission to appropriate it.

In the beginning no one treated the scheme with complete seriousness. Queen Victoria said pretty things about the idea which had been fostered by the man whom she loved almost as much as her throne.

But when a wildly unimaginable design was selected to house the Great Exhibition, domes of glass stately enough to encompass and shelter full-grown trees, then the clubs and salons of the city began to snicker. "Al's glass house," *Punch* called it, and the jokes about throwing stones grew tedious and monotonous. Still, Joseph Paxton, the creator of the design, persisted, aided and abetted by Albert and his commission of dreamers.

Here the nations of the world would exhibit their swords beaten into plowshares—if possible mechanical plowshares—by the new industrial processes. "All history points," said Prince Albert, "to the Unity of Mankind." At the "Crystal Palace," as it was now called, Albert intended to achieve on a worldwide scale that "reciprocity" which Palmerston had prevented in Europe. At home, inspiration would flow from the liberated minds of a thousand independent, self-reliant creators.

Clever England! While for over a decade the rest of Europe had been involved in senseless, bloody revolution, she had pacified her band of lunatic revolutionaries by calling cabs for them on rainy days, by opening her arms wide and even providing a desk and lamp for the little German Socialist named Karl Marx. If the English were a quiet people, they were also a polite people, for politeness meant peace, and peace enabled her industrial lions to proceed, uninterrupted, with the greatest revolution of all, the sort that invented a machine to replace a dozen men, one process to take the place of four, brave trophies of a bloodless war. That she now wanted to exhibit the spoils of her miraculous conquest was understandable.

Thus it was that one half of the nation learned of the Great Exhibition over warm fires, in the soft purple velour of private clubs, while trying on a new bonnet, or when the conversation lagged at a country house party.

The other half of the nation, the miners burrowing in the coal pits, the farmers toiling behind a team of ailing horses, the thieves and pickpockets and costermongers of the London streets, this half of England had not the slightest knowledge that anything remarkable was taking place in their capital city. How could they? Most did not read or write, and even for those who did, newspapers cost money

and as practical objects served only to insert inside a
tattered coat as extra protection against the chill wind.

A few learned about the Great Exhibition in much the
same way as Edward and John did, cutting through Hyde
Park on a December evening, having delivered a trunk to
a house on Edgware Road after they had put in a day's
labor on the great covered platform of Euston Station as
porters, carrying baggage of all shapes and sizes. They had
reported for work at six in the morning and had spent the
day hauling luggage up and down the platform of Euston.

Still the employment was welcome, for it meant that
they took home fourteen shillings a week between them,
and with no rent to pay and with Elizabeth's skillful planning, which amounted at times to genius, they could feed
themselves and about thirty regulars for whom the Common Kitchen meant the difference between dying and
living.

So it was that in the dusk of this bitter December evening, Edward walked quietly alongside John, trying to
think of something suitable to say to ease the silence
between them. Fatigue of course had taken a toll as always.
Added to the day's labor was the walk of several miles
home. Still he longed for communication, for some way to
convince the boy that manual labor did not diminish him,
that they were doing very well, in spite of everything.
Elizabeth had miraculously converted the small house in
Bermondsey into a sheltering warmth. Why couldn't John
share his pleasure at seeing the old men and women, and
many young ones as well, seated along the low benches,
their heads bent over their bowls of hot soup, a good fellowship springing up between all of them.

But apparently he couldn't and while he was no longer
openly hostile, as he had been that first day after they'd
left Oxford Street, the silences between them were growing
deeper.

For Edward, the loss of his son's support and affection
was a deep wound. And compounding this pain was the
realization that as the winter deepened, the shillings would
have to be woefully stretched to include firewood and fuel.

Now, on this evening, as they cut across the edge of
Hyde Park, Edward looked up from his assortment of
worries and saw a remarkable sight, the land beyond the
Serpentine cleared, one enormous column fixed on the right

and an army of workmen dragging heavy ropes along pegs which had been driven into the ground as though marking off a vast area.

In the dusk of evening, the sight had appeared before him with the suddenness of a mirage. He observed that John, walking a few paces ahead, had seen it as well. Now, though no words were spoken, they both cut across the newly scraped earth, heading toward a cluster of low-lying sheds which seemed to be the center of activity. Edward saw a burly, black-haired man wearing a corduroy jacket and leathern gaiters standing over a small coal fire. He was at that moment shouting instructions at a group of workers with coils of heavy rope wrapped about their necks. "Watch the cut, you bastards," he shouted angrily. "You! There! Your fill is too heavy. Back off! Back away!"

Apparently the men did not understand the commands and continued to stand in clear confusion. At that moment another man emerged from the small shed. Tall, lean, with a haughtily inquiring face, he came up behind the man in the corduroy jacket. "It would help if you would hire a few with brains," he suggested quietly.

The dark-haired man turned, enraged. "With the rush on, I hire them that first appears."

At that, the tall man drew himself up. "Do your best," he muttered and walked back into the shed.

Edward watched the frustration of both the man and the workmen for a few moments, then walked forward, his hands shoved into his pockets. "Substructure?" he inquired softly.

The man looked up as though at last someone was speaking his language. "To you, maybe," he grumbled, "and to me. But to them"—and here he stabbed a finger at the workmen—"one of the great mysteries of the world."

Edward laughed. "And what's the structure to be?"

The man ran a rough fist across his dripping nose and stared incredulously at Edward. "What's it to be?" he parroted. "My God, man, where have you been?" Now he gestured broadly with arms outstretched. "This here is to be Prince Albert's Crystal Palace it is," he entoned, a note of pride in his voice. "An Exhibition, that's what it's to be, an advertisement for British enterprise. Let 'em all come, Prince Al has said. We can do everything that they can do, and do it cheaper and better. A wonder of the world, that's what it'll be."

"If you can get the substructure laid, that is," Edward said.

The man looked across the small fire at him, sternly at first, then his weathered face softened into a smile. *"If we can get the substructure laid."*

Behind him, Edward was aware of John's impatience. He knew the boy was hungry and tired. Still he continued to watch as again the burly man shouted instructions at the workers. But apparently nothing he said made the slightest difference.

Without a word, Edward moved across the field to where the workers stood, about thirty in all. Quickly he separated them into two groups, took the coil of rope from around one fellow's neck, stooped down to the nearest peg in demonstration of what was to be done, and in the remarkably short time of about twenty minutes had the two crews working in opposite directions, the ropes stretching out in mammoth squares and rectangles, clearly marking off the shape and size of the structure.

As he walked back to the small fire, he saw the foreman's face, eyes squinted as though he were now surveying Edward in a new light. "You, there," he shouted while Edward was still a distance away. "You for hire?"

"Depends," Edward answered, warming his hands over the fire. "What's the wage?"

The man paused, his face going momentarily blank into the bargaining mask when it behooved a man to quote small and not blink. "Four shillings," he announced finally.

Edward shook his head and started away from the fire.

"A day," the man called after him.

Edward stopped. "My son, too?" he asked over his shoulder.

"Does he have a brain like you?"

"Better."

"Agreed then."

Dear God, eight shillings a day, seven days a week, food, firewood, perhaps blankets—Edward closed his eyes, then opened them and turned back to the man. "When do we start?"

"Now."

"Night labor?"

"Night and day until it's finished and the Queen herself comes to proclaim the opening."

"And when would that be?"

"May first, God willing."

Edward nodded. He looked across at John standing a distance away. Perhaps he should have conferred with him. Why was it that when the boy had been four, it had been easier for Edward to talk to him than now, at thirteen?

"John?" he began, approaching him slowly. "Four shillings a day, night labor, eight shillings plus—"

Abruptly John interrupted. "I can add, Papa," he smiled. He walked a few steps away, then looked back. "We're rich men, aren't we, Papa?"

The sarcasm in his voice was clear. Then the foreman in the corduroy jacket was upon him again with a black ledger book. "What's your name?" he demanded.

"Eden," Edward replied, still watching as John walked away. "Edward Eden."

"And the boy?"

"John Murrey Eden."

"Can you read and write?"

Edward nodded.

"The boy as well?"

Again Edward nodded.

The man grinned. "Then you're both on," he announced. "Jack Willmot's the name," he added, extending his hand. "Bad bark, no bite, if you do the work."

Edward smiled and took the hand extended to him.

"Eight-hour shifts," Willmot instructed further, "with hour intervals in between and four hours for rest until the job's done."

At this, Edward looked sharply up. Oxen in the field were not driven thus. Still the wages were good. So in spite of his fatigue after his day's labor, he started off across the field following after John, who had already taken his place with the other workers, a coil of rope about his neck.

What had Willmot called it? A Crystal Palace? A great exhibition?

No matter. To Edward and all the other workers dragging heavy ropes across the muddy field, it was four shillings a day and another chance to stave off hunger and cold and perhaps death.

Look yonder where the engines toil:
These England's arms of conquest are
The Trophies of her bloodless war:
        Brave weapons, these.
Victorious over wave and soil,
With these she sails, she weaves, she tills,
Pierces the ever-lasting hills,
        And spans the seas.

With that bit of doggerel, Thackeray prepared himself
for the first of May, 1851, and sat back to await the great
dawn.

For others, as the day approached, there was no waiting,
but increasingly feverish activity. Throughout the long
winter and early spring of 1851, Edward and John, along
with twenty-two hundred other British workingmen, had
caused a miracle to rise on the meadows of Hyde Park.

It had been hard labor, but good and most rewarding.
In six months the meadows of Hyde Park had been transformed from ordinary greenery to a spectacle which might
have been taken from the pages of the Arabian Nights.
These twenty-two hundred workers had laid the founda-
tions, maneuvered four thousand tons of ironwork into
position, raised the two thousand three hundred cast-iron
girders, the three thousand three hundred pillars, the thirty
miles of rainwater guttering, the two hundred and two
miles of sash-bars, and the eight hundred thousand feet of
glass.

Now, in the gathering shadows of dusk on April 30,
1851, Edward sat on the banks of the Serpentine and gazed
out at the incredible spectacle. The rays of the evening sun
struck the cathedral-high glass walls and caused them to
shimmer with glorious hues of pink and blue. There were
sightseers all about, a public impatient to enter the grand
hall and see what miracles Englishmen had wrought.

In this brief, quiet moment, facing one more task before
his job was done, with John lounging in the grass beside
him, it occurred to Edward that, though weary beyond
description, he'd never known such peace.

Although John appeared relaxed beside him, Edward
could see his impatience to be off for the north entrance,
where for the last few days, the boy had watched, fascinated, as wagon after wagon had arrived from the Mid-

lands bearing impressive machinery, all the mysterious inventions which had brought both a new simplicity and a new complexity to English life.

At Edward's insistence, John had reluctantly given up his vigil for a few moments' rest and a bite of cheese and roll while they waited for nightfall, for the curiosity seekers to depart, and for the arrival of the greatest invention of all, Mr. Harrison's Power Loom, which was at present on its way from Manchester on a specially constructed wagon drawn by sixteen horses, under cover of canvas, to arrive in secrecy sometime yet tonight. At that time Edward and John, along with fifty other men, would transfer it to the iron platform specially designed for its use and transport it into the Industrial Exhibit where, like the predominant jewel in a brooch, it would take its place in a proper setting.

This was the last task remaining to be done. With luck, Edward and John would be home by midnight, where that morning Elizabeth had threatened to have a hot tub waiting in which they could scour the dirt of six months' labor from their bodies and make themselves presentable for the Grand Opening.

Again Edward smiled, recalling Elizabeth's excitement that morning. She was making a new frock for herself, he knew that much, although she'd kept its design and color a secret. "With the Queen in attendance," she'd said proudly, "I must look my best."

He felt it again, a strong emotion, curiously tinged with melancholy. Why should the thought of Elizabeth sewing herself a new gown stir him?

Then it passed, and all that was important was that John was beside him, warmer and more loving these last few weeks than ever before, that out of their increased wages they had managed to share bread nightly with over fifty people who might not otherwise have had any. All that, plus the magnificent results of their labors, shimmering in the evening sun.

There it was again, that embarrassing moisture in the corners of his eyes. He wiped it quickly away and dragged himself to his feet, nudging John in passing. "Come," he said, "let's go study your machines. Perhaps you can explain them to me, for I must confess, their meaning eludes me."

John scrambled to his feet. "No mystery, Papa," he grinned. "They make men rich."

"Is that their only purpose?" Edward teased.

"Of course not."

"Then what?"

"They save time, increase productivity, and—"

He paused and Edward filled the silence, "—and make men rich."

John returned his grin. "Yes," he concurred. Suddenly he raced ahead a few yards, his youthful exuberance clearly getting the best of him. He stopped abruptly and turned about and, walking backwards, asked, "Are we really coming tomorrow, Papa, for the opening, I mean?"

"Of course we're coming," Edward called out to him.

"Elizabeth, too?"

"Try leaving her behind."

"For the whole day?"

Edward nodded, blissful in the face of his son's eagerness. "For the whole day." Then he said the words he knew John was waiting to hear. "Run along if you wish. I'll catch up in time. The North Gate, remember, at dark. Then, home."

The boy scooped his crushed hat from his head and tossed it into the air. "Home," he cried out, then raced off across the broad green lawn, dodging artfully through the crowds, on his way toward the North Gate and his shiny black pets that "made men rich."

Edward stopped to watch him as he ran, feeling a sudden loss, a sense, no doubt, of his son growing up. The boy's external character was impressive, an endless source of pride to Edward. He was a willing worker, honest, without deceit, blunt, too blunt on occasion, tall for his age, with fair hair and eyes as blue as his mother's.

As for John's interior character, of course it wasn't fully revealed as yet. He was loving, perhaps more in need of receiving love than giving it. But the signs were there and promising.

Without warning, Edward felt self-conscious, standing in the middle of the green, gazing blankly into the distance where hoardes of people gaped upward at the Crystal Palace. It was his estimate that there was about an hour remaining until nightfall.

Then he would walk and enjoy the calm evening, the

color of dying sun on green boughs, the sweet elixir of
early-blooming lilacs, and for a brief period clear his head
of labor and effort and powerful machines. His thoughts
of late had gone mysteriously back to his mother. How he
missed her. And to Eden, his thoughts had traveled there as
well.

It must be age, he thought, starting off along the winding path which led deep into the park. He set an easy pace,
his hands laced behind his back. Yes, surely age, that
peculiar and incoherent mix of nostalgia for one's past, the
place of the beginning. And he missed Daniel as well, as
he'd missed him daily since his death several years ago.
How Daniel would have loved the Crystal Palace, the excitement of the Great Exhibition. What a life they had had
together, were still having, at least in memory.

He smiled. Then he laughed softly, and suddenly caught
himself up. Passers-by were gaping, undoubtedly thinking
him balmy. What a sight he must present, a poor thin
workman with graying hair and worn clothes, walking
alone on a glorious spring evening, laughing at absolutely
nothing.

He would have been happy to explain it to them, if only
he could have explained it to himself.

Jack Willmot stood at the North Gate, staring at the
access road lined with small charcoal fires burning on
either side, the monster itself moving slowly forward,
glowing black and fiery red in the night shadows.

Now, "Move it forward," he shouted to the thirty or so
workmen who had run out to take possession of the sixteen
horses who had dragged the monster all the way from
Manchester. Still under canvas covering, the Power Loom
sat like a great inert lump while the horses strained, and
dozens of men ran alongside, shouting good-natured greetings to the six men high atop the wagon seats.

As the crew of six scrambled down, stretching, Jack
Willmot saw his own hand-picked men offer warm greetings. Let them rest a moment, he thought, before the final
effort. A good lot, all. Never before had he looked with
dread to saying goodbye to a crew.

Standing a short distance away from the massive wagon
and the talking, laughing men, he crossed his arms, mystified by the difference. In a way he wished they were just

starting the job. With what pleasure he would go through the entire six months again. He supposed that part of the difference was in the men themselves, all first-rate workmen, sharing their enthusiasm, and on occasion, for Jack had witnessed it, their bread as well.

At that moment he saw a man emerge from the shadows on the far side of the park and join the others standing in a close huddle next to the wagon. The latecomer was greeted warmly and welcomed into the circle, more than welcomed. At his appearance the circle of men opened and immediately closed again as though it had consumed him.

It was Eden. Willmot had recognized him. A strange one, that one. Jack Willmot still remembered that cold December night when Eden and his son had signed on and taken over the substructure crew. And from that day to this, the man's labors and efforts had been ceaseless. And he was no young plow either, clearly showing his rust and age.

Yet, how he had worked, and how noisily and eagerly the men clustered around him. If there was general fatigue and grumbling, Eden would set a new pace. If someone faltered, Eden would take his place. If there was hunger, Eden produced bread.

Look at them now. Eden was saying something and where moments before they had been shifting aimlessly about, now they stood with rapt attention, the only movement that of the men around the perimeter of the circle who were trying to move closer to the center.

What was it the men called him? The Prince of Eden? Jack Willmot had no idea where that foolishness had come from. He'd heard dozens of rumors concerning the man, wild tales that always grew wilder after several pints. One bloke had proclaimed that he knew it for a fact that Edward Eden once had been a very wealthy man.

Recalling that bit of nonsense, Jack Willmot smiled. He'd worked for rich men before and knew the smell and weight and appearance of money. No. While Willmot knew little of substance concerning Edward Eden, he knew most definitely that the man had never been rich.

At that moment the group laughed heartily. A few minutes earlier, many had openly grumbled to Jack Willmot about this last night's work. Now you would have thought they were attending a fete, all talking and laughing and huddled about that fixed center.

All but one. Jack Willmot had spotted him, the man's son, a good worker as well, but definitely not a chip off the original block. The lad kept to himself and now seemed more interested in what was beneath the heavy canvas on top of the wagon than in anything his father was saying.

Well, enough! Put them through their paces, then send them home for the first full night's rest they had had in several months. Now he shouted, "Lad, as long as you're up there, loosen those straps and let's put the pretty to bed, then ourselves as well."

He'd seen the boy swing atop the wagon and decided the time had come. One good last effort, and Jack Willmot's job was done. Tomorrow the grand folk would take over, the Queen and her Albert and all the fancy ladies and gentlemen in their ribbons and striped trousers. Jack Willmot smiled. He felt mildly sorry for them, those grand folks who could never share in the fellowship, the challenge, the sense of a job well done.

"Hie up with you," he shouted to the other men. "The lad can't do it all." And immediately half a dozen men hopped atop the wagon and commenced loosening the ropes interlaced across the heavy canvas. To his left a dozen others guided the winch into place, while behind him he saw about twenty all putting their shoulders to the low iron wagon onto which they would transfer the monster and roll it into the hall.

Damn, but they were good men and he vowed before the night was over to seek each of them out and see if they would be willing to work for him again. Something had made a vast difference with this crew, and while Jack Willmot couldn't identify the difference, he could feel it and wanted to retain it, and if possible, never be far removed from it.

Now pulling his gloves on, he stepped toward the wagon where the crew of eight were just loosening the final rope. As they tugged and pulled the canvas free, all activity ceased as the men stopped and gaped up at the miracle.

Mr. Harrison's Power Loom. In size it matched four pianofortes, though solidly constructed of gleaming black iron, a mass of interworking parts, pistons, bobbins, and levers, and fronting it all, two massive black rollers the length of two stalwart men.

The sense of awe was profound and shared by all.

Several men from the winch crew hopped onto the wagon and encircled the wonder, while the lad, Eden's son, was clearly transfixed. Willmot saw his face in the flickering torches. Never had he seen such a rapt expression as one hand reached timidly forward to touch the rollers.

At last Willmot came to his senses. "Well, she ain't going to hop down and move herself in, mates. Let's be about it. I'll treat you all to a pint if she's sitting where she belongs within the hour."

The offer was received with hearty enthusiasm, and within the moment, he saw all the men scrambling, all except the Eden lad, who seemed loath to leave the side of the machine.

"Clear the way," Willmot shouted. "Are the chains in place?"

One of the men shouted that they were. Good! At least they didn't have to lift her first. Now it would be a simple matter to attach the winch to the chains, lift her up, and deposit her on the iron wagon, then round up the grazing horses and let them drag her into Exhibition Hall.

Then apparently all was ready. He saw the men manning the winch standing a distance away, the heavy chain coiled round and round the drum, a bit of a miracle itself, thought Willmot, as, at a signal from the men on top of the wagon, the lever was pulled and the powerful engine roared, the drum turning, the chains pulling against the awful weight of the machine.

From all sides now he heard the men shouting, as though with their voices they might aid the giant which was beginning to rise into the air from the bed of the wagon. Willmot heard the high-pitched scream of the winch as it performed its labor, saw smoke slipping out from one side of the drum.

"Douse it!" he shouted to the crew near the winch. "Keep it wet, or she'll burn up on you." Still the Power Loom rose higher and higher, all faces upturned.

"To the left!" someone shouted. "Then leave her be."

It was suspended now at a height to clear the wagon. Willmot watched carefully as the men pushed the iron platform into place. "Not too close!" he shouted. "Give her room to swing."

The men followed his command, then continued to stand directly beneath the area where the loom would shortly be lowered. "Move back!" he cried out. Gawd! They were getting careless, and with gloomy concentration, he watched as they scrambled backward.

What was that? He smelled something then. Fire? He looked frantically about. The winch. "Water!" he cried, and again the men working the winch doused the smoke. Still there was the smell of burning in the air. They couldn't keep it suspended forever.

"Lower away," he shouted now. "Easy, not so—"

Suddenly there was a ringing in his ears, the sound growing to a mechanical scream. He glanced up and saw the Power Loom beginning to shift in its swing. Still it swung, a great, black lump, airborne and out of its element.

Had no one else seen it? The smoke from the winch was growing thicker and at that moment he saw a flame shoot out from the drum.

Gawd, no! The loom was tipping. "Get back!" he shouted, but somehow felt that the command had not been loud enough to be heard over the scream of the winch. There was a hoarse cry from atop the wagon, other voices joining it. Magnetized by the imminent catastrophy, Jack Willmot ran forward, then instantly was driven back as the monster slipped from its cradle of chains, tilting first one way, then the other, as though in that instant she had a mind of her own. As another tongue of flame shot up from the winch, Willmot saw a group of men still dangerously within the fall area, all scrambling, trying to outrace the inevitable.

"Move!" he screamed.

But then the night air was rent with a rumble; the chains slipped and there came a crash of deafening explosion as though walls were falling and ceilings. Willmot's ears were bursting with the roar and hiss of flames and the terrified shouts of the men. He closed his eyes, then quickly opened them to the sight of hovering clouds of smoke, there folding over into black masses, there drawing out and lighting up with gleaming sparks, and there the monster loom fallen to earth, its rollers set to spinning by the impact, filling the air with a prolonged scream. The heat and smoke and sound all produced on Willmot the effect of a disastrous conflagration.

All at once he saw the men rushing forward toward the

fallen loom, then in the same instant saw them draw back. Willmot held his position a distance away and felt a peculiar weakness coming from the withdrawing men.

Then he was running, pushing the men aside, and when his eyes still had not found anything to recoil from, he pushed farther in until he thought curiously that he might have to scramble over the loom itself if he wanted to see what had sent the men moving slowly backward.

He heard several voices shouting. As he passed, one spoke breathlessly, "He lingered, sir, I swear it, he lingered till them others was clear, then—"

Now he saw. Oh God, now he saw and instantly denied it and tried to turn away, but the men had crowded in behind him, as though he somehow could set it to rights, could raise the powerful loom and free the man who lay crushed beneath it.

Willmot continued to stare down. The man's face was so quiet. Willmot could not comprehend the stillness, nothing moving save for the small red trickle which slipped from the corner of his mouth and disappeared into the shadows of his neck. Now he became aware of the shocked presence of the men, a few weeping openly.

Slowly he bent down as though belatedly aware that some sort of action might still be feasible. Oh God, how mistaken was he there. The trestle was pressed into his chest, and behind it all the awesome weight of the machine itself. Beneath such a force, a man's body would be crushed as a dry leaf in winter.

Behind him he heard the brittle silence broken by a few panting groans. Someone was praying to God in a swift rapid monotone. Still Willmot crouched, staring downward with a sense of horror mingled with loss. He couldn't cry openly like some of his men were doing. He must remain aloof.

Then because he couldn't cry, he raised up suddenly and smashed both fists into the senseless machine, struck it again and again until his knuckles were bleeding and someone turned him forcibly away and directed his attention to the young boy, standing white-faced at the edge of the circle, his face drawn with shock.

Angrily Willmot shook off the hands that had interrupted his assault on the loom. Couldn't they do anything for themselves? Must he do it all? The lad was there for all to see, his need clear, his shock and disbelief equally as clear. Couldn't someone else have guided him gently forward, shown him the face of the man lying crushed beneath the loom?

But if anyone else could have done it, they didn't. The job was left to Jack Willmot, who let the boy cry for several minutes and in the youthful weeping felt life shrinking farther and farther away.

All the other men had joined them now and all stared down upon the boy, cradling his father's head in his lap, his fingers smoothing back the graying hair.

Dear God, they couldn't stand like this forever. The man was dead. Men die every day. They all were mortal. It could have been any one of them. But as Willmot tried to draw together the shattered fragments of his authority and issued a spate of orders for the men to fetch the other winch, for others to retrieve a piece of canvas in which to wrap the body, and still others to bring around his own wagon, while he was doing all this, he felt something unassailable within him. Why this man? Better if it had been himself.

Although he was not normally a man given to such perceptions, he knew that Fate had played a particularly foolish hand on this night. He looked out across the road at a distance of about twenty yards and saw the boy seated upon the ground, his head down, two men hovering over him.

Behind, he saw the second winch being dragged into place, the men working silently, angrily, the enormous chains reattached with a force that resembled rage. A few moments later the cursed loom was lifted and eased back.

He had no desire to step closer. He'd done enough. Leave it to the others. He felt dead himself. Better to stand still in helpless activity, at least until the feeling passed.

Shortly before midnight, in her low-ceilinged room beneath the attic, Elizabeth was just buttoning the last button on her new frock when outside on the empty street she heard the rattle of a wagon.

Home so soon? Edward had told her that they probably would be working most of the night. Obviously they had finished sooner than they had expected.

Good! She'd fix them both hot soup, then bully them into a warm tub. They must all look their best tomorrow. In a state of almost unbearable excitement, she started hurriedly to unbutton the new dress. It must be a surprise. How she looked forward to seeing both their faces when she appeared in the morning in something other than the worn, always soiled blue dresses, remains of her days as a volunteer in the Ragged School.

Quickly her withered hand tried to manipulate the tiny buttons and buttonholes. But she heard footsteps then on the pavement and knew she'd never make the change in time. Well, no matter. She'd give them a glimpse tonight. Perhaps the new gown would impress upon both of them that if they were to accompany her to the Great Exhibition, they must look their best.

Not generally given to vanity, she was rather pleased with what she saw in the glass. How far she'd come. And what a good life she had now. Oh, not easy, not that at all. Sometimes it seemed that all she did was peel spuds and boil joints and fill the outstretched bowls of the people who lined up outside the Common Kitchen from dawn to dusk. Oh yes, she knew fatigue now like she'd never known it before.

Still, the miracle was there, gazing back at her from the distorting mirror, a woman who could read and write and do figures, who'd raised a child, sadly not her own, though she'd managed to keep a portion of joy for herself. She scarcely had any memory at all now of the frightened little package who'd crawled across the soiled straw of the Common Cell and offered herself to Edward Eden.

Edward! She closed her eyes, finding now, as she'd always found, almost unbearable happiness in the name alone. Edward. Were angels named Edward? Or saints? They should be.

Abruptly she made a merry little turn before the glass, fascinated by the manner in which the dress whirled about her. Without looking foolish, she must try to manage a few such turns tomorrow at the Great Exhibition.

Suddenly embarrassed by her vanity, she stood still, listening. She thought she'd heard the door open downstairs, but there was no sound now. Perhaps they were playing a joke on her. Stealthily she crept to the door and opened it a crack. As always she'd left a single lamp burn-

ing on the downstairs table, and from her angle of vision
at the top of the stairs, she saw John.

"Is it you?" she called down, thinking to make a grand
descent. But first she must be certain that she had both
their attentions. "John, is it—"

At that moment, she saw another face peering up, a
man she'd never seen before in a black corduroy jacket,
with ruddy weathered face. He stood with his arm about
John's shoulder, and she saw his face take on a terrible
expression.

Moving slowly forward, Elizabeth started down the
steps. Midway down she saw four other men standing near
the door. None seemed inclined to speak.

"John?" she inquired softly, puzzled by the strange
gathering.

The boy hesitated, seemed incapable of looking at her.
He bowed his head. "There's been an accident—"

She clutched at the folds of the yellow dress. "What—"
But her breath caught.

One of the men stepped toward her as though to come
to her aid, but she drew herself up and decided to move
whether her heart was beating or not. "Where—" But again
the words choked in her throat.

There was movement then, the four men departing
through the open door. John crumpled into the chair by the
table. The man still stood with his arm about his shoulder.

But Elizabeth kept her eye on the doorway and on the
black night beyond. She felt safe as long as that doorway
was empty. If the four men would only be kind enough
not to return, she might endure, her heart might start up
again and—

Then they were there again, carrying something between
them. All at once she felt incredible relief. It wasn't Edward. Merciful God, thank You, it wasn't Edward. It was
merely a rolled piece of canvas, something heavy to be
sure, but it wasn't Edward, though it was peculiar how
gently they carried it.

Still clinging to the bannister, she stared down into the
small room at the mysterious activity, the men now with
great tenderness placing that old roll of canvas on the floor
before the fire. Feeling sudden anger, she was on the verge
of calling out, asking them kindly to remove it. Lumpy it
was, she noticed, with dark spreading stains.

The large man in the black corduroy jacket had now
moved away from John and was bending over the canvas.
Was he weeping? Why should such a strong strapping man
weep over a—

Her thoughts stopped. The man kneeling on the floor
ceased fumbling with the cord and drew back the upper
portion of the heavy canvas.

The moan commenced at the base of her throat and
climbed upward, culminating in a single howl. Then she
was moving, aware of the men retreating, but aware of
little else as at last she knelt beside the still face, thinking
that life for her, from now on, would be impossible. No
sooner had she touched the cold forehead than the coldness
spread, moved up through her fingers, across her shoulders,
lodging somewhere near the base of her skull.

Sounds floated to her from afar. Who was talking
behind her? What were they saying? Something had fallen?
And who was weeping? No matter. All she wanted to do
was carefully, lovingly catalogue his face, her fingers
brushing across his features, his eyes, nose, the line of his
jaw. How she loved him, would love him always.

Then at last she began to cry. She bent over and embraced him, lifted his face to her breast and held him
close. Someone still was talking, a gentle gruff voice utter-
ing words of comfort.

Didn't he know? Didn't they all know? There was no
comfort possible. From now on, in every street, on every
corner, inhabiting every shadow, there would be only silent
grief and loneliness. Her sun had set. There would be no
more laughter, no more walks in the park, no more quiet
moments before the fire with the shadows playing gently on
his face.

She cradled his head in her arms, and commenced rocking with him back and forth. A low, continuous moan
escaped her. She pressed as closely to him as she could, so
close that she could see the gleam of his face in the darkness.

The month of May occasionally belies its character for
merriment with unexpected fits of gloom. It had rained in
the early morning hours, but by ten o'clock on that morning of May 1, 1851, the London sky was filled with glorious sunshine. Larks were singing in the parks, and the

splendid glass palace which had risen like a miracle on the meadows of Hyde Park stood ready and waiting for the arrival of the Queen and the Royal Family and the magnificent opening which would signal to the world that England was still supreme, her strong, hardworking hand securely on the helm of the ship which she modestly labeled "All Mankind."

But on the pavement of the narrow lane in the slum district of Bermondsey, the sun did not shed its warming rays. At ten o'clock on this morning, a hollow-eyed Elizabeth watched, without feeling, as four men loaded a simple coffin into the back of the wagon. The large man, whose name she had learned was Jack Willmot, was the overseer of the procedure, as he'd overseen everything during that long nightmare.

Standing to one side, she saw the four horsemen who had arrived only moments before, again Jack Willmot's idea. He'd felt they would need escort through the city on this bustling morning so he had appointed four of his strongest men to ride alongside the wagon.

Now she shivered in the morning chill and to keep her eyes away from the coffin, she lowered her head and concentrated on the puddles left by the early morning rain. In all directions the street was so quiet. She'd hoped that some of the people would come to see him off. She knew the word had spread, had been aware, in spite of her grief, through the night of whispered conversations taking place all around her.

Yet there was no one here save for the men and Jack Willmot and herself, still wearing the yellow dress which she was to have worn to the Great Exhibition, walking proudly between Edward and John.

At this thought she looked slowly up at the young boy already seated atop the wagon, the reins in his hand. She was worried about him, but didn't know how to reach him. How could she begin to ease his loss when the emptiness within her was still so painful. When, at some point during that endless night, he'd suggested that they must take his father home, she'd felt a strong objection rising in her throat.

But on this matter, John had been adamant and vocal and had sworn before witnesses that his father had repeatedly voiced the request that if something should happen, he be taken home.

Lacking both the will and energy for argument, Elizabeth had agreed. What matter now? Again she raised her eyes to the empty street, then back to the wagon, where she saw Jack Willmot's men lacing the coffin in place.

Then she saw Willmot jump down from the wagon and walk toward her, the effects of the grim night clearly visible on his face.

"All's ready now," he said softly, touching her arm. "I've instructed the men to go the full distance. You'll have to make the journey without intervals." He lowered his head. "They'll see to fresh horses."

She nodded to everything and drew the cloak around her. "I thank you for your kindness, Mr. Willmot," she murmured. "I don't know what—"

"See to the boy," he interrupted abruptly, clearly embarrassed by her expression of gratitude. "Try to make him understand."

Make him understand what? she thought angrily. Then she checked herself. "The boy will be fine," she murmured. "He's going home. It's what he's always wanted."

Now embarrassed by the intense stares of the waiting men, she said, "Well, then," and closed the door of the house and walked rapidly to the wagon. As Willmot assisted her up, she heard him speak to John.

"Take 'em slow through the city," he warned, gesturing toward the horses. "Then give 'em their head on the road."

As Elizabeth settled herself on the high seat, she noticed John staring straight ahead. His face was a mask. Perhaps it was just as well. The journey would be long. Time for talk later.

Now she saw Jack Willmot step away from the wagon and lift his hand in salute. On the other side, the riders were just climbing onto their horses. She took a quick glance back at the small house and instantly averted her eyes. There was nothing there for her now.

She saw the horsemen take their places, two on one side, two on the other, saw John's hands tighten on the reins, and in that instant the wagon moved forward with a rattling start. Again she looked in all directions.

It did seem to her that at least a few might have come and told him goodbye. Was it asking so much? But appar-

ently it was, and as the wagon approached the corner and
swung wide for the turn, she settled back against the seat
and consoled herself with the realization that it would have
meant nothing to Edward, whether people came or not.
She lowered her head. Oh God, when would the thought
stop hurting, the awareness of what was behind her in the
coffin?

Tears again then, though they were brief compared to the
floodgates of the night. Still no relief, though. The hurt was
lodged permanently in her heart.

Thus it was that through glazed eyes she looked up and
saw a small knot of people standing on the corner just
ahead. She recognized them as residents of Bermondsey
and was grateful when the men lifted their hats as the
wagon passed. A few moments later she glanced behind,
surprised to see these few walking quietly after the
wagon. How kind of them, she thought, even to go a short
distance.

She was on the verge of pointing out their presence to
John when just ahead she spied several others, emerging
from doorways, rising from stoops where apparently they
had been waiting. Six, maybe a few more, and they too
fell silently in behind the wagon.

"John, look," she whispered and was about to direct his
attention to those behind the wagon when up ahead at the
approaching intersection she saw still more, a much larger
gathering, this one, thirty, forty, men mostly, a ragged
crew if she'd ever seen one, but all with hats removed,
their eyes wide and solemn as they too fell in, not waiting
for the wagon to pass, but coming silently forward to greet
it, then parting and taking their places at the rear.

Elizabeth sat up, suddenly alert, turning first in one
direction, then the other, as people continued to appear,
emerging from all quarters now, a never-ending stream,
spilling out of tenement doors, out of alleys and grim inner
courtyards, some on crutches, she noticed, hundreds now
was her estimate, still coming, women clutching children
by the hands, men with protective arms about the women,
all, all falling silently in behind the wagon, more people
than Elizabeth had ever seen. Now it was as though every
inhabitant from Lambeth, from Southwark were joining
them, still more appearing from off Kennington Common,
a silent, moving wave of humanity, and there, Jacob's

Island, still more appearing, men coming individually, in pairs, in groups of eight and ten, a swelling tide which, raising up from her seat, she noticed extended as far behind as she could see.

"John, look!" she gasped, clutching at the back of the seat for support.

Dear God in Heaven, still they came, every human being in the world, or so it seemed. Turning rapidly in all directions, she couldn't begin to take it all in, thousands now, surely thousands of silently marching men, women, and children, their faces, their eyes fixed on the back of the wagon, on the coffin bearing—

One of the horsemen riding nearby drew close, his plain face aglow with a smile, the first she'd seen in ever so long. "It's for him, Miss," he whispered, "for the Prince of Eden."

She nodded quickly and made no attempt to hide the tears streaming down her face. She glanced again at John, his eyes still fixed on the pavement ahead, the reins wrapped so tightly about his hands that the skin showed white.

While she wished that he might have expressed appreciation for the incredible spectacle of humanity walking silently behind him, for the moment she didn't care.

All she knew was that Edward Eden was being given a grand send-off. Very stealthily she reached her hand behind her, slipped it through the slats of the high wagon seat, and with tenderness touched the unresponding wood of the coffin.

Over her shoulder, she saw them, still coming, a gray-brown-black crowd of thousands, yet not one sound but the muffled tread of boots, and the upturned, quietly grieving faces of men whose lives had in some way been touched, changed, warmed by the Prince of Eden.

At ten forty-five on the glorious morning of May 1, 1851, the Royal Procession was forming within the high black iron gates of Buckingham Palace.

In the lead, following the dictates of history and precedence, were the Coldstream Guards. Immediately following them was the Royal Carriage, open in honor of the May sun and the special day, containing Her Royal Highness, dressed in pink and silver, wearing her Garter Ribbon and the Kohinoor Diamond, a small crown and two feathers in her hair. Also in the carriage rode Prince Albert, the dreamer of the Dream, and their two eldest children, Victoria Adelaide Mary Louise and Albert Edward, Prince of Wales.

At the head of this splendid procession rode the Commander of the First Battalion of Coldstream Guards, Colonel Nigel Stevens. His was an awesome responsibility, and from where he sat astride his horse, waiting for the procession to fall in, he ran the route in his mind: beyond the gates, one circle past the Mall, then into the Serpentine Road and a short distance beyond through the main Hyde Park gate to the doors of the Great Exhibition. A brief journey. What could go wrong?

Earlier that morning he'd noticed that thousands had already lined the Mall, hoping to get a glimpse of Her Majesty. If he'd had his way, the Royal Carriage would have been closed, not open. One couldn't be too careful.

Look! There! From where he sat at the head of the procession, he could see the trees opposite Buckingham. All seemed to have burst out suddenly into a crop of eager boys who, in spite of warnings of the police, seemed to think every tree a legitimate spying point. In vain did the constables look up and threaten the youthful branches. Mere urchins, those. But if they could climb, so could an anarchist, or an anti-royalist, a radical agitator. And London, on this great day, was full of foreigners, come to see the Great Exhibition, a few to wish England well, but more, he suspected, to wish her ill.

Still he knew what his duty was. At the first whiff of trouble, he and his men would rapidly encircle the Royal Carriage and lead it forward out of danger. If any foreign dissident had designs on the Queen, he first would have to slaughter Colonel Stevens and his seventy-five men, then wade through their blood.

Quickly now he glanced over his shoulder, taking enormous pride in himself and his men. The cream, that's what they were, top-rank. Then at that moment, still looking over his shoulder, he saw the signal from the rear guard that all was in order. He turned smartly in his saddle, raised his hand to the Keepers of the Gate in signal that the gates could now be opened. Her Majesty was ready to commence.

In the throes of an overwhelming awareness of who and what he was, he glanced briefly to the right. At first he saw nothing but the curious parting of the crowd, as though they had mistakenly thought that the Royal Procession would be moving from left to right toward Birdcage Walk and Parliament.

He looked again more closely, slowing his horse. A distinct parting it was, even the conveyances drawing close to the pavement, the crowds there looking not toward Buckingham and the Royal Carriage, but rather in the opposite direction.

It occurred to him that he should rein in his horse completely and check further, but instead he proceeded on for several yards. Out of the corner of his eye, as he was just in the process of executing the turn, he saw what appeared to be a wagon, a single wagon, followed by—

Christ! What was it? From where he sat it looked like an army, unorthodox to be sure, but hundreds, all moving silently behind the wagon, coming steadily forward. The near crowd now saw it as well and grew ominously silent.

Quickly Colonel Stevens reined his horse and thrust his hand up into the air, signaling his men to do the same. If they proceeded to move forward, they would be on direct collision course with the steadily approaching marchers. For an instant his emotions vaulted as his mind turned over the horrendous possibilities. Mobs had marched on Versailles. Was this the same?

For a moment his horse whirled rapidly as though in imitation of his whirling brain. Then he drew himself up and gave his emotions over to training. He knew where his position should be. Hurriedly he shouted to a near captain. "Take ten men and see to the nature of it!" Then sharply he brought his horse about and galloped rapidly back toward the Royal Carriage. Behind him, he heard the others following, good men, who like himself had sensed the danger and were now moving into protective position around the Royal Carriage.

As he approached, he allowed his eyes only to skim briefly over the occupants, then rapidly he took up a position directly to the right of Her Majesty. He did not speak or offer explanation concerning the delay. It was not his position to do so, though he heard a little girl's voice whisper, "Mama, what is it? Why did we stop?"

Then he heard a man's voice, faintly tinged with German. "Hush, be patient."

Still he kept his eyes straight ahead, searching for the Captain. Fortunately the Royal Carriage had not yet passed through the gates. There was at least a measure of protection, though he noticed the stillness which had fallen over the inner courtyard of Buckingham, a tense interim of waiting as all eyes apparently focused on the gates and the single wagon which was now passing directly before them. He could see it clearly from where he sat, a rough conveyance, a boy on the reins, as well as he could tell, a young woman seated beside him. Flanking the wagon on either side were four riders, and behind them, just coming into view the beginning of the silent marchers, Christ, even more than he'd first imagined, a thousand strong at least, an impressive match, if such was their inclination, for his men.

Where was the Captain?

Then, out of the corner of his eyes, he saw a small white-gloved hand, rather stout, lift from the pink and silver gown and rest itself on the edge of the carriage. The voice was high and thin and it too bore traces of a German accent. "What is it?" this voice now inquired, almost plaintively. "Who would spoil this day?"

He lowered his voice. "I'm not certain, Your Majesty. I would respectfully suggest that you—"

But at that moment he spied the Captain galloping rapidly toward him. He held his position and let the man come to him. There was a brief whispered exchange, something to do with a death, a funeral procession, then slowly he lifted his head and held his horse steady beside the Royal Carriage and waited for the invitation to speak.

"Well?" The white-gloved hand lifted slightly, then settled again into a firm grip on the side of the carriage.

"It appears to be a funeral procession of some sort, Your Majesty," he explained. "It seems that one of the workers was killed last night on the Exhibition site. I can disperse them easily enough if you so desire, Your Majesty. They are not armed. It would be a simple matter."

There was a pause. He lowered his eyes the better to see the white-gloved hand. The fingers were short, almost like a child's, though the hand itself was fleshy, the glove stretched taut. The littlest finger lifted now, a graceful

movement. "No," came the reply. "Give them their moment." Then the entire plump little hand seemed to go limp
against the edge of the carriage. "Poor man," she whispered, and Colonel Stevens heard a kind, almost maternal
mourning in the voice.

So he waited and kept a tight grip on his reins and
watched, as best he could, the ragged procession still
streaming past Buckingham Palace.

Who was the man? he wondered. Rabble, no doubt.

Give them their moment, she'd said.

As the silent mourners continued to file past, he sat
erect, keeping his eyes opened, his nerves alert. They *were*
rabble, he saw that much, all the rabble of London or so it
seemed. In a way they alarmed him, in spite of their peaceful march. There were their vast numbers, their silent,
drawn faces, the muted shuffle of their worn boots. In the
quiet moment, in the blowing of a mild wind barely per-
ceptible upon his face, he felt a mysterious depth of power
dominating the hushed crowds.

Give them their moment, he thought wryly, and hoped
that Her Majesty was more prudent than that.

Give rabble such as that a moment, and watch carefully
lest they steal an age.

In the late afternoon of May 2, 1851, having left the
mildness of spring behind in London, in a cold rain, Elizabeth looked up to see the gray silhouette of Eden Castle in
the distance.

Beside them now rode only three riders on horseback. At
Taunton that morning, the fourth had galloped ahead to
inform the inhabitants of Eden Castle that Edward Eden
was coming home.

Approaching exhaustion, Elizabeth looked with pitying
sympathy at John. Not one word had they exchanged during the entire journey. Not once had he partaken of food
or drink, and not once had he relinquished his control of
the reins although all the riders had offered repeatedly to
spell him, as had Elizabeth herself.

But apparently there was a turmoil inside his young head
that compelled him to keep silent. And silent he had been
and silent he was now as, looking up, she saw that he too
had caught his first glimpse of Eden Castle.

Suddenly she closed her eyes, unable to look at him any

longer, unable as well to view the great hulk of that castle drawing nearer. Her one thought now was to have done with it and return immediately to London. All she was bringing home was a broken shell. The spirit and memory of Edward Eden still resided in London, in the hearts of those men and women and children who had followed the wagon to the extreme western edge of the city before they had commenced to fall back. She belonged with them, and although she hadn't the faintest idea how, she fully intended to continue his work and reopen the Common Kitchen, to feed, clothe, and give shelter as best she could to anyone who came to her door in need.

Up ahead now, just emerging from the castle gates, she saw half a dozen riders on horseback, carrying lanterns in their hands. What was yet ahead of her? she wondered. Was Edward pleased to be home?

As the six riders approached, they joined the three who had accompanied them from London. Two of the men exchanged words of some sort and the third relayed a message to John. "Follow them," he shouted. "They'll show you the way."

Passing beneath the gatehouse now, Elizabeth looked up into the driving rain at the awesome facade of the castle itself. Grander than Buckingham, or so it seemed to her. Ahead she saw a small group of people moving down a flight of grand steps, all clothed in rain-wet black, a man and a woman as far as she could tell, while at the top of the stairs, inside the shelter of an arch, she saw an old woman, clutching two small children to her skirts. And at that moment, she saw as well and recognized immediately poor Miss Jennifer. In stark white she was, hiding behind one of the arches, a box of some sort clasped in her arms, a fearful expression on her face.

Elizabeth had thought that the wagon was headed toward the steps, but suddenly the lead rider veered sharply to the left and led them down a narrow lane which skirted the castle wall, the north facade of the castle looming over them. As she looked up, she saw white-faced servants in prim lace caps peering down from mullioned windows. Every window, it seemed, contained a face.

Again she shivered and drew her cloak about her though it did no good, for the cloak itself was soaked through, as was the yellow dress. As she glanced behind, she saw the man and woman following steadily behind the wagon, their heads down and covered by thick heavy black-hooded cloaks.

Turning about, she looked ahead and saw that the guardsmen were leading them toward a black iron fence which surrounded a small graveyard. The gate was open and beyond she saw a scattering of impressive marble stones, and there to the left, near the fence, she saw three gravediggers, silently standing, their spades in their hands. Then the grave itself was visible.

Through the narrow gate, John guided the horses into a small clearing on the left, brought them to a halt, then sat still for a moment, his head, rain-drenched, inclining slowly forward as though he were aware that his job was done. How she longed to speak to him, to somehow penetrate that awesome silence into which he had fallen. But she knew she couldn't and therefore didn't try and merely looked at him with eyes full of scared sympathy.

She was aware of activity at the rear of the wagon, saw the four guardsmen climbing aboard, each lifting one corner of the coffin and hoisting it down to earth. But instead of carrying it immediately to the freshly dug grave, they placed it at a spot not too distant from where the gentleman stood. The lady with him seemed to be protesting something, what, Elizabeth couldn't tell.

But she saw clearly the brief though heated conference, the gentleman insisting, his last words floating upward over the rain with perfect clarity. "It must be done. We must be certain."

Then Elizabeth saw the gentleman say something to one of the guardsmen, who in turn took from the lining of his heavy coat a piece of metal and as he slipped the metal lip beneath the coffin lid, clearly to pry it open, Elizabeth again averted her eyes.

Edward apparently must first be identified as the true Edward before they granted him the privilege of burying him in this sacred plot. Her eyes blurred by emotion and rain, she turned around in her seat and left the grisly ritual to others. Dear God, who else would it be? Who else would they drag to this dreary place? How much better, Elizabeth thought, to have buried him beside Daniel Spade in tiny St. Dunstan's graveyard. But no. John had assured her that this had been his wish.

She heard the sound of splintering wood and looked back in spite of herself to see two guardsmen lift the lid. The suspicious gentleman stepped forward. Simultaneously the lady retreated and walked rapidly away toward the iron fence, where, for a moment, she stood absolutely erect, eyes straight ahead, as though she'd laced herself into that formal pose and had vowed to let nothing penetrate.

At the instant the gentleman stepped away from the coffin with the soft announcement of, "It's him," she saw the lady reach sharply out for the fence, saw her hands grasp the iron spike, saw the second hand rise to a similar position, saw her standing now like a prisoner behind bars, her head inclining softly forward, a subtle collapse which moved Elizabeth for no other reason than at last she was glad to see that someone in this grim arena had feelings.

The collapse of the lady by the fence was very brief. As the guardsmen replaced the coffin lid, she turned back and to Elizabeth's surprise appeared to be gazing up at *her*. As yet no words had been spoken between them and Elizabeth thought for a moment that she was coming toward the wagon. But instead she seemed to hesitate, then fell slowly in beside the gentleman, both walking now behind the coffin where the guardsmen were carrying it to the grave.

Suddenly Elizabeth felt a flare of anger. If she wasn't going to be issued a bloody invitation to get down from the wagon, she'd get down without one. She'd not traveled all this distance under these terrible circumstances to sit atop a wagon and view the ritual of Edward's commitment to earth.

As she swung to the ground, she glanced back up at John. "Are you coming?" she asked, trying to stretch the stiffness out of her legs so that she might walk erect, like a lady.

Although that pale boyish face lifted and looked down on her, he gave no response.

Well, then— Slowly she turned and started walking through the gravestones, Edens all, she noticed. As she approached the open grave, she saw the lady look at her from out of the depths of the hooded cloak. She tried to read the expression on her face, but couldn't.

Then Elizabeth felt her attention being drawn to the grave, to the coffin being slowly lowered into earth. The rain, she noticed, made a peculiar sound on the coffin lid as though it were hollow. And in that instant, a new sense of loss swept over her.

No words? She glanced quickly about in search of a priest. No words at all? No one to tell the world about this man? Then although she'd vowed not to break, she bent her head over and gave in to one small moan. It sounded rude, out of place, weak, in that death yard, as though mourners and corpses alike must maintain the silence of the grave.

The coffin was lowered now, gone from sight. It was the gravediggers' turn and as these three drenched, rough-looking men stepped forward, spades in hand, Elizabeth found she could watch no longer. As the first clods of dirt struck the coffin lid, she turned slowly away and walked a distance beyond the mound of dirt, blinded by her grief, her sense that this was not the way it should be.

What was the connection between the man himself and that almost obscene ritual which was taking place behind her? And all at once, an unexpected memory from an earlier time rose up before her. She remembered Edward as she'd first seen him in the Common Cell at Newgate, recalled how he'd put his arm around her and warmed her with his own cloak. She remembered him in the banqueting hall in the house on Oxford Street, laughing, lifting the children into the air, carrying them on his shoulders. And she thought too of certain facts that again had nothing to do with what was going on behind her, of the reality of his seventeen Ragged Schools scattered throughout London which were still functioning, existing quite well now on contributions from charity and from the Union. She thought, standing in that gray, rain-swept graveyard, of the hundreds of abandoned children who had been fed, and clothed and housed and in certain instances, educated, like herself. She thought of the Common Kitchen, the door always open. She thought of his love and tenderness and kindness to all. She thought on all these things and more, and felt her heart fill, not with grief, but with gratitude that she had known such a man.

Then she could restrain herself no longer and wept openly for Edward Eden, for John, and even for the two standing rigidly beside the grave.

She looked back then at the place where the gravediggers were doing their job. Let them! The man himself had long ago escaped and now resided in thousands of human hearts. Try to contain him in mere earth and wood, she thought with a smile.

It could not be done.

Harriet stood atop the stairs outside the Great Hall, in the cold drizzling rain, feeling nothing, seeing little, and completely aware that her awesome strength was fast running out. Behind her, she was aware of James huddled in the shelter of the arch with the children. There were two now, Richard, age eight, and lovely Mary, age three, Harriet's gift to James for having dismissed the Cranfords three years ago. The dampness was bad for all of them. What in the name of God was the delay?

Annoyed, she glanced down at the wagon standing at the foot of the Great Hall steps, its wheels coated with mud from the graveyard. She saw the two in close huddle. She'd never seen the woman before today, a drowned waif really, with an injured hand of some sort. The young boy she vaguely remembered as being the same one who had accompanied Edward to the hearing several years ago in London.

Feeling profoundly sorry for both, she'd issued an invitation for them to take refuge around the fire in the servants' kitchen. They both looked weary to the point of illness. James had objected, but she'd offered the invitation anyway. They were welcome to stay as long as they liked. There would be fresh garments for them, warm food, and cots.

She'd not expected such a simple and humane gesture to be a matter for discussion. But apparently it was. So still she waited in the cold gray day, consuming what strength she had left in an attempt to keep her mind away from the fresh grave, the realization of the man they had just buried.

Edward. The name still hurt. She was in desperate need of privacy in order to stifle those thoughts that were too painful and too near to her heart.

She looked again down the steps to where the young boy and the woman were still talking. What was the problem? Nearby she saw two stewards waiting, saw a groomsman ready to lead the horses away. Behind her she heard her daughter's voice, "Mama?" She was cold no doubt and baffled by the curious interlude in the rain.

"In a minute," she soothed.

Then at last she saw the two moving toward the stairs, the woman in the lead, her injured hand carefully concealed beneath her cloak.

"Milady?" she called up, in a curiously aggressive voice. "We thank you for your kind invitation." At that moment, Harriet saw the young boy move up close beside her. He must be about fourteen, Harriet guessed, perhaps fifteen. His face bore a peculiar expression, resolution of some sort. She couldn't tell.

The woman was speaking again, her upturned face damp with rain and tears. Harriet had seen her in the graveyard turn away, weeping. "I will not be staying, milady," the woman went on. "I want to return to London right away."

Was she able? Harriet wondered. She looked done in. Yet she saw the four riders waiting for her at the gate. Surely they would be of assistance to her. Still, she felt pity for the young woman. She looked so thin and cold. Well, she had the boy and the riders to help her.

Considering it settled, Harriet was in the process of retreating back into the sheltering arch with James and the children when she heard the woman speaking again and looked back to see her climbing the stairs. Midway up she stopped as though she did not want to come any farther. "I beg your pardon, milady," she said then. "With your kind permission, the boy will stay."

Harriet turned slowly back. A peculiar request. She couldn't very well say no, for the boy was standing within earshot. "Of course," she murmured vaguely, "if he desires—"

The woman moved up another step, her face tense as though she were trying very hard to say the right thing. "The boy here," she began, looking back over her shoulder, "is Mr. Eden's son."

The word came softly over the wind and rain. "Mr. Eden's—" As Harriet tried to repeat what she thought she had heard, she found she couldn't.

The woman repeated it for her. "His son, milady. I have his papers back in London, his baptismal certificate. I'll send them right away if you wish—"

But at that moment, Harriet was not thinking of baptismal records. Instead she gazed steadfastly down upon the boy who, with matching steadfastness, returned her gaze. She saw it now, although she did not want to admit it, the similarity, the stance, the line of the jaw, the hair coloring, the eyes, especially the eyes. It might have been a young Edward staring up at her.

She looked away over the rain-drenched inner courtyard. My God, she couldn't turn him out. She owed Edward that much, that ancient debt for abandoning his first son. But who was the mother? That poor thin woman on the steps before her?

Incapable of speaking, she gave a vague nod and looked back toward James, as though for assistance. Surely he had heard the same incredible news. But if he had, it had not registered on his face. He appeared hopelessly bewildered and, clearly, in this matter, as in all other matters since the Cranfords had left, he would leave the decisions and solutions up to her.

As she turned back to the two waiting patiently at midstep, she tried to erase all traces of uneasiness from her face. "Of course, he's welcome," she said.

She continued to watch closely as the boy and the woman hurried back to the wagon, was still watching as the boy reached into the back and withdrew a small satchel. A moment later he fell into a close and loving embrace with the young woman.

Still Harriet stood watching, trying to conceal her agitation, telling herself that it was nothing, that of course their solicitor would have to launch a discreet but thorough investigation, perhaps discover the identity of the mother. There was plenty of room in the servants' hall to accommodate a fifteen-year-old boy.

At last the embrace was ending. She saw the boy hug her lightly again and assist her up onto the wagon. There was another quick kiss and a whispered exchange of some sort. Then the young woman quite expertly flicked the reins and the horses started forward, the wagon lighter now, the mud-caked wheels throwing off bits and pieces of graveyard soil.

Everything seemed to wait in the cold dusk as the boy watched the wagon pass through the gatehouse arch. And still everything waited as he seemed content merely to stand and stare toward the now empty gate. Harriet saw him bow his head, as though he'd offered a brief, silent prayer. Then those eyes, Edward's eyes, were staring up at her.

She felt the blood rush to her heart. He appeared so alone now, that young face gazing at her, his satchel at his feet, both boy and satchel dwarfed by the vast emptiness of the inner courtyard.

Clearly they couldn't stand like this all evening. Someone had to move. Behind her she heard her children fretting to be taken inside to the warmth of the sitting room fire. With an effort of will she pulled away from those intense eyes and issued a command to one of the waiting stewards. "Take him to the servants' hall," she called out. "And see that he has fresh dry clothes and something to eat."

The steward nodded and started toward the boy, his hand already outstretched for the satchel. But at the last moment, Harriet saw the boy himself scoop up the luggage and start toward the stairs. As he drew nearer, she saw that his eyes were clear, almost cheerful, not a trace anywhere of the recent melancholy parting.

Still watching her, he came closer, ever closer. Beyond him she saw the gaping steward, who appeared equally as baffled by the boy's aggressive movements.

As he came steadily upward, approaching the top of the stairs, her first impulse was to withdraw. But she held her ground and was about to kindly redirect him to the servants' door when without warning a dazzling smile broke across those young features.

He stood less than three feet from her now. "If you don't mind," he commenced, in a voice remarkable for its strength and clarity, "I prefer to reside in my father's chambers. It's a waste of time, don't you think, to get settled in one place only to have to move to another?"

Again she found that speech was beyond her and she did well to move quickly to one side as he walked past her, beneath the arch, past James and the children, into the Great Hall itself.

There he turned back. "I know the way," he announced. "I need no assistance."

He proceeded on across the Great Hall, his satchel still in his hand, when suddenly at midpoint he stopped and again looked back. "If it wouldn't be too much trouble," he asked, "a fire would be pleasant. I'm quite chilled from the day and the occasion. My father always said there was nothing worse than a May Devon rain."

Harriet followed a few steps after him. She saw him now glance lightly up at the ceiling of the Great Hall as though he were searching his mind for something.

Apparently he found it, for the smile on his face grew broader. "I believe my father told me that the fire well in his chambers required half a dozen good oak logs, approximately the length of a man's arm." He was silent a moment, assessing her. "If the steward would be so kind as to lay such a fire, I'd be most grateful."

There was not a trace of impudence on the young face, only quiet conviction. Then he turned again and proceeded slowly across the Great Hall, his head erect, shoulders back.

Harriet watched him, noted the swing of his arms, the way he carried his body, the angle of the head. Suddenly and without warning she shivered, though not from cold now, but rather from the incredible sensation that true recognition was just beyond her, that if only she could remove certain veils from her eyes, the mystery of his identity would be solved.

Now she stepped quickly forward and asked in a voice remarkable for its fearful quality, "Who are you?"

Just a few steps short of the far doorway which led into the heart of the castle, the boy stopped. Slowly he turned, an expression of quizzical impatience on his face, as though he was certain that this was old ground that had been gone over before to everyone's satisfaction. He bent over and placed his luggage on the floor by his feet, then stood erect. With visible and awesome pride, he said, "My name is John Murrey Eden. My father was Edward Eden. I have come home."

She saw him pause again, as though to see if there would be further interrogation. And at last he retrieved his luggage and disappeared into the darkened corridor on the far side of the Great Hall.

Behind her, she heard James, trying to articulate something, a protest, she assumed, though it came out as little more than sputtering. She glanced over her shoulder and saw her husband in a crouched position, clutching their children to him, as though they all were in imminent danger from an unidentified threat.

She looked back toward the empty doorway, and stood absolutely still, listening. There were a dozen passageways leading out from that corridor. It had taken her over a month to learn them all. Surely he would return in a moment and confess to being lost.

But he didn't. In fact she heard his step on the staircase now, measured, determined, moving steadily upward in the proper direction toward Edward's third-floor chambers, as though he knew the interior of vast Eden Castle as intimately, as thoroughly as he knew any place on earth.

ABOUT THE AUTHOR

Marilyn Harris was born and educated in Oklahoma and received her B.A. and M.A. degrees from the University of Oklahoma. A prolific writer, she first gained public attention with a collection of short stories, published in American and European periodicals and later in one volume, KINGS EX. She has gone on to write many books, including her popular Eden novels. She is author of the current Doubleday hardcover Warrick. Miss Harris is married to E. V. Springer, a professor at Oklahoma's Central State University. They have two children and live in Norman, Oklahoma.

Ballantine's World of
Historical Romance...

14   TA-13